MW00451824

# BAJA REDEMPTION

# BAJA REDEMPTION

## A NOVEL

*John R. Gentile*

## JOHN R. GENTILE

**Wild Spirit Books**
Tucson, Arizona

Wild Spirit Books
Tucson, Arizona
(An imprint of Wild Spirit Journeys, LLC)

Printed in the USA.

*This book is dedicated to the volunteers and activists of the Sea Shepherd Conservation Society and the Cove Monitors of Ric O'Barry's Dolphin Project who stand witness and place their lives on the line to protect whales and dolphins all over the world.*

# CAST OF CHARACTERS
### (In order of appearance)

**Macario Silvano** – whaler, son of Gustavo and Marta Silvano
**Gustavo Silvano (Tavo)** – whaler, former fishing partner of Jake Spinner
**Marta Silvano** – wife of Gustavo Silvano, mother to Macario
**Alejandro Cabrillo (Alex)** – marine biologist, Director at *Instituto de Mamíferos Marinos*
**Sandy Wainwright** – marine biologist, lead humpback whale researcher
**Paola Jiménez** – marine biologist, humpback whale researcher
**Emily Rosen** – investigative reporter, *New York Times*
**Jake Spinner** – former Army Special Forces, expatriate, part-time fishing charter operator
**Alfonso Figueroa** – Minister of Fisheries, Mexico City
**Hirokan Yoshimatsu (Hiro-san)** – high-ranking member of the Consortium, part of the Yakuza
**Susan Lawrence** – Administrative assistant to Hirokan Yoshimatsu
**Sato Izumi (Sato-san)** – lieutenant in the Consortium
**Roland Castellano (Rollie)** – Spinner's friend from Special Forces, CEO of Las Altas
**Jesús Trujillo** – fisherman, whale activist
**Carlos Palacios** – fisherman, whale activist, friend of Jesús
**Ako Kanamura (Ako-san)** – head of security for Yoshimatsu's organization, hit man
**Raúl Campos** – fisherman, goat rancher, whale activist
**Francisco Trujillo** – brother of Jesús, boat mechanic, whale activist
**Carmen Cabrillo** – wife of Alejandro Cabrillo
**Lili Cabrillo** – daughter of Alejandro Cabrillo
**Guadalupe Campos Mora** – wife of Raúl Campos, *curandera* (healer)
**Alisa Campos** – daughter of Raúl and Guadalupe
**Julio Campos** – son of Raúl and Guadalupe
**Captain Watabe** – captain of the *Shodokai Maru* whaling ship
**Alma Quintín** – Native American villager, whale activist

**Fernando Quintín** – fisherman, husband to Alma Quintín

**The Cetus Global Alliance:**

    **Graham Neely** – environmental lawyer, whale activist

    **Morgan** – whale activist

    **Brittany** – whale activist

    **Beau** – whale activist, technical support

    **Brad** – whale activist

    **Diane** – whale activist

**Dora Trujillo Sanchez** – wife of Jesús, midwife

**Arturo Ruiz** – small animal veterinarian, whale activist

**Presidente Emilio Duarte** – president of Mexico, brother-in-law of Alfonso Figueroa

**Oliver Sweet (Ollie)** – former Navy SEAL, employed by Las Altas

**Derek Robideaux (Snake)** – former Army Cavalry helicopter pilot, employed by Las Altas

**Angelina Obregón** – Administrative Director, partner of Rollie Castellano at Las Altas

Leviathan...
Upon earth there is not his like,
who is made without fear.
Will he speak soft words unto thee?
*Job 41*

# PROLOGUE

## Gulf of California, Baja California Sur, Mexico

The twenty-eight-foot *panga* cut through the slate-gray water easily. The twin Yamaha 75s kept the bow up on plane as the boat and its six occupants sped toward the island. In the east, the January sky glowed in hues of rose and tangerine, silhouetting the rugged mountains of the Baja Peninsula. Macario Silvano sat near the stern huddled against the cold breeze. Even in his slicker, the moist air and constant wind chilled him to the bone.

Macario was twenty years old with a slender build and long black hair tucked under a watch cap. He looked across the seat at his father, Gustavo, who sat hunkered down, his sweatshirt hood pulled over a faded baseball cap. His father's grim face was lined and leathery, the result of a lifetime spent fishing on the ocean. His high cheekbones, common to members of their coastal tribe, gave him an almost skeletal appearance in the early morning light.

The man in the bow, who was holding a line to keep his balance, suddenly raised a hand. The helmsman eased back on the throttle, and the panga slowed. When the man in the bow motioned with four fingers and pointed ahead, the helmsman cut the motors, and the boat began to drift.

Without a word, Macario, his father, and two other boatmen pulled long oars from the gunwales, attached them quickly and quietly to the oarlocks, and began to dip the paddles into the water. Their movements were synchronous and made no sound except for the occasional drip of water from the oars. The Japanese man standing in the panga's bow dropped the safety line and picked up an ominous-looking gun. A deadly harpoon with an explosive charge attached to the shaft now rested in his arms. Attached to the harpoon were a coiled cable and several large floats.

In the still of the pre-dawn air, Macario heard a loud whoosh in the water ahead. It reminded him of a great set of bellows he had seen at the ironworks foundry in Tepic. A moment later he heard two more massive exhalations, then another, this one lower in volume.

The helmsman, a grubby man dressed in greasy coveralls, leaned forward and said to Macario, "*Las ballenas están durmiendo.*"

Macario cast a look at the boatman, who flashed a toothless smile. Then he looked toward the source of the exhalations. In the early morning light, Macario could see fifteen-foot plumes of atomized water forming clouds against the outline of the dark island. He counted four exhalations, three large spouts and a smaller one. He felt his gut twist in anticipation.

The panga closed on the sleeping whales. Macario sensed the tension emanating from his fellow villagers. Only the harpoon man and the helmsman were strangers. They had been sent from the company.

The sound of the whales' exhalations grew louder. A smaller spout, half the volume of its mother's, followed. Macario looked off to port and saw three large backs raising and sinking together. His heart began to race as the panga drew within thirty yards of the sleeping humpbacks. The rifleman at the bow held up a hand and signaled to the oarsmen to stop rowing. They pulled their paddles in, securing them quietly. The harpooner readied his rifle, then pushed the gun's stock firmly against his shoulder as he braced his feet for the recoil.

Gustavo grabbed his son by the arm and whispered, "Keep your hands in the panga, *mijo.*" He made the sign of the cross and muttered a prayer in their native language. At the end, Macario heard his father apologize. *"Lo siento, ballenas."*

The panga drew within striking distance. One of the whales surfaced and blew, covering the occupants of the panga in a fine spray. Macario remembered that the mist exhaled from the whale's huge lungs smelled of fish, brine, and fathomless ocean.

Another whale surfaced. Midway through its exhalation, it snorted. Something was wrong.

Huge flukes lifted off the water and pounded the sea into foam. Macario heard the rifle's report, and then an explosion followed by a high-pitched scream. The sound was so visceral he thought he would vomit.

The coils of line whined; floats ripped over the side of the boat as the mortally wounded whale made a desperate run to free itself of the exploding lance. The sky glowed red in the east, casting flashes of crimson across the water. The water churned red as the great whale's life force mixed with the sea. Macario's nostrils were assaulted by the coppery smell of blood.

He looked across at his father whose weathered face, caught in the first rays of light, was wet with tears.

The matriarch lay at the surface sleeping. More correctly, she was half-sleeping. Millions of years of evolution allowed her to shut down one hemisphere of her brain to allow for sleep while keeping a watchful eye on the constantly changing ocean around her with the other.

She was a Pacific bottlenose dolphin, around thirty-five years old. Next to her was her six-month-old calf, a male who maintained close contact with her by leaning against her pectoral fin. This was her fifth calf and the second male offspring. The first male had died shortly after birth, the victim of a vicious attack by a tiger shark. That was long ago when she was an inexperienced mother. Things were different now.

The mother was distinctive in her markings. Where a typical bottlenose was slate-gray to black, she had a distinguishing mark on her forehead—just forward of her blowhole—that resembled a star pattern. Her new calf had inherited a similar physical trait. He had an array of four small white spots on his forehead resembling the cardinal points on a compass and a small white blaze on the dorsal aspect of his flukes that looked like a lightning bolt.

Nearby, eight other dolphins rested or slept. All females, they were daughters, sisters and their offspring. Once they matured, males born into this maternal subgroup had formed alliances with one to two other males. One of the matriarch's daughters, a three-year old adolescent, was the primary "auntie" for the newborn male. When the old female needed to feed, the auntie took over the duties of watching the young dolphin, having him accompany her in an echelon swimming formation, close by and just below her. The young dolphin was gregarious and inquisitive. His precociousness kept the adult dolphins on constant alert.

The lead female dolphin suddenly heard something in the deep blackness of the Gulf of California. The sea was always full of sounds, which differed from day to night—from the popping sounds of pistol shrimp on the nearby reef to vocalizations from blue striped grunts and croakers to the deep sonorous sounds of her larger cousins, the great whales. But this was something distinctive. It was the sound made by the propeller of a ship. Once, further south, she had heard it before. Her calf, awakened by the deep thrumming noise of the twin screws, twitched his flukes in fear and nuzzled closer to his mother. Alerted, the rest of the pod faced toward the disturbance.

Several of the younger dolphins vocalized. They wanted to investigate. Sometimes they would ride the bow wake of large ships. Judging by the *vibration coming from the two giant propellers, this would be one pressure wave that would be fun to ride!*

*The sound of the ship grew louder, drowning out any other sounds in the ocean around the dolphin family. The female emitted a warning whistle and the younger dolphins held back.*

*Just then the female picked up a faint taste in the water. She sampled the water again. Images danced through her mind as she attempted to separate the tastes on her tongue. Suddenly, her whole body tensed as recognition came to her. She had tasted the blood of her own kind and, in that blood, she felt the presence of great suffering.*

*She issued three sharp whistles to the family. Together, they turned and swam swiftly in the opposite direction until the sounds from the Death Ship had all but faded into the blackness.*

# 1

## La Paz, Baja California Sur, Mexico

Alejandro Cabrillo sat at his desk looking at his computer screen. The satellite image before him showed a section of Lower Baja California. Small blinking dots were interspersed around the region, forming the semblance of a travel pattern. The dots represented humpback whales that had been tagged by his team and were now being monitored. Information was being streamed via satellite regarding migratory routes, travel patterns, gathering places, and feeding sites.

The whales wintered in the southern Gulf of California near Loreto, drawn by the warmer waters of Mexico to give birth and nurture their young. This population of humpbacks moved from southern waters near Puerto Vallarta, back and forth, unlike their cousins who ranged from the colder waters of Alaska to the birthing waters of Hawaii—a round trip of more than 5,000 miles.

Alejandro sat back and stretched in his chair as he ran his fingers though his jet-black hair. The angular features of his face were made more prominent by the heavy shadow of a day's growth of beard. He leaned forward and squinted through his bifocals at the screen. He looked from the screen to the laminated pages sitting next to the computer.

"Where are you, D-7? You should be with D-5, 6, and 8."

He scrolled to another page of data, this one showing times and locations when the satellites last picked up the traveling humpbacks. Number D-7's last position was reported over a week ago, fifty miles south.

He leaned back again, still staring at the icons on the screen. It wasn't uncommon for the transmitters to be sloughed off or break down over time. The whales, because they were extremely tactile animals, were constantly in contact with one another. Although the science of tracking the huge cetaceans had made great strides, the equipment was still subject to the rigors of salt water, currents, and animal movement.

Alejandro had become the director of the *Instituto de Mamíferos Marinos* three years earlier. He had moved his wife and young daughter here from Cuernavaca after finishing his PhD in Mexico City. His chief duties were to oversee projects pertaining to whale and dolphin populations in the lower Gulf of California. He supervised four research scientists in the small center in La Paz and worked with graduate students from the United States and Canada on projects that helped to fund the institute.

Alejandro answered directly to the Department of Fisheries in Mexico City. Grant money was tight. Nearly all of the available government resources were being channeled into the ongoing and unwinnable "War on Drugs." Alejandro had come to depend on the soft monies coming in from institutions outside of Mexico. Fortunately, universities from all over the world wanted to send their enthusiastic students to study the rich waters of the Gulf of California, bringing grant money with them.

A knock on the door brought him out of his reverie. Without looking up, Alejandro said, "Yes?"

The door opened and Luisa, the department secretary and office manager, poked her head in. She was about the same age as Alejandro, pleasantly rounded, but attractively dressed in a flattering print dress. She wore her hair to her shoulders and had a ready smile.

"Alejandro, the Minister of Fisheries is on the phone and would like to speak to you. He's on line two."

A small knot formed in Alejandro's stomach. Chief Minister Alfonso Figueroa was a force to be reckoned with. From a wealthy family in Sinaloa, it was well known that he had aspired to climb the political ladder. A consummate politician, he would slap you on the back and inquire after your family, but under that veneer of congeniality Alejandro suspected that he could be ruthless in his desire to advance his own agenda. And besides, his brother-in-law was the president of Mexico. Alejandro's predecessor had fallen prey to the machinations of Figueroa a little over three years ago.

Alejandro picked up the phone. "Hello Minister! To what do I owe the pleasure of this call?"

"Just checking on your progress, Alejandro. How are you handling the crush of paperwork since you became director?"

Alejandro laughed. "It's really not that much different than pursuing my PhD. The volume is about the same. Only the content is different."

"How go the projects in the Lower Gulf?"

*Uh-oh, here it comes,* thought Alejandro. *Slash and burn the projects, direct from Mexico City.* "Um, fine. Our joint project tracking the traveling patterns of the humpbacks is revealing some promising data."

There was a short, but very distinct, pause. "When can you send me your preliminary findings? We need this information to determine funding allocation for the next fiscal year."

"I should be able to give you viable data at the end of this season—which is in about two to three months."

"In two to three months?" Figueroa sounded light-hearted, yet Alejandro heard the undertone. "We need to get all the budget information to the Ministry of Fisheries by the end of the month."

Alejandro did not dare mention the several lost signals that had occurred in the past few weeks.

"I'll put together a brief and have it in your office by the end of the week. Please remember, sir, it's only preliminary."

"Very good, Director Cabrillo." Figueroa resumed his fatherly tone. "I also beg a small favor of you, Alejandro. Next week my assistant, Felipe Muñoz, will be in La Paz. He is meeting a contingent of Japanese officials from both the fisheries ministry and the private sector. They wish to see the institute and would like to hear about your work there. I already told them you would be happy to show them around."

Alejandro flushed. *I'm a scientist, not a tour guide.* Besides, representatives from the Japanese Department of Fisheries had classically not been at the forefront for conservation of most whale species.

Alejandro sighed. "That would be fine, Minister."

"Good. I'll have Felipe call you and finalize arrangements. I'm looking forward to seeing that report." Figueroa signed off.

Alejandro stared at the receiver as if he were looking at a viper in his personal space. *"Madre de Dios."*

Luisa opened the door and stepped in. Alejandro suspected that she had been listening in on the conversation from the other side of the door.

"Get ready, Luisa. We're going to be entertaining Japanese dignitaries. I really don't have time for this."

"Maybe they're coming here for the whale meat tacos."

Alejandro smiled. "It seems odd that they would be interested in an institution that promotes conservation of marine mammals. Maybe they've seen the light."

Luisa laughed. "In your dreams. I watched *Whale Wars*. They don't quit."

"There was a time about twenty years ago when Japanese trawlers were sneaking up into the Gulf and taking everything they could get with their harpoons and nets. Whales, swordfish, dolphins, mantas, turtles, tuna. I heard they were even killing sea lions."

"To eat?"

"I guess. They think we in the west are *muy locos*. We eat cows and pigs. They don't understand the difference. One's on the land, another is bigger and swims in the sea."

Alejandro's cell phone rang. He retrieved it and saw that the name on the phone said "Sandy W."

*"Bueno. Hola,* Sandy. *¿Qué pasa?"*

Sandy Wainwright, marine biologist, was the other principal researcher on the humpback study. She had been on the project for nearly a year. Alejandro liked working with this dedicated and brilliant field biologist.

"Alejandro." The connection crackled with static. "We have a problem. We located Number D-7. Valentine. Washed up on Isla Ratón. Dead."

"You're sure it's Valentine?" Alejandro's chest felt like it was being squeezed in a vise.

"It's Valentine. We matched her flukes."

"Was the transmitter still working?"

"No. Transmitter's gone. Some local fishermen found her earlier today and called it in to us."

"Any idea about the cause of death?"

Sandy's voice caught. "Someone shot her, Alex. There's a harpoon shaft in her back."

# 2

Sandy Wainright looked at the broken shaft sticking out of the back of the young humpback whale and felt the bile rising in her throat. She walked away from the dead whale, leaving the two Mexican fishermen and her research assistant, Paola Jiménez, staring after her.

The whale had already begun to decompose. The sickly-sweet smell of rotting flesh left to bake in the semi-tropical sun made her want to retch. Bloated and lying on its left side, the abdominal contents were spread across the rocks like yards of gray rope. Bite marks on the underside and near the head indicated that night predators had been coming here to feed for several days. Nearby, on the rocky embankment, half a dozen black vultures watched warily as the newcomers walked around the kill.

Normally, Sandy would have been somewhat philosophical about this. After all, we are all recyclable, she would tell her marine biology students. But this was different. As far as she was concerned, this whale was murdered. Brutally shot with an exploding harpoon and left to die a horrible death.

Sandy moved toward the whale's diminutive dorsal fin. She crouched down on one knee and felt along the opposite side until she found what she was looking for. She twisted her fingers and produced a portion of the sensor that had been attached to Number D-7's dorsal fin nearly thirteen months ago. She took a deep breath as she stood up.

Sandy was nearly five feet ten inches tall with long brown hair, which she kept tied in a ponytail or stuffed up underneath a faded Seattle Mariners cap. Her long legs were muscular and tanned from doing strenuous fieldwork in the sun. She looked over at Paola.

"Paola, can you get some photos of the flukes? We'll need those for the record."

Paola sniffed and nodded. She spoke in Spanish to the two fishermen who helped her lift the nine-foot flukes. The fishermen strained under the enormous weight. She produced a digital SLR camera from her backpack and shot several pictures, first of the ventral side, then of the dorsal aspect of the flukes. Humpback whale flukes could be used to identify individual whales throughout their lives from the patterns of white and black coloration and the scarring, nicks, and scratches on their underside.

After taking some final measurements of the deceased whale, Sandy and Paola climbed into their eighteen-foot Zodiac Pro 5.5. The inflatable, powered by a 150 horsepower four-stroke Honda motor, had a rigid hull and a center console. The seats folded out for sleeping when the two researchers had to be out for several days.

After thanking the fishermen, the two women pushed the boat out and fired up the motor. They began heading southward down the coast while the two Mexican fishermen turned their panga north to their fishing camp.

Neither woman spoke much for most of the trip back to their base camp at Isla Santa Cruz. The campsite served as a good field station. From here, it was easier to catch up to the three groups of humpbacks who plied these waters during the winter season.

They arrived in camp just as the sun was sinking in the west behind the mountains in a wash of peach and red colors. Sandy hardly noticed the sunset. They cleaned equipment and set about making dinner. Finally, she spoke.

"Who would do such a thing?" Her words, as they left her lips, carried an immense sadness and rage.

When I asked the *pangueros*," Paola took the small cook pot from the Coleman burner, "they said they didn't know of anyone whaling in these waters."

"Did you believe them?"

"I don't know. One of them got nervous when I started asking questions. He kept looking to the other one. I think they know something but don't want to talk about it."

"Alejandro won't let this rest," Sandy's voice took on a hard edge. "I won't let this rest."

"Be careful, *hermana*. I saw something else in their eyes. It was only a brief flash, like a sudden change in a wave."

"What? What did you see, Paola?"

"Fear. They were afraid."

"What would scare a *panguero* out here? Those guys have nerves of steel."

"Whatever it is that's out there, they're scared. Scared enough to lie about something."

"I'm going to call Alejandro in the morning. See if we can arrange to have that whale towed back to the Institute in La Paz and have a necropsy performed."

# 3

## *New York Times* Building, New York City

Emily Rosen's desk could best be described as something between a post-apocalyptic smorgasbord and the bottom of the recycling bin at the end of the month in Washington D.C. Two-day-old pizza crusts that looked like they were about to take on a life of their own were intermingled with just about every color and size scrap of paper strewn across the desktop.

The desk was merely a reflection of its owner. Emily Rosen was a petite, dark- haired reporter at the *New York Times*. She wasn't into health food or into women's high fashion. She was all about the story.

She covered the political scene in New York City, and had been at her present post for five years. As a native New Yorker, she loved nothing better than tunneling into the dark underbelly of the politics of the Big Apple. This had earned her the respect of many readers who followed her weekly column, as well as the ire of many local government officials, who discovered that she had somehow managed to uncover some of their unsavory dealings in their attempts to rise to the top.

Many of the rich and powerful had her on a watch list. Most in City Hall just thought of her as a major pain in the ass.

She strode into the department on the third floor of the *Times*, dressed in her usual attire: baggy cargo pants tucked into black combat boots and a black silk shirt under a black frock coat—reminiscent of Keanu Reeves in *The Matrix*. Her ensemble was topped off with a black beret that was pulled down low over her forehead. The thirty-year-old reporter wore black-rimmed glasses and no makeup. At her desk, Rosen shuffled through several paper scraps, muttering to herself. Finally, she located a sticky note, held it up, and said, "Ha!"

A group of her colleagues stood at one of the overhead television monitors located on one of the office walls. She walked over to them.

One of the reporters at the television looked up and saw her. "Hey, Rosen. Seen the news lately?"

"Hey guys, what's up?"

Jarvis, a paunchy redheaded reporter, looked over at Rosen and made a face. "Jesus, Rosen. Nice outfit. When are we going to get a look at your legs?"

Rosen peered over the top of her glasses at Jarvis. "Jarvis, have you had a vasectomy?"

"No. Why?"

"You should really consider it. The planet's gene pool would thank you."

Several reporters sniggered. Jarvis's face went crimson.

"Fuck you," Jarvis said.

"Whatever," said Emily.

The scene on the television was near the city courthouse. Several large and not-too-friendly-looking bodyguards were escorting a man dressed in a business suit down the steps. Several reporters were crowding around with microphones. On the screen, Emily Rosen was suddenly standing in front of the man in the suit.

One of the other reporters, a tall blonde woman in black slacks and a white shirt pointed. "Look! It's Rosen."

Rosen was heard to say, "Senator Donato, can you tell me about your association with Salvatore Mischetta? What about the purported mob ties and the laundering scheme linked to those emails?"

The senator snarled. "No comment. I am a respected United States Senator. I am not—and have never been—tied to any crime syndicate. Get her out of my face!"

A bodyguard took one of his bear-sized hands and covered Rosen's face with it, then pushed her aside like some bothersome insect. She went down in a heap on the steps.

The next portion of audio was bleeped out due to some very colorful vernacular coming from Rosen.

"Do you eat with that mouth?" Jarvis asked, a sneer forming on his lips.

A man appeared at the entrance to one of the offices on the other side of the newsroom. "Rosen! My office. Now!"

The banter stopped among the group gathered at the television. All eyes turned toward Emily Rosen. Most of them weren't sympathetic. Emily shrugged, grabbed her satchel from her desk, and strode toward the editor-in-chief's office.

Charles Dickerson stood leaning over his desk, veins popping in his neck and forearms, glaring at her.

"Close the door." He was a middle-aged man with a receding hairline and wire-rimmed glasses. The thing Rosen always noticed about him was that his face took on a nearly crimson color whenever she was around him. His jacket was off, his shirtsleeves were rolled up, and he looked like he had just bitten down on something vile.

Emily closed the door behind her—not that the door would prevent Dickerson's rage from being heard outside.

"What the hell was that all about?" Dickerson gestured toward the television screen on the wall of his office. "I told you to back off from Donato!"

"Sir, you don't know how close I am to busting his balls. He's running scared right now with those emails."

"You're busting my balls, Rosen. You can't confront a U.S. senator until you have all the facts. The emails are purely conjecture."

"Sir, they are not conjecture. My source—"

"What source? Who is this source?"

Emily bit her lip, looked off into some unknown distance, then returned her gaze to Dickerson. "I can't say, sir."

"You can't go around harassing a public figure. Maybe at the *Enquirer*, but not here."

"Damn it, Charlie. You know he's dirty as well as I do. All we have to do is line up the dots."

"That's for the Attorney General to figure out, not you. You report the news once it's broken. That's your job, Rosen."

Dickerson sighed deeply, then stared at Emily. "You're too close to this story. I'm pulling you."

"What? I'm close to breaking this one wide open!"

"You're off the story. Jarvis can pick it up from here."

"Jarvis is a douche bag—uh, sir."

"You're off and that's final. You're lucky I don't pink slip you right now. I'm reassigning you. To Baja, Mexico."

"Mexico? What for?"

"We need a feature article for the Sunday travel section on the effects of cartel activity on tourism. We want a slant that implies it's actually safe to travel in Mexico again."

"This is bullshit, Charlie. I'm not a travel writer."

"You don't have to take the assignment, Rosen. You can walk right out that door, and we'll get you an escort out of the building if you don't want to do your job."

She stared at Dickerson. He met her gaze with a stony countenance. The chief editor reached into his desk drawer, retrieved two travel vouchers, and slid them across his desk. "You leave tomorrow."

Emily looked at the door for a long moment, then stepped forward and took the vouchers. She turned to leave.

"And clean up your desk before the health department closes us down."

She went back to her desk, swept the sticky notes into her satchel and tossed the old pizza crusts into the trash. Marilyn, the blonde reporter, came over.

She spoke in a hushed tone. "What happened?"

"They got to Dickerson." Rosen tossed more trash into the receptacle.

"Who? Who got to Dickerson?"

"The senator's people. He knows I'm close. Now they're assigning Jarvis. He couldn't find his pecker in the dark."

Emily slung the paper-laden satchel over her shoulder. "I've been reassigned."

"Where to?"

"Mexico," replied Rosen coldly.

"Hey, I wouldn't mind an assignment in Mexico," Marilyn said, brightening.

Emily Rosen stared at her, shook her head, and walked toward the elevator.

# 4

Jake Spinner was sleeping off a mescal drunk. He was curled in a fetal position exactly in the same spot where he had passed out the night before—on the sandy floor in the storage shack of *El Pulpo Morado*, a seaside cantina in the sleepy little fishing village of San Jacinto. If Jake had been conscious, he would have been able to enjoy hearing the gentle lapping of waves against the golden shore. Presently he was tangled in a net hammock on the floor.

A middle-aged Mexican woman carrying a bag of groceries from the village *mercado* stepped into the closet and stared down at the human wreckage. She shook her head scornfully.

"*Ay, pendejo,*" she muttered under her breath.

The man passed out on the ground might have been handsome at one time. He was dressed in a pair of cotton shorts with a worn Hawaiian shirt that hadn't been changed in days.

She stared at the scar that crossed his left cheek. It was thin and white, highlighted by a deep tan and several weeks of beard growth. His unruly dark hair was tinged with gray and dusted with specks of sand.

The woman leaned in to shake him awake, then recoiled at the smell.

"*¡Cochino!*" She nudged him with her foot. "*Señor* Jake, wake up!"

At first, the inert form did not move. She nudged him harder. For her efforts, she was rewarded with a loud and explosive snort.

"Wake up, you crazy *gringo!*"

Spinner rolled away from her.

The next nudge with her foot sent the wind rushing from Jake's lungs. She stepped back quickly as the American rolled and sat up surprisingly fast for his size and level of inebriation. Wrapped in the hammock, he resembled a hairless sea lion that had been trapped in a ghost net.

15

Spinner looked at the woman, his eyes red and unfocused. "What?" He squinted at her, and then tried to open his eyes. "Aw, shit."

"You owe me 120 pesos, *borracho*. For the groceries. And another one hundred for straightening up your place."

"Juanita, it's too god damn early for you to be yammering at me about *dinero*." Jake's voice was harsh and gravelly after a long round of alcohol and cigarettes.

"It's almost 12:00. And that is 12:00 in the daytime."

"No way. What day?"

"Tuesday."

"Are you sure?" Jake scratched his beard and then scratched his balls. "Last time I checked it was Friday."

"*Pendejo.*" She held out her hand. "*Dinero! Ahora!*"

Jake fished into the pocket of his shorts for his wallet, not an easy task considering that he was still wrapped in the hammock. When he finally did produce the wallet, Juanita snatched it from his hand and fished out several colorful bills. She tucked the bills inside her blouse and tossed the wallet at Spinner, then turned to leave. At the door, she looked back scornfully.

"You are lucky that you bring many fish back to the village. Otherwise, I think the people would have drowned you at sea a long time ago."

Juanita turned and disappeared into the brilliant light. For a brief and unbalanced moment, Jake thought she appeared angelic in her departure. That visage quickly faded as a searing pain arced across his forehead and back to the rear of his skull, replacing the brief ethereal image.

After a series of contortions that made all of his joints pop and creak painfully, he freed himself from the entangling hammock and emerged from the supply closet into the main room of El Pulpo. The cantina was virtually empty except for Maximiliano, the young bartender, and a sunburned Italian couple sitting at a table over near one of the large open windows. A cool breeze was blowing in off the Gulf of California, carrying with it the sweet smell of ocean.

The young Italian couple, upon seeing the apparition that emerged from the liquor closet, stared for a moment, slack-jawed. When Jake nodded at them, they quickly turned away. He stumbled up to the bar, barely able to maintain an upright position.

The bartender, a lanky twenty-one-year-old with earrings and long hair tied back, looked at Jake, but did not approach him.

"Max, *mi amigo*, how about a bit of the hair o' the dog that bit me?" He reached for his wallet and frowned when he realized that Juanita had taken the last of his cash.

"Son of a bitch!" Jake forced a smile. "Hey, how 'bout it, Max? I pick up my check from the government a week from Thursday."

Max shook his head slowly. "Sorry, Señor Jake. *El Jefe* says no more credit for you."

"I can have some fresh yellowtail for the kitchen tomorrow."

"El Jefe says no more fish for tequila."

"Ungrateful bastard."

Later that afternoon, Jake sat in the shade of a small cantina facing the village square. Today was market day and many of the villagers were crowded into the square, sitting at canopied booths, and selling everything from colorful cloth to cheap jewelry and chocolate covered grasshoppers. He was nursing a hangover with a Bloody Mary.

He had moved down here seven years ago for the fishing after his marriage had nosedived and his ex had taken just about everything except for his check from the VA. Maybe it was the PTSD. Maybe Jake hadn't gotten enough love from his mother and father when he was a kid. Maybe he was simply a world-class asshole. She had said she couldn't live with him anymore and moved out.

His pension wasn't much. But it was enough to keep him in a boat for fishing, a cheap place to live, and enough left over for food and drink. These days, more was dedicated to the latter.

Across the square, Jake spied a familiar figure stepping into a booth featuring knockoff jewelry and gangsta-type bling. Jake had known Macario since he was about thirteen. He had become friends with Gustavo, Macario's father, after he had hired them as fishing guides. They were from the *Kumeyaay* tribe, and their village was a couple hours north of San Jacinto. The native people from this part of Baja had a longstanding reputation as seafarers, and Gustavo Silvano knew these waters like no one else.

There had been years of tension between the Mexican government and the Kumeyaays. Treated like second-class citizens, most of the villagers lived in poverty. Since fishing had been restricted due to the falling fish stocks, their ability to earn a living had been curtailed even more.

Jake stood, finished the last of his Bloody Mary, and ambled across the square to the booth where Macario was looking at the trays on the tables. As he stepped into the booth, he saw Macario pull a wad of pesos from his front pocket and peel off several to pay for a gaudy looking necklace, the type that gang bangers would wear in East L.A.

Jake sidled up next to him. "Fishing must be real good these days," Jake said in Spanish, as he picked up an ornate silver bracelet and examined it.

Macario spun quickly, stuffing the money back into his pants pocket. "Oh, *Señor* Jake. How are you doing?"

"Apparently, not as well as you, kid." Jake didn't look directly at him.

"Papá and I had a couple of good weeks. Americans came up from La Paz and wanted to go out. They paid us well."

"What were you fishing for?"

"Mahi mahi mostly. Twice we got into schools of crevalle jacks."

"Hmm. Whereabouts did you go?"

Macario fidgeted. "Near Isla Tortuga. Did some deep water trolling up north."

Jake looked at Macario, who met his gaze and then looked away suddenly. His tribe did not make regular eye contact. In their culture it was considered rude. But Macario's quickly averted gaze spoke volumes. The kid was lying through his teeth.

"How's your dad these days?" Jake said, with a brief hint of a smile.

"He's good. Busy with the charters."

"You tell him I said hello. Tell him it's time for the three of us to go fishing again."

Jake's mind flashed briefly on the wad of cash in Macario's pocket. It was going to be a long dry week until that government check came in, but he dismissed the idea of asking Macario for a loan until next week. His pride prevented him from borrowing from his friend's son. But there was something else. Wherever Macario got this money, one thing was for certain. He didn't come by this much cash from taking gringo fishing tourists for a joyride in the Gulf.

Jake touched Macario's shoulder, making the young *indio* meet his gaze. "You're not getting into selling drugs, are you, son? That's some mean shit and you'll end up headless hanging from a streetlamp."

Macario pulled back. "No, Señor Jake. I swear! No drugs. It's from fishing!"

Jake relaxed his grip, then half-smiled. "Okay, kid. No worries. Just wanted to make sure you're safe."

Macario looked very uncomfortable, his eyes darting around the booth. "No problem. Look, I gotta go. *Mis compadres* are waiting for me."

"Tell your dad to call me." Jake made the universal sign for a telephone, placing his hand near his ear.

"I will. See you, Jake."

The young man turned on his heel and left the booth quickly.

Jake watched him disappear into the crowd of villagers milling around the square.

The kid standing behind the tables asked, "You gonna buy that bracelet, *hombre?*"

Jake tossed the bracelet back, and the kid nearly dropped it. "I already have one just like it."

As he walked toward his bungalow, Jake felt something he had not felt for a long time. The hairs on the back of his neck were standing up and his gut had tightened. Somewhere nearby, the shit was about to hit the fan.

# 5

Alejandro Cabrillo waited in a large hallway outside the doors of the Minister of Fisheries office in Mexico City. The high vaulted ceiling, tall windows and polished tile floors lent a chill to the already drafty interior. The inside of the lavish hallway had ornate decorative columns that went from floor to ceiling—a remnant from pre-revolutionary Mexico.

Alejandro sat in an old leather chair that should have been retired thirty years ago. Late afternoon sunlight filtered in through high windows creating bright panes of light across the tiles.

He had been waiting outside Director Figueroa's office for nearly forty-five minutes and was getting irritated. He had already turned in the Budget Request Form and the report about the dead whale. Now he went over his notes—twice—in preparation for their meeting. He rechecked the numbers and made sure the budgetary requests were all in order. In his hands he held the necropsy report from the lab in La Paz. He looked at the report. D-7, the whale that had affectionately been called Valentine—because she was first encountered on Valentine's Day four years ago—had died from massive blood loss and tissue destruction.

The shaft of the harpoon had penetrated the left lower lobe of her lung and had partially discharged, rupturing the surrounding tissue. Normally, the shaft would be aimed at the heart so as to hasten death and decrease the death throes the whale would suffer. This whale had died a much slower and more agonizing death.

Alejandro felt numb. The young humpback had been a favorite among the team. Early on, D-7 was an exuberant whale, often breaching and tail-lobbing near the boat. Alejandro thought back to last year when he had snorkeled next to Valentine and photographed her underwater. It was the first time he had ever been that close to a living whale. A framed picture taken by a colleague hung in his office, depicting a diminutive Alejandro finning alongside the thirty-three-foot humpback.

The door to the Minister's office opened and a slender woman dressed in a blue business suit smiled at Alejandro.

"The minister will see you now, Dr. Cabrillo."

She led him through the door into a large office with several desks placed around the room. They approached double cherrywood doors with colorful stained-glass panes. The seal for the Department of Fisheries was embossed on the doors, along with the name "Alfonso Figueroa" and "Minister of Fisheries" stenciled below the seal.

The secretary knocked gently and opened one door, letting Alejandro walk in. She closed the door behind him.

Alfonso Figueroa sat behind a huge, ornate wood desk. *Ostentatious* was Alejandro's first thought upon seeing the man behind the desk. Another man sat across from the Minister of Fisheries. He was Asian, probably Japanese. He looked serious, yet oddly amused. He wore a dark blue suit. Although smaller in frame than Figueroa, the man's carriage conveyed power.

"Ah, Alejandro. Please come in," Figueroa said as he stood. The other man stood as well.

The minister gestured toward the Asian man. "Please allow me to introduce you to Mr. Hirokan Yoshimatsu. He serves on the board for the Japanese Fishing Industry. This is Dr. Alejandro Cabrillo, who runs our research facility in La Paz."

The Asian performed a short bow. Alejandro bowed back. The businessman never took his eyes off Alejandro.

"A pleasure to meet you, sir," said Alejandro.

"I have been telling the undersecretary of the work you are doing at the facility, specifically your work with tagging and following humpback whales in the Gulf of California."

Alejandro was surprised. "Are you interested in whale conservation?"

"Of course we are." Mr. Yoshimatsu, his lips hinting at a smile, continued, "We are interested in all aspects of conservation. We want to extend these resources for as long as possible."

Alejandro bristled inwardly but hoped he could maintain a poker face since the Japanese businessman was watching him for a reaction. He smiled. "From my position, it is difficult to consider them just renewable resources."

"That is exactly why I want you to give Mr. Yoshimatsu and his colleagues a grand tour of the facility in La Paz. Perhaps if they see how you do your satellite tracking system, they can use this information to help better manage their own stocks."

Alejandro started to speak but saw that Figueroa had pinned him with a cautionary look.

He swallowed his anger and looked at Yoshimatsu. "We would be delighted to show you and your colleagues our facility."

"Very good," Yoshimatsu's smile broadened. "I will have my secretary call you to make the arrangements."

"There is an upcoming international summit for fisheries management in Kyoto this summer," Figueroa said. "I would like to open up the channels of communication between the Mexican government and our friends from Japan to find ways to preserve dwindling resources."

"We look forward to working with the Mexican government in these and many other endeavors. Now, gentlemen, if you will excuse me, I have another pressing engagement." He bowed to Figueroa. "I look forward to our next meeting, Minister." He turned to Alejandro and again bowed, this one shorter and more abrupt. "Until we meet again, Dr. Cabrillo."

The Japanese businessman turned smartly on his heel, and Figueroa rushed to open the door for him. Closing it, the Minister turned back and glared at Alejandro.

"I want you to give the gentleman from Japan and his associates every possible attention when they visit. They are to have full access to your facilities."

"But not the data! We're still in the preliminary stages of data acquisition. Turning over data to anyone at this time could not only be misleading but could endanger our project."

"Cooperation is at the forefront if we are to establish new trade relations with the Japanese." Figueroa stared at Alejandro. "I expect it from all levels. This is a top priority for you and your associates."

Alejandro could barely contain his rage. Someone had just killed one of his whales and now the Minister of Fisheries was more than willing to sell out the entire research project just so he could score points with the Japanese fishing industry.

The minister continued, "Our government budget committee has approved your budget request for the next year, Dr. Cabrillo. Congratulations. However, I have been asked to oversee the granting of funds for the tracking program. The purchase of the upgraded tracking telemetry equipment will be contingent upon the quality of your research and your cooperation with this office."

Alejandro met the Minister's gaze. "I understand, Minister."

"Good. Please keep me informed of any new developments with your missing whales."

Alejandro walked down the steps of the commanding government building and was caught up in the busy midday foot traffic of people on their way to lunch.

But now, the last thing he could think about was lunch or a siesta. He was consumed with a mixture of fury, helplessness, and worry. Figueroa was exposing his entire project. Alejandro had picked up a very bad vibe from Yoshimatsu. Whatever his intentions, conservation was not part of the Japanese businessman's plan.

Everyone knew that the Japanese had been shut down in the Antarctic for the past few years, due to the efforts of some bold campaigns by groups such as The Sea Shepherd Conservation Society. They were funded by private citizens repulsed by the heinous slaughter of whales in the Southern Ocean under the guise of scientific research. Alejandro couldn't help but think that the Japanese, insatiable in their hunger for seafood, were exploring more hidden markets with less publicity and hassle.

But he had no proof.

He pulled his cell phone from his jacket pocket and speed-dialed a number. The phone rang several times before a female voice answered.

"Hola, Sandy. How's it going?"

"You don't sound too good, Alejandro. Did the meeting not go well?"

"Well, the good news—we got the funding we asked for. Here's the bad news. Figueroa is holding hostage our request for tracking software. It depends on us kissing the asses of some Japanese dignitaries. And on top of that, we're supposed to share information from our project with the Japanese Fisheries Department. Complete transparency."

"What?" Sandy's voice rose. "Are you kidding?"

"I wish I were."

"Talk about your fox in the henhouse."

# 6

*T*he family of Pacific bottlenose dolphins swam leisurely through the blue-green waters of the Gulf of California. The matriarch and her young calf traveled in the typical echelon formation, the youngster just below her, but still close enough to use his mother's slipstream to decrease the water's resistance. Intermittently, the calf would touch his mother's pectoral fin or nuzzle her side. She responded by gently placing her pectoral fin on his. There were ten dolphins in all making up a mother-calf subgroup, including the older female and her three-month-old calf. Two of the calves born in the previous year were now rambunctious, curious adolescents.

On this calm spring morning the family was heading toward the familiar sound of a motor. It wasn't the motor that attracted them. They were going to visit the man in the boat. The old female had discovered several years ago that this human was particularly good at catching fish, and, upon investigation, discovered she could relieve the man of some of his catch. The family dined on fish they normally would not hunt. They only had to suffer the explosive noises emanating from the slow-moving human.

After eating their fill, the old female sometimes floated at the surface, watching the erratic movements of the human on the boat. He spoke abruptly, sometimes loudly, but she could not decipher his strange vocalizations. She sensed the human was deeply wounded, but that the illness was not of a physical nature.

Suddenly a flash of silver caught her attention. From the depths, a crevalle jack thrashed back and forth, a line attached to its mouth. The jack was being pulled up, but it dove and the dolphin could hear the whine of the line going tight again. The dolphin family moved in. Breakfast was waiting.

The Gulf of California appeared as a huge lake, the ocean flat without even a hint of capillary waves. The day was unseasonably warm and Jake Spinner sat back in his chair at the stern—barefoot, shirt unbuttoned, wearing cargo shorts. He had several fishing poles in steel holders on either side of the stern. In a large, metal ice chest near his feet, he already had thirty pounds of yellowtail, crevalle jacks and one mahi mahi. The mahi mahi and the yellowtail would garner him some much-needed scratch until he could pick up his check in a few days. He hadn't had a drink in over four days and he was becoming surly.

Spinner reached into the ice chest and produced a plastic Gatorade bottle filled with water. He took a swig. It bore a strong smell of fish. Jake poured some of the water onto one of his hands and wet his face. He replaced the bottle and was rewarded with a loud thump as one of the fish thrashed about, gasping to breathe.

*This Side Up* was the only lady in Spinner's life. He had purchased the 1982 Bertram 31 shortly after his divorce nine years ago. The Yamaha twin diesel engine could bring the boat to a cruising speed of twenty-three knots with a top speed of thirty-two knots on a flat sea. The cruiser had a range of 400 miles, much more advantageous than the smaller pangas the local fishermen used. The boat could comfortably carry six passengers for charters, and the cushions could be converted into open deck sleeping mats. He had modified it so meals could be prepared in the main cabin from a propane stove. The stern held built-in ice chests to handle the volume of fish his clients reeled in.

He looked over his shoulder and checked the position of the sun in the sky. Another hour and he had better head in. Even though the weather was pleasantly warm, it was still winter in Baja. As soon as the sun went down, it would get cold and Jake didn't have any cold weather clothes along on this trip. If the seas remained flat, it would be a short ride back to San Jacinto.

He lifted the fishing line and checked the mackerel on the end of the line. The Penn Bluewater Carnage rod felt balanced in his hands. He adjusted the drag on the Fathom two-speed reel and brought the rig over his shoulder. With a calculated snap of his forearm and wrist, he arced the baitfish high, twenty-five yards to the stern. The mackerel landed with a satisfying plop. Two more trolling rods stood in their holders ready to be deployed when he weighed anchor. He began reeling in slowly.

Without warning, the surface of the quiet waters erupted in a series of splashes and rooster tails. Dark gray dorsal fins cut through the water. Jake heard the familiar *phhhttt*, the explosive exhalations of a group of bottlenose dolphins circling his boat.

"Stay away from the god damn fishing lines, you guys," Jake said irritably. "I don't have enough baitfish left to feed your lazy asses!" He reeled in one of the rods and cast it out again, the mackerel flying through the air for thirty yards before it hit the surface. "Why don't you guys try something new and different for a change? Like go out and fish for yourselves?"

One of the dolphins, an old female, had a distinctive marking on her forehead. It looked like a white star that crowned the top of her melon, just in front of her blowhole. There were numerous scars across her back. A deep whitish scar curved behind her dorsal fin. Spinner wondered what battles this old girl had endured in her lifetime. Both of them bore scars from surviving on this big blue ball called Earth.

The young dolphin that swam at her side had four small white spots on its melon and a white blaze across the back of its flukes. The female and her calf lay at the surface, logging, the small dolphin nuzzling against its mother's flank. They eyed the man in the boat with curiosity. Both dolphins vocalized in that high-pitched squeal that sounded vaguely like someone was rubbing their hands across an inflated balloon.

The two dolphins continued to watch Spinner as the other members of the pod fished near his boat.

"I already told you, I don't have anything for you. Besides, where's your dignity? You're supposed to be apex predators." Jake looked at them, wondering to himself, *What the hell do you know about dignity, Spinner?*

He reached down and flipped the lid on the ice chest. Fumbling inside, he produced a freshly-caught smaller crevalle jack. He tossed it at the old scarred female. She swam over casually, nosed the fish, and then swallowed it whole. He threw the other jack to the smaller dolphin, probably Star's offspring. They always seemed to travel together. The younger dolphin nudged the fish, then took the jack in its jaws, flipped it in the air, caught it, and swallowed it.

Spinner shook his head. "Now beat it. You're scaring the fish."

He leaned back and watched them go about their day. A restless feeling had been creeping up on him the past two months. It gnawed on the periphery of his conscience when he was semi-alert, as he was today. He felt the pull of other ports, a feeling that the smaller latitudes may be the next destination in his runaway life. He heard Costa Rica was nice but had become overpopulated with retired Americans. Perhaps he should go to one of the smaller, lesser-known Central American countries. Fluent in several Middle Eastern dialects, he had easily picked up Spanish when he moved to Baja.

He hadn't always been a loner. He once had a wife and dreams and desires just like anyone else. He vaguely remembered being at the top of his class at West

Point. All of his earlier life became a blur after the explosion in Kabul. He'd been three days from being transferred back to the States after four deployments in Afghanistan. The IED had gone off less than ten feet away, killing two of his men and knocking him twenty feet into the air. When he woke up, he didn't know who or where he was. Shrapnel had pierced his gut, resulting in the removal of two feet of intestine by the trauma surgeon.

After his discharge, Jake Spinner's life had slowly unraveled. Constant headaches, flashbacks, bouts of extreme depression, and rage became more frequent and explosive. One night, he woke from a troubled sleep, grabbed his standard issue Beretta M9, walked out into the backyard, and emptied the entire magazine into a palm tree. He calmly walked back to the bedroom, placed the gun in a drawer, and went back to bed. His wife, Carolyn, was sitting bolt upright in bed, her eyes wide with terror.

The next day, while the heavily sedated and drunken Jake slept, Carolyn packed quietly, slipped out the door, and never looked back.

He had relinquished just about everything in the divorce settlement, except for his truck and his personal savings account. He still loved Carolyn but felt that she'd earned everything in the settlement. The last few years of their marriage had been hell for her. He used most of the remaining funds to buy *This Side Up*, then began a meandering exodus southward, finally making landfall near the end of the Baja Peninsula. He'd met Gustavo Silvano, a native fisherman from a local coastal tribe. Gustavo was the best fishing guide Spinner had ever known, and they soon formed a fishing charter partnership. Spinner supplied the boat and Gustavo obtained the necessary permits to operate a charter in Mexican waters. As Spinner's drinking increased, the partnership dissolved.

He shook his head, as if the movement would rid him of the old memory. What he really wanted right now was a drink. Any drink. Grain alcohol would do the trick. Hell, he might not even turn down a can of Sterno. *Jesus, Spinner, get a grip. You ain't that bad. Yet.*

Abruptly, something large hit one of the lines that trailed off the stern. The line twanged tight and then began to move. Spinner could tell by the sharp pull and the way the fish ran that he had hooked into a good-sized mahi mahi.

He bolted up from his chair and grabbed the pole. He felt the power of the fish and set the hook. Releasing the spool, he let the fish run.

"C'mon, baby." Spinner gritted his teeth. "Come to Papa."

He felt a little slack in the line and began reeling in feverishly. The fish pulled back and tried to run again. Spinner leaned into the pull and reeled again, making the fish give in by inches. He reeled again, pulled, reeled, pulled. His body leaked sweat, his nostrils picking up the acrid scent of processed alcohol leaching from his pores. Jake's arms cramped from the mahi mahi's desperate attempts to lose the hook.

He continued to pull and reel until he caught a flash of silver below the water. The mahi mahi made a brief run across the stern before making a last attempt to go deep. Spinner pulled and reeled in more line. The fish was tiring. One more good pull and it would be his. He was thinking about which restaurant would pay the top dollar for this fish. *Tonight wasn't going to be a dry night after all!*

Then the line went slack.

"What the fuck?" He reeled in quickly. A moment later he pulled a bloody fish head alongside the transom.

"Son of a bitch!" Jake pulled the head on board and stared at it. The fish had been shredded. Ragged chunks of flesh hung loosely from its gill plates. He looked at the head disgustedly, then unhooked it and flung it back into the ocean, swearing the entire time.

He turned to place the rod back in its holder. Movement at the surface caught his attention. The late afternoon sun was reflecting low on the water. He squinted and caught a flash of something on the surface. He cocked his head and saw a dolphin on its side looking up at him. In its jaws, it still held what was left of the mahi mahi.

Spinner stalked over to the gunwale and pulled loose the gaff, holding it aloft like a spear. He eyed the distance between himself and the dolphin that floated at the surface playing with the mahi mahi carcass. He brought his arm back in a poor semblance of a javelin thrower's pose. In two gulps the dolphin downed the fish. Turning on its side, it eyed Spinner and began to emit a series of high-pitched squeaks.

He hesitated. His arm relaxed and he lowered the gaff. "Oh, hell. Guess we all gotta eat sometime."

The next morning, Spinner drove over to Puerto Nacimiento, the pueblo inhabited mostly by the Kumeyaays. He had sold the two mahi mahis and had garnered enough dinero to put five bucks worth of gas in his old beat-up Chevy half-ton, buy a liter of Tecate and get a meal.

It was late morning and he was going to see Gustavo Silvano. He hadn't seen his friend in a few months. He reflected on the fact that Gustavo and his son were about the only friends he had in all four cardinal directions.

Jake arrived at the Silvano house on the outskirts of Puerto Nacimiento. It resembled all the other structures common to this small fishing village—a low-slung concrete and stucco style. The walls were thick but the windows were all open, small curtains wafting through the openings from the ocean breeze. He stepped up to the front door and knocked. A moment later, a woman answered. She had lines in her face that made her appear much older than her forty-two years. Her skin was the color of mahogany and her dark hair had streaks of gray. When she saw the visitor was Spinner, a visible frown formed on her face. A novella was blaring from a large flat-screened television behind her.

"He's in the back," she said tersely.

In his most affable voice, Spinner spoke in Spanish. "You wouldn't happen to have a cold beer in the fridge, would you, Marta? It was a parched and dusty drive over here."

Marta responded by closing the door in his face.

He felt the rush of air as the door slammed shut. *I guess not.*

He sauntered around the back of the house, past a derelict panga and several old motors on wooden stands. Old fishing poles lay against the wall and covered a warped wooden table. Various boat parts lay strewn about the yard. A flea-bitten, skinny brown dog raised its head from a torn car seat and growled as he passed. The dog was that mixture common to Mexico that had become a breed unto themselves over years of uncontrolled selection.

He found Gustavo Silvano sitting in his panga, *El Tiburón*, which was resting atop a rusty trailer. Gustavo looked up from the net he was mending and nodded at Jake. He was wearing a faded chambray shirt and jeans with well-worn tennis shoes. His arms and face were deep chestnut resembling the fine hardwood trim on a fancy sloop. His dark eyes were bright with an innate inquisitiveness.

"Hey, Tavo, *¿Cómo estás?*"

Gustavo managed a weak smile and motioned for Jake to climb up into the boat. With some effort, Spinner hoisted himself over the gunwale and flopped down, breathless, opposite his friend and fishing-guide partner.

"You need to stop drinking and join a gym," Gustavo said, without looking up.

"I'm at the top of my game," Spinner replied, still trying to catch his breath.

Gustavo grunted and went back to mending his net.

"Say, amigo, you don't happen to have anything to drink on board, do you?"

Gustavo nodded his head toward the house. "The woman says no liquor in the house."

"We're not in the house at the moment. Man, you'd think the sea had all but dried up." He pulled his old ball cap off his head, wiped his brow with his sleeve and held the cap up to block the sun. He wanted to see Gustavo's face.

"How's the guide business these days?"

"Some good days. Some bad."

"That's a nice TV you got back at your house. Fish guiding must be okay." Spinner looked at the new Yamaha 150 4-stroke attached to the stern of the panga. "That's a hell of a nice motor. When did you get that?"

"A couple of months ago. It's got 200 hours on it. Got a good deal." Gustavo faltered in his mending by half a beat, but it was enough to let Jake know that his friend was hiding something.

"I saw Macario the other day in the plaza. He was carrying a sizable wad of cash."

Gustavo stopped his net mending, staring at his calloused hands. "He told me he ran into you."

"What's he into, Tavo? He's not mixed up with the Sinaloa Cartel, is he?"

Gustavo shook his head violently. He looked into Spinner's eyes, hidden by his aviator Ray Bans. "No, Jake. No drugs. He's the *guía* for some wealthy foreign sport fishermen. They are paying both of us to take them out."

"What kind of foreigners?" Jake squinted up at the sun, then back at Gustavo.

"Asian. Chinese, I think. They don't talk to us much. One of their hombres is the contact between their group and us. He does all the talking and arranging."

"What are they fishing for?"

"They want *totoaba*, black sea bass, shark. Also, big tuna."

"Some of those are illegal. Is that why the big money?"

"*Sí.* They pay us well and ask us to look the other way."

Spinner pulled a half-burned cheroot from his shirt pocket and lit up. He stared pensively out at the blue-green ocean.

"Fisheries people in on this?"

Gustavo shrugged. "I don't think so. I think they're just a bunch of *Chinos ricos.*"

Spinner stood stiffly and stretched. "Glad to hear Macario isn't involved with the cartel. Those bastards would chew him up and shit him out dead."

After a moment, Jake turned to Gustavo. "Hey! I have an idea. Why don't you and Macario and me start running charters again? We could use *This Side Up* and show those Asians some primo fishing spots that we can get to quicker. We can fit six of them on board and split the profits three ways. Between your skills and my boat, we can't lose."

Gustavo stopped his mending and looked up at Spinner. "Jake, you're my friend. But I cannot put Marta through what she endured the last time. When you stopped showing up for charters with clients standing at the dock, we nearly lost everything. No one thought we were trustworthy or reliable."

Spinner bowed his head momentarily, then stared out at the brilliant, azure Gulf of California. "Yeah, I guess I haven't been the best of partners. But I swear to God, I'll make it work this time."

This time it was Gustavo's turn to look out to sea. "I grow tired of fishing. I have thoughts that I have committed great sins against the Ocean Mother."

"What do you mean? You're about as holy and reverent about the ocean as anyone I've ever met. And if anyone doubts that, tell them to come talk to me. I've spent weeks at a time on the water with you. Good weather and bad."

For the first time, Spinner noticed a deep sadness in Gustavo's eyes, which momentarily caught him off guard.

"Gustavo, is everything all right? You can tell me."

Gustavo bit his lip, then resumed mending his net. "No, my friend, it is nothing. Some days the weight of living bears down on you more than others."

Spinner started to clamber out of the boat but was stopped by Gustavo's hand grabbing his forearm.

"Jake, do you still have connections in *El Norte*? Can you arrange for work visas?"

Spinner turned and looked directly at his friend. "I don't know. Why?"

"Lately, Marta and I have been talking. We want Macario to know something other than this little village and the meager living that fishing brings us."

"I haven't talked to my buddy in, what, maybe three years now."

"Does he still have that restaurant?"

Jake pulled his fishing cap high onto his forehead. "I don't know, Tavo. Last time I heard, it was still up and running. You need temporary work visas."

"Macario and I could do construction. Marta could clean houses."

Gustavo lifted his head and stared at the building waves out in the Gulf of California. Spinner saw several things in his old friend's face: a mixture of sadness, remorse, and what Jake could have sworn was fear. Gustavo turned and looked at Spinner. "I think it is time for us to leave."

Jake met his gaze. "I'll see what I can do."

As Jake walked from behind the house and onto the sandy street, he passed the front window and saw movement as Marta stared at him. She pulled the curtain closed in disgust.

When he got to his truck, something down the road caught his attention. A black Ford Excursion, covered in road dust, was parked on the side of the road. Inside, two men sat watching him. Even though the glare of the windshield hampered his view, Jake could swear that the two men behind the windshield looked Asian.

For the second time in as many days, he felt the hair stand up on the back of his neck.

# 7

Emily Rosen stood in front of the entrance to the La Paz airport and stared up at the stand of tall, thin palm trees, their fronds undulating in the late afternoon breeze. She had seen palm trees in arboretums and at the New York Zoo, but this was the first time she had seen them as part of the landscape for an airport.

She looked oddly out of place, standing there dressed in Gothic black, wearing a skull tee shirt and black knee-high boots adorned with silver buckles. Her black beret was cocked to the side of her head and her black Ray Bans made her look like an aging punk rocker or Euro-trash from the Balkans. Most of the passengers who walked by her were dressed for warm weather, wearing brightly colored clothing that smacked of a rendezvous with a long stretch of sandy beach and a frosty margarita.

The first thing she did when she got outside was to light up a cigarette. The flight from New York to Los Angeles and then the connecting flight to La Paz seemed to take an eternity. She barely had enough time at LAX to grab a few quick puffs in the bathroom.

She was still stewing over her removal from her story at the *Times*. She knew there was a pretty good chance she wouldn't have a job when she went back. The senator's influence reached deep into the various institutions of the city.

Rosen took a long drag from her cigarette and looked skyward once again, shuddering. Other than the airport terminal, the palm trees were the tallest structures she could see. She felt a sense of imposing dread, like the open spaces were threatening to swallow her up in their vastness. She already missed the comfort of all the large buildings, the concrete, and all the noise and grime of the Big Apple.

It was too late in the day to get started on her new story. The only thing Rosen wanted to find right now was a comfortable bathtub and a place to link onto the internet. She pulled her iPad from her backpack and scrolled through until she found the hotel where she'd be staying. She wondered if the Los Sueños Azules had room service. She wondered if they even spoke English. She also wondered if the tales of giant cockroaches in Mexican hotels were greatly exaggerated. In New York—now we're talking cockroaches! Although she could navigate around the menu in a French restaurant, she had not spent much time learning Spanish while at NYU. She actually didn't even like Mexican food.

It was going to be a long two-week assignment.

She flagged down a taxi, a green sedan that looked wrinkled. As it pulled over to the curb, she saw that the wrinkles were actually hundreds of small dents and scratches that covered most of the side panels, hood, and fenders.

The cab driver's name was Chuy, which Emily soon learned was a nickname for Jesús. She thought it bizarre that parents would name their kid after the Messiah. She wondered what school must have been like for him.

Chuy was quite gregarious. As he wove through the late afternoon traffic at a Mr. Toad's Wild Ride pace, he kept eyeing her in the rearview mirror. He asked if she would be interested in going to the local disco that evening.

"I hate discos," she said flatly.

"It's okay. I know good places to eat. How about sports bar?"

"Jesus H. Christ," Rosen muttered.

"How you know my middle name?" Chuy whipped his head around.

"What?"

"Humberto. My middle name is Humberto."

Rosen sighed. "How long until we're at the hotel?"

The Los Sueños Azules hotel was located in downtown La Paz between a *ferretería* and a tortilla factory. Rosen wasn't sure about the ferretería. She wondered if the Mexican people had a thing for weasels. She was brought up to speed by the uppity desk clerk who informed her that a ferretería was a hardware store.

Her boss had made reservations for her at this hotel. Once rather upscale, the hotel was now at least forty years old. The furniture was outdated and tattered and the tile floors, once smooth and white, were now scuffed and dull. Her room was small and dark, with old wood paneling and a bed with a frilled bedspread depicting a green landscape from somewhere in the Mexican highlands. A small, cube-shaped television sat atop the dresser. On the wall behind the television were faded photographs of La Paz circa 1960. The room smelled of stale cigarette smoke.

She tossed her suitcase on the bed and walked over to the window. Pulling back the curtains, Rosen saw that she was looking at the adobe-stucco wall of a tortilla factory. She hadn't expected anything else from her editor, Charles Dickerson. You could say what you wanted about him, but generous wasn't a word that came to mind.

Rosen inhaled the smell of burnt flour and lard. Not bad. Even her stomach voiced its approval.

When she turned on the lights in the small bathroom, she heard a scurrying sound like hundreds of tiny feet hightailing it south. She spotted several of the biggest roaches she had ever seen. They gave her a fleeting glance, then disappeared down the shower drain.

"FUCK! Fuck! Fuck you, you little bastards! My bathroom! My shower!"

She grabbed one of the bath towels from the rack and tossed it onto the drain. She looked under the sink for some kind of insecticide, to no avail. She went back into the bedroom, located an empty vase, and placed it on the towel.

She took her shoe off and waved it at the covered drain. "I dare you to come back up."

She took a cold shower, but not by choice. The hot water heater appeared to be out of commission at the moment. Shivering, she looked between her feet at the drain, wondering if she was being watched. She dressed quickly and went down the tiled steps to the lobby.

After querying several people there and a few more on the street, Rosen was able to locate a small, open-air restaurant near the *malecón,* the boardwalk near the beach. She recognized it by the brightly colored Christmas lights the hotel clerk had told her about. She was seated outside at a small table near the water's edge.

She ate alone, but this was nothing new. She always ate alone. She looked up from her seat, the ocean breeze caressing her face. The restaurant was almost full. Most of the seated patrons were gringos, the majority being couples from the States, but she was able to discern a few Canadian accents. Everyone looked like they were having a great time.

Emily's attention was drawn to a couple sitting on the other side of the room near a window facing out to sea. The man and woman appeared to be in their late twenties or early thirties. The woman was a striking blonde, wearing a black strapless cocktail dress and heels. Her male companion wore a light blazer with a white shirt open at the neck. From the way they were leaning toward the center of the table, Emily figured they were lovers.

She felt a dull pain in her chest, a long-suppressed memory attempting to bubble up through her granite veneer. How long had it been since she and Mark had sat across from each other, staring into each other's eyes, each dressed to please the other, hanging onto the intent of every word.

She shook her head as if trying to fling the memory out of her conscious mind. *That was then, this is now,* her pragmatic mind spoke. *You got over it a long time ago.*

The waiter arrived with chips and salsa. Emily ordered a Mexican beer with her seafood enchiladas. When he delivered the bottle of Pacifico with a cold glass, she started to pour the beer into the glass, then stopped. She wiped down the lip of the bottle with her napkin and then took a draught. The last thing she needed on this shitty assignment was to wind up doing the Aztec two-step.

The beer tasted surprisingly good. She ordered another after her meal came and started to feel the combined effects of a long day on a plane. After finishing dinner, Emily decided she didn't want to experience any more of the nightlife along the malecón. She headed straight back to her hotel.

She was relieved to find that the roach armada had not resurfaced. She flipped on the television, stripped and quickly dressed in a pair of ratty sweatpants and a tee shirt. She channel-surfed until she landed on a local news program. It was all in Spanish. She was about to give up on trying to correlate the rapid-fire Spanish with the images that danced before her eyes when something on the television caught her attention. Footage of large whales breaching and slapping their tails at the surface of the ocean mesmerized her. Emily had never seen a whale in the wild. A tall, handsome man was being interviewed by the reporter. The caption under his image read, *"Alejandro Cabrillo, Director, Instituto de Mamíferos Marinos La Paz."*

More whale images appeared. Mexican fishermen were interviewed. Then an image of a whale carcass appeared, beached on a sandy stretch of shoreline. Black objects were hopping over its back. When the camera was able to zoom in, Rosen realized the black objects were vultures feasting on the beached whale.

She was riveted to the screen. When the images turned to another story, she stared into empty space. Tomorrow, after she did her information gathering for her bullshit assignment, she was going to pay a visit to the institute.

Emily Rosen wanted to see a whale.

She was not destined to have whale dreams. Soon after she turned out the light, the couple in the next room were going for the Guinness Book of Records. The bed kept banging against the wall in an annoyingly steady cadence. The only good thing was that she learned some colorful new words in Spanish.

After nearly two hours of this, she turned on the light, sat up in bed and sighed deeply. Movement out of the corner of her eye caused her to look toward the bathroom. A cockroach stared at her, then scurried back into the darkness.

Rosen swung her legs out of bed and picked up one of her black combat boots. She walked toward the bathroom, raising the shoe above her head.

"Okay, you little fuckers. Let's dance."

# 8

Hirokan Yoshimatsu sat in a sauna, leaning against the cedar wall, his eyes closed. From the rise and fall of his chest, he appeared to be asleep. He was naked except for a towel draped over his hips. A naked, statuesque blonde woman walked over to a rack of heated stones. In the reddish light, the sweat glistening from her skin made her appear to flow across the floor. She splashed water on the heated stones and a fresh cloud of steam erupted into the closed room.

Yoshimatsu was a man who did not require much sleep. Most nights he averaged two to three hours. He had trained himself many years ago in the art of meditation and was able to completely rejuvenate himself with a twenty-minute session.

The woman joined him on the bench. A soft chime sounded somewhere outside, and she stood once more. This time, she opened the door and slipped out of the sauna. Yoshimatsu did not move nor open his eyes, but he was aware of the woman's exit.

They had met on his first trip to Mexico City at a government function at the Mexico City Hilton. Susan Lawrence had been the assistant to one of the U.S. oil CEOs sent down to negotiate with the Mexican government regarding drilling permits in Mexican waters. Yoshimatsu had convinced her to come to work for him. Since the nature of his business called for him to spend a great deal of time away from his home and family in Tokyo, Susan was the one who helped him keep his affairs in order.

She reappeared with a glass of sake on a small tray and a cell phone. This time she was clad in a short, flowered robe.

"I'm sorry to disturb you, Hiro-san. It's Tokyo."

Yoshimatsu opened his eyes slowly and gazed at her. With two fingers, he untied the sash on her robe and exposed her breasts. He traced his finger along the curve of one breast until it found her nipple. She smiled invitingly at him.

"Do you want me to have them call back?"

Hirokan sighed, then smiled. "No. I will take this call."

She set the tray down next to him, took his finger in her mouth and looked at him invitingly. She retied her robe and left the sauna.

He took a sip of sake, closing his eyes as the liquid lit a smoldering trail of warmth down his throat. He picked up the cell phone and punched the speakerphone.

"Hello, Sato-san, it is good to hear from you."

"Greetings my old friend. I am hoping the waters of Mexico have not been disagreeable to you."

The voice on the other end of the phone was one of measured cheerfulness but carried an undertone of little tolerance for prolonged banter. Yoshimatsu was fine with that. He had never been one for small talk.

"The hospitality of our hosts is only exceeded by the fine cuisine and luxurious accommodations. But yes, I am managing to somehow survive in this wilderness, Sato-san."

"How goes the project?"

"Our hosts in Mexico City are most gracious. They are providing us access to all data and research. Tomorrow I will meet with one of the directors and he will be telling me about his project."

"Do you expect any problems?"

"I always anticipate problems," Yoshimatsu said evenly. "That is why there will be no problems. Our contact has assured me that the field staff will cooperate with our project."

"That is good to hear, Hiro-san. The Sea Shepherd Conservation Society has all but closed down our Antarctic operation. The Australian government is looking to increase the no fishing zone by 2,000 miles southward in the Reserve. The world is watching down there. We need a place to play our hand quietly for a while."

"We should be able to carry out operations here without the eyes of the world scrutinizing our every move."

"You seem very confident of this, Hiro-san. What makes you so sure?"

"Because," Yoshimatsu paused for emphasis, "we have another advantage that our fleet in the Southern Ocean does not have."

"And what is that?"

"We have the full support of the Mexican Department of Fisheries. My contact in Mexico City has assured me of this. He has enlisted various contractors to assist us in our endeavor."

"Impressive. What is the strength of the resistance in Mexico?"

"The media and the populace are more concerned with the cartel wars. The environmental groups are a small faction of the political spectrum. They will not pose a problem to our endeavor."

There was a pause on the other end of the line. Yoshimatsu sensed that Sato was weighing his colleague's confidence levels, searching for any hint of false bravado. Even though an air of formality and politeness appeared to be the foundation of the organization, failures were dealt with severely and harshly. Yoshimatsu had not risen to this level because of his bravado. He was a man of his word—and deed.

"How is the operation with the indigenous population?" Sato asked. "How is their output?"

"Each team from the village is averaging two kills per week. There are three teams currently. We have recruited ten from the village for our international operations. They are good workers and keep to themselves mostly."

"Some of our agents on the site say there is dissension among the villagers. Can you remark on this?"

"I have not heard of any dissension." A slight edge crept into Yoshimatsu's voice. "They are happy to be paid as much as we are paying them. They're able to buy televisions, groceries, and iPads. We will have no problems with the loyalties of the villagers."

"When do you anticipate concluding this harvest?"

"The resource will be available for another five to six weeks before leaving these waters for the open ocean. I believe we will have access to several blue whales, but we need to make adjustments with the crews due to the immensity of the resource."

Yoshimatsu could hear Sato sigh on the other end of the phone. Sato would love nothing more than to take credit for Yoshimatsu's efforts.

"It would appear that you have the situation well in hand, Hiro-san. By the way, how is your family?"

Yoshimatsu knew this to be more than just casual conversation. It was a veiled threat that, if failure was to occur, the organization always had the family to use as leverage.

"They are well, Sato-san. The boy starts university at Cambridge next fall. My daughter is top in her class at her school and first violin in the orchestra."

"Ah, very good. You must be very proud of them."

"They are good children. Their mother has taught them well."

"Well, my friend, when can I next expect to hear from you?"

"I will give you an update within the next five days, after we launch the next phase of the operation," Yoshimatsu said.

"Until then, Hiro-san."

"Until then, my friend."

Yoshimatsu disconnected the phone and placed it on the bench next to him. He leaned back against the heated cedar wall slats, closed his eyes and smiled. After next week, Sato Izumi would no longer be in a position of leverage. Yoshimatsu would have his position secured. This pleased him greatly.

The door of the sauna opened and Susan reappeared with fresh drinks on a tray. She set the tray down next to Yoshimatsu, then undid the tie to her robe, letting it fall to the floor. "How did the meeting go?"

# 9

Another whale had gone missing yesterday. The signal had abruptly stopped at 4:17 am, Pacific Standard Time. A frantic Sandy had awakened Alejandro from a deep sleep with a phone call. The humpback's location was one-hundred miles due north in the channel. This news put Alejandro in no mood to pander to a wealthy, arrogant, Japanese industrialist this morning. He strongly suspected what the Japanese contingent were here for. And Yoshimatsu knew that he was suspicious. Alejandro was filled with impotent rage.

He had been to the International Whaling Commission meetings in Tokyo two years before. The Japanese whalers were calculating and ruthless, employing every means of political subterfuge to curry favor among participating nations and gain leverage. In a brash statement, the Japanese Minister of Fisheries had said that Japan was on a mission to hunt down every last whale in the ocean. Whales and dolphins were seen as pests, taking much needed fish intended for a dependent island nation. The Japanese contingent was especially adept at swaying the votes of emerging nations, or, as Alejandro interpreted, desperate Third World nations seeking to build up their infrastructure at the expense of the environment. For their votes, the Dominican Republic was rewarded with a chicken processing center and Vanuatu a chemical processing plant.

And the Japanese knew they could do it. They could do it because loopholes were woven into the IWC charter like buoys woven into a fishing net. They could do it because of the immense amount of trade leverage that they held over the West like a giant scimitar. As much as Mexico, the United States, and most of Europe disparaged the archaic and brutal slaughter of whales and dolphins, they were relegated to damage control, keeping the Japanese and a few other nations from decimating populations to their breaking points.

Alejandro walked out to the front room of the Marine Mammal Institute which served as the Marine Museum in La Paz. Various educational displays were artistically arranged around the rotunda.

He had dressed in a sport coat and tie this morning, the most formal attire he owned. He never felt comfortable in a tie. He was a field biologist, for God's sake.

Alejandro observed a large, black, stretch limousine pull up to the curb of the Institute. A moment later, a stocky Japanese man dressed in black opened the door.

Yoshimatsu followed and then three more similarly dressed men wearing dark sunglasses entered. The entourage walked directly toward Alejandro. Yoshimatsu was smiling slightly, but Alejandro knew it was not a friendly smile. He stopped in front of Alejandro and performed a perfunctory bow.

Alejandro bowed back. "Mr. Yoshimatsu, we welcome you and your colleagues to our institute."

"Thank you for opening your facility to us. I look forward to productive exchanges of information between our two governments."

*Yeah, some exchange,* thought Alejandro. *We give you information and you give us the finger.*

If you and your associates are ready," Alejandro said, "we will take a short tour of the institute and then show you our methods of data collection." The words felt like glass shards in his mouth.

As they walked, Alejandro explained about the displays and their significance to the region. Yoshimatsu nodded his head, "Yes, most interesting," as Alejandro pointed out the various projects aimed at conservation and preservation of the indigenous populations of marine mammals. At some level, he had a faint hope that Yoshimatsu would appreciate the significance of their conservation efforts.

They had stopped in front of a display that had been set up by a group of local school children depicting the effects of whaling. The display ranged from artwork submitted by the students to letters penned to the Minister of Fisheries asking for protection of all the whales in the Gulf of California. When Yoshimatsu's underlings saw this they began chattering excitedly, sniggering. Yoshimatsu's face flashed a brief hint of a smile, then went deadpan.

Alejandro kept his anger in check. "I'm sorry. I see nothing humorous about the indiscriminate slaughter of whales and dolphins. There are many people in Mexico who believe these animals deserve to be protected for their children and their children's children."

Yoshimatsu cast a hard stare at his subordinates who immediately went silent.

"Many apologies, Dr. Cabrillo. My associates come from a long line of proud fishermen. Many of their fathers and grandfathers, like my own, had to hunt whales in order to survive. After the bombs were dropped on Hiroshima and

Nagasaki, there was no food, no protein. Many more Japanese would have died from starvation if our fishermen had not gone back out to sea."

The two men looked at each other, Yoshimatsu's stare unflinching, until Alejandro had to avert his gaze.

"Please, if you will, we would like to see the laboratory now."

In the lab, Alejandro explained how they collected data. "We locate the whales through observation by researchers and the fishermen. We apply radio telemetry transmitters to the whales. The images are downloaded twice a day from a live stream. We're receiving signals from satellites unless there are atmospheric disturbances."

"How many whales are you currently monitoring?"

Alejandro hesitated. It was a slight catch on his part, but the pause was long enough for Yoshimatsu's eyebrows to rise ever so slightly.

"Originally, there were thirty-six individuals being monitored." Alejandro tried to control the tightness in his throat. "We have lost three so far and two more whales' signals went off telemetry in the last seventy-two hours."

Yoshimatsu was thoughtful. "To what do you attribute the disappearances, Dr. Cabrillo?"

"I can only speculate on six of the seven individuals. One of the whales was discovered washed up on a beach by some local fisherman. The shaft of an exploding harpoon was sticking out of its back."

"Poachers?" If Yoshimatsu's face showed any emotion, Alejandro was unable to discern it.

"Local fishermen do not normally take large whales. Most cetacean deaths are due to incidental catches, drowning in gill nets. Whaling is illegal in Mexican waters."

"Are there ways to patrol these waters to ensure the whales' safety?"

"There's the Mexican Navy. But they're spread thin. Most of their resources are directed toward stopping shipments of drugs throughout the Gulf of California. On a local level, there's very little enforcement for protection of endangered species."

Yoshimatsu flashed Alejandro the briefest of smiles. "Dr. Cabrillo, you have been most helpful to us. I believe we can adopt some of your techniques and apply them to our research efforts back in Japan. I would like to have copies of your data as examples to present to my esteemed colleagues back in Tokyo."

Alejandro thought fast. "We will prepare a file for you."

Yoshimatsu bowed. "I thank you."

They walked back to the main rotunda. Yoshimatsu thanked Alejandro once more for his cooperation, then turned and headed for the door. The Japanese contingent nodded as each passed him on their way out. Alejandro could only stare after them, silently cursing himself for promising to deliver raw data.

He felt as low he could remember feeling in his entire adult life. He barely noticed the petite woman dressed in black, wearing a beret and dark sunglasses, inspecting the displays along one wall.

"Excuse me. Do you work here?" The voice was distinctly American with an edginess to the dialect that smacked of East Coast. Alejandro recognized that cadence from several trips to New York to attend marine mammal conferences. He snapped back to the present and looked at the woman.

Her clothing was mannish, as was her style of gait. She didn't look like any of the typical American tourists who walked into the museum. In fact, she didn't look at all comfortable in her body.

"Yes, I work here. How can I help you?"

She approached him, removed her sunglasses and looked directly into his eyes.

"Bingo. You're the one I saw on television last night." She stuck out her hand. "Emily Rosen, *New York Times*. I was wondering if I might ask you some questions."

# 10

Gustavo Silvano walked into the kitchen and found Marta scrubbing an old cast iron skillet. Woven baskets she had designed hung over the kitchen window and elsewhere around the spartan room. Before the cartels had scared off the tourists, Marta had done a brisk business selling her baskets. During cruise ship season she would take her wares down to La Paz and wait at the pier as the eager gringos disembarked.

He walked over to the modest dining room table and sat down heavily in the chair. He continued to watch her as she worked.

"You are quieter than usual," she said. Without looking up, she continued to vigorously scrub the bottom of the pan.

When he didn't respond, she turned and faced him. He could see the concern in her eyes.

Gustavo gestured to the chair. "Come. Sit with me."

She wiped her hands on her apron and took the chair next to her husband.

Gustavo looked into his wife's cocoa-colored eyes. They were still bright—eyes that reflected the intelligence and strength of the woman behind them.

"I have been thinking a great deal lately," said Gustavo. "I did not want to waste words until I had a clear picture of what I wanted to say." He placed a weathered hand on top of hers. "I have been speaking with Jake Spinner," he continued. When Marta scowled, Gustavo held up his other hand. "Wait. Hear me out."

"He is nothing but trouble, Gustavo," Marta said, her voice almost a hiss. "He will come to no good end."

"It is no longer possible for us to stay here," Gustavo said evenly. "Jake can help us in El Norte. He has a friend who can find us work, get us work visas and help us find a place to live."

Marta looked shocked at her husband's remark. "Move? Move to El Norte! What are you saying?"

"Things are bad here. They are going to get worse."

45

"I thought you said your new employers were paying you well," Marta gestured to the big screen television. "And what about the new motor for your boat?"

Gustavo shook his head. "They are *hombres muy malos*. They do the devil's work."

"I thought you said they wanted you to fish."

"It's not fishing!" Gustavo snapped. "Slaughtering las ballenas is not fishing!"

"They pay you well to do your job and to keep your mouth shut. If it wasn't them, it would be someone else. At least our tribe gets to share in the profits of the hunt. Isn't that part of the Indigenous Act?"

"Marta, at night when I dream, I still hear the death screams of the mother whales and their babies. Since I was seven, I was taught by my father there are certain things that are considered sacred. This isn't respect for the sea and the ones who dwell there. It is murder. And I have been a willful participant. But no longer. *El Jefe* wants all of the hunters to increase our kills. Their hunger to kill the whales is unending."

Marta looked into her husband's eyes. Behind the deep sadness and remorse, she saw something she hadn't seen before. "You are frightened of something. There is something you're not telling me."

"Santiago has not been seen for over three weeks. He told a group of us he no longer wanted to do the devil's work."

"I thought everyone said he went to the mainland to work."

Gustavo shook his head. "Santiago had no reason to go to the mainland. He told me he was thinking about going to the local authorities in the Fisheries Ministry."

"Do you think something happened to him?"

"I can't say for certain. His panga sits behind his house on a trailer. When he was not working for the *Japonés,* he would use his panga to fish."

"Surely, there must be some other explanation. Perhaps he took his money and went to Mexico City for a vacation."

"Several of us have been talking. There are those of us who think Santiago may have been silenced. He was going to break the contract."

They both turned as the back door opened and Macario strode in. He was dressed all in black. His hair was slicked back and pulled into a ponytail. Expensive silver-tipped cowboy boots adorned his feet. Gustavo's heart sank as the realization hit him.

Macario shifted his gaze back and forth between his parents and saw the worried looks on their faces.

"Hey, what's going on?" Macario asked.

Gustavo took a deep breath, then looked directly at his son. "Your mother and I have been talking. We think it is time for us to head north. Jake Spinner has friends up there who can employ us and find us a place to live. For a while."

"What are you talking about?" Macario was incredulous. "We're making good money here! We can have things we never had before."

Gustavo reached out and grabbed his son's shoulder. "It's blood money. There is no good that can come from killing whales. Our village is cursed now. The whales have watched over us for hundreds of years. What we do to them now is like tearing the heart out of Ocean Mother."

Macario pulled away vehemently. "That's old-time Indian bullshit!" He gestured in a sweeping motion. "Everyone is living better because of the whaling. Look around you."

"Why don't you ask Santiago if he is living better. He didn't want to do this anymore. They killed him."

"What are you talking about? Everyone knows Santiago went to Mexico City." Macario's eyes were defiant, but Gustavo thought he caught a glimpse of doubt, or even fear lurking deep within. Macario was doing what all the others in the village had done—what Gustavo himself had wanted to do: believe that Santiago left of his own volition.

"They didn't kill him," Macario insisted. "They wouldn't do that." This time the tone of certainty had dropped from his voice.

Gustavo stepped over to the kitchen sink and pulled back the curtain. "Look out there, Macario. What do you think those men are doing parked there? They're watching us! You, me, your mother."

"It's your fault. You're the one stirring up trouble."

Marta interjected, "Are you listening to yourself, Macario? You need to listen to your father. As long as you live in this house, you will obey your parents."

Macario stared at his mother coldly. "Then I guess I don't live here anymore."

He walked to the back door, opened it and stopped midway. He turned and faced his parents. "Going up to *El Norte* to wash dishes in a restaurant for gringos will not improve our lives. I think I'll stay here and take my chances." He turned and slammed the door behind him.

"Macario!" Marta pleaded. "Come back! We have to stick together."

Gustavo touched her shoulder. "Macario is young. Full of ambition. He has tasted things he only dreamed of before. I will talk to him."

Marta looked at her husband. "When are we going to leave?"

"I will to talk to Jake Spinner again. Jake has spoken to a *compadre* of his from the war. He's arranging for travel papers and work visas to be drawn up for us. I'll see if he has heard anything from El Norte."

"I don't trust him, Tavo. He's a drunkard! He's only out for one person—Jake Spinner."

"You don't know him like I do, Marta. Yes, he has problems. Problems from the wars. Underneath the tequila lies the heart of a good man."

"That heart no longer beats. I can't believe we are trusting our lives to a man whose only concern is where his next drink is coming from."

Jake Spinner was sleeping off a half-bottle of El Patrón when his cell phone rang. Somewhere in a tequila-induced dream, he heard reggae music followed by a distant bell. Sometime later, with his head pounding as if someone had taken an eight-pound sledgehammer to it, he replayed the message.

Even in his state, Jake picked up on the subtle, quiet desperation in Gustavo's voice.

# 11

Sandy Wainright squinted against the bright sun and stepped into the cool air-conditioned comfort of *El Museo de Mamíferos Marinos*. It took a moment for her eyes to adjust to the unlit room. She was dressed in a pair of quick-dry shorts and a white long-sleeved shirt, the tails tied around her slender waist. An old, ratty backpack with salt stains was slung over one shoulder.

She made her way to the back of the museum, opened an old wooden door and went into the set of rooms that served as the administrative and research offices of the institute. Sandy and Paola, the newest additions to the team, shared an office. Though a bit cramped, the room had an air conditioner, a three-level bookcase and space enough to accommodate two computers. On one wall was a large array of black and white photographs of humpback whale flukes. Identification numbers and sighting dates, as well as familiar names, were listed under each photo.

Sandy heard voices coming from the conference room at the end of the hall. She dropped her pack off at her desk and walked the length of the hallway. She knocked twice and poked her head in. Alejandro was sitting at the conference table with a petite woman. She was dressed all in black: black beret, black tee shirt with an image of Che Guevara on the front, black parachute pants, and black lace-up boots. Alejandro and the woman looked up.

"Oh, Sandy, I'm glad you're here," Alejandro said. "Come in. I'd like you to meet Emily Rosen, from the *New York Times*."

Sandy extended her hand and Emily took it. The woman's grip was surprisingly strong. "Hello. It's nice to meet you, Emily."

Sandy was struck by how pale Emily's skin was against the black clothing she wore. She wondered if this was a New York thing.

"Emily is here on assignment and wants to do a story about the whales and our research here at the institute," said Alejandro.

"Originally, I came down here to do a piece on the effects of cartel activity on tourism, but this is a much more interesting topic. Besides, I've never seen a live whale."

Sandy took a seat opposite her. "This is a good time of year to see whales. We have about sixteen species of whales and dolphins that frequent the waters from Loreto to Cabo San Lucas."

"I was telling Alejandro that I saw a news story on your whale beachings and disappearances. This would make a great second page story in the *Times*. I'd been considering doing a story about the research you do here with the whales and how it applies to conservation and tourism, but this is the real story."

A shadow passed across Sandy's face. She turned her gaze from Emily Rosen to Alejandro. Although she tried to remain impassive, the look on her face was one of mistrust. It was only a fraction of a second, but it was not lost on Rosen. Years of covering the mean streets of New York had honed her intuitive skills to a razor's edge.

Alejandro nodded. "It's okay, Sandy. She's one of the good ones."

Sandy's shoulders were still tense, but she managed a weak smile. "Anything you can do for conservation awareness for these whales would be greatly appreciated."

Rosen produced a small tape recorder from her black satchel and set it on the table. "Mind if I record this?"

"What for?"

"I can recall most events verbatim. This is just for legal purposes. Protects us from misstatements."

Sandy fidgeted in her chair. "Well, okay then. Let's do this."

Rosen pressed a button on the tape recorder. "The date is March 7th. First interview with Alejandro Cabrillo, director of the institute, and Sandy Wainwright, lead biologist."

Alejandro and Sandy explained the radio tracking techniques to Rosen.

Alejandro said, "At this time we're still looking into the causative factors in the whales' beachings and disappearances."

"A harpoon embedded in one of the whales is a pretty good explanation," Rosen said. "Anyone hunting whales down here?"

"Mexico's waters are off-limits to any commercial whaling activities and have been since the early 1980s," Alejandro said. "As far as we know, that whale could have lost its tracking tag and gone out into international waters where it was shot. It could have come back here to die or just been washed up with the winds and tides."

"Why would anyone want to kill a whale?"

"For food," Sandy interjected. "Countries like Japan, Norway, Iceland, the Faroe Islands, and, to a lesser extent, indigenous cultures consider whale meat a part of their traditional diet. They believe it is their birthright, their heritage, to kill whales."

"But don't they realize they are exterminating an intelligent species?"

"They think we're hypocrites," Sandy said. "We kill and consume billions of cows and pigs every year in the Western world. They don't see any difference."

"They could argue that point," said Emily.

"What it comes down to," emotion evident in Sandy's voice, "is brain size to body size. Proportionally, whales and dolphins are up there with humans with large brain-to-body ratios. These brains have been developing for over fifty-million years. We've had ours for only a couple of million. We're systematically annihilating a sentient race before we've even learned much about their lives, including how they communicate."

"Scientists are rethinking models of intelligence versus instinct," Alejandro said. "There is a growing movement in the scientific field that is coming to terms with the idea of 'a nation among nations,' that human beings are not the only ones capable of sentience."

"What we're trying to do here," Alejandro said, "is preserve species for future generations. We're just barely scratching the surface of the lives of these animals. The more that we humans learn about these whales, the more inclined people will be to want to save them. We feel this is important for our children and our children's children."

When they concluded the interview, Emily turned off her tape recorder and slid it into her black satchel. She looked at Sandy and Alejandro. "Thank you for taking the time to be interviewed. I'll probably have a lot more questions once I start to write this up. Would it be possible to schedule another interview at your convenience?"

Alejandro turned to face Sandy. "I was thinking of having Ms. Rosen go out with you and Paola to see firsthand what we do here at the institute. Do you think you two can make enough room for Emily in the inflatable?"

Sandy shot a quick glance at him. The question was not a request.

Rosen's eyes grew wide. "Me? With you, on the water?"

"That's where the whales live," said Alejandro.

"How close are we going to be to them?" Her gaze darted back and forth between them.

"That depends on whether we need to gather tissue or fecal samples. Sometimes, we're within three to six feet of them. Occasionally, they're curious and come over to check out the boat," Sandy responded.

"And how big are they?"

"Full grown humpbacks are about fifty-five feet and sixty tons," said Sandy. "That's bigger than a New York City bus."

"Okay," said Rosen. "Now that's big."

Sandy said. "Ever spent much time on open water?"

"I've been to the beach at Coney Island."

"It can get pretty rough out at sea, especially in the afternoons when the winds pick up. Prepare for sun and wind. You're going to get wet. And take your Meclizine."

"What's that?"

"Sea sickness medication. You take it an hour before you go out. Tomorrow at the pier. Slip 16. It's the gray, rigid-hull inflatable. We head out at five a.m."

"Five a.m. It's still dark then."

"Won't be when we get to the whales," a half smile crossing Sandy's face.

"Right." Rosen picked up her satchel and slung it over her shoulder. She walked to the door, then turned and faced Alejandro and Sandy. "They—the whales—they don't like kosher, do they?"

"I don't think so," said Alejandro.

"Just a thought." Rosen bit her lower lip. She slipped out the door.

Sandy turned her gaze toward Alejandro. He felt her eyes burning holes in the side of his face. "What?"

"Really? Do you really think this is going to be helpful?"

"Right now, a little public relations for the whales may be exactly what we need," Alejandro said.

Sandy heaved a great sigh. "This should be interesting."

# 12

Jake listened to the voicemail again. He couldn't remember a time in the seven years he'd known Gustavo that his old friend's voice had sounded so— he tried to put his finger on it—full of dread and apprehension. Gustavo had always been unflappable. Time and again they had weathered rough seas, winter storms, intense heat, breakdowns at sea, even a run-in with drug smugglers. He'd never flinched, his only emotion being a brief smile and the question posed: *"Are we having fun yet?"*

Jake got up from his small table and went to his dilapidated refrigerator. Today was a particularly hot day and the inside of the bungalow was stuffy and humid. He opened the refrigerator and stared into the nearly empty space. On the shelf were two cans of Tecate beer, some moldy cheese, and a couple of *bolillos*, Mexican rolls that had to be a week old. He stuck his head into the refrigerator to feel the marginal coolness the refrigerator generated.

These last few days, his stomach had been giving him fits. After his last binge, he had vomited up blood. The cramps had subsided some since this morning and he figured he needed to get something in his stomach that wasn't percentage-proofed. He grabbed a beer and rolled the cool can around on his forehead. He closed his eyes for a moment, trying to clear his mind. The demons had returned. He couldn't believe he was still having flashbacks.

Another wave of pain passed through his gut, this time nearly doubling him over. When the spasm passed, it left him weak and breathless. A voice in the back of his head began speaking. Jake had come to call the voice "his evil twin." Lately, the voice had been getting louder, more constant, more insistent.

*Drink a beer, pal. It'll make your stomach feel better.*

"Shut the fuck up."

*Don't be a douche. One of those Tecates won't hurt you.*

He grabbed his head and screamed. He slammed the refrigerator door and flung the beer can across the small kitchen. It exploded in a frothy burst against the far wall.

*Why don't you just shoot yourself, Spinner? It would be much kinder.*

He remained bent over and gasping for several minutes. Finally, with great effort he walked his hands up his thighs until he stood nearly erect. He thought about his old semi-auto tucked away under the floorboards in his bedroom. He didn't think anyone would miss him. Spinner had pretty much had enough of this ride anyway. He had no family. He'd used up all favors with friends and old Army buddies.

He squared his shoulders and again pulled open the refrigerator door. Reaching inside, he grabbed the moldy cheese and the stale bolillos and staggered to the table. With shaking hands, he cut away the mold on the cheese and bread and made himself a sandwich.

It wasn't the worst thing he had ever eaten, but lately his memory didn't reach back very far.

After the sandwich, the stomach pain subsided. For now, the voice in his head was quiet. Jake opened the Mexican cell phone and played Gustavo's message again.

Gustavo was clearly afraid of something. Jake was feeling like a shit right now because he hadn't followed through procuring work visas with his friend for Gustavo and his family.

*You were busy, Spinner,* spoke the voice from somewhere in the cobwebs.

"Christ!" He proceeded to punch in Gustavo's number.

After several rings, the call went to message. He called again and listened to the message. He looked at the phone and disconnected.

His gut began to roil again. This time he knew it wasn't from the booze. With shaking hands, he punched in a number.

"Castellano." The gravelly voice that answered on the other end brought back a flood of memories.

"Rollie. It's me, Jake."

"Spinner, you crazy bastard. You're still alive?"

"Some would argue that point."

Roland "Rollie" Castellano had been in Special Forces with Spinner. They had done more tours than they cared to count, had buried most of their comrades and both had been seriously wounded. Rollie had lost a leg below the knee from a mortar blast a month before his tour ended. Jake had been the one who ran through enemy fire to carry him to safety. In Special Forces, Rollie had developed a reputation for being able to procure things, both legal and circumspect.

"I need a favor, Rollie. I have a friend who needs to go stateside. I need work permits and travel visas for a male and female and their twenty-year-old son. I was hoping you still had a connection with that restaurant in Tucson."

"When do you need them?" Rollie's voice was flat.

"Yesterday."

"I figured you were gonna say that. Gimme two days and I'll get back to you. I'll put a call in to my friend in Tucson." There was a pause. "I don't suppose you plan on paying for this, do you, Spinner?"

"My friends are good for it. Just don't gouge them on the price, okay? They're friends."

"You don't have any friends, Spinner. I was your last one. And I don't like you anymore."

"Call me when everything's in place. And Rollie, time is of the essence here."

"Always is. I'll call you when I have something."

Castellano got the personal information from Jake, then hung up. Jake looked at the phone, then tossed it on the table. He knew he had used up all his favors from his former friend and comrade-in-arms. Rollie had bailed Jake out on so many occasions that Spinner was hard pressed to remember one incident from the next. Apparently, though, there was a ceiling on the value of saving a life.

When Jake's nerves had steadied to the point where he could run a stick shift, he drove his old green Chevy truck to Puerto Nacimiento. He needed to talk to Gustavo face-to-face and get some money up front to pay for the visas.

The air conditioner in Jake's truck had gone belly up several years before. By the time he'd made the hot, dusty drive through the desert to the pueblo, he was parched. The only thing he could think about was an ice-cold beer.

He pulled into Puerto Nacimiento in the mid-afternoon. At this time of day, the streets of the villages on the peninsula were quiet because most residents went indoors or retired to *palapas* on the beach to escape the afternoon heat.

He parked the old pickup in front of Gustavo's house. Gustavo's rusted red Nissan pickup, normally parked under a palapa beside the concrete house, wasn't there. Stiffly, he got out of his truck and walked to the front door. He half expected Marta to open the curtain and curse him out. He knocked on the worn wooden door. No answer. He put his good ear up to the door and tried to listen for sounds coming from within. No sound of radio or television. Then he pounded on the door.

"Gustavo! Marta! It's me, Jake. I need to talk with you. If you're in there, open up!"

Jake tried peering into several windows, but all the curtains were drawn. He went around to the back. The first thing he noticed was that Gustavo's trailer and panga were missing.

*They must be out fishing,* thought Jake. *Strange. Marta usually doesn't go with him.* He wondered if the family had taken a few days off and gone to the fish camp. That seemed odd since Gustavo and Macario were busy running fishing charters for the wealthy Asian tourists.

Jake heard a low growl coming from a rickety wooden shed attached to the back of the house. He walked over, peered in, then stepped into the darkness. It took a moment for his eyes to adjust. He heard the growl again, this time coming from underneath a dilapidated wooden workbench. He leaned down and saw the shape of a dog under the lower shelf. It growled again, followed by a whine.

"It's okay, fella. I'm not going to hurt you." He slowly held out his hand, palm down. "Come on out, let's have a look at you."

The dog was visibly shaking. Jake recognized the animal as the one that was always sleeping in the old chair alongside Gustavo's house. Jake had never before seen the dog react to anyone passing by.

"What's got you spooked, boy?" Jake backed up a step. Bending down like this in the hot and stuffy shed, Jake's head began to swim. He stood and placed his hand against the wall to keep from falling. The dog retreated back under the shelf. Looking right, Jake noticed an array of fishing poles and tackle stacked against the wall of the shed. Most of the gear was old and non-functional—spin casting rods with broken reels, rods missing sections or eyelets. But one fishing rod caught his eye. He grabbed it, examined it, then stepped out of the shed for a closer look at the rod and reel.

It was Gustavo's favorite rig. It wasn't fancy—a Shimano open-face deep-sea reel and a fiberglass pole. Jake had offered to buy it from Gustavo several times after fishing ventures where Gustavo consistently landed larger fish and more fish than Jake did. Gustavo had laughed at him.

*"It's not how big your pole is, Jake. It's how you use it."*

*That's odd,* Jake thought. *If Gustavo went fishing in his own panga, why would he leave his favorite rig behind?*

He held the fishing rod, feeling its weight and balance as if there were some message waiting to be divined from the rig. He finally returned it to the shed and walked out into the hot sun. When he rounded the side of the house, movement in the front window of the house across the dusty street caught his attention.

Someone had been watching him, then quickly closed the curtain. Jake ambled across the street to the house.

His eyes were drawn to a black Ford Excursion, which was parked about a hundred yards away. The sun reflected off the windshield, obscuring any of the occupants within. Thoughts flashed through his tequila-soaked brain as he approached the house. *Where was Marta? She didn't usually accompany Gustavo on his fishing trips—she was prone to seasickness. And what about Macario? Had he gone with his father? And why had they taken their small panga if they were working for the wealthy Asian patrons?* There were far too many questions and the sight of that SUV parked at the end of the street set off alarm bells in Jake's head.

He approached the front door and rapped loudly. No one came. He knocked again, even louder. The door opened and a small man with skin like old leather chaps, dark with deep creases, gazed at him. *"¿Qué pasa?"*

*"Estoy buscando a Gustavo Silvano. ¿Usted sabe adonde está?"*

*"No sé,"* the pescador said. *"Yo pienso que está pescando."*

*"¿Cuándo?"*

*"No sé,"* replied the small fisherman.

The man's eyes shifted down the road. Jake heard the sound of a vehicle starting up. He turned and saw the SUV moving slowly toward them. He looked back at the fisherman. The look in his eyes confirmed Jake's suspicions. The fisherman was terrified.

The fisherman's glance darted once more to the black Excursion, then he said, *"No puedo ayudario, Señor,"* and he shut the door in Jake's face.

Jake turned and walked back toward his truck. Approaching the bed, he saw a dark form huddled in the bed of the pickup next to his spare tire.

"Oh no you don't. I don't want no god damn *playa* mutt following me around. Besides, you're Gustavo's dog. C'mon, get out."

The dog retreated back against the tire. The SUV stopped several feet behind Spinner's truck. The doors opened and two very large men in suit coats got out. The dog bared its teeth, emitting a low throaty growl. Jake turned and leaned against the tailgate. He lit a cigarette, inhaled, then blew the smoke skyward.

The men wore reflecting sunglasses, but Jake could tell they were Asian. Judging by the bulges on the left sides of their jackets, Jake surmised they were both packing heat.

"Nice jackets," said Jake.

The larger of the two men stepped forward and, in stilted English, asked, "What is your business here?"

Jake looked at the two men. "I'm here looking for a friend. What's your business here?"

The two men assumed an aggressive stance, standing side by side. Jake's addled brain began calculating where and when to land the punches.

The big man demanded, "Who? Who you look for?"

"Gustavo. Gustavo Silvano. What's it to you?"

"He gone fishing," said the second Asian man.

"Did he take your boss?" Jake asked.

"Time for you to leave," said the larger of the two men. His hand moved to the inside of his jacket.

Jake raised both hands. "Okay, okay. I'm leaving."

He walked around to the cab of the truck, feeling the gazes of the two thugs on his back like laser pointers from a rifle. He climbed in and turned the ignition. This time, it caught on the first revolution. He jammed it into gear and spun the tires, coating the two men in a fine layer of road dust. They looked like characters out of a peyote dream. The truck lurched forward and accelerated.

"Welcome to Mexico, douche bags."

# 13

Emily Rosen stood at the bow of the rigid inflatable, her 35mm Canon digital camera held in both hands, peering ahead intensely at the roiling water. Thirty yards off the bow a circular stream of bubbles was rising to the surface, covering an area three times the size of the inflatable. Above her, brown pelicans, royal terns, and blue-footed boobies circled, awaiting the bounty that was at hand.

"Get ready." Sandy pointed from the steering console. "Here they come."

Emily raised the camera to her eye and focused on the bubble stream. Behind her, Paola steadied the video camera and began recording. Emily heard a soft beep as the video camera was activated.

The water exploded as three huge mouths opened at the surface, scooping up thousands of small anchovies that had been trapped by the bubble net. The sight of the feeding lunge was so forceful and overwhelming that Rosen almost fell over backward.

But she didn't. Years of shooting pictures on the mean streets of New York kept her hand steady. The colossal whales closed their gaping maws, sending water shooting out the sides, along with some struggling anchovies that had escaped the humpback's lunge. The staccato whir of Rosen's camera caught the spectacle at ten frames per second. As if on cue, the sea birds dove around the whales' heads, hitting the water like bullets, scooping up the hapless schooling fish.

The behemoths slid back into the blue-green water, leaving a large circular print on the surface that quickly spread in an ever-widening circle. Some of the birds took flight, some squabbled over the remaining stunned and dying anchovies.

"Did you get that, Paola?"

Paola turned to her friend. "Got it."

Rosen turned around and faced Sandy and Paola. Her look was one of awe, excitement, and childlike wonder all rolled into one.

"That . . . was humpback bubble net feeding." Sandy was smiling big. "Happens very rarely down in these waters. Not many people get to see that."

Emily looked back at the whales' expanding fluke print. "Holy fucking shit!"

Sandy and Paola burst into laughter.

Paola asked, "Is that the New York response to a religious experience?"

"Oh—my—God! That was the most amazing thing I've ever seen."

"Did you get it on camera?" Sandy asked.

Rosen hit the playback button on the camera and scrolled the images quickly. Grinning, she looked up and said, "Yep. Got the whole sequence."

"Good. You owe us a beer when we get back to port," Sandy said.

"A beer? Are you kidding? I'm talking a four-course dinner when we get back."

"Won't argue with that." Sandy turned to Paola. "Did you get the GPS coordinates?" She looked at her wristwatch. "The time is 4:33 p.m."

Paola produced a handheld GPS from a dry box. She then spoke the coordinates into a portable tape recorder she kept in her shirt pocket.

A quarter of a mile away, the humpbacks surfaced, blowing loudly, the mist from their spouts hanging momentarily in the golden light of late afternoon.

"So—what just happened?" Rosen set her camera down, took out her own tape recorder and looked at Sandy. "Was that some form of cooperative fishing?"

"Absolutely. Normally, they do it in their summer feeding grounds. Alaska mainly. This group may not make that long of a journey. That may be why we saw it here."

"Walk me through how they do it."

"When a group of humpbacks comes across a bait ball," said Paola, "one of the whales acts as the netter. He or she will circle the ball of sardines or anchovies and begin emitting a steady stream of bubbles from her blowhole. This frightens the fish and causes them to bunch together in an even tighter ball. After the whale completes the bubble circle, the other whales swim up through it, forcing the fish to the surface. Opening their mouths, they can take in hundreds of gallons of fish-filled water at once. They close their mouths, forcing the excess water out through baleen. They use their tongues to lick the fish from the baleen."

"Is one whale the designated netter?"

"From the studies I've seen on bubble netting in Alaska, it appears to be a shared task." Sandy turned the ignition and the motor came to life. "Let's see where this group is going." The inflatable began moving.

"We saw three whales feeding. How many can do it at a time?"

"I've seen as many as ten up in Alaska." Sandy talked loudly over the engine noise. "Most of the time, I think the group size is like the one we saw today."

They followed the humpbacks for another two hours as the three adults and one adolescent whale swam leisurely northward along the Baja coastline. Paola photographed the undersides of each whale's flukes to obtain an identification, explaining to Rosen how they were identified.

Rosen fired off a series of shots as one of the humpbacks arched her back and dove deep, revealing the intricate pattern of markings and scars on the underside of her twelve-foot flukes.

"That one we call Minerva," said Sandy, throttling down the motor and slowing the boat near the giant fluke print that expanded before them. "She's Athena's calf, who is also in this group. Minnie is easily identified by the twin Rorschach patterns on the tips of her flukes."

Rosen nodded. "Yes, I saw them. So, every whale has a different pattern on its tail—I mean flukes?"

"That's right. We match the photos of individuals and record where they're picked up by satellite tracking. We then have an ongoing data base of their comings and goings in the Gulf."

The whales reappeared this time nearly a half-mile away. Several seconds later, the women heard the distant whoosh of air coming from their blowholes.

Sandy turned to Paola. "I think we're about done here. Sun's going down anyway. What do you think, Paola? San Esteban Cove? I think I can get us there in twenty minutes."

Rosen stopped wiping her camera gear and looked up in alarm. "Wait a minute. San Esteban Cove? You mean we're not going back to La Paz tonight?"

"Too far and too dangerous in the dark," said Sandy. "Lots of exposed rocks that could put a big hole in the boat."

"Besides, we're already out here," said Paola. "We can pick up early tomorrow where we left off today."

"Let me get this straight." Rosen looked around uncomfortably. "We're going to spend the night out here? On this?"

"Sure." Paola grinned. "The bench seats flatten out into beds. And we have sleeping bags stowed in the forward compartment. And wait till you see what I cook up for dinner tonight."

Rosen stared at her. "What about bathrooms?"

"Three-hundred-sixty degrees. Bathroom with a view." Sandy waved her arm in the direction of the cove. "Take your pick."

"Jewish women from Brooklyn don't camp on boats," Emily muttered.

Sandy and Paola laughed.

"C'mon, Rosen, think of it as a girls' sleepover. On a boat," Sandy said. "Besides, now you'll get the full experience."

"It will make for a better story," said Paola.

"It's already a hell of a story," Rosen said indignantly.

They arrived at San Esteban Cove shortly after sunset. After checking the depth finder, Sandy set anchor in the middle of the cove about a hundred yards from shore.

"Why so far out? We're more exposed out here."

"Exactly," said Sandy. "Out here we'll pick up some of the breezes coming off the water. Keeps the mosquitoes and no-see-ums away."

"No-see-ums?"

"Little biting gnats. They can raise a welt and make you itch so you won't get any sleep," said Paola.

"Okay. Sleep out here. Good plan."

Paola went forward to the storage compartment located at the bow of the boat. She produced a box containing a small propane stove, and various pots and plastic dishes. Sandy went aft and reached into a metal cooler, retrieving three cans of Pacifico. She handed one to Paola and another to Rosen. Emily studied the label on the can for a moment, then looked inquiringly at Sandy.

"No. There is no wine in the cooler." A wry smile lit up Sandy's face. She popped the tab on her own beer. "Beer is all we're serving at this bar tonight."

Rosen popped open her own beer. "Well, in that case, here's to the whales. Long may they swim."

"I'll drink to that," said Sandy.

"Damn." Rosen looked at the label again. "I don't normally like beer. But this tastes great."

"As Doc Ricketts used to say," said Sandy, "Nothin' like that first sip of beer."

"Who's Doc Ricketts?"

"Famous marine biologist and researcher back in the '40s." He and John Steinbeck hung out. The main character in *Cannery Row* is based on the real-life persona of Doc Ed Ricketts."

Paola stashed the rest of the research equipment. "If you get the chance, you should check out *The Log from the Sea of Cortez*. It chronicles a trip Steinbeck and Ricketts took traveling down the length of Baja by boat."

Rosen pulled her tape recorder out, clicked it on and spoke into it. "Check out *The Log from the Sea of Cortez* and *Cannery Row* by John Steinbeck."

Sandy took another sip from her beer, closed her eyes, and held the cold can against her neck. "Mmm. That feels good." She took another swallow and looked at Rosen. "I went online and checked you out."

Rosen's eyebrows rose slightly. "Yeah? Checking to see if I was legit?"

"That. And general curiosity. You're one hell of an investigative journalist and writer."

"Thanks."

"And from your portfolio, I got the impression you can be a real thorn in the side of those in power who play fast and loose with the truth."

Rosen smiled. "I have been blessed or cursed, depending on what day it is, to have a very tightly wound bullshit meter. It has a tendency to peg to the right real fast."

"You seem to have carved out a niche in the political arena of New York," Sandy said. "Why a story about tourism in Baja?"

Rosen let out a long breath. She looked down at the floorboards for a moment before she spoke. "I was getting too close to some nefarious dealings involving a prominent senator from New York. I have it from pretty good sources that he has ties to organized crime. Money laundering, racketeering. It's a shopping list of betrayal of the public trust."

"So your boss pulled you from the story and sent you to sunny Mexico."

Emily shrugged. "That about says it all. Between you, Paola, the whales, and me, I think the editor is somehow on the senator's payroll. I think as soon as I finish this assignment, I'm going to be pink-slipped when I get back."

"What are you going to do?"

Rosen half-smiled. "I don't know. Maybe write an exposé about two adventurous women who are trying to save whales. Now, that would be a story."

Sandy leaned forward and clinked her can to Rosen's. "Glad to have you aboard."

Sandy and Paola set about preparing the dinner. In short order, they served up plates of bean and cheese burritos with fresh pico de gallo salsa. Paola handed Rosen a plate with two burritos and a generous helping of salsa.

"What are we eating tonight?" Rosen studied the plate of food.

"Bean and cheese burritos," said Paola.

"Wait a minute. Is this a good idea? I mean three of us on a small boat? Eating beans?"

Sandy laughed. "Hey, it's an open-air boat. Just don't light any matches."

Later, after the dinner plates had been cleaned and the cookware stowed in the forward compartment, Paola fired up the propane stove once more and prepared tea by the light of a propane lantern. Handing Rosen a cup of steaming Earl Grey, she said, "A researcher's idea of a nightcap."

Rosen took the cup from her and brought it to her lips. A chill had settled on the water, and the warm cup felt good on her hands.

"That's really weird," said Rosen.

Paola seemed surprised. "What's that? You don't like tea?"

"No. It's amazing. We ate simple meals tonight. Yet I feel like I have just eaten in the finest New York restaurant. Everything tasted so good!"

Sandy chuckled. "Being on the water all day long will do that to you. Wait till you get a taste of tomorrow's fare."

"And what, may I ask, would this *haute cuisine* be?"

"The finest peanut butter and jelly sandwiches on the planet," Sandy said.

"Really? PB and J?"

"You'll see."

Paola turned the lantern off and the women, each in their own sleeping bag, were enveloped in the deepening darkness. Silence reigned for several minutes as they gazed at the sky dome filled with stars.

"My God," Emily said, "I've never seen a sky like this."

Sandy smiled. "Kinda takes your breath away, doesn't it?"

A flash arced across the sky and disappeared below a set of low-lying hills on the Baja coastline, briefly illuminating the desert landscape of *cardónes* and palo verde trees.

"Wow!" Rosen said. "Check out that meteor."

"I think it's tonight, or tomorrow morning there's supposed to be a meteor shower in the western sky," Paola said. "Around 4:00 a.m., I think."

"You can stay up and wait for it, Emily," said Sandy.

"No thanks," said Rosen. "Never thought I'd say this, but this bench feels pretty comfortable right now."

Another silence followed. Sandy closed her eyes and was beginning to nod off when Rosen broke the silence.

"So, who do you think is killing the whales?"

Sandy and Paola reflected for a moment. Finally, Sandy let out a long sigh. "We honestly don't know at this time. We haven't had any incidents of illegal whaling for over twenty years, since a Korean trawler came up the Gulf and took everything from whales to swordfish to giant mantas. At that time, the Mexican government mobilized the Navy and chased them out."

"A few of the indigenous tribes along the coast can still hunt a whale under the subsistence fishing clause outlined by the IWC," Paola said. "But the ruling states that they're only allowed to take one per year. To my knowledge, I don't know of any of the local tribes who are invoking this law."

Rosen frowned. "IWC?"

"The International Whaling Commission," Sandy said. "They're the world's governing body on regulating whaling throughout the oceans. They determine the quotas for hunts that the whaling nations are supposed to follow."

Rosen, following the thread, said, "Supposed to follow?"

"It originally was set up to protect whales and dolphins worldwide. It's become a giant political machine, full of corruption and vote-buying from smaller non-whaling nations by the big consortia to push their own agendas and increase the quotas."

"Who are the big players?" Rosen turned and raised up on one elbow.

"Japan, Norway, Iceland, South Korea, Greenland, the Faroe Islands, Portugal, a few islands in Indonesia, and the Grenadines," said Sandy. "All told, including the U.S., which allows subsistence whaling by First Nations in California, Washington, Oregon, and Alaska, there are currently about eleven countries hunting whales."

"What the larger whaling nations do essentially," Paola enjoined, "is to curry the favor of the smaller non-whaling nations to buy votes. So, for example, they may offer one of the smaller non-whaling commonwealths in the Caribbean a chicken or fish processing plant in exchange for their vote to continue whaling."

"Sounds insidious." Rosen stifled a yawn.

"It is." Sandy's voice rose as she spoke. "The IWC is supposed to be the body that protects the endangered whales. A few years ago, several biologists went undercover and infiltrated the restaurants and markets in Japan, mainly Tokyo. DNA testing of the meat samples they procured in the markets and restaurants revealed that it came from critically endangered species. Blue, sperm, humpback, and right whales were all being sold for consumption, collected under the guise of 'scientific whaling.' The world's whale populations," Sandy continued, "are being stressed to the breaking point. Relentless hunting in their summer feeding grounds, the constant bombardment of their environment by boat and ship sounds, and now this new threat, the Navy LFA Sonar System."

"What's LFA Sonar?"

"It stands for Low Frequency Active Sonar. The Navy blankets the ocean with extremely loud low frequency pulses that are damaging whale navigation systems. It causes hemorrhaging in brain tissue, pulmonary embolisms, and all kinds of nasty stuff."

"Why is the Navy using this?"

"It's supposed to be the optimal means of locating enemy submarine activity. But nothing has proven it even works—other than to kill large groups of cetaceans." Sandy sounded bitter.

"My money's on one of the bigger players in the game," Emily said. "When we get back, I'm going to do a little digging of my own."

The women gazed up at a brilliant star-filled night, the Milky Way illuminating the Baja sky. Rosen looked toward the horizon; the stars reflected on the water as far as she could see. At the end of her focal gaze, the ocean and sky appeared as one.

Emily nestled into her sleeping bag listening to the night sounds. Occasionally, she would hear a splash in the distance, most likely fish leaping. Somewhere, in the hills beyond the cove, a pack of coyotes yipped and barked in a high-pitched cacophony for several minutes. Once, she heard the distinctive bark of a sea lion on the prowl in the cove.

Sandy awoke from a dream she was having about swimming with whales. The humpback family was all around her, turning in beautifully choreographed pirouettes. In this dream, the songs echoed through her in the endless blue water and she could understand the meaning of each coda. She was eye-to-eye with a giant female when she heard a loud report. The whales disappeared in a burst of bubbles.

She opened her eyes and sat up blinking.

"Did you hear that?" Paola was also sitting up.

"I thought I was dreaming. What was it?"

"Fireworks, maybe?"

"That sounded like gunfire," said Rosen.

# 14

Jesús Trujillo and Carlos Palacios were paralleling the shoreline heading back to their fishing camp on San Vicente when they saw the remains of the panga. It was lying on its side on an outcropping of sharp volcanic rock. The tide was coming in, slamming the twenty-five-foot vessel against the rocks. Jesús turned their panga toward the wreck but had to fight against the backwash to maintain a safe distance. The waters here were treacherous. One wrong move and the bottom of your boat could be shredded.

The men noticed flotsam washed up on the black rocks and floating in the water around the ruined vessel. Drawing as close as they dared, they recognized the name on the bow—*El Tiburón*. Both men looked at each other in surprise. They conversed in Spanish.

"That's Gustavo Silvano's boat," said Carlos. "What's it doing way down here?"

"And where's Gustavo?" Jesús scanned the shoreline.

From where they idled, the pangueros could see a gaping hole in *El Tiburón's* port side bow.

"Bring me in closer," said Carlos.

"The tide is coming in. I'll drop you off and then move back."

Carlos nodded and assumed a position at the bow of their panga. Jesús gave the throttle a little gas and the boat moved forward. Carlos pointed ahead, calling out the rock formations just under the surface. Right before the panga touched the lava outcropping, Jesús eased off the throttle, allowing it to coast the last few feet. Carlos jumped out, almost losing his balance on the sharp, slick rocks. The wiry Mexican fisherman turned and pushed against the boat, slowing its forward progress. With one more push, he sent it backward as Jesús throttled in reverse.

Carlos bent and picked up a shredded life preserver. He looked it over, then set it on the hull of the capsized boat. He worked his way around the vessel, stepping carefully to avoid falling. He retrieved several more objects from the rocks and the shallow water: a sodden sweatshirt, a broken ice chest and more shredded life vests.

"See anything?" Jesús called over the sound of the surf crashing on the rocks.

Carlos shook his head. He made a circular motion with his hand indicating that he was going to expand his search.

He found the body about thirty yards from where the boat was grounded. It was lying face down in a rocky tide pool. The man's skin was badly abraded and bruised. There were numerous cuts and lacerations all over his back and head. A trio of shore crabs balanced on the man's back, picking at a freshly opened wound.

"*Dios mío,*" murmured Carlos. He waved his hands overhead and yelled, "He's here!"

He waded into the pool and cursed at the crabs, who slipped into the water at his approach. Upon closer inspection, he saw that the body had been in the water for a while. The corpse was bloated and whitish. He turned it over.

The man's eyes were gone—empty sockets burning an image into Carlos's brain that he would take to his grave. The skin on the face, chest, and upper arms had been abraded until there was only raw flesh showing.

By now, Jesús had maneuvered the panga closer to where Carlos was bent over the corpse.

"Is it Gustavo?"

"I don't know. Maybe. The body has been ravaged by the rocks and scavengers."

"I'll call it in."

Carlos nodded. He looked down at the corpse and said a silent prayer over the dead man. He crossed himself. He wondered how, if this truly was Gustavo Silvano, he had come to such a horrific end. Gustavo was considered one of the most skillful fishermen in Baja del Sur.

*The sea favors no one*, he thought as he watched Jesús bring the panga in.

The shower in Emily Rosen's unadorned hotel room was nothing to write home about. But to her, it felt as luxurious as a spa. What made this shower especially pleasurable was that the water was hot, washing away the two days of salt caked to her skin from her voyage to see the whales.

The past few days seemed like a dream. Stepping out of the shower, Rosen felt like she was still on the boat, rocking with the waves. When they had first reached the dock, she'd almost fallen over when she stepped onto the pier. She looked at her sunburned face and forearms in the mirror.

Every time she closed her eyes, images of whale flukes arched, then disappeared into the blue water. She heard their exhalations, imagined the subtle fish smell on their breath.

She remembered sitting at sunset, the water reflecting a silver light as whale number twenty-one, Lucy, floated at the surface with her calf. The female would roll onto her back, exposing her fifteen-foot-long pectoral fin dotted with barnacles. Her youngster would nuzzle against her mother's belly as Lucy gently lowered her pectoral fin over the baby's back.

That's when Rosen got hooked.

She had a good start on her new mission to write about whale research and the impact these enigmatic animals had on humans. But she was missing the thread that would elevate this story to another level.

She needed to find out who was killing these whales.

Rosen contemplated getting into her sweats and catching some early evening Mexican news. Her stomach growled, reminding her that she hadn't eaten since noon. She seriously doubted that her less-than-five-star hotel had a room service menu, much less a café. Donning the cleanest pair of black jeans she could find and a black sweatshirt, she set out in search of another La Paz culinary experience.

She entertained the idea of calling Sandy and Paola and asking them to join her. She really wanted to discuss the last few days on the boat with the two marine biologists. She liked them; they were intelligent, passionate, and funny. She pulled out her cell phone and dialed Sandy's number.

Sandy answered on the fourth ring. *"Bueno."*

"Hey, it's me. I was just going to grab a bite and thought maybe you and Paola might like to come along."

"Hey, Emily. We'd love to, but we need to enter this data tonight while it's still fresh. How about tomorrow night?"

"That works for me. Oh, and I'm buying."

"You're on! We'll catch up tomorrow about time and location."

"Sandy?"

"Yes?"

"Thanks again for the last two days. It was the most amazing experience I've ever had."

Sandy laughed. "Well, you can thank us by writing a hell of a story."

"Count on it."

After she disconnected, Rosen walked toward the malecón, the esplanade that wound along the western end of the city, bordering the bay. Up and down the boardwalk, brightly lit restaurants with large menus beckoned hungry tourists and locals alike. She stopped in front of La Roca, one of the busier establishments, and read the menu on a wooden sandwich board. She went inside and was soon ushered to a small table near a window overlooking the bay. The lights from the harbor illuminated the sailboats and schooners moored offshore.

The crowd was noisy and garrulous. Rosen looked around the restaurant, picking out the gringos right away. There was a smattering of locals, but this was definitely where the *turistas nortemericanos* went for food and drink. At the bar, the crowd was three deep. Several overhead televisions blared various sports, from baseball to NASCAR to golf.

Rosen studied the menu until a young Latino man dressed in a white shirt, black apron, and black pants sauntered up to her table. He was slender, well-muscled, and looked like a younger version of Antonio Banderas.

"Something to drink, miss?" He spoke loudly over the din.

"I'd like a glass of chardonnay. What do you recommend?"

The waiter pointed to a selection on the menu. "I sell a lot of these."

"Where's Tecate?"

"Baja del Norte, Baja's wine country."

"What the hell. I'll try it."

She settled on pan-seared mahi mahi with steamed vegetables. The waiter retreated to place her order and left her to people watch. She noticed the crowd tonight appeared younger, more boisterous than in other restaurants. She felt a strange feeling building inside of her. She realized it was agitation. After being on the ocean for several days with just the sounds of whales and seabirds, the noisy restaurant seemed an affront to her senses. Her thoughts soon led her to gaze out at the peaceful bay.

Rosen soon recognized another source of her agitation. She wanted desperately to *tell someone* about what she had just experienced out on the ocean with the whales. Something had happened to her on that boat. Something was different. She abhorred all of the new-age thinking about whales and dolphins having the ability to cure humans of diseases, or that they were the direct descendants of the former residents of Atlantis. But somehow, these whales touched something deep in her core, a visceral feeling of huge size and power, yet a profound sense of a gentle, knowing presence.

Her thoughts flashed to Mark, her former lover of seven years. She wanted to tell him about what she'd seen, what she'd felt. He would understand. He understood her. *At least,* she thought, *he did at one time . . . .*

Emily shook her head, trying to fling away the memory. That was a long time ago. In the end, their stubbornness and unwillingness to compromise had created a schism larger than the Gulf of California.

Suddenly she felt something else she hadn't experienced in a long time. Her eyes were wet. Grabbing her napkin, she dabbed at them and sniffed once. When she looked up the handsome young waiter was standing over her. She quickly cleared her throat and straightened.

"A gentleman at the bar wishes to buy you a drink."

"If I accept, do I have to talk to him?" Rosen activated her personal force field.

The waiter just shrugged. "Another chardonnay?"

"Sure. Why not."

When the waiter returned with the wine, she scanned the bar until she made eye contact with a middle-aged man sitting at the far end. She raised her glass in a gesture of thanks and took a swallow.

Moments later, he wove his way over to her table. From the way he navigated, he had already had a few too many. The smell of his cloyingly sweet cologne reached the table before he did. Rosen imagined sea gulls dropping out of the sky, asphyxiated from the overpowering fragrance.

Emily did a mental eye-roll. *Here we go again.*

"Mind if I join you?"

"I'm sorry. I didn't think conversation came with the wine. But thank you for the drink."

The man sat opposite her at the table. He was in his late forties to early fifties, well-tanned, with graying blond hair, and well on his way to an expansive middle-age paunch. He wore a large Rolex watch and had several gold chains visible in the open neck of his Hawaiian shirt. Rosen guessed he had made a killing in the last stock market boom and had taken his gains and headed south.

"Sure. You look like you could use some company." The man smiled, a predatory kind of grin. His eyes were red-rimmed, a product of either too much time in the sun, too much liquor, or a combination of both. He leaned across the table, already invading Rosen's personal space.

"Really? And what kind of look is that?"

"Well . . . you're sitting alone. And you don't look like you're from around here."

Emily looked around the crowded bar. "Who does?"

"I'm Trent Lahane," the stranger said, extending his hand. "And you are?"

"Emily Rogers." His handshake was not memorable.

"Nice to meet you, Emily. Down here on vacation?"

"Not exactly. I'm thinking about purchasing some property here."

Trent suddenly brightened. "Really? I happen to be in real estate." He produced a card from the breast pocket of his Hawaiian shirt. "I can hook you up with some pretty fabulous property."

He handed her the card. She studied it. At the top it read, "Lahane Investment Properties. Specializing in Your Dream in Paradise."

"So, Emily, what are you looking for?" Trent gave her a used-car smile.

Rosen smiled. "I'm looking for some ocean-front property. Something not too ostentatious, up to 3,000 square feet, secluded, with high walls and lots of landscaping."

"I think I might have something that'll interest you. Great views—360 degrees and the beach is just a half block away." He moved his chair around the table so he was sitting next to her.

"You don't understand." Rosen felt herself wanting to pull back. "I want a place right *on the beach*. I want to hear the waves lapping up against the shore."

Lahane placed his hand on Rosen's forearm. "What line of work are you in?"

"Architect. I design and build assisted living facilities all along the eastern seaboard." It was everything Rosen could do to keep a straight face. She was definitely on a roll. "Ever hear of the 'God's Waiting Room' franchise?' We have sixteen facilities from Florida to New Jersey." She took another mouthful of wine.

Lahane was definitely interested now. "Yeah, I have heard of you. I think I saw an article about you in *Business Week*."

She almost spit out her wine.

"I can see you living down here, Emily," Lahane was oblivious to her body language. His hand stroked the top of hers. Rosen pulled it back.

The waiter returned with her seafood meal and set it before her. It smelled wonderful. She realized she was famished.

"If you'll excuse me." She dug into her food. "I haven't eaten a thing since this morning and I'm starving." She placed a forkful of the succulent fish in her mouth and closed her eyes while she chewed.

"No problem. Don't mind me. Hey, Emily, I was thinking. How 'bout after you finish your dinner we go back to my boat? I've got some great wines, a full bar, and some killer tunes." He pointed out to the harbor. "It's that sweet trimaran anchored out there in the bay. I think you need to join me."

Emily followed the line of his finger until her gaze rested on a large sleek boat anchored about one hundred yards offshore.

"Nice boat. That's a long swim."

"I have a dingy tied up at the dock."

"I'm sure you do. Thanks for the offer. But I have an early morning presentation."

"Just one drink, sweetheart? I'll have you back before midnight. I'm a really nice guy once you get to know me." He leaned over and placed an arm around her shoulders.

*Persistent bastard,* Emily thought. *No problem with a distorted self-image here.* She felt a sudden anger build in her, realizing that there were actually women out there who would fall for this asshole's line of bullshit.

"What do you say?"

She looked over her glasses at Trent. "What do I say to what?"

"Having a drink on my boat. Come on, Emily. It's Mexico. Lighten up. Let your hair down. Have some fun. Admit it. Secretly, you know you want to go."

"Like I said, Trent, I have an appointment in the morning."

He placed his hand on her thigh and began sliding it up. "I can show you a real good time."

Emily placed the fork down near her plate, then removed Lahane's hand from her thigh. She then removed her glasses and set them on the table. "I'm not sure what to think about you, Trent. I can't tell if you're just drunk, oblivious, or just have a bad case of the permanent stupids. I told you I wasn't interested in going out to your boat. Not tonight, not tomorrow, and no time in the foreseeable future. And another thing, Trent. I think buying women drinks and then luring them back to your boat is nothing short of predatory. So, thanks for the drink, and no thanks for the extended evening."

"Fuck you, bitch!" Lahane stood quickly and glared down at her. He tottered slightly, but then regained his balance. "I was just doing you a favor."

"Have a nice life, Trent." Rosen replaced her glasses and picked up her fork.

Lahane turned to leave, then spun back. "I told you, I'm a nice guy. See my buddies at the bar? We had a bet and I lost. The loser had to weed out the homeliest woman in the place and give her a mercy fuck. I wasn't going to tell you. I was going to let you think that you were something special. But you ain't shit."

Rosen looked up at his face, twisted into a leering grin. He looked back toward the bar, where three other drunks were laughing uproariously.

The young waiter walked up to Lahane. "Señor. It's time for you to leave the restaurant."

Lahane stared at him. "And what the fuck are you going to do about it?"

"Me? Nothing," said the waiter, without taking his gaze off Lahane. "But the chief of police is my uncle, and he's sitting at that table over there." The waiter nodded toward a burly man at another table. "He'll do something about it. The inside of his jail is not a pleasant place. Unless you care to see it, I suggest that you and your compadres leave. Now."

Lahane looked back and forth between the waiter and the man on the other side of the restaurant. His mouth twisted and contorted as he tried to find the words. He turned and stumbled toward the bar, rejoining his three friends. A moment later, they walked out.

"I am very sorry for this," said the waiter.

Rosen was trembling.

"Are you okay, miss?"

Emily forced a smile. "Yeah, I'm fine. Thanks. For what you did."

"What can I bring you? It is 'on the house,' as you Americans say."

"Just the check, please."

The waiter was apologetic. "Would you like me to wrap up the rest of your meal?"

"No. Just the check. Thanks."

She pulled several bills from the backpack and laid them on the table.

"Is that enough?"

"It is too much, *Señorita*. I will bring you change."

Emily shook her head. "That's okay. Thank you."

She felt as if all eyes in the restaurant were on her as she got up from the table. She couldn't remember the last time she had felt such mortifying embarrassment. She nodded to the waiter and forced a wan smile. After she walked by, she suddenly turned back around and looked at the waiter once again. "*¿Por favor?*"

"Yes?"

"Was that man across the bar really your uncle and the chief of police?"

The waiter smiled slightly. "Could be."

Rosen decided against a stroll along the malecón and walked quickly back to her hotel room. She tossed her backpack on the bed. She absentmindedly reached for the remote, turned the television on, and channel-surfed. She ended up watching a Mexican *novela* that was right in the middle of some lover's crisis.

Moments later, the tears came. How, she wondered, could one of the most glorious experiences of her life be tainted by such base rudeness. Memories of her former life and relationship came flooding back to her—memories of things she could have said, things she could have done. She told herself it didn't matter. Mark had too many things that just annoyed the shit out of her, but she couldn't remember right now what those annoying traits were.

Emily Rosen couldn't sleep. She tried to clear her mind of everything except the images of whales. She tossed and turned for what seemed like an eternity before she sat upright in bed. She reached for her cell phone and tried to recall the area code for dialing long distance from Mexico. After several failed attempts she heard the phone ringing. Mark answered on the sixth ring.

"H'lo," came the sleepy voice from far away.

"Hey. It's me, Emily. Just wanted to check in and find out if you were all right."

"Rosen? What time is it?"

Rosen looked at her watch. It read 11:20. What was it? Three—no four—hours time difference to New York City. "Hey, I just thought you might still be up."

Mark let out a long sigh over the phone. "It's 3:20 here."

"Sorry. I just wanted to let you know I'm in Mexico. For the past two days, I've been out on the ocean with whales. It was absolutely amazing. You would have loved it."

"Mexico? You're in Mexico?"

Emily heard another sleepy voice in the background. A female voice. "Honey? Who's calling?"

"No one, babe. Just go back to sleep." Mark cleared his throat and then spoke. "I'm glad for you, Emily. But you can't call me anymore. I've moved on. You should, too."

"I just wanted to . . ."

"Good luck to you, Emily." Mark hung up.

Rosen leaned against the headboard, staring at the screen on her cell phone. "Those whales. Boy, they were something to see."

She looked up and grabbed the remote. She channel-surfed for a moment and was about to turn it off when she landed on a local Mexican news station out of La Paz. There were images of Mexican police, *federales,* and a body lying under a shroud at the docks. Two local fishermen were being interviewed by the police. From what she could make out, the fishermen had recovered the body of another fisherman at sea. The newscaster said the name of the dead man was being withheld until next of kin could be contacted.

Rosen felt a flicker of interest in this news piece. What was the dead guy's story? Sandy had told her that the Gulf of California could lull you into a state of complacency, then kill you before you blinked. She shuddered involuntarily, turned off the television, then the light, and crawled under the covers, hoping sleep would come soon.

# 15

Jake Spinner was sitting at El Pulpo Morado in San Jacinto nursing a Bloody Mary. The old dog that had recently adopted him lay curled at his feet, much to the chagrin of the bar's management. Since the dog had jumped into the back of his truck, it had not let Jake out of his sight. It was nearly noon and he had already spent the better part of the morning walking the dock, asking the locals if anyone had seen Gustavo Silvano. No one had seen Gustavo or his son Macario for at least a week. Some said that they heard that the father and son team had gone over to the mainland to find work.

His attention was drawn to the television screen over the bar. The newscast was from La Paz. The federales and Cruz Rojas personnel were attending to an accident scene at the docks.

He stared disbelievingly at the television, feeling his gut turn inside out. A dead fisherman had been recovered by two pangueros cruising the coast north of La Paz. An inert figure covered in a shroud was being loaded into an ambulance while a small crowd of onlookers stood by. When the cameras panned to the recovered panga, Jake felt like a knife had just been shoved between his ribs.

On the bow of the panga was the name *El Tiburón*.

"Shit!" Spinner said loudly. He got up from his stool, walked behind the bar and turned up the volume. Max, the bartender, came hurrying over.

"Señor Jake, no one is allowed behind the bar. Especially you."

When Max saw the look of fury and pain in Jake's cold blue eyes, he immediately took a step back. Jake turned and looked at the television. The camera panned back to the reporter, a well-dressed young *Latina* who was saying that the name of the deceased was being withheld pending notification of relatives.

The reporter next interviewed the two fishermen. They described where they found the grounded boat. They said that region of coastline was treacherous.

76

Jake turned from the television, reached into his shirt pocket, and tossed a bill on the bar. Without another word, he left the bar with the dog padding at his heels. Max heard Jake's pickup roar to life. He caught a glimpse of a cloud of dust as Jake's beater spun out of the parking lot.

Spinner made it to La Paz in less than three hours and went directly to the police station. It was late in the day and the main room was crowded with people, many sitting in chairs waiting dourly for their turns to plead their case. Ceiling fans overhead were working overtime, but the air inside was stifling. He approached the desk and asked for the officer in charge of the dead fisherman who had been recovered earlier. The clerk motioned for Jake to take a seat against the wall and someone would be with him shortly.

Nearly an hour later, Jake felt like he was crawling out of his skin. He needed a drink. Being in close proximity to all these people pegged his anxiety to the near-breaking point. Finally, a portly policeman approached him and stood in front of him.

"You are here about the dead fisherman?" He spoke in rapid-fire Spanish.

Jake stood up. "Yes."

"You are family?" The policeman peered over his glasses at Jake.

"A friend. Has anyone identified the deceased?"

"Only members of the immediate family can be allowed in for identification purposes. You are not family."

"Look." Jake's already thin veil of patience was evaporating by the second. "If it is my friend, I can identify him for you. Is he the only victim? Were more bodies recovered at the site?"

"I cannot answer your questions at this time. A statement will be issued by the medical examiner pending notification of next of kin."

"Just answer me this then. Was there anyone else recovered?"

"This interview is over."

"Interview? What interview?" Jake fished his wallet out of the rear pocket of his jeans and produced several bills.

The policeman looked at him as if he were some speck of dirt on his shoe, but Jake saw something else in the policeman's eye. He looked beyond Jake for a millisecond, but it was enough for Jake to recognize acknowledgment.

He turned around. Standing at the back of the room was one of the Japanese thugs who had confronted him back at Gustavo's place. The large Asian man could have been looking at Jake, but his eyes were hidden by dark wrap-around sunglasses.

"Looks like someone already beat me to it," Jake said, palming the bills and sticking them back in his pocket.

He turned and walked out of the police station. Passing the Japanese behemoth, Jake muttered, "How's the fishing, *Gordo*?"

He drove down to the docks as the sun was dipping into the sea, creating a brilliant golden fireball in the west. He was hoping to catch up with the two *pangueros* before they headed north. There were only three places where the locals liked to grab a shot and a bite. Jake had been in all three cantinas at given times in various states of altered consciousness.

He finally caught up to the two fishermen at the last one. They were sitting at the bar with two empty plates in front of them, along with a half-dozen empty Pacífico bottles. They wore greasy hats, old sweaters, and had the rough hands and deeply lined faces of men who made their living on the water.

Jake pulled up a stool next to the older of the two fishermen. He ordered three Pacíficos and then addressed them in Spanish.

"My name is Jake Spinner. Gustavo Silvano was a friend of mine. We fished the mid-Gulf for over seven years together. That was his panga that was recovered. I've been trying to locate him, and I'm afraid he's dead."

The older fisherman turned his steely gaze on Jake. "I knew Gustavo. He spoke of you, Jake Spinner. He said you drink too much."

"That sounds like Gustavo."

The round of beers arrived. Carlos and Jesús looked at the cold brews. Carlos gave Jake a disparaging look. "What is this to you? You are a gringo. Gringos don't care what happens to *indios*."

The older man held up his hand. "Carlos, he was a friend of Gustavo's. Gustavo spoke well of him." Jesús turned back to face Jake. "What do you hope to gain from this?"

"I need to know if the body that you brought in was Gustavo Silvano. I have reason to believe he was murdered. And if that's so, I aim to find the people who killed him."

The panga drivers' heads whipped around to face Jake.

Carlos asked, "Murder? Why would anyone want to kill Gustavo? He was a fisherman."

"Do you think he was trafficking for the cartels?" Jesús asked.

Jake shook his head. "I don't think so. But I did see Macario, Gustavo's son, flashing around a lot of cash in the marketplace in San Jacinto. He was hiding something. A week ago, Gustavo asked me if I could arrange passage for him, his wife, and son to El Norte. Something had gone badly for him here." Jake took a deep breath then exhaled. "What I want to know, given your best guess and memory, did the body look like Gustavo?"

"The body was so badly battered and . . . " Carlos trailed off, then took a long draught from his bottle.

"The body was the same height as Gustavo," said Jesús. "Roughly the same build. The body had been in the water for a very long time. He was already decomposing and the scavengers had already been working on him."

Carlos looked uncomfortable. "Have you tried to view the body at the morgue?"

"Only family members," Jake said sourly. "But I don't think the rest of his family is going to come forward any time soon."

"Why is that?" Jesús cast a suspicious glance at Jake.

"Because I have a bad feeling that they may have been murdered as well."

Carlos and Jesús each made the sign of the cross. "May God rest their souls," said Jesús.

They sat at the bar silently for a moment, each man lost in his thoughts. Finally, Jake broke the silence. "Did you see any evidence of a struggle? Any articles of clothing that could have belonged to a woman or another man?"

Carlos shook his head. "No. We saw no clothing or items that could have belonged to a woman. There were only the barest of supplies in or around the boat.

"See any fishing gear? Rods, reels?"

Jesús was thoughtful. "That is strange. There was no tackle anywhere on the boat or on the rocks. We checked the area."

Jake finished his beer and set it next to the other bottles on the bar. "Another beer?"

"No, thank you," said Jesús. "It's a long boat ride to our fishing camp."

"Fishing camp?" Jake said, as if a light bulb had gone off in his head. "Where's your fishing camp?"

"It is at San Vicente, about twenty kilometers south of Playa Escondida," said Jesús. "Do you know of it?"

Jake nodded. "Been by it many times over the years. I heard there was a good boat mechanic living there."

"Sí," said Carlos. "That is my brother, Francisco."

"Wait," said Jesús, turning to face Carlos. "Do you remember the man had strange markings on his wrists and ankles?"

Jake's eyes widened.

"Yes," said Carlos, "On both ankles. Both wrists," said Carlos. "We thought they were strange marks. It didn't look like damage from the reefs. It looked like—"

"Rope marks," Jake finished.

Jesús nodded. "The marks were the same on the ankles and wrists."

Jake's gaze hardened. Carlos and Jesús could feel the palpable rage emanating from Jake's core, causing them to flinch slightly.

"One more question," Jake said in a measured tone. "Have you been approached by any foreigners? Possibly Chinese or Japanese?"

Jesús shook his head. "No, Señor. But there were two very large Asian men dressed in expensive clothes and wearing sunglasses, standing in the crowd at the docks. They were hard to miss. They stood above the rest of the crowd."

Jake stood stiffly. "*Muchas gracias.*" He laid a 200 peso note on the bar. "For petrol and food for the ride home."

Carlos asked, "Should we go to the police station and tell them?"

"Just go back home to San Vicente," Jake said flatly. "You'll be a whole lot safer."

He turned and walked out of the cantina.

# 16

Hiro Yoshimatsu looked at the great expanse of ocean in front of him. From his penthouse suite on the seventh floor of the finest hotel in Cabo San Lucas, Yoshimatsu had all the amenities he desired and could still be within an hour's flight to La Paz. He could easily coordinate the operation from here. La Paz just seemed a bit too quaint for his tastes.

Dressed in a white shirt and white pants, he was sitting in an ornate, cushioned rattan chair under a large umbrella on the patio of the penthouse. In a bucket next to him were several bottles of chilled Bohemia beer. On the table was a large silver platter loaded with shrimp, lobster, and ahi tuna. In a lounge chair several feet away, Susan lay on her stomach, catching a tan. She was naked, wanting to avoid tan lines. Next to her were several phones, the largest being the direct line to the front desk.

Yoshimatsu was studying the data that had been provided by Alejandro Cabrillo. Many of the notations were of no use to him. But there was sufficient data from telemetry that provided positions of groups of whales in the Gulf at certain times that would improve the efficiency and productivity of the hunts.

The phone next to Susan rang. She picked it up on the second ring. "Yes? Please send him up. Thank you."

She swung out of the lounger and deftly put on her bathing suit and a sheer overshirt. She looked at Yoshimatsu. "Excuse me, Hiro-san, but Mr. Kanamura is on his way up."

Yoshimatsu did not look up from his papers. "Very good. Please let him in when he arrives and show him out here."

Moments later, Susan led Ako Kanamura onto the patio. He bowed deeply when he faced Yoshimatsu.

As Chief of Security for Yoshimatsu's organization, Kanamura was the enforcer who made sure all operations ran smoothly. He was dedicated to Yoshimatsu and would stop at nothing to carry out his boss's directives. Kanamura was also a highly skilled assassin specializing in martial arts with a particular penchant for Samurai swords. Yoshimatsu recognized that every operation involved many potential problems. He was masterful at seeing the potential problems before they happened, and Kanamura was his instrument to carry out the necessary adjustments.

"Ah, my good friend Ako, I have been waiting to hear your report. Would you care for drink?"

Kanamura nodded. He was dressed in a dark suit and tie. He was large for a Japanese man, well-muscled, and moved with the grace of a leopard. He bore a ragged scar on the right side of his face, that began just above his brow and ended near his jawline. His expression never changed, yet when Susan gazed at him, she felt a dark energy emanate from him.

She disappeared inside, returning with a carafe of sake and small sake glasses. He accepted the delicate bowl of warmed sake and bowed slightly. Yoshimatsu looked at Susan and spoke softly. "Leave us for now."

She nodded and walked back into the penthouse. Yoshimatsu turned back to Kanamura.

"How go the preparations for the drive?"

Kanamura took a sip of his sake, then said, "We are on schedule for three days from now. The fishermen from the village have almost completed the barricade and set up the containment pens. The transport vehicles that will move the live animals will arrive in two days and we will have them on site before the drive even starts."

"Very good. Captain Watabe has reassured me that his banger crews are very skilled at herding dolphins and small whales."

"We will be ready on our end," said Kanamura.

Yoshimatsu brought the sake to his lips. He looked out over the water. "I understand there were some loose ends with the fisherman and his family."

Kanamura shifted nervously on his feet, looked down briefly, then back at his boss. "The Mexicans were sloppy in their execution of the plan, sir. The problem of the disloyal fisherman and his wife has been solved, but they were unable to locate the son. Even under extreme interrogation, the couple would not reveal the whereabouts of their hotheaded son. The wrecked boat seemed to be a good setup at the time. I think the men that Minister Figueroa recommended from the cartel were inefficient and lacked discretion in executing the operation."

"I will speak with the minister on this. Your job, Ako-san, is to make sure everything runs according to plan. I do not want any surprises."

Kanamura bowed his head in deference. "Understood, Sir."

"Continue, please."

"Unfortunately, we have been unable to locate the son, Macario Silvano. We have been interrogating other members of the village. No one appears to know where he is."

"That is most disturbing news, Ako. What about his friends?"

"They all say the same thing. Macario has gone over to the mainland. He has a girlfriend there. They do not know when he is coming back. They assured me that he would return in time for the next hunt."

"We must find him before he exposes our operation. Sooner or later, the younger Silvano will have to return to his village. Make sure your men are ready when he does. Keep someone posted on the house."

Kanamura nodded. "There is another problem, sir."

Yoshimatsu's gaze hardened. "Tread softly, Ako-san. Those are words I do not want to hear."

"An American has been snooping around the village. We first observed him nearly two weeks ago when he came to the fisherman's house. They conversed for a while in the back, sitting in a boat. When we inquired who he was, Gustavo said that he was just another tourist looking for a charter. The next time we encountered the American was three days ago. He showed up again at the Silvano house. We asked him his business and he became belligerent. Yesterday, he appeared at the police station wanting to identify the body."

"I want you to find out about this American."

"I already have taken the liberty, Hiro-San." He handed the folder to Yoshimatsu who nodded and opened it. As he read, Kanamura recited the details.

"His name is Jake Spinner. He is forty years old, former Army Special Forces, three tours in Iraq, two in Afghanistan. He was a specialist in explosives and infiltration behind enemy lines. Wounded in his last tour, he spent eight months in a hospital in Germany."

"Any family?" Yoshimatsu continued to peruse the document. "A person who has family members is a much easier opponent to leverage."

"He was married once. To one Carolyn Bainbridge. They have been divorced for nine years. No children. Parents deceased. One sister. Deceased."

"We will have to find another way to dissuade him."

"As you will see in the file, Hiro-san, he has had—how shall we say—numerous difficulties adjusting to civilian life. Multiple arrests for disorderly conduct, public drunkenness, some questionable business dealings with tourists looking to book fishing charters. He appears to be tolerated, at best, in the village of San Jacinto."

"A man, once he loses his honor, is no longer a man."

"What will you have me do with him?"

"I want the furor from the press to fade away. An American dying in Mexico is big news. Keep an eye on him. I want no more surprises."

Kanamura nodded again. "I will have one of my men follow him."

"No. I will speak with Figueroa. One of the locals would blend into the crowd better. But he will answer to you."

"As you wish, sir. Is there anything else?"

Yoshimatsu smiled. "Ako, come sit with me and I will show you the data Minister Figueroa organized for us. GPS points for whale congregations in the lower and middle Gulf. It will streamline our operation and improve our catch rate."

# 17

Sandy Wainright's eyes were beginning to blur. She had been staring at the computer screen for nearly three hours and the data were looking like hieroglyphics. It had been difficult for her to concentrate over the last few days. After she and Alejandro had completed the alternate coordinates for the humpbacks' locations in the Gulf, she had waited for the ax to fall. If their duplicity was exposed, their research would be discontinued and they would lose their positions.

The signal for the whale, a seventeen-year-old male identified as J-6, had dropped off somewhere in the southern quadrant, about fifty miles southeast of Cabo San Lucas. "Rooster"—as he came to be known by the researchers—had a propensity for carving huge rooster tails with his flukes while he played at the surface. This was something he did every time the research boat was in the vicinity. Part of the reason for this behavior was due to his naturally ebullient nature. The other, Sandy suspected, was due to an incident that had occurred nearly two years ago.

While looking for humpbacks in Loreto Bay, Sandy and Paola were alerted by fishermen that there was a young whale trapped in gill nets. It was floundering at the surface on the east side of Isla Montserrat. When they arrived, they found the humpback barely moving, its breath labored and rapid. Its flukes were trapped in wads of netting and rope, almost completely immobilizing the exhausted whale.

They spent the next three hours cutting the monofilament netting. Since neither one of them had thought of bringing a wetsuit, each took a turn climbing into the chilly February water to slice segments of gill netting away from the flukes while the other maneuvered the boat around the nearly helpless humpback. Some of the gill net had become deeply and painfully enmeshed in the whale's skin, and Sandy tugged at a length to slice it away.

What astonished her was that this huge whale was calmly allowing her to cut the net and pull off the deadly mesh that had immobilized him. After two hours, Sandy could no longer feel her hands and feet. Her numb hands could no longer work the handles of the surgical scissors. She took one final breath and went after the last shred of netting. This remnant had a buoy attached to it and when Sandy cut though the last segment, the buoy popped to the surface and the rest of the netting drifted slowly toward the bottom.

At first the whale didn't move. Sandy held onto the gunwale, too exhausted to swim.

"C'mon baby, move those flukes! You can do it!"

The young humpback remained stationary. She feared it was going to drown.

Paola leaned over the side and held out her hand. "Sandy, your lips are blue. Get back in the boat. Now!"

"Let me try something." Sandy let go of the boat and swam out to the listless whale. She positioned herself at the whale's flank. She pulled her knees in and gently pushed her feet against the whale. "Move your ass!"

Surprised, the whale flinched. Sandy backpedaled. Then the flukes swept downward, then upward, tentatively at first. Then a stronger beat. Downward, then up. The strokes grew larger as the whale disappeared into the blue-green water. Sandy swam back to the boat. With all of her strength sapped by the cold water, Paola had to help her into the boat.

Paola wrapped Sandy in beach towels. All of a sudden, fifty yards off the starboard bow, the water exploded. The young humpback began to breach, almost bringing his forty-five-foot body completely out of the water. He landed with a resounding splash. The whale repeated this performance for nearly thirty minutes before disappearing in the distance.

Both women laughed with joy.

Paola said, "I believe Rooster just said, 'Thank you.'"

The memory caused Sandy to brush a tear from her cheek. Part of her wanted to believe that the young rambunctious whale had shaken the transmitter loose with his boisterous surface behavior. Transmitters had a tendency to either fall off or malfunction over time. Ocean water and fifty-five-ton whales were hard on tracking devices. But deep in her heart, she feared the worst. Rooster, whale J-6, had most likely been killed by poachers.

Wainright now suspected that the Japanese contingent had something to do with the whale disappearances. Mexico had banned whaling anywhere in and around its coastal waters for nearly twenty years. There was strong public support for whale conservation and protection of critical habitats. Sandy wondered why the Mexican Fisheries Department would now allow access to the Japanese to vital data that could expose the populations of humpbacks to illegal hunting. Sandy felt it would be important for her to work with Alejandro to falsify the data regarding the whales' locations.

Alejandro, Sandy, and Paola made inquiries up and down the coast. They asked fisherman, boaters, SCUBA divers, and even the Mexican Navy if they had seen any large processing ships offshore, or even beyond the international boundary. No one had reported anything.

Someone was killing whales. Sooner or later, Sandy was going to find out who.

It was late. She had just gotten into bed when there was a loud knock on the door. Throwing a ratty robe over her sweatpants and tee shirt, she padded over.

"Who's there?"

"Raúl Campos, Señorita."

Raúl Campos was one of the local fishermen who had, on many occasions, assisted Sandy and Paola in their research, locating pods of whales and reporting on their activities while he was setting his lobster traps. He had been skeptical about the work of the institute. Initially, he believed that the researchers were only out to prevent the fishermen from earning a living. Over time, he had become a passionate supporter of both the whales and the institute. Sometimes, he acted as spokesman and informal go-between for the researchers and the group of fishermen who fished the waters south of La Paz to Los Cabos.

Sandy opened the door. Raúl stood before her, his cap in his hands. He was dressed in yellow fishing waders with suspenders over an old knit sweater. Though in his mid-forties, the toll from the years of sea wind and saltwater made him appear much older.

"Señorita Sandy, it is important I speak with you."

Sandy ushered him in but left the door open. "What is it Raúl?"

"If it is what I think it is, then something terrible is about to happen."

She closed the door and sat down at the table. She motioned him to sit.

Raúl took a seat and leaned forward. He looked at her through bloodshot eyes. "I have been fishing in the north for the last few weeks. The lobster catch south of La Paz has been meager for the past two months. There is a cove north of here, three hours by panga, called San Mateo. In the past I have had good luck there."

"I know of this cove. Go on."

"There are very few who visit the cove. There are only the remnants of an old fishing camp. Today there was much activity. There were refrigerator trucks on the beach. Many men were on the shore and several boats were anchored at the entrance."

Sandy felt her gut begin to churn. "Did you see what they were doing?"

"When I brought my panga in for a closer look, I was intercepted by one of the boats. There was a *Mexicano* who looked like a federale. He told me to move along. He held some kind of a machine gun over his shoulder. When I asked him what they were fishing for, he pointed the gun at me and told me it was none of my business."

"What do you think was in that cove?" Sandy dreaded the answer.

"Señorita Sandy, I could not see very well because of the angle of the sun, but my ears heard. I heard the breaths of many dolphins."

"Oh, my God. Are you sure, Raúl?"

"Sí. My ears are still good. I heard many breaths at once. And they sounded like they were breathing hard."

"I can't believe this is happening." Sandy stood and began to pace. She then turned to Raúl and said, "Can you take me there?"

Raúl shook his head vigorously. "No, Señorita Sandy. It is too risky to approach from the sea. These men are *muy peligrosos!*"

"Then can you show me how to get there by land?"

Raúl stared at Sandy as if he were looking straight through her. After a moment, he looked out the window, his brow deeply furrowed. "The road is bad. You have to go over a mountain to get to the *bahía*. The track is rocky and steep. Many four-wheel-drive vehicles have gotten stranded there."

"Raúl, we need your help," Sandy pleaded. "The dolphins need your help."

The fisherman let out a long, ragged breath. "Sí. I will show you to the road."

"Thank you." Sandy went to the counter and picked up her cell phone. She hit the speed dial for Paola.

"¿Qué pasa, *chica?*" Paola said after the second ring.

"You need to get over here pronto. Something horrible is about to happen."

"What's going on?'

"Raúl Campos is here. He was out near San Mateo Cove today." Sandy relayed the information to Paola.

"¡Dios mío! Does Alejandro know?"

"Not yet. You're the first one I called. He's next on the list."

"I'll be right there."

The phone seemed to ring forever before a sleepy voice answered. "Qué pasa?"

"Alejandro, sorry to bother you at this hour," Sandy's voice was tense. "I have Raúl Campos here with me. He saw men with guns at San Mateo Cove today.

There were nets closing off the cove and refrigerator trucks parked on the shore. He said there were lots of dolphins trapped behind the nets."

"What? Is he sure?" Alejandro's voice was thick from sleep.

"Yes. He's sure. Alex, I think they're going to slaughter dolphins."

Sandy heard a muffled voice in the background. Alejandro said, "It's okay, *mi amo*. Go back to sleep." To Sandy, he said, "How long will it take us to get to San Mateo?"

"A boat won't work," said Sandy. "They have guns. Probably three to four hours by truck. Raúl says the approach over land is rough."

"I'll be there in thirty minutes. Don't let Raúl leave."

"He's not going anywhere. Alejandro, should I call Emily Rosen?"

There was a pause on the other end of the line. Finally, Alejandro said, "Yes, call her. If this is really going to happen, then we need to have it documented by someone other than us. Someone with press credentials."

Sandy went to her backpack and located Emily's business card. She dialed the New York cell phone number. Rosen picked up. "This better be good."

"Emily, this is Sandy. Something terrible is about to happen. We need you and your camera over here now."

"What's up?"

"We think a bunch of dolphins are about to be slaughtered."

"I'm on my way." After Sandy gave her directions, Emily's phone went silent.

An hour later, Alejandro, Paola, Emily, and Raúl sat around Sandy's kitchen table. Half empty coffee cups and topo maps and charts lay before them. Sandy grabbed the coffee pot and refilled everyone's cup. The faces around the table were grim.

Alejandro's eyes were still puffy from sleep. "I must ask you, Raúl. Are local fishermen involved in this hunt?"

Raúl's gaze hardened. "No, Señor. The men I saw at San Mateo were not from here. The hombre who chased me off with a gun looked like a federale."

"I mean no offense. I'm just trying to get an idea of who we're up against." He grabbed Raúl gently by the shoulder. "You've always been a trusted friend to the institute. How do you think they got refrigerator trucks over that pass?"

Raúl shrugged. "I don't know. The men could have removed rocks to allow passage. I think they will have the road to San Mateo guarded as well. We should approach the bay from here." He pointed to the map. "We will have to hike in. I know of an animal trail that will lead us to a place where we can observe without being seen."

Rosen asked, "Shouldn't we contact someone? Greenpeace or some organization like that?"

Sandy shook her head. "By the time we contact them and they get down here, the kill will be long over. You're our best bet, Emily."

"No pressure."

"Once we get there, what are we going to do?" Paola looked nervous.

"We're going to document. That is all," said Alejandro. "I don't want anyone risking their life unnecessarily. Our job is to record any and all events, no matter how hard they are to watch. That's the only way we can stop this from happening again."

"Alejandro, shouldn't you contact the Mexican Navy?" Rosen asked.

"Right now, we don't know who is behind this. I have some suspicions, but I don't know who is aligned with whom at this point. I don't even know if we can trust the Mexican Navy." He turned to Raúl. "What do we need to bring?"

"Water. Lots of water. Those rocks get hot during the day. We may be in for a long wait. And food. Once we're there, it's a long walk back to the trucks."

Alejandro looked at the members of the group. "This is going to be dangerous. These men might shoot at us if we're discovered. If anyone—for any reason—feels uncomfortable doing this, now is the time to speak. No one will think ill of you if you don't want to go." He looked around the table at his colleagues. He could see fear underlying the determination in everyone's eyes.

"Don't sugar coat it like that for us, Alejandro," Rosen said, a half-smile etching her lips. "I'm in."

"Me too," said Sandy.

Paola nodded.

Alejandro looked around the group, sighed deeply, and then said, "We leave in thirty minutes. Pack only what you need and be quick."

# 18

Jake Spinner knew he was being watched. He sat in the dark in his small bungalow on the beach. The undeniable tingling sensation at the back of his neck had returned. That feeling of impending dread was back, that feeling that had saved his life more times than he could count during his deployments to the Middle East.

Jake stood and moved slowly toward the window and peered between the drawn curtains. The dusty street was empty this time of night. One lone streetlamp about half a block down bathed the narrow street in an amber light. From where he stood, the curtains blocked most of his view, but he dared not move them. He was hoping his stalkers were thinking he wasn't home.

He had slipped in through the back door an hour earlier. His cover had almost been blown when he nearly tripped over the dog that had been curled up on the straw mat in front of the door. The dog whined several times when Jake closed the door on him. Jake tried several times to hush the dog, but to no avail. Finally, Spinner grabbed him by the scruff of the neck and pulled him into the house.

Two days had passed and still no word about the whereabouts of Marta or Macario Silvano. An idea had been brewing in Jake's addled brain. Something kept gnawing at him ever since he had spoken with the two fishermen at the docks who had discovered Gustavo's body. He needed to check out the old fishing camp he had set up with Gustavo. It was in a remote location several hours north of San Jacinto. Along with Gustavo and Macario, he had established the camp six years ago and built a small *palapa* with a storage shack for supplies on subsequent trips. The shack held ice chests, extra fishing equipment, and canned goods for times when the fishing wasn't so good.

It was just a hunch, but Macario could have figured it was the one place where he wouldn't be found. Hell, it's where he would have gone if he needed to disappear for a while.

In the distance, Jake heard a car engine start up. A vehicle was approaching. He could hear the sounds of rolling tires grinding against sand. The dog lifted his head and let out a low menacing growl.

Jake put a finger to his lips. "Shhhh! Shut up, damn it."

The dog cocked his head.

The dog laid his ears back, turned, and stared at the door. Jake drew back against the wall. A dark SUV pulled slowly in front of his bungalow and then kept going. He could only get a glimpse of it. The car windows were darkened, but he suspected it was the same vehicle he'd seen at Gustavo's house. It paused for a moment. Jake instinctively lowered himself to the floor in anticipation of a hail of bullets spewing out of the SUV.

After a moment the vehicle rolled forward until he could no longer see or hear it. He was reasonably sure the vehicle hadn't gone far. He went through the house in the dark and gathered some water and canned food and threw them, along with a change of clothes, in an old duffel. Lastly, he quietly pushed his bed to the side. Under an old throw rug was a three-foot-square cutout that had a small metal ring in the center. He lifted the wooden piece and placed it to the side. Always paranoid, Jake had cut out the opening in the floor to hide his personal items. This crawl space provided him a quick escape from the bungalow if he needed to make a hasty retreat. He lay down on the floor, reached in, and lifted out an old army surplus ammo box. Unlocking the box, he fished out his service Beretta and several magazines. He tossed these in the duffel and listened again.

The dog let out another throaty growl. Jake was about to shush him again when he saw a shadow pass in front of the window. He retrieved the pistol and then crawled along the floor to get a better view of both the front and back entrances.

Somewhere in Jake's brain an alarm sounded. He knew he had to get out of the house. He went to the opening in the floor and tossed the duffel into it. He crawled along the floor until he was able to grab the dog by the scruff of the neck. He pushed the dog down through the opening and with some effort squeezed himself through. Before ducking down into the crawlspace, he pulled the rug back into place over the hole.

Suddenly the house erupted in a hail of lead and shattered glass as automatic weapons lit up the still night. Chunks of wood and adobe tore from its foundation. Jake figured there were two shooters firing AK-47s. The assailants were laying down a steady stream of fire from top to bottom. He heard bullets crunching into the concrete foundation at the front of the house. That was the only thing preventing him from becoming Swiss cheese in his current location. He and the dog belly-crawled toward the rear of the foundation where a worn plank was the only thing that separated them from the outside world.

The firing continued. Spinner peered through the crack in the wood to see if any of the assailants had decided to surround him. It seemed they were having too good a time leveling the front of the bungalow at the moment. He turned his body to get enough flex in his hip and kicked the worn board outward. The terrified dog was frozen in place. Jake reached back and grabbed the dog again and pulled. They squirmed out from underneath the house and took off at a dead run for the nearby pier where Jake's boat was moored.

He was gasping for breath when he reached the pier. He tossed his duffel into the boat and untied the mooring lines. The dog wasted no time. He dove headlong onto the boat and went below deck. Spinner gave him a disparaging look but kept looking over his shoulder to see if he was being followed. He heard shouting, he saw house lights go on, and the neighborhood woke up in alarm.

Jake vaulted into the boat and ran to the console. Fumbling in his pocket he found the ignition keys and clumsily slid them in. The engine coughed to life after the third turn. He throttled the boat backward and swung out into the open sea. He gunned the throttle and the boat jumped forward. He was determined to put as much water between him and his assailants as quickly as possible.

The next morning Jake was still wired when the sun began to show color in the east. His mind kept replaying the events of the past few days. Why had he been targeted for a hit? Was he getting too close to discovering the truth about Gustavo's death? One thing was for sure—someone was willing to expend a lot of lead to keep him from nosing around.

He was roughly three miles offshore, on a heading for his old fishing camp. The water surface was silver and flat like a lake, disturbed at times as shoals of small baitfish leapt from the water at the boat's approach. He was making good time. With luck and with no one else taking pot shots at him, he would get to the fishing camp around noon.

He realized he was very hungry. He hadn't eaten since yesterday afternoon. He throttled down, put the transmission in neutral, then went below deck to forage for something to eat. Pickings were slim in the galley. He hadn't had a chance to restock before his hasty departure from San Jacinto. He finally located a package of stale tortillas and some cheese in the refrigerator that had morphed into a new life form. He cut away most of the green mold until he was left with a small square of passable yellow cheese. "Lot of penicillin here," Spinner said, forgetting that penicillin was cultivated on bread, not cheese.

In an overhead cupboard, he discovered an unopened can of refried beans. He fired up the propane stove, heated the refried beans and prepared himself some burritos. He took the two burritos back to the wheel and began devouring one. A whimper near his feet caused him to look down. The dog was looking up at him, drool dripping from his muzzle, eyes beseeching.

"What?" Spinner, annoyed, looked down at the dog. "Not now. I'm eating."

The dog tentatively raised a paw and gently patted his leg. He whined again.

"Aw, shit." Spinner tore off a chunk of burrito and handed it to the dog, who snapped it up like a shark taking a baitfish.

"Easy, pal," said Jake. "You expect to get any more of my meal, you're going to have to show some table manners." Spinner tore off another chunk of burrito and handed it to him. "Now, gently."

The dog lunged forward and grabbed the morsel from Jake's fingertips. He had to pull his hand away quickly for fear that the dog couldn't discriminate between burrito and fingers.

"We're going to have to work on this, you and me," Jake pointed his finger at the dog, then back at himself.

He ended up giving the dog most of the second burrito. He hoped the dog's digestive system was up to the challenge. Otherwise, it was going to be a long trip to the fishing camp.

Surprisingly, Jake encountered no other boat traffic while he motored out. Usually, he could count on seeing at least a few pangas hugging the coastline. This section of the Gulf of California was eerily deserted today. As the boat droned along, Spinner ruminated on how his life had spiraled down to the point that he was now homeless and broke and his only companion was a flatulent, flea-ridden mutt that really didn't like him much. It had been nearly two days since any liquor had passed his lips. Sobriety had not brought clarity. Jake's mind wrestled with the events of the past few weeks.

Why would anyone want Gustavo and his family killed? Jake thought back to that day in the mercado when he saw Macario sporting major bling and flashing the wad of bills. And then there were the new amenities at Gustavo's house. What had they gotten into? And why were they killed for it? So far, Marta's body had not been found. Neither had Macario's. Perhaps Gustavo, realizing imminent danger, had sent his wife and son over to the mainland.

Spinner found his thoughts drifting back over the years to his former wife, Carolyn. Before his deployment, he had been like any other starry-eyed lover—

every day was a glorious adventure. They were young, strong, and beautiful, and they faced the world like they owned it. Jake wondered how Carolyn's life had turned out. The last correspondence he had received from her was brief. She was living on the East Coast, had remarried, and had one child, a boy, with another on the way. She wanted no further contact with him but wished him well.

He felt a deep pang rumble through his gut. He could have tossed it off to withdrawal from the alcohol—maybe it was. But he knew it went far beyond the physical manifestations of addiction. His very soul was sick, and he had no idea how to make it better.

At a little past noon, he pulled into the shallow cove where the fishing camp was located. No boats were visible in the small bay and the camp looked deserted. He eased the boat through the shallow cyan water and turned off the motor when he was about twenty yards from shore. He used the automatic lift to lever the motor up so as not to drag it on the sandy bottom. Grabbing the bowline, he jumped overboard into waist deep water and walked to the shore where he tied the line to a large rock outcropping.

The dog, seeing his human traveling companion abandoning ship, frantically paced back and forth on deck, whining loudly. Spinner looked back. "Well, you want to come ashore, jump. I'm not carryin' your sorry ass."

The dog paced more frenetically, his whines morphing into desperate barks.

"Jesus Christ, you'd think someone was killing you." He waded out toward the boat and the panicked dog. "Come on! Here boy! Jump!"

The dog responded by becoming more agitated. Spinner got to the bow and reached for him. The dog pulled away, terrified.

"C'mon, Dog. I got you. It's going to be okay."

He reached out with one hand, coaxing the dog toward him. Tentatively, the dog approached and sniffed his hand. When he moved closer, Jake grabbed him by the scruff and attempted to pull the dog toward him. Forty pounds of desperate dog leapt toward him, hitting him hard in the chest and driving him backward and under the water.

Jake came up sputtering. "Son of a bitch!" He stumbled around in the shallows until his feet found purchase, and he dragged himself to the shoreline. He flopped down at the water's edge to catch his breath. He pulled off one shoe, then the other and emptied the water and sand from them. The dog was now happily bounding up and down the shoreline, obviously glad to be on solid ground. He came back, shook vigorously and began to lick the salt off Jake's face.

"Knock it off! I know where that mouth's been."

After Jake got his wind back, he stood stiffly and began to look around. There was no sign of disturbance on the beach. It appeared as if no one had set foot on this shore for a while. Behind him, there was a lone fishing shack at the entrance to a sandy arroyo. Jake and Gustavo had built it five years ago. Never luxurious, it had recently fallen into disrepair from the effects of wind and storms. He trudged up to the rickety wooden building with its corrugated tin roof.

He heard the dog barking off in the distance behind one of the dunes. He made a mental note of the direction the barking was coming from. Spinner pushed the ill-fitting wooden door open. It took time for his eyes to adjust to the darkness of the shack after being on a blindingly bright white sand beach.

Someone had slept here recently. In the far corner of the shack was a rusty bed frame topped with a pile of worn blankets in disarray. An old wooden table stood in the middle of the sand floor. On the table, there was a nearly empty bottle of *habañero* salsa and some salt and pepper shakers. Near a window, a makeshift sink was stacked up with dirty plates. Empty cans that had once held peaches and refried beans were lined up behind the sink. Movement on the lip of one of the cans caught Jake's attention. He squinted at the can, then scowled when he realized it was a very large and nasty looking scorpion.

The sand floor had recently been tamped down and swept. Near the bed, he found one print in the sand. He recognized the footprint and could even tell the make of the shoes: high-end Nike basketball shoes.

He lifted the lid of an old rusty ice chest. Brownish water filled the lower third. Several unopened bottles of beer and cans of soda floated in the swill. He reached inside and retrieved a warm Pacífico. From the rear pocket of his cargo shorts, he produced an old Swiss Army knife. He popped the cap on the bottle. He then wiped the lip of the bottle on his shirt before taking a long pull.

The beer was warm. But it was a beer—the first he'd had in nearly three days. He turned and walked out the door toward the dunes.

He saw the boat after rounding the first dune. It was a small panga with a seventy-five-horse Yamaha motor. Both the motor and the panga had seen better days. Jake marveled at how the boatman had gotten the boat and motor up onto the beach. He looked down to see several cylindrical-shaped ribs from a *cardón* cactus. Nearby, a rusty hand-crank winch was attached to the scarred stump of a mesquite tree. He shook his head and a thin smile crossed his parched lips as he realized the boat had been rolled up on the cactus ribs. He removed the cover from the motor, reached inside and deftly took out the fuel line, sticking it in his pocket.

He felt that odd prickly sensation at the back of his neck. As dulled as his senses had become, he knew this feeling well.

"C'mon out, Macario. It's me, Jake."

He took a swallow from the bottle of beer, then dropped it onto the sand. In one deft move, he spun around as an assailant thrust a long spear at him. He blocked the parry and pulled the spear away from his attacker. He spun the weapon into play thwacking the attacker in the ribs. Macario went down with a grunt of pain.

Jake looked down at Macario who was writhing in the sand.

"Never sneak up on a guy who has PTSD. It could get you killed."

"I didn't know it was you," Macario said through clenched teeth.

"Who the hell did you think it was?"

Jake stuck out his hand and helped Macario to his feet. "You okay?"

"I think so. I'll tell you after I get my breath back."

Jake looked at the weapon the young fisherman had brandished. It was about six feet long with a retro-curved blade near the point. The other end was a weighted and wrapped handle. It was more than just a spear. It was a harpoon.

"Where'd you get the frog sticker?" Jake said, hefting the weight of the harpoon in one hand.

"Long story."

"It was a long trip. I got time. C'mon, let's get out of the sun."

Back at the fishing shack, Jake sat in a rotting plastic chair, drinking another beer. Macario sat opposite him on the bed, his head in his hands.

"I don't believe you. They can't be dead."

"I'm sorry, Macario. I wish they weren't. And we still don't know for sure about your mom."

Macario looked up, his eyes red and swollen. "You took the word of two fishermen. So, where's my mother's body?"

"I don't know. They haven't been able to locate her. They found *El Tiburón*. Your father's things were scattered around the reef."

"My father would never run his boat aground there," Macario said vehemently. "He's been by that reef hundreds of times. I think it was someone else. Someone else must have stolen his boat and ran it onto the reef and died."

"I wish that were true, son. But you and I both know that it's not." Spinner looked down at the floor, allowing Macario to absorb the twenty-megaton hydrogen bomb that he had just dropped on him.

Finally, Spinner looked up, his blue eyes penetrating. "Macario, I'm going to ask you some questions. I believe your mom and dad were murdered for something they knew. If these bad guys find you, you are probably next on the list for fish-food. Who are these Asians that have been hanging around Puerto Nacimiento?"

Macario looked up beseechingly at Jake. Tears carved dirty tracks down his face. "They wanted to leave. They wanted to go to El Norte. But I didn't want to leave. The money was good, and our lives were getting better. It's my fault they're dead."

Jake felt a sudden sharp stab of guilt. "You're not to blame, Macario. I was supposed to make arrangements to get you all to the states. I was supposed to get you and your parents out of Mexico."

An uncomfortable silence ensued.

Jake finally spoke. "Macario, were you working for the drug cartels? Were you and your dad *burreros*?

Macario shook his head violently. "No! We weren't hauling drugs!"

"Where'd the money come from?"

"We were hired to fish."

"Don't bullshit me, god damn it!" Jake's eyes flashed gray. "What was the game? What's the connection to the Asians?"

Macario lowered his head. "Several months ago, two men came to our village. We were told they were from a Japanese fishing syndicate. They said the Japanese people eat lots of whale meat and we would be paid well if they could fish in our waters. They contracted the village to hunt whales for them. They swore the village to secrecy and said that all of us had to cooperate or they would go elsewhere. Some of the men from the village were recruited to work on processing ships in Chile, and others went to a place called the Southern Ocean. The pay was good. Very good. My father did not want me participating in the hunts. But I wanted to. With the thought of that much money, we became drunk with greed."

"When did they show up in the village?"

"Four months ago, I think. At first, we never saw the Japanese. There were Mexicano overseers who supplied the boats and exploding harpoons. We were paid 4,800 pesos per man, per catch. We hunted the whales by night. Most of the time, we found them sleeping. He looked down, a blush of shame moving across his face. "They were easy to kill."

"How did you deliver the whales?"

"Refrigerator trucks would meet us at a deserted beach. They would butcher the whales on the beach. They were very efficient. Sometimes we dragged the dead whales to a large processing ship that waited in the gulf in the middle of the night."

Jake stood stiffly, stretched his back, and walked over to the sink where the harpoon leaned against the cabinet. He picked it up and sighted down the shaft. "You ever use this?"

Macario looked at his hands. Jake saw a fresh tear splatter on the sand between his Nikes. "Twice. I've killed two young whales. I can still hear their screams in my sleep."

"I'm surprised Gustavo went along with this." Jake set the harpoon down. "Your father always had a deep respect for the whales. He spoke reverently of them when they traveled near our boat."

"My father was very upset with the killings. He never would throw a harpoon. He was sad. He said he had committed a great sin against Ocean Mother and the whales. That's when he said we were going to have to leave."

"Did he try to back out of the contract?"

"He went to talk to them one night to tell them he didn't want to participate in the hunts anymore. When he came back home, he said it was dangerous for us to stay and we must make a plan to leave."

"Your village has been fishing these waters for hundreds of years. There must have been others who didn't want to participate in the hunts."

"There were some who protested. Days, maybe a week later, we never saw them again. The overseers said they had taken jobs on the mainland or gone to work on the large factory ships in the south."

Spinner walked over to the ice chest and removed another warm beer. He popped the cap and flopped down in the faded plastic chair once more. "What do you think happened to them?"

Macario shook his head. "At first, I believed them. I didn't want to believe anything else. Now, I think they were killed."

"Why did you come out here? Did your father tell you to go?"

Macario stood and began to pace. "He called me on my cell phone. He said there wasn't much time. He told me to go to Ramón Torres and borrow his panga. My father told me to come to the fishing camp. He and my mother would meet up with me soon." The young man walked to the open doorway. He gazed out at the waters of the gulf. The afternoon winds were picking up speed, whipping up whitecaps in the channel. "They never came."

Jake took a swallow of beer, grimaced, then set it down on the table. He wiped his mouth on his bare forearm and walked over to where Macario stood.

"I'm going to get to the bottom of this, Macario. I'm going to find out who killed your mom and dad."

"I'm coming with you, Jake. I want to see the face of the murderer as I drive that harpoon deep into his chest!"

"You ain't going anywhere, pal. You're going to sit it out here, while I try and sort this thing.

"No way am I staying here! My parents are dead! I can use a gun, Jake. I know how to shoot."

"You haven't got a clue what you're up against, kid. Before I came here, someone did a drive-by on my casita and nearly leveled it with a shitload of bullets. All because I was asking too many questions. These aren't your garden-variety street corner thugs. They're pros and they've maybe got someone in your government backing them. You'll just get in the way at the least and, at the worst, you'll get yourself and probably me killed in the process. You hang here until I can figure how to get you out of Mexico for a while."

"You can't make me stay here! You have no authority over me."

"You're right. I can't make you stay here. But it's going to be a long paddle back to Puerto Nacimiento." Jake held up the six-inch piece of clear plastic fuel line he had removed from the motor earlier.

"You bastard! Give that to me! You have no right!" Macario's eyes were wild with hate.

"Your parents got killed because I failed them. I'm not making the same mistake again."

Macario looked like he was going to lunge at Spinner. Tears streamed down his face; his fists balled at his side. Then he bolted out the door and ran into the dunes. Jake thought about going after the boy, then decided to let him cool off.

It was late when Macario came back to the shack. Spinner was passed out on the rickety bed. He stirred several times when Macario clattered some plates while making his dinner. He stood at the sink and stared at Spinner.

Spinner half-laid on the bed frame with one foot on the floor. When he snorted in his sleep, Macario froze. He took a moment to gaze upon the ruin that Spinner had become. He flashed on the memory of a much younger Jake Spinner: newly arrived in Puerto Nacimiento, lean, tanned, and full of vitality. He and his father had watched Spinner's alcohol-fueled descent into Hell.

Macario felt a great hollowness. The only emotion that beat in his chest now was a bitter acidic hatred. He needed to hold onto it, to embrace it fully, for it would drive him away from here to find his parents' killers. And when he found them, he'd make them pay. Right now, he needed to get out of here. All he needed was a fast boat. Jake's boat.

He moved slowly toward the inert form, positioning himself so he'd be able to reach down into Spinner's pocket with minimal disturbance. He crouched down next to Spinner and moved his hand toward the pocket. Holding his breath, he slipped three fingers into it. Spinner didn't move. Macario inched his fingers down further. The tip of one finger brushed against the keys. Another inch and he could pinch the keys between two fingers.

Instantly, Macario felt a vise-like grip on his wrist. He cried out in pain. Spinner opened his eyes and looked up at him.

"You're gonna have to be a lot faster than that if you're planning on taking down the guys who killed your parents. They'll chew you up and shit you out dead." Jake released Macario, who sunk down to the floor holding his throbbing wrist.

"You son of a bitch! I think you broke my wrist!"

"If I had broken your wrist, you'd be in so much pain you couldn't see straight, much less speak." Jake said. "I'm not going to talk to you about this again. You're staying here." Spinner got up from the bed. "You need to get some sleep, kid."

Macario rose quickly and slunk out of the shack.

*He's right*, Spinner thought. *I really am an asshole.*

Jake trudged up the beach to the fishing shack as the first light of dawn lit up the Gulf of California in a vermilion hue. His arms were full of fishing tackle and various kitchen items from his galley. Entering the shack, he leaned the fishing rod against the table and placed the other supplies on the counter. Macario lay asleep in the corner, the blankets pulled over his head. Jake set about preparing coffee and a breakfast of leftover fish tacos and beans.

As the coffee aroma filled the tiny shack, Macario began to stir. He sat up in bed, his dark eyes red-rimmed and swollen.

Jake poured two cups of black coffee. He set one on the table for Macario. "There's some cans of beans and a bag of rice on the counter. In the box there are salt, pepper, flour, hot sauce, and some utensils. If you dig up some clams or scavenge some turbo snails, you can catch some tasty rockfish from shore. I'm leaving you my fishing rod and tackle box. If you value your hide, don't lose them. And watch the drag on the reel. It can be touchy at times."

Macario reached across and grabbed the tin coffee cup. He took a sip and regarded Spinner sullenly. "When are you coming back?"

Spinner sighed deeply and looked out the door at the pre-dawn sky. "I don't know. A couple of days at the most. I need to talk to some people. I need to make arrangements to get you to a safe place. I let your parents down. I won't let that happen to you. Just hang tight here until I get back." Spinner turned back and looked into Macario's eyes. "You have to trust me. I won't rest until I find who killed your folks. I owe that to them. I owe it to you."

The dog suddenly appeared at the doorway. Its fur was matted and coated in something greasy. It barked once then assumed a play bow position.

"I brought your dog," said Jake. He made a face and recoiled. "Christ, what did you roll in?

"That's not my dog," Macario said.

"He is now."

# 19

They arrived at the base of the hill in the dark. They parked the two vehicles in an arroyo near a stand of palo blanco trees and got out, donning their packs. From where Emily Rosen stood, it was going to be a steep climb up through cactus, rocks and thorn bushes to the viewpoint Raúl had described. She felt the straps from her backpack dig deeply into her shoulders, the weight of her camera gear, water, and food pulling her down.

They stood in front of Raúl's old Chevy pickup. Everyone was dressed in warm clothing and wool caps. The night air was chilly and a steady breeze blew off the water from the other side of the hill. Raúl spoke quietly but urgently.

"Be careful when using your flashlight. Point it at the ground at your feet. At the top of the hill, we'll walk by the light from the stars. Out here at night, it's very easy to spot the light coming from flashlights."

In the diffused light from Alejandro's flashlight, everyone looked grim. The tension among the members was palpable. Rosen herself felt a gut-churning anxiety—the anticipation of being in the middle of a newsworthy story which could turn deadly.

"Move slowly and stay together," Raúl continued. "Keep talking to a minimum. The sound of voices carries a long way on the wind."

"How close will we be?" The reporter wanted to know.

Raúl looked directly at her. "Close enough."

Rosen heard something scuttle into a bush in the dark and panned her flashlight a few feet ahead.

"Don't do that," said Raúl.

"I heard something. What if there's a snake out there?"

"Not this time of day," Sandy said. "Too cold."

Alejandro shouldered his pack. He looked at Raúl. "Let's do this. Lead on."

They walked single file up a rocky trail ending at the top of the arroyo. The ground inclined quickly and Rosen could see they were following an old game trail. The trail thinned out and they picked their way over loose rock and around clumps of cactus. Raúl moved slowly and deliberately, retracing his steps when he lost sight of the trail. They began moving up the hill following a set of switchbacks. Although the night air was cool, Emily felt the sweat building under her backpack. Her breathing became labored. She couldn't remember the last time she'd been to a gym.

Raúl called for a break. Rosen shucked herself out of the pack and took out her water bottle.

Sandy asked, "You okay?"

Rosen wiped her brow with her sleeve. "I guess chasing down cabs in New York City doesn't count as aerobic exercise."

"It's getting light in the east. We should be on top within the hour," said Raúl.

"That's one hell of a hill," Rosen said.

By the time they reached the summit, every member of the party had slipped on loose rock and fallen. All except Raúl. Rosen was now sporting parallel scratches on her forearm from falling into the spines of a catclaw acacia. Paola had twisted her ankle when she stepped on a pile of loose rocks that gave way. Alejandro and Sandy each hit the dirt once, but other than bruised pride, they were unscathed. Just before they reached the summit, Raúl gave the signal to kill the flashlights.

Rosen stopped and placed her hands on her knees, breathing heavily. Alejandro sidled up next to her. "Are you okay?"

She waved him off. "Fine. I just need a minute."

When she'd caught her breath, she stepped forward to where Raúl stood and realized she was standing on a cliff that was at least 1,000 feet above San Mateo Cove. Up here, there were enough places to hunker down and plenty of vantage points unseen from below.

Once Rosen got her bearings, she heard the distant hum of a generator. She saw lights strung around the cove. Near the shore were two large semi-tractor trailer trucks, along with several smaller trucks with canvas covers. Half a dozen tents, lit from within, were near the shoreline. She noticed some flickering lights out on the water near the entrance to the cove.

Rosen pointed to the row of lights that spanned the entrance to the cove. "What's that?"

"It looks like they built a catwalk across the entrance to the cove." Raúl wasn't even winded from the climb. "Somehow, they've fenced the dolphins in. Look, there are floats at the top. There has to be mesh netting below, keeping the dolphins from escaping."

Rosen reached into her backpack and retrieved her Canon 1DX MK II digital camera with a 100-400 mm zoom lens. She focused her lens. Movement in the center of the cove caught her attention, and she saw the water was churning. It was still too dark to see clearly.

Alejandro, Sandy, and Paola came and stood next to her. Alejandro was holding a high-definition video camera. Sandy also held a 35 mm Canon SLR camera.

"Can you see anything?" Alejandro asked.

"Nothing yet," said Rosen. "It looks like the surface of the water is being disturbed."

"I think we're going to have to count on you to get the shots," Sandy said to Rosen. "Alejandro's video camera doesn't have the reach to get clear footage. Besides, it's too dark now. My lens may fall short too."

"I have an extra 2X teleconverter in the pack," Rosen said. "You're welcome to use it. It's in the front zip pocket."

"Thanks." Sandy reached for Rosen's backpack and soon had the teleconverter attached. She came back and sat with Alejandro and Rosen. Paola joined them.

Alejandro looked around the small group. "Remember, we're here to record events. No matter how bad it gets down there, as I fear it will, we can't shout out or make ourselves visible. I have no idea who orchestrated this hunt, but I will find out. If we have to put this on an international stage to bring attention to the slaughter of marine mammals here in the gulf, then so be it. I think if we can find out who's behind this hunt, we'll also discover who's killing the humpbacks."

They all found places hidden from view along the cliff and positioned themselves, waiting with dread for the coming dawn.

Rosen laid out her camera gear in front of her. She mounted the camera with long lens on the tripod and checked her pockets for extra batteries and flash cards. From her vantage point, she had a clear view of the entire cove all the way back to the refrigerator trucks. She checked her watch: 4:47. Sunrise would be around 6:15.

She removed her gloves and blew on her cold hands to relieve some of the stiffness. She felt extremely uneasy. She'd seen footage of whales being slaughtered on television before. She had even seen a documentary about a small group of Japanese in a place called Taiji who had been performing a grisly ritual of rounding up herds of dolphins and killing the ones that did not make the cut for marine parks and aquariums. After what she had experienced the other day in the boat with Sandy and Paola, she wondered if she could remain a detached observer.

Rosen could hear voices carried on the breeze, voices of men talking and laughing. As the sky in the east began to flush a deep crimson, she attempted to focus her lens in the poor light. Several pangas were tied up near shore. She noticed increased activity at the periphery of the cove. People were moving about. Some were loading boats.

The surface of the water in the cove was alive. Rosen suddenly realized that the cove was packed with dolphins, nervously thrashing and pushing against one another. She could barely make out the black outlines of dorsal fins as the dolphins moved forward, nearly beaching themselves.

She looked up from the viewfinder to the water below.

"My God!" She turned to Sandy, who was peering through binoculars.

Sandy returned the look. "Can you see them?" Her voice was strained.

Rosen nodded. They all knew what was going to happen next.

Rosen sighted through the viewfinder once more. She remembered the words of that song by Bruce Cockburn, "If I Had a Rocket Launcher."

At first light, the camp sprang into action. Men climbed into the pangas and sped out to the catwalk at the entrance, paying no attention to the hapless dolphins in their path. They dropped several men off at different places along the catwalk and then positioned others on both sides of the lagoon and along the shore. Other men began laying out large plastic tarps on the shoreline, just above the tide zone.

Rosen detached the lens and placed a teleconverter onto the camera body. Although the light was still too dim for photos, she could use the lens like a telescope to assess the action.

In a voice that wasn't a whisper, she said, "Holy shit!"

Alejandro asked, "What is it?"

"Those two guys on the edge of the cove are carrying assault rifles."

His finger to his lips, Raúl hissed, "Shhhhh!"

As the sun peeked over the mountains in the east, three pangas moved into position at the entrance to the cove at equal distances. There were four men in each boat: a driver, two at the gunwales who held long spear-like objects, and another at the bow. A length of pipe was attached to each bow and these extended down into the water. Each man at the bow held a mallet.

On cue, the three boats began moving slowly forward. The men at the bow of each boat began banging on the pipes with the mallets. From Rosen's vantage point the clanging was loud. In the water, it must have been deafening. She cringed every time the mallet struck the pipe. Panicked by the barrage of sound, the herd of dolphins erupted into flight straight toward the shoreline where the men waited with spears and flensing knives.

"Oh, God, please no. Oh, God. I can't watch this." Paola turned away and buried her head in her hands.

Rosen began firing away, the shutter clicking in bursts like a machine gun, as she captured image after image of the hunt. Through the viewfinder she saw dolphins, mostly mothers and calves, swim desperately up to shore and beach themselves, only to be clubbed and speared by the whalers. Some of the younger dolphins were separated from their mothers and hauled onto the beach. The mothers were slaughtered where they were stranded. The young dolphins were placed in slings and carried by several whalers to transport trucks that were parked near the shoreline.

"Bastards!" Sandy said. "They're killing the mothers and taking the babies away."

The boats pressed on, mowing down dolphins in their wake. The whalers standing along the gunnels poked and prodded the dolphins forward. Several wounded dolphins attempted to swim back toward the nets but were crushed by the oncoming stampede.

Sandy's face was stained with tears. "Today, I'm ashamed to call myself human."

And the sea ran red.

# 20

*The little dolphin with the star pattern on his forehead swam frantically back and forth along the inside of the barricade. All around him the ocean was filled with the terrified calls of hundreds of his kind. He had been separated from his mother and auntie when the earsplitting clanging noises started. In the panic, one of his cousins had been crushed under the weight of dolphins fleeing into the shallows. He had managed to get back to the barricade and now swam frantically back and forth, calling for his mother. The smell of blood filled the water, a scent that nearly paralyzed him. Panicked dolphins bulleted past him. Some bore gashes on their bodies from wounds they received in the shallows. The water tasted of fear and death. When he tried to surface near the barricade, men with poles beat the water to drive him back. Where was the rest of his family?*

The dawn sky lit up the horizon in a deep rose color, reflecting veins of red and silver light across the waters of the Gulf of California. As Spinner's boat tracked across the flat sea, his mind was racing. The events of the past twenty-four hours had assaulted his psyche as if he were back on the battlefield. He had only caught a few hours of sleep since he had escaped his bullet-ridden house. Still sleep deprived, he was having difficulty processing the fact that someone was trying to kill him.

As he cruised back toward San Jacinto, he still had no clue what his next move would be. He knew the Japanese thugs he had seen in Puerto Nacimiento and the federales were just hired muscle. Spinner needed to know who pulled their strings. He suspected that if the Japanese were illegally hunting whales in the gulf, then someone at the local or national level of the Mexican government was turning a blind eye.

He knew he couldn't show his face in San Jacinto. If the attackers were as professional as Jake thought they were, they would have checked the house for a body. No body means no kill. They would still be looking for him. He figured he had used up all of his favors in the sleepy little seaside town.

That irritating voice kept niggling at his brain. *This isn't your fight, Jake. Just leave and head south. Gustavo's dead, and, what the hell—that's Mexico, baby.*

His worldly possessions had dwindled down to a battered fishing boat, some miscellaneous fishing gear, a couple of changes of clothes, and a very illegal pistol. *Let's face it—your prospects aren't good.*

Spinner shook his head to rid himself of the voice. Perhaps a shred of loyalty to a man who had been his closest friend for more than seven years was the only remnant of his abandoned moral character. That was the reason Jake knew he had to stay. He had nothing left to lose. He would bring down the men who murdered Gustavo.

A disturbance on the water up ahead caught Jake's attention. He thought it was a large marlin or sailfish charging baitfish at the surface. And here he was, with no time to deploy his rod and reel. Suddenly, a lone dolphin arced clear over the bow of his boat in a fantastic leap, landing headfirst in the water on the port side. He had seen dolphins leaping in front of his boat before, but this one had come dangerously close to landing on the boat.

The dolphin leapt across the bow again, this time higher, nearly shooting over Jake's head. It landed with a splash on the starboard side. He realized it was the female dolphin that had always dogged his boat, looking for fish to take from his line. Something wasn't right.

He slowed the motor to idle and peered over the side. The female dolphin surfaced near him. She was vocalizing and, to Jake, the squeals and whistles sounded frantic.

"Where's your calf, old girl?" He looked around. There were clearly no other dolphins in the immediate area. "Where's the rest of your family?"

Jake didn't know all that much about the social lives of dolphins, but he did know that they traveled in tight-knit family groups. This was not normal behavior.

The female drew closer, her vocalizations and whistles becoming louder and more emphatic. Suddenly, she began beating the water with her flukes. She whipped the water into chop, soaking him in the process. The tail lobs were faster and more forceful. Then the dolphin kicked once and took off, porpoising toward the distant shore. When Spinner did not follow, she came back. She beat the water into froth once more with her powerful flukes. When she shot forward again in the direction of the peninsula, realization came to Spinner.

"You want me to follow you?"

He needed to get back on course to San Jacinto. But something was horribly wrong with that dolphin.

Spinner got behind the wheel and accelerated. The female dolphin took off like a shot, porpoising in six- to eight-foot leaps across the flat sea. Spinner accelerated the boat so he could keep her in his sight. She appeared to be heading for a section of rocky coastline about five miles distant. He looked down at the boat's speedometer. The dolphin was easily swimming at nearly twenty-five knots. Mile after mile, her leaps devoured stretches of water. She was a dolphin on a mission.

As he drew closer to the coastline, Spinner was able to recognize some features of this part of the Baja peninsula. He remembered there was a hidden cove here but couldn't recall the name of it. It appeared the female dolphin was heading toward that cove.

When he was within a half mile of it, he slowed the boat to get his binoculars out. He scanned the rugged shoreline. Boats were in the cove, but something was blocking the front of the cove. What appeared to be a string of buoys was stretched from one side to the other. Thick support ropes were attached to the rocks that rose above on both sides.

"What the hell?"

Spinner slowed the boat and raised his binoculars. Two men were standing on the catwalk. They each carried large spears with deadly looking points. He could make out a makeshift walkway—a series of narrow planks that extended across the cove supported by floats. One of the men turned and saw Jake approach. He yelled to the others and they began shouting and waving him off. They were speaking rapid-fire Spanish. Spinner couldn't make out what they were saying, but he suspected he wasn't being invited over for a *huevos rancheros* breakfast.

Spinner saw the female dolphin reappear on the outside of the net. She was porpoising frantically along its length, stopping frequently to spy-hop to locate her family. A man raised a spear overhead and thrust it at her. Anticipating the attack, the female dove quickly out of the way.

*The old female spun away from the spear's deadly point. She heard the plaintive cries of her calf. She vocalized her signature whistle repeatedly, trying to discern his call from the din of terrified dolphins crying out. Then she heard a faint, plaintive cry, her offspring's signature distress call, a variation of her own signature whistle. A moment later, she was joined by the rest of her pod, who had been skirting the barricade calling to the younger dolphins trapped behind the nets.*

*The frightened members gathered around the old female, vocalizing frantically. The dolphin family moved as a group along the perimeter of the barricade, searching for a breach and calling to the young male still behind the deadly nets. Suddenly, the female sensed movement from the human she had led here. He was moving his boat closer to the barricade. She and the other dolphins swam toward him.*

Jake drew the boat closer to the barricade until he was within several feet of the walkway. "Hey, guys, what's up?" He moved his hand to his gun which was tucked under the console.

One of the men came forward. He yelled at Spinner in Spanish.

"This is a restricted area! You must leave now!"

"Why is it restricted? What do you have in there?"

"Leave now!" The man whacked Spinner's boat with the spear.

"Don't touch my boat, man." Spinner's voice was menacing.

The man pointed the spear at Spinner. *"¡Vete, pendejo!"* He rapped the rail again, scraping paint off the bow with the spear point.

Spinner put the motor into reverse and backed away. The men continued to stare at him. Movement on the shoreline caught his attention. Something was wrong with the color of the water. It was crimson. Spinner brought his binoculars up to his face and saw the source of the blood. Bodies of dolphins lay on the beach, blood staining the white sand. More dolphins thrashed in the shallows as men waded out and slashed at them with flensing knives. Several men were carrying slings with dolphins inside and loading them onto covered trucks parked at the back of the cove.

Spinner saw why the female dolphin had led him here. Her offspring was swimming frantically back and forth on the other side of the net. He recognized the distinctive white star pattern on the little calf's melon. Several other members of the pod were tracking the matriarch's movements on the opposite side of the net. The men were trying to prod the dolphins back toward shore.

Something inside of Spinner snapped.

"Fuck this."

He gunned the boat and sped forward, aiming at the center of the barricade and the man who had threatened him. The two men looked surprised, then panicked when they saw that the crazy gringo wasn't going to stop.

Spinner hit the barricade with a resounding splintering of wood, sending the whaler flying ten feet and landing on his back in the water with a great splash.

"I told you," Spinner said to the sputtering man in the water, "never touch my boat."

Spinner hit the throttle and went into full reverse. He backed up and then gunned the engine. The boat shot forward and hit the barricade again, this time punching a hole in it. The second whaler lost his footing and went into the water. Spinner put the motor in neutral, then grabbing his old Ka-Bar knife from under the console, jumped down onto the narrow walkway. He found where the nets were tied and began ripping and tearing at them. He needed to open up a big enough hole to drive the boat in and herd the dolphins out.

Out of the corner of his eye, Jake saw a whaler coming at him. He grabbed another length of netting and sliced through it. He spun around just in time to see the point of the spear flash by his face. Losing his balance, he landed on the platform on his rear and almost toppled into the water.

His attacker was Asian. His clothes were stained in blood. His face had a maniacal look, crazed from the sight and smell of gore. The flensing knife was heavy—the whaler was having trouble wielding it while maintaining his balance.

The man came at Spinner as he stood up. Jake half-turned his body as the knifepoint barely grazed him, tearing his shirt. He grabbed the shaft of the knife and yanked the attacker toward him. The man lost his balance and stumbled directly into Jake's fist. The whaler's nose erupted in a spurt of blood. He cried out and fell into the water. He came up sputtering. Spinner went back to hacking away at the nets with a vengeance.

By now, the activity at the mouth of the inlet had caught the attention of whalers from both ends of the cove. Two of them walked the catwalk unsteadily toward Jake. The pangas had stopped herding dolphins and focused on the intruder. Men shouted orders from shore, and boats turned around and bore down on him.

Spinner grabbed a section of rope and netting, went back to his boat, and tied the rope from the buoys around the bow's anchor mount. He clambered aboard and turned over the ignition. The motor stalled. He tried it again. Nothing. The pangas were closing the distance. He glanced up to see several men in each boat, all armed with clubs and knives.

"Shit. Come on, come on!" He turned the ignition again.

The motor roared to life and he hit reverse. The boat throttled backward and the rope twanged taut. There was a great CRACK as a large section of the catwalk and netting tore away. The opening was large enough for his boat. He jumped to the bow and threw off the rope. He looked up to see a group of dolphins shoot through the opening. It was the old female leading her family group out, the star-faced baby at her flank. Other animals massed toward the opening. Spinner had to get through before the pangas got here and blocked any escape route for the dolphins.

Up on the cliff face, the researchers watched in stunned silence as the savage butchery played out below them. Sandy turned to Alejandro. "Alejandro, we need to do something!"

Alejandro stared at Sandy and Paola. "No! They'll kill us!"

"He's right," said Raúl. "They've got guns. They don't want witnesses."

Rosen kept shooting images, switching between video and photo formats. Everything was automatic now. As a photojournalist, she had seen and photographed the worst of humanity in the underbelly of New York City, but this was the most heinous thing she had ever witnessed. It was a crime against nature. She knew the images of this brutal slaughter would haunt her for the rest of her life.

Movement at another part of the cove caught her attention. A lone man had just used his boat to ram the barricade at the entrance to the cove. He was fighting off one of the whalers who was attacking him with a long flensing knife.

"Hey? You guys need to see this," Rosen switched over to video.

"What is it?" Alejandro moved to her side.

"There's some guy in a Hawaiian shirt down there, kicking ass and taking names. He just rammed the barricade with his boat and knocked out two of the whalers."

"What?" Sandy turned back toward the cove. The researchers grabbed their binoculars and moved to the edge of the cliff.

"Holy shit!" Rosen exclaimed. "He's going in. And here come the bad guys."

They watched through the lenses of their binoculars and cameras as the lone boatman sped into the cove of death.

Spinner throttled forward through the gap and threw the wheel to the right. His ill-conceived plan was to skirt along the border of the small bay and maneuver the boat between the whalers and the shoreline, while herding the dolphins back through the opening in the barrier.

The men in the pangas had other ideas.

He veered to starboard just in time to avoid colliding with the first panga. It missed his boat by inches and slammed into the barricade, pitching the whaler poised with a harpoon at the bow headlong into the water. Spinner performed a quick turn into the cove sending a rooster tail of water into the air.

Over the roar of the motor, Jake heard a sharp report. Bullets stitched a path through the water and tore into the hull of his boat. The starboard gunwale erupted as a hail of wood splinters and fiberglass filled the air.

"Shit!" Spinner veered the boat again and performed a series of quick course changes to make himself less of a target. He caught a glimpse of the gunman standing on the rocks at the north end of the cove. Since when did whalers carry automatic weapons? From the staccato report, the gun sounded like an AK-47.

Jake turned the boat toward the middle of the cove. The second panga was right on his stern and gaining quickly. Those dolphins that weren't bleeding out or in shock, took off in a huge charge, swimming for their lives. Jake saw they were headed for the opening in the barricade.

Spinner felt a jolt as the panga slammed into his port side. He veered to the right to get some separation. A whaler was perched on the bow, knife in hand, ready to leap onto Jake's boat. Jake did a double take when he saw that the man was one of Gustavo's neighbors from Puerto Nacimiento. The man had fear in his eyes as he made ready to jump into Jake's boat. He caught a quick glimpse of an Asian man in the back of the boat, shouting orders. Due to the close proximity of the two vessels, the guard with the AK-47 had momentarily stopped shooting.

The panga angled in again and the whaler jumped. Spinner yanked the wheel to starboard and the man bounced off his stern and catapulted into the sea. Ahead he saw panicked dolphins milling around, unsure of which direction to run. They parted as Spinner's boat sped past them.

Another whaler, a Mexican, moved into the position the last hapless attacker had occupied. He held a semi-automatic pistol. As the whaler stood on the bow, readying himself for the jump, Spinner took the offensive.

He veered into the boat. The impact knocked the second assailant off his feet, but he fell into Spinner's boat. The pistol clattered behind the motor sump and the whaler scrambled after it. Spinner had no choice. He leapt on the man as his own boat veered out of control. The two men tussled as the Mexican attempted to kick Spinner in the groin. Spinner deflected the man's leg and punched him hard in the face. The man came at him again, catching Spinner with a glancing blow to his jaw. Spinner jackhammered him with a blow to the gut followed by a wicked right cross that sent him backward over the back seat and into the motor well.

The boat was speeding toward the rocks. Spinner lurched forward and grabbed the wheel. An armed guard on the opposite side of the cove opened up on him with an automatic rifle. He turned the wheel violently to avoid the hail of bullets, heading toward the barricade once again. He turned to see the whaler in the back scrambling for the pistol. Spinner jumped to the back. Just as the assailant brought the pistol to bear, Spinner blocked the man's shooting arm. The shot went wild. Spinner then landed a crashing blow to the whaler's nose, launching him off the back of the boat.

He got back to the wheel too late. The boat hit the barricade and went airborne. Spinner pitched forward, hitting his head on the windshield. He scrambled back to the wheel as the firing from the rocks continued. He glanced back. There were now two gaping openings in the barricades. Dolphins swarmed for the breaches in the barrier, swimming towards freedom and the open sea. Spinner checked to see if he had any fresh holes in him. As he sped away, he reached under the console and produced his Beretta just in case he was being followed. He chanced a look behind. The two pangas had broken off their pursuit. Most of the dolphins had broken free of the barricade and were moving away from the death cove at a breakneck pace. He hoped the female and her family had survived.

He surveyed the damage to his boat. Most of the damage was above the water line. There was a leak somewhere and his motor didn't sound too good. He guessed one of the slugs had hit its mark. He may have fractured the fiberglass at the bow. He hoped he could limp it back to town, or at least to a friendly fishing camp. He needed to get back to Macario as soon as possible. The young man was impatient and angry. He wouldn't sit still for long. Jake had to keep it together long enough to make arrangements to get the kid out of the area and out of harm's way.

He looked down at his hands. They were shaking uncontrollably. In the space of two days, he'd been shot at twice. A flood of nightmare images danced in his mind's eye. He figured he was in for some rough days ahead.

He picked up movement on the cliff above the cove and instantly recoiled. If the whalers had an armed guard posted up there, he was toast. He decided that it wouldn't be a good idea to stick around and find out what the contingent on the cliff was doing up there. He needed to put some serious distance between himself and the whalers.

As he sped away, his ears told him the motor wasn't going to last long.

# 21

Alejandro and Sandy stood up. They instantly became visible to the group of angry whalers below. A bullet ricocheted off the rocks in front of Sandy. Only after she heard the report of the gun seconds later did she realize someone was shooting at her.

"Get down! Get down!" Raúl yanked Sandy back forcefully and pulled her behind a large boulder.

The rest of the group retreated from the edge. All except Rosen, who was lying prone on the edge of the cliff recording the pandemonium in the inlet below.

"We have to leave," said Raúl. "Now! They can't come up this way, but they'll know where we are. ¡Vámanos!"

Raúl darted forward and grabbed Rosen's backpack and tripod. She crawled backwards away from the edge and scrambled back to the shelter of the rocks. She heard shouting from far below and vehicle motors starting up. Hastily she stuffed the camera into the backpack and attempted to tie the tripod on the back. Raúl saw her fumbling with the straps and grabbed it. "I got this. Go."

The three researchers and Rosen started running down the trail with Raúl bringing up the rear. Several times they had to slow their descent on the trail's loose scrabble. A twisted ankle now could mean death.

Below they could see their vehicles, still somewhat obscured in the arroyo. It looked like it was still a long way off. Because Rosen's pack was loaded with camera equipment, she was top-heavy. Once, she pitched forward, unable to stop her momentum. Raúl's hand shot out and grabbed her pack strap, preventing her from toppling headfirst into a thicket of prickly pear cactus.

"Thanks," Rosen said breathlessly.

Raúl nodded and pointed down the trail. "That way."

They arrived at the vehicles, winded and sweating. A fine coat of dust kicked up by the helter-skelter run down the hill had caked their faces and arms. Rosen tossed her pack into the back seat of Alejandro's SUV and jumped in.

Alejandro got in and fired up the vehicle. "Buckle up everyone. This is going to be a rough ride."

Sandy looked across the seat at him. "Whatever you do, don't get us stuck."

Alejandro held up a hand. "I know! I know!"

Raúl started his truck and pulled ahead of Alejandro's vehicle. As they bounced along the dirt track, a dust cloud trailed the two vehicles.

Sandy kept looking back toward the mountain that separated them from the whalers. "I don't see anything yet." Her words were lost as the vehicle squealed loudly when it hit a pothole.

Alejandro glanced back. "Keep an eye out for a dust cloud."

"Who was that guy?" Sandy yelled, as Alejandro ground through the gears, downshifting into another arroyo.

"I don't know. Maybe Raúl knows him. We'll ask when we get back."

*If we get back*, Rosen thought. She turned around and looked back in the direction they had come. So far, no telltale signs of a dust cloud in the west. "I don't see anyone following."

Alejandro was having difficulty keeping up with Raúl's truck. Even though his Toyota 4Runner had more horsepower than Raúl's old beat up Chevy, Raúl was much better at driving through sand and desert scrub.

The sand track converged into a wider road that was mostly washboard. He pushed the accelerator down and all the occupants felt the bone-jarring ride as they tried to put distance between themselves and the whalers. After nearly an hour of being thrown about the inside of the vehicle, they arrived at the main road, a two-lane blacktop with some fair-sized potholes. Alejandro fishtailed onto the pavement until the tires caught.

As they careened onto the blacktop, Rosen turned around again and looked to the west. She saw a cloud of dust rising in the late morning light, moving toward them.

"Pedal to the metal, Alejandro. They're coming."

"No need to say it twice," Alejandro gunned the engine and they sped south towards La Paz.

Later, road-weary and battered, they convened at Sandy's house. Sandy went to the refrigerator and produced five cold beers and a pitcher of lemonade. She brought out a basket of fruit, cheese, and bolillos and set them on the table. Everyone grabbed a cold Pacífico.

Alejandro looked pointedly at Rosen. "Did you get all that recorded?"

Rosen nodded. "Every minute."

Sandy took a swallow of beer. "Raúl, any idea who the guy in the boat was?"

Raúl's eyes looked haunted. "His name is Jake Spinner. A gringo fisherman who lives in San Jacinto." Raúl paused and took a swig from his bottle. "He's called *El Borracho* by the local *pescadores*."

"In my book, he's a hero," said Rosen. "That took some *chutzpah* to crash that barricade and free those dolphins."

"He is *muy loco*," said Raúl.

"Do you know where I can find him?" Emily asked. "I want to interview him for my story."

Raúl shook his head. "No sé. I don't know. But San Jacinto is not a large pueblo. I've heard he catches fish for the local restaurants. That would be a good place to start. He used to fish with an indio from Puerto Nacimiento named Gustavo, but I heard last week that Gustavo was found dead. His boat and his body were discovered on a reef north of here."

Rosen pulled out a battered notebook from her backpack and scribbled Gustavo's name in it. "Got a last name?"

Raúl scratched his stubbled chin. He looked like he had aged ten years since early this morning.

"I'm not sure. I only met him briefly once. Lo siento."

"Wait a minute," Rosen said, looking up abruptly. "Wasn't there something on the local news station about the fisherman who drowned? Was that Gustavo?"

"No sé," said Raúl. "I was out at sea fishing at that time."

*Was there a connection between the death of this Gustavo character and Spinner arriving at the dolphin hunt?* Rosen scribbled into her notebook. She wrote Spinner's name and circled it, then wrote Gustavo's name and circled it. Lastly, she wrote out the word dolphins, circled it, and connected all three names together by a line.

"What are you thinking, Emily?" Sandy noticed no one had touched the food.

"Not sure. I need to speak with this Spinner guy."

"*Es muy peligroso.*" Raúl took a deep breath. "Those men who organized the hunt will be looking for Spinner. They'll look in the same places you'll look. I think they'll kill you if they can."

"I've done this kind of thing before," said Rosen, meeting Raúl's concerned gaze. "Only instead of the thugs being mob guys in New York, these are poachers in Baja."

"They saw us!" Paola spoke up, her first words since the slaughter at the cove. "They shot at us!" Fresh tears appeared at the corners of her eyes. Sandy moved to comfort her friend and colleague.

"Don't take them lightly," admonished Raúl. "You can be killed just as easily in Mexico as you can in New York."

"Wait a minute." Alejandro stood up quickly. He looked directly at Sandy and Paola. "Why didn't I notice this before?"

"What?" Sandy was startled at his quick movement.

"Banger boats. Those pangas were fitted with pipes and the whalers beat them with mallets to scare the dolphins and herd them into shore. That's a technique used in Japan to drive whales and dolphins to shore so they can kill them. They're called banger boats. The practice is called the *oikomiryou*, the "drive hunt." Mexican fishermen don't normally use that technique."

"Mexican fishermen don't usually kill dolphins," Sandy said. "Do you think that Figueroa is involved?"

Alejandro continued, caught up in his own momentum. "Seems kind of suspicious that a contingent of Japanese fishing executives appears in La Paz and requests information about our whale census and locations and then a group of whalers trap a bunch of dolphins and use methods similar to a Japanese whale hunt."

"Why would the Japanese want to hunt whales in Mexico?" Paola slowly regained some of her composure. "The Gulf of California is a narrow sea. Surely, they'd be spotted by fishermen, ferry crews, or the Mexican Navy. It would be extremely difficult to hide a factory ship in the Gulf of California."

Alejandro began pacing back and forth in the kitchen. He stopped in his tracks. He took off his baseball cap and ran his fingers through his hair. "Unless . . . " He looked at Sandy and Paola. "Unless someone who's in a position of power has turned a blind eye and is letting them carry out whaling here. Think about it." Alejandro resumed his pacing. "Several months ago, we start seeing some of our whales disappear off the grid. Then we get a call from Figueroa telling us to cooperate with this contingency of Japanese fishing executives who are looking to streamline their operations in Japan. Figueroa wants us to surrender our data to them. And now, the slaughter at the cove that we were witness to this morning . . . "

Rosen, who had been sitting at the table, head down writing in her notebook, looked up. "Why would the Japanese carry out high profile whaling here in Mexico? Aren't they focusing their whaling activities in Antarctica?"

Alejandro turned his gaze to her. "Recently, the World Court at the Hague has revoked the fishing permits for the Japanese to take whales in the Southern Ocean. The Court deemed the Japanese were not conducting 'scientific research.'" Alejandro made the sign for quotation marks with his fingers. "The whalers were down there purely to bring whale meat to the Japanese markets. They were killing the whales in an established sanctuary. The Court finally upheld what the Sea Shepherd Conservation Society and the governments of Australia and New Zealand had been telling the world for years."

"Yeah, but why Mexico?" Rosen asked. "Like Paola said, the Gulf of California is not that big a place."

"Supply and demand. The gulf has more species of whales traveling here throughout the year than any other body of water in the world."

There was a moment of awkward silence as each member at the table contemplated the weight of Alejandro's statements.

Sandy broke the silence. "What are we going to do?"

"We need to find out who's behind this and make it stop," Alejandro said, his dark eyes burning with an intensity Sandy had not seen before.

Sandy scoffed. "How are we going to do that? March into Minister Figueroa's office and demand that he close down the whaling operations? After he fires us and dissolves the humpback ID program, he'll laugh us out of the office."

Alejandro looked frustrated. "I know it seems impossible, but there must be a way we can bring this to the correct authorities, whether it be within or outside of the jurisdiction of the Mexican government."

The room erupted into a heated discussion with everyone talking at once.

Finally, Rosen spoke up, her voice rising over the din. "Can I say something?"

Everyone stopped talking. All eyes turned to her.

"I've had a little experience in dealing with government cover-ups and conspiracies. This is classic David versus Goliath and I can tell you right now, it's not looking good for David. Goliath is well funded and they believe in their blackest of hearts that they are entitled to take whatever they want. Before we proceed, I have a question for all of you. An important question." She made eye contact with each one before continuing. "Are you prepared to give up your jobs by going after the whalers? Once you start uncovering dirt on these guys, there's no going back. Best-case scenario, we expose them and their operation for who they are. Worst case scenario, we lose our livelihoods, not to mention the distinct possibility that we maybe even lose our lives. When you're talking millions of dollars, people can do some pretty heinous things."

Alejandro looked at Rosen, a hint of a smile crossing his lips. "I noticed you used the word "we" when you were speaking of bringing these guys down."

"Did I?" Rosen grinned. "Even though it's against my better judgment, I've had my fill of David and Goliath scenarios."

"I don't believe that for a minute," said Sandy.

Rosen sighed. She looked around the room, appraising the other members of the team.

"Oh, hell. I didn't want to write a piece about Mexican tourism anyway." Her gaze grew sharp. "I just need to know that I'm not going to be thrown under the bus when things go nuclear. I'm going to start digging and we're all about to go down the rabbit hole. If there's anyone who's feeling squeamish about this, I need to know before I start asking questions." Rosen looked around the table. Her eyes met theirs. No one broke eye contact.

"Okay, then. I'm going to call my boss and see if I can switch out stories. With the footage and photos I have, this could be page two in the *Times,* maybe even headline material. I can't think of a better way to smoke out rats than to expose them to the light of day."

Alejandro leaned on the table. "Okay. I propose we meet here again tonight after we've had time to get some rest, eat, and begin to formulate a plan of attack. We have to assume that the whalers don't know who we are. But we have to be careful. Sandy, Paola, and I will go back to the institute and secure all our data. Emily will follow up on the drowned fisherman story and see if we can get some coverage with her newspaper." He looked at Raúl. "Thank you for helping us. You have done so much, my friend. We can't ask you to do any more."

Raúl looked down at his hands, then brought his gaze to bear on Alejandro and the others. "I've been fishing these waters all my life. My father and his father fished them before me. What I saw today broke my heart. My grandfather used to talk to the dolphins. They would lead him to the fish. They worked together. They were his friends. I will help Señorita Emily locate the gringo fisherman. There are places that I can go unnoticed where she can't."

Alejandro nodded. "*Muchas gracias, amigo.*"

"Well, all right," said Emily. "Let's get dirty."

Rosen arrived back at her hotel room, exhausted, sore, and in need of a shower. She squirmed out of her backpack and set it on the bed. She checked her watch. It was nearly 4:30 in the afternoon. That would make it 7:30 in the Big Apple. There was a good chance that her editor-in-chief, Charles Dickerson, would still be working. She'd make the call now, hoping to catch him before he went out to entertain the rich and famous of Manhattan.

"Dickerson."

"Charlie, it's Emily Rosen. I'm calling from La Paz."

"Where's my story, Rosen?"

"Charlie, that's what I'm calling about. There really wasn't any story about tourism and the cartels. But I discovered something that could make front page. There are illegal whale hunts going on down here. We were at a cove today and I saw hundreds of dolphins being slaughtered. When the whalers saw us, they shot at us. I managed to get some good photos and some video. Charlie, this is one hell of a story and I want to follow up on it."

Dickerson exploded. "God damn it, Rosen! I sent you down to Mexico on a simple assignment to put together an exposé on how the drug cartels are influencing the tourist trade in Mexico. But no, you have to go off on your own!"

"This *is* the story, Charlie. The other story was fluff and you know it!"

"This is your M.O., Rosen. You're a loose cannon. You think you can make your own rules as you go. When I give you an assignment, I expect you to follow through with it."

"Charlie, what I saw today was horrific. It will shake the foundation for conservation in the United States and Mexico. There are some big players involved here with corruption probably going to the highest levels in two governments."

"Everything is always a conspiracy with you, Rosen."

"C'mon, Charlie, give me a shot at this."

Emily heard a deep sigh on the other end of the line. "I've been meeting with the board of directors. The board has unanimously decided that your journalistic methods and investigative reporting are not up to *New York Times* standards."

"What are you saying?"

"A decision has been reached. I regret to inform you that your services as a reporter are no longer required at this news organization."

"You're firing me?"

"You left me no choice, Emily. You've been on thin ice for a while, and now you've deliberately disregarded my assignment."

Emily sat on the bed, the weight of the day bearing down on her. There was silence on the other end.

"They got to you, didn't they?"

"I don't know what you're talking about," Dickerson said coldly.

"The senator's people. They got to you. What did they have on you, Charlie?"

"You'll receive two weeks' severance pay. Use the return ticket to come home, or pursue your whale hunt, or whatever. I don't care. Good luck to you, Emily."

The line went dead.

Rosen stared at the phone as her numbed brain tried to sort out what had just happened. She suddenly realized that this had been Dickerson's plan all along. Why else would he have assigned his top political reporter to a travel piece?

Movement at the bathroom door caught her attention. She looked up to see the largest cockroach she had ever encountered staring at her, antennae waving.

"Cock-sucking roach." She grabbed her shoe and leapt after the insect. The roach, seeing movement, retreated into the bathroom. It scuttled for the drain in the shower, but Rosen blocked its escape with a foot over the drain cover. The roach backed into the corner of the shower. Rosen raised her right hand, ready to deal it a deadly blow with her boot and crush the life out of the vermin. With antennae waving, the roach cocked its head slightly, regarding its attacker.

An image came to Rosen's mind. It was the image of a bloody beach with corpses of dolphins lying in rows and dying dolphins bleeding out in the shallows in a froth of red. She sat down hard, lowered the boot, and began to sob.

# 22

Chief Minister Alfonso Figueroa was at a formal dinner in Mexico City when he got the call. His assistant strode into the grand ballroom and walked briskly to the head table where he sat with other Mexican government officials. He leaned in as the Chief Minister was telling a joke to an attractive woman seated to his right.

"Sir, Mr. Yoshimatsu would like to speak to you."

Figueroa gave him an irritated look. "Did he say what for?"

"He said it was urgent, sir."

"I'll be with him momentarily." He turned back to the woman, smiled and said, "Please excuse me, my dear. A matter of some importance has just come up. I'll be back as soon as possible. I'll finish my story then. Oh, yes, and please tell the waiter that I will have the dessert."

The woman smiled at him as he stood.

Outside the grand ballroom of the hotel, Figueroa walked to where his assistant stood. The assistant handed him a cell phone.

"Minister, my apologies for the disturbance at this time of the evening," said Yoshimatsu. Figueroa noted a coldness in his voice. "We have a new development with the operation in Baja. I must speak to you in person as soon as possible."

"Can it wait until tomorrow?"

"It cannot. I am sending a plane for you tonight. It will be at the airport by 12:30. Make sure you are on it." The line went dead. Figueroa felt a sudden sense of dread.

He handed the phone back to his assistant. "Pack my things and prepare the car. I'll be flying out tonight."

Hiro Yoshimatsu stood, hands clasped behind his back, on the veranda of his penthouse suite facing out toward the ocean. There was a chill breeze coming off the Gulf of California, but he didn't feel it.

He was enraged and had the overwhelming urge to hit something or someone. But to look at him, one would think he was the epitome of control and constraint. Susan stood several feet behind him and could tell from the distended veins in his neck that he was about to explode.

"Hiro-san, Mr. Kanamura will be here within the hour. He said the cleanup took longer than he had expected."

Yoshimatsu sighed heavily. "I grow weary of these excuses. It appears that I am forced to deal with incompetents."

"Yes, sir." The cell phone was still in her hand. "Minister Figueroa's plane is scheduled to arrive on time. I've dispatched a driver to pick him up at the airport."

Yoshimatsu nodded, almost imperceptibly. She wanted to go to him, to try and console him at this time of stress, but she knew better. She didn't want to get between Yoshimatsu's rage and those who angered him. Susan knew Yoshimatsu all too well. She knew when to console, and she knew when to walk the official line.

"Hiro-san, is there anything I can do for you right now?"

Yoshimatsu unclasped his hands from behind his back and waved in dismissal.

"I'll be in the living room if you need anything." Susan retreated back into the penthouse where the air was not supercharged.

Kanamura arrived first, followed by Figueroa several minutes later. Several of Kanamura's lieutenants were in attendance, among them the two assassins from the village who had been charged to eliminate Spinner. All faces in the room were grim except for Kanamura's. His was unreadable, almost surreally calm. Yoshimatsu was still facing out to sea, his eyes closed as if he were summoning some force from the ocean itself. Finally, he turned around and faced his subordinates.

"In the past days, we have had numerous failures in the implementation of our project," he began. "I have summoned all of you here tonight so that you can explain to me how this happened. I want to hear about San Mateo Cove and how the hunt was compromised."

Kanamura stepped forward and bowed to Yoshimatsu. "Sir, I have spoken with my men who were the acting security guards on the hunt. Apparently, a lone man in a cruiser crashed the barricade and cut the nets. He then drove through the cove, herding the dolphins out. As a result, we lost at least eighty percent of the catch. Several of the men suffered broken ribs and contusions. Because our cover was compromised, we had to move quickly and shut down the operation."

"Eighty percent," Yoshimatsu let the words hang in the air. "And who was this man, the one who crashed the barricade and freed the dolphins?"

Kanamura looked directly at the two assassins. "We ran the registration on his boat. It is registered to Jake Spinner."

One of the assassins, a burly Asian named Maro Sakei flushed a deep shade of crimson. "That's impossible! No one could have survived the firepower that we poured into that shack."

Yoshimatsu's jaw clenched. "Did you see the body?"

The second assassin, a tall slender Japanese man with a pockmarked face stammered, "Well, uh, sir—"

"Did you find a body?" Yoshimatsu's voice rose, cold as ice.

The men lowered their heads.

"What did you say? I could not hear you."

"No. Sir. There was no body," said Sakei.

Yoshimatsu stared at the men, then turned to Figueroa. "Do you not know that when one part of the chain breaks, another link soon comes apart? If Spinner had been eliminated as was the plan," he faced the assassins now, "I would not have lost eighty percent of my product!"

Yoshimatsu walked back to the veranda and stared out at the sea. "We had a lucrative contract with the Chinese government to supply their aquariums and ocean parks with young bottlenose dolphins. Each animal would bring in between 150,000 and 200,000 dollars to our company. Now I must tell our buyers in Beijing that I will not be able to deliver the product on the date we had agreed upon."

He turned slowly and faced the gathering of his subordinates. His face had regained a look of passivity. "The chain of command is only as strong as the weakest link."

He walked directly toward the two project managers of San Mateo. Reaching into the pocket of his linen jacket, he produced a 9mm Glock semi-automatic and shot Sakei between the eyes from three feet away, spattering his own suit with blood. The big man was jerked backward and slid on the white tile floor, leaving a trail of blood and gore in his wake.

Figueroa, who was standing behind and off to the side, was instantly splattered with bits of brain and skull fragments. The Minister of Fisheries began to retch.

Yoshimatsu stood quietly gazing around the room at the shocked and fearful faces. The only face that was passive besides Yoshimatsu's was the expressionless face of Kanamura.

"This organization will not tolerate failure. Do not fail me again."

Two security guards appeared with a plastic bag, but Yoshimatsu waved them off.

He turned to Figueroa, who was now wiping his face and hair with a bar towel.

"Minister Figueroa," Yoshimatsu began in his businessman's voice. "There are several matters we must discuss."

Figueroa looked panic-stricken, staring at Yoshimatsu's jacket pocket. "Y—y—yes?"

"The data you have provided me and my colleagues is flawed."

"I—I don't understand," said Figueroa.

"The GPS points from the institute that were supposed to show where we could locate the whales is wrong."

"How could it be wrong?"

"I sent men in helicopters to the coordinates supplied by your research team. In all of the locations, they did not see one whale. Even the spotter plane I had sent up came up empty. How can that be? All of those GPS coordinates and not one whale sighting?"

Figueroa's face blushed deep crimson. "Many apologies, Mr. Yoshimatsu. The whales can move hundreds of miles each day."

"Your choice of employees is questionable. Make sure your people at the institute are forthcoming. I want you to organize a manhunt from the Mexican side. I want this Jake Spinner brought before me."

"How will I do that? Spinner is an American. His embassy will ask questions if he's found dead. Reporters from the United States will flock down here."

"I have read the history on this man. He will not be missed. This is Mexico. Mr. Spinner could have been caught up in some cartel activity that took a bad turn."

"You want me to involve the federal police?"

Yoshimatsu nodded. "If necessary, the Mexican Navy." Yoshimatsu motioned to the two security guards who brought a shower curtain and rolled the bloody corpse into it.

"An example must be set. The people of Puerto Nacimiento must know that insubordination at any level will be dealt with harshly. Jake Spinner will be that example."

"Begging Mr. Yoshimatsu's forgiveness," Figueroa said. "But if we have the federales and the Navy, more attention will be brought to this area than we want."

"That is when you become creative in who you hire for the job. I am sure there are those in your reach—well-trained soldiers who will hire out to the highest bidder. I have read of men like this. I believe you call them the '*Zetas*.'"

Figueroa's eyes grew wide. "They are dangerous mercenaries with loyalties to no one."

"They are loyal to one entity," Yoshimatsu said. "They will swear allegiance to those who pay them the most. Our time here is drawing to a close. It is your highest priority to facilitate this matter before the whales leave and the curtain is raised to the world on what is happening here."

Figueroa bowed. "It will be taken care of, Mr. Yoshimatsu."

The two security guards removed the corpse and Yoshimatsu motioned to the men in the room. "Gentlemen, you are all excused." He looked at Kanamura who nodded slightly. Figueroa quickly left the room.

As the group dispersed, Yoshimatsu went to the wet bar and poured out two glasses of Scotch whiskey. He handed one to Kanamura and beckoned him to sit on the sofa. Susan entered the room with a fresh change of clothes for Yoshimatsu, who stripped and donned a dark pair of slacks and a pressed white shirt, open at the collar. He sat opposite Kanamura, who was sipping his drink.

"Tell me what happened at the cove."

"It seems Spinner was working alone." Kanamura's voice devoid of any emotion. "The men said he used his boat as a battering ram and collapsed the barricade in two places. He then drove through the lagoon and herded the animals out the breaches."

Yoshimatsu took a swig of his whiskey. "It seems we have underestimated this Spinner."

"I think he just got lucky. Reports from the men who were there said his actions were erratic, unplanned. I believe he was able to capitalize on the chaos of the hunt."

"What I am wondering," Yoshimatsu held up his glass and swirled the amber liquid, "was what Jake Spinner was doing out there in the first place? San Mateo Cove is very remote. I think he happened on the cove by accident. He has been inquiring relentlessly about Gustavo Silvano. He must be looking for Gustavo's son, Macario. If he can get Macario to turn on us, our operation will be in grave danger."

"Do you think he is hiding the Silvano boy around there? That would be a long shot."

"Think about it, Ako. Where would you go if you knew people were after you? He has not surfaced in Puerto Nacimiento or San Jacinto. What better place for a young fisherman to hide than along the rugged coast of Baja? I think we have been looking for young Silvano in the wrong places."

Kanamura nodded. "I will put the word out and have our men begin patrolling the roads and checking into the fishing camps."

"We must prevent him from speaking out. The success of our project requires that silence be maintained. Macario Silvano must be found and dealt with before he can get to those who can make trouble for us."

"I will have the search expanded. Hiro-san, there is another problem."

Yoshimatsu's eyes narrowed. "Be careful of the words you choose next, Ako. I have heard enough problems for one day."

Kanamura shifted slightly in his chair, the only hint that revealed his apprehension at what he was about to divulge to his superior. "There were observers at the cove today."

Yoshimatsu looked up from the rim of his glass. "What? Who were they?"

"We don't know yet. They were above the cove standing on the edge of a cliff."

"How many were there?"

"No one was certain. At least two. They left quickly when they were spotted. We tried to follow their tracks, but they were gone by the time our men got to the other side of the mountain."

Yoshimatsu threw his glass against the wall behind Kanamura. Shattered glass rained down on Kanamura's head. A sliver gashed the side of his face, producing a small trickle of red.

Yoshimatsu looked at Kanamura with cold rage. "Perhaps I terminated the wrong associate. Tell me why I shouldn't shoot you right here."

Kanamura looked directly into his superior's eyes. "I told you, Hiro-san. By allowing Figueroa to bring in local contractors, we are dangerously exposed. Someone on the Mexican side leaked information. I do not believe this man Spinner was part of a coordinated effort to stop the hunt. His methods were too erratic. He either was tipped off by someone or accidentally stumbled on the cove during the culling."

"Then who were the others?" Yoshimatsu almost spat the words.

"The cities and villages along this coast are not large," said Kanamura. "We will find them all—Macario Silvano, Jake Spinner, and the spies on the cliff."

He leaned forward in the chair. "Hiro-san, you and I have worked together for a long time. I have always delivered for you."

"It is not your loyalty I question."

"We are in Mexico. There are factors here that we have not planned for. In the Southern Ocean, we knew the nature of our adversaries. It has not yet been revealed whom we are dealing with here. Let me do my job, Hiro-san. I will deliver Silvano, Spinner, and the trespassers to you myself."

Yoshimatsu looked at Kanamura, his gaze colder than the Southern Ocean. "See that you do, my friend. If you fail, our friendship means nothing. You know the price of failure."

Kanamura returned his gaze. He nodded slowly, once. "I understand, sir. I do not wish to end up like Maro Sakei."

# 23

By the time Spinner was able to find a safe anchor to begin repairs, he was well into a full-blown episode of the shakes. Being low on food and water didn't help his already dispirited and declining condition. Two things drove him on: he needed to contact Castellano to begin making arrangements to get Macario out of country and he needed to have a fully functioning boat.

Jake pulled into the fishing camp of San Vicente. His foggy brain remembered that Carlos and Jesús, the two fishermen who had found Gustavo, lived and worked here. He hoped the brother of Jesús was still in the business of repairing boats.

Spinner was barely able to tie the boat to an anchor line. The motor was coughing and smoking and reverse gear was no longer working. His vision was blurring and he kept hearing echoes of anguished voices and gunfire.

A panga left the beach and motored out toward where Jake lay anchored. He barely recognized Jesús at the bow. He assumed the man at the tiller was Jesús's brother, the mechanic.

The two men in the panga came alongside of *This Side Up* and stared, open-mouthed, at the ruined boat before them.

Jesús whistled. "Who have you been fighting? The Sinaloa Cartel?"

The man at the tiller started to laugh until he got a good look at the human wreckage piloting the boat.

"Señor Jake," said Jesús. "What happened to you?"

"Long story," said Jake, nearly doubling over. "Can you fix her? I need to have her running as soon as possible."

"Jake, this is my brother Francisco," said Jesús. "He's *un mecánico muy bueno*."

"Francisco," Jake acknowledged.

"Hand me the bowline," said Jesús.

Spinner stumbled forward and tossed the line over to Jesús, who secured it to a cleat on the stern of his boat.

"Can you get cell phone service?" Spinner rasped.

"Sí. Although it's better in the morning and at night," replied Jesús.

"I might have to borrow your phone. I'm pretty sure my battery is about done."

Jesús nodded. "We need to get you to shore, Señor Jake. Are you hurt?"

Spinner shook his head. "I'm okay."

Jake's hands were shaking so badly that he could barely hold onto the railing. His vision had narrowed to a small area in front of him and voices were ringing. He had to keep it together long enough to call Castellano.

Once his boat was pulled into the shallows, he transferred over to Jesús's boat for the final leg to the beach. When they got to the beach, he stepped off, fell forward onto his knees, then went face down into the water. Jesús jumped over the side and quickly pulled him up and onto the beach.

"Damn it," Spinner muttered weakly. He fumbled in his shorts pocket for his cell phone. It was wet. Jesús quickly dried it off on his handkerchief.

Spinner fumbled with the numbers on the keypad and managed to get Castellano's number inputted after the third try.

"Castellano."

"Rollie, it's me, Jake."

"Spinner, you sound like shit."

"I don't have much time. My cell phone's about to crap out on me. Do you remember when I asked you to book passage for the Silvano family?"

"Yeah, but I never heard back from you."

"Well, I screwed up good, Rollie. Because of me, my friends got murdered."

"Oh, Christ, Spinner. What happened?"

"A Japanese syndicate is down here hunting whales. They recruited local villagers to do their dirty work. When the indios wanted out, they were killed. I believe that's what happened to Gustavo and his wife. I found their son hiding out at our old fishing camp. I need you to arrange passage out of Mexico for Macario until things cool down. If those assholes get a hold of him, he's fish bait."

"Two exit visas?"

"Just one." Jake doubled over in agony as a lightning bolt of pain drove through him.

"God damn it, Spinner. You need to get the fuck out of there. If those syndicate guys wasted your friend, they won't think twice about clocking you."

Through gritted teeth, Spinner managed to say, "Not yet." He dropped the phone, fell to the sand, and writhed in agony.

"Jake? You still with me? Where are you now?"

Jesús picked up the phone and said, "Jake's not able to come to the phone right now. Please wait."

It took several minutes before the pain subsided and Jake came back on the line.

"I'm at a fishing camp. Need to get my boat repaired. All shot up. I'll bring the kid in when she's seaworthy again."

"You're in no shape to do this, Jake," Castellano said. "Let it go."

"I'm not done yet! Not until I find out who killed Gustavo and Marta." He was hit by another wave of pain. Through gritted teeth he said, "Just do this for me, Rollie. Last time I ask for anything."

"We both know that's bullshit." There was a brief pause, then, "I'll have the necessary documents ready in twenty-four hours."

"Thanks, Rollie. I owe you one."

"You owe me a lot more than one. Do you have ordnance to hold you until the job is done?"

Before Jake could answer, his cell phone went dead.

The next twelve hours were a descent into hell. Bouts of delirium followed by episodes of severe nausea and vomiting left him completely helpless. To keep Spinner from hurting himself, Jesús carried him to an empty shack and placed him on a cot with a blanket to ride out the storm that wracked his head and body.

In a series of cascading nightmares, Spinner was running across bloody battlefields from Afghanistan to Somalia. Bullets like a thousand stinging wasps pierced his flesh, but he kept running. The ground was churned into flying clods of dirt; trees splintered into sharp projectiles. Everywhere he ran, he heard the screams of the wounded and dying.

At one point, in a brief moment of near lucidity, Spinner searched for his pistol in a desperate attempt to stop the nightmares once and for all. The gun was no longer in the waistband of his shorts and he was too weak and sick to go searching for it.

When Spinner came to, the shack was bathed in darkness. Voices drifted in the night behind the steady beat of water against the shore. He tried to stand but stumbled and fell to his knees. All his joints were on fire, and he had a splitting headache. His stomach was still churning, the aftermath of the inner maelstrom that had battered and beaten him. He emerged from the shack and saw a group of men gathered around a large campfire. He caught the smell of cooked fish and almost retched on the spot. Shakily, he made his way to the fire.

Jesús looked up from his conversation with Francisco and Carlos. He came over and guided Spinner to a rickety chair.

"How long have I been out?" Spinner's voice was a harsh rasp.

"Fifteen hours," said Jesús.

"Fifteen hours?" Spinner tried to stand. "I need to get back to Macario."

"You're not going anywhere, Señor Jake. He went to the fire and pulled a blackened pot away from the flames. He scooped out a bowl of steaming soup. "The boat's not ready. You're still too weak to travel."

"I gotta get back. They're looking for the kid."

"Your boat needs a few more things," said Francisco. "I'll have it ready to go in the morning. I had to stop working. We ran out of propane for the lamps. He nodded toward the boat. "You really know how to wreck a boat, Señor."

Jesús and Francisco saw a look of dread cross the American's face.

"You need to eat." Jesús handed him the full bowl. "It's lentil soup."

Spinner took it and looked at the contents of his bowl. He looked up at Jesús. "Right now, I could use a drink."

"That's all that we have," Jesús lied.

Spinner tentatively spooned out some soup, gulped once and let it run down his throat. His stomach lurched once, then went still. "That's not bad," he said and downed another spoonful. Moments later, he had finished the bowl.

"Thanks. For watching my back."

"*De nada.*"

"Look guys, I can't pay you for repairs yet. I won't get another check from the government for two weeks."

"That's okay, Señor Jake." Jesús grinned, the fire illuminating his stained teeth. "We know where you live."

"Not anymore. The bastards blew up my house."

Francisco, Carlos, and Jesús looked at Jake, then at each other. "Señor, we think it's very dangerous to be around you," said Francisco.

"Anyone comes snooping around, you don't know me. It'll save you a lot of grief."

The next morning, Francisco finished the final repairs a few hours after the sun came up. Jake got behind the wheel and fired up the motor. It ran rougher than before, but passable, especially considering Francisco had to work miracles to get the boat seaworthy. Spinner made ready to return to the fishing camp to retrieve Macario. Jesús presented him with lunch bags filled with fruits and cooked fish. He then produced Spinner's gun and handed it to him.

"You told me to hold onto this. Until you were ready."

Jake was overwhelmed. "Muchas gracias. For everything." These men had next to nothing, yet they had helped him in his worst hours. Jake remembered why he had come to care about these people of the desert sea. It was their kindness, spirit and resiliency.

"*Buena suerte*," said Jesús. "I hope you can find the killers of Gustavo and his wife and bring them to justice."

Spinner nodded. "Gotta go. There's a trigger-happy kid out there looking for revenge. I need to get to him before the bad guys do."

He backed out into deeper water, then turned the boat around and waved back at the fishermen as he accelerated out of the cove.

Little did he know that he was already too late.

# 24

Macario Silvano lasted for nearly eight hours before blind rage and guilt compelled him to defy Jake Spinner's orders. He couldn't stay here any longer. He was determined to find the killers.

He searched through the camp hoping he'd find an extra fuel line somewhere. His effort proved fruitless. Spinner had taken steps to make sure that Macario would have to stay put until he returned. What Jake didn't know was that Macario not only knew the Gulf of California well, but he was also adept at traveling the deserts of the Baja Peninsula.

He spent the day gathering supplies and water and packing as much food into his backpack as he might need. He decided against carrying any canned goods as they would weigh him down too much. Macario made enough dried fish burritos to last two days. He packed three liters of water and a change of clothes. He still had some money tucked in his sock, but it wasn't nearly as much as he would have liked. He hadn't worked in several weeks and was beginning to feel the pinch.

He needed to move fast. To avoid detection, he decided to travel at night on back roads and cross country. Once he got to the one highway that spanned the length of Baja, he could hitch a ride to the city.

The dog was lying near him while he rummaged around for supplies. Macario looked at the dog and sighed. Where he was going there was no way for a dog to tag along. The dog would have to fend for itself—at least until Spinner came back. After all, it was Spinner's dog.

Macario grew more eager to get on the road as the sun dropped below the mountains in the west. Navigation through the desert to the highway would be relatively easy for him in the light of the waxing moon.

He was haunted by thoughts of his parents. Perhaps if he hadn't been so adamantly opposed to his parents' plan to leave the village, they'd still be alive today. He felt a crushing weight in his chest. Because of his greed and selfishness, his parents were dead. He wiped away hot tears that stained his chiseled brown cheeks. The guilt soon morphed into searing hatred, that rage which causes normally sane men to perform insane deeds.

In La Paz, Macario knew a young man who could get him a gun. As children, they had played and fished together in the village. When Alberto turned fifteen, he had moved to Ensenada with his family and soon became part of a gang. After several gang members were gunned down by a rival gang, Alberto migrated back south, stopping briefly in their village to see old friends. He had tried to convince Macario to come with him to La Paz, but Macario declined. Alberto said if he wanted a change of scenery or needed a weapon, to come see him.

The moon rose above the cordillera as Macario shouldered his pack. He took one last look at the derelict fishing shack, performing a mental checklist of all the things he was taking and what he was leaving behind. Macario set off, heading in a southwesterly direction toward the road, and then south to La Paz.

As he topped the last dune before dropping into the desert scrub, he heard a bark. The dog was sprinting across the dunes toward him.

Macario turned around. "No! Go back!"

The dog slowed to a trot, then stopped. He cocked his head, then followed after Macario again. Macario took a few steps toward the dog and waved his arms. "Get out of here! ¡Vete!"

The dog stopped, its tail lowered and ears flattened back. It then took several tentative steps forward.

Macario kicked sand toward the dog. Waving his arms, he ran at the dog again. The dog finally took off running, his tail between his legs.

"No, Dog! Go with Spinner!"

From a safe distance, the dog sat on his haunches and regarded the young man. He cocked his head and let out a low whimper. Macario turned and began walking through the desert. When he next turned around, the dog was nowhere to be seen.

He set a brisk pace across the rocky terrain. The rising moon created long, pumice-colored shadows that made avoiding pitfalls and rocks easy. Macario figured if he could keep up this pace, he could make it to the road by mid-morning tomorrow. There was always a steady stream of trucks driving south to La Paz and Cabo. Picking up a ride south shouldn't pose a problem. With a little luck, he would be in La Paz by tomorrow night.

After three hours of steady walking, Macario stopped and wriggled out of his pack. Even though a cool breeze wafted gently across the peninsula, he was sweating profusely. He actually felt a chill go through his body as he sat on a flat rock and sipped water from a plastic bottle. He didn't rest for long. Killing was on his mind.

He still had no plan. He had heard a rumor. One of the villagers had overheard one of the supervisors talking about a meeting in La Paz. It wasn't much, but it was a place to start. Once there, he could have Alberto start asking around. Macario would hang around the wharves and docks and, sooner or later, he'd see one of the overseers. He'd hang back and blend in with the crowd until the jefes inadvertently led him to the ones who had given the orders to terminate his parents. Energized, Macario jumped up, donned his pack, and set off again through the moonlit desert.

It was after midnight when he realized he was being followed. At first, it was just an odd sensation, a general sense of unease that superseded his anger and fatigue. Then he thought that the dog had been following him all along. Several times he turned around and looked behind him. The moon was high overhead now, and the shadows contracted.

He continued walking ahead toward a series of low-lying hills. It was then he saw the coyotes. At first, he could only see them at the periphery of his vision. Whenever he turned his head to look, the coyotes would vanish into the shadows like wraiths. He quickened his pace. He finally got so he had to rotate his head slightly while walking so he could see the desert canids better. He guessed there to be six of them—three adults and three smaller ones. The pack was thirty to forty yards behind him and off to the side. If Macario stopped, the coyotes stopped. If he walked briskly, they trotted along matching his pace. After several miles of this, Macario became increasingly agitated. He only had a hunting knife in his backpack for protection. The coyotes had grown more brazen and closed the distance to about twenty yards. Several times he could hear low growls and whines above the sound of his own breathing.

Macario turned around abruptly, raising his arms and waving wildly while yelling at the top of his lungs.

"Go away! Get out of here!" He ran directly at the stunned coyotes. They turned tail and ran into the desert, blending in with the night shadows. Satisfied he was no longer being followed, Macario turned around and set a course for the low hills to the south.

By the time he reached the foothills, his legs ached and his feet were sore. He knew he had developed some new blisters on his toes. Expensive Nikes worked great on a basketball court but were terrible for an extended hike over rocky desert. He stopped by a stand of palo blanco trees and dropped his pack in the dirt. The white trunks reflected in the moonlight, giving the trees a skeletal appearance. He sat down, leaning against the trunk of a tree and took several swigs from his water bottle.

His eyelids were heavy, and he wanted to sleep. By his best reckoning, he'd been walking for nearly seven hours without much rest. He'd been fueled by adrenalin and dark energy, but now some of it was flagging due to fatigue. He experienced a brief moment of fear when he remembered Spinner's words: *You're going to have to be a lot faster if you plan on taking down the guys who killed your parents. They'll chew you up and shit you out dead.*

Macario felt tendrils of doubt creep into his mind and, for the first time, he experienced a visceral fear that he could die. Maybe Spinner was right. But Spinner shouldn't have left him back there at the fishing camp. Spinner was treating him as if he were a child.

He didn't see how that useless old borracho was going to bring his parents' murderers to justice. Jake Spinner was good at two things: fishing and drinking. His father had told him that at one time Spinner had been a heroic warrior, a soldier in his country's armed forces. But now he suffered from some disease that was like battlefield sickness. Macario recalled several times at the fishing camp when Spinner had gone crazy after too much tequila.

Maybe he should have left Jake a note—just something that said he was all right and would catch up with him later. But he didn't want Spinner following him. He had enough to worry about without having to contend with the gringo.

Before dawn, Macario left the hills and was walking through a cardón forest. The moon was sinking in the west now, and the shadows cast by the giant cacti were long and ominous. As far as he could see, the silhouettes of the desert sentinels stretched toward the horizon. If it weren't for the stars and the faint light to the east, he would have gotten disoriented.

He was exhausted. He wanted to lie down, close his eyes, and sleep. But he kept walking, trudging through the loose desert sand. He was afraid that if he stopped to rest for too long his resolve would collapse. The highway shouldn't be far from here. Once he got a ride, he could sleep in the back of some pickup truck all the way into La Paz.

Shortly after 5:00 a.m., he saw the lights from a vehicle a mile or so ahead, followed by the sound of a diesel motor straining as the driver downshifted into a turn. He picked up his pace in spite of the fact that his feet were on fire.

By the time he reached the highway, it was deserted. He began walking southbound, anticipating the arrival of the next big rig full of vegetables or livestock that would give him a lift to his final destination.

When he heard the sound of the first semi's approach, he stopped walking and turned and faced up the road. When the lights of the eighteen-wheeler illuminated him, Macario began waving his arms wildly. The semi roared past, the draft almost lifting him off his feet.

Two more semis and a passenger vehicle passed him on the road. Maybe people were nervous about picking up hitchhikers along this isolated stretch of road. Macario was about to give up and drop into an arroyo for some much-needed sleep when the lights of another vehicle approached. As they bathed him in halogen brightness, he waved his arms like a windmill. To his amazement, the vehicle slowed and pulled off to the side of the road twenty yards ahead of him. Macario sprinted toward the black SUV and went to the passenger's side. The rear door swung open and Macario unleashed his pack and got into the back seat.

"Muchas gracias, amigos! I'm going to La Paz."

There were three men in the vehicle, two in the front seat and another, who looked vaguely familiar, in the back seat next to him. He was grinning at Macario in a sinister way.

The man in the front passenger seat turned around. "We've been looking for you, Macario."

Macario recognized Kanamura. He felt the bile rise in his throat. He hit the door and tried to bolt out of the SUV. A strong hand caught him by the shirt collar. He felt an excruciating pain at the base of his neck; then everything went black.

# 25

**D**r. Alejandro Cabrillo slipped the key into the service door behind the *Instituto de Mamíferos Marinos* while Sandy Wainright looked cautiously in all directions. Most of La Paz was asleep.

"I never thought we'd be breaking into the institute." Sandy held the flashlight while Alejandro wiggled the key in the rusty lock.

"Think of it as performing a security check."

"Something tells me that you might have done something like this in your youth."

Alejandro's smile was barely visible in the low light from the flashlight. "I probably would have made more money as an international jewel thief. But that job requires a lot of scaling tall buildings, and I'm scared of heights."

He jiggled the door handle, and the back door opened with a groan. The researchers slipped inside, closing the door behind them. Alejandro produced a flashlight from his back pocket. As they walked briskly down the corridor, he said, "Download the data you need from the main computer in the lab. I'll meet you there in a few minutes."

"I'm not sure what to take and what to leave."

"Anything that looks like it could compromise the whales," Alejandro replied.

"Well, that just about covers everything we've archived."

"Any data pertaining to travel patterns, aggregations, sighting dates. Just grab it. Leave the altered data. After you download the original data onto a flash drive, delete it. And don't dawdle."

"This is scary as hell," Sandy whispered as she headed toward the laboratory, and Alejandro moved toward his office. He fired up his computer and waited for what seemed an eternity for it to boot up. Once in, he scrolled through all the files that had been compiled since the inception of the humpback project four years ago. He could understand Sandy's frustration. There were many files of information here revealing the humpback's traveling and aggregation patterns. He removed a flash drive from his pocket and plugged it into one of the side ports on his Mac. While downloading, he scanned the room to see if there was anything here that he should take along.

When the download was complete, Alejandro stuck the flash drive inside his sock. He highlighted the file names of valid data and punched the "delete" key, shut down the computer, and proceeded to the laboratory.

When he got to the lab, the room was bathed in darkness except for the bluish reflection on Sandy's face from the computer screen. Her brow was deeply lined as she leaned toward the screen. He pulled a chair close to her and sat down.

"I can't believe we have to do this," she said angrily. "They have no right to our data. We've put our hearts and souls into this project. And now we're just supposed to turn it over."

"It's not over yet. We're going to get to the bottom of this. Besides, we have the *New York Times* on our side."

"Alex, I'm done."

Just as she shut down the computer, the laboratory was bathed in harsh light. Sandy gave a little yelp.

"Hello! What's this?" The voice came from behind them. They spun around to see Minister Alfonso Figueroa standing there, his eyebrows raised in question. Next to him stood a sleepy looking security guard, and behind him a large formidable looking man wearing a suit, one hand held inside his jacket. Figueroa was dressed in a formal dinner jacket, white shirt open at the collar.

"Working a bit late tonight, aren't we? Or is this when researchers begin their day?"

Alejandro and Sandy stood. "Minister Figueroa." Alejandro attempted to regain his composure. "We were just collating some data that we needed to input."

"In the dark? Why would you work in the dark?"

"We were just closing up," said Sandy, "when I remembered something that we needed to input. So, I turned the computer on again and entered the data."

"Working on a computer screen in the dark can be bad for your eyes." Figueroa's tone was mildly sarcastic.

Alejandro asked, "To what do we owe the honor of this visit, sir?"

"I believe there is a serious problem with the data. I came here as soon as I found out. We have provided Mr. Yoshimatsu and his colleagues with inaccurate data. Perhaps there are inconsistencies with your instruments or your measurement techniques. We must clear this matter up. Our future relationship with the Japanese government may be compromised unless I can see the data and figure out what is wrong."

"Minister Figueroa, why would you think there is anything wrong with our data?"

"They informed me that the coordinates were not accurate. When they flew over the designated coordinates, no whales were seen at all. None of the coordinates revealed any animals. Not one. How is that possible?"

"Whales are constantly on the move," said Sandy. "They're looking for food and mates."

"Recently, we have lost the signals from several of our humpbacks," said Alejandro. "That could be a possible explanation."

"What does that mean?"

"It means we are no longer getting satellite data sent to us. This could mean the whales have left the area, the transmitters could have fallen off, or worst case, the whales may have died.

"We recovered one humpback with a harpoon still in it," said Sandy.

Alejandro gave Sandy a sidelong glance.

Figueroa stared at Sandy. "A harpoon? Are you quite certain, Miss Wainwright?"

Sandy returned his gaze. "Absolutely. If someone is hunting them, then I would say the whales probably left for safer waters."

"This is the first I have heard of any such incident. I will need to know the date and the location of this dead whale."

"I will send you the date and GPS locations today," Sandy said.

"I'm sorry, Minister Figueroa. It's not our intention to be insubordinate or disrespectful. But we find it somewhat strange and disturbing that our whales have been disappearing over the last few months. We have to admit, we are uncomfortable sharing our information with the Japanese."

"I find it troubling, Director Cabrillo, that you have repeatedly referred to them as 'our whales.' These are resources that you're studying. They're under the direct supervision of the Department of Fisheries. They are not your personal pets."

"I fully understand that, sir. But we've poured our hearts, our sweat, and even some of our personal finances into this project to make it a success. We only have the best interests of the whales in mind."

"The Japanese dignitaries are only interested in being better able to manage their own dwindling stocks using the latest methods that we employ. I would think you would be elated over this chance to share information about the conservation of a species. I will not compromise any future relations between our two governments based on conjecture and possibly flawed data."

"Minister, I—"

"I will have my staff review your data again. And I want to see you both in my La Paz office on Monday at 8:00 a.m. Sharp."

Alejandro and Sandy stared at him, too stunned to speak.

Figueroa glared at the researchers as if he were weighing what to do next. Alejandro saw the Minister's eyes shift down to Alejandro's hands, then to his backpack. For a moment he thought Figueroa was going to confiscate their backpacks. Fortunately, none of the information was in them. They had agreed to hide the flash drives in other more personal places.

He motioned to the security guard. "Please escort Dr. Cabrillo and Miss Wainwright out."

As they walked away, Sandy caught a look from Figueroa's bodyguard that sent a chill down her spine. Once outside, the security guard closed the door and locked it behind them. Alejandro said, "Follow me."

They both got into their vehicles and parked a block away from the institute. Sneaking back, they hid themselves across the street behind a hedge of bougainvillea that gave them a better vantage point to the institute.

Moments later, the door opened and Figueroa and the two men emerged. They carried all three computers and quickly placed them in Figueroa's SUV.

"I can't believe this shit," Sandy whispered. "They're hijacking our computers."

Figueroa and the others got into the SUV and drove away.

"Lucky that we still have our laptops," said Alejandro. "That was way too close."

"What now?"

"We're going to have to play this out, that's all."

"I noticed you didn't say anything about the dolphin hunt yesterday."

"I don't want anyone to know that we were there," Alejandro said. "Remember, they were shooting at us."

They began walking briskly toward the vehicles. "Call the others," Alejandro said. "Tell them the meeting has to be moved. We can't meet at any of our houses. Maybe Raúl knows a place where we won't be seen."

"Right. What are you going to do?"

"I'm going to go back to my house and awaken my wife and daughter. I'm going to make sure they're on their way to her mother's house before the sun comes up." He turned and looked at her, the lines in his forehead deep with worry. "I have a very bad feeling about all of this."

The sun was just coming up, and the light coming through the curtains over the sink was ethereal. Alejandro sat at his kitchen table, nursing a cup of black coffee. Sleep had eluded him. His restlessness had awakened his wife, Carmen, who sensed that something was wrong.

"Alex, are you okay? You got home really late last night." She rubbed his shoulder.

"I want you to pack some things. I want you and Lili to go to your mother's house for a few days."

"What is it, Alejandro? Why would you send us away?"

"It's probably nothing, *mi amor*. We have to straighten some things out about what happened at the San Mateo Cove."

"You're a terrible liar, Alejandro Cabrillo. Tell me what's going on."

He placed his hand on top of hers. "There's something I didn't tell you. The other day at San Mateo, the whalers were shooting at us."

Carmen put her hand to her mouth. "¡Dios mío! They shot at you? Why didn't you tell me?"

"I was still processing. At the time, I didn't want to upset you."

"Well, I'm upset now!"

"I'm sorry, Carmen. We have reason to believe this is not a random act. There are too many coincidences, and there may be involvement at higher levels than we thought. I would feel better if you and Lili would leave La Paz for a few days. At least until we can get some answers."

"I'm not leaving without you!" Carmen said, tears welling in her deep brown eyes. "We all go to my mother's or not at all!"

"I can't leave yet. I have to finish what I started. I can't focus on the project if I know that you and Lili may be in danger."

"Is it worth your life, Alejandro? Is it worth tearing our family apart?"

Alejandro hung his head. After a moment he looked at his wife of ten years. She saw that his eyes were moist now. "I must do this. All I need is a few days to get some information out to the media. The others on the project are depending on me. We're going public with video footage and photos. When this happens, I want you and Lili to be in a safe place. I swear to you on the graves of my ancestors that I will join you both in a few days."

"Why don't you just turn everything over to Minister Figueroa? He's in a position to do something about this horrible thing."

"Carmen, I have reason to believe that Minister Figueroa might be involved."

Her eyes grew wide. "The Minister of Fisheries involved in illegal whaling? No one will believe that, Alejandro. What you're saying is occupational suicide.

You'll be fired if you accuse him of this. Besides, his brother-in-law is the president of Mexico."

"I'm not accusing him of anything. Yet. But once the photos and the video go public, and everything is out in the open, we should have a better idea who's behind this."

Alejandro walked into Figueroa's La Paz office at five minutes to eight on Monday morning. The whale biologist looked like hell. He hadn't shaved since the incident at San Mateo. His eyes were red and puffy from stress and lack of sleep. His clothing was rumpled. Figueroa motioned for Alejandro to come in. The Minister of Fisheries, although dressed in a fresh business suit, looked equally worn and haggard.

"Where is Miss Wainright?"

"She sends her apologies. She's not feeling well today, so she stayed home."

Figueroa hesitated. "If she goes into the lab today, she will see that your computers are not there. I have taken it upon myself to remove the computers and check your whale population and location data."

Alejandro looked directly into the minister's eyes. "You took our computers?"

"I needed to determine that the data on your computers correlated with the data that you gave the Japanese contingency. The data are identical."

"Of course it is, sir. Why would you question that?" Alejandro hoped Figueroa wasn't as adept at spotting a lie as his wife Carmen was.

He gave Alejandro an apologetic smile. "The computers will be returned to your lab this afternoon. I still find it very odd and disconcerting that their spotter helicopter did not find any whales. Not one. Does that not seem strange to you, Dr. Cabrillo?"

"No, sir. Whales are very intelligent animals. They move around a lot under normal circumstances. If someone is killing whales in the Gulf of California, it would not surprise me that they most likely have left the area."

"Then where would they go?"

"That is hard to say, sir. Possibly south." Alejandro drew in a deep breath, then exhaled. "What I find disconcerting, sir, is that the Japanese did not bother to consult with our team about aerial surveys before they undertook them on their own. We could have saved them a lot of trouble."

"They are a very polite society. They informed me that they did not wish to impose on you and your fellow researchers. They had the data and wanted to see for themselves."

"The helicopters may scare the whales away from an area. Besides, why are they harassing these whales? We've given them all the information they should need."

"They didn't observe any animals anyway." Figueroa leaned forward on his desk. "In the future, I expect a concerted effort from your team to fully cooperate with our guests regarding their conservation efforts. I would advise none of you to speak to anyone about the harpooned whale until I have a chance to investigate the matter further. I'm taking you at your word, Alejandro. I need to hear from you that you will abide by my request."

Alejandro nodded. "Yes, sir. I'll tell the others."

Figueroa sat back in his chair. The meeting was over. The tension in the room was apparent. Alejandro smiled weakly, stood, and walked toward the door. As he left, Figueroa said, "Dr. Cabrillo, how's your family?"

Alejandro turned around and stared at him. "They're fine, sir."

"That's good. The family is everything. It's very important in these uncertain times to keep your loved ones close." Figueroa's gaze was pleasant, but his eyes held no emotion.

Even though Alejandro had been sweating throughout the meeting, a cold chill now permeated his body. There was no missing the veiled threat. "Thank you, sir. I will."

# 26

Jake Spinner knew the fishing camp was deserted even before he set foot on shore. Call it a feeling, but he knew Macario was no longer there. Still, he anchored in the shallows and waded ashore. He saw that the panga was untouched. The young man had not even tried to get it working. When he stepped inside the shack, the first thing he noticed was the rod and reel he had left with Macario.

"Shit," he muttered. He looked around and found more evidence that Macario had packed up quickly. *The damn fool took off cross-country.* Jake's addled brain hadn't factored in the possibility that Macario would light out on foot and cross the desert, in all likelihood, in the dark.

Spinner heard a noise from outside near the shack. Nerves still ragged from the encounter at the cove, he pulled his semi-automatic from the back of his cargo shorts. Stepping outside into the glare of the afternoon sun, Spinner performed a quick assay. He heard the sound again and spun toward the source, pistol raised. It was coming from the woodpile behind the shack.

"I have a headache and an itchy finger. Better show yourself."

He heard a whimper, and Dog appeared from under a pile of brush. He approached Jake timidly, ears down and tail between his legs.

"Damn dog. You were supposed to watch out for Macario until I got back."

The dog came close and rolled on his back. Spinner wanted to kick the dog for not keeping track of Macario, but then he realized it was his own lack of planning that had caused him to lose track of the kid.

As if on cue, the dog sprang up and took off toward the dunes. When it got to the top of the first dune, it turned around and barked sharply at Jake. Spinner stuck the pistol back in his waistband and followed the dog. On top of the dune, the dog was standing next to a set of footprints that looked like they were the size and type made by Nike basketball shoes. The footprints appeared

148

to be heading west toward the highway. The dog yipped once again and took off following the footprints.

Spinner called the dog back. "He's long gone by now."

He began trudging back the way he'd come. When Dog whined once, Spinner looked back. "Well, you coming or not?"

The dog looked back across the expanse of desert, now shimmering in the hot afternoon sun. He whined again, then turned back and trotted after Jake.

After retrieving his fishing rod and loading the dog onto the boat, he set a course for San Vicente. Jake needed to do something with Dog. Where he was going, he couldn't be dragging a dune mutt all over Baja Sur. He finally decided to impose on Jesús and Carlos one more time.

Jake accelerated *This Side Up* to a full plane and mentally checked off possible places where Macario might go. He just hoped he wasn't too late.

# 27

The dirt road to Raúl's *ranchito* took on a surreal appearance. Tall cardón cacti, reaching up to a violet sky glittering with countless stars gave Emily Rosen the impression that she was driving through an alien landscape. The giant cacti resembled an army of silent sentinels waiting for a signal to wake up and march. Emily was nervous; she was comfortable in subways and had no problem hailing a taxi at three o'clock in the morning in the big city. But she disliked driving. The rental car, a Ford Focus, kept bottoming out in the arroyos, and several times she'd scraped the oil pan on protruding rocks in the middle of the track. The ugly grating sound of metal on rock further heightened her anxiety.

They had decided to arrive separately. After his confrontational visit with Figueroa, Alejandro was particularly adamant about arriving separately. There was something in his voice that Rosen recognized from years on the beat— Alejandro was scared.

After several wrong turns that ended in brush-filled arroyos, Rosen backtracked, driving slowly, her face nearly touching the windshield. She glanced at her watch. She had already been on this track for over an hour; she should have been at Raúl's house fifteen minutes ago.

She wasn't sure why she was still here. Yesterday, someone had shot at her. In all her years as a journalist, she had been threatened countless times, even pushed and shoved around on rare occasions. Hearing bullets ricocheting off rocks and making little spurts of dirt explode when they hit nearby had created such a visceral feeling in her that she hadn't slept last night.

Rosen wondered if she and the others could actually make a difference. Corruption was corruption, but this wasn't the Big Apple. This was Mexico. She was way out of her element. Because she'd been fired, she'd lost her primary means of getting this story out to the world.

She climbed a hill and came around a sharp turn. She gasped reflexively and slammed on the brakes. A dozen pairs of eyes, glowing yellow in the headlights, were staring at her.

"Jesus Christ!" She caught her breath.

The goats regarded her passively, then began moving off the road and into the desert. Rosen heard the bells attached to their necks above the intermittent bleating. After she recovered her composure, she realized she was close. With her heart still hammering in her chest she drove slowly forward. Soon Raúl's ranchito came into view. She parked next to Alejandro's truck, got out of her car, and walked toward the small ranch-style house. Before she even got to the door, her nostrils were treated to the most wonderful smells coming from inside the house. Her stomach gurgled. She realized she hadn't eaten anything since noon. She knocked and Raúl let her in.

Rosen stepped into a large kitchen that befitted a ranch. The others were sitting around a large rough-cut wooden table. Various dishes were laid out with beer and pitchers of *agua de jamaica,* a tea brewed from hibiscus flowers. A short, robust Mexican woman dressed in jeans and a tee shirt looked up from stirring a pot of beans. On her hip, she held a toddler with the blackest hair and biggest brown eyes Rosen had ever seen. The woman smiled at her.

"Emily, this is *mi esposa,* Guadalupe," said Raúl.

Guadalupe looked roughly around Rosen's age, but her skin was weathered and her hands calloused from a life working on a ranch.

"*¡Mucho gusto!*" Guadalupe smiled broadly. She spoke rapidly in Spanish, something that Rosen didn't understand.

"It's nice to meet you."

"She said it's an honor to have a famous writer from New York come to our *casa,*" said Raúl.

"I don't know about the famous part, but I can't remember when I smelled such wonderful aromas coming out of a kitchen."

Raúl interpreted and Guadalupe broke out into a huge, white-toothed grin.

"And this is my son, Julio," Raúl said. He touched his son's head affectionately.

Standing at the counter cutting vegetables was a slender girl Rosen guessed to be about eleven or twelve. Her long silky hair was woven into a braid. She smiled shyly at Rosen, then went back to her work. Raúl walked over and stood behind her, placing his hands gently on her shoulders.

"And this is Alisa, my daughter. She wants to go to university one day and study to be a scientist."

Rosen came over and held out her hand to Alisa. "Mucho gusto, Alisa." The young girl took her hand and shook it. "Do you speak English?"

"Sí—I mean, yes." Alisa, blushed.

"What do you want to study?" Emily asked.

"Biology, I think."

"You go, girl! Don't let go of your dreams and you'll get there."

The young girl smiled at Emily. "Muchas gracias!"

Rosen admired these people. Even though the nature of their business was deadly serious, it was still important to rekindle familial bonds and forge friendships over food and drink. As Guadalupe placed serving platters of roasted fish and dried meat on the table, Rosen licked her lips and hoped she wasn't openly salivating. When Alisa delivered a basket of hot steaming flour tortillas, Rosen could barely contain herself.

When the platter of meat came around to her, Emily looked closely at the food. "So, what is this? It smells great."

*"Birria de cabra,"* said Raúl. "Dried roasted goat."

Rosen's mind flashed on the eyes that had greeted her as she drove into the ranch earlier. She hesitated, then forked a small amount onto her plate. She wasn't inclined to eat goat, but she didn't want to offend her hosts. She passed the platter on to Sandy, who passed it to Paola and ultimately to Alejandro, who served himself a generous portion. When the plate of *pescado a la plancha* came around, Rosen wasn't shy and forked a large piece onto her plate.

As they ate, Rosen couldn't hold back any longer. "I have an announcement to make." She looked down, then at everyone seated at the table. "I was fired today. I no longer work at the *Times.*"

Sandy's face registered shock. "They fired you? Why?"

Rosen shook her head. "I should have seen it coming. The assignment in Mexico. The bogus story. My boss was looking for an excuse to get rid of me. I can't prove it, but I think the senator I was doing the investigation on made my editor an offer he couldn't refuse."

"That's terrible," said Paola. "I'm sorry."

"It seems corruption is not exclusive to Mexico," Alejandro said bitterly.

Rosen forced a small smile. "You don't know the half of it. Look, you guys. Before, I had the *Times* to bring to the table. Now, I don't have squat. If you want me to duck out . . ."

"No way!" Sandy paused. "Unless you want out."

Rosen inhaled deeply, then exhaled a long, ragged breath. "Yesterday, someone shot at me. No one's ever done that to me before. I've never been that frightened in my life. This morning I was strongly tempted to call a cab and catch the next flight to anywhere. But whenever I closed my eyes, I saw the dolphins in that cove. And it enrages me. That rage is far stronger than any fear."

She looked at the group. "I want to try and tap into some resources I have in the media. There are other venues besides the *Times*."

Sandy looked concerned. "Do you have any connections with environmental or conservation groups? Any leads we could follow?"

"All of you are much better connected to those groups than I am. But I'll send you any and all contacts I have with environmental journalists in the major media outlets."

"We have to be particularly careful with inquiries here in Mexico," said Alejandro. "Minister Figueroa will exercise his position to discredit us and confiscate our data."

"Who does he answer to?" Rosen grabbed another tortilla. "Oh man, these tortillas are fantastic! How far up the chain do you think the corruption goes?"

"He answers to the Undersecretary of Resources in Mexico City," said Alejandro, "who sits on the President's Council. Besides that, Figueroa's sister is married to the President of Mexico."

Emily asked, "Do you think Figueroa's dirty?"

Alejandro shrugged. "If we approach him with this, and he is involved, it'll all be over before we even get started."

"Damned if you do. Damned if you don't."

"Exactly. What we need is someone who can dig deeper. Someone from the outside who's not connected to this project and doesn't have ties to any institution."

Rosen smiled. "Thought you'd never ask. I'll follow that lead ASAP." She looked at Raúl. "Can you get me in contact with this guy Spinner? What's his game anyway? Why would an ex-pat drunk try to take down an entire operation and get shot at in the process?"

Raúl folded his hands and placed them on the table. "I have been asking around San Jacinto. It seems the house that Spinner lived in was recently destroyed. Rumor has it that he was involved in a drug deal gone bad, and the cartel shot up his house with automatic weapons."

"So Spinner's on the run," said Rosen. "That's going to make him harder to find."

"I don't know him well. He's a very difficult man. I heard that he and Gustavo used to guide fishing charters until Spinner's drinking got out of control."

Paola asked, "Do you think there's a correlation between Silvano's death, Spinner's house being razed, and the incident at San Mateo Cove? It could all just be a coincidence."

Rosen spoke up. "In my business, we say there are no coincidences."

"Tomorrow we'll go to San Jacinto and ask around," Raúl said. "If he's there, someone will know where to find him."

"In the meantime," Alejandro, directed his attention to Sandy. "Could you contact your colleagues up at Santa Cruz? Perhaps they'll have some connections with conservation groups."

"Of course. What about Sea Shepherd Conservation Society, Greenpeace, or Earth Island? When should we release the footage to them?"

"If you release that footage now," Rosen said, "before we know who the major players are, they'll go underground so fast they won't even leave a dust cloud. Hold off for a little while longer until we can track down some leads."

Paola spoke up. "What about Figueroa? I think he's very suspicious of us. You said it yourself, Alejandro. He did everything to intimidate you short of threatening you outright. And I think that question about your family was a poorly disguised threat. Once he looks at that video, we'll all be in danger."

Alejandro looked troubled. "Right now, all he knows is that we discovered a harpooned whale. He suspects that our data may have been altered, but he has no proof."

"Once that video is released," said Rosen, "we all become targets."

"Emily is right," said Raúl. "I think it is safer here. Use our home as your base of operations."

# 28

J ake Spinner opened his eyes and immediately regretted it. The bright
sunlight filtering through the slats of the building caused a searing pain to
shoot to the back of his head. He felt as if the pain was going to exit his skull and
leave a twelve-inch hole in the wall behind him. He groaned and closed his eyes.

When he opened them again, he waited until they could adjust to the light.
He looked down at an empty bottle of *Herradura Añejo* tequila and several
empty bottles of Tecate. In his left hand, he still clutched the Beretta.

*A hell of a lot of good this would have done me if we had surprise visitors.*

When he was able to orient himself, he realized that he was lying in the
supply shack of the El Pulpo Morado Cantina. *My home away from home.*

It smelled like stale beer and old sweat, overlaid with the cloying stench of
mold. Spinner's stomach roiled once, momentarily taking his mind away from
the pain in his head.

Two days ago, he had arrived back in the quaint fishing village of San Jacinto.
His first priority was to conceal *This Side Up.* He contacted Manny Gonzalez,
who rented out spaces in several old, large warehouses located near the end of the
harbor. Boats could be stored on a month per month basis. He parked his boat
and slipped Manny what cash he had, promising the balance within a few days.

He had exhausted every possibility for places to hide out while he searched
the streets for Macario Silvano. Everywhere Jake went, he was met with
apprehension and fear. Many of the locals wouldn't speak with him. Others
would promptly close the door in his face saying, *"¡Eres muy peligroso!"*

Even Juanita, who used to work for him, refused to help him. When she had
tried to close the door on him, Spinner placed his foot between the door and
the frame and forced his way in. He noticed that it was not disgust or revulsion
in her eyes when he showed up at her door. She was terrified.

"You must leave, Jake. Men, they come looking for you."

"What men?"

"*Los Japonés.*" Juanita looked out her window. "They came here asking questions. They pushed me down. In my own house!"

"When was this?"

"Two days ago. You need to leave now! They are hombres muy malos."

"Juanita, I need a place to hide until I can find Macario. He's in danger."

"Get out! If they see me talking to you, God knows what they'll do to me." She pushed him hard against his chest. "Get out!"

Finally, Jake had found Maximiliano at the El Pulpo Morado and pleaded his case. At first, the bartender was loath to let him take up residence in the storage shack again, but after Jake had explained that he was searching for Macario Silvano, Max acquiesced. The Asian thugs had entered the cantina and made veiled threats to Max. They suspected he was withholding information regarding the whereabouts of Spinner. Even though Spinner wasn't one of his favorite people, Max bristled at the idea of foreigners coming into his bar and threatening him. Macario Silvano was a friend. But friend or no friend, Max gave Spinner two days to do his business and then leave.

Spinner realized today was the second day, and he was no closer to finding out where Macario had gone. Fearing the worst, his scattered mind was running in all directions. With considerable mental effort, he forced his demons back down.

He didn't know why he had gotten drunk last night but for the previous two days his stomach had been on fire. He shouldn't have left Macario alone out there at the fish camp. Hell, he would have lit out the first chance he had if he was in Macario's shoes. Jake cursed himself for his lack of focus. There was a time when he could think four or five moves ahead of his enemies. Now, he was lucky if he could stumble along and not get hit by a Mexican taxi.

A makeshift plastic sink and wash area stood askew at the back of the shed. A thin stream of brownish water ran from the rusty spigot. He stumbled over the stacks of empty Tecate cases and grabbed hold of the rickety sink. The water smelled stale, almost brackish. After a moment, he closed his mouth tightly and splashed a handful of the brown water on his face. It felt warm and gritty.

After drying his face with his shirttail, he sat on a stack of beer cases and put his head in his hands, contemplating his next move. He had exhausted all his contacts and leads in San Jacinto. No one had seen Macario Silvano for over a week. He wondered if the boy had headed for La Paz. Spinner hazily remembered that a boyhood friend of Macario's lived there. *What was his name?* Wait, something like—Alberto?

"Shit," muttered Spinner, recalling that Alberto had left Puerto Nacimiento to join a gang.

Just as Spinner was thinking the day couldn't get any worse, someone rapped on the door of the storage shack.

They had arrived shortly after sunrise. The first place they drove past was Spinner's old residence. A chill ran up Emily's spine when she saw the bullet-riddled casita.

All morning, Rosen and Raúl had walked up and down the malecón, asking questions of the locals about where they could locate Jake Spinner. Many times, they were met with looks of disgust, even anger. Several fishermen they queried cursed Spinner, informing Rosen and Raúl that the drunken bastard still owed them money. It appeared that this Spinner character was not exactly a pillar of his community.

It wasn't until Raúl located a very old fisherman sitting on the beach under a canvas tarp mending his nets that their luck changed. He sat down in the sand with the man and, for several moments, neither spoke. Rosen thought this fisherman was older than time itself. His craggy face, dark brown from years in the sun, was lined with deep creases. His shoulder length hair was completely white. His back was bowed from years working on a boat, and his bare legs were bandied. His hands were gnarled and calloused. Rosen wanted to pull her camera out of her satchel and shoot a photo of that aged face, but she dared not, having learned when not to get into someone's personal space.

Raúl and the old fisherman spoke briefly, followed by another stretch of silence, with both men staring solemnly out to sea. When Raúl motioned to Emily, the old man looked at her, his gray eyes a strong contrast to his dark features. It was a quick look, but she felt as if the ancient fisherman was peering through her. A shudder ran up her spine.

Raúl shook the old man's hand, uncrossed his legs, and stood. He reached into his pocket, produced two one-hundred-peso notes, and handed them to the fisherman. The fisherman nodded, then went back to mending his nets. Raúl walked toward Emily. "Let's go."

Rosen fell in step with him. "That old guy is amazing. How old is he?"

"He was fishing when my father was a boy. And he's fishing still."

"Did he know anything about Spinner?"

"He said Spinner sleeps with the purple octopus."

Rosen stopped in her tracks. "What? Spinner's dead? Is that the Mexican version of the Godfather—sleeps with the fish?"

Raúl smiled. "He knows that Spinner is being hunted by men who ask questions along the beach. Spinner is very much alive. Come with me."

Emily Rosen sat in Raúl's truck parked outside of a cantina. She stared up at the large sign above the *cantina*. "El Pulpo Morado." The Purple Octopus. Rosen felt the anxiety building inside of her. She couldn't shake the feeling that they were being watched. Every few moments she turned her head and peered down the street in both directions. This time of day, the streets were becoming more active, with locals and tourists moving along the malecón, entering and leaving shops and restaurants. She did not notice anyone or anything that seemed out of order. That fact heightened her anxiety. She looked at her watch. Raúl had been gone now for nearly five minutes. It seemed like an hour.

The Pulpo Murado Cantina didn't look very busy. Rosen wondered what information Raúl was extracting from the occupants of the cantina. It seemed odd that Spinner would hide in such an open, obvious place. Raúl stepped out of the cantina, squinting against the glare of the noonday sun. He walked briskly to the truck, got in, and closed the door.

"Spinner's in the storage shack behind El Pulpo," said Raúl. "Apparently, we're not the first to come looking for him. The bartender said he's crazy and unpredictable."

Rosen touched Raúl's well-muscled arm. "Let me go in and talk to him. I won't present a threat to him."

"Señorita Emily, he's been drinking. You don't know what he could do."

"If he sees us both, he's going to run. I can get him to listen to me."

Raúl stared at her, sizing up the mental toughness of this petite woman from the eastern U.S.

"It's okay, Raúl. I can do this. Where I come from, this kind of stuff is just another day in the burg."

"I don't believe that is completely true. In his state, he could shoot you."

"Trust me, I got this."

Raúl lifted Emily's hand and squeezed it. "Your mouth speaks bravely, but your hands tell another story." Emily pulled her hand away, not realizing that she'd been shaking.

"I'm okay. You go into the bar and have a cold one. I'll give you a heads up when we're ready to come out."

Raúl turned his gaze from Emily and stared at the supply shack for a long time. Finally, he let out a deep sigh. "I'll be watching you from the back door of El Pulpo. Anything goes wrong, you yell as loud as you can."

"Don't worry. I have a real big mouth when I want to make a point." She looked at the storage building, took a deep breath, and squared her shoulders. "Here goes."

She opened the truck door and walked toward the cantina. She stepped inside, looked around, then made her way to the side door that led to the supply shack. A moment later, Raúl exited the truck and walked toward El Pulpo Morado. As he entered the cantina, he nearly collided with a man wearing an old straw cowboy hat pulled low over his eyes. The man gave him a furtive glance and walked briskly down the sidewalk.

Raúl moved toward the bar and found a seat with a view of the supply shack. The man with the *sombrero* turned a corner and walked a short distance to where a black Ford Excursion sat parked along the side street. The darkened driver's side window rolled down, and Sombrero Man spoke to the Asian driver and pointed down the street. The driver nodded, rolled the window back up, and started the ignition. The black SUV began moving slowly down the street toward El Pulpo Morado.

As Rosen walked toward the storage shack, she saw that a large piece of corrugated sheet metal covered a space that once was a window. Outside the door stood weathered plastic crates full of empty Mexican beer bottles. On the other side, a worn broom and wet mop leaned against the flimsy building, their state of deterioration an indication that they had not been used for cleaning for a long time.

Stepping up to the door, she took another deep breath and composed herself. She reached up tentatively, her fist poised for several seconds, then rapped on the door quietly.

She held her breath and waited. No sound came from inside. After what seemed an eternity, she knocked again, this time a little louder and more insistently.

Emily cleared her throat, which had suddenly gone dry. "Mr. Spinner? My name is Emily Rosen. I'm a reporter for the *New York Times*. I was wondering if I might have a—"

Suddenly the door flew open as if it were being ripped from its hinges. A disheveled man in a ratty Hawaiian shirt appeared, an ominous-looking gun leveled directly at her head.

# 29

"What the fuck are you doing here? Who sent you?"

"I just wanted to ask you a few questions about—"

Spinner grabbed Rosen roughly by the arm and pulled her inside.

"Hey! You can't do that!"

"Shut up!" Spinner peered out the door to the left and the right. He quickly closed and locked it from the inside. He turned and faced Emily Rosen, who was quickly losing the battle at remaining calm.

Spinner pointed the gun at her. "Lady, right now my bullshit meter is sitting on a hair trigger. I'm going to ask you again, one last time. Who sent you?"

Rosen stared down the muzzle of the semiautomatic. The bore of the gun looked enormous from this perspective. She began speaking in an even tone. "No one sent me. My name is Emily Rosen. I'm from *The New York Times*. I'm doing a story about whales in Baja. Several other researchers and I heard about a dolphin hunt and went to film it. We saw you at San Mateo Cove. We saw you break up the dolphin hunt. I just wanted to find out why you did it."

"None of your god damn business. How did you find out I was here?"

"Some old fisherman down the beach gave us a clue, and we tracked it to here." This guy did not look very stable, and to make matters worse, he reeked of alcohol. Even though Emily was scared half out of her wits, the trained reporter in her took over observing the desperate character standing in front of her. Spinner was tall, probably around six feet, and at one time might have been called handsome. His dark hair was greasy and uncombed, with strands hanging in his face. His blue eyes were tinged with red; his eyelids were puffy. His face hadn't seen a razor in weeks, and his clothes were disheveled.

"Not good enough, little sister. Which old man?"

"The old fisherman who mends nets near the dock."

"I know that old man. He doesn't speak a lick of English. Who are you working with? Talk, god damn it!"

"I could talk more coherently if you weren't pointing that damn gun at my face." Rosen's anger overrode her fear. "Raúl Campos. He talked to the old fisherman." She motioned with a movement of her head toward the door. "He's outside. In the bar."

Spinner's wild eyes moved from Emily to the door and back again. "Shit! You may have just gotten all three of us killed."

Spinner lowered the gun and began gathering together his meager belongings. He pushed past Rosen and pulled a worn canvas duffel from under a cot in the corner.

"I was hoping you could help us out, Mr. Spinner. Someone is killing whales in the Gulf and we think you may have an idea who it is."

"What? Lady, I have no idea what you're talking about," Spinner gave Emily a hard gaze. "Someone killed a friend of mine and then shot my house to shit. I don't give a damn about a bunch of whales."

He was about to brush past her and started out the door when he heard the creak of a footstep on a floorboard outside. Spinner froze.

Raúl didn't see the two men approach until it was too late. They stepped into the cantina and performed a quick survey of the occupants of El Pulpo Morado. One man wore the uniform of a federale. The other wore a dark suit and looked Asian. Both were large and muscular. They turned and left. Raúl saw them pass by the front window on their way to the storage shack out back. He knew most of the local federales, but this one was a stranger. Raúl's eyes met Maximiliano's who nodded, placed the glass he was wiping on the sink below the bar and moved toward the opposite end. Raúl looked around for something to defend himself. He watched as the two men approached the shack. He walked to the wall near the pool table and pulled the heaviest cue he could find from the rack.

It was so subtle it seemed nearly insignificant. Even though Spinner's senses had been numbed by age and years of alcohol, his survival instincts instantly kicked in. He saw a puff of dust come through a crack in the wall of the supply shack.

A sharp voice from inside the bar broke the silence just as the door was hammered inward.

"Rosen! Watch out!" Raúl yelled.

The federale came through the door of the shack first, bringing his 9mm semi-automatic to bear. Instinctively, Spinner shoved Rosen behind a stack of wooden beer cases and dove for the floor as the Mexican opened up, a stitch of bullets chinking into the wall behind them. Spinner rolled and came up on his stomach between the beer cases. He fired two shots, hitting the assassin in the chest. The Mexican assailant flew backward, crashing into the Asian man as he attempted to storm the door. Spinner rolled again as the Asian fired wildly into the shack. He was firing an uzi and the shack erupted in a rain of splintering wood, glass, and plastic.

Suddenly, the firing stopped. Spinner chanced a look around his marginal barrier and saw Raúl, standing over the Asian who was face down in the sand. In his hand, Raúl held half of a broken pool cue.

Emily Rosen came out slowly from behind a stack of beer cases, her clothes and hair coated in a layer of dust. Her right cheek was oozing blood from a small gash caused by flying glass. In the distance the sounds of sirens started up and grew louder.

"We need to leave," said Raúl. "Now!"

Spinner removed the sunglasses from the dead federale. "You know him?"

"No."

He retrieved the dead federale's wallet and rifled through it. He pocketed the IDs and credit cards then tossed the wallet aside but stopped when he saw something on the dead man's forearm. He rolled the arm over to expose a tattoo of a laughing skull with the letter "Z" behind it. A knife pierced the top of the skull.

"This guy's one of the Zetas. I should have known."

Spinner moved over to the unconscious Asian assassin. He reached into the man's breast pocket and located the wallet. He looked at both IDs. "What's a Zeta doing with a Japanese hit man?" He pocketed the IDs and credit cards.

"We need to leave." Raúl grabbed Emily by the arm, who stood in a mute state of shock. He began leading her away. "You can't stay here, Jake. You won't get your answers here. We have information, and you have information. We can help each other."

"That's just fucking great. First you lead them to me. They damn near killed all of us! Next, you're going to help me. I think I'll take my chances here. You guys are bad news."

The approaching sirens grew louder.

"You won't be able to find Gustavo's killer if you're in prison, Jake."

Spinner looked angrily at Raúl, then down at the dead man. "Fuck."

He tucked his pistol into the waistband of his shorts and followed Raúl and Rosen into an alley between the shops of the malecón.

# 30

Raúl's truck slid through several narrow alleys and side streets and finally emerged on the outskirts of San Jacinto. The *barrio* they drove through was a bleak landscape of rundown homes surrounded by car parts, old pangas, broken motors, and tin roofs. A layer of dust hung in the air like the desperation of suffocated dreams.

Spinner, who had been quiet until now, slammed his hand into the dash. "What the hell were you two thinking? You led those two straight to me!"

Rosen, still in a state of shock, exploded. "You're out of your mind! You didn't have to shoot him!"

"I wouldn't have had to shoot him if you hadn't led him to my front door! That asshole was no federale. He was one of the Zetas."

"What's a Zeta?"

"Mercs. Mercenaries. Originally trained at Fort Benning. They were supposed to be inserted into the jungles and cities of Columbia to bring down the drug cartels. They found out the other side pays better. Hombres muy malos. I'd like to know what they're doing running around Puerto Nacimiento with a bunch of Asian thugs."

Raúl asked, "You saw them in Puerto Nacimiento?"

"Yeah." Spinner glanced over his shoulder. "Just drop me off at the edge of town. I can make it from there."

Rosen looked down and saw that Spinner's hands were shaking. "Where are you going to go? You can't get away on foot." She had a sudden overwhelming feeling of nausea. She motioned to Raúl. "Stop the truck."

She covered her mouth with one hand and dove across Spinner, reaching for the door handle. She flung the door open and retched violently, some of the effluent splashing onto Spinner's bare legs.

"Aw, Christ, lady," Spinner said disgustedly.

Raúl slowed the truck, and Rosen climbed over Spinner and stood on the side of the road, her hands on her knees. After several minutes, she wiped her mouth on her sleeve and walked back to the truck. This time, Spinner got out to let her climb back in.

"I need to ask you some questions." She looked Spinner squarely in the eye. "Then you go your way, we'll go ours. I just watched a man get shot who was trying to kill you. And I don't think it was just because you broke up a dolphin hunt. I don't believe in coincidences. I think there's a connection here, and you may be able to help us connect the dots."

"Those bastards killed a friend of mine," Jake growled. "I was getting too close. Asking too many questions. If they see you with me, then you're dead too. And there's not a damn thing I can do to help you."

Rosen said, "We were there. At the cove. They shot at us too."

Spinner turned his head and looked at her. "You were on the cliff?"

"That's right. Got the whole god damn thing on video. We're going to go public with it."

"My advice to you, Missy, is to drop me off, go straight to the nearest airport, and get your ass out of Mexico. They play by different rules down here. You stay, you're going to be a statistic."

Rosen turned on Spinner. "Missy? Missy?! What planet did you just fall off? This is the second time in a week that someone has shot at me. These guys aren't nickel and dime. They're well financed and, judging by the muscle that's been showing up, both at the cove and in town, I'd say we have some Asians working with Zeta mercenaries looking to make a score here."

Spinner looked at Rosen, his gaze narrowing. Behind his alcoholic haze, she saw something that unnerved her. This man had killed before. And he was willing to do it again.

"I don't believe in coincidences either," Spinner said. "Those Asian guys show up, and my friend and his wife end up dead. I'm going to find out who had Gustavo and his wife killed."

"And then what?" Emily said.

"I'm going to kill them."

"They put people in jail for that. Or worse."

Spinner looked at her dead pan. "That's the thing, Miss *New York Times*. I just don't give a shit."

"Jake, please help us," Raúl said. "Just give us time enough to answer a few questions, and I'll drive you anywhere you want to go."

Spinner stared straight ahead, the midday sun casting the edge of town and the mountains beyond in a washed-out sepia tone. "I haven't eaten in two days. You want to talk? I need some food."

Raúl gave a half smile. "I know just the place."

By the time they arrived at the Campos ranchito, the late afternoon sun was already dipping below the Sierra de la Giganta, creating a golden landscape with cardón cactus casting long shadows across the ground. While they drove through the mountains, Emily called Alejandro on her cell phone and informed him that they had located Jake Spinner. He was to contact Sandy and Paola and they'd meet at the ranchito after dark. As they entered the property, the greeting party of several dozen goats parted to let the truck pass through.

Raúl had called his wife to inform her that they were about to have houseguests again. He also told her to break out some of his old clothes, the ones he had worn when he was much heavier. When Spinner looked at him, Raúl shrugged. "Lo siento, Señor Jake. I know Guadalupe will not let you into her kitchen until you—ah—clean up some."

"That's just damn spiffy. Blow my cover, nearly get me shot, and now you want me to take a bath."

"Jesus, Spinner, those goats smell better than you do," Rosen said. "I've been holding my breath for nearly an hour and a half."

Spinner scowled. "I don't smell anything."

Guadalupe met them at the door with a pair of folded jeans, a clean white shirt, a towel, a razor, and a bar of soap. When she saw Spinner, she cast a sidelong look at her sheepish-looking husband.

*I'll bet she's going to give Raúl an earful later*, Rosen thought.

Spinner took the bundle hesitatingly from Guadalupe and then Raúl led him behind the main house to a workroom that had a sink. Spinner, grumbling the whole while, closed the door behind him.

When Raúl entered the kitchen, he found Emily and Guadalupe sitting at the kitchen table drinking jamaica. From the looks of it, Emily had been trying to explain the course of events that had transpired during the afternoon. Raúl went to the refrigerator and poured himself a glass of the hibiscus tea and then sat down next to his wife. She stared at him for a moment, then punched his shoulder.

"Ow! What was that for, woman?"

Guadalupe began speaking Spanish in rapid-fire sentences. "Are you loco? You could have gotten yourself killed!"

"There were no problems," Raúl tried to remain nonchalant.

"No problems! He shot a man! You could have been shot! And now you bring him here where he can be followed. What about me? What about the children? You've put us all in danger!"

"Jake Spinner has information that may be necessary to our investigation," Raúl said unapologetically. "Lupe, as soon as we get the information we need, I'll take him to where he needs to go and drop him off."

Guadalupe got up from the table, looking down at her husband scornfully. "After dinner, he leaves. We're not safe as long as he's here." She went to a cupboard and retrieved two bottles, one being tequila and the other sotol. She set the bottles down forcefully in front of Raúl, causing him to wince.

"Hide these where he won't find them," Guadalupe commanded. "I know about this Jake Spinner."

Guadalupe said something under her breath and stalked out of the kitchen. Rosen heard the screen door open and close.

"I'm sorry, Raúl," said Rosen in a low voice. "I couldn't lie to her. She knew I was pretty shaken."

"She sees through people," Raúl said tiredly. "Many see it as a gift. Sometimes, it makes me crazy." He stood up, grabbed a bottle in each hand, and walked out the back door.

Rosen looked down at her hands. They were still trembling from the incident at the storage shack. If Spinner had not pushed her down, she would have taken that bullet designated for him. For a drunk, he could move pretty fast. Still, she had a hard time classifying him or his act as chivalrous. He just didn't seem the type. From their initial meeting, her first impression was a man drowning in his own self-absorption. And one thing Rosen was good at: her first impressions were usually right on.

She was surprised that she wasn't as frightened as she thought she should have been. Instead, replacing that visceral fear was another feeling—anger. She was furious that people had been trying to kill her. Fighting back with a gun was not an option. But she had words. She could string words together to make others angry. She knew how to slice, impale, shoot, and explode those on the wrong side with a stroke on a keyboard.

And that's exactly what she was going to do.

Raúl returned and joined her at the table. He looked at Rosen. "Are you okay?"

She gave him an icy look. "No. No one shoots at me twice and gets away with it."

"They weren't shooting at you, little sister." Jake Spinner stood in the doorway, wearing Raúl's old clothes. The pants were high water since Spinner's legs were considerably longer than Raúl's. The off-white shirt was a bit tight, and he wore it with the top two buttons unfastened. His hair was wet, and he had attempted to shave but had given up after scraping his neck, leaving a few small bloody patches above his collar line. Rosen saw that his eyes were deep blue, like stretches of water in the Gulf. She hadn't before noticed the whitish scar that ran part of the length of his tanned left cheek. He held the dirty clothes he'd been wearing. Raúl jumped up and took the soiled bundle from him. He wrinkled his nose as the smell hit him head on. "Guadalupe will wash these for you." He disappeared behind Jake and went out the door.

Spinner was still looking at Rosen. Uncomfortable, she averted her gaze. "I guess I should thank you for saving my life."

"You'll excuse me if I don't thank you for nearly getting me killed."

Rosen stood, looking directly up at him. "We didn't know that people were trying to kill you. And stop calling me "little sister." It's Rosen or Emily."

Her chilling gaze matched his, and it was Spinner who ultimately averted his gaze. "I need a drink."

"I'll bet you do."

"Now what's that supposed to mean?"

Rosen looked down. "Nothing."

He put his hands on the table and leaned forward. "Lady, I don't want to be here any longer than you want me here. You want to ask questions, then ask away. The sooner we finish this, the sooner I can leave and get on with my business."

"We have to wait. Until the others get here."

"What others?"

"The biologists I was with on the cliff that day you broke through the barricade. They'll have questions for you, I think."

"Oh, Christ on a bike. This is why I bought a boat."

When Raúl returned, Spinner looked up and, nearly snarling, said, "Anything to drink around here? I'm going to need something strong if I have to talk to a bunch of eggheads."

Raúl shrugged. "Lo siento, Señor Jake. We only have agua de jamaica, té, o café, bien fuerte."

"Just shoot me now."

Guadalupe and their daughter Alisa came back into the kitchen. Alisa carried a basket of freshly picked vegetables, and Guadalupe placed a plate of fresh chicken meat on the counter. She pulled a large black pot from under the counter, added some water to it, and turned on the stove. Alisa began slicing the vegetables into a large heap on a cutting board. Guadalupe sliced the chicken meat into small chunks on another cutting board.

"What's for dinner?" Emily asked, trying to cut through the heavy tension in the room.

"*Pollo asado y calabecitas*," Guadalupe didn't smile. Rosen thought that Guadalupe was slicing the chicken with a little more vigor than was required for the task.

Outside, there was the sound of vehicles approaching and the crunch of tires on gravel as they came to a stop. Raúl excused himself and went to the door. Spinner saw a tall, lean Mexican man in his mid-thirties trailing behind an American woman and a Latina. The American woman could have been an athlete. She was tanned, and her arms and legs were well-muscled and sinewy. The Latina was also attractive, but Spinner sensed that she was self-conscious about her looks by the way she carried herself.

Rosen stood. "Everyone, this is Jake Spinner. Jake, this is Alejandro Cabrillo, Director of the Marine Mammal Institute in La Paz."

Alejandro stepped forward, his hand extended. "Mr. Spinner, it's a pleasure to meet you. What you did at San Mateo Cove the other day was incredible!"

Spinner looked at Alejandro's hand, then up at him. "Yeah, well."

Rosen looked increasingly flustered. "This is Sandy Wainright and Paola Jiménez. They're heading up the study on humpback whales in the Gulf."

Paola looked nervous. Sandy smiled uncomfortably. "Thank you for what you did the other day."

Spinner looked all four of them over. Rosen could see that he'd already formed an opinion.

"Three scientists, a reporter, and goat farmer. Not exactly the Avengers," Spinner said tiredly. "Come on and sit down. Let's get this over with." He poured himself a glass of jamaica, took a swallow, and made a face.

The five sat at the table. Alejandro spoke. "Mr. Spinner, can I ask you how you found out about the slaughter at San Mateo Cove?"

"I didn't. And Mr. Spinner was my father's name. He's dead. Spinner works just fine." He took another drink of jamaica. Rosen saw that his hands still had a slight tremor as he brought the glass to his lips. He saw her looking at him and quickly set the glass back on the table. "No one told me about what was going on at the cove. I was led there by a dolphin. Some of her family members were trapped behind the barricade."

He looked up to see the group staring at him, with looks ranging from slack-jawed astonishment to total disbelief.

"You asked."

Sandy leaned forward. "Did these dolphins know you?"

"They've fished around my boat for years. Been stealing fish off my lines for as long as I can remember."

"That's amazing," said Sandy. "Those dolphins actually asked you for help?"

"I think I was the only one in the neighborhood at the time. We don't have any particular bond or relationship. I was out looking for the son of my former partner. I think my partner Gustavo and his wife were murdered by the same guys that ran that operation at the cove. The same ones that ambushed us at the shack. Now, their son has come up missing."

Raúl exchanged a worried look with Guadalupe. "Macario?"

Spinner nodded.

"Mr. Spin—uh, Jake," queried Alejandro. "Did you get a good look at any of the men on the barricade?"

Spinner gave Alejandro a disgusted look. "Yeah, I got plenty of good looks. Tends to happen when people are trying to kill you in close quarters. You could say we became intimately connected. They were Japanese with a few indios from Gustavo's village of Puerto Nacimiento. There were others there, wearing uniforms. They looked like federales, but after what I saw at El Pulpo, I think the Asians are in cahoots with the Zetas. Macario said the men in his village had been conscripted to hunt whales."

The researchers stared at each other.

Paola asked, "Zetas, as in *Las Zetas*?"

"Those boys will do just about anything if the price is right," said Spinner.

"Exploiting the loophole in the subsistence whaling clause of the IWC," said Alejandro to Sandy and Paola.

Spinner asked, "What's the IWC?"

"It's the International Whaling Commission," said Alejandro. "The governing body that monitors whaling activities around the globe, sets quotas, and directs conservation of whale species worldwide."

Spinner asked, "Who's exploiting the loophole?"

"The Japanese mostly," said Sandy. "A few other nations, Norway, Iceland, Portugal, China, and the Faroe Islands are still killing whales by defying the quotas and exploiting loopholes in the regulations."

Sandy looked at Alejandro. "Do you think Yoshimatsu has anything to do with this?"

"Seems suspicious that Yoshimatsu shows up here with Minister Figueroa, and then we not only have whales disappearing, but now there's a highly organized dolphin hunt. And the participants were Japanese, mercenaries, and members of a coastal tribe," said Sandy. "Jake, are you sure the men were Japanese?"

Spinner spoke a couple of sentences in Japanese. "I know the difference between Japanese and Mandarin."

The group that was gathered around the table stared at him blankly.

"A long time ago, I spoke Arabic, Kurdish, Dari, Pashto, and a few more," he said in English. "More recently, Spanish. They were Japanese."

He reached across the table, snagged one of the researcher's notebooks, and tore out a blank page. He grabbed one of the pencils that lay on the table in front of Rosen. "I'm borrowing one of your pencils. Now, who is this Yoshimatsu and who's Figueroa?"

"Figueroa is the Minister of Fisheries," said Paola. "Unfortunately, he is also the brother-in-law to the president of Mexico."

"Yoshimatsu supposedly serves on the Japanese Fisheries board," interjected Alejandro. "I was told there was to be a joint commission to share ideas and strategies to promote more sustainable fishing practices both here and in Japan."

"Did you believe that bullshit?" Spinner scribbled the names on the paper, then circled them.

Alejandro blushed. "Well, no. I was very suspicious. Especially when Minister Figueroa ordered me to turn over all of our research data to the Japanese group."

Guadalupe and Alisa dished up plates of pollo asado and calabacitas with rice and onions topped with goat cheese. Alisa served them to the guests. Then came the platters of potatoes, roasted chiles, and onions on the table, along with a deep bowl of refried beans and a steaming basket of fresh flour tortillas. When the young girl placed the plate in front of Spinner, she stepped back quickly. Spinner looked up, smiled slightly, and said, "Thank you."

*At least he's not a total asshole*, Rosen thought.

Rosen watched as Spinner attacked his food. While he chewed, he raised his head and closed his eyes, looking as if he were in the throes of ecstasy.

"Damn, that could very well be the best meal I have ever eaten," Spinner declared between bites. In short order, he had scraped his plate clean while the others were still on their first servings. He held up his plate to Guadalupe. "*¿Más, por favor?*"

Guadalupe quickly snatched the plate from him and refilled it with a heaping second helping. Alisa brought the plate to him, and he took it from her before she was able to put it down. "Gracias."

"We can't give that video to Figueroa," said Paola. "If they find out who was standing on that cliff, God knows what they might do."

"I think it should go public," said Rosen. "The more people who see it, the more the whalers are going to be looking over their shoulders."

Spinner looked up, chewing thoughtfully. He swallowed and chased the mouthful with a swig of water. "You guys asked me to come here to give you my take on this. Here it is." He looked directly at each member of the group. "Take your family members and get the hell out of Dodge. These pendajos aren't going to stop until they get what they want. And they won't think twice about killing you or using your families for leverage."

"Now, you're scaring me." Sandy looked stricken.

"You should be terrified. All of you. If this Figueroa is connected to the Japanese, then basically you're working against corruption at the highest levels. He has every available arm of the military and federal police at his disposal. You won't see it coming. Maybe one day your wife and kids are stopped at a traffic light, and some guy dressed like a policeman comes up and blows them all away. Or they kidnap your family to get at you. It's a noble cause trying to save the whales, but it won't keep you or your families safe."

"So why aren't you leaving Baja?" Rosen asked. "Revenge?"

"My friend and partner Gustavo and his wife Marta were drowned at sea. Gustavo's body was nearly unrecognizable. From the wounds on his wrist and ankles, I think he was dragged through the water until the reefs flayed all the skin from his body. His wife's body hasn't been recovered, and I think the bastards have their son, Macario. So, yeah, revenge works for me."

"So, you won't even consider saving yourself?" Rosen's tone was bitter.

Spinner looked at her, the corners of his mouth curling into a half-smile. "No one lives forever. Besides, I'm different from the rest of you in one important respect—I have nothing to lose."

There was a moment of silence at the table as members of the group shifted uncomfortably in their seats. Finally, Alejandro broke the silence. "After we release this video, there's a good chance they'll come after us—if they find out who we are. We'll probably be fired or, at the very least, suspended. Figueroa will probably shut down the institute and confiscate all our equipment and data. I have discussed this predicament with my wife and daughter. They've agreed to move to her parents' house on the mainland for now."

"Not far enough," said Spinner. "There's no place safe in Mexico. Get them on a plane to the states tonight if you're going to follow this foolishness to its end."

Raúl placed his hands on the table and leaned forward. He looked directly at Spinner, then the rest of the group. "My family has been fishing *el Golfo de California* for generations. We have the blood of Spaniards and the indios running through our veins. We will not run." Guadalupe and Alisa joined their father at his side.

Alejandro looked directly at Spinner. "If I were to back down from this, I wouldn't be able to look into my daughter's eyes when she asks me, 'Papá, why didn't you do something?'"

"This scares the hell out of me," Sandy said, "but it's something I have to do."

"Count me in." Paola was resolute.

"I'm going to need access to an internet connection," Rosen said. "I'm going to start digging dirt on Figueroa and Yoshimatsu and follow the money trail. This is what I'm good at. By the time I get done with these dirtbags, they'll be a household name."

All the members of the group looked at Spinner. He ran his hands through his hair and looked slowly around the table. "You're all crazier than I am."

"I seriously doubt that," said Rosen.

# 31

Macario Silvano awoke in blackness to a sharp pain in his right ankle. He kicked out with his other foot and connected with a soft, furry presence. The rat squealed and scurried out of harm's way, issuing a vicious hiss. The rats were getting braver now. Once they'd figured out he couldn't see, they were able to access the meager meals that his captors infrequently provided. The meals were horrible and so were the smells in this place. His nostrils were constantly assaulted by the smell of rancid meat.

Macario didn't know how long he'd been imprisoned. He had no visual information to mark the passage of time. He did know this much—he was being held captive on a very large boat. Above the smell of decaying flesh, Macario recognized the briny scent of salt water. The walls of his prison were iron and produced a hollow sound like an old gong when he kicked at them with his foot.

Something was different. The loud thrumming of the giant engines had suddenly gone quiet. He looked around his damp surroundings, straining his eyes in the darkness. He could feel the large rat's presence nearby. Macario was hungry, thirsty, and scared. At first, he'd cried out, cursing his captors. There was no response. Occasionally, a small light would appear from above and a bag of food and a plastic bottle of water would be lowered down. He had never seen or spoken to any of his tormentors.

Recently, despair had overtaken his feelings of grief and rage. In the perpetual darkness, his bravado had slunk away like one of the rats. He should have listened to Jake. Spinner had wanted to get him to safety. But no, Macario wouldn't rest until the deaths of his mother and father were avenged. He knew he was probably going to die. Then what were they waiting for? Right now, he was ready to die. Anything was better than this. His joints ached. His mouth felt swollen and parched, and there was a constant knot of hunger and fear roiling in his stomach.

The worst thing was the confinement. Macario had spent most of his life outdoors. When he was twelve, he spent two weeks on his first solo fishing trip in the gulf. His father had taught him well. He could service the outboard on the panga and set a line. He could navigate the treacherous coastline at night by marking the positions of the stars and watching for familiar headlands in the light cast by those stars. There were times when he had to ride out eight-foot seas. He sheltered in protected coves on islands miles from the mainland. He survived on what he caught along shorelines and drank water he found in pools, or *tinajas,* on the islands.

Back then, he was able to set his course by the movement of the sun and moon, by following currents, and by feeling the direction of wind on his face. Then he'd always had a reference point. Here there was nothing but the stench and darkness. It was all closing in on him.

His despondency was interrupted by a loud grating sound coming from overhead. A shaft of light speared through the opening, temporarily blinding him and causing several large rats to scurry back into the shadows. A sound like metal sliding on metal made his teeth clench. He shielded his eyes from the intense light and, after several seconds, through squinted eyelids, he was able to see a metal ladder being lowered. One by one, two men descended the ladder and walked toward him. For the briefest of moments, Macario thought he was about to be released. They each grabbed one of his arms and pulled him roughly to his feet

"Where am I?" He was unable to hide the fear in his voice. "Where are you taking me?"

One of the men produced a burlap sack and pulled it over Macario's head fastening it tightly around his neck. "Shut up."

He was led forward to where the ladder stood. His hands were placed on the rungs, and one of the men said, "Up. And don't fall."

Climbing up the ladder proved to be a monumental effort. He must have lain in that hold for longer than he'd thought. His legs were sluggish and his arms felt like they couldn't support his weight.

He stumbled out onto a steel deck, his hands and knees scraping on the metal surface. His nostrils picked up another smell that didn't register to his dulled senses right away. He was pulled roughly to his feet and marched forward. He could feel the breeze on his arms and legs and knew he was outside. Around him he heard the sounds of men working. They were speaking a language he didn't recognize at first. As he was prodded along, he realized that he was hearing a Japanese dialect. Suddenly his olfactory memory kicked in, and he realized what the malodorous scent was. It was blood. The realization caused his stomach to lurch violently.

He was led inside a room and, at one point, his head was pushed down to guide him through a small space. He was forced to sit in a metal chair and told not to move. His captors left the room, a large metal door clanging shut signaling their retreat. Macario could see light through the fabric of the burlap. He tentatively lifted the sack from his head.

He was in a small, bare cabin. In front of him was a heavy oval doorway with no portal. The floor was covered in blue plastic, similar to the plastic tarps that he and the other fishermen had used on the beaches to cover their fishing shacks.

The hatch door opened, and a large Asian man dressed in black entered. He moved with the grace of a large cat. His dark eyes fixed on Macario. In one hand he carried a plate of food, in the other a bottle of Coca-Cola. Ako Kanamura pulled a folding chair from the wall near the hatch, flipped it open, and sat down opposite him. He slid the food and soda across to the young man.

"Eat. You must be hungry," the man said in a quiet, relaxed voice. He nodded toward the food. On the plate was a sandwich with meat of some sort, potato chips, and a Hershey's candy bar. Macario eyed the food hungrily, then looked up at his captor.

"What do you want from me?"

"We just want to ask you a few questions. That is all. If we are satisfied with your answers, then you are free to go. Now, eat your sandwich."

Macario grabbed the sandwich and began stuffing it in his mouth. He grabbed the bottle and took two long gulps of Coke. The big Asian man watched him, expressionless.

When Macario had finished the last of the chips and the candy bar, he took a final swig from the Coca-Cola bottle. He wiped his mouth with his sleeve. "Thank you."

The man removed the plate and bottle and set them on the floor, never taking his eyes off the young indio. Macario noticed something about those eyes. They were empty, like looking down into the ocean on a starless night.

"When are you going to let me go?"

"I have some questions for you," said Kanamura. "Your answers will determine your freedom."

"Did you kill my parents?" Macario said, his eyes flashing with hate.

Kanamura's hand reached out so fast, it only registered as a blur. In the next instant Macario found himself on the floor, his mouth bloody.

"You weren't listening," said Kanamura quietly. "I ask the questions." He stood up, walked over to where Macario lay on the floor, picked him up by the collar, and flung him back into the chair. Kanamura went back to his chair and sat. Reaching in his jacket pocket, he produced a photograph and slid it across the table to Macario. It was a grainy picture of Jake Spinner at the wheel of his boat.

"Do you know this man?"

Macario touched his split lip. "Jake Spinner."

"What is your relationship to him?"

"Nothing. I have no relationship with him. He's El Borracho, a drunk who used to fish with my father."

Macario felt a sudden sharp pain in his knee as his patella was driven into his femur. He cried out and crumpled to the floor once more.

"This is not going well," Kanamura said tiredly. "We know you were with Spinner recently. We know he has been snooping around your house, and we know you are going to tell me exactly how I can find him."

Macario rocked back and forth on the floor, his hands cradling his damaged knee. Tears of pain and fear welled in his eyes. "I don't know where he is! I swear it!"

Kanamura reached into his pocket and produced Macario's cell phone. "Call him."

"I don't think he has a working cell phone. I don't think I even saved his number," Macario said between gritted teeth.

"Call him."

Macario picked up the phone and tried to slide it open, but he was having difficulty because his hands were shaking so badly. He finally located Jake Spinner's number. He fumbled several times before he was able to make the call. The Mexican operator said the number was no longer in service. Damn that Spinner! If Macario knew anything about Jake, he knew that he probably hadn't paid his cell phone bill.

"It's not a working number anymore," said Macario.

Kanamura took the phone from him. "That is too bad for you," he said, standing up and walking around the table.

# 32

Emily Rosen stepped out into the cool night air. She walked to one of the nearby corrals and leaned against it, gazing at the magnificent stars that looked close enough to touch. She still couldn't get over how clear and unfettered the skies were in the west. She was able to recognize the Milky Way as a giant band of stars that spread into the south, like a celestial cloud.

Tomorrow, she'd make her way back to La Paz where there was a working library and numerous places with Wi-Fi. She needed to go online and do what she did best—dig dirt on Yoshimatsu and Figueroa. Find out how the Japanese are connected to the Mexican Minister of Fisheries. She still had some favors to call in from certain members of the State Department. There was a fair chance that her contacts may have seen Yoshimatsu show up on their radar at one time or another.

"Pretty, isn't it?" The voice came from behind her. She spun around to see a large figure sitting on a rickety chair in the shadows, a lit cigarette in his mouth.

"Damn it, Spinner, you scared the crap out of me! You shouldn't be sneaking up on people like that."

"I believe I was here first. Always a good idea to know what's in front of you and what's behind you."

Rosen turned away in disgust. "Whatever."

She heard the chair creak and a moment later he stood next to her. He looked skyward. "That is some sky."

"Yeah, some sky," An uncomfortable moment followed until finally she couldn't stand it any longer. "Where to next, Mr. Spinner?"

Jake took a long pull on his cigarette. She watched the billow of smoke leave his mouth and dissipate into the shadows.

"Not sure. I need to get to the source. And right now, San Jacinto is too hot for my comfort level. In the last week, I've had my house and my boat shot up, been targeted by two assassins, and I'm still no closer to finding Gustavo's killers than I was a week ago. On top of everything else, Gustavo's kid is missing, and that little voice in my head tells me he's in deep shit right now."

"Did you ever stop to think that by combining forces, we can all get more accomplished than by going it alone?" Rosen turned and looked at him. "I'm pretty good at my job. I have ways of getting information on people that others can't. I've made a career of it. I may be able to find out things that'll help you in your quest to find Macario and maybe bring the murderers to justice."

Spinner snorted. "Groucho Marx once said, 'I would never join any club that would have me as a member.'"

His attention was drawn to a meteor that arced across the western sky and disappeared below the Sierra de la Giganta.

"That one hit the ground." He turned toward her. "Look, Ms. Rosen. I once went around tilting at windmills. I even believed in a cause. Believe it or not, I was once a leader of men. I watched everyone I ever cared about get killed or maimed for life. And when the smoke cleared and the bodies were counted and bagged, it didn't make one damn bit of difference at all."

"So, you're going to stand there and tell me that when all of those animals were being slaughtered at the cove, that you felt nothing?"

"We all die, Ms. Rosen. If you're lucky, you get to choose the time and place."

Rosen turned and walked back toward the ranch house. After several steps, she turned and looked at him. "You're full of shit, Spinner. Either that or you're already dead, but you're just too stubborn or stupid to lie down."

She walked back to the house and disappeared into the light from the door. Jake thought about what the feisty young New Yorker had just said to him. Maybe she was right. Maybe he was just a hollowed-out husk of humanity waiting for the next desert wind to blow him into eternal dust.

He turned back to watch the stars, wishing he could find a drink. It had been several days since he had tasted liquor. The last time he drank, the stomach pains were unbearable. He dimly remembered writhing around on the floor most of the night in the storage shack of El Pulpo Morado. Tonight was the first time he'd eaten a decent meal in months. Even though he was the antagonistic presence, the ambiance in Guadalupe's and Raúl's kitchen was something he hadn't experienced for a long time: a sense of place.

Jake heard the sound of laughter coming from the house and saw a diminutive figure run out into the dark, followed by a laughing Raúl. Father scooped up son and buried his face in the boy's belly, prompting another bout of happy squeals. In the diffused light cast by the kitchen, Raúl looked up and saw Jake watching him. He set Julio down and told him to go back inside. He walked to where Jake leaned against the corral.

"I hear you won't be staying," Raúl said. "It's too late to travel tonight. Tomorrow, I'll take you where you want to go."

"Much obliged. And tell your missus that I appreciate the meal."

Raúl looked at Jake and smiled. "You're not getting off that easy. Tell her yourself."

"I was hoping to spare her any more discomfort. I know my being here makes her and everyone else nervous."

"Guadalupe is a strong woman. She had to be strong to make a life with me. But she has another quality that I admire greatly. She's kind and would never turn a stranger in need away from our door."

Spinner bit down on his lip and looked at the ground. "I'm no charity case." He turned and leaned against the corral again, lifting his head and staring at the canopy of twinkling stars.

"No. You just looked like you could use a home-cooked meal." Raúl assumed the same leaning position and looked skyward. "Where will you go, Señor Jake?"

Jake removed a pack of cigarettes from his shirt pocket and produced a match. He dragged the match across the rough wood of the corral and it flared. He lit the cigarette, took a long pull, and exhaled into the night air.

"I reckon I'll head down to La Paz. There's a chance Macario went down there to connect up with one of his old friends from the village. I want to get to him before he does something stupid."

"And then what?"

"I'm going to find his parents' killers."

Raúl closed his eyes and drew in a deep breath of desert air. "I guess we all need a cause, Señor Jake. Even if it's one that leads into darkness." He turned and looked at Spinner. "Señorita Rosen is going to La Paz tomorrow. I'll ask her if she can take you. If not, then I will."

He began walking back toward the ranch house. Spinner, who was now staring straight ahead, said, "Is it worth it?"

Raúl stopped in his tracks and turned slowly back to face him. "Yes. Yes, it is. *Buenas noches*, Señor Jake."

Spinner spent the night in the workroom on a cot with a worn mattress. Sometime in the middle of the night he awakened, his teeth chattering. He wasn't sure if it was the temperature inside the old workroom or if he was still dealing with the effects of trying to dry out. He felt the chill of the mountain air seeping through the cracks in the door and the poorly sealed window. He drifted back into a fitful sleep of horrific dreams. In the nightmares he was floating on a blood-red sea, full of the mutilated bodies of dolphins and whales struggling to keep their heads out of water, bleeding from numerous deep lacerations, their cries piercing his senses to the core. Forms appeared in the black water, ghostly at first, then becoming more defined as they drifted toward him. Three bodies floated and bobbed in front of him, their faces pulled back in the horrible rictus of death. Gustavo, Marta, and Macario stared at him from eyeless sockets.

He snapped awake, crying out. His body was bathed in a cold sweat, and he rolled into a fetal position. He felt something being draped over him. Jake looked up to see a form bending over him, covering him with a blanket.

*"Tome esto,"* said Guadalupe. She helped Spinner sit up and held a cup of something to his lips. He reflexively grabbed it and took a drink. He doubled over into a paroxysm of coughing. Guadalupe stood by patiently until it subsided.

"Más," she said, holding the cup to his lips. Spinner took another swig of the herbal medicine. She helped him back onto the cot, pulled the blanket over his shoulders, and walked toward the door. She barely heard the raspy voice coming from the form on the cot.

"Thank you."

When Spinner awoke the next morning, something was different. He sat up and looked around. The storage room was exactly as he remembered it from last night. He realized that his head wasn't throbbing. He looked down at his hands. The tremors had nearly stopped. He swung his bare legs out of the cot and placed his feet on the cool cement floor. He worked his toes up and down, then pressed the balls of his feet into the floor, feeling the sensation course up his legs.

"I'll be damned."

There was a soft knock at the door. "Señor Jake? *Desayuno,*" spoke the young Alisa.

He continued to stare at his hands. "Yeah. Breakfast. Be there in a minute." He stood and realized he felt better than he had in a long time. His addled brain registered that Guadalupe had entered the storage room and given him something to drink in the middle of the night. Until now, he had passed it off as just another segment in a long line of distorted dream images that neither made sense nor gave him much respite these days. But last night was different. He suddenly realized that, after he'd been given the concoction, he slept deeply, unfettered by nightmares.

After washing up and dressing, he went to the kitchen and found the group already seated and passing plates around the table, while Guadalupe and Alisa hovered over them like bees around a flower.

The odd entourage looked up.

"Buenas días," said Raúl cheerfully. "Did you sleep well, Jake?"

Spinner forced a sheepish smile. "Too good. Thanks."

"Sit down and eat before the food gets cold," Raúl said as Guadalupe appeared with a steaming pot of black *Café Combate*. She poured him a cup, and he was almost knocked back by the delightfully strong aroma. A plate of eggs and chorizo came around, and his salivary glands began working overtime. He dug into his breakfast like a man on a mission.

Alejandro looked around the table. "All right everyone, let's go over our assignments one more time. First, make sure everyone has each other's cell phone numbers. It's imperative that we maintain communication throughout these next few days." He turned to Sandy and Paola, who were sitting to his right.

Sandy, are you and Paola clear on what you're to do?"

"I'm going to make contact with as many U.S. and international animal rights and conservation groups as possible to enlist any assistance they can give us." Sandy was matter-of-fact. "I'll send a copy of the video to the major conservation groups."

Alejandro nodded. "Paola?"

Paola shifted in her chair. She looked at Alejandro. "I'm going to do the same here in Mexico. I'll be contacting the Mexican conservation groups and will try to contact the president of Mexico to get the video to him."

"Be especially careful, Paola," cautioned Alejandro. "We have no idea how far up the corruption goes. If you're able to contact the president, do not agree to meet with him or any other member of his cabinet until you communicate with us. Then we'll decide what to do as a group. We have limited time to use the video."

"Don't worry. You'll be the first one I call."

Alejandro turned his attention to Emily Rosen, who was busy inputting information into her laptop. "Emily?"

Rosen looked over her glasses. "Oh, sorry. I'm going to La Paz and will set up an information-gathering site. With access to the local library and the internet, I should be able to come up with some information that will be helpful to the cause. My cell phone will be on twenty-four-seven. If you come up with anything, no matter how insignificant, let me know. It may be another piece of the puzzle."

"I want everyone to check in daily," Alejandro said. "Is between 5:00 and 6:00 p.m. agreeable to everyone?"

They all nodded.

"Okay, then. Everyone, be safe. Don't take any unnecessary chances. Don't run down evidence without letting the rest of the team know what you are planning to do." He looked around the room one last time. "Good luck to all of us."

As the group stood and began to disperse, Jake walked over to where Guadalupe stood at the kitchen sink finishing up the last of the breakfast dishes. She turned and looked up at the tall man with dark features. He looked better today. His eyes were brighter. There was some color coming back into his sallow cheeks.

Jake spoke in Spanish. "I wanted to thank you for your hospitality." He looked into her soft brown eyes. "Thank you for feeding me and allowing me to sit at your table with you and your family. You reminded me that there are still good things in this world. And thank you for the medicine. For the first time in a very long time, I awakened without feeling like someone was driving a spike through my head. *¡Muchísimas gracias!*"

Guadalupe smiled and took hold of Jake's large calloused hands and spoke, "*Vaya con Dios*, Señor Jake."

He smiled. Guadalupe knew that at one time that smile would have broken hearts. And, for the briefest of moments, she saw a faint light at the very furthest depths of his deep blue eyes.

He turned and walked past Raúl, who was standing at the doorway. Raúl smiled and nodded at Spinner as he stepped out into the bright clear morning. Spinner saw Rosen standing next to her car talking to Alejandro, Sandy, and Paola. Spinner noticed that Rosen seemed uncomfortable. They all walked to their respective vehicles, all except Alejandro, who approached Spinner.

"Jake, it was nice to meet you," Alejandro said, extending his hand. "I hope you find what you're searching for."

Jake shook the institute director's hand, sensing that the man genuinely meant what he said.

"Good luck to all of you. I admire your courage."

"Are you sure we can't convince you to stick around?" A wry smile crossed Alejandro's lips. "A man of your steady nerve could be of great help to our cause."

"My nerves are anything but steady. But thanks for the offer just the same. In another time, another place, I might have jumped on your bandwagon. I'm going to be going into a very dark place. I don't want to drag others down that hole with me."

"Well, good luck, Jake." Alejandro nodded, then turned on his heel and walked back to his truck.

Spinner saw that Rosen was putting the last of her things into her rental car. He walked toward her. "I heard you're heading to La Paz today. Mind if I tag along?"

She looked over the top of the vehicle at Spinner. Dark sunglasses shielded her eyes. "I kinda prefer to be alone."

"I could use a ride to La Paz."

She lifted her glasses and stared at him. Finally, she looked back at the ranch house and sighed. "What the hell. Get in."

Spinner went around to the passenger side and opened the door. He was about to slip inside when Rosen said, "We're splitting the gas. Fifty-fifty."

He threw up his hands in mock surrender. "You're the boss."

She fired up the car and backed out slowly. Just as she was about to pull forward, Raúl came running up carrying several objects in his arms. He leaned into the passenger window. In his arms were Spinner's old clothes, cleaned and folded, and a small bag tied with string.

"You forgot your clothes."

Spinner started to peel off his shirt in the car.

"No. Keep them. Those were clothes I wore when I was *muy gordo*." He handed Spinner the small paper bag. "Guadalupe says to mix this with tea or hot water when you're feeling bad. It will help you to sleep."

Spinner took the bag. "Tell your wife that her kindness has touched my heart. Thank you."

"*Adiós*, Jake Spinner."

"Thank you," said Emily. "For everything."

"*Ten cuidado, Señorita*," said Raúl. "With God's grace we'll see each other again under better circumstances."

Rosen and Spinner didn't speak for some time. The tension inside the rental vehicle was so thick you could almost cut it. Rosen cranked up the radio, and the throbbing pulse of *banda* music poured from the car speakers. Spinner looked out the window and took in the rough country. On his right, the spine of the Sierra de la Giganta Mountains thrust upward into the morning sky, dipping down in places so that the dark rock contrasted with the cerulean blue sea beyond. A vast cardón cactus forest stretched out from the road all the way to the base of the rugged mountains. Jake had heard these giants were the largest cacti in the world. They stood like giant spiky sentinels, guarding whatever secrets the great mountains were hiding.

Finally, realizing that his agitation was mounting, Spinner broke the silence.

"So, how did you get mixed up in all of this, Ms. Rosen?"

Emily's hands tightened on the steering wheel. "I said you could have a ride. Glib conversation wasn't part of the deal. And stop calling me Ms. Rosen. It's Rosen or Emily to my friends." She gave Spinner a sharp look. "Though we're definitely not friends."

Spinner pulled back, squinting at her. "Okay, Emily. Just thought I'd make a little conversation to pass the time. It's a long drive to La Paz."

"You really are one irritating individual."

"I hear that a lot."

She sighed and relaxed her hands on the wheel. "I was sent here to cover a story about the effects of drug cartel activity on tourism."

"That's a long way from chasing down a bunch of whale poachers."

"I didn't do the story. It was a bullshit attempt by my editor to get me out of the way from the story I was breaking about corruption and money laundering by a prominent U.S. senator."

"Hit some chords, did you? So, how did you get involved with the others?"

"One night in my hotel room, I saw a news piece about a dead whale that had been harpooned. Alejandro was being interviewed, and I thought that would be a much better story to tell. There was also a piece about a dead fisherman being found. Your friend?"

Spinner nodded grimly. "Gustavo Silvano. My fishing partner and friend for more than seven years."

Rosen saw a brief flash of pain in Spinner's eyes.

"What did your editor do when you said you wanted to cover the whale killings?"

"He told me not to come back."

"You're doing this on your own?"

"Yeah, I guess so. After I met Alejandro, he introduced me to Sandy and Paola. They invited me out on their boat for several days to see how they studied the whales." She turned and looked directly at him. "Having a whale blow snot in my face was a moment I won't ever forget. After I saw what those bastards did to those poor animals in that cove, I decided that I needed to do something."

Spinner turned his gaze back to the Baja landscape that sped by the window. "What's your plan when you get to La Paz?"

"I'm going to tap into some sources I have. Even though I'm no longer at the *Times*, I still have a few contacts out there in positions of influence that owe me a favor or two. I'm going to do some digging on the Minister of Fisheries and see how far up the chain his influence goes. And then I'm going to find out exactly who these Japanese businessmen are and how they might be connected to the Fisheries Department."

"That's a pretty tall order. What makes you think you can come up with any usable information on these guys? These people are good at what they do and even better at covering their tracks. Besides, this isn't New York City. It's Baja, Mexico. You're playing by a whole different set of rules down here."

"Sooner or later, Spinner, they all slip up. Even the slickest of them will always leave a trail of breadcrumbs behind. And I'm pretty damn good at finding breadcrumbs."

"Okay, so let's say—for conversation's sake—that you find out who's killing the whales. Then what? Report them? Most times these guys get a slap on the wrist. The Japanese have been going all over the world for years taking whales and other animals illegally. What's new?"

"I believe that the general population will find this so revolting that they'll place immense pressure on those who support and condone these acts of butchery."

Spinner half-smiled. "I guess we all have to have a cause."

Rosen turned sharply toward him. "You know damn well that your friend could have been murdered by these same people. I would think that would be motivation enough to at least look into this a little further."

Spinner bit down on his lip and turned his gaze back out the window. For a moment, she thought that he might go postal on her. She watched as he clenched his fists and pushed them into his thighs. The veins in his neck stood out, as if he'd been overcome by some sudden, intense pain. Just as quickly, the darkness in his face passed.

"We may be going after the same people. But the end game couldn't be more opposite. You want to bring these assholes to justice. I just want them dead."

"Judge, jury, and executioner," Rosen said sarcastically. "Maybe you've been off-planet for a while, but this is the twenty-first century. That's just not how things get done." Her tone softened. "Look, you obviously know a lot more about combat and defense than any of us. Maybe some of those skills can be put to good use to throw the whalers off and smoke out the perpetrators of your friends' murderers."

"My services are not for hire. And you're all extremely naïve if you think these guys are going to roll over just because you apply pressure through the media. They don't care. They'll make you and your friends disappear, your families disappear. I can't do anything to stop that."

"I saw what you did at the cove and back in San Jacinto. I think you could be a formidable force if you were . . . "

Spinner turned his head and faced Rosen, his craggy features hard. "If I was what? Sober?"

"I didn't say that." Rosen looked straight ahead.

"You don't need to. I heard it loud and clear."

Rosen slammed on the brakes and the rental car nearly fishtailed before skidding to a stop. "God damn it, Spinner! I don't give a shit about your past! Who you were, who you are now, it's all the same to me. The bottom line is we just left a group of people who are going to put their lives—and possibly their families' lives—on the line. I don't think you're the type to let innocent people get hurt or killed if you can help it. Like it or not, you cast your vote when you destroyed that barricade at the cove."

Spinner opened the door and stepped out onto the blacktop. He walked to the side of the road and stopped, gazing out over a vast desert valley filled with cardón cacti, palo blanco trees, and creosote bushes. Rosen considered reaching over, closing the passenger door, and putting the pedal to the floor to put as much distance as possible between her and Jake Spinner.

As she watched him pull a pack of cigarettes from his shirt pocket and light one up, she wondered how he had come to this point in his life. In another lifetime, he must have been a functioning human being. He had alluded to being a soldier where men under his command had died. Was that it? Haunted by the ghosts of his past? She had seen him react with lightning speed when the assassin had broken into the storage building. If he was that quick then, Rosen shuddered to think how formidable he would be if he were sober.

He tossed the cigarette butt onto the pavement, ground it out with his shoe, and walked back to the rental car. Sliding into the passenger seat, he cut his gaze to Rosen.

He held up one finger. "First, if I think at any time that you science-oids are pissing in the wind, I can terminate this association without any notice. I'm not sitting around with a bunch of geeks and singing Kumbaya." He held up a second finger. "Second, if your way of bringing these bastards to justice doesn't work, then I reserve the right to deal with them my way." He held up a third finger. "Finally, any activities that involve covert operations will be orchestrated by me. I'll have the final say in field operations that deal with aggression from the outside."

Rosen stared at him, her face devoid of emotion, as he ticked off the last of his demands. "Are you finished?"

Spinner looked flummoxed. "Well, uh, yeah. I'm through. For now."

"Good. Then close the damn door and buckle up."

# 33

Hirokan Yoshimatsu stepped from the Bell 407GX Executive helicopter onto the lighted landing pad of the whaling ship, *Shodokai Maru*. He was greeted by Ako Kanamura and the first officer and led to the bridge. As soon as Yoshimatsu stepped onto the deck of the 23,000-ton vessel, his nostrils were assaulted with the stench of brine, blood, and putrefying flesh. He passed by the open processing area that was one level below him. Workers dressed in yellow waterproof suits were using high-powered sprayers to scrub the decks of blood and viscera from the last whale processed. Several were pushing a wheeled cart loaded with wheelbarrow-sized chunks of freshly flensed whale meat.

"Which type of whale was that," Yoshimatsu asked.

"Blue whale," said the First Officer. "Eighty-five feet."

Yoshimatsu nodded. He turned his next question to Kanamura. "Any new information from our guest?"

"He doesn't know anything. Otherwise, he would have told me by now."

"Were you able to make contact with Spinner?"

"Apparently Spinner pays little attention to things like keeping cell phones activated. We have been unable to contact him thus far."

"Keep trying. We have something he wants."

The three men proceeded to the bridge where Captain Watabe, a short burly man with a wispy black beard and a lined face, greeted them. Watabe had been with the Consortium for seven years. Originally, he had captained a smaller trawler in the waters off Thailand where young men were kidnapped to work as slaves in the shrimp industry. Many of these men would stay at sea for years at a time, unable to get back home. Many were murdered and dumped overboard if they complained or if their work flagged. He bowed ceremoniously to Yoshimatsu, who returned the bow with less flare.

"Welcome aboard, sir," said the Captain. "My ship and crew are at your service."

"Thank you, Captain Watabe. I look forward to touring the ship again. I would also like to discuss upcoming operations, including the next dolphin hunt. We have a site established and need to discuss the nature of *Shodokai Maru's* role in the upcoming venture."

The Captain nodded. "We will be ready, sir. With Mr. Kanamura organizing the ground personnel, we will deploy the banger boats at your signal."

"Very good. Mr. Kanamura will provide you with the coordinates. We will also be requiring your assistance to transport the materials for the floating booms. Mr. Kanamura will oversee construction and security for the site."

"Everything will be ready, sir." Watabe bowed once more.

Yoshimatsu clasped his hands behind his back, turning his gaze out to sea. "How has the hunt been progressing?"

"Very well, sir. Two finbacks three days ago, and today we located a fully mature blue whale."

Yes, I saw the processing being completed below. Your efficiency is most impressive."

Watabe suddenly looked uncomfortable. "There is a minor problem that has come to my attention, sir."

"Mr. Yoshimatsu does not like to hear about problems." Kanamura stared at the Captain.

"What problems?" Yoshimatsu spoke with measured calmness.

"Three of our indigenous workers who man the banger boats have deserted. They did not show up for their shift for the last two days."

Yoshimatsu turned to Kanamura. "Did you know about this?"

The look on Kanamura's face—a look of surprise coupled with underlying anger—told Yoshimatsu that his first lieutenant had just been blindsided. "No, Hiro-san. I was not informed."

"You are charged with maintaining the security in the village. I believe it is time that they be reminded of their contract and commitment to our cause."

"It will be done, sir." Kanamura cast a malevolent glance at Watabe, who flinched slightly.

Yoshimatsu stepped onto the exposed flybridge. He placed his hands on the rail and stared at the indigo sea spread before him. Low on the horizon, a waning moon was rising over the jagged desert peaks in the east. He overheard Kanamura discussing the communication protocols with Captain Watabe. A moment later, Kanamura joined him on the open deck.

"We have to be careful, Ako-san. We have a limited window for success here. The tides are already beginning to turn."

"I understand, Hiro-san. I will double my efforts to maintain order and compel compliance from the indigenous workers."

"After the completion of the next dolphin hunt, it will be time for us to leave these waters for now. Minister Figueroa has promised us the next two weeks to complete our venture. After that, he cannot guarantee our safety."

"Are there any new developments on the data from the director's computer?" Kanamura inquired.

"The data are the same. That tells me that the whales have been moving around, the researchers' data are inaccurate—or they falsified the GPS readings and numbers of whales. I am leaning toward the latter."

"Perhaps it is time that I had a conversation with the good doctor."

"Oh, I think he will be most cooperative," said Yoshimatsu confidently. "He loves his job and wants to remain in that position. Minister Figueroa has made it abundantly clear that Director Cabrillo has more to lose than a position at the institute."

"What about Spinner?"

"Yoshimatsu, looked directly at Kanamura. "That, my friend is your job. Jake Spinner has cost me a great deal of money and lost time. I want you to locate him and bring him to me. He needs to learn that no one goes against the Consortium. After that, do what you will with him."

"I believe we have obtained all of the useful information from the young fisherman, Macario. Would you like me to dispose of him?"

"No. Not yet. He may still serve us in some capacity. Keep trying to contact Jake Spinner. If Spinner knows Macario is still alive, he will come looking for him. And that will be his downfall."

# 34

The sun had just appeared over the mountains when Alejandro pulled his truck into the loading zone at the La Paz International Airport. He retrieved the two suitcases out of the truck bed. An attractive young woman with long black hair dressed in fashionable jeans, a white shirt, and a tan jacket got out of the passenger side. She was helping a young girl with a small pink backpack. The girl was about ten. She looked a lot like her mother, but she had Alejandro's deep brown eyes.

"Carmen, do you have the tickets?" Alejandro hoisted the two suitcases onto the curb.

"Yes, I have the tickets!" His wife was irritated. "Lili, stay close to me."

"I'm going to park the truck and I'll be right in."

They had awakened early to get ready. The tension in their home was apparent as Carmen and Lili finished packing. After breakfast, the normally grounded Carmen lost it and yelled at her husband.

"You're being irresponsible to us and to yourself! You're putting yourself in needless danger. And for what? The whales? You could die, and what will become of Lili and me? Your priorities are all wrong."

Alejandro sat on the edge of the bed, looking miserable. "We have already talked about this, Carmen. I have an obligation: to the whales, to the researchers and to the institute. I cannot, in good conscience, stand by and watch these men decimate our Gulf of California."

"What about us? What about your obligation to your family?"

"That's why I'm sending you someplace safe—until this is over and the men who committed these crimes are either in jail or expelled from Mexico."

"No one will think you're a coward if you leave with your family. They'd understand."

"Yes, they might understand. But the person I have to see every day in the mirror for the rest of my life will know the truth."

He parked the truck and entered the terminal. He found Carmen and Lili near the front of the line. He couldn't remember feeling this sad and frightened before.

He took his place in the line next to Carmen and Lili. His daughter wrapped both arms around her father's waist and held him tight. He hugged his daughter close to him. "Everything is going to be fine, mija," he said, in the most convincing voice he could muster. She buried her head in her father's side and began to cry quietly. The ticketing agent beckoned them forward.

The ticketing agent greeted her. "Your destination today?"

"Cuernavaca," said Carmen.

"How many will be traveling?"

Carmen didn't look at Alejandro. "Two."

They did not speak as they walked toward the security checkpoint. They stopped, and Alejandro dropped to one knee and faced Lili. He wiped her tears from her cheeks. "Before you know it, you'll both be back here and we can get back to our lives. In the meantime, I want you to keep up with your school lessons on your computer and listen to your mamá."

Lili nodded. "I'll miss you, Papá." She buried her head in his shoulder.

Alejandro stood up and looked at Carmen. "I don't want us to part being mad at each other."

Carmen embraced him. "You be careful. I love you."

He held her tightly. "I'll call you every chance I get."

She pulled back and looked into his eyes, forcing a smile. "And you'd better not go and get yourself killed, because you'll have to answer to me if you do."

He watched as they made their way through the security line, his daughter looking back at him intermittently as they stepped through to the secure area. Lili raised her hand to wave at him one more time before they disappeared.

As Alejandro drove away from the airport, his cell phone rang. He checked the number. It was Sandy.

"Did Carmen and Lili get off all right?"

"They just went through security. Their plane leaves at 7:40."

"Are you okay?"

"Yes. I'm fine."

"You don't sound fine."

"That was just about the hardest thing I've ever done."

"I'm sorry. That must be hard. What time are you meeting with Figueroa?"

"Ten."

"I was thinking, that maybe it would be better if all three of us meet with him. You know, safety in numbers."

"No. He has no idea who has access to this information right now. The last thing we need to do is put three of the major players in the same room with him at once."

"Are you going to carry a tape recorder?"

"I don't know if I can pull that off in time. My guess is that he'll have his security staff with him, and they won't take any chances that I might be wired."

"We're going to need to know exactly when you go in, and if you're not out by a certain time, we need to get the police in there."

"No police, Sandy. They may be working with Figueroa."

There was a pause on the other end of the line. Sandy exhaled. "I got a call from Rosen about twenty minutes ago. Spinner's in."

Alejandro straightened up in his seat. "What changed his mind?"

"She didn't say. She said he could be a problem."

"I agree our unlikely colleague could be a loose cannon."

"Ya think?"

"Ask Rosen to get a working cell phone for him. We need to be able to contact him quickly if necessary. Were you able to contact Greenpeace?"

"I have a phone interview this afternoon at 2:00 our time. Alex, I don't like this one bit. Someone should be going in there with you. I don't trust Figueroa further than I can throw him."

"Sandy, I'll be fine. The worst he can do to me—to us—is to suspend us. Once this story gets to the press, it will reflect very badly on his administration if news got out that he'd been assisting illegal whale hunting in Mexican waters."

"I'd still feel better if you'd at least have Spinner watch your back. He's pretty handy when the feces hit the fan."

"Mr. Jake Spinner may be of help to us, but now is not the time. Remember, Figueroa has no idea who was at the cove and who saw what. The recording he's going to receive will have none of our faces or voices on it."

"Okay. Just make damn sure you call us as soon as you get out."

"Sandy, you'll be the first one I call. Good luck with Greenpeace."

Alejandro drove to his modest single-story home, four blocks in from the malecón. He shaved and showered and then dressed in a pair of black jeans, white shirt, and sport coat. He tried to eat some breakfast, but found he was too nervous to eat anything other than a handful of nuts and a banana.

He retrieved the flash drive from the desk in his office and pocketed it. He and Sandy had edited the original recording, eliminating any voiceovers or images of those present on the cliff. The original footage had been recorded while Jake Spinner had laid waste to the barricade and freed the dolphins. That had also been edited out. What was left on the video was just the raw footage of the slaughter. He drained the last of his coffee and left the house.

He arrived at La Posada Hotel where the Minister of Fisheries stayed when he had business in La Paz. Located on the malecón, the hotel was frequented by both Mexican government officials and tourists. It was five stories high and boasted a circular palm-lined driveway with a large pool between the hotel and the ocean. Alejandro parked on the malecón and walked up the driveway and into the expansive lobby. He went to the front desk and was directed to the fifth-floor suite where the Minister of Fisheries was ensconced.

As soon as he stepped into the elevator and the door closed, his first thought was to press the "DOOR OPEN" button and get the hell out of there. He had never really cared much for confrontations. He was a shy person at heart, always trying to find the middle ground when conflicts arose. However, there didn't seem to be any middle ground in this situation.

The elevator stopped on the fifth floor. Alejandro stepped into the lavish hallway and looked for room 525. He closed his eyes, took a deep breath to compose himself, then knocked on the door.

A large Mexican man dressed in a dark suit answered. Alejandro recognized Figueroa's personal bodyguard from the other night at the institute. He was as tall as Alejandro but had a good eighty pounds on him. The bodyguard looked Alejandro up and down like a prizefighter assessing his opponent.

"Alejandro Cabrillo to see the Minister of Fisheries," Alejandro said, in a confident-sounding tone.

"You are expected," said the man gruffly. He opened the door and let Alejandro in. "Wait," he said, holding out an arm. He performed a pat down on Alejandro.

Alejandro was incredulous. "What? Why would I carry a gun?"

"Everyone must undergo a security check before entering. The Minister will see you now. Follow me."

Alejandro was led down a short hallway that opened up into a vast living room with a large, rectangular cherrywood table in the center. The suite had a panoramic view of the Gulf of California with Isla Espiritu Santo outlined in the distance. White couches and overstuffed chairs were neatly arranged around the room. On one wall there was a huge flat screen television. Against the far wall was a fully stocked bar. Minister Alfonso Figueroa entered the room from one of the large bedrooms off to the right. He was wearing a suit coat over a white shirt with dark slacks and black shoes. He looked tired and angry.

"Thank you for coming, Dr. Cabrillo," he said, without much warmth. He gestured to two overstuffed chairs near the window. "Something to drink?"

"No, thank you."

The bodyguard immediately brought a drink and placed it on the small table in front of Figueroa.

"There is a matter I wish to discuss with you." Figueroa sighed. "Repeated attempts by our Japanese friends to locate the whales have been met with frustration. Every trip thus far has not revealed any whales at all. In the spirit of cooperation between our two governments, I would like you and Señoritas Wainwright and Jiménez to lead an excursion to find the whales. In turn, you can discuss with our esteemed guests your research techniques and your data analysis. Our visitors are willing to charter a larger boat to accommodate the increased number of people."

Alejandro's brow furrowed. "You want us to lead an expedition to find the humpbacks? I will not do that."

"This is not a request."

"I'm sorry, sir," said Alejandro. "But I can't do that. I speak for Sandy and Paola as well."

Figueroa stared at Alejandro. "Be very careful, Dr. Cabrillo. Your next words could determine your fate at the institute."

Alejandro reached into his jacket pocket and produced a flash drive. He placed it on the table and slid it across to Figueroa.

Figueroa picked it up and examined it. "What's on this?"

"Something you should see."

Figueroa inserted the flash drive into his desktop computer. A moment later, images of the dolphin slaughter at the cove flashed across his screen. Alejandro saw Figueroa's face flush and the veins on his neck distend.

"Where did you get this?"

"Some local fishermen shot this footage and gave it to me."

Figueroa's eyes narrowed. "Who are these fishermen?"

"I'm sorry, Minister Figueroa. They never told me their names. I believe they want to remain anonymous."

Figueroa leaned toward the scientist. "It seems odd to me that a couple of fishermen would seek you out to tell you about this hunt. How did they know it was going to take place?'

Alejandro shrugged. "I can't answer that, Minister. They came to my home in the dark of night. They wore hooded sweatshirts and caps and gave me the video."

"I don't think you understand, Dr. Cabrillo. This has just become a government matter of the highest priority. Your ultimate cooperation is mandated by the highest levels of this office in Mexico City. Permission to study these whales is a great honor."

Alejandro looked levelly at the Fisheries Minister. "Again, my apologies. The technique the whalers are using is identical to the technique used to drive whales to slaughter in Taiji, Japan. I suspect that the Japanese may be using this practice here in Baja to catch dolphins."

"That's an outlandish accusation!"

"I also have reason to believe that one of the local fishermen may have been murdered by the same people who have been hunting whales—and possibly killing those dolphins. How could I possibly trust these people?"

"What proof do you have?"

"I don't have any at this time. Other than this video. But we believe it is important and urgent enough for your office to investigate."

"Investigate what? A fisherman drowned. They drown all the time. The Gulf of California is a very dangerous place." Figueroa turned the flash drive over and over in his fingers. "Perhaps your colleagues might be more helpful."

"You'd get the same information from them. They only know what they saw on this video."

Figueroa leaned back, never taking his eyes off Alejandro. "Since you will not cooperate, I have no choice but to suspend you from your directorship, effective immediately, pending further investigation into this matter."

Alejandro looked shocked. "On what grounds am I being suspended, sir?"

"Failure to cooperate fully with this office."

"I've given you the information you asked for."

"Have you? No whales were found at any of the study sites listed. All I have from you is a grainy video. The Department of Fisheries will conduct a thorough study of the facts. In the meantime, until further notice, I'm suspending all further research at the institute."

"You're closing the institute?" Alejandro was incredulous. "Why?"

"You have no idea the far-reaching implications your accusations will have. This administration will not jeopardize future relations with our trading partners based on some wild conjectures and a homemade video of poor quality."

"We've only brought this to your attention because a gross injustice is being done! At the very least, someone is stealing our natural resources for their own gain. Doesn't that make you want to investigate this?"

"After a careful review of the data, we will determine whether there's just cause to pursue this matter." Figueroa was dismissive. "In the meantime, you and your colleagues are to pursue this no further. If you do, none of you will be able to work in this country again. This meeting is over." He motioned to his large bodyguard. "Show Dr. Cabrillo out."

Alejandro stood, his face red, feeling his pulse pounding in his neck.

Figueroa's eyes moved to the guard, who stood menacingly over Alejandro.

"Your time is up," said the personal bodyguard.

Alejandro walked out with the bodyguard right behind him. After he was sure that Alejandro had entered the elevator, the bodyguard walked back into the large living room and announced, "He's gone, sir."

Figueroa picked up his cell phone and punched in a series of numbers. After a few seconds, he spoke into the phone. "Cabrillo just left. He showed me a video of the hunt at San Mateo Cove. I'm suspicious that he was there. No, I do not believe he's telling us everything." There was a pause as Figueroa listened to the voice at the other end. "Yes, I have suspended him. I don't believe that will deter him." Another pause. "Very well. Just make sure that it doesn't get traced back to this office."

# 35

Emily Rosen and Jake Spinner had an uneventful drive from the Raúl's ranchito back to La Paz. Upon their arrival, she changed hotels to another part of the city on advice from Spinner. He told her that, from now on, no one was to travel the same path twice. Originally, she had thought his paranoia was fueled by years of excessive alcohol consumption. After the altercation she'd witnessed at El Pulpo Morado, she couldn't argue with Spinner's logic, however twisted it might seem.

After checking in, she drove Spinner to another hotel within walking distance of hers. Although Spinner's lodging was more spartan than her new digs, it was definitely a step up from the store room at El Pulpo. Rosen returned to her hotel, hoping to take advantage of the free Wi-Fi to contact media colleagues in the states who might be able to help, while Spinner was impatient to track down some possible leads to Macario's whereabouts.

Rosen awakened early the next morning, brought back into reality quicker than she would have liked by the sound of two cats making ugly at each other outside her window. This hotel room was a vast improvement over the last one. It was immaculate and very comfortable. She rolled out of bed and parted the curtains that opened up onto a small courtyard. The sun hadn't risen yet, and the gray early morning light gave a muted tone to the flowers, plants, and stones.

She showered and dressed, sat down at a polished mesquite table, and turned on the Talavera-style lamp. She opened her laptop and logged in. The hotel claimed they had a Wi-Fi connection, but last night she had been unable to get a signal. She hoped that this morning, at this hour, most people would still be in bed. She needed to connect with some East Coast people before it got much later. She checked her watch. 5:30. In New York, the day would've already started. Her contact would've been at work for nearly two hours.

Bertrand Hollis was a former assistant to the U.S. Ambassador to Japan. He had left the office after his boss had been replaced, and he had formed his own

197

think tank. Six years ago, Emily had helped clear his name in a high-profile cyber attack on the embassy. Her diligent investigating uncovered a network that had collaborated with a department within the embassy. Bertrand had spent most of his life in the Far East, was fluent in Mandarin and Japanese and knew the major players on the chessboard of Asian politics and commerce.

At 6:08 a.m., she sent him an email. At 6:12, her cell phone rang. She looked at the LED readout and saw that it was a long number with a familiar prefix.

She set the phone on speaker. "Hello, Bertrand."

"Hello, Emily. How's life in the trenches?"

"Still waist deep in it, Bert. As long as it doesn't get past my chin, I think I'm okay."

There was a deep, rumbling laugh on the other end of the line. "Rosen, I've missed your pieces lately in the *Times*. I'm hoping you haven't been transferred to the restaurant guide section. You'd scare all the chefs half to death."

She smiled at the thought. "Well actually, Bert, it's worse. I'm currently down in sunny Mexico, Baja Sur, to be exact. My editor sent me down here a few weeks ago to cover some bullshit story about the effect of the drug cartels on the tourist trade."

There was a pause on the other end. "You're kidding, aren't you?"

"Wish I were. He took me off the story I was developing about Senator Donato's ties to organized crime."

"Someone got to your editor. When can you go back?"

"I can't. I'm no longer employed by the *Times*."

"What? No! I'm very sorry to hear that, Emily."

"It's okay. I'm doing some freelance investigating right now, which brings me to why I called you."

"This should be interesting," said Hollis.

Rosen spoke quickly and emphatically, knowing that Bertrand Hollis was a very busy man. She told him about the institute and the work of Alejandro, Sandy, and Paola, and about how some unknown outside entity was killing whales and dolphins indiscriminately. She told him about the dolphin slaughter at the cove and that a group of Japanese was behind the hunt at the inlet.

He listened quietly until Emily finished. "Good God, Rosen. What have you gotten yourself into?"

"Here's where I need to ask a favor of you. Ever hear of a Japanese businessman named Hiro Yoshimatsu?"

Rosen heard Hollis pull in a sharp breath through his teeth. "Maybe you should think about trying the restaurant beat for a while, Emily. Hiro Yoshimatsu is a very influential person. He's also very dangerous. Ever hear of the Yakuza?"

"The Japanese Mafia?"

"Right. Yoshimatsu has roots with the Yakuza that go back a long way. He worked his way up to the top and is now considered a wealthy, respectable businessman who has the ear of the Emperor. His ties with the Yakuza began with drugs and prostitution, black market acquisitions, and arms. Now, he's considered one of the most powerful men in Japan, overseeing shipping and commerce in different areas of Japan's economy."

"He's here in Baja. He's been to the Institute of Marine Mammals in La Paz. We think he's behind the whales and dolphins disappearing. There's also been at least one murder. Bert, I need your help. I need as much information on Yoshimatsu as you can give me. You worked that side of the world for a long time. You know who I should talk to. I just need a scent trail to follow."

"Rosen, Donato is a stroll through the park compared to Yoshimatsu. You have no idea what you're getting into." There was a distinct edge to his voice.

"Bert, I have to do something. If you'd seen what I saw at that cove, you'd know I couldn't live with myself if I just let it go. Every time I close my eyes, I see those poor animals being cut and slashed and bleeding to death in the shallows. Please. One more time, Bert. And I promise I'll never bother you again."

Hollis paused for a moment. The only sound coming over the phone was a tap-tap-tapping which Rosen guessed was a pencil on a hardwood desktop.

"I don't think you can win this one, Emily. You have no idea how connected this guy is. He has heads of governments on speed dial in his cell phone."

"I need to do this."

Hollis sighed. "I'll send you what I know. I'll also send you links to some other investigations that have been aimed at our industrialist."

"Thanks, Bertrand. I owe you one."

"You don't owe me anything, Rosen. Just watch your back and don't trust anyone. With these guys, you never see it coming."

Hollis clicked off and Rosen stared at her phone. She turned to her computer and began typing. Forty minutes later, a ding emanating from her computer announced she had an email. It was a message from Bertrand Hollis.

Jake Spinner awakened from a fitful sleep feeling exhausted. In his erratic and convoluted dreams, he moved from one dreamscape to the next, his pursuers close at hand. Once, he awoke with a sharp gasp, sitting bolt upright in bed in his rundown hotel room. In the dream, he was trying to locate Macario, who was crying out in pain somewhere, but Jake couldn't see him through the ether. Somewhere in the inky fog ahead of him, he heard the tortured screams of others. The screams were piercing, but he somehow knew that the desperate voices were those of Rosen, Alejandro, Sandy, and Paola. The screams morphed into an alien wail emanating from many different points in the fog. It was the sound of whales and dolphins dying. Suddenly the fog turned from an inky black to deep crimson. That's when Spinner nearly flew out of the bed.

He sat on the edge of the bed, running his hands through the tangled mop of his hair. He shook his head violently side to side, a reflexive gesture to clear the visions from his ravaged mind. He realized that, although still horrible, his dream content had changed. All of his previous nightmares had centered on his comrades in Afghanistan, how they died, and how he was unable to save them. This hellscape had thrust him into the present with a vengeance.

He stretched and without thinking, flopped onto the floor and began counting off push-ups. He made it to twenty-one before he collapsed in a heap.

He rolled onto his back and stared up at the ceiling, his breath coming in rasps.

"Jesus, Spinner. Twenty-one god damn push-ups. You used to do 200 without breaking a sweat. What the hell happened to you?"

The night before, he had purchased a cheap razor, along with a few other toiletries that he could afford. He got up and shaved—a painful experience in itself. Then he showered and dressed. All the while a gnawing feeling told him that Macario wasn't in La Paz. Still, he needed to check out Macario's friend to see if he had even made it here. He had to find Alberto. Macario had told Jake the name of the neighborhood where Alberto had last lived. He would spend this morning combing through Barrio Ledezma. Under duress, he had agreed to touch base with Rosen around noon. He sensed that the fiery easterner could be a major pain in the ass if someone crossed her. It was then he realized he hadn't bothered to reinstate his cell phone service.

As he left the hotel, Spinner checked the streets in both directions and, feeling satisfied that he wasn't being watched, moved down the street in the shadows. Two blocks away he found an open street vendor and bought a burrito. Munching on it as he walked, he arrived in Barrio Ledezma just as the morning sun was lighting up the tops of the palm trees along the boulevard.

Luckily, Alberto Cortina wasn't hard to find. Several inquiries led Jake to discover that Alberto was a small-time gang leader in the barrio. He was the proverbial big fish in a very small pond. He ran a small-scale operation of drugs, prostitution, and fenced goods—mostly pirated electronics. Spinner learned that Alberto wanted into the big leagues in the worst way but was just waiting for the right opportunity to arise.

He found the address, a shabby, run-down white stucco house on a dirt street. Vines and bushes that hadn't seen a landscaper's trimming tool in a very long time, hung over the wrought iron fence. On the covered porch, a filthy worn sofa and two overstuffed chairs looked like they should have been hauled to the dump years ago. He felt the cold weight of the Beretta against the small of his back, under his shirt.

Spinner walked up the two stone steps and rapped on the door. He waited for what seemed an interminable amount of time before he heard a groggy voice say in Spanish, "Who's there?"

Spinner answered in Spanish. "I'm here to see Alberto. My name is Jake Spinner."

"He's not here. Go away."

"Not until I speak with Alberto. A friend of his is in trouble. I need to warn him." Spinner heard shuffling and objects being moved behind the door. Suddenly, it flew open and he was looking down the barrel of a pump shotgun. A wiry, shirtless Mexican with a shaved head and multiple tattoos, pointed the weapon at him.

"I told you, gringo, he's not here. What? Are you stupid?"

Spinner held up his hands. "I don't want any trouble. I just need to speak with Alberto. It's about Macario Silvano. He's a friend of Alberto's and he is in danger."

"We don't know no Macario," sneered the little man, pushing the barrel of the shotgun into Jake's chest. Jake stepped back a half step. Sensing movement behind him, he glanced around to see that four more gangbangers had converged on him from both sides of the house. All were armed.

"I don't want any trouble. I just want to talk to Alberto."

"You already have trouble, pendejo." The shirtless man again prodded Spinner in the chest.

The wiry Latino barely noticed the change in Spinner's eyes. In the next instant Spinner grabbed the barrel, twisted the shotgun out of his hands, and cracked him in the jaw with the butt end. The little thug flew back against the wall and crumpled to the floor. Spinner had the shotgun pointed at the other four before they could react.

"I'm going to ask you one more time. Where's Alberto?"

"I'm right here." Alberto stepped out from inside the house. He was a big man, around six feet with a paunch and a tank top which revealed biceps that had seen a good deal of time at a gym. His entire upper torso was tattooed.

"That was pretty fast for an old man. Who are you?"

"Jake Spinner. Macario's dad was my fishing partner. He and Marta, his wife, were murdered, and I think the guys that killed them are going after Macario now."

Alberto looked at Spinner through bloodshot eyes. His eyes widened in recognition. "Hey. I know you. I remember you from when I was a kid in Puerto Nacimiento."

"Has Macario been here?" Jake's patience was wearing thin.

"No, hombre. He called me several weeks ago. He said he was coming to La Paz. He said he needed my help. But he never showed."

"When did you last talk to him?"

Alberto scratched his stubbled chin. "Seven to ten days ago, maybe two weeks."

"Did he say what he wanted?"

"Yeah. He wanted to buy a gun."

Spinner lowered the shotgun. "If he shows up, tell him to call me." Spinner pulled a stub of a pencil from his shirt pocket and wrote a number on the wall.

"Why should he trust you?" Alberto asked sarcastically.

"Because I'm all he's got. If you care at all for your friend, you gotta tell him to contact me. It's his only chance." He ejected all of the shotgun shells onto the porch and handed the gun to Alberto. Jake motioned toward the downed hoodlum, now groaning in pain. "Tell your boy that next time, he shouldn't stand so close."

Spinner walked down the two steps between the four hoods who were glaring at him. They looked to Alberto for direction, but he shook his head. Spinner felt the five sets of eyes on him as he walked slowly away. He hoped that the young gang members hadn't seen his hands shaking.

Rosen put her laptop in her satchel, and stretched her aching shoulders and neck. She'd been sitting at the computer for nearly five hours with only one bathroom break. Bertram Hollis had sent to her a mountain of information about Hirokan Yoshimatsu. Between the actual articles and the related links, she had enough to compile an impressive file on the Japanese tycoon.

She stood up and nearly lost her balance, her legs having gone to sleep. She grabbed the edge of the table and gingerly danced back and forth on each foot until the intense numbness subsided.

She looked at her watch. It was 1:00 p.m. and she was famished. Where the hell was Spinner? He was supposed to show up an hour ago. She didn't know whether to be angry or worried. More than likely, he was sleeping off a drunk in some flophouse. On the other hand, what if he ran into trouble when he went looking for Macario's friend? Spinner had said the guy was looking to climb the cartel ladder. Rosen couldn't even call him.

At 1:30, she packed her backpack and left the room. To hell with Spinner. She needed to eat. Rosen took the stairs to the first floor and walked through the lobby. She put on her sunglasses and stepped out into the warm afternoon sun. She looked up and down the street for a suitable restaurant. Nothing in the immediate vicinity sounded or looked very good. She felt the pull of the Gulf of California and began walking toward the malecón.

Rosen gasped suddenly when a tall man sidled up next to her.

"Damn it, Spinner! You scared the shit out of me!"

"You're not paying attention, Rosen." He pointed to his eyes with two fingers. "Three hundred-sixty degrees at all times. And always watch your six."

Rosen stopped and punched a finger into Spinner's chest. "Where the hell have you been? You were supposed to check in over two hours ago."

"I found Alberto." There was irritation and a hint of worry in his voice. "Macario hasn't been there."

"Do you think he's telling the truth?"

"Yeah, I think so. The last time he heard from Macario was nearly two weeks ago. He wanted Alberto to find him a gun."

"Oh, God. Is there somewhere else he might have gone?" Rosen suddenly realized the implication of what Spinner had just said.

"He's a local kid. La Paz is like the Big Apple to him. He doesn't have a vehicle, can't go home, and sure doesn't know his way around a big city. My gut tells me he's been picked up."

Rosen walked briskly while Spinner kept pace. He said, "Where we going now?"

"I'm going to get something to eat."

"Good idea. I could eat."

"As soon as we've eaten, we're going to get you cell phone service." She made the phone gesture with her hand and held it to her ear. "E.T. needs to phone home."

They ended up at a seafood restaurant that was situated over the water near the harbor. Rosen wanted to sit outside, so they were led to a table on the patio that was next to the water. From their seats they could see numerous sailboats and motor yachts at anchor, gently rocking in the aquamarine-colored sea.

Spinner looked uncomfortable. Rosen peered over her menu at him. "Is something wrong?"

Spinner's gaze darted around the restaurant. "Ah, well, Rosen, this joint may be a little rich for my blood. Maybe I'd better wait for you outside."

"Relax, Spinner. I've got lunch covered."

"I'm good for it. Really, I am. After I get my monthly check."

"Don't worry about it. I still have some of my stipend left from my former editor." Rosen stared at him. "This covers food. No liquor."

Spinner looked stricken. "Not even a beer?"

"If I'm buying, it's iced tea, Coke, or water. I need you working on all cylinders."

"You sure know how to take the fun out of a romantic dining experience."

The waiter approached the table, and Rosen ordered two soft drinks while Spinner looked irritated. He left menus, and Rosen perused hers while Spinner looked around the restaurant. No Asians or federales were to be seen. Over at one corner of the bar were three Americans hitting on some young women. From the way they were talking and carrying on, there was enough liquor and testosterone for Spinner to deduce that the Americans probably came from one or more of those boats anchored just beyond the harbor.

He turned his attention to the menu and soon landed on his choice. The waiter returned with the drinks a few minutes later and Emily ordered the pan-seared mahi mahi. Spinner wanted the half-pound cheeseburger with fries.

Rosen teased, "What? No fish?"

"I eat enough fish."

After the waiter had left, Spinner said, "So, what did you find out?"

Rosen reached into her satchel and produced her notebook and a pen. "Well, it seems our Mr. Yoshimatsu has a very long and very colorful history. He was orphaned when he was seven, moved around with different relatives until he was twelve, then took to the streets of Tokyo. Did the usual aspiring gang banger rise to stardom. Worked running numbers, then drugs, then graduated to prostitution and human smuggling rings. The Yakuza took notice of him and brought him into the fold. He was a quick study and moved up the ladder rapidly, supposedly because of his street smarts and ruthlessness. It seems a lot of his adversaries never saw him coming. A lot of his opponents ended up missing."

"A real philanthropist."

"It gets worse. It wasn't long before he convinced the Yakuza that there was a fortune to be made in the shipping business. He was set up as the regional head of the Yokohama district and soon found out how to conduct his operations on an international scale, mostly through Hong Kong and Thailand. He's been on Interpol's person of interest list for a long time, but has never given the authorities enough for an indictment. In the past twenty years, he's amassed a fortune—mostly in shipping. Some of his shadow companies include illegal shrimp fishing in Thailand where the workers are literally kidnapped and taken to sea for years, working as slaves. If they refuse to work or get sick, they're thrown overboard. A lot of these shrimp end up in big box stores in the States and Canada."

"And I'll bet they're all shadow companies that can't be traced to Yoshimatsu or his cartel," Spinner sipped his Coke and made a sour face. "How the hell can people drink this shit?"

"Tea would be better for you. His shipping business includes small fleets that he contracts all over the globe. I even found evidence of whaling operations in Antarctica and shark finning operations in the Philippines and Costa Rica."

"That might explain why he showed up recently in Baja."

"Not really his style. I'm not sure why he's overseeing day-to-day operations. I think there might be a shake up going on in the Yakuza hierarchy. Environmental groups and public opinion have been gathering more momentum, forcing him and his fleets to look for different markets."

"Do you think he's worked a deal with the Mexican government?"

"Why else would he be here? This guy's worked hard over the years to make himself look legitimate. There's more than a few Japanese VIPs that reside in his little black book. What I don't get is why he came out in the open. Part of his success and ability to stay away from the international enforcers is that he maintains an insular presence. He's got so many legal firewalls through his corporate connections that a crack team of lawyers would still be at it in twenty years—if that's all they did."

"Something has to be up. The stakes must have suddenly been raised for him to show up at one of his operations."

Rosen took off her glasses and set them on the table. She rubbed the bridge of her nose and blinked. "Which begs the big question. What in hell are we doing?"

"Don't let stature throw you off, Rosen. He's still a scumbag and he can be taken down, just like any man. You just have to find his weak point."

Their food arrived and Spinner dove in like a man possessed.

Rosen, mildly disgusted as her companion attacked the cheeseburger with a vengeance, asked, "When did you last eat?"

"This morning."

The noise from the bar was getting louder and Rosen glanced over to see what was going on.

She almost choked on her mahi mahi when she recognized the guy who had humiliated her that night a few weeks before. Spinner saw rage cloud her face, and he stopped mid-bite.

"What's the matter? You look like you're about to puke."

She caught herself and attempted to regain her composure. "Nothing. Nothing's the matter."

Spinner turned his gaze to the threesome at the bar, then back to Rosen, studying her.

"What?" She was annoyed.

Spinner shrugged and took another bite of his burger, washing it down with a swig of Coke. "This burger sure is good. Only thing that would make it better would be a cold Pacífico."

"No, damn it. I've had enough with drunks for one lifetime."

Her retort caught Spinner by surprise, and he sat back in his chair. "Okay. Okay. Just kidding."

He looked up to see one of the three men approach. He was a tall, well-tanned American with wavy bleached hair, wearing a blue polo shirt and white cargo shorts with deck shoes. He was a few inches taller than Spinner and, judging by the way he was walking, Spinner could tell he had probably already downed two or three martinis. His two friends followed close behind, one a stocky, curly-haired, semi-balding guy who looked like he lifted weights. The other guy looked like a Wall Street investor, medium build with every hair in place. Spinner had seen guys like these a hundred times in San Jacinto when he ran fishing charters. He had little use for them even when they were paying customers. In the bars and streets of the village, he avoided them at every chance.

"Well, well, well. Look who we have here," said the tall blonde man. "It's the architect from New York."

Spinner saw Rosen look up and visibly cringe. Her face went crimson, and she turned back to face Spinner.

Trent Lahane spoke. "Still looking for that house on the beach?"

"You know this guy?" Spinner squinted up at him.

"Only in passing," Rosen said. "Why don't you just go away, Lahane. I'm enjoying my lunch."

Lahane cast a disparaging look at Spinner, then at Rosen. He leaned on the table and smiled. "Well, I have to say I'm surprised. But I guess it's true. In this world there's someone for everyone. I'm just not sure who set their sights lower."

Spinner's eyes flashed gray. Lahane saw this nearly imperceptible change and took his hands off the table.

"No, Spinner. Let it go," Rosen gave Spinner a hard look. "We don't want any attention brought to us here. Not now."

Lahane smiled, a lecherous look on his face. "C'mon, boys. I think these lovebirds want to be left alone."

They moved back toward the bar and ordered more drinks. Lahane looked over at Rosen several times and raised his glass to her. She picked at her food, unable to finish the rest of the meal. Spinner wiped up the last dab of ketchup on his plate with the two remaining fries. He pushed the plate away and looked at her.

"Want to talk about it?"

"No."

The waiter came around and picked up their plates. He asked if they wanted dessert, to which Rosen gave a curt shake of her head. When the check came, she reached into her satchel and placed the exact amount and a tip in pesos on the plastic tray. She stood and Spinner followed her out. He noted Lahane's sneering smile as they went out the front door.

Once outside the restaurant, they began to walk along the malecón. Spinner suddenly stopped. "I forgot something. Be right back." He turned and walked back into the restaurant. Rosen leaned against the rail overlooking the water, feeling the full brunt of another humiliation.

A commotion broke out in the restaurant, followed by shouting and the thud of flesh being hit. Rosen looked up in time to see Trent Lahane flying head first through a doorway, careening off a table, then flipping over the rail and crashing into the sea. He came up sputtering, his nose bleeding. In short order, a second, and then a third, drunk flew through the door and over the rail. Spinner exited the restaurant and walked briskly toward her.

"Feel better?" Rosen asked.

"Yeah. I think so."

"Great job of keeping a low profile."

"I don't think we'll be able to dine there again anytime soon," Jake said.

# 36

Raúl Campos drove his truck down a dusty sand track toward the shimmering azure sea in the distance. It was mid-afternoon and he had already covered nearly sixty miles of coastline. His plan had been to visit the outlying fishing camps to see if he could muster a coalition of fishermen who either had been approached by the Consortium or had witnessed other acts of whale slaughter or illegal fishing. He needed to find others who would be willing to corroborate the evidence that they had compiled against the Japanese. So far, the only thing he had to show for his efforts was a sore back and a coating of dust from driving the back roads of the peninsula.

Most of the fishermen that Raúl had been able to locate seemed to know nothing. If they knew something, they were feigning ignorance. He thought he could see fear in their eyes. Getting the locals to cooperate with him was going to be difficult.

He eased his truck down an embankment into a dry arroyo and downshifted to climb up the other side. He went through an open gate in an old barbed wire fence. The sand track became deeper as he drew closer to the small bay. A low-lying brick building covered with a palm frond roof stood back from the quiet stretch of beach. A dusty old Nissan Sentra was parked under a palo verde tree and several old pangas lay on their sides in the front yard. A rickety wooden table near the water's edge was covered with monofilament fishing netting in chiffon-like piles. Middens of brick-and-cranberry-colored scallop shells lined the seashore.

He honked once to announce his arrival and parked near the Nissan. He got out and stretched his cramped legs and back, then walked to the front door of Fernando Quintín's house. Fernando was a reclusive fisherman who was rumored to employ questionable fishing practices. Most of the fishermen in this part of the gulf belonged to a cooperative. They self-regulated their catches voluntarily for the sake of conservation and sustainability. Fernando had been approached several times to join the cooperative, but had declined.

He had married a native woman from Puerto Nacimiento who still had ties to the village. Raúl tried to remember her name. Alma, he thought. He hoped Fernando and his wife might have a connection to someone in Puerto Naciamiento who could give him some insight. But in his mind, he was afraid he'd arrived at another dead end. The indios of Puerto Nacimiento didn't like the interference of the Mexicanos.

Fernando Quintín emerged before Raúl could knock. He was only a few years older than Raúl, but he looked ancient. His skin resembled old dried leather, his eyes carried a yellowish tint, and he was missing most of his teeth. He wore a threadbare tee shirt—the printing long since faded—and a pair of stained khakis. He walked with a bandy-legged lurch, his legs abnormally bowed. He didn't say anything but lifted his chin in recognition of Raúl.

"Hola, Fernando. ¿Cómo esta?"

"Hola, Raúl Campos," he said, lisping through toothless gums. "It is long way to come for a social visit."

"The road was hot and dusty, Fernando. I would enjoy a drink, if you could spare it, and a few words if you're willing."

Fernando motioned inside the cool darkness. "Come in and sit down."

Raúl stepped inside the small concrete structure. It took several seconds for his eyes to adjust to the light. A diminutive dark-skinned woman with long black hair was nursing a small boy at the rickety kitchen table. *"Mi esposa*, Alma," Fernando said.

"Mucho gusto," said Raúl. "What's the boy's name?"

"Israel," said Alma.

Raúl nodded in approval.

Fernando motioned for him to sit. "My wife and I have no secrets," he said. "What you say to me, you can say to her."

He poured a cup of coffee from the propane stove and placed it in front of Raúl, then sat down.

Fernando stroked his young son's hair and touched his cheek. "So, Raúl Campos, what brings you to this lonely stretch of beach?"

Raúl took a sip of coffee. It was bitter and had probably been sitting on the stove since morning.

"I came here today to ask you and Alma about the strangers that have come to these waters to hunt whales. I wanted to know if you knew anything about them or their activities."

Fernando and Alma exchanged quick glances. He said, "Why are you interested in this matter?"

Raúl looked down at his clasped hands on the table. He appeared to be gathering strength for what he was about to say. He looked up, his gaze drifting between them. "I've grown up on this coast as you have. In my lifetime, I've seen many of the fish and animals from these waters that we share disappear or decrease in numbers—so much that now we can no longer sustain ourselves as a people. Recently, men came from across the sea and herded many dolphins into a cove and slaughtered them without mercy. Many of the great whales are being killed while they sleep to be sold as a delicacy in Asian markets. There are those of us who feel that this wanton slaughter is wrong, a crime against the sea and against the people who call Baja their home."

"Why did you seek us out?" Fernando was defensive.

"Because you fish these waters every day." Raúl's gaze focused on Alma. "And because you're from Puerto Nacimiento, where it is believed some of the villagers are working for the Asians."

"We know nothing about these Asian fishermen," said Fernando. "You made a long, hot trip for nothing."

"I mean no disrespect," said Raúl. "I'm only seeking information." He stood to leave. "Thank you for the coffee."

As he turned to leave, Alma spoke. "Wait. There's something you need to hear."

Raúl stopped at the door and turned around. Fernando glared at his wife.

"Tell him nothing, woman!" Fernando snapped. "You don't know who he answers to."

"We need to tell someone!" Alma shot back. "I can't live like this anymore."

"Whatever you say to me, I will not reveal the source." Raúl tentatively approached the table and Alma gestured for him to sit back down.

"You could get us all killed," Fernando said bitterly.

"This has to stop." Alma looked directly at Raúl, her face a mask of worry and fear. "My brother's gone missing. We haven't talked to him in nearly two weeks. Some of the other villagers in Puerto Nacimiento say he went to the mainland for work, but I know my brother. He wouldn't leave like that. The last time I saw him, he told me about another hunt that the village was told they must perform. There is to be another hunting operation, this one bigger than the last. He was very afraid. He was told that villagers who had gone missing had taken work elsewhere with the company, but he believed they were killed for trying to leave."

"When is this hunt to take place?" Raúl's heart was pounding.

"I—I don't know for sure. He said within the next few weeks."

"You've already said too much, Alma. You're endangering the baby and you and me."

"I think they killed my brother," Alma's eyes welled with tears. "He told me he had to get away from them, that what they were doing was a crime against God."

"Did he know where the hunt is to take place?"

"He didn't know. Los Jefes don't tell the fishermen until close to the day."

"What's your brother's name?" Raúl asked.

"Santiago. Santiago Garza. Please don't talk to the federales. We don't trust them."

"Neither do I," said Raúl. "I have other sources who may be able to assist. We know what these men are doing. We know about their upcoming hunt, and we want to stop it before it happens."

"What do you want from us?" Fernando stood and crossed his arms.

"You can move freely through the village because of your family ties, right, Alma?"

"That's too dangerous!" Fernando's voice rose.

"'Nando, I think they killed Santiago. I still have family in the village. You know that!" She turned to face Raúl. "What do you want me to do?"

"I don't want you to risk your lives for this. Don't ask questions. Use your eyes and ears to watch and listen. If you ask questions you'll come under suspicion." Raúl produced a cheap cell phone that he had picked up in town and slid it across the table. "My number is in the phone. Just punch in 26 and I should get it. No matter how trivial the information seems, it may lead us to something important."

"How are you going to stop these men?" Alma asked. "I think they answer to more powerful men somewhere else."

"We have contacts in the international community, not just in Mexico. We have information that has already been made public. As we speak, groups are making their way to Baja to join in the fight."

Alma fixed her gaze on Raúl, studying him. Usually, indigenous peoples did not engage in overt eye contact. Raúl concluded that Alma was looking for the truth.

"I believe you, Raúl Campos. We'll do what we can," she said.

# 37

Alejandro Cabrillo drove north on Highway One towards Insurgentes, about a three-and-a-half-hour drive from La Paz. He was going to meet with an old colleague, Victor Esposito, who would provide him with internet access and connections to colleagues in the United States and Canada. He and Victor had worked together on a project just after graduate school, performing a preliminary census of humpback whales in the area around Cabo San Lucas. They had speculated that the whales moved back and forth between mainland Mexico and southern Baja, a shorter version of the Alaska/Hawaii migration for the West Coast humpback population. This initial study had led Alejandro to his current project and a directorship at the institute. Victor had gone on to study the natural history of gray whales in Magdalena Bay and was a professor at the local college.

Alejandro was still in a state of shock. He had gone into the meeting with Figueroa knowing that suspension could be one of the possible outcomes, but he wasn't prepared for how this would impact him. Because of him, Sandy and Paola were also on suspension, and the institute was closed until further notice. They would all be lucky if they weren't blacklisted by the Mexican government. Marine biology positions were hard to find, and a directorship of an institute was a once-in-a-lifetime opportunity. Right now, Alejandro saw his professional career going over a very steep precipice.

Once the video went live, he wondered if he'd be able to return to La Paz. He suspected Figueroa was somehow connected to the group of Japanese that were exploiting the waters around Baja del Sur. Every fiber of his being told him so, but they were a long way from connecting the dots. Although the hunt was similar to slaughters that had taken place in Taiji, Japan, he had no positive proof linking Yoshimatsu to the hunt at San Mateo Cove. At the very least, the Minister of Fisheries had turned a blind eye to the activities of the Japanese group.

The traffic was light this late morning other than the occasional eighteen-wheeler carrying produce and supplies to La Paz and Cabo San Lucas. Alejandro found the rhythm of the two-lane highway helped to un-knot the tightness that had been churning in his stomach since his confrontation with Figueroa earlier that morning.

He was having second thoughts. What he wanted right now more than anything was to be with his wife and daughter. The grand crusade of saving whales and exposing their hunters seemed to pale. Nothing was as important as family. For the first time, the hard realization hit him. He might never see Carmen and Lili again. Maybe Spinner was right. Maybe getting Carmen and Lili out of the country for a while was the wisest move. Once he got the flash drive to the right people, he would join his family.

He realized that he hadn't checked in with the others since his meeting with Figueroa. After the dust-up with the Minister of Fisheries and his bodyguard, he realized he needed time to prepare himself to break the bad news to Sandy and Paola.

He wracked his brain to see if there was another way that he could have handled the situation. From the beginning, the Minister had stonewalled them. Why had Figueroa brought the Japanese representatives to the institute and demanded data on humpback whale distribution and movement? When he thought about the carnage he had seen at the cove, he burned with rage.

He retrieved his cell phone, called Sandy, and keyed the speaker function.

"Alex, are you all right?"

"I'm okay. The meeting with Figueroa didn't go well. He had his bodyguard escort me out of the office. More like threw me out."

"Since when does a Minister of Fisheries have bodyguards?"

"My thoughts exactly. I gave him the doctored flash drive, but he didn't buy it. I don't think he believes the story about the fishermen taking the video and delivering it to us. I asked him directly about the presence of the Japanese contingent and told him how I thought there might be a correlation between their presence here and the sudden killing of whales and dolphins. When I mentioned that a dead local fisherman may have had ties to this group, he got really angry."

"What did he say?"

"He suspended us, Sandy. And he closed the institute until further notice, pending investigation."

A moment of silence followed on the other end of the line as Sandy absorbed the full impact of Alejandro's statement. "Well, I'm not surprised. In fact, I half expected this."

"Sandy, I'm so sorry. I've been trying to figure out if there was another way to handle this. I told Figueroa that none of us had anything to do with the incident at San Mateo. I was hoping you and Paola would be spared this."

"Alejandro, stop beating yourself up. Figueroa is just looking to get us out of the way. We all went into this knowing full well that we could lose our jobs."

"Right now, I'm wondering just how far up the chain of command this goes. I wonder if the president is privy to this information."

"That's the 64,000-dollar question," said Sandy. "Where are you now?"

"On my way to Insurgentes to talk to Victor Esposito. He's going to help me network with the other researchers in Mexico, and he also has connections with Woods Hole and the Scripps Institute."

"Do you trust him?"

"We go back a long way, Sandy. I believe Victor's a good man."

"I hope so." Sandy paused. "Oh hell, Alejandro. I'm sorry. I shouldn't have said that. Guess I'm just getting paranoid."

"These days, I don't blame you at all."

"Do you want me to call Paola and let her know?"

"No. I'll call her. It's my job. Sandy, where are you right now?"

"I'm driving back to my house to pick up some things. I've been at the library using their Wi-Fi. The connection at my house kinda sucks."

"Be careful, Sandy. I think Figueroa is dangerous. Who knows what he's up to?"

"I will, Alex. Call me back at five?"

"Will do. Good luck."

Alejandro disconnected and set the cell phone on the console. He was now climbing steadily, the road winding upward in a series of switchbacks passing through the spine of the Sierra de la Giganta range. The call to Paola would have to wait until he got past this treacherous stretch of highway.

Movement in his rearview mirror caught his attention. A large black SUV was approaching at a speed not prudent on a narrow winding highway. The Ford Excursion was soon close behind. He tapped the brakes lightly, hoping the tailgater would get the hint. It continued to dog Alejandro's bumper. He looked again and saw that the windows were dark. He couldn't see the driver. He slowed his Toyota 4Runner and turned on the left turn signal, indicating that the black SUV could pass him if they wanted to. He was surprised when the SUV rammed his rear bumper.

Alejandro lurched ahead and the Excursion slammed into his rear bumper again. He punched the accelerator and sped ahead turning the wheel, the tires squealing angrily as he came upon a hairpin turn. He glanced in the rearview mirror. The black SUV had dropped back and was now concealed by the steep slope of the mountainside.

He pushed the Toyota as fast as he dared around the series of tight curves. He was hoping the last collision had damaged the SUV and that they wouldn't be able to pursue him. His heart was racing in his chest. He rounded a corner and was looking at a straight stretch of road when the black Excursion again appeared. It was accelerating, getting larger in the mirror. Soon it was dogging his bumper again. He braced for another impact but was surprised when it sped up on a curve and pulled parallel to him. He tried to accelerate ahead, but the SUV had more power.

Suddenly, he felt the impact of metal grating against metal. The Toyota's tires screeched as Alejandro pulled hard to keep on the curve. In the next instant the 4Runner was launched over the edge. He saw a white cloud as his airbag deployed in his face, knocking him backward in his seat.

In the instant before crashing into the arroyo, his thoughts were of Carmen and Lili.

# 38

Sandy Wainright pulled up to her small cottage and knew immediately that something was wrong. The front door was ajar. She sat in her car and stared at the partially open door, trying to decide whether she should go in or run.

She had just returned from her cell phone meeting with César Domínguez, the local representative and spokesperson for Greenpeace Mexico. They had talked for over an hour, Sandy outlining in detail what she witnessed at San Mateo Cove. As she recounted the horrendous story, she had to stop several times, choked up by the memory of the carnage she'd witnessed.

She shut off the motor and reached under her driver's seat, her hand wrapping around a tire iron she carried for road emergencies and protection. She got out of the car and walked tentatively toward the partially open door. As she got closer, she saw that the door was hanging slightly askew and there was splintered wood where the deadbolt used to be. She reached for her phone and hit the speed dial for Paola.

It took several rings before Paola answered. "Sandy? Is everything all right?"

"Hang on. I need you to be on the phone while I go into my house. Someone forced the door."

"Oh, God. Sandy, don't go in there! Wait until we can get Alejandro or Raúl there."

"I'm going in." She mustered as much bravado as she could, feeling like her heart was in her throat. "Stay on the line and get ready to make the call."

Sandy pushed the door aside. It swung inward with a sickening scraping sound. *So much for a surprise entrance.* Clutching the tire iron with one hand and the cell phone to her ear with the other, she said quietly, "I'm in."

She walked down a narrow hallway that led to a small living room. When she entered, the sight that greeted her sucked the air from her lungs.

"Someone trashed my house."

"Sandy! Get out of there!"

The living room looked like a tornado had touched down. The furniture was upended. Huge rents were torn in the sofa and chairs, as if they'd been eviscerated by some very large animal. Research papers were scattered everywhere. Pictures were ripped off the wall, the frames and glass shattered.

"Oh, my God," Sandy said, her voice choking.

"What? What is it?"

"The bastards trashed my house."

"Just get out of there, please. They may still be there."

Sandy's hand tightened on the tire iron. A boiling rage grew in her, and she walked toward the back of the house. "I hope so."

When she got back to her office the damage was similar. The computer had been smashed, and the monitor was on the floor. All of her music CDs were strewn around the room, some smashed into shards. Books had been pulled down from shelves.

When she got to her bedroom, she couldn't hold back the tears of rage anymore. Her mattress was ripped down the middle, the dresser drawers were standing open. Piles of her clothes and personal items covered the floor. She looked at the disaster that was once her neat little house, too numb to speak.

"Sandy? Talk to me! What's going on there?"

Finally, she answered, "They're gone, Paola. They're gone."

She found herself shaking badly. She looked dumbly at the havoc and destruction all about her. She knew what they'd been looking for as soon as she'd entered her house. She looked at the pillaged room and realized that if she'd been there when the intruders arrived, she wouldn't be standing. She would be dead. But she still had the data and the flash drive and her laptop . . .

"I can't stay here anymore. Have you got room?"

"Of course. Get out of there as fast as you can."

"I'll just grab a few things. I'll see you shortly."

Sandy hung up so quickly that Paola thought the intruders might have returned. She called back but got Sandy's voice mail. Forty-five minutes later a frantic Paola went to the door when she heard a vehicle pull up in front of her house.

Sandy got out, retrieved a small backpack from the back seat, and forced a weak smile.

"Are you okay?"

"Yeah. I'm fine."

They hugged for a long minute.

"I—I can't go back there. I feel as if I've been violated."

"Thank God you weren't there when they came."

"I can't remember when I've felt that much fear and rage at the same time. Part of my brain wanted them to still be there. I wanted to bash someone's skull in."

"Let's get you inside, Sandy. You're still shaking."

Paola led her into the vibrantly colored kitchen. The savory smell of tortillas cooling on the stove filled the air. Sandy sat at the table while Paola made her a cup of tea.

Sandy was finally able to talk and recount what she'd found when she got home and how her fear had morphed into dark fury. She reached into her shirt and pulled out a small cloth passport holder on a string around her neck.

"This is what they were looking for. The original recording." She motioned to her backpack. "I still have it on my laptop."

Paola asked, "Did you have it copied anywhere at home?"

"No. Something told me to wipe it from my desktop computer. I'm glad I listened to that little voice."

Paola went to the kitchen counter and picked up her cell phone.

"What are you doing?" Sandy asked, still in a fog.

She began punching in numbers. "I'm calling the others. They need to know."

Sandy looked suddenly stricken. "Did Alejandro call you?"

Paola stopped mid-dial. "No. Was he supposed to?"

"He said he was going to call you to let you know that we've been suspended until further notice."

Paola suddenly went pale. "What? We're fired?"

"Essentially. I can't believe he didn't call you."

"It's not like Alejandro to shirk responsibility."

Suddenly, a look passed between them. "Oh, God," Paola said, her eyes wide. "Do you think . . . ?"

"Call him. Now."

An hour later, Rosen and Spinner sat with Sandy at Paola's kitchen table. Repeated calls to Alejandro's cell phone had gone to his voice mail.

Rosen looked across the table at Sandy, who at the moment was nursing a shot of tequila with a beer chaser. Although her surface composure was relatively calm, her unfocused eyes indicated that she was still pretty traumatized.

Rosen caught Spinner longingly eyeing Sandy's drinks. "Spinner. Focus."

Spinner gave Rosen an irritated look and turned back to Sandy. "Did you see anyone hanging around the outside of your house? A car or something that seemed not to belong there?"

Sandy shook her head slowly, her attention snapping back to the present. "I don't think so. But I have to admit, I had a pretty bad case of tunnel vision when I stepped into that house."

"You're a better woman than me," said Rosen. "I wouldn't have gone in there for love nor money."

Spinner walked to the kitchen window and peered out. "I'll be right back." He went out the front door and walked up and down the street, looking for anyone or anything that looked suspicious. When he returned, he said, "It's clear. Doesn't look like you were followed, Sandy."

Paola asked, "What do we do now?"

"They're upping the game," said Spinner. "It's not safe here now."

"What've you heard from your contacts?" Rosen directed her query to Sandy.

Sandy took a sip of tequila and then a swallow of beer. "I contacted Rick Moody from Greenpeace today. I sent him a downloaded copy of the video. He's sending it out nationwide. I also contacted the Sea Shepherd Conservation Society but haven't gotten a response yet. I think they're down in the Southern Ocean right now chasing down the Japanese whaling fleet." She looked at Rosen. "Any luck with your contact in the State Department?"

"Yeah. It seems our esteemed friend Hiro Yoshimatsu has quite a long and sordid history. He's been meticulous about covering his tracks under the pretense of being a business tycoon. He's nearly bulletproof."

Paola asked, "Are you saying he can't be touched?"

No," said Emily. "No one is invincible. Politicians and giants of industry can all crumble and fall. We just need to know the right brick to remove to set it all in motion."

Spinner stood and again looked out the window. Rosen could see that he was agitated. "Where the hell are Raúl and Alex? When's the last time anyone talked to them?"

"I spoke with Alejandro this morning," said Sandy. "He called before his meeting with the Minister of Fisheries. He called again after he left. He was okay, except to tell me we'd all been suspended. Said he was going to Insurgentes to check on a few leads. I haven't been able to reach Raúl all day."

"This doesn't make me feel all warm and fuzzy inside," Spinner said. "I thought we were to be in contact every few hours."

Rosen shot Spinner an incredulous look. "And this is coming from a man who, up until an hour ago, didn't have a working cell phone."

Spinner held up his cell phone. "I am now officially plugged in."

Rosen rolled her eyes. "What we're going to have to do is indisputably tie Yoshimatsu to the hunt at San Mateo Cove and to the slaughter of part of the resident humpback population. There may not be enough international clout to put him behind bars, but at least he'll be exposed and marked for the bastard he is."

"Spinner, for God's sake!" Rosen said irritably. "Would you please sit down. You're making everyone nervous with your fidgeting."

Spinner sat down roughly. He had that feeling again. Like everything was about to go to shit very soon. He felt vulnerable here. Right now, he was probably at the top of the local federale's list for most undesirable person in the region. And here he sat, smack dab in the middle of La Paz. Hell yes, he was fidgety.

Sandy asked, "Anything turn up in your search for Macario?"

"He never made it to his gangbanger friends," Spinner said. "I'm basically back to square one."

"We need to keep following up on our leads," said Rosen. "Any chance the environmental groups can get people down here? If we can get some other bodies down here, we can cover a lot more ground."

Spinner shook his head. "It all sounds good on paper, but remember, this is Mexico. Depending on who's pulling the strings, civil disobedience down here can go south pretty quickly."

"That's right," Sandy agreed. "Remember what happened in Oaxaca a few years ago with the student protests?"

Jake's cell phone started ringing. The occupants of the room were instantly stunned into silence.

# 39

Spinner looked at his cell phone as if he didn't really believe he was getting a call. "Spinner."

He heard a click on the other end, then a deep voice with a slight Asian accent spoke. "Mr. Spinner, you are a very difficult man to contact."

Spinner hit the speaker button and set the phone on the table. "Who is this?"

"My name is not important. What is important is that we have something you want."

There was a sound that resembled feet being dragged across a floor followed by something being bumped against the phone. "Jake?" The voice was raspy and laden with terror.

All the blood drained from Jake's face. "Macario?" Rosen saw deep pain cross over his face like a black cloud moving across a desert landscape. "Are you all right?"

"I—I'm sorry, Jake. I should've listened to you."

"Don't worry, kid. I'm going to get you out of there."

"Jake, don't . . ."

The Asian voice came back on. "As you hear, Mr. Spinner, you have placed us in a most difficult position. You have cost us a great deal of money by disrupting our operation here."

Spinner thought the speaker's English was good. It bore only traces of an accent. He guessed the man on the other end of the line had learned his English in Britain, or perhaps one of the Commonwealth nations.

"Let the kid go. He's no threat to you. I know what you want."

"How very astute of you, Mr. Spinner. If you want to see your young friend alive again, you will come to Pier 23 in La Paz, tomorrow, 12:00 midnight."

Rosen started to open her mouth to protest. Spinner drew his hand across his own throat to silence her. His eyes were wild with wrath. Rosen sat back, biting her lip.

"What's my guarantee that you're going to let Macario go?"

"I am a man of my word. If you cooperate with us fully, he will be released unharmed. As you say, he poses no threat to us. We only want you."

Spinner was looking at the phone now. "Fair enough. I'll be there."

"Come alone. Do not make any attempts to contact the authorities. If you try to deceive us, Macario will suffer."

"I get the message. I'll be there. Alone. I don't care what you do to me. Just let Macario go."

"A life for a life, Jake. That is honorable." The phone went dead.

Spinner looked up. The faces around the table were registering various levels of shock and horror.

Rosen was the first to speak. "Are you out of your fucking mind?"

Spinner returned the phone to the front pocket of his shorts. "Yeah, I guess I am."

"Spinner, they're going to kill both of you!" Rosen said. "You can't save Macario. He put himself in this position when he didn't follow your instructions."

Spinner cast a hard glance at her, then turned away. "I fucked up. I should have been sober when we had a chance to get Macario and his folks out of Mexico. I have to meet with them. If there's the smallest chance that Macario can be released, then that's a chance I'm willing to gamble my life on."

"Jake, we need you here," said Sandy plaintively. "You're the only one who has any experience dealing with men like these."

"Stay the course," said Spinner. "You'll get a lot more accomplished by exposing these poachers to the media than I will trying to stop them by force."

Spinner stood, his knees creaking. "Look. We haven't heard from Alejandro and Raúl for several hours. I think you should be focusing your energies on contacting them. I'm going out for a walk."

He disappeared into the white light of midday. Sandy and Paola stared after him. Rosen, fuming, stood quickly and stomped out the door.

Outside, Spinner walked to the end of the street, then turned and walked toward the ocean. He stood in the sand staring into the west. Rosen caught up to him.

"You selfish son of a bitch!" She stared up into his craggy face. "It's all about you, isn't it?"

"I'm not having this conversation with you, Rosen."

She punched him hard in the chest, causing his eyes to go wide in surprise. For the briefest moment, she saw a flash of anger cross his face, then it was gone.

"You're not getting off that easy. You're a coward and you know it. So you fucked up. You were drunk and your friends died. You are not drunk now."

"They're going to kill him," Spinner said matter-of-factly. "You're right. He's probably a dead man already. But I have to try to see if I can get him out of there. I owe it to Gustavo and Marta."

She turned away from him. "What a waste. They're going to kill you both, Jake. And for what? Some misplaced sense of duty? Did you ever think you might be of more help to Macario and honor the memory of his parents by seeing this thing through? By exposing those who murdered your friends?"

"If there was any other way out of this, I'd take it. But who else? I can't call the authorities. They probably picked Macario up and delivered him all nice and neat to the Yakuza. Besides, there's not that much of me left to kill."

"You are one hard-headed bastard."

"If anyone can bring these assholes down, it's you, Rosen. Once I got my phone charged, I looked you up online. I've seen some of your work. Your words cut deeper than any knife or bullet. Contact your people and write your ass off."

Rosen turned to walk back to the house when she saw Sandy running toward them. As she drew closer, Spinner saw that her eyes were wild.

"It's Alejandro." Sandy could barely get the words out. "He's been in an accident."

As they walked briskly back toward the bungalow, Spinner fired questions at Sandy.

"Who called you?"

"A Dr. Mendoza. He works the emergency room at the hospital in Insurgentes. Alejandro asked him to call me before he passed out."

"What happened?"

"Before he lost consciousness, Alejandro told the doctor that someone forced him off the road."

"Shit. That means that someone knew that Alejandro was on that road. Do you know anything about who his contact is?"

"Only that they used to work together at the institute and went to graduate school together."

"They're tightening the noose. Sandy, how bad is he?"

Sandy stopped suddenly and stared straight ahead. "Oh, my God. We have to call his wife."

Jake stopped and grabbed her by the shoulders. "Sandy, I need you to focus right now. I need to know how bad his injuries are."

Her eyes fluttered, and she shook her head slightly as if to free herself from some horrible image. "The doc said he has a punctured lung, several broken ribs, a fractured clavicle, and a fractured lower right leg. He suffered a pneumothorax and a lot of lacerations to his face."

They fell in step once more and headed for Paola's casa. Sandy sat at the table, the cell phone in front of her. She looked stricken and her hands were shaking.

Spinner asked her, "Who brought him in?"

"The doctor said a family saw the wreck in the arroyo as they headed in the opposite direction. They phoned the hospital at Insurgentes, and an ambulance was dispatched."

Spinner ran both hands through his hair, then looked around the room, "Where the hell is Raúl?"

"He was supposed to check in over an hour ago," said Sandy. A look of horror passed over her face. "Do you think—?"

"No. Don't go there," said Jake. "Can you try and get him on the cell phone? We need to bring him in."

She swallowed hard and said, "Right away." She stepped away to make the call.

Spinner looked at Rosen. His face was like stone. "I need to borrow your car."

"Like hell you will. I'm driving."

"The hell you are. There's nothing those sons of bitches would like any better than to catch several of us together in the same place. Then it's really game over. I'm betting that whoever ran Alejandro off the road will want to come back and finish the job."

Rosen took a defiant stance. "Spinner, I'm not going to argue with you. You can ride in my car or else take a god damn bus. I'm going to Insurgentes with or without you."

"You have to stick to the plan. We don't need another loose cannon here. I want the three of you to go back to Raúl's and sit tight until I can get Alejandro out of there."

"This plan hasn't worked out so well up to now," Rosen said sharply. "We have one of our team in critical care at a hospital, you're going on a suicide mission tomorrow night and, so far, none of our efforts have done anything to deter these scumbags." Rosen shifted her weight forward. "Besides, two sets of eyes are always better than one."

"Oh, Christ." He knew he wasn't going to win his one. He could try and retrieve his truck, but that would take precious time. He needed to be on the road now.

Sandy held her cell phone out to him. "Jake, I have Raúl on the phone."

Spinner kept glaring at Rosen. "I need to speak to him." He walked over and took the cell from Sandy.

"Amigo, I need you to get back here pronto."

"What happened, Jake?"

"I think Alejandro got bushwhacked on his way to Insurgentes. If they find out he's still alive, my money says that they'll come back and finish the job. I'm leaving for Insurgentes as soon as we hang up."

"What do you need me to do?"

"I need you to take Sandy and Paola back to your ranch and lay low until I can get Alejandro out of there and safe again."

"What about Emily?" Raúl asked. "Where is she?"

Spinner glared at Rosen. "She's insisted on going with me."

"Jake, I think something big is about to go down. I spoke to a fisherman's wife who lives half a day up the coast. She told me that there's another dolphin hunt planned."

"When? Where?"

"She didn't know. Soon. Maybe next week or the week after."

"That's just great," said Jake. "They're planning another kill, and we're sitting on our thumbs here."

"The fisherman's wife is originally from Puerto Nacimiento. She's going to keep her eyes and ears open for us."

"Do you trust her?"

"I think the whalers killed her brother."

There was a brief yet heavy silence between them. "Get back here as soon as you can, Raúl. I need you to get the team to high ground."

"What are you going to do when you get to Insurgentes?"

"No clue. I'm making this shit up as I go."

"Buena suerte, Jake."

Spinner hung up. He turned to Sandy and Paola. "Pack only what you need. As soon as Raúl gets here, move out!"

Jake handed the cell phone back to Sandy, and went to the corner where his duffel bag lay against the wall. He scooped it up, then emptied the contents on the kitchen table. Rosen was surprised to see the array of weird and totally incongruous items that lay spread before them. A key ring with several keys attached, a military service ring, an assortment of medals and bars, dog tags, some underwear, tee shirts, and the item that Jake had been looking for, an extra magazine for his Beretta. He picked it up, counted the cartridges, then looked at Rosen.

"Fifteen rounds. We get in a firefight, it's gonna be over before it starts." He pocketed the magazine and put all of the items back into the duffel. Rosen kept watching his face. He glanced at her sheepishly, then went back to repacking the bag.

By the time Raúl arrived, Spinner was fit to be tied. He'd stood watch silently at the kitchen window. Rosen had tried to engage him in conversation, but when he turned his face toward her, she saw instantly that he was in a very dark place. He turned away and resumed his window vigil until he saw Raúl's truck pull up.

"Time to go, Rosen," he said irritably.

Raúl walked in, a look of deep concern on his weathered face. "Are you all right?" He embraced Sandy and then Paola.

"Okay." Sandy said, her voice rough. "It's been a hell of a day."

He pulled back. "Any more news of Alejandro?"

Sandy shook her head. "Just the doctor's call."

Spinner slung the duffel over his shoulder and walked toward the door. He caught Raúl's gaze. "We'll bring him back," Spinner said, without emotion.

Rosen grabbed her pack and followed. As she passed Sandy and Paola, they hugged her. "Be careful, Emily," Sandy said.

"I'll call you as soon as I know something." Rosen followed Spinner out the door.

They didn't speak for a long time. The day's events had spiraled into a maelstrom of tragedy and confusion. The Consortium's retaliation had been swift and well-orchestrated. Spinner and Rosen both knew that the whalers had seen the small band on the top of the cliff that fateful day at the cove. It wasn't a huge intellectual leap to place Sandy and Paola at the scene with Alejandro as well. As of yet, Raúl and Rosen were still relatively unknown entities. Spinner felt only slight relief that they'd find sanctuary at Raúl's ranchito in the mountains. Sooner or later, because of his inquiries up and down the Baja coast, Raúl's identity would be revealed.

"I think you should conduct your investigation from outside of Baja," Spinner said finally.

Rosen, who was lost in her own thoughts, snapped back, and turned her gaze toward Spinner. "What?"

"You have the footage. You can probably do more damage from the States than you can from here."

"Spinner, you heard what Raúl said. Those bastards are planning another hunt. I don't know about you, but the image of the last hunt is still festering in my brain. I'm not going anywhere."

"They're going to kill you and the others! Get out while you can."

"If you care so much for our welfare, why are you going to walk into the lion's den? Why don't you stick around and help us through this?"

Spinner rolled his eyes. "Here we go again."

"I don't even know why I bother talking to you," Rosen's voice cracked with emotion. "You blame yourself for your friend's death. Those murderers are going to kill you. You're on a suicide mission, and you don't know if either you or Macario is likely to survive." Rosen squinted, then strained her eyes to see ahead in the blinding late afternoon light.

He glared at her, then looked down at his hands. If any one of his former comrades from Special Forces had called him out like this, Spinner would have rearranged their faces. But here was this fiery woman, small in stature, but gargantuan in chutzpah, calling him out.

"You're lucky you're a woman. If you were a man, I'd . . . "

"Oh, please. Don't let that stop you. I'm sick to death of you macho jerks. The world would be a lot safer place if there wasn't so much damn testosterone floating around poisoning everything."

They drove on for a long time without speaking. They were in the mountains now, the road angling upward. After rounding several corners and dropping into a low area, they saw federal vehicles and a tow truck near the edge of an arroyo. They recognized Alejandro's 4Runner, or what was left of it. The front end had folded into the firewall like an accordion, and the windshield was shattered. The front suspension was bent, and one of the wheels was missing. Rosen began to slow down.

"Don't stop. Keep going. Don't turn around to look."

"Don't you think we should stop and see what happened?"

"We don't know who those federales work for. Besides, I got all the information I needed."

Rosen looked at him. "What was that?"

"I wouldn't have seen it if you hadn't slowed down. As we came off that curve, there were two sets of parallel burn tracks, then they converged, with one set going off to the right into the arroyo." He turned and looked at Rosen's face, which had gone ashen with the sudden realization.

"Someone ran Alejandro off the road." Spinner's face was stony. "These guys aren't going to quit until every one of us is silenced."

# 40

Alejandro thought he was having a very bad nightmare. He remembered seeing ghostly faces peering down at him. Someone was trying to take something from him but he couldn't stop him. His hands were restrained. He tried to speak, but his words were gibberish. The man looked down at him and smiled cruelly. He awoke to a crushing pain in his shoulder and leg. He tried to move, but could only cry out. He passed out from the pain. Later, when he regained consciousness, three people were standing over him, their faces grim. Their images were blurred, but they looked to be a family: a man, a woman and a little girl. Was he seeing himself, Carmen and Lili? A thought suddenly came to him. *Am I dead?*

Then the searing pain was back. Worse than that, Alejandro couldn't draw a breath. He felt as if his ribcage had collapsed. He heard voices. He heard an irritating buzzing sound. A moment later, he was able to breathe shallowly.

The next time he awoke, four people wearing white were carrying him up a hill. *Angels?* He tried to lift his head, but some force held him back. His arms and legs would not move, no matter how much he willed them.

In the ambulance, someone bent over his face and said they were going to give him something to help with the pain. He drifted into sleep, dreaming fitfully of his wife and daughter. They were in danger. He needed to let them know.

He could no longer distinguish the dream state from reality. The next time he opened his eyes, he was staring at a white ceiling with a very bright light. A face with a blue mask appeared in his field of vision. The man sounded very far away. Alejandro could barely make out the words he spoke. *"Is there someone you wish us to contact?"*

His lips were so parched he could barely form the words for fear his face would crack. When he spoke, the voice that came from his lips did not sound like his. With great effort he first spoke the names of his wife and daughter, then

Sandy Wainright. The doctor nodded and said he'd look up the numbers on Alejandro's cell phone.

A mask was placed over Alejandro's face. He heard the sound of oxygen being pumped into his lungs. He felt the heaviness in his chest lift just a little. He thought he heard the doctor say, "We're going to have to set that leg," and he made a vain attempt to lift his head and look at his throbbing right leg. His head felt like it weighed one-hundred pounds. He put his head back and winced at the accompanying pain in his clavicle.

He felt a sharp sensation in his arm, then waves of sleep washed over him. Within seconds he went to a place beyond dreams.

Spinner had been staring out across the desert for some time without speaking. He was trying to think of every possible scenario that they might encounter once they reached the hospital at Insurgentes. The worst-case scenario was that assassins from the Consortium had already been there. Most likely, Alejandro had been rushed to surgery to eliminate the pneumothorax and repair his fractured leg. He'd probably be in recovery for at least two hours before being moved to a room. Jake figured he could keep an eye on him until he could be safely moved. One thing Spinner felt with conviction was that the longer Alejandro stayed in that hospital, the less likely he'd be walking out alive.

"You've been awfully quiet, Spinner," Rosen said, bringing him back to the present. "Care to let me in on your thoughts?"

"Just weighing our options once we get to the hospital. And I don't like any of them."

"Are we going to try to spring him?"

"That depends on how bad he is. If they have the pneumothorax controlled, then how drugged he is will determine if we can move him. If the Consortium is as well connected as you say, then it won't be long before Alejandro has visitors. And I don't think they'll be bearing flowers and get-well cards."

"Do you really think they'll come after him?"

"They came after me. They believe Alejandro was there on the cliff above the cove. The one thing these guys don't like is loose ends."

"I just hope we're not too late."

"That makes two of us."

Rosen looked at her hands on the steering wheel. They were trembling slightly. She felt a certain degree of paranoia when she was attempting to break the story on Senator Donato. She always felt like she was being watched—and followed. But this was different. This time she felt like she and the others were being hunted. Hunted by a group of ruthless businessmen who valued profit over human life. She recalled instances of Americans in Third World countries who disappeared and were never heard from again. She now understood how easily that could happen.

"Rosen, you're going to choke the life out of that steering wheel." Spinner cast his gaze at Emily's white knuckles on the wheel. "You're not going to flip out on me now, are you?"

"No. I'm fine," Rosen lied. "I just wish we had a plan."

"A plan would be nice. At this point I'm open to suggestions."

"Spinner?"

Spinner lifted his chin toward Rosen. "Hmm?"

"Have you ever been scared? I mean truly terrified?"

He turned away and stared down the empty highway, breathing deeply. "Every damn day."

Darkness had fallen by the time they arrived at the hospital. It was small by U.S. standards, a single level building that had four adjoining wings. The emergency room was located at the center of the north side of the complex at one of the main entrances. The front was well lit with a circular drive and a covered canopy. Several *Cruz Roja* ambulances were parked out along the curb. Spinner made a mental note of the two attendants who were leaning against one of the ambulances smoking cigarettes.

"How about we do a little drive-by before we go in with guns blazing?"

Spinner pointed to his head. "You read my mind. Take a short spin through the parking lot first."

"What are you looking for?"

"In Puerto Jacinto, gunmen in a couple of black SUVs flattened my house, and I've seen them parked near Gustavo's house. My guess is they haven't upgraded to the next best car at the rental car place."

Emily drove up and down the half-full lot while Spinner noted the make and license plates of each car they passed. They continued to circle the facility.

"Anything look familiar?"

"I don't recognize any of them. But that doesn't mean a whole lot. My memory isn't what it used to be."

"Well, no black SUVs. That's a good sign. What's next?"

"I saw a service entrance near the back side of the hospital. I'm going to try and get Alejandro through those doors. Park the car near that door and keep watch while I get him. If anybody shows up who looks the least bit suspicious, call me."

Rosen looked him up and down. Her mouth turned downward. "Maybe I should go in and get Alejandro. You kind of —um—stand out."

"What are you talking about?"

"Your mode of dress, Spinner. You look like a street person. They're not going to let you past the lobby."

Spinner glared at her. "What? And they're going to let a short New York princess who parades around in retro Goth pass through? You're batshit crazy."

"Christ, Spinner, I can't believe I'm taking heat from a guy who, if he's feeling ambitious, changes his shirt once a week."

"No matter how much you sweet talk me, Rosen, I'm still going in. You can't lift Alejandro if he can't walk, which I suspect is the case."

Rosen paused. She stared angrily at him, then turned away. God, he could push her buttons. She had never met a man more exasperating than Jake Spinner.

"Look, Rosen, I need your help on this one. I don't want the Consortium thugs surprising me while I'm trying to get Alejandro out the door. With you as my early warning system, we have a chance to get him out."

Rosen sat staring straight ahead, her hands clenched tightly on the wheel. She could see in her peripheral vision that Spinner was looking intently at her.

"You're still an asshole."

"Duly noted. What time do you have?"

Rosen looked at her wristwatch. "It's 8:12."

Spinner quickly reset his own watch. "If I'm not back by 8:30, get your ass outa Dodge. If we're not here by then, we're probably not coming. Don't wait, don't come looking for us."

"So, you're going to just walk in there and hope you can locate Alejandro without raising suspicion?"

"Something like that. Okay, stop the car here." He held his hand out to Rosen. "Give me your cell phone." She gave him a sideways glance. "I'm going to program my number into your phone." Rosen reached into her backpack. She handed it to Spinner who quickly punched a series of numbers into the keypad, then handed it back to her.

"If you need to call me fast, hit number seven. If I don't pick up the first time, then I'm in the middle of something. Let me know where the bad guys are and what they're doing."

Emily nodded. "Got it. What if they cover the service door?"

Spinner looked irritated. "Then we go to Plan B."

"What's Plan B?"

"Hell, I don't even know what Plan A is. I'll get back to you on that one."

"God help us." Rosen shook her head.

"You've got until 8:30. After that, you turn into a pumpkin." Spinner stepped out into the night.

"Spinner!" Emily called out in a hoarse whisper.

He turned abruptly.

"Good luck!" He nodded, turned, and walked briskly toward the emergency room entrance.

He skirted the entrance, avoiding the bright lights and security cameras. There were enough shadows that he could bypass the two attendants without being seen. From behind a pillar, he was able to look into the lobby. The emergency room was half full. It was then that Jake Spinner decided to develop a case of severe respiratory distress.

He stood up to his full height and walked in. After a few feet he doubled over into the worst fit of coughing that he could summon. He stumbled toward the admissions desk, hacking and wheezing. The nurse, a young woman in her early twenties, looked up in alarm at the man who held one hand over his mouth while he clutched his chest with the other.

By holding his breath at first, then coughing violently, Spinner managed to turn the color of his face a deep crimson. With all the years of smoking and drinking, it wasn't all that hard for him to sound like he was drowning in his own phlegm. He tried to speak, but only half phrases escaped his lips.

The other patients were clearly disturbed by this gringo's symptoms. With each coughing spasm, many recoiled or moved to another seat, clearly fearful of contracting whatever malady the poor wretch had.

Jake made the universal sign for choking with his hands on his throat as he coughed. The panicked admissions clerk, not knowing what to do next, motioned for him to follow her. She led him to a curtained booth near the rear exit door of the ER. He made a mental note of the exit. As he pretended to hack up a giant hairball, the clerk excused herself and said she'd be back with the paperwork after the doctor had seen him.

Spinner kept on coughing until her footsteps had disappeared. He waited a minute and then peered cautiously through the curtain. There were several curtained-off booths with family members gathered around patients. No one was looking his way. Nearby was a rack where medical coats were hanging. Spinner stepped out of the booth, put one on, and disappeared through the rear door.

In the hallway, he began to cough, this time for real. His throat and vocal cords were raw from his recent charade. When he was finally able to draw a deep breath, he began walking down the hallway.

He had spent considerable time in hospitals over the years. While in Special Forces, he had become adept at familiarizing himself with environments at a glance. He instinctively knew that after admission through the ER, med-surg wasn't far off, and recovery was right around the corner from that. He came to an intersection in the hallway, looked at the signs and turned left.

Emily Rosen grew more anxious with each passing minute. Though it had only been five minutes since Spinner had entered the emergency department, it seemed to her that time had come to a screeching halt. She looked at her watch, then scanned the parking lot again. Nothing had changed since she'd begun her vigil. Other than a hospital employee leaving through an exit door and walking to her car, the parking lot was quiet.

She wanted to call Spinner, to see if he'd found Alejandro. He'd been specific. Don't call unless it was a dire emergency. Her mind wrestled with many emotions. Underlying everything was that dull fear that gnawed at her—that she and the others were on a fool's mission, and the only outcome was going to be a lonely death in a foreign country.

Her thoughts went back to Jake. Within twenty-four hours, he'd most likely be dead. He knew, as did everyone else, that the whalers wouldn't let Spinner or Macario remain alive. She wondered what he'd been like before his life had spiraled out of control. She wondered about the forces that had brought the motley group of scientists, a fisherman, a journalist, and an ex-pat together. She thought about her own journey to this time and place. A thought flashed through her mind that brought her clarity. She was meant to be here! She'd been dropped into the middle of a war zone, and she was the designated correspondent. It wasn't a war over politics or boundaries. It was a war against nature.

A large vehicle entered the parking lot. Emily sat up in her seat and took notice, her heart racing. It was a black SUV. It turned its beams down and cruised around slowly.

"Shit."

She strained her eyes but couldn't see any of the vehicle's occupants. She glanced a quick look over the steering wheel and noticed that there was a long silver streak down the length of the side panel and part of the front bumper was crumpled. She realized the black SUV had to be the one that ran Alejandro off the road. She hunkered down quickly as it passed in front of her. The vehicle moved on toward the emergency room entrance. Rosen hit the speed dial for Spinner's phone.

Spinner slipped past the nurse's station. He saw the twin doors and a sign in Spanish for "Recovery." Approaching footsteps caused him to duck around the corner and hide in a recessed alcove. A portly attendant was focused on a clipboard and failed to notice the large shadow plastered against the wall of the alcove.

After the sound of the nurse aide's footsteps had faded, Spinner came out of hiding and looked quickly in both directions before opening one of the double doors and slipping in.

Alejandro was in that space between sleeping and wakefulness. His visions varied from the four white walls of his recovery room to nightmare images of being pursued by hideous forms in the dark. Once the images of his wife and daughter beckoned to him from a distant shore. The sea that separated them was stained a deep crimson from dead and dying whales and dolphins.

Alejandro cried out, calling for Carmen and Lili to get away from this place. He tried to reach for them but was stopped by a wash of pain in his ribs.

"Alejandro?"

He heard his name being called. It seemed distant, like he was standing at the bottom of a very deep well. Was it Carmen? She sounded so far away. He struggled to open his eyes. He could barely make out a pinpoint of light above him. Ever so slowly, the light grew larger. Soon he could make out the shape of a face looking down at him. The face became larger, more in focus.

"Alejandro, it's me, Jake."

Alejandro's eyes opened wide and he looked wildly around the room. He looked back at Spinner. "Am I in hell?"

Spinner grinned. "Not quite yet."

Spinner's phone buzzed. Alejandro looked at him quizzically, trying to determine why Spinner was making such a strange sound. Spinner retrieved the phone from his pocket. "Talk to me."

"Jake, we have company. They're walking toward the front ER entrance right now."

"How many?"

"Three. Two big Asians and a Mexican in a federales uniform."

"Don't let them see you move. We're on our way." Spinner hung up. He looked at Alejandro whose face was a mask of pain and confusion.

"We need to go, Alejandro. Now. Can you move?"

Alejandro nodded. "My leg is pretty banged up."

"You ain't walking out of here." Spinner went to the back of the room and returned seconds later with a wheelchair. With great effort, he was able to assist

Alejandro from the bed and lower him into the wheelchair. He unhooked the IV from the stand and placed the bag in Alejandro's lap. He spun out the footrest and placed Alejandro's broken leg on it.

Alejandro reached up and grabbed Spinner's biceps with his good arm. "Jake, they got my laptop." His face was a mask of pain. "They have the full video and the original humpback data. I have just put you and everyone else in grave danger."

"Not now, Alex. Hang on. We're going for a ride."

He rolled the wheelchair to the door, stepped out, checked the hallway quickly, then moved Alejandro toward the back door of the hospital. Spinner walked quickly, checking over his shoulder every few seconds.

They came to an intersection and Spinner skidded to a stop, temporarily disoriented. With Alejandro staring at him wide-eyed, Spinner looked hastily down each of the corridors.

"That one, I think," Alejandro pointed to the corridor on the right.

Spinner looked back and forth between the two corridors, trying to visualize how the hospital had looked from the outside. "You think?"

"Better than staying here."

"Good point." Spinner turned the wheelchair down the right corridor.

The three men approached the front desk, the federale in the lead. He inquired about the accident victim who'd been brought in several hours ago. When the nurse asked the nature of their business and wanted to see identification, the federale got angry.

"He is a suspect in a criminal investigation. Tell us where he is or I'll have you relieved from your position!"

The young clerk looked around nervously, then said, "He's in Recovery. Section B, Room 3."

One of the Asians demanded, "Which way?"

The nurse pointed through the ER doors. "Through the back door and to the left. Right at the next corridor."

Quickly the men pushed through the large doors and hurried into the hospital.

Spinner located a door that had a red exit sign above it. He pushed Alejandro toward it and glanced behind him. They were coming fast. He could feel it.

When he opened the door, he felt a blast of humid air against his face. Spinner was looking at an empty parking lot. A lone yellow light illuminated the back lot. He looked at his watch. It was 8:31. Rosen was nowhere to be seen.

"Shit!" Spinner looked around, his eyes wild. Had they gone to the wrong exit? He thought he heard a commotion coming from somewhere in the hospital, angry voices shouting orders.

Just then there was a squeal of tires, and blinding lights appeared from around the corner as Rosen's car careened toward Spinner and Alejandro.

"I think this might be our ride," Spinner said.

Rosen's car came to a screeching halt. Spinner flung open the back door.

"Spinner, you idiot! Wrong door!"

"Aw, crap. Not my fault!"

"Don't look at me," said Alejandro drowsily. "I just had surgery."

Alejandro cried out in pain as Spinner lifted him from the wheelchair and set him in the back seat of Rosen's rental car. He guided his injured leg in and closed the door after placing the IV bag next to Alejandro. "Hold that bag overhead for a minute until I get in."

"Let's go! Let's go!"

Spinner ran around to the passenger side and slid into the seat. "Like a bat out of hell, Rosen."

She punched the accelerator, and the rental car's tires screamed as they struggled to find purchase on the asphalt. The tires smoked as the car jettisoned into the night.

They drove for ten minutes, Rosen constantly checking the rearview mirror for approaching lights. She checked the speedometer. Seventy miles per hour. On this road, at night, anything faster would be suicide. "Do you think we gave them the slip?" Rosen asked.

"They were right on our ass," said Spinner. He was half-turned in his seat, holding Alejandro's IV bag suspended over his head, while gazing at the road behind them. "They're coming."

"I can't believe you went to the wrong door, Spinner. I thought you Special Forces guys were infallible."

"So, shoot me."

"I'm not going to have to." Rosen looked in the rearview mirror at Alejandro. "Alex, how're you holding up?"

"Surprisingly well. My leg doesn't hurt too bad. But it still hurts to take a deep breath."

"You're not going to be a happy camper when that IV drip runs out," said Spinner. "Right now, the morphine in that bag is keeping your pain at bay. We're going to need to get something to carry you over."

Worried, Rosen asked, "What's next, Jake?"

"There's a pullout after a bridge a couple of miles ahead that I saw on the way in. It goes under the highway. Pull the car under and shut it down. Let's see if we have company."

"Why," asked an exasperated Rosen, "would we want to wait for them to catch up with us?" .

"Because I'd rather have them speeding in front of us trying to catch a phantom than to slowly close the gap between us and ride right up our ass."

"I think this is a very bad idea."

"Trust me. I've done this stuff before."

"That doesn't make me feel better."

Moments later, they crossed a concrete bridge, and Rosen slowed the car.

"There's the turn off," said Spinner. "On the left."

The road dropped quickly, and Rosen found herself bumping over large stones at a twenty-five-degree angle while cat claw acacia scraped across the body of the rental car. Alejandro cried out in pain several times as the rental car lurched over rocks sticking up in the road.

"Sorry! Sorry, Alex," said Emily.

"No worries," Alejandro said through gritted teeth.

The car's oil pan scraped across a large boulder in the middle of the track. Rosen almost lost control, barely avoiding a collision with an elephant tree.

"There goes my deposit," said Rosen.

"Just a little desert pin-striping," said Spinner. "Now you'll blend in with the rest of the vehicles down here."

At the bottom, Rosen found a stand of palo blanco trees and parked between the ghostly white trunks, still giving them a view of the road above them. She shut off the engine and killed the lights. They sat in silence in the humid night air. The only sound was insects buzzing outside the car.

"What if they see us down here? We'll be sitting ducks."

"I'm counting on them being focused on the road ahead. I don't figure they'll think we doubled back on them."

"That's a big—," Rosen began, but Spinner shushed her.

"Car's coming."

Emily drew in a deep breath and held it. The sound of the approaching vehicle grew louder. Soon the bridge was illuminated from the distant lights of an approaching vehicle.

The black SUV passed overhead quickly. Spinner guessed it was going well over seventy-five miles per hour. On this road at night, there was a good chance that these assholes could fly off a ledge anywhere up ahead, but he doubted the universe would be that benevolent.

"Let's give them a little space," said Spinner.

"How long?"

"Give it fifteen, maybe twenty should do it."

After what seemed an eternity, Spinner looked up. "Okay, let's go."

After some precarious moves to get the car turned around, Emily pointed the vehicle up the rocky slope and soon crested onto the turnoff. She looked ahead and pulled onto the highway.

"Looking good," said Spinner.

As they drove down the road toward La Paz, Rosen looked over at Spinner, who still held the IV bag over Alejandro. The young biologist had drifted off into a dead sleep.

"I had my doubts, Spinner. But you did it. It worked."

"Hell, even a blind squirrel finds a few acorns occasionally. We're not home yet."

# 41

By midnight, they arrived at the ranch. Raúl and the others were waiting for them. Spinner had called ahead and told them to be ready for Alejandro.

"He's going to need pain killers," Spinner had told Raúl on the cell. "He's down to the dregs of his morphine drip. I don't think I can make it into La Paz in time and hit up Alberto for some black market Oxycontin."

"Don't worry, Jake. I have mi esposa working on that right now."

Alejandro was in and out of consciousness, the net result of the morphine and the aftereffects of the anesthesia.

By the time Rosen pulled up, Sandy, Paola, and Raúl were standing in front of the house, looking anxious. She had barely stopped when Spinner flew out of the passenger's seat and ripped open the rear door of the rental car.

"Give me a hand here! Raúl, bring me a chair!"

Raúl hurried inside. Spinner got in the back seat to support Alejandro's back. Sandy could see the distress in her mentor and friend's face. Raúl returned with one of the chairs from the kitchen table.

"I'm going to help slide him into the chair," said Spinner. "Raúl, support his broken leg. Sandy, Paola, stand by if he needs it."

Alejandro was now long-sitting on the rear seat with Jake supporting him from behind.

"On the count of three," said Spinner. "One . . . two . . . three!" Alejandro cried out as Spinner and the others lifted and pulled him to the end of the seat.

"Sorry, Alex," said Spinner. "One more move and we'll have you in the chair."

Alejandro waved them off. "It's okay. Do what you have to do."

"One more time," Spinner braced a foot on the floor of the rental car. "On three. One . . . two . . . three!" He felt the strain in his low back as he lifted the researcher. Alejandro sucked in his breath to keep from screaming. They moved Alejandro onto the kitchen chair with no small amount of jostling.

"Okay, okay," said Spinner breathlessly. "Raúl, you and I on either side of the chair. Sandy and Paola, support his legs."

Moments later, Alejandro was sitting in Guadalupe Campos Mora's kitchen. She and her daughter were a whirlwind of activity, gathering pillows for support and trying to make him comfortable.

Sandy hugged Alejandro. Alejandro responded by putting his arm weakly around her and patting her on the back. Paola joined in. All three seemed frozen in time as they just held each other.

Guadalupe approached Alejandro with a mug of foul-smelling fluid. "Drink this," she said. "It will lessen the pain in your legs and ribs."

Alejandro made a face as the mug passed beneath his nostrils. He looked beseechingly at her, then back at the rest of the group. He forced a wan smile. "Well, bottoms up." He threw back the liquid and immediately went into the dry heaves.

"Hold it down, Alejandro," said Guadalupe, as she massaged between his shoulder blades until he was able to regain his composure.

"Whatever she gives you, you drink it," said Spinner. "Take it from me. She's a *curandera*."

Guadalupe beamed. Raúl went to the refrigerator and brought out three bottles of Pacífico. He handed one to Rosen and the other to Spinner. They clinked bottles and Spinner took a long pull. He closed his eyes as the cold beer flowed down his throat. Rosen looked at him and was about to say something but checked herself.

"That," said Spinner wiping his mouth on his sleeve, "was just about the best beer I've ever had."

Raúl asked, "So they came to finish the job?"

Spinner nodded. "Two Asians and a Mexican dressed like a federale. My guess: another Zeta assassin. Or these guys have at least one branch of the police in their pockets."

"Did they see you leave?"

Spinner took another swig from the bottle. "I don't think so. We were out of the parking lot before they came out the door. That is unless they copied down license plate numbers as they rolled through the parking lot." He looked at Emily.

"I don't think so," she said somewhat unconvincingly. "They were on the move and didn't stop at any of the parked vehicles. The windows were pretty much blacked out so I couldn't see what was going on."

"Unless they were shooting videos on their iPhones to check on later."

"Oh, crap! Do you think?" Emily looked worried.

"Try to keep a low profile with that car," said Spinner. "If you need to go somewhere, use Raúl's or Sandy's."

"We must get Alejandro to bed," said Guadalupe. "He must sleep now."

"I'm okay, I think—for now," said Alejandro, as he painfully attempted to shift his weight on the chair. "I think we need to talk about what to do next."

"What you're going to do next," Sandy said sternly, "is to follow Guadalupe's orders to the letter. To bed with you."

Alejandro was about to protest, but Spinner and Raúl had already taken their cues and lifted the chair to move Alejandro to the children's bedroom. As they settled him on the bed, Rosen appeared at the bedroom door.

"Thank you," Alejandro sounded sleepy. "I am so sorry to have put you all in so much danger."

"Not your fault, Alex," said Spinner.

"Get some sleep, Alex," said Emily. "We need you back with the group as soon as you're up to it."

Alejandro closed his eyes. "I lost my cell phone. Can someone please call Carmen and Lili for me and let them know that I'm all right?"

"I'll do you one better," said Emily. "When you wake up, I'll give you my phone and you can call them yourself."

Alejandro nodded and forced a smile. "Thanks. That would be good."

They turned the light off and went back to the kitchen. By now Jorge was up, awakened by the din of activity. Alisa assisted Guadalupe in preparing plates of food for everyone.

When they were seated at the table, Rosen addressed the group. "They got Alejandro's laptop."

"Oh, my God," said Paola. "That means they have the original humpback data and the unedited video!"

Rosen nodded.

"They're going to be able to ID all of us," said Sandy.

"The stakes just got a lot higher," said Spinner. "Now they know who they're up against."

Paola asked, "What are we going to do?"

"The smart thing would be to get everyone across the border. They'll have all your faces plastered on every television, newspaper, and police station in Baja," said Spinner. "But I have a feeling you're not going to do the smart thing."

"Spinner, we can't just let them get away with this!" Sandy said hotly. "They damn near killed Alejandro!"

"We have to make sure this video goes public," said Emily.

Exasperated, Spinner turned to Raúl. "Can you please talk to these women. I guess my voice carries at a frequency they can't hear."

"Oh, we can hear you just fine, Spinner," said Rosen. "Yeah, so they upped the ante. We're not folding."

Raúl shrugged. "There are some arguments you just can't win, Jake."

Spinner grumbled something under his breath and took a large bite of chorizo.

While they ate, Raúl filled them in on the whalers' plans for the next dolphin and whale drive. He told them about Fernando and Alma Quintín and said that Alma would be relaying any information from the village.

Between bites, Spinner asked, "Do you trust her?"

"More than I trust her husband. He has a reputation for illegal fishing. He takes fish in the off-season. She has a brother who worked for the whalers. The brother hasn't been heard from for two weeks now. She thinks he might be dead."

Spinner stopped chewing for a moment and stared at Raúl. "They can't keep disappearing people and not expect the villagers to rise up and expose their operation."

"Several people flee Puerto Nacimiento each week," said Raúl.

"Those are the people we need to talk to. If you could find them." Spinner waved a fork at Sandy and Paola. "If we can get a date for that next hunt, can you contact your friends at—what?"

Sandy said, "Sea Shepherd Society?"

"Yeah. Those guys aren't afraid to run their boats between the whales and the whalers. If Alma can give us a date and location, we can send the coordinates."

Rosen asked, "Can they legally enter Mexican waters?"

"Never stopped them before," said Sandy.

Spinner asked, "Any response on the video?"

"Nothing yet," said Sandy. "We should be hearing something today. I'll be checking my sources in a few hours."

"I'll call my sources as well," said Emily. "If the video goes viral, it could do one of two things. It will make the whalers go away or they may go deeper with their operation and move to another area of the Gulf."

"Find the whales, you'll find the whalers," said Spinner.

When the children had been put to bed in their parent's room, Guadalupe finished up the kitchen cleanup. Spinner and Raúl were the last two seated at the table. Guadalupe kissed her husband on the forehead and bade them goodnight.

Raúl's face was lined with worry. "Jake, do you know what you're going to do when you meet with the whalers?"

"I haven't a clue. More than likely, they'll take me to where Macario is and then kill us both. From what I could gather, these guys like spectacle. They're going to make an example of us."

Raúl looked at his weatherworn hands, struggling for something to say. "Are you sure there is nothing that we can do to help you and Macario?"

"They said I was to come alone." Spinner sat back and regarded the Mexican fisherman. "Don't be going all soft on me, Raúl. If it's any consolation, the best part of me died a long time ago. My body just hasn't gotten that memo yet."

"You getting killed serves no purpose at all."

"Don't count me dead yet," said Spinner, a bitter smile crossing his lips. "I've been in a lot worse situations than this. At the very least, I might be able to disrupt their operations—if only for a little while—until you and the others can expose these bastards. If I get real lucky, maybe I can find a way to get both of us out of there."

"I think you're a very brave man," Raúl said. "But you're also muy loco."

"I think one begets the other. Raúl, I need you to do me a favor," He got up and went to the small table near the phone and retrieved a slip of paper and a pencil. He jotted down a number and slid it across to Raúl.

"He's a friend," continued Spinner. "Name's Castellano. Lives on the mainland. If things get real bad, call him. Give him a day or two. Tell him you're a friend of mine, and you need exit visas. Everyone. You, Guadalupe, the kids, and those four whale warriors. Castellano will help you all get the hell out of here."

"Jake, I don't think I can—"

"Do this for me, amigo. If it goes to hell tonight, there's nothing stopping those guys from putting a bullet in your heads and feeding you to the fish. I need to know that you'll take care of this." Spinner looked directly at Raúl. His gaze was unsettling.

Raúl nodded. "I'll take care of it, Jake."

Emily Rosen awoke from a fitful sleep. She'd been dreaming. In the dream, she was being chased down stark, white hospital corridors by some unknown menace. Every turn she took was a wrong one. Every door she went through she thought would be her last. She tried to turn over and go back to sleep, but her mind began to race.

So far, attempts had been made on the lives of every member of their group. Spinner had already survived three attempts on his life. Alejandro had narrowly escaped being killed in a car wreck, and if it hadn't been for Spinner, he would've been one of those names on a police blotter. Sandy's house had been ransacked. They had all taken fire at San Mateo Cove.

She had suppressed her fear and anxiety throughout the entire ordeal. When she tried to sleep, all of the angst came back in a flood. She swung her legs out and sat on the edge of the bed for several minutes, rubbing her eyes and trying to make some sense of the insanity into which they'd been hurled.

She made a mental note of the things she had to do today. Her contact, Bertrand Hollis, needed to be pushed. She constantly worried about her cell phone charge. The video needed to be posted today. That needed to be done in La Paz. She dreaded the idea of going back to La Paz. Too easy to be seen there.

Rosen got up from her single bed in the bunkhouse and walked to the window. The first gray light of morning was creeping in through the faded print curtains.

She opened the window and was moved by the view of the corral with mountains veiled in a deep purple haze to the east. A corona of light appeared behind the jagged peaks. Movement near the corral diverted her attention. Someone was sitting at the corral, his back to her, legs propped up on a wooden chair. She caught the brief flare of a cigarette and instantly knew who it was.

She was still frustrated with Spinner for his decision to meet with the whalers. She understood why he'd made the decision but didn't want him to die. The whalers were using Macario for bait. Once they had Spinner, they would kill Macario and undoubtedly get rid of the bothersome American.

Underneath his somewhat crude and minimally hygienic exterior, she knew he had principles. She had seen glimpses of his damaged soul during their times in the car and during interactions with Raúl's family.

She stopped herself, shaking her head violently, as if to rid herself of some horrid nightmare. *Jesus, Rosen. You're not falling for him! He's a train wreck. And besides that, come this time tomorrow, he'll most likely be dead.*

She knew that going back to sleep was out of the question. Her mind was going a million miles an hour. She dressed and grabbed a blanket from the bed, and walked outside into the chill air.

"Couldn't sleep either?" Spinner said, before Rosen had even arrived at the corral.

"How did you know it was me?"

"I've been hanging around you for a while, Rosen. It wasn't hard to learn the cadence of your footsteps. Did you know that you land a little flat-footed on your right? There's a bit of a slap as your foot hits the ground."

Rosen looked down at her foot. "I don't slap my foot when I walk!"

Spinner said, "Look at the heel of your right shoe. It wears more than the heel on the left."

Rosen stopped short. "How did you know that?"

"In my former line of work, you learned these things. If you didn't, you'd end up with your throat cut or a bullet to the back of your brain."

"Couldn't shut my mind down."

Spinner took his feet off the chair and moved it next to him. "Have a seat. In a few minutes, they'll be the best seats in the house."

She sat in the chair and gazed into the east. The sky was a deepening crimson behind the Sierra de la Giganta mountain range. A cool breeze blew out of the east. She felt a chill and pulled the blanket around her shoulders.

"It's beautiful."

"Red sky at morning, sailors take warning."

Rosen looked at him. "What does that mean?"

"Old mariner's saying. Red sky at dawn means there's a storm coming."

They sat quietly for a while, each lost in their own thoughts. Rosen suddenly realized she was comfortable with that; just the act of sitting here with someone watching a beautiful Mexican sunrise unfold felt . . . good.

"I never did thank you for what you did back at the restaurant a few days ago. It doesn't happen often, but I was at a loss for words when Lahane approached me. He was trying to get me on his boat. He had tried to pick me up one night when I first got here. It was my own fault. He was throwing out more bullshit than a stockyard, and I jumped in and fed him back more. When I called him on it, he said some pretty ugly things. Under normal circumstances, I wouldn't give a rat's ass what a guy like Lahane's opinion was, but . . . well, let's just say my life was at a pretty low ebb on more than one front."

Spinner looked straight ahead while she was speaking. When she finished, he looked at her intently, then turned his gaze back to the sky, which was now lit up in hues of peach, mauve, and eggshell blue.

"Well, aren't you going to say something?"

"There are Lahanes all over the planet. They get off on diminishing other people because their lives are so pointless and pathetic. They have a gift though. They can smell people at weak moments. That's when they strike."

"So you think I looked vulnerable?"

Now Spinner looked directly at her. "You're a beautiful woman, Emily. You try to hide it. Your mode of dress, your hard, exterior shell—they're all part of your disguise."

"Spinner, that's not true!"

He held up his hand. "You know it's true. I know this to be true because you and I are cut from the same cloth. We're both running from something."

"You're full of shit, Spinner."

"Am I? Come on, Rosen. I'd bet good money that at one time you probably turned every head in a room. Something happened to you to make you go all Goth. Whatever that guy did to you, fuck him. He's worse off for leaving you."

"Spinner, why the hell do you think it was a guy?"

"It usually is something like that. I saw you at the restaurant. I saw how you looked at couples sitting at tables. At one time, you lived in that world, too."

She faced ahead, biting her lip. "You know, it's amazing. Every time I sit down and talk to you, you just end up pissing me off."

"Like I said, we all have a gift. That's mine."

Rosen suddenly smirked. "There's got to be some universal irony out there. I'm sitting here getting fashion advice from a guy who looks like a refugee from a Jimmy Buffet concert." She burst out laughing. Spinner stared at her, offended, then broke into a hearty laugh.

The sun's rays crept over the peaks, bathing them in a golden light. Desert animals began stirring; ravens called from the mesquite bosque. A Gila woodpecker sounded off somewhere behind the house. One by one, the goats began bleating and a rooster crowed. Rosen looked around her, absorbing all the sights, sounds, and smells of the desert morning.

"Spinner, I just wanted you to know. I understand why you feel compelled to try to save Macario. I think it is amazingly brave and devoted to try to get him back, despite the odds. But we wanted to let you know that we care about your well-being."

Spinner grinned. "We?"

"Yes, we. All of us. We need your guidance. You know how to deal with these people."

"You guys don't need me. You have everything you need to burn these murdering bastards good. You just have to watch your backs."

"Would it make any difference if I asked you to stay?"

Spinner regarded her for a moment. "In another time, another place, I'd say yes. But I have to square the ledger for my friends. I know you all think I'm nuts. But they were about the only family I had. I owe Macario that much."

# 42

"Damn it! I can't get a signal," Rosen said. She held her cell phone in her hand as she walked to the kitchen table where the rest of the group was gathered.

"Neither could I," said Sandy. "What are we going to do? We need Wi-Fi."

Spinner looked at Raúl. "How far to the nearest internet connection?"

"Insurgentes."

Spinner sighed. "I don't want to risk going back to Insurgentes or La Paz. After last night, there's going to be some pissed off bad guys on the road."

Sandy said, "We don't have any options."

"We'll just have to be careful," said Rosen.

Paola nodded. "Let's do this."

Spinner turned to Raúl. "Can I borrow your truck?"

"I'll drive."

Spinner made a face. "What is it with you guys? Doesn't anybody trust me with their vehicle?"

Everyone spoke in unison, "No!"

"Two sets of eyes are better than one." Raúl, smirked. "Besides, Lupe and the children are taking good care of Alejandro. I'm not needed around here."

"Your goats need tending."

"No, they pretty much take care of themselves, Jake."

"Fine. We'll all just pack into your truck like it's Cinco de Mayo. Christ on a bike. You people don't listen to anyone, do you?"

"Look who's talking." Rosen was grinning. "Get over it, Spinner. We're all going."

Raúl perked up. "I know of a great taco stand in Insurgentes. Their *adobado* tacos—*muy sabrosos.*"

Spinner shrugged. "Good place for a last meal. Insurgentes it is."

"Hey! I want to go too!" A voice came from the back bedroom.

They all moved toward the room where Alejandro sat propped up in the bed. The three women rushed in and gathered around the bed. Raúl and Spinner stayed at the entrance and leaned in to listen. Alejandro looked better today than he had the night before, but he still looked frightful. His eye sockets were purple, and there was a crust of dried blood on his forehead. A deep purplish bruise went from his neck, across his chest and down his arm. The toes of his right foot were deep red. They looked like tiny sausages.

"You're not going anywhere," chided Sandy. "Your job, whether you accept it or not, is to heal."

"I need to contact Carmen and Lili." A look of deep concern etched across Alejandro's face. "They'll be worried about me. They might even try to return."

"I'll call them for you, Alex." Sandy took his good hand. "We'll take care of it. I promise. As soon as we get the phones charged up, we'll call Carmen and Lili."

Rosen asked him, "How're you feeling today?"

"Alive," replied Alejandro. "Anything after that would be conjecture."

Sandy said, "Is there anyone you want us to contact besides your wife and daughter?"

"I never was able to connect with Victor Esposito. Maybe you can call him too."

"How well do you know this Esposito?" Spinner asked.

"I would trust him with my life. Please let him know I'm fine," Alejandro said. "I feel as if I've let you all down. Now I can't even hold up my end."

"This room is now central command," said Sandy. "And you're in charge. You'll orchestrate all of our actions from here. What we need right now is your brain, Alejandro."

Alejandro nodded reluctantly. "Be careful out there."

Sandy smiled. "Alex, we'll be back before you know it. And we'll make the call to Carmen and Lili."

"Please don't tell her how bad I am. She'll try to come back here. I don't want them anywhere near this place. It's too dangerous."

"I'll spin it as best I can."

They filed out of the bedroom and went out to Raúl's truck. Even though it had an extended cab, it was still going to be a very cramped ride.

"Where's Raúl?" Spinner asked.

"He said he had to get something," Paola said, "and he'd be right back."

Spinner turned to see Raúl approach, carrying something covered in an old Mexican blanket. "What's that?"

"Just in case we run into any trouble."

"Let's see it."

Raúl pulled away the blanket, revealing an old rifle. Spinner studied it.

"That's a Krag-Jørgensen 30-40 and, if I'm not mistaken, it's one of the original 1895 models. My friend Castellano would pay a lot of money for that piece."

"This gun has been in my family for four generations," Raúl said proudly. "My great-grandfather fought alongside Pancho Villa in the Revolution with this rifle. He taught my grandfather to shoot, who, in turn, taught my father, who then taught me."

"It's a beauty. Amazingly well preserved." Jake gave Raúl a wry smile. "Problem is the bad guys have automatic weapons. Question is, can you hit anything with it?"

Raúl returned the smile. "Do you see the string of tin cans hanging between the two palo blanco trees on the hill behind me?"

Spinner squinted into the sun. "You mean the two trees that are about seventy-five yards from here on top of that hill?"

Raúl dropped the blanket, turned quickly and brought the rifle up to his shoulder. He squeezed off four quick shots, making each of the cans on the line jump.

Spinner looked back at him, grinning. "Remind me to never piss you off."

"Jesus Christ," said Rosen. "I've gone back to Deadwood. Can we please get in the truck before I suffocate from testosterone poisoning?"

On the drive to Insurgentes, the atmosphere inside the truck was somber. There was some small talk between the women, mostly in an attempt to distract themselves from the inevitability of Spinner leaving the group to most likely end up dead.

Finally, it was Paola who addressed the elephant in the truck. "Jake, I know you have to do this because he is the son of your friends, and you feel you let them down. But isn't there some other way? Isn't there someone out there who you can turn to for help? Can't we do something to help?"

"I don't like this anymore than any of you. And no, there is no one else who can go in my place. The cavalry isn't coming over the horizon at the last minute to save the day. That's the way it is."

Paola turned to Raúl. "Raúl, I want you to hit Spinner over the head with your gun when he's not looking. Then we can tie him up until this thing blows over."

"That wouldn't do any good. It would probably just break the gun."

Spinner forced a half smile. "I appreciate the sentiment—I think."

"Don't waste your breath." Rosen sounded bitter. "I already tried to talk some sense into him. You'd get a better response from one of Raúl's goats."

"With him gone and Alejandro all banged up," Sandy said, "how are we going to keep the Consortium off our backs?"

"Hey! I'm still here, in case you haven't noticed," Spinner said. "Besides, why is everyone already counting me dead? Did it ever occur to you that I might have a plan?"

"I truly doubt that," Emily countered. She turned toward Spinner. "Okay, Sergeant York, let's hear it."

Spinner bit his lip, a series of wrinkles crossing his tanned forehead. "It's a work in process. I haven't worked out all the minutiae just yet."

"You don't really have a plan, do you, Jake?"

He scowled. "Well, not exactly. But do you think for a moment I'm going to lie down and let those pendejos take Macario and me down without a fight? I appreciate what you guys are trying to do for me. The truth of the matter is, if I don't go, that kid is going to die all by himself, and I might as well put a gun in my mouth and pull the trigger. At least this way, Macario might have a slim chance."

"This is insane," said Rosen.

When they reached Insurgentes, they charged cell phones at the internet cafe. Sandy contacted Alejandro's wife and spent several anxious minutes trying to calm Carmen, who was nearly frantic when she found out Alejandro had been injured. Sandy reassured Carmen that Alejandro would call her later when there was a signal back at the ranchito.

# 43

Ako Kanamura took out his cell phone and hit speed dial. It rang once, and Yoshimatsu picked up.

"Yes?"

"I have Cabrillo's laptop, Hiro-san, and I have been going over the video. It is a different version than the one that Cabrillo gave Figueroa."

"How so?"

"The video Figueroa received was edited. This one was not. This one has audio. The other did not. I have identified four other voices besides Cabrillo's. Two are likely to be the female researchers. There is a male voice with a Mexican accent and another woman's voice. She has an accent common to the eastern seaboard of the United States. Possibly New York or Massachusetts."

"What else?"

"Jake Spinner is also on the video. It shows him breaking up the hunt, and there is a final shot of him driving his boat away. Spinner could have been working with the group."

"Do we have reason to believe they have left the area?"

"We don't know yet. Perhaps this would be a good time to have Director Figueroa place some of his operatives at the harbor and at the airport."

"What about Cabrillo?" Yoshimatsu's voice was acidic.

"He was left for dead on the highway by one of my men and one of the federal police on loan from Figueroa. A crowd was gathering around the crash, so they could not finish the job. Cabrillo was taken to the hospital in Insurgentes and underwent surgery. By the time my agents got there, someone had taken him from the hospital."

There was a moment of heavy silence on the other end of the phone. "Was it Spinner?"

"When we interrogated the hospital staff, several employees said they remembered a tall American in a Hawaiian shirt who had entered the Emergency Room. Then he disappeared. By the time our team got there, Cabrillo was gone."

"What about Cabrillo's family?"

"They left on a plane for Mexico City three days ago. We lost their trail there."

Yoshimatsu swore. "Tonight, when Spinner comes in, I will be there. I want you to question him in the manner that only you can. I will find out where the rest of them are hiding. If we can get to Cabrillo's family, Cabrillo will surface quickly. When are you going to contact Spinner?"

"I will contact him shortly with the instructions," said Kanamura.

"Make sure there are no mistakes. Your life depends on it."

"Before tonight is over, Hiro-san, Jake Spinner will sing like a bird. He will reveal more than he ever thought he knew."

"That is, if he shows up."

"Oh, he will be there. He thinks he is about to give his life for the son of his best friend," Kanamura said.

"I want this episode put to rest. I want no more interference before and up to the next scheduled hunt. I want those responsible for the video and the incident at the cove to be taken care of, once and for all."

"One more thing, Hiro-san. You were right about the data. The researchers altered the data regarding the humpbacks. I have the original data from Cabrillo's computer."

Hirokan Yoshimatsu hung up and placed the cell phone on the table in front of him. He stared out at the turquoise waters of the Gulf of California from his penthouse suite.

He would be glad when this nasty business was concluded in the next few weeks. He was astounded and dismayed at the absolute incompetence of the locals in the handling of sensitive matters. He was beginning to doubt Figueroa's competence. The disposal of Alejandro Cabrillo should have been simple and final. Back in Tokyo, the dispatch of an enemy was done quickly, silently, and efficiently.

Susan walked onto the patio carrying a phone on a tray with a cold Bohemia beer and a frosted glass. "Hiro-san, it's the director of the Beijing Aquarium. He wants to know if you'll be able to deliver the bottlenose dolphins he had requested earlier. Do you want to take the call?"

Yoshimatsu motioned for the phone and put it to is ear. "Hello, Mr. Li. It is good to hear from you."

"Honorable Mr. Yoshimatsu, thank you for taking my call. I was wondering if you had been able to procure the four young bottlenose dolphins we had requested. Our original date was two weeks ago and we were beginning to wonder..."

"I apologize for the inconvenience, Mr. Li. We ran into some difficulties during the procurement process. We have another collection scheduled in the next few weeks, and then we will be able to fill your order."

"I assume you have received the wire transfer we agreed upon," said Mr. Li.

"Yes. Half the amount of our agreed upon price of $1,000,000 for four young, healthy bottlenose dolphins. The remainder to be paid upon delivery."

"Thank you, Mr. Yoshimatsu. Our display tanks are fully operational. Our trainers are standing by, ready to start. We just need some dolphins."

"You will have your dolphins in short order, Mr. Li. I will be on hand to make sure that you get the best specimens we have."

Yoshimatsu signed off and handed the phone to Susan. She was looking at him, her face lined with concern.

"Hiro-san, did I hear you say that you'll be at the hunt? Do you think you should risk the exposure?"

Yoshimatsu sighed deeply.

"Sato is trying to position himself with the board. He has poisoned them with lies about me. He has planted seeds of doubt about whether I am capable of completing the task. The board wants to send him here to assess the situation and make any necessary adjustments." He looked up at Susan, a deep rage simmering behind his normally impassive eyes. "I will attend the hunt and supervise all operations from a nearby launch."

"I worry for your safety. Out there in the open, you're vulnerable. What if Figueroa turns on you? You said yourself that he's of weak character."

"The only one that concerns me is Jake Spinner. As of midnight tonight, he will no longer present a problem."

"What of the others?"

Yoshimatsu shrugged. "Once they lose their leader, they will crumble and break ranks. They are scientists, not warriors, and by the time they regroup— if they do—we will be long out of the country. Next year, we believe we have enough influence to induce the powers that be to reinstate the limited hunting agreement in the Southern Ocean."

Yoshimatsu's cell phone rang again. He picked it up and inspected the number on the face. "It's my wife."

"I'll give you some privacy." Susan picked up the tray with the beer bottle and glass.

"I will not be long," Yoshimatsu said, squeezing her hand. He clicked on and spoke cheerfully in Japanese, "Kimi, my dearest wife, how are you today?"

# 44

Emily Rosen sat in the small cubicle in the Café Damiana in Insurgentes typing madly. The internet café was not fancy like those she had frequented stateside. There was a small counter near the back that offered coffee and soft drinks. A sign above an empty dish read, "Empanadas."

Sandy Wainright worked at the station next to Rosen. Both women wore earbuds since they were using Skype. Paola sat at another table on the other side of the room. The women were nervous, but they felt comfortable enough to perform their tasks, knowing that Spinner and Raúl stood guard outside.

The first thing Rosen discovered when she opened up her internet account was several emails with attachments from Bertrand Hollis. He had sent her three more files with dossiers on Hirokan Yoshimatsu. She quickly downloaded the attachments to her desktop, stopping only for a few minutes to peruse the contents. She could go through the documents later at the ranch. There were people she needed to contact first.

She punched numbers into her cell phone and, after a few problems getting an outside long-distance number, she heard the phone ring on the other end. A moment later, an abrupt voice answered, "CNN News Desk. Micheala Schroeder speaking."

"Mica, this is Emily Rosen."

"Emily? Where the hell have you been? I thought Senator Donato's people had gotten to you, and you were on the bottom of the East River or in a Jersey landfill."

"You're not that far off. I'm in Baja California Sur. Charlie Dickerson reassigned me."

"He what?"

"He sent me down here to cover the effects of the drug cartels on tourism in Mexico."

"That's bullshit," said Schroeder. "Someone wanted you out of there because you were getting close."

"My guess."

"That really pisses me off. I thought between the two of us we were going to take that son of a bitch down."

"That's your fight for now, Mica. Dickerson terminated me and I'm 4,000 miles away. But I need to talk to you about something else. Are you in a secure location?"

"Sure. My office."

"Good. I'm sending you something right now. I have to shrink the file some so it'll send, so hang on a bit. Let me know when you get it." Rosen moved the document from her laptop to another file and then sent it. Her computer registered an audible ding indicating the message had been sent.

"Rosen, tell me what's going on."

"I need you to see the video first."

"But, what the—?"

"Just trust me. I don't have a lot of time to explain."

Rosen waited for what seemed an eternity. Finally, Michaela said, "I just got it."

"I didn't send you the whole recording. It's nearly ninety minutes long. But this will give you an idea."

On the other end of the line, Rosen heard Schroeder punching characters on her keyboard. Another interminable pause and she said, "It's running."

A minute went by, then two. Rosen heard a gasp on the other end and "Oh—my—God. Where did this take place?"

"Gulf of California. Keep watching," said Emily.

"I don't think I can."

Moments later, Schroeder spoke again. "How did you get this?"

Rosen went on to explain how she had met the researchers who were studying whales in Baja and how a local fisherman had discovered the hunt at the cove.

"Jesus, who is that guy?"

"You must be at the part where the hunt is broken up. I can't tell you his name right now. Everyone down here is looking for him. And it's not just him. Right now, I've gone underground with the researchers."

"Are people after you?"

"Apparently, there are people out there who will kill to get hold of this video. Several locals have been murdered already. I believe it goes all the way up to top tier Mexican officials who are colluding with some really nasty foreign cartels. I have reason to believe it's a Japanese crime syndicate, the Yakuza, working with some mercenaries, but I don't have proof yet."

"Jesus, Rosen. If I run this, I'm going to need some more facts on the ground. I can't go pointing fingers at Japanese crime syndicates in collusion with corrupt Mexican government officials until I have substantive proof."

"Look, Mica, we're on a timeline here. We have it on pretty good information that another hunt is scheduled soon. These guys are sneaky as hell. Once they conduct the kill, they'll be history. After that, none of this will matter. They don't leave a lot of tracks, but the body count is piling up—both human and cetacean. I'm convinced that local villagers have been conscripted to work with the Asians and, if they're disloyal or faint of heart, they'll be disappeared."

"You never cease to amaze me, Rosen. Wherever the shit hits the fan, you always seem to implant yourself firmly in front of it."

"Yeah, well, it's time to point that fan at someone else for a change," Rosen said. "This one goes deep for me, Mica. Deeper than any story I've ever covered."

"Emily, in order to run this, I'm going to have to put a name behind it. Are you willing to take that risk, given your present predicament?"

"Right now, I'm *persona non grata* at the *Times*. I have no news organization to back me up. That's why I'm calling you. The researchers are contacting environmental groups in the states and worldwide to garner support, maybe even get some bodies down here to at least bear witness. We just may scare them enough to call off the next hunt and leave, at least for the time being."

There was a long silence on the other end. Rosen assumed Schroeder was focused on the video. Michaela had been one of the investigative reporters who had broken the original story on the abuse of captive orcas by Marine Life Fun Park. Her piece had inspired a controversial documentary that had sparked a worldwide debate about the morality of sequestering whales for human entertainment. Finally, she spoke. "I have no words for this. This is humanity at its lowest."

"I wondered why those activists would put themselves between the whales and the ships firing exploding harpoons," Emily said. "Once I saw them in their world and gazed into the eye of a whale, something happened to me. Something profound. I can't explain it. But I'd give my life to save them."

"I hope that's not a self-fulfilling prophecy," said Schroeder somberly. "Emily, can you send me the entire video? I'll get it to the editing department, and we'll see what we can come up with. I'm going to need regular updates as this story breaks, okay? Can you access media?"

"We have spotty reception in the hills. To get out communications, we'll have to drop down to the cities on the coast. We have to be careful. One of our team was nearly killed by these guys when he was trying to meet with another researcher."

"God, Rosen. You need to get out of there! I just don't want you to end up on a missing person's list. Let's see if we can mount a media blitz from here."

"This story is far from over. If it's the last thing I do, I'm going to make sure there's no second hunt. Don't worry, Mica. I'll get you reports as often as I can. I'm uploading the long version as we speak. It'll take a while to load."

"I'll make sure this goes public. Keep me posted. And you stay safe, Emily."

"Safe is never where I lived."

"Silly me. Had a sudden and unusual slip of raw emotion."

"I'll be in touch."

As soon as she hung up, she went back to her contact list, suddenly remembering a brief encounter with a reporter from the BBC who covered human-interest stories. It was a bit of a stretch, but the more she thought about it, "chumming" the media wasn't such a bad idea. She found the number and placed the call.

Sandy Wainright took a deep breath and steadied herself for her fourth call. This one was going to a small non-profit based out of San Francisco. She had already spoken to Sea Shepherd Conservation Society, Greenpeace, and the World Wildlife Fund, and she'd sent each organization a copy of the video. All had promised they would run it and get it to as many media outlets as possible, but they were noncommittal about sending people to the Gulf of California to organize protests and stop the hunt. Most of their personnel were tied up in other parts of the world.

The Sea Shepherd organization was caught between two campaigns running simultaneously: one in the Galapagos preventing the Chinese fleet from illegal shark fishing and the other in the Southern Ocean where the activists were risking their lives putting themselves between the whales and the Japanese whaling fleet. Greenpeace's Ocean Division was focused on the Faroe Islands, anticipating the yearly pilot whale slaughter conducted by the locals. The WWF would view the video and take it under advisement with its board of directors. In the end, they were sympathetic, but no one believed they had the resources or the ability to mobilize in time.

After the third call, Sandy felt truly alone. She was coming to the realization that, although people sincerely wanted to help and thought the hunt was heinous and abhorrent, they were hesitant about jumping into a full-blown protest in a foreign country. On some level Sandy understood this. But she also knew that time was of the essence. In a week, maybe two, none of this would matter anymore. The hunters would be gone, and there would be no trace of their having been there other than some bloodstained rocks and sand on a remote beach somewhere along the Baja coast.

Her next call was picked up by a pleasant-sounding man. "Cetus Global Alliance. This is Graham Neely."

"Hi, Graham. My name is Sandy Wainright. I'm a marine biologist and humpback whale researcher working at the Institute for Marine Mammal Research in Baja California Sur. Do you have a few minutes? I need to tell you about a dire situation down here in the Gulf of California."

"Sure," said Graham. "What can I help you with?"

Sandy went on to detail the disappearance of several individual humpback whales in her study and the bloody massacre of dolphins they had witnessed at the San Mateo Cove. She also explained her theory—that there was corruption that went to the top levels of the Mexican government.

"I have something you need to see. I'm emailing it to you now."

Moments later, Graham acknowledged that he had received the attachment. She waited while he downloaded the video to his computer.

"Holy shit!" Graham exclaimed. "Are the dates and times correct?"

"Yes."

"My God. This looks like Taiji."

"Funny you should say that. There were Japanese whalers down there among the locals. The way they rounded up those dolphins was almost exactly like the hunt in Taiji."

"Sandy, I want to jot down some notes while I watch this. It's amazing that you got this footage."

"Once they saw us, they began shooting at us. That comes near the end."

"They shot at you?"

"Some locals have disappeared, and we're suspicious they may have been killed. We have reason to believe that another hunt is in the works."

"When?"

"We don't know for sure. But soon. This needs to be moved on. Now."

Sandy provided Graham with the GPS coordinates of the cove and her own contact information. Suddenly Graham said, "Wait a minute. What the—? Who is that guy?"

"I'm not at liberty to say right now. There's a lot of people down here who would like to see him dead."

"Is he working with you?" Graham asked.

"Not really. Only on a temporary, peripheral basis."

"Damn. We could use a guy like that at Cetus. He's got some balls."

"Look, Graham, I didn't give you the video so you could recruit another activist," said Sandy testily. "Everyone on our team is hiding out right now. Someone tried to kill the institute's director. We need help and we need it now. Next week is too late."

"Okay! Okay! Sorry. Sandy, I need to contact our administrator and find out what he wants to do. Right now, the majority of our personnel are up in Canada and Alaska trying to prevent a mining concern from operating near some major tributaries that are critical salmon spawning areas."

"Sounds like you guys are doing great work. Graham, we're really desperate here. This is urgent. Is there any way you could help us out?"

"Look. Are you in a place where I can call you back? I need to contact some people."

"Right now, we're exposed. We risk being seen every time we venture down out of the hills. Do you have a pen handy?"

Sandy gave Graham her cell phone number along with Raúl's.

"I'll try to get back to you within the next hour."

"We're sitting on a ticking time bomb, Graham. Whatever you do, get that video out to the public. The more people who see it the better the chances are that the whalers will have to postpone the hunt."

"Sandy, I promise you, I'll be in touch within the hour."

She hung up and stared at her computer before complaining to Rosen. "Damn it! No go on Sea Shepherd, Greenpeace, or WWF! Everyone is committed elsewhere around the planet. And then my last call was to a small environmental group based out of San Francisco that I never even heard of before."

"What are they called?"

"Cetus Global Alliance," replied Sandy.

Rosen began typing in her computer. "Did he get the video?"

"Yeah, he got the video."

Rosen looked up from her computer. "It appears that they've only been a non-profit entity for about six months. Not a long list of volunteers and donors."

"My luck. All the major hitters are out at sea, and I got the rookie who was charged with minding the store."

Jake Spinner squinted into the hot afternoon sun. It was that time of day when the sun cast its harshest light, giving everything a washed out, almost flat, appearance. He was getting more agitated by the minute. They had already been here too long. Fifteen minutes earlier, Rosen had come out and informed him that they needed more time to receive the callbacks they had requested. Raúl went to look for the stand that sold the adobado tacos. Now Jake was beginning to worry about him. He breathed a sigh of relief when Raúl appeared from around a corner, carrying Styrofoam containers and bottles of Coca-Cola.

"Sorry, Jake. The taco stand moved to another street." They carried their meals over to a rusted metal table with two spindly chairs next to the internet café. Spinner sat down and bit into his taco.

Between mouthfuls, Raúl asked, "How much longer?"

"We should have left for the ranch forty-five minutes ago. I'm getting that prickly sensation at the back of my neck again. That's not good."

Raúl was about to respond when Spinner's cell phone rang. The two men looked at each other with apprehension, guessing who the caller could be. Spinner swallowed his food and answered. "Spinner."

"You have been busy, Jake Spinner," said the Asian voice on the other end.

Spinner's eyes narrowed. "Excuse me?"

"Rescuing Alejandro Cabrillo from the hospital in Insurgentes was a bold move. But it will all be for nothing. Eventually, I will track them all down and, when I do, there is nothing that you can do for any of them."

"I have no idea what the hell you're talking about. I don't know any Alejandro Cabrillo."

"We saw you on their security video in the hospital. You are not difficult to find. Your shabby mode of dress and your sloppy execution of plans leaves a trail only a fool would not recognize."

"You're the second person in two days who's commented on my mode of dress. I find that in very poor taste."

"I very much look forward to our meeting, Jake. We have many things to discuss. In fact, we have five topics to discuss. I know that you will be happy to enlighten me."

"Five topics? I'm not really that good of a conversationalist."

"Oh, you will be, my friend. You will be."

"Just leave the kid alone. I'll give you what you want."

"Midnight tonight. Slip 23 at the main pier in La Paz. Come alone. If we suspect that you are being followed, Macario Silvano dies. And you get no absolution."

"I heard you the first time." Spinner was working hard to reign in his anger. "I'll be there."

The line went dead. He stared at the phone, then looked up at Raúl. "They know that we sprung Alex. I'm dead sure he's going to torture me until I give up all the names and locations of the rest of the group."

"What are you going to do, Jake?"

Spinner poked at the last adobado taco. He wasn't hungry anymore. He pushed the container away. "In Afghanistan I was captured and tortured by the Taliban. After six weeks, they damn near broke me. One more session and I would have caved."

"What happened?"

"The weather cleared enough for a drone strike. The missile killed five of them. The rest scattered. One of the villagers came and found me. They helped get me back to my unit. The thing is, I was a lot younger and stronger then. I'm not sure I have what it takes anymore to withstand their interrogation. After tonight, you may want to get your family and the rest of the group away from this part of the world."

Raúl nodded solemnly. "I understand."

Sandy's phone rang and she looked at the number. Graham was on the line.

"Hi, Graham. What have you got?"

"I sent the video to all of our operatives currently out in the field. It's now streaming to all our members and donors and at least twenty news organizations around the world. Within eight hours, it'll be broadcast all over the planet via social media."

"Thanks, Graham. That's great. What about getting some support down here?"

There was a pause on the other end. Sandy felt her gut tighten in anticipation.

"I'm sorry, Sandy. We're a small NGO. All of our resources are stretched pretty thin as it is. Right now is the height of the killing season."

"We're in the height of a killing season down here! We need bodies to stop these guys."

"I'm sorry, Sandy, but you don't even know where the next hunt will take place. By the time we get a boat outfitted with volunteers and equipment the whale hunters will already be gone."

Sandy fought back her anger and frustration. "That's it? That's your final answer?"

"Sandy, I'm sorry, but I'm—"

"Have you ever seen dolphins speared to death, panicked into crushing each other to get away from the harpoons? It's pretty horrible, Graham."

"I did a brief stint with Sea Shepherds a while back. I've only been with Cetus for a couple of months," he said defensively. "I haven't seen that."

"I hope you never have to see it. That memory's been burned into my psyche forever, and I wish someone would just take it away."

There was another uncomfortable pause. Finally, Graham spoke. "I might have an idea. Give me a couple of days to follow up. I'll call you as soon as I know."

"What is it? You have something?"

"I can't say yet. I have to check in with a few people. I'll call you back as soon as I have something."

"Okay, Graham. Thanks."

"Don't thank me yet. I'm not making any promises. This is a long shot at best."

Spinner stuck his head inside the door of the café. "Time to go."

# 45

After their return to the ranch, Spinner kept to himself for the rest of the day. He didn't want to see the hangdog looks on the faces of the researchers, and he didn't want to hear how he was "needed" as part of the team. He especially did not want to run into Emily Rosen. He had decided that if this were to be his last twenty-three hours on the planet, he didn't need a dressing-down from the East Coast reporter.

He played out as many different scenarios as his addled brain could conjure. It would have been nice to have some intel about the layout of his final destination. Was it a ship? A building? He assumed that he was going to be delivered to the location from a boat that would be waiting at Slip 23 at the pier.

A Maasai warrior had once told him, "Be as familiar with your new location as you are with the place you live." Spinner had always been exacting in his memorization of the surrounding terrain and buildings and cognizant of every possible outcome. Tonight's scenario was completely out of reach of his mind's eye. He might have one, maybe two opportunities to do some damage before he was taken out. The gnawing feeling at the back of the brain came with a New York accent. Rosen was right, much as he hated to admit it. Macario might already be dead. He was just walking into the executioner's chamber, easy as that.

Spinner changed from his worn Hawaiian shirt and shorts to long sleeve white shirt and khakis. He went through his meager belongings and stared long and hard at his pistol and combat knife. He would be relieved of these as soon as he boarded. There was a time when Spinner could use any available object at hand and turn it into a lethal weapon. He had once killed a terrorist with a spoon. He was counting on the fact that his enemies would underestimate him due to his looks and age.

Raúl appeared at the door. The two men regarded each other for the briefest of moments. "Guadalupe wants you to come to the table for dinner."

263

Spinner flashed a half-smile. "I can't believe I'm going to say this, my friend, but I don't have much of an appetite right now."

"You should eat something, Jake. To keep up your strength. Besides if you don't eat, you'll offend the cook."

Jake grunted a laugh. "I'll be along shortly."

Raúl turned to leave.

"Raúl—" Jake handed him the pistol and the knife. "They're going to relieve me of these as soon as I show up."

"Jake, I cannot accept these. They're—"

"I'd rather turn them over to you now than surrender them to those murdering bastards."

The Mexican fisherman looked directly at Jake. "I'll hold them for you."

Just then, Alisa and Julio burst into the room and grabbed Jake by the hands. "Señor Jake! Señor Jake! Mamá wants you to come to dinner!" They began pulling him toward the door.

"Better go along with it, Jake." Raúl smiled at the American. "Mí esposa, Guadalupe, is a force of nature."

Spinner sat at the table between Alisa and Julio. The rest of the crew was already seated. They were quiet, but Spinner caught them stealing furtive glances at him. The meal consisted of green corn tamales, rice, beans, and *calabacitas*. After his first bite he decided to finish the meal, not only to please Guadalupe, but because every man deserves a last meal.

He glanced around the room. The stress of the last few days was evident in everyone's faces. They made small talk about the video, who they talked to that day, and who they still needed to contact. Sandy turned her attention to Emily, who hadn't spoken throughout the meal. She was looking down while she pushed a pile of beans and rice around on her plate.

"Emily, how soon do you think CNN can get the video on network news?"

When she didn't answer, Sandy said again, "Rosen?"

Rosen looked up, her gaze somewhere far away.

"I'm sorry, what did you say?"

"I was asking about CNN. When do you think the network will run the video?"

"Oh. Um—" She looked around the room, settling on Jake Spinner. "I can't do this." She stood. "Excuse me." She turned and left the table.

"I don't want you to go away, Señor Jake!" Alisa blurted out. She leaned against his shoulder and, for the first time that Raúl could remember, he saw Jake Spinner's blue eyes mist over. Spinner awkwardly touched the little girl's head, attempting to console her. She looked toward her father, pleading, "Papá, tell Señor Jake we want him to stay here." Raúl nodded in understanding.

Spinner pushed his plate away and placed his napkin on the table next to it. He looked toward Guadalupe. In Spanish, he said, "The meal was excellent. If you all would please excuse me, I have some things to take care of."

He found Rosen standing at the corral looking toward the west. The air had cooled, and the sky in the west was a painting of peach, violet, and red. She leaned against the corral, staring straight ahead. Around them, the goats were settling in for the night, the coyotes howled in the distance, and a Great Horned Owl called from the bosque of mesquite trees in the arroyo. It was time for the creature shift change in the *barranca*.

Neither spoke for a while, partly because of the stunning desert sunset unfolding before them, but mostly because of the chasm of discomfort that stretched between them. What can you say to someone who's going to walk into oblivion in a few hours? Rosen was never one for small talk anyway, but she couldn't remember a more uncomfortable moment than this.

Finally, unable to withstand the tension in the air, Spinner reached into his shirt pocket and produced a crumpled pack of cigarettes, tapped one out of the pack and lit it up. He drew in a deep breath and blew the smoke skyward.

He regarded the cigarette. "I always thought these things were going to be the death of me."

Rosen fought back the lump building in her throat. She glared at him once, then turned away quickly. "Go away. I don't need this in my life."

"Rosen, I—"

"You don't need to explain anything to me, Jake Spinner. You're no different than all the rest of the men I've met in my life. Sure, you can dress it up and paint it to look like you're doing something brave and noble, but in the end, it's just another act of self-absorption. That's what you men do well—you just leave. Even if you're driving a runaway car into oblivion, it's still easier than sticking around and making a difference."

Emily turned to face him. "You're all just cowards. Except for Raúl and Alejandro. They're staying to fight for what they believe in. They're staying because of family and others who need them. And they're putting their lives on the line for a greater cause. Because they're connected to this place, the ocean, and the whales."

Spinner dropped the cigarette on the ground and crushed it with his foot. "You're right, Emily. I am a coward. I only wish I were able to measure up to Raúl and Alejandro. I had my chance once. I blew it. Now it's down to damage control. I should have been there for Gustavo, Marta, and Macario. I should have gotten them out of the country when I had the chance. Instead, I got drunk. Now two of my friends are dead and psychopaths are holding their only son. So, you're right, Rosen. I'm a coward—the worst kind. I have no right to call people like you friends. You and the others are what I should have aspired to become, but I took a wrong turn somewhere and couldn't find my way back. Now I have one more thing to do. Out there is a scared kid who knows he's about to die unless I show up. I'm not going to disappoint him again."

Rosen cleared her throat. "I don't think I can do this by myself. She gazed into the distance. "I'm afraid my actions are going to get these people killed."

"Stay the course, Emily. You have much more power than you think you do. You have the ability to reach millions. Your voice and the voices of the others can bring about change. What you did today was an act of extreme courage. You rang the bell. The world will listen to you."

"What time do you have to leave?"

Spinner sighed. "Around ten. We need time to get out of the hills, and then—"

Rosen spun suddenly and kissed Spinner hard on the lips, her hands cradling his grizzled face. He nearly stumbled backward, clearly unprepared. She turned abruptly and walked off, leaving him looking dazed.

Spinner placed the last few things in an old backpack provided by Raúl. Most of the items in the pack were for Macario: a change of clothes, food that Guadalupe had prepared, several bottles of water. Perhaps it was just wishful thinking that Macario would still be alive. He looked at his watch. Nearly time to go.

He shouldered the pack and walked out of his room toward the main house looking for Raúl. Everyone was standing outside. Alejandro leaned on a pair of crutches. Emily Rosen was conspicuously absent.

"I was hoping we could avoid goodbyes," he said to Raúl. "I thought you were going to keep this on the down low."

Raúl shrugged. "With so many people in one house, it's impossible to keep a secret."

One by one the members of the team came up to Spinner. The women and children hugged him, including Guadalupe. Most didn't speak.

He walked over to Alejandro and shook his hand. "Take good care of yourself and your family, Alex. You're a good man." He turned and faced everyone. "Hey, it's been an honor and a privilege to know you folks. Being in your company makes me feel that there might be some hope for this planet."

Raúl looked at him. "Ready?"

Spinner looked at the gathering one last time. He forced a weak smile and nodded. "Yeah. Let's go."

Nearing Raúl's truck, they spotted a petite figure leaning against the tailgate, her camera bag slung over her shoulder.

Spinner frowned. "What the hell do you think you're doing?"

"I thought I'd come along. Proper send off and all."

"That's why you have your camera rig? No way, Rosen. They said no one comes with me. If they see you, they'll kill you and Macario. I won't let you do that."

"Spinner, they won't see me. I can find a place where I'm hidden. I'll get a shot of you getting on that boat. We need to record this."

"No, god damn it!" Spinner turned to Raúl. "What did you tell her?"

"She's right, Jake. We need to have a record of you getting on that boat. If you're never seen again, then all we have is our word against theirs."

"Why do you people have to make everything so damn complicated?"

"They won't see us, Jake," Raúl said. "I promise you."

Spinner looked back and forth between the two of them. "I suppose if I refuse, I'm going to have to find my own transportation into town?"

"Something like that," replied Rosen.

Spinner shook his head. "The universe is punishing me. I just know it. Only here have I found people more pig-headed stubborn than me."

"Some of *El Ranchito de las Cabras* is rubbing off on the guests, I think," said Rosen.

"Oh, the stubborn goat thing happened long before you all landed here," said Spinner bitterly.

Their faces were lit in the pale blue glow of the dashboard light as they drove down from the mountains toward La Paz. They hardly spoke. Each seemed lost in thought. As much as she hated to admit it, Rosen was going to miss the grizzled ex-pat who sat next to her, staring out the window into the darkness. Once, their hands brushed against each other, ever so briefly. She felt a surge in her chest, but quickly shifted position so they no longer touched.

"If you find the location of the next hunt," said Spinner, who was staring straight ahead, "it's going to get ugly fast. They're going to be ready for you. And this time they'll all be packing. The world will be watching when it goes down. There's a good chance that some of you may die for your cause."

"Jesus, Spinner, I wish you'd stop sugarcoating everything," said Rosen. "Hey, none of us just fell off the tortilla truck."

"I'm just saying. Any of those green do-gooders that decide to come down here need to know what's at stake."

"They already know what's at stake."

"Raúl, I'm counting on you to keep the rest of these heroes from doing something stupid." Spinner glared at Rosen.

"Of course, Jake."

On the outskirts of La Paz, Spinner ordered Raúl to divert to side roads and avoid busy thoroughfares. Raúl veered the truck through one barrio after the next until they could see the lights of the malecón in the distance. Rosen felt her gut tighten as they drew closer to their destination.

About a mile from the waterfront, Jake said, "Stop here."

Raúl pulled the truck over to the side of the road on a darkened street with single story houses on both sides. The only sign of life was a stray cat wandering under a yellowed streetlight a block away.

"Are you sure?" Raúl leaned on the steering wheel. "I can get you closer without being seen."

"This'll do, amigo," said Spinner. He opened the door, slid out of the truck, and retrieved his pack from the back seat.

Rosen stared straight ahead, not wanting to meet his gaze.

He went around to the driver's side and held out his hand to Raúl. "Thank you for showing me what family means. Take good care of yourself and Guadalupe and the kids." He looked at Rosen. "For what it's worth—I've never met a finer group of people in my life. Good luck."

He turned and began to walk away.

"Jake! Wait!" Rosen climbed out of the truck and ran to him. She threw her arms around his neck and hugged him fiercely. Spinner hugged her back.

"You're the spark, Emily," Spinner whispered into her ear. "You can stop these bastards. Tell your story to the world."

"Spinner, I never did—"

Spinner released his grip and held Rosen at arm's length. "It's going to be okay." A crooked grin crossed his grizzled face. "Raúl! Both of you, be careful. Don't get seen."

Raúl nodded solemnly. Spinner turned and walked into the darkness, his figure fading into the inky night. Rosen stood and watched him go until she could no longer see his outline. She turned and ran back to the truck.

"Raúl, I need you to get me down to the pier. Somewhere near Slip 23 where we won't be seen."

"Señorita, you heard what Jake said. It's too dangerous."

"I know what he said. Look, Raúl. There's a high probability that Jake Spinner won't be alive tomorrow. I don't want his death to be in vain. Someone needs to record him getting on that boat."

Raúl sighed deeply. He drummed his fingers on the steering wheel, looking toward the lights of the malecón.

He turned the ignition of the truck. "I think I know of a place where you can get the photo."

Rosen touched his arm. "Thank you."

"First sign of trouble, photo or not, we're leaving."

The truck lurched forward and headed in the direction of the pier.

Spinner walked briskly toward the malecón. He carried a generic retractable pen in one shirt pocket. On the inside of his canvas belt, he had hidden several paper clips and a razor blade. In the sole of one huarache, he hid a small knife. Not much of a defense, but in close quarters one or several of these objects might come in handy.

At first Spinner kept looking over his shoulder to see if he was being followed. He didn't think Raúl would follow him, but he knew that Emily Rosen would do as she damn well pleased. On some level, Jake understood this.

As he drew closer to the pier, he was surprised at how calm he was. In fact, he couldn't remember the last time he had such clarity of mind. It was a calmness born of resolve—and sobriety. All he could do was to focus on this exact moment. From here to the denouement, his only assignment was to deal with the present situation—and react when the time called for it.

He walked along a series of streets that wound down toward the pier. At this time of night, the houses and small businesses were shuttered and dark. He rounded a corner, and the malecón came into view. He walked past more closed shops. On the next street a cantina was still open, salsa music blaring from speakers. A few inebriated American tourists lingered at the bar, while the weary bartender wiped down glasses.

Spinner walked past most of the lit portion of the malecón. The pier was located at the end of the street, near the industrial section. Slip 23, which was empty, was in the second section of boat slips. He checked his watch: 11:55. He looked up and down the slips for any signs of life. There were several boats tied up at adjoining slips, mostly commercial fishing trawlers and a few trimarans. He clambered down a short ladder and stood on the wooden platform.

The drone of a motor caught his attention. It was growing louder. Another moment passed before a twenty-foot launch with twin outboards approached the slip. It decelerated quickly and eased in. There were three men aboard. They were all dressed in black and wore watch caps and sunglasses. In the dim light, Spinner saw that two of them carried Uzis. The driver had a semi-auto holstered on his right hip.

Two of the men jumped out of the boat, their Uzis pointed at him.

"You had better be Jake Spinner," the man in the boat said.

Spinner could see that the man was well- muscled, and he moved with the grace of a panther. He recognized the voice. It was the voice from the phone call.

"I'm Spinner."

The tall man motioned with his machine pistol. "Hands up."

Spinner held his hands up. The shorter man patted him down. The other man kept the gun pointed at Spinner's chest. The search was thorough. He was relieved of his backpack, and his pockets were searched. The ink pen was removed and tossed aside.

"He's clean," said the shorter one. "No wires, no weapons."

"In the boat," said the taller man, motioning with his pistol.

Spinner climbed into the launch and was instructed to sit at the stern. The short man placed a hood over his head. They sat opposite him, weapons pointed at his chest. The driver fired up the twin outboards, backed the launch away from the slip, then accelerated into the night.

Half a block away, from a warehouse rooftop, Emily Rosen focused the camera on Spinner. The light was bad, so she quickly adjusted the camera's ISO to a low light setting. The photos would invariably be grainy, but some record was better than none.

When the assailant placed the hood over Spinner's head, Rosen let out a gasp. She feared he was going to be assassinated on the spot. Rosen felt a sense of dread as the launch disappeared into the darkness.

Raúl placed a gentle hand on Rosen's shoulder. "Come, Emily. We need to leave. It's not safe to linger here."

# 46

Without any reference points to draw upon, Spinner had no idea how far they'd traveled. The boatman kept up a punishing pace, the bow of the launch pounding the chop. Jake deduced they were probably heading northeast. The wind blew out of the west this time of year and the boatman was taking the waves nearly head on. He was feeling the chill from the spray as it shot back from the bow, drenching his clothes.

After what seemed like an interminable stretch of time, Jake noticed a change in pitch of the twin outboards. The launch began to decelerate. Soon, he heard the sound of voices yelling out orders in Japanese above the sounds of the motors. He noticed something else. Something assaulted his sense of smell and left a coppery taste in his mouth. It was the distinctive smell of blood. A lot of blood. He had been brought to the mothership. The launch bumped against something hard and unforgiving. The hood was pulled off his head, and he was looking at the black hull of an enormous ship. A steel ladder rose up the side to nearly twenty feet above him. He felt the prod of a weapon in the small of his back.

"Up there," the tall captor said. "Move."

Spinner tried to catch a glance at his captor, but a sharper prod to his kidneys told him to get moving. He grabbed the ladder and began to climb slowly. The rungs were slick with seawater. Several times his feet nearly slipped out from under him as he ascended. When he reached the top of the ladder, he was hauled over the rail and pulled roughly to standing by three men, all dressed in black.

The deck was expansive. He passed an opening in the top deck that revealed a lower processing deck. The lights were dimmed, but he could still see shadows of red-brown stains on the steel decks. Men in hardhats and hazmat suits hosed the decks and moved large rolling containers. Spinner looked up and caught a quick glimpse of the wheelhouse. Several men stood at the railing staring down at them. They soon went back inside. As the guard pushed him forward, he saw a platform not far from the wheelhouse. He thought he saw the glint of a helicopter blade. Spinner looked off to one side and noticed an opening in the stanchions. He mentally ticked off the distance from one beam to the next.

As he was marched by the open deck, he saw a life preserver attached to the railing. The words on the life preserver were in Japanese characters on the top half and English on the bottom half. Even though the lettering was inverted, Spinner mentally reversed the words and repeated the name several times in his mind. *Shodokai Maru*.

He was taken to the stern by the three armed men. The taller of his captors walked forward, removing his watch cap. His face was angular, his hair jet-black and tied in a ponytail. A prominent puckered scar lined the right side of his face. He walked up to Spinner, stopping within inches. He looked into Spinner's eyes without blinking. This was the face of someone who enjoyed doling out pain in measured quantities. Spinner returned the stare, his own face impassive.

After a protracted silence, the man spoke. "So, you are Jake Spinner, the one who has become a distraction to us," said Kanamura.

A slight grin crossed Spinner's lips. "Only a distraction?"

"I will admit it. You have surprised me more than once." He leaned forward, closed his eyes and inhaled. "Is that fear I smell?"

"Probably some bad adobado I ate. Can't handle the Mexican food like I used to."

Kanamura's eyes snapped open. "I am looking forward to a long and revealing discussion with you about *things*, Jake Spinner. At the end of our conversation, I believe you will have eagerly answered all my questions."

"I spent six weeks being tortured by the Taliban," Spinner didn't break his gaze with Kanamura. "You got no game."

"Enough!" The sharp voice came from the shadows. A Japanese man dressed in a business suit, stepped forward. He was slightly shorter than Spinner and looked to be a few years older. Only the gray at his temples gave away his years.

Kanamura glared at Spinner, then backed up slowly to flank his boss.

"You must be Yoshimatsu," Spinner said

Yoshimatsu showed only the briefest sign of surprise, which registered as a slight flicker in his eyes. "You have been doing your homework, Mr. Spinner. Or perhaps, it is your colleagues that have managed to identify me."

"I work alone."

"Mr. Spinner. I did not get to this station in life without a certain amount of preparation and diligence. We know you are not working alone."

"Where's Macario? I held up my end of the deal. You want what I know? Let me see the kid."

Yoshimatsu turned to Kanamura. "Bring him."

Kanamura nodded and walked into the shadows.

"You have cost me a great deal of money and time," Yoshimatsu said, his voice sounding tired. "What do you think I should do with you?"

"Well, you could just drop Macario and me off at the nearest island, but I don't think you're going to do that. Let the kid go. He can't hurt you. He's scared shitless. He won't talk."

Kanamura appeared again, this time dragging a figure with him. He pushed the young man down onto his knees just at the edge of the light. It was Macario.

Spinner almost didn't recognize him. His eyes were nearly closed. The deep bruises around the sockets gave him a spectral appearance. His clothes were bloodstained and filthy. Spinner caught a glimpse of bare, battered feet. He was overpowered with rage. "Oh, god, kid."

Macario looked up at Jake, trying to focus through swollen eyes. "Jake? Jake?"

"It's me, Macario. I'm here to take you home."

"Jake, I should have listened to you," Tears streamed down Macario's cheeks.

Spinner looked at Yoshimatsu. "I said I'd tell you everything. Put the kid in a boat and turn him loose."

Yoshimatsu lifted Macario's chin and looked down at him. "Mr. Spinner. I am a businessman. I work in a very competitive world. In order for the wheels of a machine to turn in synchrony, every one of the cogs must play their part. Your young friend broke the agreement I have with the village, just as his parents had." He let Macario's head drop. The kid was barely able to remain upright.

Yoshimatsu smiled thinly. "Frankly, I am surprised you took us up on our offer. Surely you did not believe that I was ever going to let either of you go. How would I look to my men if I showed you and the boy mercy? My clients are awaiting their prizes in China, Japan, and the Middle East. Do you know how much a dolphin sells for in Dubai, Mr. Spinner?"

Spinner felt the prod of the machine pistol in his kidney. "You kill the kid, you get nothing from me. I'm not afraid of dying."

"That is exactly what makes you so dangerous. The only thing that leverages men like you is sentiment. Why do you think you came here tonight? Did you honestly believe that we would bargain with you? I will extract the information from you about whom you are working with and how we can find them. My colleague, Mr. Kanamura here, is a lifelong devotee of the administration of pain and the prolongation of the dying process. He has forgotten more about applied means of coercion than you have ever learned."

"Yeah, he already told me what a bad boy he is."

"Allow him to show you," Yoshimatsu said and stepped aside.

Kanamura stepped forward, a blade appearing in his hand. In one deft move he lifted Macario's head by the hair and drew the blade across his throat. A fountain of blood gushed forth and Macario began to thrash on the deck, his head lolling grotesquely forward.

Spinner screamed, "No!"

Spinner felt the pressure from the barrel of the machine pistol ease up just slightly. The two captors were momentarily distracted by the writhing figure on the deck. Jake spun, his hand blocking the machine pistol as the assailant fired wildly. His free hand hit the man in the face. A blow from his elbow followed in lightening succession. Spinner wrenched the Uzi away and sprayed the second assailant with a burst of rounds. The man flew backward in a bloody heap.

Yoshimatsu shouted, "Kill him!"

Spinner pulled the stunned assailant in front of him as the rest of his captors recovered. He laid down a steady burst of fire as he began backing up. Kanamura grabbed Yoshimatsu and pulled him behind a metal storage container just before a spray of bullets ricocheted off of it. The other men hesitated, not wanting to shoot through their comrade to get to Spinner.

He looked up and saw Kanamura aiming at him. Spinner felt the assailant's body lurch as two slugs slammed into him. Spinner returned fire, causing Kanamura to retreat behind the container. Two more slugs hit the now dead assailant. Spinner sprayed the deck with the last of the magazine and flung the dead crewman to the side.

He turned and ran. He headed toward an opening in the railing on the deck. He sprinted for all he was worth, hoping that the darkness and the angle of his body would keep him from being hit. Bullets whizzed by his head as he pumped his arms furiously.

The first slug caught him high on his left shoulder torquing his body and causing him to almost stumble. He reached the edge and launched himself into space. The second slug found its mark in the flesh on his right side. He didn't feel much pain, but he knew he had been hit. As he fell toward the black sea below, two thoughts flashed through his brain. *Take a deep breath and get down fast.* He had two—maybe three—seconds to get far enough under water to avoid the hail of bullets that would surely come.

The impact and the shock of the cold water nearly drove the air from his lungs. He pulled downward and then reversed course suddenly, swimming as hard as he could toward the hull of the death ship. Instinctively he knew that the men above would not want to aim their fire too close to the hull.

Spinner touched the barnacle-encrusted hull just as the water exploded in a storm of bullets seeking a target. *Phhttt! Phhttt!* Streams of cavitation bubbles formed all around him as the bullets rained down.

His lungs were burning, but he didn't dare swim away from the hull. Swimming underneath to the other side was not an option. He knew he was fairly close to the stern, so he started pulling himself along the hull in that direction. He could still hear the sound of projectiles tearing through the water. He reached the stern as his chest felt like it would burst. He kicked toward the surface and came up as close to the hull as he could. He grabbed two quick breaths and kicked down again. He swam past the twin propellers and headed away from the whaling ship.

On board, Kanamura barked orders to the men as they fired a barrage into the inky waters. Yoshimatsu stood near the railing watching the spectacle.

Kanamura walked up and down the railing searching the sea for any sign of Jake Spinner. He finally told the men to cease their firing. Walking over to Yoshimatsu, he said, "I know I hit him at least once, possibly twice. There is no way he could have survived the barrage from the deck. Even if he did, the nearest landfall is twenty miles away. In these seas, he will not last more than a few hours."

"Gather all available men," Yoshimatsu said. "Launch the boats."

"Hiro-san, I don't think—"

"I want to see the body! Bring me the corpse of Jake Spinner!"

Spinner performed slow, steady strokes to put as much distance as possible between himself and the whaling ship. His legs were tiring in the cold water and his painful left shoulder was barely working. He was losing blood and would soon go into shock if he didn't do something fast.

He stopped paddling and lay on his back, floating on the rolling waves. He pulled a shirttail up to his mouth and tore at the fibers. He tore until he was able to rip three strips from the cotton shirt. With one, he plugged the small hole in the front of his left shoulder. The bullet had passed completely through. With difficulty, he plugged the back of his shoulder with the second strip of cloth. With considerable effort he groped behind his back until he could feel the small entrance wound just above his waist. He winced as he worked the cloth into the hole to staunch the flow of blood.

Out of sight of the whaling ship, Spinner attempted to get his bearings. The waves were three-to-four-foot rollers, and he had to keep his head up when the waves crested. Spinner couldn't see any land. He turned his attention to the night sky. The ocean around him was dimly lit by the brilliance of millions of stars overhead. He found Polaris easily, then Betelgeuse visible to the west. From there he had a rough idea which way to go. He paddled slowly and deliberately in a southwest direction, keeping the North Star on his right.

That little voice in his head told him that he probably wasn't going to make it. For one thing, he could bleed out. And then there was the issue of leaking body fluids into the sea. He knew it wouldn't be long before he received some unwelcome company. A chill ran down the length of his spine. The thought of being eaten alive produced a visceral emotion of terror and revulsion. Then Spinner smiled inwardly. *Payback's a bitch, Jake.* He had made a living from landing a lot of fish in the last seven years. He laughed at the thought that a large, hungry shark was literally going to bite him in the ass. Universal karma. His only hope was that there was still enough residual alcohol marinating in his system to make the sharks seek out a less toxic meal.

The scene of Macario's death played over and over in his mind. He kept mentally searching for what he could have done differently. He pictured the knife blade slashing across Macario's throat and the look of surprise and pain in the boy's eyes before they rolled back in his head. A wave of guilt enveloped him. Gustavo. Marta. And now Macario. All dead. Because he was irresponsible.

Sometimes simple revenge is enough fuel to keep a person going. If he lived through this, he vowed he'd hunt down Yoshimatsu and Kanamura.

His thoughts turned to Emily Rosen. She was an enigma. Of all the women he had met, she was the smartest, the bravest, and the most exasperating. If he could see her now, he'd tell her she was right—and possibly get his chops busted. Suddenly, Jake Spinner had a realization. He didn't want to die out here. He had another reason besides revenge to keep swimming. He desperately wanted to tell Rosen that she was right about him. He turned on his belly, and began to paddle toward the west with renewed energy. In the distance, he heard the faint sound of motors.

Hours later, Spinner noticed both of his legs had gone numb and he was shivering. Hypothermia was setting in due to loss of blood and prolonged exposure to cold water.

Something brushed against his leg. The sharks had found him.

# 47

*T*he female bottlenose dolphin rested in a cove on the lee side of a small island called Isla Roca. The rest of her family was gathered around her at the surface. Most of the other members of her maternal subgroup were asleep. Or at least partially asleep. Her calf, the juvenile male with the star pattern on his rostrum, slept at her side, his pectoral fin touching hers for periodic reassurance. The matriarch scanned the immediate area around the subgroup, and feeling confident there was no imminent threat, allowed herself to doze.

Suddenly, she snapped fully awake, alerted to a disturbance in the void. It was almost like a taste in the water, a disruption of the fluid balance. She projected her sonar but didn't receive a response. They had not heard the death ship for a long time, but she knew where it was.

Her calf fidgeted, now aware that his mother was agitated. He nuzzled her, patting her pectoral fin nervously with his own. She focused her senses once more. Almost imperceptibly, she picked up the taste of something that confused her. Then, with a perception that had been honed for some forty million years, she knew there was a man in the water. And she knew by the beat of his heart who that man was. He was injured and bleeding. Larger hunters were coming for the man. They, too, had tasted the blood in the water.

The matriarch issued a series of distress calls to the rest of the family. Her sisters and their calves awakened and began vocalizing in high-pitched, agitated tones. She conveyed her intentions to the others, and with two powerful thrusts of her flukes, the old female shot toward open water, her calf in echelon position at her flank. The rest of the pod fanned out in a chevron formation toward the disturbance ahead.

Spinner sculled slowly in a circle, following the silhouette of the black dorsal fin in the dim starlight. Several feet behind, he saw the vertical tip of the caudal fin moving back and forth in the water. He estimated the distance between the dorsal and caudal fins and surmised that the shark was between ten and twelve feet long. Great whites had been spotted out here occasionally, but they were usually subadults, migrating from their birthplace in the deep water off the Midriff Islands. Spinner figured that, based on the shark's size and the fact it was traveling alone, it was probably a tiger. That wasn't good news.

If he could keep the shark in front of him, he might have a chance to punch and kick at it when it came in for the kill. It was going to be a futile defense. Weakened by loss of blood and shivering from the onset of hypothermia, his reflexes were dulled and his muscles were sluggish. The shark didn't seem to want a frontal attack. It accelerated and circled quickly behind him. He spun in the water just in time to avoid its head. The rough hide of the shark brushed against his leg, abrading the cloth of his pants. He instinctively let out a cry and drew in his arms and legs to make himself a smaller target. This would have the secondary effect of giving his blows a bit more force. The shark circled again and then charged, but Spinner was able to meet it head on. He watched the dorsal fin approach and at the last second punched as hard as he could.

His fist connected with the shark's head just under the eye. Surprised that it had been struck, the shark spun quickly, thrashed the water with its large tail and disappeared. Jake's hopes soared. Maybe the tiger shark had had enough.

But it reappeared suddenly. It was less than fifteen feet away and still circling. "Come on, you son of a bitch. Finish this!"

But it was in no hurry. Sensing that its prey was losing strength, the tiger shark was fully prepared to wait and watch from a safe distance. Soon, its prey would be too weak to move.

Spinner was having a hard time keeping his eyes open. The elements and his wounds were sapping the last of his already drained reserves. Through increasingly blurred vision, he watched the tiger shark circle, then disappear for a time. He wasn't sure how long it was gone. Everything was moving in slow motion now. At one point, his sluggish brain told him that the shark had lost interest.

Spinner felt his head lolling to the side, and he shook himself awake. He slapped his face with his hand just in time to see the tiger shark accelerate toward him. Its nose caught him in the chest, lifting him out of the water. He saw rows of jagged teeth before driving his fist into the great fish's eye socket. The shark thrashed and broke off its charge. Spinner went under. Panicked, he clawed his way back to the surface.

He coughed up water and almost went down again. His arms no longer worked, and his legs felt like lead weights, pulling him downward. Even in his flagging state of consciousness, he knew the next charge would be the last. He knew the shark sensed this as well. Spinner watched as the huge predator angled in toward him.

Images flashed through his brain. Visions of his parents, his life as a boy, lovers and friends, his fallen comrades. All passed before him in an ethereal haze. The haze lifted as a great bulk accelerated toward him.

The water exploded in front of him. Spinner thought he heard the dull thud of two large, fleshy bodies colliding. He caught a glimpse of the shark's flank as it rolled violently away from him. Then he heard something else. The water was suddenly filled with the sound of whistles and high-pitched squeals. Just then, small curved dorsal fins surrounded him, forming a protective net. He felt strange vibrations penetrating his arms, chest, back, abdomen, and legs. The feeling was not unpleasant, just eerie. He felt like he was being scanned. He could no longer keep his eyes open. He rolled forward, face down in the black water.

The images returned like vapors. Spinner now dwelt in that world between life and death. He was vaguely aware he was moving. From time to time, his eyes would open and he would see shiny black backs all around him and underneath him, buoying him up. One smooth fusiform shape would sink down, only to be replaced by another, maintaining the continuity of the flotilla. The sensation felt like riding on a living mattress. All around him, explosive exhalations broke the stillness of the night. Strangely enough, he no longer felt cold.

He drifted off, carried along in a dreamscape. There were voices all around him. But they weren't human voices. What surprised him, even in this dream state, was that he actually understood what they were saying. It wasn't a language that you spoke or heard, yet there was the image in his head, as clear as if someone had just spoken it to him.

The old female dolphin that had led him to San Mateo cove, swam next to him in his dream. She spoke in a language that was older than time—yet somehow, he understood her. Now he knew every one of the members of the maternal subgroup, their affiliation and their family history. He began to separate out the voices as the old matriarch helped direct his thoughts. The images would melt away into the ether, only to be replaced by another series of images.

His band of brothers was standing before him, shrouded in an ethereal mist. They were all younger, clean shaven, and dressed in battle fatigues. They were all grinning at him. These were not like his prior visions of maimed and screaming comrades dying before his eyes that had plagued him for so long. These men were vibrant and full of life. One by one, each member of his unit nodded to him and then turned and walked back into the mist.

Out of the mist a woman's face began to materialize. As Spinner strained to see through the fog, the image began to clear. It was Emily Rosen. She, too, was smiling. And then she said, "You die, Spinner, and I am going to kick your ass."

He thought it was only fitting that Rosen would be here busting his chops and setting him straight. *She is a force.* He found himself wishing he could say something to her. He didn't know what. Every time they came together, they just ended up pissing each other off. Emily's smiling face suddenly expressed fear and then horror. She and the others were in trouble. Their lives were in grave danger. The whalers were coming for them. There would be blood.

His dreams morphed into a nightmare landscape. He gazed across a crimson ocean. The struggling forms of dolphins and whales, bleeding and dying, were everywhere. Men with large flensing knives and harpoons stabbed at the water. The whales' screams drowned out all thoughts. Spinner was paralyzed—he could not come to their aid.

When he awoke, he knew he was near the end. He no longer felt the cold, nor the pain from his wounds. He turned his head enough to catch a glimpse of stars overhead. In the east the light was beginning to break. He looked around. He was in the center of a flotilla of dolphins, churning slowly through the sea. The air was punctuated with the regular sound of their explosive exhalations. With each spout, plumes of greenish bioluminescence hung briefly in the thick air. His hands were forward, grasping the dorsal fins of two parallel dolphins. The dolphins were packed tightly around him. The raft of dolphins undulated in one synchronous movement. A magic carpet ride, ocean style. A smile etched his parched blue lips.

*I'll be damned. If only those researchers and Rosen could see me now! Stick that in your notebooks, science geeks.*

He closed his eyes for several moments. He was about to drift back into sleep when he felt a presence close at hand. He opened one eye and found himself looking into the face of a very young dolphin. He recognized the four white spots on the little dolphin's head reminding him of a constellation. The calf studied Spinner with one eye, an eye filled with curiosity and—what else? The little dolphin moved his flukes vigorously, then rolled over slightly and placed its tiny pectoral fin flat on Jake's forearm. The gesture was deliberate and not lost on him. His eyes began to sting and he knew the source wasn't the saline brine he had been immersed in for so many hours.

Jesús Trujillo awoke to the dog barking. He lay in his bunk on his back and stared at the palm frond-thatched ceiling barely visible in the pre-dawn light. He yawned, swung his legs over the edge of the wooden bed and sat up. His wife, Dora, was still asleep on the other side of the bed, facing away from him. He stood slowly and stretched out his back, feeling tendons and ligaments complain loudly.

It had been an exhausting five days. He and Carlos had been fishing farther up the coast than they had ever ventured before. They had to go further away from their normal fishing grounds to find enough fish. This meant camping on strange beaches and sleeping in the panga. He was glad when they pulled into the fishing camp late last night. The promise of his own bed and lying next to his wife had never felt so good. He walked to the kitchen sink, poured water into a blackened cook pot and lit the propane burner.

The dog barked again. This time its yips were more emphatic. Spinner had left the dog here after he had limped his boat into the fishing camp for repairs. Jesús had pleaded with Spinner to take the dog with him, but the *Americano loco* said he didn't know where he was going to be from one day to the next. Once he found Macario, he'd come back for the dog. That was nearly two weeks ago.

"Jesús, it's so early," said Dora, her voice muffled by the pillow she had pulled over her head. "Can't you quiet that dog?"

"Something has got him excited," said Jesús. "Perhaps that family of coyotes has returned."

"Jesús! Shut that dog up!"

He pulled on a pair of jeans and slid his feet into sandals. He walked to the door when he heard his wife say, "I curse Jake Spinner for leaving that dog with us!"

Jesús stood in the doorway and shrugged. He really didn't mind the dog at all. He stepped out into the cold morning air and looked down the beach. He could barely see the dog in the pre-dawn light. It was frantically running back and forth, barking at something in the surf line. Jesús thought about fixing a cup of coffee and taking it with him as he walked the beach. Dora put an end to that thought.

"Today, Jesús!"

"Ay, woman. I've been at sea for five days. I haven't even gotten my land legs back yet."

Jesús grabbed his jacket off a hook on the wall and stepped outside. He felt the cold damp air against his face and shivered slightly. He regretted getting out of his warm bed. He began walking toward the source of the disturbance. The dog ran down to the water's edge, barked, and paced. No coyotes were in sight.

He saw something in the shallows—several dorsal fins moving back and forth. At first, he thought the dolphins were aiding one of their stranded family members. It wasn't until he was almost upon them that he realized the object floating in the water wasn't another dolphin. He saw wet black hair matted on a skull, and he realized he was looking at a man. He ran into the foot-deep water and stood over the sodden figure. Jesús's breath caught in his throat. He was looking at Jake Spinner—or what was left of him.

The dolphins remained dangerously close, risking being stranded in the shallow water. Jesús watched their erratic behavior. *Did the dolphins bring him here?* He turned his attention back to Spinner. The crazy gringo's face was devoid of color. He had been in the water for a long time. His lips were blue. There was blood on his shirt.

Jesús dragged the inert body to the water's edge.

"Dios mío." Jesús said softly. He held Spinner's head and torso above the water and turned toward the fishing shacks. "Carlos! Wake up! Get down here!"

Jesús leaned down and checked Spinner's pulse, then put his head on Spinner's chest. He could barely hear any breathing.

"Señor Jake! Señor Jake! Can you hear me?" Jesús shook Spinner by the shoulders. Spinner groaned softly when Jesús grabbed his left shoulder. He turned Spinner enough to see a piece of bloodstained rag stuffed into a small hole in his shoulder.

Carlos stumbled, shirtless, out of his shack. He held a hand up to shield his eyes.

Jesús shouted, "Get down here now! And bring blankets!"

Carlos stared at his friend uncomprehendingly for a moment, then shot inside. He emerged a few minutes later carrying an armful of blankets. When he drew nearer, he looked at the dolphins, then at the limp form in Jesús's arms.

"It's Spinner," said Jesús. "He's been shot. Help me get him up on the beach."

Together, the two men carried Spinner to where the sand was nearly dry. Jesús stripped off his coat and placed it over Spinner's chest. They laid him gently on a blanket, then proceeded to cover him with the rest.

"We need to bring up his body temperature," said Jesús, "or he'll die."

The dog approached whining nervously. Recognizing Spinner, he began to enthusiastically lick his face. Carlos shooed the dog away.

"Stay with him. I'll wake Dora," Jesús said. "Then we'll move him up to the house."

Carlos nodded. He looked seaward at the dolphins that continued to swim slowly back and forth just offshore. "Do you think they brought him here?

"I don't know. There's no sign of a boat. But they seem to be waiting for something." Jesús sprinted up the beach to his fishing shack. He burst in the door and faced his wife in the kitchen.

"Dora, heat as much water as you can."

"What is it, Jesús?"

"Jake Spinner came back for his dog."

# 48

The video was first picked up by an obscure station in Vermont which ran it on the six o'clock news. At 10:00 a.m., a news station in New York City aired the video. A station in Los Angeles soon picked it up. Seattle followed, then Portland aired the piece on their evening news.

Within twelve hours, the video had been aired in Ireland, Great Britain, and France. The recording of the slaughter at the cove began streaming on the internet. By the next morning, it was appearing on social media throughout Mexico. Within twenty-four hours of the first airing, it had amassed nearly half a million views worldwide. A groundswell was in the making.

From his suite above the city of La Paz, Hirokan Yoshimatsu knew that their time frame had to be moved up. He had seen Figueroa interviewed on Mexican television regarding the video of the dolphin slaughter. The Minister of Fisheries stated to a group of reporters that his office was launching an investigation to determine who was responsible. Presently, they were looking into the authenticity of the video. Figueroa said that if the video was found to be authentic, then the perpetrators of this crime would be brought to justice. The hidden message Figueroa sent to Yoshimatsu was that the operation was on borrowed time. The next hunt had to take place very soon.

Yoshimatsu wasn't comfortable with disorder. He stared out from the terrace overlooking the city. The sun was peeking over the mountains, casting everything below in a golden light. Things were in chaos. The search for Spinner's body had been futile. Three crews of men in launches had scoured the area for several hours to no avail. He had a feeling of foreboding, an emotion that was foreign to him. He tried to reassure himself that Spinner had been twenty miles from shore when he leapt from the ship and, as best they could tell, had taken two slugs on the way down. Even if he'd survived the fall, no one could last that long in cold water with wounds. There were many predators that lived in the ocean that would be drawn to a bleeding man.

Kanamura had informed him that seven more whalers had deserted the hunt. The indios had become sullen and fearful. When Kanamura and his enforcers went to the whalers' homes, he found their houses in disarray and their personal effects missing.

Yoshimatsu's cell phone rang. He knew who it was before he pulled it from his jacket pocket. "Hello Sato-san. It has been a while since we last spoke."

"Yes, my esteemed friend. It has been too long. I wanted to call you and see how you are progressing with the plans for the next procurement."

"Everything is in order." Yoshimatsu's tone gave away no emotion. "We are moving up the timetable in order to deliver the products to our buyers in an expedited fashion."

"That's good. Our buyers grow concerned that we will not be able to make the deliveries as promised. They are worried that something will happen to ruin the harvest."

"Everything is under control."

"The board of directors is concerned." Sato Izumi sounded smug. "We have heard rumors of unrest among the indigenous people, and there are reports of increased desertions."

"That is all they are—rumors. We have our transport trucks on standby, our boom crews ready with all the necessary materials, and the chaser boats are awaiting my command."

"This morning, the board discovered a most disturbing video on the internet. It showed a dolphin hunt being disrupted and broken up by one man in a boat. This is of great concern to the board. Certain members are questioning whether you are fit for the task of carrying out the next hunt."

Yoshimatsu was seething. It was everything he could do to maintain his air of steely calm. He knew that Sato was attempting a power grab.

"The one who disrupted the last hunt has been dealt with. The others that are responsible for the video are in hiding. It is only a matter of time before my contacts find them and they are silenced. It is unfortunate that this video was released, but it will not matter. My contacts will deflect any unwanted attention until the operation is complete."

"I am glad to hear that, Hiro-san. I wanted to let you know that the board of advisors has asked me to come there and observe the operation firsthand. They want a full report. I will be arriving in thirty-six hours."

"There is no need for you to come. You will only draw more attention. I have this under complete control."

The hesitancy in his tone pleased Sato greatly. It was not easy to catch Yoshimatsu off guard. "I am afraid the board has insisted. Do not worry, my friend. I will be, how do the Americans say, 'Like the fly upon the wall.' I wish to offer my assistance in any way that I can. Everyone in the Consortium wants you to be successful in this great endeavor."

"I will arrange for your transport from the airport." Yoshimatsu, regained his composure. "I value any assistance you can give."

"From the ship we can oversee the operation and bring it to a successful conclusion. I look forward to our meeting." Sato clicked off.

Yoshimatsu stared at the phone. Then, in a fit of rage, he turned and flung it against the wall, shattering the device into pieces. Susan had entered the room and was barely able to avoid some of the flying fragments.

She didn't say a word, just stood and waited for her boss to speak. Finally, Yoshimatsu turned away from her and again stared out at the sunrise on the bay.

"Get me Kanamura."

# 49

Rosen and the two researchers were worried about returning to either Insurgentes or La Paz, so they drove all the way to Loreto. Raúl had argued with them that going to an internet café was dangerous and foolhardy given the present situation, but the three would not be dissuaded. Raúl soon realized he was no match in a battle of wills with these three strong women.

Raúl carried Jake's semi-auto tucked in the back of his waistband and concealed by his shirttail. He had checked out the café before allowing the women to enter. A back door led to an alley between buildings. After reconnoitering the street and the alley, he signaled to the women that it is was safe to enter.

Sandy, Paola, and Rosen worked on their laptops while Raúl sat at small table near the entrance, keeping watch. They not only had internet access, but also were able to make cell phone connections. Rosen was conducting an interview with a BBC station in London. Paola followed up with contacts that Alejandro had given her, including colleagues in Mexico and the United States who could lend their voices to their cause. She had emailed the video to all of them, requesting any assistance they could provide to halt the upcoming hunt.

The problem was that no one knew exactly when the hunt was to be. Raúl had not heard from Alma Quintín, his contact in Puerto Nacimiento. He worried that Alma had lost her nerve or worse.

Sandy scrolled through her email and stopped when she saw Graham Neely's name. The email was all in caps: "CALL ME WHEN YOU GET THIS MESSAGE!"

She reached for her phone on the desk and punched in Graham's number in the States. He picked up almost immediately.

"Sandy?"

"Yep. It's me, Graham. What have you got?"

"I sent the video to a bunch of enviro groups. Sea Shepherd Conservation Society, Greenpeace, WWF, Defenders, and the Humane Society are posting it."

"That's great. Any chance any of them can get down here and give us a hand. One of our group is banged up pretty badly, and we think they might have killed another."

"Holy shit. Who was it?"

Sandy hesitated for a moment. She felt her throat tighten up. "Jake Spinner, the guy from the video."

"Oh my God."

"We need support down here, Graham. Can you convince any of the organizations to send some volunteers?"

"They all asked the same question, Sandy. When's the next hunt?"

"I don't know, damn it! They're hunkered down for now due to the publicity out there. But they're not going to leave. Not until they get what they came for."

"For what it's worth, I managed to get hold of a thirty-foot catamaran that a friend of a friend has moored in Cabo San Lucas. Six of us are flying out to Cabo day after tomorrow."

"One boat." The disappointment was evident in her voice. "If there is any chance—any chance at all—of getting more people down here . . . "

"Look. These people are doing this on their own dime. They're about to risk their lives for your cause. We're doing the best we can."

"I'm sorry, Graham. Every one of us is wound pretty tight right now. We appreciate any and all help you can give."

"No worries. With a little luck, we'll be in La Paz in a couple of days. I just hope we're not too late."

"Me, too. . . . Graham?"

"Yes?"

"Thanks. Thanks for doing this."

"See you soon. Call me if you hear the timetable has been moved up."

"I will."

Graham clicked off.

Raúl left his station at the front of the café and walked back to where the three women were sitting. "We need to go. We've been here too long."

The ride back to the ranchito was quiet. No one felt like making small talk. Since their time in the café had been limited, each of them had worked to prioritize which contacts were the most urgent. They had all performed their tasks for the day: retrieved emails, answered emails, and made the calls that had to be made.

Emily Rosen stared out the window, her head leaning against the glass. She felt like she was slogging through a slow-moving dream. She still couldn't believe that Jake Spinner was dead. She felt a hollowness that wouldn't go away. Part of her was still pissed at Spinner for deserting them. But more than that, she found herself missing him. For the first time since she had arrived, Emily thought about packing it all up and catching the first northbound plane she could find.

The group had initiated a media event. The video was turning up in television newsrooms around Europe and the United States, and it had even been aired in Australia. Hopefully, the public outcry would be so great that it would reverberate in the government halls of Mexico City. At this time, only a presidential order could stop the imminent slaughter. Rosen hoped upon hope that the president of Mexico would respond quickly and forcefully to bring this lunacy to a grinding halt.

An idea for an exposé was gelling in her mind. She had been compiling information since she signed on with the researchers. The elements of a story began to take shape. Ideas and phrases, fragments of sentences, all began to swirl in a maelstrom in her brain. She was hoping for some kind of cohesiveness to her thoughts, but knew she was distracted over the death of Spinner. Now was the time for grieving, but she knew that a prolonged bereavement was a luxury that the ticking clock would not allow.

They arrived at the ranch in the early afternoon. Alejandro was sitting outside next to the front door, his injured leg propped up on a chair. Over the last two days, his mobility had improved: he could now transfer himself in and out of bed and was able to hobble to the bathroom using crutches. He looked relieved to see his colleagues again.

Sandy walked up to him and gave him a hug then kissed him on one cheek "That's from Lili." She kissed him on the other cheek. "That's from Carmen."

Alejandro blushed. "Are they okay?"

"They miss you, Alex. Very much. Carmen didn't understand why you didn't have the doctor call her first. I told her you were worried about their safety and also trying to warn us of the danger to the team. They're glad you're in a safe place."

"For now," said Raúl, as he walked past them.

"Lili got on the phone. She told me she's very proud of her papá. She wants you to save all the dolphins."

Alejandro turned his head away for a moment, overcome with emotion. When he turned back, he looked at Sandy and grabbed her hands. "Thank you. Thank you for contacting my family."

Sandy nodded. "Want to hear who we connected with today, Director Cabrillo?"

"I'm all ears. Let's go inside and talk. Besides, lunch is almost ready."

Alejandro put his leg down and attempted to stand. Sandy reached out to support him. "No, I can do this." Painfully, he stood up, placed the crutches under his arms and hobbled into the house.

Guadalupe and Alisa brought to the table plates of beans, rice, and flour tortillas followed by *pollo a la barbacoa*. Young Julio carried his own plate and sat next to his father. He was at that age where he mimicked everything his father did. They all dug in hungrily. Except Rosen. She stared at the empty seat across from her.

"So, what do we have?" Alejandro looked around the table. His gaze landed on Sandy. "You start, Sandy."

"Well, the good news: the Cetus Global Alliance is sending a group down here. They'll be here in three days."

"Never heard of them. How many boats?" Alejandro queried.

"That's the bad news. One boat. They're picking up a catamaran in La Paz."

"A catamaran? This isn't a regatta."

"That's all they have—a skeleton crew and a borrowed boat. They've only been an NGO for six months or so."

"One boat and a catamaran are not going to stop anyone," said Raúl. "Who knows how many boats they'll use to herd the dolphins. We're going to need more boats."

Alejandro asked, "Do you think we can count on the help of some of the local fishermen?"

"We have to be careful," replied Raúl. "Most of the fishermen I know are good men. But even good men can be turned if it means a better life for them and their families. We approach one who is not sympathetic to our cause, we'll end up having a visit from men with guns."

Alejandro's face showed concern. "Yes. Yes, I see what you mean."

"At this point, I don't know if we can trust Fernando and Alma Quintín," said Raúl. "Fernando has a long history of questionable fishing practices. They are poor and could be easily influenced by the promise of more money." Raúl turned and wiped Julio's mouth from a smattering of beans that had leaked out from his burrito. "I'll continue to try and recruit the fishermen that I've known to be honest men."

Alejandro sighed, then turned his attention to Paola. "Were you able to connect with the contacts I gave you?"

"Yes. I've sent copies of the video to the *Instituto de Nacional de Ecologia* and to the Attorney General for Environmental Protection. They said they'd get back to us."

"Now, that's something. As soon as we find out when the next hunt is, we need to let them know as quickly as possible, so they can mobilize. Good work, Paola."

Alejandro looked at Rosen. "What have you got, Emily?"

Rosen had been staring out the kitchen window toward the corral. "What? Oh. I'm sorry. My contacts continue to send the video out. My contact at CNN got it slotted into the evening news last night. I just learned that it's been aired in Australia. I received more info on Yoshimatsu and his involvement with the Yakuza."

Paola asked, "How is he connected to the Yakuza?"

"Think Japanese mafia," said Rosen. "They're into a lot of the same practices as the mafia in the U.S. They have a particularly extensive shipping network headed by Yoshimatsu that specializes in illegal fishing practices, the worldwide distribution of contraband, including the selling of whale meat and the illegal dolphin trade for theme parks. Their connections go deep into every industrialized nation, including the United States."

Paola eyes grew wide. "The United States is obtaining illegal dolphins?"

"From what I've seen, the paperwork goes through shadowy holding companies that are difficult to trace, most of them belonging to the Consortium, as that branch of the Yakuza is called." Rosen looked around the room. "I have enough info on this guy Yoshimatsu to burn him if we can connect him to the hunt. But here's the rub—putting him next to those whalers is going to be nearly impossible. Yoshimatsu doesn't make a lot of mistakes."

By the flatness in Rosen's voice, Alejandro could tell that she was distracted and disheartened. He couldn't blame her. Even though they all knew that Spinner had willingly gone to his death yesterday, the stark reality of his murder was still sinking in for all of the team.

After lunch Rosen retired to the bunkhouse, crawled into her bunk and leaned against the wall. She stared into her laptop, scrolling through the info that she had attempted to organize into the beginnings of a detailed exposé. Part of her wished she had an internet connection, but she had no idea who to talk to about her feelings. Hell, she couldn't even explain what she was feeling. She had broken one of her key tenets of investigative reporting—don't get emotionally involved. In order to write an objective piece of journalism, she needed to be detached. That had gone out the window after she'd spent time among the whales and gotten to know the researchers, Raúl and his family— and Spinner. In her anguish, she felt the sudden urge to turn her back on it all.

Suddenly Paola burst in, eyes wide. "Emily! You need to come quick!"

"What?" Rosen swung her legs out of the bunk.

"Spinner's alive!"

# 50

"How bad is he?" Raúl asked, holding the phone to his ear, dreading the answer Jesús was about to give.

"Está muy mal," said Jesús. "He was shot twice, and as best as we can guess, he was in the water for six to eight hours."

Rosen and Paola rushed in. "Is it true?" Rosen asked, her voice shaky. "Is he okay?"

Raúl held up a hand to quiet her. The air around the room was thick with tension. All eyes focused on him.

"He's lost a lot of blood," continued Jesús in Spanish. "He's too weak to make the trip in to La Paz."

"How did he make it to your fishing camp?" Raúl asked.

"You would not believe me if I told you."

"He didn't swim there, did he? Not with two bullets in him."

"We think the dolphins brought him here. They left him in the shallows where we found him early this morning. They've been hanging around just off the beach since we pulled him out."

"Dios mío." Raúl lowered the phone. He looked as if he had just seen a spirit. He looked around the room at the anxious faces that were hanging on his every word. He drew a deep breath. "Spinner's alive, but barely so."

There were gasps in the room followed by a barrage of questions from everyone. Raúl held up a hand to quiet them. "Let me hear what Jesús has to say."

"*Necesita un médico ahora mismo,*" Jesús said. "Can you bring a doctor? He needs his wounds tended, and I'm sure he needs a transfusion."

"Blood type!" Rosen exclaimed. "What's his blood type?"

Raúl looked at Rosen, then spoke into the phone again. "Did you ask Jake what his blood type is?"

"Sí," said Jesús. "He woke up long enough to tell us that he is O positive."

293

Raúl looked crestfallen. "We may have difficulty finding a doctor who is willing to go out there. The federales may be keeping an eye on the hospitals."

"Whoever you bring, you'd better hurry. Jake Spinner is on borrowed time. I need to sign off, Raúl. My battery is low."

"Call me if anything happens. I'll call you as soon as we have medical assistance and are on the water."

"Buena suerte," said Jesús and clicked off.

The room exploded in a cacophony of raised voices, all asking questions and seeking information. Raúl held up both hands to silence them. "We don't have much time. Jake Spinner needs a doctor right now. I have to go into La Paz and see if I can convince one to go out to Jesús's fishing camp."

"I'm coming with you," said Emily.

Alejandro asked, "What's his blood type?"

"O positive," said Raúl. "That's what Jake told Jesús before he passed out."

"I'm O positive," said Rosen.

"Me, too," added Sandy.

Raúl looked back and forth between them. "All right. One problem solved. We need to leave immediately and go into La Paz. I'll phone ahead and see if one of my friends can ready my boat. Bring only what you need. We leave in twenty minutes."

"I must tell you, Señorita Emily," Raúl said, touching her shoulder. "Jesús said that Señor Jake is . . . " Raúl struggled to find the right words. "He may not make it. He was shot twice and was in the water for a long time."

"Well, I guess we're wasting time sitting around here jawing. I'll be ready in ten minutes."

Guadalupe gave Alisa the task of preparing food for their trip while she hastily put together a medicinal bundle from the pantry for Raúl to take with him. Alejandro caught glimpses of jars filled with herbs and strange liquids. Guadalupe's hands glided over them, selecting key ones and placing them on the counter nearby. Within several minutes she had a dozen bottles lined up. She contemplated them, then eliminated six of the concoctions. She called Raúl over and in rapid-fire Spanish instructed him in the application and dosage of each of the medicines.

Rosen threw together a change of clothes and, out of force of habit, grabbed her camera, laptop, her notebook, and pens. She tossed everything in her backpack and went back to the kitchen. The bagged food and medicines were sitting on the table.

Raúl came in carrying foul weather gear and water, followed by Sandy, her backpack slung over one shoulder. He went to the counter and gathered up the two sacks.

"Here. I can carry something," Rosen stepped in and took the two sacks from him.

Raúl knelt down and hugged Alisa. "I'll be back soon. He kissed her on the forehead.

In a small voice, Alisa asked, "Papá, is Señor Jake going to be okay?"

"I don't know, mija," Raúl said, putting her at arm's length and looking into her large brown eyes. "Señor Jake *es un hombre muy fuerte.* But he's hurt and needs medical help. I promise you, we'll do all that we can."

He looked past Alisa at Guadalupe. He could see the emotion in her eyes. He went to her and she touched his cheek. He hugged her and Julio.

"I'll be back as soon as I can." He broke the embrace and turned back to Emily and Sandy. "Ready?"

They both nodded. The three of them started for the door.

"Good luck," said Alejandro.

"Vayan con Dios," Paola said.

Their search for a doctor was an exercise in frustration and futility. The main hospital in La Paz may as well have been an impenetrable fortress, Rosen thought. No one in the emergency department offered to help and when Rosen asked about doctors in residency assisting them, the response from the administrator was terse and final. No one could be spared to make a four-hour boat trip. The patient had to be brought in to receive treatment. Looking around the various sections of the hospital, they noticed what appeared to be the beefed-up presence of federales.

After trying another private hospital without any luck, they turned to urgent care facilities. There were only three in the city. At the third clinic, when Raúl pleaded their case to a young doctor, she was sympathetic, but could offer no assistance. She was constrained by long hours at her job.

Seeing the looks of defeat on their faces, she was moved.

As Sandy, Emily, and Raúl shuffled out of the clinic, the doctor said, "Wait!"

She scribbled something on a prescription pad and handed it to Raúl. "His name is Arturo Ruíz. We went to medical school together in Grenada. He didn't like medicine so he went back to school. But he had training as a trauma surgeon."

"What did he go back to school for?" Rosen asked.

"Veterinary Medicine," replied the doctor. "Small animals, mostly."

"Oh, my God," said Sandy.

"Look. I don't even know if he'll agree to do this," said the doctor. "But from what you tell me, your friend's time is short. He may be your only option."

Raúl looked at the piece of paper, then back at the young internist. "Thank you. We'll give him a call."

Twenty minutes later, they were sitting in the small, but comfortable, home of Arturo Ruíz. He appeared to be in his mid-thirties, medium height and build, with curly black hair. He was dressed in a pair of jeans and a white button-down shirt. He led them to his living room and had them all take a seat. Raúl explained how they had found him. Each one of them filled in the story of the whale hunt leading up to the disappearance of Jake Spinner. Arturo didn't say anything but nodded throughout. Once, when Alejandro's name was mentioned, Arturo lit up. "I've met Alejandro. He's doing great work at the institute."

"Not right now," said Sandy. "The whalers ran him off the road and came to finish him off at the hospital. Luckily, Emily and Jake, uh—the man who needs your help—rescued him before the assassins could."

Arturo looked genuinely disturbed. "These men. The whalers. They are muy malo?"

"Sí," said Raúl. "They have no regard for life, whether it be human or animal."

Arturo looked at his hands then turned his gaze back to his guests. "I haven't performed surgery on a human being since I did a residency in trauma. I'm afraid my skills fall far short of what your friend needs. If I operated on him, I could be the cause of his ultimate demise. Surely, there must be someone else who can help."

"You don't understand," Rosen said, desperation in her voice. "You're our last hope. No one else would help us. And every minute that we're still in La Paz is one more minute off Jake Spinner's life."

Rosen saw that Arturo was still hedging. "I assume you're a vet now because of a passion for working with animals."

Arturo met Emily's gaze. "Sí. I wanted to help those without a voice."

"We watched Jake Spinner break through a barrier and single-handedly free over a hundred dolphins that were about to be slaughtered for their meat."

"Mexico does not sanction the killing of marine mammals in her waters," Arturo said indignantly.

"Oh. Really?" Rosen pull her laptop from her backpack and opened it. She brought up the video and played it. Arturo watched and the three of them saw the look of horror grow on his face.

"How could anyone allow this to happen?" He shook his head.

Sandy rubbed two fingers against her thumb. "Money. Plain and simple. Someone's dirty in the Mexican government, and they're in cahoots with members of the Japanese mafia."

When it came to the part where Jake crashed the barrier, Arturo sat back in his chair and blew out a long, ragged breath. "He's either very brave or certifiably insane."

"Equal amounts of both," said Rosen.

"How will you get to him?"

"There's only one way," Raúl said. "By boat."

"I was afraid you were going to say that," said Arturo. He sighed. "At one time, I dreamt of being *un biólogo marino*, but I had to give up that dream. You see, I get seasick. It's horrible."

"Then you won't help us?"

"I didn't say that, Señorita Rosen. I'm letting you know this to prepare you for what will promise to be a most unpleasant trip."

Sandy needed confirmation. "Then you'll do it?"

"I need a few minutes to organize some equipment. And I need to stop by my clinic. Your friend, Jake Spinner—you don't happen to know his blood type, do you?"

"O positive," said Emily. "You have two compatible and willing donors right here."

Arturo stood. "I'll meet you down at the pier in forty-five minutes."

"Please hurry," said Emily. "Every minute counts."

Within the hour, Raúl had loaded and fueled the boat and Emily and Sandy were settled into the front two seats. They all watched nervously for the arrival of the veterinarian. Raúl also kept a watchful eye on the comings and goings of people on the pier. So far, he had not spied any federales or men of Asian descent prowling about.

Just when Rosen began seriously entertaining thoughts that the small animal vet would bail on them, they saw a figure hastily weave his way through the crowd walking along the malecón. He reached the pier and Rosen saw that he carried two large metal cases. His backpack was slung over his back with several pole-like projections sticking above his head like some bizarre type of plumage. He stopped and looked up and down the line of boats tied at the many slips until he spotted them, walking as rapidly as he could walk, given his heavy burden.

Movement from the pier caught Raúl's attention. A life on the ocean had enhanced his ability to look at a seascape and recognize when something wasn't right. A ripple on the water's surface could indicate a school of fish suddenly changing course, or that same ripple could signal barely submerged rocks that could rip out the bottom of your hull. It was this sixth sense that focused his eyes on two men in the crowd on the malecón. They were looking right at him and the others in the boat. Their attention turned to the veterinarian rushing down the stairs to the slips. Raúl noticed these two men stood out from the other tourists and fishermen—a large Asian dressed in a dark suit and his partner, a uniformed federale.

"We're about to have company." Raúl fired up the engine and yelled to Sandy, "Cast off the bowline!"

Sandy and Emily looked at him, their faces registering confusion until they saw the two large men pushing their way through the crowd to get to them. Sandy ran forward and quickly untied the bowline.

Rosen looked at Arturo. "Run! Hurry!" She pointed past him at the two approaching assailants. Arturo looked over his shoulder and broke into a stumbling run. He reached the slip just as the two men jumped down onto the boardwalk. He handed the cases over to Sandy and Rosen, then jumped into the boat. Raúl slammed the throttle into reverse, and the launch lurched backward, nearly spilling Arturo into the water. Only Sandy's hand on his belt loop kept the veterinarian from going overboard. Raúl shifted the throttle into forward and the boat roared ahead. The federale and the Asian brandished pistols.

"Keep your heads down!" Raúl yelled.

Raúl zigzagged the boat and aimed toward two large sailboats moored in the middle of the harbor. He veered the boat between the two craft and surged out the other side, pointing the boat to the northwest and not looking back.

# 51

Arturo's prediction that it would be a very long trip turned out to be a self-fulfilling prophecy. The winds had been steadily building as they motored up the coast. Soon Arturo was reduced to leaning over the gunwale and emptying the contents of his stomach until there was nothing left. Rosen had heard about people turning green from motion sickness, and he definitely had. She felt genuine sympathy for him. He looked absolutely miserable.

Conversation had been minimal. Everyone was too worried about what they'd find when they arrived at San Vicente fishing camp. The sun was low on the horizon. This meant performing surgery by flashlight or propane lantern, definitely not optimal conditions. As they pulled into the cove, two figures ran down to the waterline.

Rosen heard the hiss of sand on the hull as Raúl guided the boat onto the beach. He lifted the engine as one of the men waded out to keep the boat from broaching on the incoming surf. Sandy handed the bowline to the second man, who ran it up the beach and wrapped it around a large angular boulder. Rosen jumped onto the sand and turned to take one of the cases from Arturo. The veterinarian stumbled toward the bow and handed the second case to one of the fishermen. Raúl helped the unsteady Arturo off the boat. The vet immediately crossed himself.

"How is he?" Raúl asked Jesús.

"He hasn't been awake for several hours. "He turned to Arturo who looked like he had just disembarked from the boat ride from Hell. "Are you the doctor?"

Arturo looked up at the two fishermen. "In a manner of speaking. Arturo Ruiz, small animal vet."

Jesús looked incredulously at Raúl. "It's a very long story and we're wasting time. Where is he?"

"Follow me," said Carlos.

None of them was prepared for what they saw when they entered Carlos's ramshackle home. Spinner was lying on a cot, wrapped in blankets. His ashen face was shiny with sweat. Rosen rushed to his side and knelt down.

"Spinner! Can you hear me?" She shook him gently as her eyes welled with tears. He moaned something incomprehensible. His eyes fluttered open briefly, then closed.

Arturo stepped forward. "I'm going to need to see the wounds." He motioned to Jesús and Carlos. "Here. Help me turn him." Together, they managed to move Spinner onto his side. Spinner grunted in pain but didn't wake up. Arturo studied the wounds in Spinner's shoulder and side. He pulled on a pair of sterile gloves and gently probed the wounds.

"He got lucky here," said Arturo as he examined the exit in the front of his left shoulder. "It looks like a flesh wound. Mostly the middle deltoid and a part of the teres minor. No major damage here. Doesn't look like any major blood vessels or nerves were affected."

Next, he turned his attention to the hole in Spinner's right side. He saw that there was no exit wound. That meant the bullet was still lodged inside somewhere. That wasn't good news. He inspected the skin around the wound and noticed a deep, purplish blotch running along Spinner's lower rib cage. Ruíz palpated along the rib and found a jagged portion of the rib beneath his finger.

"I can't say for sure, but judging by the discoloration along the rib here, I think the bullet fractured his rib and is lodged somewhere nearby." Arturo looked at Jesús and Carlos. "Have you noticed him coughing up any blood?"

"No," said Jesús. "When we first brought him in, he coughed up some seawater, but no blood."

Arturo removed his gloves and went to one of the metal cases. He opened the case and stared at the surgical instruments. *Had he brought the right ones?* His stomach was still doing flip-flops. He couldn't tell if the queasiness was due to the difficult boat ride or the dreaded anticipation of performing surgery on the semi-conscious human lying in front of him. He took a deep breath. And to think what he had originally planned for this day was to watch Mexico take on Brazil in World Cup soccer.

He motioned to Rosen. "See those extensions sticking out of my pack? Those are the poles for the IV lines. I need you and Sandy to set those up for me."

Rosen went over to the pack and pulled the metal extensions free. She handed one to Sandy and they began assembling the pieces.

"I'm going to need a free arm and a unit of blood from each of you soon." Arturo looked to Jesús and Carlos. "I'll be needing an assistant to help me with the surgery."

Carlos and Jesús looked nervously at the veterinarian, then at each other. "Señor," said Carlos, "I don't think we—"

"I can assist," said Rosen. "Just tell me what to do."

"No, Emily. You are already helping by giving blood. You might be lightheaded after we draw blood from you. I need to have someone assisting me who's fully awake."

From the back room, two women emerged. The younger of the two, a dark-skinned woman with her hair tied in a braid and wearing a traditional peasant blouse and a long skirt, appraised Arturo momentarily and then spoke. "My name is Dora Trujillo Sánchez. I am the wife of Jesús. I have helped deliver many babies up and down this coast. I can assist you."

"You are a midwife?"

"Sí, Señor."

"Your help will be greatly appreciated."

Arturo requested that everyone not directly involved with the surgery leave the room. Rosen and Sandy were seated at the rough-hewn kitchen table. Arturo inserted needles in both of their arms. A flow of deep red blood began. Rosen watched, fascinated as her vital fluid flowed into the IV bag. She looked from the bag to Spinner as Arturo and Dora draped and prepared him for surgery. At one point, she noticed Sandy's free hand resting on hers. Sandy gave Rosen's hand a squeeze.

"He's going to be okay, Em. We just have to believe it."

Rosen swallowed hard and nodded, unable to speak.

A few moments later, Arturo returned to the table and disconnected both of the lines from the women. "Make sure you drink something soon, preferably some juice, or at the very least, water."

He went back to Spinner and did his best to sterilize the surgical field. He looked at Dora and took a deep breath. "Ready?"

"Sí." She nodded her head

Spinner was on an IV drip that delivered anesthesia. Per Arturo's instructions, Dora set out the surgical instruments. Arturo decided to go after the bullet first. He picked up the scalpel, took three deep breaths, and made a small incision just below the ribcage.

Time stood still for Rosen. The minutes felt like hours. How long had Spinner been under? She felt as if she were in some disjointed dream where none of the surrounding scenery made any sense. She was sitting at a table in a Mexican fishing *cabaña* but was looking at a make-shift surgical theater. The lighting in the building was eerie. The cot was bathed in the harsh white light of the lanterns, but she and Sandy were in the shadows at the periphery of the lanterns' illumination. She remembered seeing Arturo holding up a bloody forceps with a small red object between the teeth. The bullet had been removed. Several times, she'd felt lightheaded. Sandy reached into her backpack and drew out two small cartons of *jugo de manzana*. Rosen downed one and immediately felt better.

"Damn it!" Arturo swore once.

Rosen and Sandy came to full alert.

"Sorry. We're okay here. Lost the end of the suture for a moment."

"Please. Don't do that to me," said Rosen.

An hour later, Arturo stood erect and removed his surgical mask. His face and arms were shiny with sweat, and his shirt was soaked through. He walked over to the table and looked down at Emily and Sandy. "That is one lucky *hombre*. Both of those bullets could have been fatal. Someone was watching out for him."

Rosen asked, "Is he going to be okay?"

"If he doesn't get a secondary infection, I think he'll be okay. The next twenty-four hours will tell. He's on his second unit of blood right now. We'll see how that goes, but I wouldn't go out and celebrate with some shots of tequila. I still may need to tap a vein."

Rosen stood. "Can I sit with him?"

Arturo nodded." Yes. I'm going to step out for a while to get some fresh air. Call me if his breathing changes, or you see something that doesn't seem right."

"I will." Rosen touched Arturo's arm. "Thank you, Doctor Ruíz."

"Don't thank me yet."

Arturo walked over to where Dora was cleaning up and placing the instruments back in their respective cases. He touched her on the shoulder and said something in Spanish that Rosen couldn't hear, but the look of gratitude on Dora's face said it all.

Emily found a wooden chair and dragged it to where Spinner lay sleeping. She sat next to him and studied his face. His face was drawn, and he seemed smaller than she remembered him from a few days ago. She watched the slow rise and fall of his chest. She then placed her hand over his and leaned forward toward the cot.

"Come on, Jake. You can do this."

It was dark outside when Arturo stepped into the cool night air. A sliver of moon hung in the west, and overhead the canopy of stars looked close enough to touch. A little way down the beach, figures huddled around a bonfire. Arturo trudged over toward them. He felt bone weary. He stepped carefully in the sand. One careless step and he would spend the rest of the night face down in the sand, too exhausted to get up.

As he drew closer, he recognized Raúl, Sandy, Jesús, and Carlos, their faces illuminated by the flames. Another younger man stood next to Carlos. Everyone had a bottle of beer in hand.

As the veterinarian appeared in the light, the others looked his way and greeted him warmly.

"Hey, Doc," said Sandy. "Care for a tepid cerveza?"

"Best offer I've had all day."

Carlos reached into a rusted ice chest and produced a bottle of Pacífico. He popped the cap, and it was passed along until it found Arturo's hands.

"Gracias," said Arturo. In unison, the entire group raised their bottles to him in a toast.

"Thank you," said Sandy. "For coming out here and saving Jake's life when no one else would."

Heartfelt thanks were spoken from the group to a blushing Arturo. He took a long pull from the bottle, closed his eyes and let the warm beer slide slowly and deliciously down his throat. "That is the nectar of the gods."

"Dr. Ruíz," said Jesús. "This is my brother Francisco."

The two men shook hands.

"He's the best boat mechanic in Baja del Sur," Jesús continued. To Francisco he said, "and this is the best doctor on this side of Baja!"

Arturo grinned. "I might be the only doctor on this side of Baja." Deflecting their attention from him, Arturo said to Jesús, "I couldn't have done this without the help of your wife, Dora. *Ella es una mujer de corazón muy fuerte.*"

Jesús was beaming. He clinked his bottle with Arturo's.

Ruíz downed the last of his beer. Carlos went to reach for another from the ice chest, but Arturo held up one hand. "No, gracias. I'd better check on the patient and I can barely keep my eyes open now."

Jesús took the empty beer bottle from the vet. "We have an extra cot in our casita. You would honor us by sleeping there tonight."

"Thank you, but I need to keep an eye on the patient. The next twenty-four hours are critical."

If you're too tired, you're not going to be any good to Spinner," interjected Sandy. "We can take shifts and keep watch. If anything comes up, we'll come and roust you right quick."

Arturo relented. He knew the gringa was right. He was all used up.

"Come, Dr Ruiz. Let's get you fed and then you can sleep," said Jesús.

When Emily Rosen awoke, it was barely light in the fishing shack. She felt an immediate sharp pain in her neck and realized she'd been sleeping curled up in the rickety chair. She painfully unfolded herself, stretched, and yawned. Her clothes felt damp, and her mouth felt like all of her teeth were wearing little sweaters. When she focused her gaze on Spinner, she almost leapt out of the chair. His eyes were open and he was looking at her.

"You're awake!"

"Couldn't sleep," Spinner said hoarsely. "Your snoring woke me up."

"Bullshit, Spinner. I don't snore."

Spinner smiled weakly, then closed his eyes again. "Where am I?"

"The fishing camp at San Vicente."

Spinner's eyes shot open. He looked around, attempted to raise his head, then grimaced as a bolt of pain shot through his ravaged body. Rosen put a hand on his forearm. "Relax, Jake. You've had a hell of a few days."

The taut muscles in Spinner's neck gradually relaxed, and his breathing returned to near normal. He opened his eyes again and looked down to see Rosen's hand on top of his. Another smile etched his parched lips. "Glad you're here."

"I'm going to go get the doc. I think he'd like to see how his handiwork turned out." She removed her hand and stood stiffly. "I'll be right back."

As she opened the door to step outside, Spinner called to her.

"Hey?"

She turned around.

"I need to pee. I don't think I can do it myself."

Rosen stared at him for a couple of seconds, then stepped back inside and closed the door. "You're going to owe me big time, Jake Spinner."

Doc Ruíz was awakened, and he quickly got up to check on his patient. Jake was conscious and talking. Everyone wanted to see him, but Arturo limited the visitors to Emily and Sandy. Spinner was still groggy and in a lot of pain, although he wouldn't admit it. Ruíz surreptitiously adjusted the morphine drip and soon Spinner was sleeping soundly again.

Rosen walked over to where Arturo was pulling four-by-four-inch gauze bandages out of one of the metal cases. He looked more rested and had managed to get cleaned up a little.

"Doc, I was wondering if you could spare me for a few minutes. I'd like to wash up and get something to eat."

"No problem. There's a shower stall behind Jesús's house. Unfortunately, there's only one temperature to the water."

"Let me guess—refreshing?"

"You could say that."

Rosen went outside to look for Sandy. She spied her down near the water's edge standing with Raúl and Jesús. The morning sun cast a silvery glow to the nearly flat seas. The dog was running circles around them, but their attention was focused out on the water. Emily trudged through the sand and, as she got closer, she could see what had gotten their attention.

Twenty yards out, curved dorsal fins moved slowly back and forth. Occasionally a head would peek out of the water revealing a searching eye.

Rosen asked, "Bottlenose?"

"Good eye, Em," said Sandy. "I just heard the most fantastic story. You need to hear this. Would you mind repeating it, Jesús?"

Sandy translated as Jesús spoke. "The other day I was awakened by the dog's barking. I went outside and saw something in the shallows. When I got closer, I saw the dolphins. They had pushed Señor Jake near to the beach so he wouldn't drown. They risked stranding themselves but managed to get him into the shallows."

"The dolphins brought him here?" Rosen was incredulous.

"I think so," said Jesús. "What's very strange is that they've been hanging around ever since they brought him in, swimming slowly back and forth just offshore."

Rosen saw one of the larger dolphins surface. She had a white blaze across her melon and an old deep scar running along the trailing edge of her dorsal fin. Swimming next to her was a much younger dolphin, who repeatedly poked his head out of the water, revealing several small white markings on his forehead.

"When I was a boy, my father told me stories," said Raúl. "He told me about pescadores being washed overboard during storms and then being rescued by groups of dolphins and returned to shore."

"Ay, I have heard similar stories," interjected Jesús. "But I've never seen dolphins acting like this. Why are they still hanging around?"

Rosen couldn't take her eyes off the dolphins. "They're waiting for Spinner."

Sandy stared at Rosen, then turned her gaze back to the milling dolphins. "There are many accounts, going back to the time of ancient Greece where scholars documented humans being rescued at sea by dolphins. The dolphins were so revered by the Greeks that killing or harming a dolphin was deemed a criminal act, punishable by death. As a scientist, I've been trained not to anthropomorphize. In other words, I'm not supposed to assign human characteristics to non-human animals. Lately, scientific research is revealing that animal brains have the capacity for emotion, altruism, and culture. If the dolphins are waiting to see if Spinner is okay, this adds more fuel to the existence of sentience in other species.

"I know one thing," said Rosen. "When Spinner wakes up, he's got some 'splainin' to do."

# 52

Sato Izumi entered the penthouse suite accompanied by two very large, sinister-looking men dressed in black suits. Susan met the entourage at the door. She smiled warmly and said, "Welcome, gentlemen. I hope you had a good flight. I'm Susan Lawrence." She was dressed in a dark blue business suit and heels.

She performed a traditional bow of respect, which Sato reciprocated with a half-bow. Susan had never met him before and was surprised to see that he was a tall, wiry man with a bald pate, and glasses that gave him a fish-eyed look. Yoshimatsu had told her, in a private moment, that he was a very, very dangerous man.

Sato looked around the room, nodding as his eyes took in the posh surroundings of the penthouse suite. His gaze returned to Susan. "My good friend, Hiro-san, always surrounds himself with things of beauty. I see he has not lost his touch."

Susan blushed just enough for Sato to notice, but quickly recovered. "Mr. Yoshimatsu will be with you momentarily. In the meantime, may I prepare you something to drink?"

Sato walked over to the bar and looked at the lineup of expensive liquors.

"Yes. I will have the Jameson's. No ice, please."

She looked at the two henchmen. They were both well over six feet, their necks bulging out of the tops of their expensive dress shirts. They could easily have been mistaken for football players, but Susan knew that they had not been recruited for their prowess in sports.

The two men looked at Sato. "Thank you, Miss Lawrence," Sato said, a thin smile crossing his lips. "Unfortunately, my colleagues are—as you Americans say—'still on the clock.'"

Just as she was serving the whiskey to Sato Izumi, Yoshimatsu strolled into the room. He was wearing a white silk suit, white shoes, and a silk ocean-blue

307

shirt. His face was tanned and he looked like he had just stepped off a yacht. He approached Sato, smiling. They bowed deeply to each other.

"It is good to see you, my friend," said Yoshimatsu. "You are looking well."

Susan knew this must be particularly difficult for Yoshimatsu. She knew damn well that her boss was not glad to see Izumi at all. The undercurrent of disdain that each man held for the other was palpable. If Susan hadn't known Yoshimatsu as well as she did, she would have believed the two old colleagues were getting together after a long absence.

She turned to Yoshimatsu. "Sir, may I bring you something to drink?"

"Gin and tonic, thank you, Susan." He turned his attention back to Izumi. "I trust you had a good flight, Sato-san?"

"Uneventful, my friend." He glanced briefly at Susan as she brought the cocktail over to Yoshimatsu.

"It is one of life's little pleasures, being able to find a bit of paradise in the Third World," said Yoshimatsu. "Come, we will sit on the veranda. It is a most beautiful night."

As they walked to the patio, Yoshimatsu said, "I have taken the liberty to order us dinner. I hope you don't mind."

"On the contrary, dinner sounds divine. Will the lovely Miss Lawrence be joining us?"

Susan handed Yoshimatsu his cocktail and caught the slightest look of irritation in his dark eyes. "Of course. That is," he said, turning to Susan and smiling, "if you would honor us with your presence this evening, Susan?"

She didn't miss a beat. "I would be honored, sir."

They sat and made small talk for a while. A short time later, the front door buzzed and Susan got up to let the room service attendants in. Two large carts approached the table pushed by waiters dressed in white. The carts were laden with generous arrangements of local seafood, including spiny lobster, octopus, and black sea bass.

"Also, a special fish for you to sample tonight," said Yoshimatsu. "This fish is a species endemic to the Upper Gulf. It is called totoaba, a rare delicacy."

Izumi's eyebrows arched. "Isn't this the fish prized for its swim bladder and sold on the market for $50,000 per kilo?"

Yoshimatsu nodded. "I am impressed by your knowledge, Sato-san. The chefs have prepared it in a most delicate wine sauce."

One of the waiters produced a bottle of Dom Pérignon and presented it to Yoshimatsu. He nodded and the attendant uncorked the bottle. As they dined, the conversation turned from the cuisine and culture of Mexico to talk of the two men's families. Because it was in Japanese, Susan was excluded from much of the conversation. Even though her grasp of the Japanese language was limited, she suspected each was playing a very subtle—yet methodical—verbal chess game with the other, waiting, watching, and listening for the other to reveal his hand.

There was a lull in the conversation. "So, tell me about the operation," Sato said, as he reached forward and speared another chunk of totoaba. "How is the planning coming along?"

Yoshimatsu smiled thinly. "Everything is in order. I am awaiting the confirmation of the cargo trucks from Tijuana. Our contact here has made arrangements for undisturbed passage once the cargo is picked up. We have two large semis equipped with freezers for long range hauling and preservation. We also have eight smaller trucks that have been outfitted for live animal transport."

"Where are the trucks going?"

"Different ports on the mainland of Mexico. They will be crossing to the mainland by ferry and then on to several airports with international connections."

"What about the ship? Is there not room to haul the meat back in the ship's freezers?"

Yoshimatsu poured himself another glass of champagne. He took a sip. "The venture here has exceeded our expectations. The freezers in the ship are full of whale meat, swordfish, tuna, and mahi mahi. I believe we also have several thousand pounds of manta rays that have been processed.

Sato's eyebrows rose slightly. "I thought that the debacle at San Mateo Cove had left you short of your quota."

Yoshimatsu laughed. "No. We were just not able to fill most of the order for live animals from San Mateo. We still have orders for thirty-two dolphins, fifteen pilot whales, and eight sea lions. Most of the buyers are from China and Russia, but there are several buyers from the Arab Emirates. The United States is moving away from dolphinariums, but the Russians and Chinese will stand in long lines to see these animals perform."

Susan saw a slight change in the balance of power that was like a rope being pulled taut. Sato set his knife and fork down, then drained the last of his *Dom Perignon.*

"How will you process the new catch?" Izumi patted his mouth with his napkin.

"We process the animals on-site. A rendering station will be set up where workers will move the processed meat into the refrigerator trucks. The smaller trucks have been equipped with slings and holding tanks for the live animals that are to be transported."

Yoshimatsu leaned back and took a sip of champagne, all the while looking over the rim of his glass at Sato. "As you can see, my good friend, you made a long trip for nothing. Everything here is under control and proceeding as planned."

Izumi leaned forward and placed both hands on the table. "The Consortium is concerned that everything is not under control, Hiro-san. That is why I am here, and that is why I will be here until the hunt is concluded."

The two men stared at each other for a few seconds until Susan broke the silence. "Gentlemen, may I suggest an after-dinner aperitif and a cigar?"

"Yes." Yoshimatsu smiled cordially. "I believe that an aperitif and a good smoke would be in order."

They retired to the two overstuffed white sofas, while Susan left to ring up the wait staff. She brought the men brandies and a box of fine Cuban cigars. Moments later, two waiters came and picked up the empty trays and plates.

After Susan closed the door behind the departing wait staff, she walked back over to where Yoshimatsu sat. "If that's all, sir, I'll be in the next room."

"Thank you, Susan."

Sato Izumi stood and took Susan's hand. "Thank you for the delightful meal and the pleasure of your company, Miss Lawrence. I hope we will meet again before the operation is concluded." He bowed to her, and she bowed back.

Once Susan had left the room, Izumi took another sip of his brandy. "She is a valuable asset to you, Hiro-san. Devoted and efficient. I could use someone like her."

Yoshimatsu leaned forward and regarded Izumi, his dark eyes burning with an intensity that caught Sato off guard. "You forgot something, Sato-san. You forgot the attribute that I most value. Loyalty. Once this venture is completed, we will have established a new market for whale meat. I would have you convey this message for me, but that will not be necessary. Once the ship returns with a full cargo hold of whale meat and the vendors have received their animals, it will be clear to the board who should be running the shipping division."

Izumi sat back and blew a puff of blue smoke toward the ceiling. "Tell me about this contact, this Minister Figueroa. Can he be trusted to deliver?"

"To date, he has done all that he said he would." Yoshimatsu settled back in the sofa cushions.

"From your last report, it would seem that he has a problem with finding competent personnel. You had blamed the problem at San Mateo Cove on a breach in security on the part of the Mexican cartel personnel. What is to say that this will not happen again?"

"We have contained all threats that presented themselves. We are close to surpassing our objectives. I have full confidence in the minister's ability to control his people."

"Yes, but can you control yours?" Izumi asked, his gaze narrowing. "I hear that desertions among the indigenous workers are occurring with more regularity and in greater numbers."

"Ako Kanamura and his security team have the local village under control. We have sufficient numbers of the indigenous available and ready for the final hunt."

Yoshimatsu leaned forward, his gaze penetrating. "There is *nothing* that will stop us from completing this hunt. We are a finely oiled machine that neither the Mexican government, the activists, nor the local villagers can stop. That also includes interference from within the Consortium. If you insist on staying to the end, you will be witness to all that I have said."

# 53

Rosen found Sandy sitting on a cot in Carlos's house. The marine biologist was checking her cell phone for messages. Her laptop was opened on the blankets. She looked up at Rosen and gave her a brief smile.

"Hey, Em. How's Spinner?"

"Sleeping, right now. Arturo has him on some pretty strong meds. I think he's going to be okay."

"How are you holding up, Rosen?"

"I'm okay. A bit frazzled. The last few days have been a blur. It seems like we've jumped from one emotional roller coaster to another without changing cars."

Sandy laughed. "That about sums it up. The good news—with all the stuff that's gone down out here, at least now we have a cell phone connection. I just spoke to Alejandro and Paola a little while ago. They were very happy to hear that Spinner's still alive. Alejandro's moving around better and says he's going stir crazy. He wants to come to the fishing camp."

"What did you tell him?"

"I told him we're in a holding pattern until we see signs of improvement from Spinner. Arturo doesn't want him moved for several days. In the meantime, we have no idea when and where the whalers are going to strike next. With both Alejandro and Spinner sidelined, I'm not sure what kind of organized resistance we can mount against those bastards."

"Have you heard from that guy Graham from the Cetus Alliance?"

"No. Last time I talked to him they were getting ready to drive down to Cabo. I figure it's going to take them four to five days from San Francisco to Cabo. He said they may try to catch a flight, but that's an expense they didn't plan for."

"Has Raúl heard from the woman from Puerto Nacimiento?" She was fidgeting with her hair—a movement not lost on Sandy.

"No, and it's making him crazy. He thinks the hunt is going to go down soon. And unless we can get some idea where it's going to be, Yoshimatsu and his murderous bunch will be in and gone before we even get organized."

Sandy noticed that Rosen suddenly looked uncomfortable. "Rosen, are you okay?"

"I know this is going to sound weird, given our location and situation, but I was wondering if I could ask you a favor?"

"Sure, Emily. Anything."

"I was kinda wanting to get cleaned up a little. You didn't happen to bring along a pair of scissors? I don't need much." She touched her cheek and pulled at a strand of hair hanging in her face."

Sandy grinned. "Let me see what I can do."

Jake Spinner was sitting propped up in the cot when Rosen entered. He was struggling with two pillows, trying vainly to get them positioned behind his back.

"Spinner, what the hell do you think you're doing?"

"I need to sit up. My damn shoulder is killing me."

"Here, let me help you. You're going to tear your stitches wide open."

She supported Spinner with one hand while she placed the pillows behind his back, then eased him back onto the cot, avoiding contact with his injured shoulder.

"Thanks." Spinner, closed his eyes for a moment. Several moments later, he opened them again, his facial muscles relaxing after the pain subsided.

"How are you feeling?"

"Better, I think." Spinner shifted his weight on the cot and grimaced. "My birth certificate apparently has not yet expired, but I feel like my parts warranty is a little shaky."

"Are you hungry?"

"I could eat something." He looked at Rosen, cocking his head slightly. "Rosen, there's something different about you."

Rosen felt the blush move up her neck and into her face. "What?"

"I can't pinpoint it, but you look damn good!"

She looked down. "It's the drugs you're on. Don't bullshit me, Spinner."

"I'm not. You're . . . beautiful."

Their hands were now touching. He squeezed hers.

"Dora has some chicken soup she made up today. It's really good. I could bring you a bowl."

Spinner nodded. "That would be great."

"I'll be right back."

She returned several minutes later with a steaming metal bowl and several flour tortillas on a worn wooden tray. "You want the tortillas in the soup?"

"Sounds good."

Emily broke up the tortilla into bite-sized pieces and placed them in the soup. She put a cloth around Spinner's neck and spooned out soup with a chunk of chicken in it. She brought the spoon up to Spinner's lips. "Careful. It's hot."

He opened his mouth and slurped at the spoon. He let it sit in his mouth for a brief moment, then swallowed slowly. He closed his eyes, anticipating that the food might not stay down. "That really is good."

Rosen fed Spinner several more spoonfuls before he held up his good hand indicating that he'd had enough for now. He leaned back and closed his eyes. "Thank you."

Rosen set the wooden tray on a chair. "You feeling strong enough to talk?"

Spinner did not open his eyes. "Sure."

"There's a family of bottlenose dolphins cruising up and down just offshore. They appeared the morning you washed up on the beach and they haven't left yet. Care to enlighten me?"

Spinner opened his eyes and looked at her. Those deep blue eyes carried an emotional pain that went far beyond any physical injury Spinner had incurred.

"I couldn't save him. They murdered Macario right in front of me." His eyes became moist as he stared beyond Emily, reliving the horrible moment.

"Oh, Jake, I'm so sorry." She squeezed his hand tightly for several minutes until he was able to speak again.

"They took me to the whaling ship. You were all right on. Yoshimatsu was there. He's the brains behind the operation. Just about everyone I saw on board was Japanese, except for a few that might have been Zetas. If there were any of the local indios on board, they were below decks."

"How did you get away? I find it just short of a miracle that I'm sitting here talking to you."

"After they killed Macario, one of the thugs drawing down on me got just a little too close. I grabbed his gun and killed him and a couple more. I made a run for the stern and jumped. That's when I got these." He wagged his injured shoulder slightly, wincing.

"After I hit the water, I got away from that ship as fast as I could swim. I don't know how long I was drifting in the water, bleeding. A tiger shark found me sometime during the night and circled me for what seemed like an eternity, waiting for me to bleed out."

Rosen was staring at Spinner now, her eyes wide. "Oh, my God! You just lived my worst nightmare. What did you do?"

"I managed to punch and kick it in the nose a couple of times. But it was patient. When I was nearly passed out, it made its move and came in for the kill. That's when the dolphins showed up." Spinner shook his head. "I don't know how or why they came when they did, but they kicked that shark's ass. The next thing I know I'm lying on the backs of a bunch of dolphins and we're moving through the water."

"How did they manage to keep you afloat?"

"It was the damndest thing! They kept rotating individuals in and out, and they swam so close together that they formed a living, moving raft. They undulated in perfect synchrony, never breaking rhythm. I don't remember what it was like being in my mother's womb, but this is about as close as I'm ever going to come, I think."

Spinner saw that Rosen was looking at him in a way he hadn't seen before. Her eyes brimmed with tears, and she squeezed his hand again.

"That's the most amazing thing I've ever heard."

"What was even more amazing was that, before they came, I was nearly hypothermic. I don't remember being cold after they put me on their backs." He half-smiled, closed his eyes again and leaned back onto the pillows.

"Do you need to rest?"

"No. I need to tell this while it's still fresh. I don't trust my memory like I did in the old days."

She brought a cup of water to his lips and said, "Here. Drink some. Arturo wants you to force liquids."

"Hell, I already drank half the Gulf of California."

"That doesn't count. Drink."

Spinner leaned in and took a sip of water. He leaned back and smiled. "Not salty enough. Who's Arturo?"

"He's the doc who put you back together. He came out here in the eleventh hour. He's the reason you're still among the living."

"Where in hell did you find a surgeon in this part of Mexico?"

Rosen smiled sheepishly. "He's not exactly a surgeon. Of humans anyway."

Spinner looked at her, confusion etched on his craggy face. "What?"

"He's a small animal vet, Spinner. He was all we could find."

"Jesus. Just my luck." He eyed Rosen suspiciously. "He didn't neuter me while I was out, did he?"

Rosen laughed. "No. But he did leave strict instructions. You misbehave and it's the cone of shame for you."

Now, it was Spinner's turn to laugh, an act that didn't end well. He arched his back, clutching his bandaged side. It took several moments before the pain subsided.

"That's it, Spinner. This talk is over for now. You need to rest."

"I'm okay. Just give me a minute. I need to finish my story," he said between clenched teeth.

"You're a stubborn man, Jake Spinner." Part of her wanted him to lie back and sleep, but she wanted to hear the rest of the story.

"Okay, got it. Laughter is temporarily on hold." He took a deep breath and exhaled slowly. Again, his gaze was focused beyond the plywood walls of the fishing shack.

"When I first hit the water, the only image that was burned into my brain was watching Macario bleed out on the deck of that whaler. With every stroke, I wanted revenge. I wanted to live for one reason only. I was going to kill Yoshimatsu and the rest of his band of murderers. That drove me on. I think it's what initially kept me going."

He shifted his gaze back to Rosen. "But then something happened. I think I was at my lowest ebb. Probably close to dying. I lost track of what was real and what was a dream. That's when I heard them."

"Heard who?"

"The dolphins. They spoke to me. But it wasn't in words. I know this sounds crazy, but it was more a feeling than an actual auditory experience. It was as if I were hearing them from here." He tapped his sternum. "They scanned me, all of them. I felt their sonar pulse in my chest. It was like they were discovering my essence. And, in turn, I knew about them. It was like they spoke in many voices, yet they were one voice. A thread of an image was passed to me by one dolphin, followed by another in the group and then another. I saw every image distinctly. I knew how many calves the old female had birthed, how many in her family had died. And I sensed a great wave of confusion in the family. They don't understand why we kill them. They said we're the keepers. We guard the secret."

Spinner was speaking as if he were far away, remembering the moment. Rosen's expression was one of awe, bewilderment, and a touch of fear.

"What secret? What are we keeping secret?"

"I'm not sure." Spinner, turned his gaze back to her. "But I intend to ask them next chance I get."

"Spinner, I think it's time for you to rest. Arturo's going to kick my ass if he finds out I've kept you awake this long."

He closed his eyes, and she watched the even rise and fall of his chest. She sat with him a few moments longer, thinking about what he'd just said to her. Her mind was reeling. She thought that he could have been hallucinating, that all of this was his descent into a bizarre dreamscape induced by hypothermia and loss of blood. But then why were the dolphins still out there, swimming back and forth? Like they were waiting to see if he was going to pull through. She wanted very badly to tell this to the others, at least Sandy. She was just about to stand when Spinner stirred slightly.

"There was another reason." His voice was a whisper.

"What was that?"

"When I was out there floating, I was fueled by anger and revenge. They were my reasons to live, but those two emotions couldn't sustain me. That's when something else took over, something much stronger." He opened his eyes and looked directly into hers. "I needed to make it back. I wanted to see you again."

Tears rolled down Rosen's cheeks. He lifted a hand and brushed one of the tears away. She leaned down and kissed him on the lips, gently at first, then with more feeling.

"Get some sleep, Jake. I'll be here when you wake up."

The next morning, Spinner awakened before the sun was up. As promised, Rosen was asleep in the wooden chair next to his cot. He was restless and the pain meds had worn off. He really felt like he needed to take the pressure off his back. Painfully, he swung his legs over the edge of the cot and brought himself to a sitting position. He really wanted to stand up. He tried shifting weight to his legs and attempted to stand.

Rosen's eyes snapped open, and she looked momentarily disoriented until she saw what Spinner was attempting to do. She rose from the chair quickly and grabbed Spinner by his good arm as his legs collapsed. She helped him back onto the cot.

"Can't leave you alone for a minute, can I? Spinner, what were you thinking?"

"For God's sake, Rosen. I needed to get out of that position. The pain meds have worn off, and now, besides my shoulder and ribs, my back's killing me!"

"Next time, just wake me up and I will help you. Stop being so damn stubborn."

Spinner lay back on the cot, closed his eyes and breathed through clenched teeth until the pain subsided.

"How're you doing there, Ace?"

"Okay. I'm good."

"I can see that you're a man who doesn't ask for help much. That's about to change—at least for now. I'm going to go find Arturo and get you some meds. Be back in a minute."

Moments later, Rosen returned with several pills and gave them to Jake. She handed him a water bottle and watched him put the pain medication into his mouth. "Wash them down with this," she said.

Spinner swallowed. "Thanks."

"I'll be back with some breakfast in a while. Try and get some sleep." She stood and turned to leave.

"Hey?"

Rosen turned. "Yes?"

"Can you check and see if the dolphins are still there?"

"The sun is just now coming up. I'll check, but I may not be able to see them—even if they are." She pointed a finger at him. "Sit! Stay!"

"Very funny."

Once outside, she looked down the stretch of beach and focused on the water. The sun was peeking over the Sierra in the east, casting a silvery glow on the water. She heard the explosive blasts of the dolphins' exhalations, but from her perspective, it was difficult to see the slate-gray dorsal fins against the quicksilver-colored ocean. Amazingly, the dolphins were still here. She heard a splash and saw the rise and fall of two dorsal fins. She turned and trudged back to the fishing shack. The inhabitants of the camp were beginning to stir.

When she got back, Spinner looked like he was sleeping again. Her stomach reminded her that she had not eaten anything substantial in nearly twenty-four hours. She stepped closer to the cot and heard Spinner gently snoring. *A good time to grab a bite and get cleaned up a little,* she thought.

When she got to Jesús's shack, his wife Dora was busy at the stove. The delicious smells of hot coffee, chorizo, and flour tortillas filled the warm room. Already seated around the table were Sandy, Arturo, and Raúl. Carlos's wife, Cecelia, helped Dora fix breakfast.

Looking over the brim of his coffee cup, Arturo asked, "How's the patient this morning?"

"I think he's going to make it, doc. He's back to his usual irascible self."

"Did he tell you how he got here?" Sandy asked.

Rosen poured herself a cup of black coffee. She held it in both hands and closed her eyes, enjoying the heat that came off the cup. She opened her eyes and said, "You guys are not going to believe this story."

By the time breakfast was served, Carlos and Francisco had joined the group. They were all electrified by Rosen's accounting of Spinner's rescue by the dolphins. Their faces registered a mix of emotions from disbelief to awe to reverence. Once Raúl, who had been translating, crossed himself.

When Rosen finished the tale, no one spoke for several moments. Arturo got up and poured himself another cup of coffee. He turned to Sandy and Raúl. "I'd like to offer my services to the cause. Do you think you might have need of a small animal vet?"

"Hell, yes," said Sandy. "We'd be honored to have you join the group."

"Be careful what you wish for," said Raúl, smiling and giving him a high five. "Associating with a group like this can be hazardous to your health."

After breakfast, Rosen brought a cup of coffee and a plate of food back to the shack where Spinner rested. When she stepped through the door, she was surprised to see him sitting on the edge of the cot.

"You hungry?" Rosen asked.

"Not now. Did you see the dolphins?"

"Yes. They're out there. They never left."

He placed his hand on the chair and tried to stand, then cried out in pain.

"What the hell are you doing, Spinner?"

"I gotta go outside. Now."

"You're in no condition to stand, let alone walk down the beach," Rosen said angrily. "Get back in bed, Jake."

Slowly, and with great difficulty, Spinner stood up.

"Rosen, I have to go. They won't leave unless they see me." He looked at her, his face lined with pain. "I could use an assist."

"You bust a stitch, I'm going to kick your ass."

"Duly noted, Nurse Ratched. Here, give me a shoulder."

She set the food and coffee down on the table. He draped his good arm around her shoulder, and she helped support him. "Let me get Raúl and Jesús. They can carry you down to the beach."

"No. I can walk."

She looked up at him. "I don't know why I waste my breath."

"I'm ready."

For the first few steps, Spinner was leaning so hard on Rosen she thought they were both going to go down in a heap. His face went pale, and he looked like he was going to puke. By the time they reached the door, he was putting more weight on his legs, but still leaning strongly on her for support.

"Hang on for a second." Spinner's voice was hoarse. "I need to catch my breath." He closed his eyes and breathed deeply for a full minute. "Okay."

They walked slowly down the gradual incline of the beach, stopping every twenty to thirty feet for Spinner to rest. Rosen noticed that as they drew closer to the water's edge, the dolphins became energized, swimming rapidly to and fro, peeking their heads out of the water. She wasn't alone in her observation. From the shacks and beyond the boat repair dock, people appeared and watched their progress down to the shoreline. Raúl and Jesús rushed to help. Spinner held up a hand, signaling that he was okay. One by one, the residents of the fishing camp walked in silence down the sandy incline toward the water, watching Jake's unsteady steps and the dolphins' reactions.

He stood at the water's edge, resting. Then he closed his eyes and bowed his head, gathering his strength. "I'm going out, Em. I think I'll be okay from here."

"Oh, no you don't." Rosen kicked off her shoes and tossed them up higher on the beach.

Spinner looked at Rosen, smiled, then stepped into the water and walked slowly and stiffly toward the energized dolphins. He reached mid-thigh depth and stopped. From Rosen's vantage point, the dolphins looked a lot bigger than she'd imagined. Sandy had told her that these cetaceans were eight feet of muscle and blubber and weighed in at nearly six hundred pounds. With one snap of their flukes, they could easily send both her and Spinner flying.

The dolphin family approached them, slowing their speed as they swam closer. Rosen spotted an older dolphin with a white blaze on her melon. Next to her swam a smaller dolphin that had a white star pattern of four spots on his forehead. The dolphins surrounded them, logging at the surface, their eyes fixed on the couple. Rosen heard the high-pitched whistles and squeaks emitted from their blowholes. It was as if all of them were greeting Spinner.

"Hey, guys," Spinner said softly.

He bent stiffly and held his hand over the water. The dolphins, beginning with the old female, swam up and brushed against his outstretched hand. Rosen marveled at how gentle the animals were as they approached, as if they sensed that he was wounded. The old scarred female floated up to him and lay on her side, her eye regarding the two humans. Spinner ran his hand along her side and rested it just behind her pectoral fin. She moved off to one side while the other dolphins each came up and greeted Spinner. Finally, the little dolphin, who had been hanging back, swam up and brushed against his hand.

Rosen dared not speak. She didn't want to do anything to interrupt the unfolding events. She wasn't afraid anymore, but she felt she was in the presence of some strange and powerful force. Tears came to her eyes. This was a feeling she'd never experienced before. It was one of those timeless moments. She didn't want it to end.

Then the matriarch issued a series of whistles and, with one powerful downward motion of her flukes, turned around and headed out to sea. One by one, the rest of the family followed. Spinner straightened up slowly, his hand still extended toward the dolphins. Just then, the little dolphin with the star pattern leapt from the water in a grand leap and came down head first without a splash. A moment later, the pod was gone.

Rosen turned her gaze from the sea back to Spinner. She could see the misting in his eyes as well. He blinked several times, turned to her, and smiled.

She hugged him. "I think I know what the secret is." Her voice was partially muffled with her face against his good shoulder.

"Yeah. Me too."

As they trudged back to the beach, she supported him like a human crutch. A small crowd stood and waited for them at the water's edge. Rosen saw that Sandy had tears in her eyes. Everyone was looking expectantly at Spinner. He limped up to the crowd and they folded in on him. One by one, everyone in the group hugged Spinner—very gently. Finally, he came face to face with a grinning Arturo Ruiz.

"Señorita Rosen was right about you, Señor Spinner. You are a man who does not listen well."

"You must be the doc." Spinner extended his good hand. "Thanks for bringing me back from the brink."

"How are you feeling?"

"Well, I'm not going to be howling at the moon anytime soon," Spinner paused, then added, "Or will I?"

Arturo laughed and turned to Emily. "He's going to be fine."

Spinner surveyed the group, a look of deep gratitude etched into his face. "Thank you. Everyone."

"What's our next move, Jake?" Raúl asked.

Spinner looked at him, his jaw set. "We're going to stop a whale hunt."

# 54

Over the next three days, the fishing camp became a blur of activity. A constant sense of anxiety—like the buzz of a circling mosquito—made everyone edgy. Alejandro and Sandy had decided that the fishing camp would be the best location for conducting preparatory operations against the whalers. Raúl and Jesús agreed that they would dispatch two pangas to San Jacinto to bring Alejandro and Paola back. Alejandro was now walking with a cane and he refused to be stuck at Raúl's goat farm any longer. Raúl's wife, Guadalupe, also insisted on coming out with the children. As much as he tried to dissuade her, her mind was made up. Her sister and her sister's husband could watch the Ranchito de las Cabras for a few days.

Spinner appeared to be getting stronger every day. With the help of Guadalupe's naturopathic remedies, he was able to cut his medication intake in half. He was now able to transfer in and out of bed without help and he was walking on the beach—albeit slowly—two to three times a day. During most of the organizational meetings in Carlos's shack, Spinner sat quietly. At one point he spoke up.

"You're going to need a power source if this is going to be a command center." He looked around the shack. "Anyone seen my duffel?"

"It's here," said Rosen, reaching behind a stack of wooden crates. She brought the duffel over to him, and he reached inside with his good hand producing a set of keys. Jake tossed them to Raúl.

"At the docks in San Jacinto is a small warehouse at the end of Calle Salvatierra. My boat is trailered inside with a bunch of camping supplies and gear. There's also a small generator that should be sufficient to supply electricity for computers and cell phones. Fill every available container you can find with gasoline and stow it on the boat. Bring anything else that could be useful."

Raúl asked, "Is your boat seaworthy? I saw what you did to it at San Mateo."

"It's seaworthy," replied Francisco. "I fixed it."

"That's good," said Raúl. "Now we have three boats."

"Don't kid yourself," Spinner said. "Three boats aren't going to be enough."

"From what we saw last time," said Emily, "the whalers had federales helping them. Those guys had guns and they were shooting at us. What's to stop them from doing the same thing this time?"

"Count on it. They won't be denied their prize a second time. We have a small window to disrupt their operation. The only thing we have on our side is that they don't know we're out here. And that's the way it's going to stay until the last minute."

Sandy spoke up. "Raúl, any word from Alma Quintín?"

"Nothing. I am beginning to think that she's been frightened off or coerced into silence by her husband. I may have to find another source."

"It's too dangerous to go anywhere near Puerto Nacimiento," Sandy said. "After what they attempted to do to Spinner, it would be nothing to them to kill you and scatter body parts up and down the coastline. I think Guadalupe might have something to say about that."

Spinner, stood up from the table and stretched painfully. "I think it's a safe bet that Yoshimatsu is clamping down on the villagers of Puerto Nacimiento. After the fiasco at San Mateo Cove, they're going to ramp up security. Watch out for federales, possibly naval patrols." He walked to the doorway and looked outside. There were several pangas sitting on the beach. Raúl's boat was moored off a buoy several yards off shore.

"A lot more boat activity around here lately." Spinner turned back toward the group, his gaze focused on Jesús. "Any chance we can stow the pangas behind the dunes when they're not in use? Might keep the federales off our asses."

Jesús nodded. "Si, Jake. That will not be a problem."

"Once we confront the fleet, how do we defend ourselves?" Raúl looked from Jesús to Spinner. "If what you say is true, we'll be outmanned and outgunned. You can't come to a gunfight with knives, pickaxes, and gaffs."

Spinner ran his fingers through his thick black hair. "I don't know, Raúl. I'm working on it." He cast a look at Rosen that she knew all too well. He was fresh out of ideas.

The tension in the room ramped up when a cell phone's ring broke the silence. Sandy reached into her pocket and quickly looked at the LED readout.

"I need to take this." She stood suddenly and walked out the door. "Hey, Graham. Where are you?"

Minutes later, Sandy walked back into the fishing shack and came to the table. "That was Graham Neely, the Cetus Alliance guy. He and his group are in La Paz. They're re-supplying their boat, the *La Serena*, and can be here tomorrow. I asked him if there was room for a few extra passengers. He said they could pick up Alejandro and Paola."

"We still need Spinner's boat," said Raúl. He looked at Jesús. "We'll leave at first light. We should be able to pick up equipment and supplies, launch the boat, and be back by tomorrow night."

"I'd like to come, too," volunteered Francisco. "You never know when you might need a mechanic."

Jesús nodded with pride at his brother.

The group meeting broke up, and everyone moved off to continue daily routines and preparations. Spinner, wearing a light cotton shirt and khaki pants, his left arm still hanging in a sling, managed to wrap a worn blanket around his shoulders and walked out into the late afternoon sunshine. The shadows were growing longer on the dunes behind the camp as the setting sun cast the rippling sand in a golden glow. He began walking slowly down the beach toward the water's edge, his lined face accentuated by the fading light.

"Care for some company?" A familiar voice behind him spoke. He turned to see Rosen walking down the slope toward him. "Or do you need some down time?"

Spinner smiled. "Company's always appreciated."

She met him and grabbed hold of his right arm. Neither spoke. A flock of brown pelicans along with blue-footed and brown boobies circled and hovered in the peach-colored sky. Several pelicans simultaneously folded in their wings, compressed their necks, and transformed their bodies into avian missiles. They plunged into the water, some returning to the surface with a wriggling mullet in their beaks. *ZIP! ZIP! ZIP!* A squadron of boobies hit the water like tracers, then bobbed back to the surface flapping clumsily until they were airborne once again.

Spinner abruptly dropped his blanket onto the sand and removed his sling. He took several deep breaths, lifting his arms over head, the left one more gingerly.

"What are you doing, Jake?" Rosen looked sideways at him.

"I need to do something. I've been lying around too long."

"Are you kidding? You just had major surgery!"

"I'm okay, Rosen. I just need to move a little." With that, he took off at a light jog down the beach. He made it about fifty feet before he stopped and dropped to his knees.

"Jake!" Rosen sprinted to him. When she got to him, he was breathing heavily, his hand clutching his right side. She, too, dropped to her knees and supported him. "Spinner, do you have a death wish? Or are you just an idiot? If you have a death wish, tell me now. I'm not going to watch you kill yourself."

He shook his head violently and held up his hand. "Moment."

When his breathing returned to near normal, Spinner said, "We're walking into a bloodbath. The whalers and their crooked compadres are going to kill a lot of innocent people. I can't let that happen."

"Hemorrhaging your wounds is not exactly the best way to help our cause."

"Rosen, I don't know what to do. If I procure weapons for the group, that gives the Mexican government license to shoot and kill, even though it's those who are pointing the guns who are corrupt. I commend the group's valor, but they're not soldiers. Raúl is right. We're outmanned and outgunned. They're going to kick our collective asses."

"Spinner, for Christ's sake. You just had surgery. Give yourself a couple of days to recuperate."

"We don't have that luxury, Em. These bastards could line up a hunt tomorrow and we wouldn't know it was going down. We don't have a reliable source, and we don't have a ready response in place."

"You can't do this by yourself, Jake. Wait until Alejandro and Paola get here and we have a chance to meet as a complete group. We'll figure out something."

He turned his head and looked directly into her eyes. "I couldn't handle it if something happened to you or the others."

She touched his cheek and kissed him. "I love you, Jake Spinner. God help me, but I do."

Spinner was up early the next morning to see Jesús, Raúl, and Francisco off. In the pre-dawn chill, he stood at the shoreline next to Jesús's panga while they loaded fuel and equipment. He was wrapped in an old Mexican blanket, but was still shivering. Immobility and the loss of blood had left him more susceptible to cold in the mornings.

Raúl produced Spinner's pistol from his backpack and held it out to him. "I took good care of it, Jake. It's time to return it to its rightful owner."

Jake eyed the semi-auto. "Not yet, my friend. Keep it for now. Just in case you run into trouble in San Jacinto."

Raúl nodded and slipped the gun back into his backpack. "If everything goes well, we should be back by early evening."

"Stay on your toes. Especially around the docks."

"I've already found that out. But we have three sets of eyes to keep watch."

"Remember, they may recognize my boat from the video. If it looks dicey, launch after dark."

Raúl grinned. "Jake, I appreciate the advice, but I think we know what we're doing."

"Yeah, I guess you do. Sorry."

"Don't worry. You just keep working on the plan to attack the cove."

"Yeah, the plan," Spinner said grimly. Jesús climbed into the panga and assumed his position at the tiller. Raúl and Francisco pushed the boat into deeper water and then climbed in. Spinner waved to them. "¡Vayan con Dios!"

They waved back and turned toward the sea. The boat disappeared into the darkness, and the sound of the motors faded.

Emily Rosen awakened with a start. Even from a deep sleep, she knew something was not right. She had pulled her cot next to Spinner's several days ago to keep a close watch on him. What woke her were not the sounds of someone in distress, but the absence of any sound at all. She had gotten used to the rhythm of Spinner's breathing. Her heart began to race as she turned quickly to face his cot. It was empty, and his blanket was missing. She grabbed her flashlight and scanned the shack. Spinner wasn't there.

She jumped out of bed and dressed quickly. She pulled her jacket on and rushed out the door. Staring down the stretch of beach, she saw no one. The sun was still behind the mountains in the east, so visibility was not at its best for spotting someone walking along the shoreline. She did notice that one of the pangas was missing. An ominous thought came to mind. What if Spinner had decided to take off and do something desperate?

She walked the distance to Jesús's shack and saw that the door was already open. A light shone from the inside. Arturo was sitting at the rough-hewn kitchen table, a cup of black coffee cradled in his hands. He looked half asleep. Dora was at the kitchen counter preparing breakfast. She wore a pair of faded jeans and a white tee shirt, oblivious to the chill in the room. When she saw Rosen, she smiled.

"Buenas días, Emily," she said cheerfully. "Hay café."

"Has anyone seen Spinner?" Rosen blurted.

Arturo's eyes opened wide. "Is there something wrong?"

"I woke up and he wasn't in his cot. He didn't go with Raúl and Jesús, did he?"

Arturo's expression went from stunned surprise to worry. "I don't think so." He turned to Dora and spoke in Spanish. "¿Spinner *se fue con Jesús y los demás?*"

Dora shook her head. "*No. No creo.*"

You don't think he went with them, do you?" Arturo asked Rosen. "That would be really—"

"Stupid," Rosen finished for him. "He's worried about what's going to happen to everyone in the upcoming hunt. I'm afraid he's going to go all Rambo on us and try to do it himself."

Rosen turned to leave.

"Hang on, I'll come with you." Arturo rose from the table.

He and Emily began to walk down the long stretch of beach. The light from the sun backlit the mountain range, while a breeze out of the east chilled their faces. It wasn't long before Emily spotted a set of large footprints leading down the beach. Another set of tracks, those of an animal, accompanied them. The tracks traced the shoreline, then started up the beach and into the dunes. At the summit of the tallest dune a lone figure sat—a blanket wrapped around him. A dog sat next to him. Both of them stared out to sea.

"Thank God," said Arturo.

Rosen glared at Spinner as the sun peaked over the horizon, bathing him and Dog in an ethereal golden light. "He may not have to wait until the Yakuza try to kill him. I may beat them to the punch."

Arturo grinned. "Ah, true love is in the air."

She gave him a sidelong glance and began to trudge up the beach. Arturo turned to go back to the fishing shack for his coffee.

By the time she reached the top of the dune she was breathless. Dog bounded toward her and jumped around in a circle, tail wagging furiously. After Rosen relented and patted the enthusiastic canine between the ears, the dog dutifully walked to Spinner's other side and sat on his haunches.

"Spinner, you damn near gave me a heart attack," she said between breaths. "I woke up and you weren't there. I thought for a moment that you went with Raúl and the others."

"Why in hell would I do that? You said yourself that I'm in no shape to be moving around much."

"Yeah, so I find you sitting on top of the tallest dune in sight. Keep it up, Spinner. Yoshimatsu and the whalers are going to be the least of your worries if you keep ignoring Arturo's orders."

Spinner smiled briefly. Then his face turned to stone. "I couldn't sleep." He stared out at the silvery flat sea. "I came up here to think."

She flopped down beside him, turned to look at his face and saw the lines of worry etched on it. "Dora's got breakfast almost on the table. You might think better if you had something in your stomach."

"Maybe later. Not all that hungry right now."

"You know, contrary to popular belief, I've been told that I'm a pretty good listener. Do you want to talk about it?"

Spinner took several long breaths, his eyes still fixed on the ocean before them. The pause lasted long enough for Rosen to think that he wasn't going to answer. When at last he began to speak, his voice was soft and metered. "I was in command of a company in Afghanistan. We were on a mission in Anbar Province. Our orders were to infiltrate behind the Taliban's lines and neutralize two of their upper echelon commanders. We were provided with intel that said we could intercept their convoy between two insurgent camps."

Rosen looked at him intently.

"Turns out it was bad intel. We walked right into the middle of an ambush. The firefight lasted sixteen hours. We used up all our ammunition. I lost half the company that day. The rest of us were wounded and barely got out under cover of darkness."

For several moments, neither one of them spoke. Finally, Rosen said, "It sounds like the situation was out of your control. You did the best you could with the information you had."

He turned his face toward her. "Until recently, I saw the faces of all of those men every time I closed my eyes to sleep. Their ghosts haunted me relentlessly, and I had one thought—they died because of decisions that I made. The dream is still there, but the faces have changed. Now when I dream, I see the faces of Alejandro, Raúl, Paola, Sandy, and . . . you. I can't—and won't—let that happen again."

Rosen bristled. "Spinner, every one of us is here of our own volition. They're all committed to the cause, because this is their home. They're fighting for what they think is right. They know full well what's at stake here."

"Yoshimatsu has armed all the whalers with automatic weapons. Besides, even if we had the firepower, Yoshimatsu has the federales or Zetas in his pocket. Take your pick. There's nothing to stop them from laying down a line of fire on a bunch of crazy eco-activists with only a few weapons. He has the law—if you want to call it that—on his side." He turned back and stared out at the shimmering water, a vista so peaceful that it seemed almost sacrilegious to speak of death and dying. "I don't know how to get around that one, Em."

"Stop beating yourself up. You don't have to go solo. Later today, Alejandro, Paola, and the Cetus Alliance group will be arriving. Between all of us, I think we can come up with a good plan." She kissed him on his unshaven cheek and stood.

"You're a good man, Jake Spinner. I'm going to get some breakfast. I'll bring a plate up to you in a little while."

He was about to protest, but Rosen raised her hand. "No arguments, Spinner. I need you—no, we all need you—to be a functioning human being real soon. So get over it."

"Why is it that I get the feeling that I'm not going to win a lot of arguments with you?" A wry smile etched the corners of his mouth.

She walked several feet down the dune, then turned back and faced him.

"Oh, I was wondering. Do you remember the name of the whaling ship where they took you?"

Spinner screwed up his face in thought. "The *Shodokai Maru*," he said after a moment's contemplation.

Rosen smiled. "I'll see you later, Spinner."

A discernible tension hung over the fishing camp like an invisible cloud. Everyone busied themselves in any way they could. Until Raúl returned with the generator, there was no way to recharge electronics. Sandy and Rosen had only limited access to the internet from their laptops due to low batteries and an erratic signal from Carlos's satellite dish.

The newly gathered whale warriors all had a premonition that the hunt would be going down any day now. Rosen felt an overpowering sense of frustration building as the days wore on. As far as they knew, Raúl still had not heard from Alma Quintín. Rosen hadn't heard from any of her contacts for days either. The video had gone out and had been played across the globe. Was it just that television viewers had been so numbed by all the violence that they were in a state of apathetic inaction?

She wanted to go up to the top of the dune and sit with Spinner. He was still there, staring out to sea with Dog dutifully sitting next to him. It looked like he hadn't moved for hours. She had delivered breakfast five hours ago. For all she knew, Spinner had given the meal to the dog just to be obstinate.

In order to quell some of her building frustration, she took to her computer. She sat under a tarp near Jesús's shack, still able to get a view of Spinner every so often. Right now, there was enough of a signal that she could access the internet, although she didn't know for how long. She typed in the words *Shodokai Maru* and began her search. For nearly an hour she worked feverishly, taking notes as she went. After considerable cross-referencing, she found what she was looking for.

"What do you think Spinner is doing up there?" Emily turned and saw Sandy standing next to her, her hand shielding her eyes from the glare of the sun off the dunes.

"Trying to come up with some plan that doesn't end with all of us getting killed."

"No pressure there, eh? How long do you think he'll stay up there?"

"No telling. Either until he figures out a plan or gets hungry." Rosen checked her watch. "Six hours since he had breakfast."

"Maybe you should go check on him."

"He'll come down when he's ready."

"You care for him, don't you?" Sandy's face was lit with a grand smile.

Rosen shook her head. "Didn't see that one coming. In a million years, I never figured I'd fall for a burned-out ex-pat with PTSD who tends to leave a wake of destruction wherever he goes."

"I think you two make a cute couple." Unable to contain herself, Sandy burst into laughter.

Rosen looked at her scornfully. "Cute? We're not cute."

Dora came out of the shack and waved to them, then pointed out to sea. They turned their attention seaward and saw a large trimaran rounding the point, making its way toward the cove. Several people were standing on the deck waving. The rest were hauling the sail and preparing to anchor.

"I believe that would be Cetus World Alliance," Sandy said.

Once the anchor was set, the group offloaded the inflatable and motored to shore. As they slid up onto the beach, a tall, lean man with a beard jumped out and secured the bowline to a boulder while the rest of the group disembarked.

There were six of them, three women and three men. Sandy observed that they looked surprisingly young. The bearded man appeared to be in charge. Sandy and Rosen walked down to the beach to meet them.

"Sandy?" The young man smiled as he strode toward her. He was lanky but well-muscled, with long, frizzy hair woven into dreadlocks. His eyes were a deep blue, the color of an ocean grotto. He wore cargo shorts and a faded chambray shirt.

"You must be Graham," Sandy stepped forward with her hand extended. They shook hands. "Thanks for coming. This is Emily Rosen. She's the one who shot the video."

Graham shook Emily's hand. "Nice work, Emily. We have the video streaming all over the world."

He waved the rest of his entourage over, introducing them. Rosen tried to assign each name to a face. There was Brad, a handsome young man who looked like a stereotypical California surfer. Morgan was a tall, twenty-something redhead with freckles and glasses. Beau was also in his early twenties, had glasses, and short, curly hair. He looked like a first-year student from Berkeley. Diane and Brittany were blondes who looked like they'd be more comfortable in a sorority soirée than chasing down a bunch of murderous whalers. Rosen shuddered to think what Spinner would say upon meeting this group.

As they walked up the beach, Graham asked Sandy, "What's the latest on the hunt?"

"Still in a holding pattern. We're waiting to hear from a key informant who has ties to the village. Raúl won't be back until tonight. He went to San Jacinto to pick up another boat and supplies."

"What do you need from us right now?"

"Does that boat have a good working battery?" Sandy queried. "We need to charge our laptops and cell phones."

"Done."

"We're probably not going to have a group meeting until tomorrow morning. The rest of the group may not be back until late, depending on what kind of trouble they run into." They arrived at Carlos's fishing shack. "Come inside. Dora and Cecilia will have fresh coffee, and there are homemade flour tortillas and beans in your foreseeable future."

"We have a bunch of food supplies that we want to donate to the cause. We can unload them when we take you out to the boat."

"That will make Cecilia and Dora very happy."

As the group filed into the fishing shack Rosen passed Sandy and whispered, "Spinner's going to love this."

# 55

The sun had just slipped behind the mountains in the west when Rosen decided that Spinner had been up on that dune long enough. He had missed his last two medication dosages and the afternoon meal. Besides, the temperature was dropping quickly with a steady breeze out of the west.

When she gazed up at the dune, neither Spinner nor Dog was visible. For a moment she worried that he'd passed out somewhere, but figured that Dog would have come back and found someone if that had been the case. She zipped up her jacket and pulled her collar up to stave off the effects of the chill wind. As she walked in the direction of the dunes, she spied two figures—one human, the other canid—in the distance, walking along the water's edge.

Spinner threw something into the surf. Dog bounded out and retrieved it. Rosen marveled at how quickly Spinner had bounced back. Anyone else would still be lying on a cot. She wasn't sure where that kind of mental toughness came from. Was it inherent in his persona or was it his finely-honed military training? Emily suspected it was a combination of both. Nature and nurture at their deadliest.

She caught up with him several moments later. He was holding a length of cardón cactus rib that had Dog's full attention. He flung the stick into the water, and the dog plunged after it. He winced from the motion.

"Hey." Spinner grinned at her.

"Hey. Not a bad throw—for a guy just back from the dead."

"This is my good arm."

She walked up to him and kissed him. They lingered in that state for a moment. Rosen was mildly surprised at how normal it felt.

"Well?"

"Well what?"

"Come on, Spinner. You've been sitting up on that dune all damn day. And I know you weren't up there writing love sonnets."

He smirked. "You never know, Rosen. Be careful what you wish for. I could have been composing a haiku for you."

"Right. So, what's the plan? I know you were hatching something to stop the whale hunt."

Spinner's face grew dark. "No matter how I turn it over, Em, I haven't been able to come up with a plan where someone isn't going to get killed or hurt." Dog returned with the stick and dropped it at his feet. He picked it up and tossed it again. The dog was relentless in his pursuit.

"How do you feel about a little road trip?" Spinner asked, still watching Dog.

"Spinner, we're hours, maybe days away from the whale hunt. And you want to go on a road trip?"

"I need to talk to an old friend from the unit. He's over on the mainland. He might be able to help our cause."

"Have you talked to him?"

"Not yet. Last time I talked to him, he was pissed off at me."

"That doesn't surprise me. How's he going to help us?" She clearly didn't look happy about traveling over to the mainland with a deadly hunt looming.

"He's a man who can get things," Spinner replied matter-of-factly.

"Things? What kind of things?"

"Well, let's just say that he deals in things you won't find at a typical supermercado."

Rosen looked at him. "When do you want to go?"

"After the meeting."

Rosen sighed. "I sure hope you know what you're doing."

"That makes two of us."

They walked back toward the fishing shacks. Spinner looked out onto the water at the trimaran anchored off-shore. "Looks like the reinforcements have arrived. What's your take on them?"

"I just met them a little while ago." Rosen avoided his gaze. "They seem kinda young."

They walked toward Carlos's shack. "You know, Em, I haven't had a drink for a couple of weeks. Funny, I don't feel an overwhelming urge."

"I want you to hold onto that thought," Rosen said, as she swung the door open.

"Children," Spinner muttered under his breath when he came face to face with the new arrivals. "We're going into a war with children." The new arrivals stared at the tall, disheveled man who looked like he'd been dragged behind a truck for twenty miles through a scrub desert.

Sandy stepped up with Graham Neely beside her. The look of disdain on Spinner's face was not lost on her. "Oh, uh, Jake Spinner, I want you to meet Graham Neely from Cetus World Alliance."

Graham stared at the big man, his bearded face slack-jawed. "You're him. The guy on the video." He took Jake's hand and pumped it furiously. "You have some serious chutzpah, dude."

"Uh, well—"

"I heard you were dead," continued Graham.

"I've been told that a lot lately."

Graham motioned for the rest of the group to come forward, and introductions were made. Rosen could see Spinner's agitation level rising with each introduction. After Brittany, the young blonde, introduced herself, Spinner eyed the group, then sighed. He turned back to Rosen and Sandy.

"I can't do this. This is a train wreck waiting to happen."

"Wait, Jake," implored Sandy. "They volunteered to come down here and risk their lives. At least give them a shot."

Spinner looked at her angrily. "This isn't spring break in Fort Lauderdale. In a couple of days, we're going to be placing ourselves between a mass of panicked whales and dolphins and some really nasty people who will kill anything or anyone who gets in their way. I'm sorry, you guys, I really am. But you made a long trip for nothing." He held up his hands. "I can't be responsible for your safety."

"We're not leaving," said Graham, facing Spinner. "No one asked you to assume responsibility for any of us. We're not asking anything from anyone. Each one of us came down here aware of the potential danger. Near Ensenada, I asked if anyone wanted out. Every one of them said they were in for the long haul."

Spinner lifted his shirt, revealing an angry-looking bruise with a stitched-up wound on his side. "There's another one just like it on my left shoulder," he said. The young people looked terrified.

"Still want in?"

Graham met Spinner's gaze directly. "Hell, yeah."

Spinner shook his head. He looked at Rosen. "I think I need that drink now." He turned and walked out of the fishing shack into the gray dusk, Dog following at his heels.

Rosen smiled weakly at Graham and the others. "Don't mind him. He's always like this."

Once outside and away from the others, Spinner reached into his pocket and retrieved his iPhone. He punched in the number and waited. A familiar voice picked up after the third ring.

"Castellano."

"Rollie, it's me, Jake."

Around 8:30 that night, Dora came into Carlos's shack and announced that Jesús and the others were about thirty minutes out. The incoming group would be hungry, wet, and tired. She and Cecilia started preparing another meal for the weary travelers. Soon the shack warmed to the smell of grilled tortillas and fried fish.

Spinner was seated at the wooden table with Rosen. Across from them sat Arturo, a stubble of dark beard on his face, his deep brown eyes bright. Sandy sat on the end answering questions from Graham about the day at the cove and her research. The rest of Graham's group had returned to the trimaran to get some sleep. Spinner noticed that Graham was a good listener, interjecting questions at the appropriate times.

Shortly the sounds of motors began to grow louder as two boats rounded the point. Spinner recognized the twin engines of his trawler and felt a familiar tug in his gut. It had been a long time since he'd set foot on the deck of his boat. Behind *This Side Up,* a thick line towed the rigid hull inflatable used by Sandy and Paola.

Paola was the first one through the door. She rushed over and hugged Sandy fiercely, then Rosen. She eventually got around to Spinner, who winced when she embraced him.

Alejandro limped in through the door, bracing himself on a cane. Spinner stood slowly and walked to him. He looked thinner than he had remembered. He had a good start on a full beard. They grinned at each other, then grasped each other's hands.

"Am I glad to see you," said Alejandro.

"You too, Alex. How's the leg?"

Alejandro wiggled his lower leg. "No salsa dancing for a while, but I'm getting around. It helps when your host is a curandera. I look forward to hearing about your escape."

"Where'd you acquire the RIB?" Spinner asked.

"Oh, that." Alejandro grinned. "It's an anonymous donation from the Minister of Fisheries. Paola and Sandy tell me it's quite maneuverable."

"A welcome addition to our little fleet," Spinner clapped Alex on the back.

Guadalupe came in next with Alisa at her side and Julio in her arms. The boy was still asleep. When Alisa saw Jake, she cried out, "Señor Jake," and ran to him. Spinner crouched down and hugged her with his good arm. He felt a rush of unexpected emotion. He looked up to see Guadalupe smiling at him.

"They told me you were dead," Alisa said, her head buried in his chest. "I didn't believe them."

"I'm so glad to see all of you again."

"Papá says that you can talk with dolphins." She pulled away and looked him straight in the eyes.

He cast a sideways glance at Raúl, who had just walked in. Raúl smiled wearily. "He said that, did he?"

Alisa nodded. "Can you teach me to speak with them, Señor Jake?"

"I don't know if I can really speak to them. But once this is all over, we can sure give it a try." Sandy and Rosen looked at Spinner, crouched down talking to the young girl.

"He continues to amaze," Sandy said. "Who'd a thunk it?"

"Yeah, who'd a thunk it," Rosen said.

Spinner stood slowly and walked over to Raúl and Guadalupe who were tending to a cranky Julio, who had just awakened. Jake shook Raúl's hand, and Guadalupe kissed Jake on cheek.

"Any trouble?"

"No," replied Raúl. "In fact, we saw no one. No federales at the port, no one. It's like they all evaporated."

"Any word from the Quintín woman?"

"*Nada*. I think it might be time to pay her a visit." Raúl took the fussing boy from Guadalupe. "Care to ride along?"

Spinner shook his head. "As long as we're still in a holding pattern, I'm going to see an old friend who might be able to even up the odds a bit."

Raúl and Guadalupe were soon seated at the table with the others and eating a hot dinner of Veracruz-style fish, rice, and beans. Spinner leaned against a wooden post. He looked wrung-out.

"I think we should let everyone get a good night's sleep before we meet as a group," said Rosen. "I think if I removed that pole, you'd fall flat on your face."

"I'm not sure what's more exhausting—mending after being shot or the mental exhaustion that comes from trying to work out a plan that doesn't get us all killed." He walked over to where Alejandro sat with Sandy, Paola, and Graham. "Okay with you if we call for the meeting after breakfast? I think tonight we're not firing on all cylinders."

Alejandro nodded. "Yes." Looking at the others seated around him, he asked, "Everyone okay with that?"

"It's been a long day," said Paola. "I can barely keep my eyes open now."

"See you all in the morning." As Spinner walked out the door, Rosen cast a strange look at him. "Where are you going? Your cot is over there."

Jake turned back and faced her, his faced etched in fatigue. "Em, I've imposed long enough on Carlos and his family. My boat's out there and it has a comfortable bunk. He eyed her askance. "Ever slept on a boat before?"

"Sure. Lots of times," she lied, grinning. "But never with you."

# 56

In his hotel room in Bogota, Colombia, Presidente Emilio Duarte, president of Mexico, finally saw the video of the slaughter at the cove. He was on the last stop to endorse a trade deal that had involved travel to seven Latin American countries in two weeks. He was dead tired and had decided to watch a bit of late-night news to lull him to sleep when the TV reporter announced the hunt of a large group of dolphins in a remote lagoon in Baja California Sur, Mexico.

He snapped awake in time to catch the last piece of footage of a lone individual breaking through the barricade and the chaos that followed. He watched with rising anger as the event unfolded. By the time the video concluded, he was on the phone awakening his chief of staff.

President Duarte fumed. "Why have I not been informed of this?"

"This is the first time I've heard of it, Excellency." The chief of staff was trying to sound wide awake. "Give me a moment, sir. I'll retrieve the piece on my laptop."

"Wake the others. I want everyone in my suite in twenty minutes."

One of the president's aides found the video on YouTube and linked it from his laptop to the television in the suite's living room. President Duarte and his staff watched the video. During the final scene, the cabinet members grew tense. President Duarte was no longer looking at the television. His gaze moved among the six in the room.

When the video froze on the last frame, there was a brief moment of uncomfortable silence before Duarte spoke.

"Why didn't I hear about this incident before now?"

"Sir, I believe that—"

Duarte raised a hand and cut his senior aide off abruptly.

"This is on the international news," he continued, his voice rising. "Mexico doesn't need this kind of publicity."

He began to pace back and forth, his face red, his eyes wild. "And yet, someone else knew about this hunt and went to break it up. And unless my eyes are playing tricks on me, there were uniformed federal police participating in this debacle."

He turned to his chief aide. "Who are these people?"

The senior aide looked at the floor. "At this time, Excellency, we do not know, but I promise you, we will have all the information about these people before breakfast."

"Contact Figueroa. As Minister of Fisheries, he should know something about this incident."

It was common knowledge in his administration that there was no love lost between President Duarte and his brother-in law. The First Lady's powerful political family in Mexico City had been able to leverage Duarte into appointing the ambitious Figueroa to his present position.

Duarte went to the window and stared into the night. After what seemed an interminable moment, he spoke.

"I want names. Who organized this hunt? Where did it take place? Who ordered the federal police support? What are the Japanese doing running a whaling operation in Mexican waters?" He turned back to the members of his Cabinet, stone-faced. "Make no mistake. If you can't answer these questions for me, your next position will be cleaning out the toilets in the Capitol Building!" He turned back to the window.

"Leave me."

As the cabinet members rose to leave, Duarte said, "Except you, Esteban."

The chief of staff stopped in his tracks. When the others had left and closed the door behind them, Esteban Hernandez stood at attention, waiting for the inevitable verbal barrage that was about to come his way. After an agonizing silence, Duarte spoke.

"I want you personally to talk to Alfonso Figueroa. Find out what he knows about this incident. Listen to how he answers your questions. Notice his tone."

"I'll be cautious in my queries, Excellency," said Esteban.

"And one more thing. I want you to find out the identity of the man who drove the boat into the cove and disrupted the hunt."

"It will be done, Excellency."

Esteban Hernández strode out of the room, fully aware that whatever information he was able to provide in the next few hours would determine his livelihood for the rest of his natural life.

Figueroa was in a deep sleep when the phone call came. His wife snorted as he rolled toward the bedside table. He picked up the phone on the third ring.

"Yes?"

"Hernández here. Something has come up."

"What is it?" Figueroa suddenly came alert.

"Have you seen the video?"

"Video? What video?"

"The video of the dolphin hunt in Baja. Surely this couldn't have slipped your attention. It's already gone viral."

"Oh, that. Yes, I've seen it. My people are looking into it right now," he lied.

"El Presidente wants to know why he wasn't informed of this matter as it happened. He wants to know what the federal police were doing at the scene."

"As I said, we're looking at the situation very closely. We're trying to determine who conducted the hunt and if certain federales were bribed to assist whoever is illegally killing these animals. Right now, we have reason to believe that a contingent from a small coastal tribe may be the culprits."

Figueroa felt the sweat running down his armpits and soaking his pajamas. He had hoped the Consortium would have finished with this dirty business by now. Originally, the plan had been to conduct the whale hunt while the president was off in South America. Since Spinner had disrupted the hunt, all of the plans had gone to hell. More of the indios were deserting the village every day. They were still waiting for the transport trucks. On top of everything else, the scouting boats had been unable to locate many dolphins and whales in the past week.

Efforts to locate Alejandro Cabrillo and the two women researchers had been unsuccessful. They were still out there somewhere, and the Consortium's inability to locate them disturbed Figueroa greatly. Yoshimatsu had promised him that the witnesses would be silenced. Figueroa took some small amount of solace in knowing that at least Jake Spinner would no longer present a problem.

"His Excellency wishes to speak to you." It was more of a command than a request. "Contact him now, Minister Figueroa."

President Duarte's cabinet reconvened at 6:30 the following morning. They met in the conference room that was attached to the suite the president occupied. The members entered and quickly found their seats. There was a nervous buzz as they conversed. The room went silent when President Duarte entered.

"What do we have?" Duarte asked, as he strode to the head of the table and sat. He looked intently at those seated around the table, making direct eye contact with each member. "Please enlighten me."

Hernández was the first to speak. "Sir, we have some information on the hunt. To the best of our knowledge, there appears to be a small indigenous fishing village at Puerto Nacimiento that is collaborating with an outside Asian group to procure small whales and dolphins."

"Who made this arrangement?"

"We think it was brokered between a Japanese group and the fishermen themselves," said Hernández. "The fishermen are hired to herd the whales and dolphins into a cove where the animals can be processed." Hernández picked up a remote and the video appeared on the television screen at the end of the room opposite Duarte. He froze the frame. "As you can see here, sir, they herd the animals into the shallows where the whalers kill and then butcher them. Those vehicles appear to be refrigerator trucks where the meat is probably stored. There are smaller transport trucks lined up as well. It appears some of the dolphins and whales are separated, taken alive and transferred to these vehicles in slings, as you can see here. We surmise that these are to be sold to various marine parks and aquaria."

"The indios don't have the resources to bring in trucks like these," Duarte said angrily. "The financing and planning are coming from somewhere else. Are the cartels involved?"

"We haven't been able to corroborate that, sir," said Hernández.

"Then is it the Japanese?"

"We think so. But the Japanese Consulate in Mexico City denies any intrusion by the Japanese whaling fleet."

"Freeze the video," Duarte saw something on the screen that caught his attention. "Right there."

Hernández froze the frame and the entire room was looking at an armed federale, standing guard near the butchering tarps on the shoreline.

"What I want to know is, on whose authority were the federal police placed on duty here?" The veins in Duarte's neck were visible.

"We haven't been able to determine the source of their deployment, Mr. President. But it appears the orders came from somewhere within your administration."

Duarte steepled his fingers and stared into space. For a moment, the only sound that could be heard was the air conditioning kicking in. Hernández held his breath, preparing himself for the inevitable tirade that was to follow.

"I spoke to the Minister of Fisheries moments ago," said Duarte, his voice measured. "He assured me that the mastermind behind the hunt will be exposed soon by him and his staff." He looked up at the members seated around the table. "I want Minister Figueroa's every movement accounted for. Where he goes, who he talks to, phone conversations."

The cabinet members looked somber and a bit apprehensive. They were about to investigate the President's brother-in-law for corruption and collusion with a foreign entity. The implications of what they might discover could have profound repercussions throughout Duarte's administration.

"This information goes no further than this room. Are we clear?"

"We understand," replied Hernández.

"I want you to find out the identities of the individuals or group who shot this video. If they're still in the country, bring them to me."

"We were able to track down one of the photographers," said an aide who sat opposite Hernández. "I traced one of the leads back to the *Los Angeles Times*. They informed me the video was shot by Emily Rosen, a former *New York Times* reporter."

Duarte asked, "Is she still in Mexico?"

"According to *Migración* she entered using her passport on March 5th. There's no record of her leaving."

"Any ideas on where she might be?"

"At this time, she remains a person of interest," said the aide, his voice trailing off.

Duarte's face was red. Hernández reflected that, if the president kept this up, he would die of a heart attack or a stroke before his term was completed.

"Who was the man who disrupted the hunt? Do we have any intel on him?"

"We were able to isolate frames from the video and then expand the image to get an ID on the boat," said another aide at the end of the table. "The boat is registered to one Jacob Spinner, American. He is former military, living in Baja California Sur. He lives off his pension and charters his boat out to gringo fishermen. Interestingly, the last house where he lived in San Jacinto was the target of a drive-by shooting. The house was nearly leveled, but no bodies were recovered."

"So, is it safe to assume that Mr. Jacob Spinner is still at large?" Duarte asked acidly.

The aide looked like he wanted to melt into the chair. "Yes, he has not been located, Mr. President."

Duarte stood and leaned forward, knuckles on the table. "Find them!"

# 57

Hirokan Yoshimatsu set the cell phone down on the table. He let out a deep sigh and walked out onto the veranda. Ako Kanamura had been sitting on the couch, going over security reports from his men who were stationed at Puerto Nacimiento. He noticed the deep concern on his superior's face. He placed the documents on the glass table and joined him outside. Sato Izumi, who had been on another call, saw Yoshimatsu hang up and spoke quietly into his own cell phone.

Yoshimatsu stood at the railing looking out over the harbor. The morning sun bathed the port in a golden glow. Ships sparkled in the sun like jewels as they gently bobbed in the small waves.

"We have to move up the timetable." Yoshimatsu did not turn around. "It seems our friend Figueroa is losing his nerve."

"What happened?"

"The President has seen the video. He wants to know who is backing our operation and who allowed us to hunt in their waters."

"I thought he said his brother-in-law would not present any problems."

"Perhaps he does not like any operation where he does not share a hand in the profits," replied Sato Izumi, who had just joined them on the terrace. "Maybe you approached the wrong man with your proposal."

"As of today," Kanamura said guardedly, "six families have deserted the village. They leave mostly at night, taking only the clothes on their backs. The number of participating fishermen has been cut in half."

"We will have to make up the difference with crew members from the *Shodokai Maru*," said Yoshimatsu.

Sato frowned. "Do you think that is wise? Leaving only a skeleton crew on board?"

"I assure you, Sato, that we have more than enough men to complete the operation."

"What about the transport trucks?"

"They are standing by awaiting my command," said Yoshimatsu. "They can be mobilized within twelve hours from Tijuana."

He turned to Kanamura. "Tell the villagers they will be paid double for this hunt. If they are still hesitant, then make the necessary demonstrations to ensure their loyalty and participation."

Kanamura nodded. "It will be done, sir."

"What are you going to do about Figueroa? It seems the Minister of Fisheries has become a liability to us."

"The Minister of Fisheries has received partial payment for his part in this operation," Yoshimatsu said. "He will receive his final payment once we are safely out of Mexico. Once the search boats have located a large pod of dolphins, we will move them to the designated processing area. The villagers should not be told of the location until the last possible moment. I want to avoid interference from any activists or the prying eyes of President Duarte's administration."

Yoshimatsu turned to face Sato. "You and I will be present to supervise the operation. It will be executed with flawless precision. The separation, processing, and transport will be completed, and we will be headed back to Yokohama within twelve hours of commencement."

"I admire your resolve and hope that your optimism will be rewarded," said Sato.

"Kanamura-san, tell Sato how you will maintain the loyalty of the remaining villagers?"

Kanamura's face remained passive. "At times, contractors need to be reminded of their ongoing commitment to our project. A public demonstration will be carried out that should be sufficient to keep their minds on the final phase of the project. We make an example of one of the more—how do you say?—vocal members of the village. Nothing too excessive, just a reminder of what could happen should their loyalties flag."

# 58

The air inside of the small fishing shack was humid and stuffy, even though the morning air was chilly. The room was packed with all the recent arrivals to San Vicente camp. After breakfast, the group crowded into the small space for the meeting that Alejandro Cabrillo had called. Conversations were animated, although there was obvious tension. Alejandro sat in a folding chair against the far wall. He still looked frail, and his eyes were dulled from the pain. He spoke quietly to Raúl. Sandy sat on his left, conversing with Graham Neely and the five volunteers. Except for Graham, everyone from the small group looked nervous and out of place. Off to the side, Spinner leaned against a wall, his arms folded, looking across the room. Standing beside him, Emily Rosen sensed that he was about to go off.

"Is it warm in here or is it just me?" Rosen looked around the crowded room.

Spinner fidgeted, shifting his weight from one leg to the other. "I'm not sure what good this is going to do. We don't have any usable intel on when and where the whalers are going to strike."

"Do you think Alma lost her nerve?"

"My guess. It's one thing to stand up for your principles. Sounds real good until the ones who are bullying you start killing your neighbors."

Alejandro reached for a metal spoon from the table and banged on a dented coffee pot. Instantly the room went quiet, and all eyes turned to the former director of the marine institute.

"Okay, let's get started. I think everyone has had a chance to meet. I want to thank all of you for coming out for this cause." He looked around the room, his face somber. "Every one of you has come here for a reason. Many of you make your living from the ocean. Some of us study the ocean and its inhabitants in hopes of conserving the magnificent species for our children and grandchildren. Some of you come to fight and lend your voices to those who can't raise their own—the animals who are at the tip of the whalers' harpoons."

He paused and took a drink of water. Clearing his throat, he spoke again. "We are not just up against a group of whalers. Someone in the Mexican government has not only allowed these hunters into our waters, but has also provided protection to them by a contingent of our federal police. Our task is especially dangerous."

Alejandro stopped speaking for several seconds, recalling a recent painful memory. "We've been informed that another hunt is to take place very soon. I would like several members of our group to speak about the plan for the upcoming hunt. Raúl Campos will tell you about progress in learning the location of the impending drive."

Raúl looked nervously at Alejandro, nodded, and began to speak. "As of today, we have no word from our contact in Puerto Nacimiento. I tried to reach her yesterday. If and when she does contact us, we'll only have a small window of opportunity to organize our attack. I've asked several of the fishermen in outlying areas to watch out for any new construction or activity in some of the coves up and down the coastline. So far, there's nothing to report."

Arturo's hand shot up. "Are there other members of the village who can be contacted?"

Raúl shook his head. "From what I've been told by our contact, the villagers' movements are being closely monitored by the whalers. No one from the outside has been allowed in or out of Puerto Nacimiento. Some of the locals have deserted the village and either moved inland or across to the mainland. I'm worried that our informant has either been found out or has lost her nerve."

Graham raised his hand. Raúl acknowledged him. The tall young man stood, looked around the room and said, "I think I've met most of you. I'm Graham Neely from Cetus Alliance." He turned back and faced Raúl. "What about sending out patrols to recon the areas up and down the coast? We have enough boats to cover a fair stretch of coastline."

Raúl answered him. "Yes, we have the boats. Our problem is there's far too much coastline and not enough fuel to reach all areas. We need to have a specific target. Another thing—and this is important—we don't want to be observed."

Alejandro spoke. "Until we can get a confirmation from our contact in Puerto Nacimiento, we're in a holding pattern. Graham, could you tell us about some of the defensive techniques employed by Cetus Alliance?"

Graham cleared his throat. "Most of our tactics are to place ourselves between the whales and the whalers. Anything we can do to keep them from getting off a shot. We've brought substances that, when combined and packaged, become noxious irritants. We launch them or throw them onto the whalers' boats. The smell becomes so overwhelmingly foul that the whalers get nauseous and have to stop what they're doing."

"Let me get this straight." Spinner was unable to hide the sarcasm in his voice. "You're going to go up against men armed with AK-47s by throwing stink bombs?"

"Well, we have launchers that we can use for increased range," Graham said defensively.

"Oh, Christ,"

"These methods are very effective at deterring the Japanese whaling fleet in the Southern Ocean," said Graham.

"How many times have you deployed this method?"

Graham shifted his weight uncomfortably. "Well . . . none of us has actually done this before. We received instructions when we signed on. It's worked before for the Sea Shepherds."

"This is a really bad idea." Spinner sounded angry. "All this will do is piss them off and get some of us killed. You don't understand these guys. They don't answer to any government or regulating body. They will not hesitate to shoot you. I can say this from personal experience."

Alejandro raised his hand in an effort to restore order. "Then what do you propose, Jake?"

"Hell, I don't know. I've been wrestling with this ever since I got to San Vicente. No matter how this plays out, the prospects for our group aren't great: a wooden box or a concrete cell. I don't care for either one of those options."

Rosen asked, "What about cutting them off at the source? Can we take the attack to the mother whaling ship?"

"We have to find it first," said Spinner. "Someone knows how to keep that ship pretty well hidden from view."

"I can find it," said Beau, the young activist from Cetus.

All eyes in the room turned toward the spectacled nerd.

Beau looked around the room nervously, made an awkward attempt at an engaging smile, then looked down at the floor. "If I can pick up a signal from a satellite, I should be able to get a real time picture of the Gulf of California. Locating the mother ship shouldn't be too much of a problem. I just need some basic specs on the ship and I should be able to match it up."

Rosen spoke. "I think I can help you on that one, Beau." She produced her notebook and began to read from her notes. "*Shodokai Maru*, commissioned in 1961 as a Japanese fish meal processor. Sold to China for scrap in 1986. Shows up again in 1994 as a whaling ship registered in Liberia. Single hull, double prop, 23,326 gross registered tons, length 325 feet, top speed of 15.5 knots, cruises at 13.5 knots, with a crew of thirty-two. Oh, and a recent ship's manifest shows a stop in Pichilingue to pick up temporary import permits."

Everyone in the crowded room was staring at Rosen, including Spinner, his mouth agape.

"How did you get this information?"

"This is what I do every damn day, Jake. I dig for information, cross reference, and follow up on leads."

"When were you going to tell me this?"

Rosen looked slightly sheepish. "Now? I needed to do something while you were contemplating your navel up on the dune."

"Never mind." Spinner stepped forward, his brow raised, looking directly at Beau. "Wait a minute. You have the ability to locate the whaling ship?"

"Sure." Beau shrugged. "That's if I can link into a satellite overhead."

"You may have just become my new best friend. Say you can make the connection. Then how difficult is it to track the ship?"

"That depends on how much large ship traffic is present in the gulf."

"Most of the larger freighters come into La Paz at Pichilingue," said Alejandro. "Mostly freighters and oil tankers. Ferries run regularly from La Paz and Cabo San Lucas to the mainland, so they should be fairly easy to discern."

"That's the best news I've heard all day," Spinner said. "What do you need?"

"Enough juice to make a connection," said Beau. "That's about it."

Spinner looked to Alejandro. "Alex?"

Alejandro nodded. "Yes. From now on, our first priority is to divert all available resources to get that satellite feed. If you need to use electronics, clear it with us first."

The room broke into a cacophony of voices. Alejandro banged on the metal pot to restore order. Spinner turned back to face Rosen. He shook his head.

"Damn good job on finding the intel on that ship, Em. Next time though, a little more communication between you and me might be a good thing."

"Sorry, Jake. I was going to tell you, but you weren't in the mood to hear it."

"I think it's time we broke into our designated groups," said Alejandro. "Logistics will meet in this corner, the assault teams outside. Graham and his crew want to demonstrate the use of the non-lethal weapons."

Spinner started walking toward the door when Sandy intercepted him. The look on her face told him that he was about to receive an earful.

"What the hell crawled up your ass and died? The Cetus Alliance are just here to help us! The least you can do is hear them out. Who knows? They might come up with something—like Beau just did—to help our cause."

"Contrary to popular opinion, none of you people are expendable," Spinner shot back. "Right now, we have no intel, no location, and no plan. About the only thing we have—and that's sketchy at best—is a kid with a computer who may be able to locate the mother ship."

"Look, Spinner, I know you're used to doing things the way the military taught you, but this isn't the military. It's just a bunch of people trying to do the right thing. Can you cut them some slack? They're scared half to death of you."

Sudden realization hit him like a cold slap in the face. The anger in his eyes faded and he heaved a deep sigh. He nodded slightly. "You're right. I'm not being helpful." He turned and walked out into the sunshine.

Sandy and Rosen watched him leave. "Do you think I was too harsh?" Sandy asked.

"He'll be all right. Spinner's got a sore spot about bad intel. He lost most of his unit in Afghanistan. He doesn't want to do a repeat of that with us."

"Oh, my God," said Sandy. "I didn't know."

"And he doesn't want you to know. He's just frustrated right now because we don't have nearly enough info to push forward on this."

The assault group convened outside. Alejandro stayed inside to coordinate the logistics crew with three members of the group.

Morgan, the statuesque redhead with glasses was helping Graham demonstrate the manufacture of the stink bombs that they were going to hurl at the banger boats. Rosen looked around at the anxious group. Everyone was listening intently to Graham's instructions on how to prepare the bombs.

"This is butyric acid," he said, holding up a glass jar about the size of a mason jar. "It has a real nasty smell when it hits. It's been deployed using various delivery systems with some success."

Rosen asked, "What does it smell like?"

Graham walked over to where she stood and cracked the lid. Her face pinched into a grimace, and she backpedaled. "Ugh! It smells like puke!"

"Makes for some real uncomfortable rides when you're in rough seas."

"How," asked Arturo, "do you throw the jar and hit the target when you're traveling at high speeds?"

"It's a bit of a learning curve. Having a good arm helps," said Graham. "We're working on some other delivery systems as well." He held up a set of rubber tubing with a canvas patch attached between the two cords. "This is a Zamboni launcher. Essentially, a very large sling shot."

Rosen smiled and leaned in toward Sandy. "I didn't know our tactics would come straight from the Old Testament."

"Ssshhh!" Sandy said, stifling a laugh.

"Come to think of it, Graham bears a striking resemblance to David," Rosen grinned at Sandy and nudged her with an elbow.

"I'll have Morgan step up and demonstrate a couple of throws so you can get an idea," Graham said. "Then we'll launch a few empty jars to show you how the launcher works." He looked around until he spotted a battered half-sheet piece of plywood that leaned against the side of Jesús's shack. He pulled out a permanent ink marker and drew a circle on the face of the plywood. He picked up the plywood square, turned to Morgan and said, "Tell me when."

Graham trudged toward the dune. Murmurs arose from the gathered crowd as he paced off each step. Spinner, who had been listening from the back of the group, stepped forward, his interest piqued.

"That's good," said Morgan. She picked up one of jars that had been filled with water. She eyed the target nearly ninety feet away, then squared her shoulders and took two deep breaths. Her left arm was a blur of movement as she wound up and snapped it forward. She let out a small *whoosh* from her lungs as she released the jar.

The glass jar exploded on the plywood inside the circle drawn by Graham. A shower of shards caught rays from the sun like tiny prisms. A gasp went up from the gathered crowd.

"Great shot," said Rosen.

"Like I said, it doesn't hurt to have an arm," said Graham.

Spinner was impressed. "Where'd you learn to throw like that?"

"University of Arizona. Varsity softball for four years," Morgan replied.

"Can you do that again?"

"Sure." Morgan retrieved another water-filled glass jar.

"This time, move," said Spinner.

She turned and looked at him her brow furrowed. "Move? What do you mean, *move*?"

"I want to see if you can hit a moving target," said Spinner. "You're going to be on a moving boat throwing it at another moving boat. Possibly in rough seas."

She nodded and backed off and to the side. She closed her eyes and breathed deeply. Suddenly she turned quickly and began to sprint back to where she had originally stood, then leapt into the air and launched the jar in a wicked overhand. It rocketed downward and smashed against the lower right quarter of the circle.

The crowd erupted into hoots and cheers. Morgan turned defiantly and faced Spinner. "I also played two-person beach volleyball every summer in Newport Beach."

Spinner grinned. "Nice arm."

Graham went on to discuss deployment of the Zamboni launcher. The assault team broke into smaller groups to practice. Spinner was surprised to see that Paola, who normally stood in the background, proved to have a formidable arm. Graham picked her to be one of the throwers. There would be two on each team. One would hand the bottles of butyric acid to the thrower who would launch them until one found its mark. Both throwers and loaders would prepare the noxious projectiles, an equal nausea opportunity for all.

Spinner and Raúl talked to the group designated to be the boat drivers. The fishermen who made a daily living handling boats in difficult conditions would be the best. That meant that Jesús, Carlos, and Francisco would strike at the heart of the whalers' juggernaut. Sandy was the fourth driver. Spinner chose her because of her boat-handling skills in rough seas and her experience avoiding collisions with fifty-five-ton moving animals.

"Okay, everyone. Listen up," Spinner commanded. "You've all seen the video and the set-up the whalers used before in San Mateo Cove. I think it's a pretty good bet that they're going to set up the same type of structure. A net is stretched across the cove secured by a wooden planking system that serves as a catwalk. The whalers can use this vantage point to keep the dolphins in the cove and drive them toward the beach where the flensers will finish them off."

Spinner picked up a stick and drew an outline of a cove in the sand. Next, he traced a curved line that ran from one point of the entrance of the cove to the opposite side. He drew an X on each point and two more on the line designating the net catwalk.

"The Xs indicate guards with guns. Remember, this was what I saw at the last hunt. I wouldn't be surprised if they doubled the guards after what happened at San Mateo. This is what you have to avoid."

"How are we supposed to take down those nets? We saw your boat after the last hunt," said Carlos. "It was barely seaworthy after you rammed the catwalk."

Spinner's face flushed slightly. "Francisco, do you think we can retro-fit the bows of the sturdier boats with something—some kind of device that will shred netting and break up the catwalk?"

Francisco looked at Spinner quizzically, his handsome brown face serious. Then he broke into a smile revealing even white teeth. "I think I might be able to come up with something, Jake."

"Three boats will attack the nets," said Raúl. "The other boats will go after the launches that are herding the dolphins back to the cove."

"Sandy will be leading this group," interjected Spinner. "You drivers have to make sure you don't get bunched up. Get in, toss a few stink bombs, and then move out of range."

"Float like a butterfly," said Sandy.

"Sting like one hell of a big bee," said Spinner.

After the meeting, Arturo walked up to Jake. Spinner grinned at him. "Hey, Doc. How's the field hospital coming along?"

"I turned that duty over to Dora," said Arturo. "I've got a new job for the hunt."

"What's that?"

"I'm going to be reloading for Paola. We're getting our timing down pretty good."

"Good. Just keep your head down, Doc. We're a little shy on medical assistance out here."

Raúl, Sandy, and Graham approached Spinner and Rosen.

"I owe you an apology, Graham," Spinner extended his hand. "I think you and your people have some particular talents that will definitely help the operation."

Graham looked genuinely surprised. "Uh, thanks, Jake. We just want to help any way we can."

Sandy looked at Jake, her tone serious. "Thanks for recommending me to be a driver, Jake. I won't let you or the others down."

"No need to thank me. From what I hear, there's no one on this beach who knows that boat better than you."

Spinner looked at the people gathered around him. He let out a long breath, then spoke. "I have to leave for a while."

The looks on everyone's faces went from surprise to dismay. Sandy looked as if he'd just plunged a knife between her ribs. "What?"

"Spinner, the hunt could be any day," said Raúl. "Where are you going?"

"I have to go to the mainland. I need to talk to someone who may be able to up the ante in our favor."

"You'll never be able to get back in time," said Arturo. "It's at least a two-day trip to get there and back."

"With any luck, I'll be back in thirty-six hours."

"I can't believe you're walking out on us now," said Sandy. "What if the hunt is called for tomorrow?"

"I'm a phone call away. Keep me in the loop."

"Yeah," said Graham, unable to hide his agitation and frustration. "What if the hunt's tomorrow? You said it yourself, Spinner. You've been there. We need your experience."

"There was nothing planned about what I did at San Mateo. I was making it up as I went."

Raúl asked, "What's so important that you have to go now?"

"We need an edge. Right now, we don't have one." He looked from one activist to the other. "I want to see if there's a way to stop these guys once and for all. I want to put that whaling ship on the bottom of the Gulf of California."

"Just how," asked Rosen, "do you propose to do that?"

"That's why I have to go to Sinaloa." Jake turned to Raúl. "First thing you hear from the Quintín woman, you call me and I'll get my ass back here." He looked around at the group, meeting everyone's gazes. "I promise."

"When are you leaving?" Sandy was still unresolved about his seemingly hair-brained plan.

"As soon as I gather a few things."

Spinner turned to walk away. Rosen fell into step beside him.

"Where the hell do you think you're going?" Spinner cast a sidelong glance at her.

"Coming with you, Spinner. Someone has to make sure you get your ass back here before the fireworks begin."

Over the sounds of the waves crashing on the beach and the generator humming behind Jesús's house, Emily heard a distant thumping that seemed to be growing louder.

Suddenly, the camp broke into bedlam as a Bell 205 cargo helicopter appeared from around the point. It banked and then headed straight for the group on the beach.

Someone yelled, "Run for cover!" Most of them began scattering in all directions. All except Raúl, Graham, and Sandy, who stood their ground.

Spinner turned and faced the descending helicopter, beach sand stinging his face and arms.

"Who the hell is that?" Rosen yelled over the din, shielding her face from the blasting sand.

"That's our ride."

# 59

Before the rotor stopped spinning, a figure climbed out of the seat and approached them in a bent-over posture. Once clear from the rotating blades, the man straightened up to his full height. Rosen was looking at the largest black man she had ever seen. His head was shaved; he wore camo BDUs, desert boots, and a tight khaki tee shirt that revealed cordlike muscles beneath. The giant trotted up to Spinner and Rosen.

"Jake Spinner?"

Spinner nodded.

"Oliver Sweet." The man extended his hand. "Mr. Castellano sent us. You ready to go?"

"Got room for one more?" Spinner pointed to Emily.

"No problem."

Spinner turned to Rosen. "Grab whatever you need, and be back here in five. Just the basics."

Rosen glared at Jake. "Spinner, next time a little warning might be nice." She took off at a run toward the fishing shack to retrieve her laptop and a few items of clothing. Spinner grabbed his old duffel that he had left out in anticipation of the impending transport.

"Go on, climb aboard," said Sweet. "I'll make sure the lady gets on."

Spinner walked quickly to the Bell, its rotor gradually spinning down. As he waited for Rosen, Sweet leaned in and said, "Mr. Castellano was right. We'd have no problems recognizing you."

"What did he tell you?"

"Not much. Something about 120 clicks of bad Mexican road."

Spinner cast Sweet a sideways glance and was about to ask the big man what exactly he meant when Rosen sprinted up, carrying her backpack slung over one shoulder.

"All aboard," said Sweet, picking Rosen up bodily and setting her down on the platform of the helicopter's cabin.

"Hey! What the hell do you think you're doing?"

"First step is a bit of a reach, miss. Just trying to move things along."

"Next time ask before you grab." Rosen's gaze was fierce, causing the big man to pause briefly.

Spinner swung up into the helicopter, wincing as he lifted his body weight. Once inside, Sweet made sure they were both strapped into their seats. The pilot, his face and eyes masked by a helmet and reflective military-style Ray-Bans, turned and faced them. He had at least a week's worth of beard growth and a smile that hinted at someone who had danced in and out of the near side of batshit crazy for a long time.

"I'm Derek Robideaux. But my friends call me 'Snake.'"

"Great," said Rosen, rolling her eyes.

"You don't have any problems flying over water, do ya?" Snake gave Rosen a diabolical grin that caused her stomach to lurch.

"No problem. As long as we're flying over it and not crashing into it. I have a big problem with that."

Snake gave her the thumbs up sign. "Excellent! We're on the same page."

Rosen looked over at Spinner, who was studying the cockpit electronics. "Spinner?"

Jake turned his gaze toward her, a smile forming at the corners of his mouth. He shrugged.

"Nice friends," said Rosen.

"They may not be much in the area of social graces, but I'll bet they're good to have around when the feces hit the fan."

Snake throttled up and the rotors began to spin until they were a blur overhead. Rosen felt the helicopter lurch to the side, then lift off the beach. She gazed out and saw the looks of concern on the others' faces.

They flew low and fast over the Gulf of California. Rosen was mesmerized by the long rollers that passed 1,500 feet beneath the helicopter's skids. She reflected on all the events that had led up to this day. It seemed like months since she had landed at the airport in La Paz, but it only was just over three weeks ago. New York seemed light years away. She knew her life had taken a turn that she'd never anticipated but now couldn't imagine being anywhere else.

At one point, Spinner clasped her hand and gave it a squeeze. "You okay?"

She looked at his tanned, craggy face, and into his blue eyes, squeezed back, and smiled. "Yeah. I'm good."

Snake spoke from the microphone and announced, "Mainland's coming into sight. We're going to start climbing."

Rosen looked out the port window and saw the green-blue gulf waters below. White sand beach stretched before them. The helicopter began to climb into mountains. Emily saw a carpet of deep green. Moments later, as the helicopter lifted above the canopy, the thick aroma of loamy earth and decomposing vegetation assaulted her senses.

After passing between two forested mountain peaks, the helicopter lurched downward, following the angle of the mountain. They leveled out and an open patch in the jungle appeared ahead. Rosen peered down and saw several buildings arranged in a pentagon and connected by pathways. A stream ran between two of the buildings with a small wooden bridge spanning it. All of the paths connected to a large central building, white with a layered red tile roof. The hacienda shone like a red ruby in a field of emeralds.

Several people dressed in uniforms and armed with automatic rifles walked the pathways with guard dogs.

When the helicopter touched down, two men who were dressed like Oliver Sweet approached. They stood just past the whirling rotors in postures of relaxed attention. Snake throttled down the engines, unsnapped his harness and turned around, his devilish grin still evident.

"Welcome to Las Altas, kids," Snake said. "BTW, what happens at Las Altas . . ."

Rosen unsnapped her harness. ". . . stays at Las Altas?"

"Hey! You're all right, Rosen."

The two men acknowledged Sweet. The older one, a stern looking man with a crew cut, asked, "Any problems?"

"No problems," said Sweet.

"Mr. Castellano is waiting at the house."

Sweet nodded. He turned to Rosen and Spinner. "This way, folks."

They followed him across the compound to the large hacienda. They walked up a series of steps composed of colorful tiles to a veranda that wrapped around the entire building. A concrete ramp off to the side angled gradually toward the porch. The two front doors were heavy, of dark wood carved in ancient Mayan designs. Two armed men stood on either side. They nodded to Sweet and opened the double doors.

Rosen found herself in the middle of a huge atrium. A fig tree, its corrugated trunk nearly ten feet across, grew up through the ceiling. Two macaws sat on one of the lower branches, squawking and nodding enthusiastically.

"That's amazing." Rosen marveled at the enormous tree. She noticed other birds flitting in and out of the canopy.

"Yeah," said Sweet. "Mr. Castellano had the house built around that tree. If you look around, he's left most of the old growth trees intact."

"Are those birds pets?"

"Nope. They drop in every morning from the canopy. They discovered that there's a bounty of fruit and nuts to be had here. They're military macaws, so they fit right in. And this is where I leave you for a while. Nice to meet you both."

They shook Sweet's hand. "Thanks," Spinner said. "Thanks for the assist."

"Oh, I have a feeling our paths are going to cross again, sooner rather than later." Oliver emitted a baritone laugh.

An attractive Latina walked toward them. She was dressed in a peasant blouse with a flowered skirt. In her hair she wore a single white orchid behind her right ear.

"Mr. Spinner, I'm Angelina Obregón, Director of Operations here at Las Altas." She extended her hand. "I hope you had a nice trip." Her English was precise and flawless.

"Fast," said Spinner. "And uneventful." He turned to Emily. "This is Emily Rosen." Rosen shook hands with Angelina.

"Welcome, Miss Rosen. If you'll please follow me, I'll escort you to the great room where you can relax and have a drink. Mr. Castellano will be with you shortly."

She led them down a hallway adorned with paintings by Frida Kahlo, Diego Rivera, and José Clemente Orozco. A bronze bust of a jaguar's head with its mouth open rested on a pedestal next to another ornately carved wooden door.

Angelina ushered them inside. The room had a large picture window that revealed a landscape of jungle and mountains. A stream flowed in an ambling course across a field. A flock of white ibises waded along its shoreline. Along another wall was a bookcase filled with books covering many different topics. Along the opposite wall was a fully-stocked bar. Comfortable overstuffed leather chairs and a deep brown leather sofa faced the expansive view.

"Oh, my God," said Rosen. "I think I just died and went to heaven."

Angelina smiled. "May I fix you a drink?"

"Do you by chance have any lemonade? With ice?"

"Of course. And for you, Mr. Spinner?"

Spinner examined the bar's row upon row of ornate bottles. He felt a strong pull toward a drink. It felt like a long time since any liquor had passed his lips. Out of the corner of his eye, he saw Rosen studying him. He turned back to Angelina. "I'll have what she's having."

"Very good. Please make yourselves comfortable while I order the refreshments." She speed-dialed a number on her cell phone. Moments later an attendant arrived carrying a tray with a pitcher of lemonade and two frosty glasses filled with ice. The accompanying fruit platter of freshly cut mangos, figs, melons, and guava made Rosen's mouth water.

Emily couldn't remember when something had tasted so good and slaked her thirst so well. She had to force herself to keep from gulping the ice-cold lemonade down. Spinner rolled the cold glass across his forehead, closing his eyes, then downed the lemonade in three gulps.

The door opened, and a man wheeled himself into the room. He had long gray hair tied in a ponytail and a short cropped gray beard. He wore a white cotton *guayabera* shirt, faded jeans, and huaraches. As he drew closer, Rosen could see that his facial features weren't symmetrical. Part of his right hand was missing.

"As I live and breathe, it's Jake Spinner, back from the dead." Rollie Castellano rolled his wheelchair forward with an ease that suggested that he had spent a lot of time mastering this form of mobility.

"Hello, Rollie," Jake said, grinning. "You look good."

"You're still a lousy liar, Spinner." He looked toward Rosen. "Emily Rosen, I'm Roland Castellano. My friends call me Rollie." He extended his good hand and Rosen took it.

"Nice to meet you, Rollie."

"I've followed your column in the *Times*. You're a hell of an investigative reporter. Top shelf stuff." He hooked a thumb toward Spinner. "How'd you end up with this derelict?"

"Long story." Emily looked at Spinner.

Castellano's eyebrows rose slightly. "I'm looking forward to hearing the tale." He regarded his former comrade, his eyes coming to rest on the glass of lemonade in Spinner's hand. "Little thinner than the last time I saw you, Jake. But better than I expected." Castellano spun the wheelchair around and faced Angelina. "I think my friends might be hungry after their long trip. I believe a light lunch would be in order."

"I will tell the chefs." Angelina turned away and spoke into her cell phone in Spanish.

"I suspect that this isn't a social call," Rollie said, turning back to his guests.

"Rollie, I . . . we need your help," said Spinner. "In a couple of days, a lot of good people and a great number of whales and dolphins are going to be killed."

"Ah, this'll be a grand topic for the table, don't you think? In the meantime, let's head onto the back veranda where we can enjoy the scenery."

They followed him to the veranda overlooking the grounds. There was a lovely view of the stream where it widened into a small pool. Along the bank, a large form lay sprawled, motionless. At first, Rosen thought the object was a large brown log. Suddenly the log's mouth opened in a yawn, revealing a gaping maw full of teeth.

"That's a big alligator," Rosen said.

"American crocodile, actually," Castellano said offhandedly. "She comes up here from the river and suns herself on the grounds."

"Is she dangerous?"

"Only if you're a small white poodle. As one of our clients found out while on an unsupervised stroll about the grounds."

Rosen looked at Rollie. His face was expressionless, but his eyes were sparkling.

"I'll keep that in mind."

Rosen felt her tension melt away as she sat at a large round table covered in a white tablecloth. "This is a beautiful estate. How big is it?"

"The property is approximately 230 acres. Only what you see in front of you has been developed. Other than security devices, the jungle has been left in its original state. We even have a jaguar that moves in and out of the compound periodically."

"It's nice to see you believe in conservation," said Rosen.

"Don't kid yourself. I'm no tree hugger. I just believe in 'Live and let live.'"

A team of men and women, dressed in white linen, brought in trays of food and pitchers of drinks. The plates were filled with brightly colored vegetables, fruits, and salads. The main course was the last to be set on the table.

"I hope you like shrimp," Rollie said.

On the large platter were the largest shrimp Rosen had ever seen. They had been grilled in butter and *guajillo* sauce.

"Are you sure those are shrimp? Where I come from, they'd be classified as lobsters."

While they dined, Spinner brought Castellano up to speed on how the Japanese cartel had conscripted the indigenous people to hunt whales for them, which led to the murder of Gustavo and his family. Rosen punctuated Spinner's discourse with what she had witnessed from the cliff as the dolphins were driven to the slaughter. When Spinner recounted what had happened once he boarded the Japanese whaling ship, Castellano held up his hand.

"Wait a minute. Are you telling me the Japanese brought a full-size whaling ship up into the Gulf?"

"Ever hear of the *Shodokai Maru*?" Spinner asked, setting his fork down. He reached over and poured another glass of lemonade.

Castellano shook his head. "No, but that doesn't mean anything. It's not easy to hide something like that in a contained body of water like the Gulf of California. Sounds like they're plugged into someone in the Mexican administration."

"We suspect that it's the Minister of Fisheries, Alfonso Figueroa, who's in league with the Japanese whalers," said Rosen.

Castellano looked up suddenly at Angelina, then shifted his gaze back to Rosen.

"You mean Alfonso Figueroa who is brother-in-law to the president of Mexico?"

"One and the same," said Emily.

"He has some nasty friends in his little black book. Ties to the military and federal police and a questionable connection to the Sinaloa Cartel. Want some advice?"

"That depends," said Spinner.

"I think you should walk away from this one, Jake. If it's Figueroa's operation, you're walking into a shitstorm."

"Too late to walk away. Rollie, we need your help. These guys have automatic weapons. We have slingshots and stink bombs."

"We don't even know where his brother-in-law stands on this." Castellano let out a big sigh. "I'm in a somewhat delicate position here, Jake. Las Altas is allowed to operate here under the auspices of the Mexican government. If what you're saying is true, then we could be jeopardizing our relationship with this administration by assisting you and your cause."

"I understand, Rollie. Under normal circumstances, I wouldn't even ask."

"I didn't say I wouldn't do it." Castellano bit down on his lip and stared out onto the lush grounds of the compound. He shook his head slowly. "I never could talk you out of anything once you made up your mind." He drained the last of his margarita, then looked at Spinner and Rosen. "After lunch, let's take a walk. I want to show you something."

# 60

After lunch, Rosen turned on her laptop and showed Castellano the video of the slaughter at the cove. He watched it intently, becoming increasingly angry as the killing progressed. When he saw the part where Spinner crashed his boat through the barricade, Castellano remarked, "Well, it appears your penchant for shooting from the hip hasn't changed all that much."

"I warned that guy, never touch my boat."

When the video concluded, Castellano sat back in his chair and looked at Rosen. "Emily, you have a lot of chutzpah. You kept that camera rolling while those poachers were taking shots at you. My hat's off to you."

"Think you might be able to help us?"

He looked at his guests. "Feel up to a little stroll?"

"Right now, I feel like I could take a siesta," said Spinner. "I'm as full as a tick."

"How about we do this, Angelina will show you to your room where you can freshen up a bit, even take a snooze. I'll send someone to come and get you. Say, around four. That work for you two?"

Spinner looked at Rosen. "Fine by me. What do you say, Em?"

"I wouldn't mind a hot shower. I think these clothes are about to walk off me."

Castellano appraised her from head to foot. She felt her face flush. He said, "I'd guess you to be a size eight."

"Uh, well, yes. I fluctuate between a six and an eight."

"Angelina, can you check the stores and see what we have on hand that would fit Ms. Rosen."

She nodded. "Yes. I believe we can find something comfortable. Now, if you'll both please follow me, I'll show you to your room."

They were taken to a spacious room located near the northwest corner of the hacienda. It was a masterpiece of softly colorful walls accented with beautiful Mexican tile work. The large bathroom had a walk-in shower and a step-down spa, both ornately tiled. The grand picture window had a view of the jungle and the rising green hills beyond. Large white cumulus clouds gathered at the tops of the mountains, contrasting with the deep cerulean sky and the forest green.

Rosen couldn't remember seeing any vista more breathtaking. Her eyes widened. "Now I definitely know I died and went to heaven."

"There are fresh towels in that closet, and robes are hanging on the inside door," Angelina said. "If you need us for anything, there's a house phone on the wall. Now, if there's nothing else, I'll leave you to your rest."

"Thank you, Angelina. It's been a long time since I've been able to wallow in luxury."

After Angelina left, Spinner wandered around the room for several minutes. As if on cue, their eyes met. Rosen smiled at Spinner. "So, what do you think?"

"Nice crib." Spinner shifted uncomfortably. "Rosen, are you okay with this?" He gestured around the room.

"Oh yeah, I'm more than okay with this."

"I mean, Em, are you okay with us? Here? Together?"

Rosen smiled again, this time a smile that spoke of an invitation. "I want to take a shower. Care to join me?"

They made love in the shower, their bodies fused together in the swirling steam. Tentative at first, they began to gently explore each other as the hot water washed away the pain and terror of the last few weeks. For the first time in as long as he could remember, Spinner felt good. Life was good again. He realized how isolated he had become. He reached up and held Emily's face in his hands.

"Thank you." He kissed her—a long, ardent kiss. She moved against him until they were pushed against the far wall of the shower. He lifted her and she wrapped her legs around his waist. As he entered her, she moaned and bit his ear.

"Welcome back to the world, Jake." She pulled him close.

They were lying on the bed when there was a soft knock at the door. Rosen flew out of bed and threw open the closet, tossing Spinner a luxuriant white robe. She quickly slipped into a robe of her own. "Door's open."

Angelina walked in pushing a cart with clothing hanging from the bar. "I hope I didn't disturb you."

"No. Not at all." Rosen's face was slightly red. "Please come in."

"I have several ensembles for you to look at, Miss Rosen. I think we have the right size."

"They're beautiful. And please call me Emily."

"Very well, Emily." Angelina smiled at her. "I have several pairs of pants and shirts for you to try on as well, Mr. Spinner."

"Jake, please. You must have picked out those threads for me, Angelina. If my memory serves me well, Rollie was never a slave to fashion."

"Actually, Rollie picked these clothes out for you himself."

Spinner laughed. "Just when you think you have someone pegged."

"Is four o'clock still good for you."

"Oh, yeah," said Spinner. "Four o'clock is good." He looked at Rosen.

"Works for me," she said.

When they walked into the great room, Castellano, now seated in an electric wheelchair, looked up from one of his computers. "Now, I'd call that an improvement."

Emily Rosen was transformed. She wore a white blouse over a black tank top with white linen pants and sandals. Her hair was styled and swept back and she wore just enough makeup to bring out the accents of her deep green eyes. Rollie noted that Spinner was having a hard time keeping his eyes off her. He was dressed in a pair of jeans with a long-sleeved, white linen shirt that he wore untucked and huaraches on his feet. His dark hair was slicked back.

"You both clean up pretty good," Rollie observed, smiling.

Rosen walked up and kissed Castellano on the cheek. "Thank you, Rollie. I can't believe how pampered I feel."

He activated the wheelchair and came from behind the desk. "Ready for a little adventure?"

They walked along with him as he maneuvered the wheelchair from the great room into the hall. Outside, he took the ramp that led from the house to the main path, Rosen and Spinner flanking him on either side. The late afternoon air was still and humid, and the buzz of insects and squawking of exotic birds provided a rainforest symphony.

They arrived several minutes later on the other side of the compound at a large, one-story brick building located in a small copse of trees. The building had no windows, and, at first, Spinner guessed it to be some type of storage facility. Two armed guards carrying assault rifles stood in front of a steel door.

Spinner grinned. "Is this where you keep the gold?"

"Not quite." Castellano nodded to the two guards. One of the armed men activated a button on a keypad he carried, and the great door slid open. "I think you're going to like this, Spinner."

They entered an open room sparsely furnished with desks and computers. Several men and women sat at the computers, inputting data. He nodded to people as he passed.

"Hell of an office pool, Rollie," said Spinner.

"This way." Rollie manipulated the joystick on his wheelchair and headed toward another metal door at the back of the room. The door slid open silently. Castellano smiled and waved them in. "Let's go shopping."

They descended two floors. When the door opened, Spinner was looking at a large room. Another armed guard, a tall black man greeted them. "Hello, Mr. Castellano. Haven't seen you in a while."

"Hello, Reggie. I brought some friends down today. Jake Spinner and Emily Rosen. They may be in the market for some trinkets, souvenirs from their stay at Las Altas."

Reggie laughed, a booming laugh that echoed in the large room. "I think we just might have something you may like." He winked, turned, and opened a door that led into another room that was caged in with heavy steel mesh.

As they went through the door, Rosen found herself looking at row upon row of shelves and racks in perfect order with every conceivable weapon. One rack displayed automatic and semiautomatic rifles. Another was solely devoted to handguns of every shape, size and caliber.

"Jesus Christ." Emily's voice was low. "This is an armory."

Spinner looked around the weapon-filled room. "Okay, I'm impressed."

Rosen turned back to Castellano. "Just what do you do, Rollie?"

"Oh, I have my hands in several pies. One of them happens to be a contract security business. After my discharge from the Army, I spent a very long time in VA hospitals and rehab centers trying to get back to some semblance of a life. I ran into a lot of vets who were lost, either from injuries, PTSD, alcohol, or drugs. Some had become addicted to the adrenaline of combat and felt they had no ability to function in the civilian world. Over time, I put together a group of vets who would take on assignments in different places on the planet."

"You guys are mercenaries?"

"Mercenaries sell their skills to the highest bidders. Here at Las Altas, we consider our association a band of brothers, a working organization that tries to leave the planet a little better than we found it."

"So, do you topple governments, assassinate rulers, and incite *coups d' état?*" Rosen studied Castellano's deep brown eyes.

"I can assure you, Emily, we're very discriminating. We've seen the fumbling of the CIA—even dealt with them a few times. All too often, the avoidance of collateral damage is never given its due importance. Many of the local governments are much worse. We work below the radar. Perhaps a family member of a very high-ranking political figure has been kidnapped, and the person in power contracts us to find their loved one. Things like that."

Rosen glanced at Reggie before shifting her gaze back to Rollie. "So, you're telling me that all these men and women served with you and Jake?"

Castellano's eyes darkened, and he furrowed his brow. "Sadly, that's not the case. Spinner and I are the only ones left from our unit. Most of these folks come to us by recommendation. We have a fairly stringent recruiting regimen, including physical, psychological, and personality batteries that each applicant must undergo."

Rosen turned and looked up at Reggie. "How long have you been here, Reggie?"

"Four years, ma'am. I served two tours in Afghanistan with the Marines. After I got out, I felt like I just didn't fit in anywhere. I learned about Las Altas from a buddy in the Corps, applied, and got lucky. Best job I've ever had."

Castellano laughed. "Reggie, you may not know this, but you're being grilled by one of the best investigative reporters in the business."

Emily found herself blushing.

Reggie's smile was ear-to-ear. "How'd I do, Boss?"

Castellano held up his good hand and rocked it back and forth.

"Well, then I'd best get back to work. Now, if you'll please follow me."

He led them up and down aisle after aisle of ordnance. One rack contained dozens of AK-47s, M-16s, and Steyr AUGS. Spinner stopped and picked up an M4 fitted with an optical sight. He ejected the magazine and reinserted it, cocked the firing mechanism and sighted through the scope. It slightly unnerved Rosen to see how comfortable he was with the weapon.

Castellano looked directly at Spinner. "What do you think?"

"I don't know, Rollie. Most of the activists are either scientists, fishermen, or college kids. I'd bet none of them have ever fired anything like this before." Spinner turned to face Castellano. "The whalers and their Zeta lackeys will be packing automatic weapons. I'm just afraid that if the activists are armed with this, the whalers and their henchmen will feel justified mowing them all down."

"You said yourself that their only ordnance is stink bombs. I don't call those favorable odds."

"I know. I know. I just haven't figured out yet what might work. We need something to level the playing field."

"What about sending along some support? We could send in a team to neutralize any armed resistance if it arises," said Castellano.

Spinner stared at Castellano. "Rollie, you don't understand. We can't pay you, and I'm not sure how your people would feel about trying to shut down a whale hunt."

"I'll go," volunteered Reggie. "One thing pisses me off more than just about anything is cruelty to animals."

"Thanks, Reggie. That's mighty kind of you to offer."

They made their way down several more aisles, while Spinner searched for something—anything—that could tip the balance in their favor. They worked their way to the back of the last aisle when he spied several crates lying on a bottom shelf. He leaned in and studied the writing on the wooden crates.

"Mind if I take a look?"

"Be my guest."

Spinner pulled a box off the shelf and onto the floor. Reggie handed him his KA-BAR combat knife and Spinner pried the lid off. He pulled out a small rounded object slightly larger than his fist. He tested the weight in his hand and palmed it.

"CS tear gas grenades," he said, studying the grenade. "This just might work."

"Beats a stink bomb any day," said Castellano.

Spinner stared at the tear gas grenade for a moment, then placed it back in the crate. As they continued on to the end of the row, he saw a canvas tarp covering a large square palette. He placed a hand on top of the tarp. Underneath his fingers, he felt contours that bore the shape of small bricks.

"What have we here?" Spinner's voice hinted at some unforeseen mischief.

Reggie grinned conspiratorially. "Oh, you wouldn't like that at all, Captain Spinner."

Spinner rolled the tarp back and let out a low whistle. Stacked on the palette were bricks of C4 explosive, each one wrapped in a protective covering. The stack of explosives measured five-by-five-by-four feet.

Spinner deftly lifted one of the bricks and examined it. "Reggie, how much C4 do you think you have here?"

"Oh, I don't know, sir. Enough to take out four city blocks. Or a good size whaling vessel."

Rosen looked back and forth between the three men. "Are you nuts? You're not thinking about blowing up the whaling ship? That's insane."

Spinner turned to Castellano. "Rollie, can I get a look on your computer at the schematic of the *Shodokai Maru*? Maybe if I could get an idea of her layout, I could figure out where I could set charges for maximum effect."

"That part's not the problem, Jake. This isn't a one-man job. And chances are, you wouldn't be able to get within a mile of this boat before they cut you up for shark bait."

"Been there, done that, got the tee-shirt. What about a night run?"

"You still have to do the approach," said Castellano. "You can't get in and out by yourself."

"That's right, Spinner. You need to listen to your friend Rollie." Rosen was becoming increasingly exasperated. "You left me once to go on a suicide mission. I'll be damned if I'm going to go through that again."

"Em, if we don't stop that ship, it's going to go somewhere else and do this all over again. More people and more whales will die. It has to stop. Now."

Castellano turned his chair around. "Come on. Follow me. We have one more stop to make."

They bade Reggie goodbye and made their way back to the elevator. Rosen said nothing to Spinner, but the tension between them was obvious. Right now, what she wanted was to push Spinner's head against the wall. Maybe a hard knock would drive some sense into that thick skull of his.

The door opened up to a darkened room. Covering much of the far wall, a huge lighted screen displayed a map of the world laid out Cartesian style. Lights of varying colors appeared in designated countries and arcs curved across the map. On desktops, computer screens aired news feeds from different parts of the world. Seated at the desks in the room were nearly two dozen people working at the computers. Everywhere he looked, Jake saw state-of-the-art equipment designed to track targets all over the globe. The room was abuzz with conversations, many in languages other than English. Rosen looked around with a mixture of incredulity and anxiety.

"What is this place?" She looked at Rollie.

"Central Command. Or, as we affectionately refer to it, Geek Central."

"You sure didn't let any moss grow under your feet," Spinner said.

"Come over here," said Castellano. "I want you to meet someone."

He wheeled over to where a petite blonde woman sat at a terminal. She wore a headset over her shoulder length hair.

"This is Anika Probst. Anika is one of our communications specialists. We stole her away from the Dutch security force. Anika, this is Emily Rosen and Jake Spinner. The young woman spun in her chair and smiled brightly. "It is a pleasure to meet you both."

"Anika, my friends want to locate something."

She shifted her gaze to Spinner. "What are you looking for?"

"A ship."

"Last known location?"

"Gulf of California."

Anika tapped quickly into her computer, and a map of the Gulf of California appeared. "What kind of ship?"

"It's a Japanese whaling ship," Spinner replied. "The *Shodokai Maru*."

Probst went to another screen and tapped *Shodokai Maru* into the keyboard. When nothing showed up on her screen, she tried another tack. Her search yielded no results. "I'm not pulling anything up on this ship. It's like a ghost ship."

"Mind if I try something?" Rosen asked.

Anika cast a glance at Castellano. He nodded.

"Be my guest," Anika said, sliding her chair backward. She stood and allowed Rosen to sidle in.

Spinner watched as Rosen's fingers flew over the keys. A moment later, the schematic of the Japanese whaler appeared on her screen.

"That's her." Spinner leaned in.

"I'm impressed," said Anika.

Spinner looked at Rosen and winked.

Rosen scrolled down and located an icon for the ship's specifications. The specs were written in Japanese. "I can't help you from here." Rosen stood to allow Anika to assume her seat once again.

"That's okay." Anika slid into the chair and scrolled slowly as she studied the Japanese characters.

"Hmm," she said. "According to this, this ship was decommissioned eight years ago and has been designated as scrap."

"Wow. You read Japanese?" Rosen said. "Now I'm really impressed."

"Oh, that ship is still out there. Believe me," said Spinner.

Probst smiled, then entered the physical dimensions of the ship into the computer and waited. Seconds later, on the screen, a greenish outline appeared near the middle of the Gulf. The boat was located off the coast of one of the Midriff Islands.

Anika enhanced the image. The image of the whaling vessel resolved to the point where people could be distinguished on the deck.

"That's amazing," said Rosen.

Spinner felt his heartbeat quicken and a deep rage begin to churn within. "Can you keep tabs on her?"

"No problem."

"Let's get a printout of that," said Castellano. "I want to see port, starboard, fore, and aft views."

"Right away, Mr. Castellano."

Ten minutes later, Anika Probst presented four rolled documents to Castellano.

"Thank you, Anika."

"Yes, thank you very much," said Spinner. "Anika, can I ask you one more question?"

"Absolutely."

"Can you track that ship once it starts moving?"

"Piece of cake, Mr. Spinner."

"What about setting up a live feed to another unit in the field?"

"No problem. Just give me the link and we can have it up in no time."

Spinner nodded and smiled. "Thanks. We'll be in touch."

Anika turned to look at Castellano and tipped her head toward Rosen. "I think you should hire her, boss."

"I'll take that under consideration, Anika." Castellano smiled.

Back at the main house, Spinner, Rosen, and Castellano went to the library. Rosen had not spoken in a while. Both men knew she was seething. Spinner was laying the schematics for the *Shodokai Maru* on a large, cherrywood table when Rosen spoke up softly.

"We need to talk. Outside. Please."

Spinner saw the anger in her eyes. "Okay."

He followed her outside into the hallway when she suddenly turned on him. "What the hell do you think you're doing, Spinner? I'm beginning to think you have an obsession with terminating yourself."

"C'mon, Em. I'm not going to get myself killed. Look, this is the kind of shit I did all the time. It was my job, and I was good at it."

"That was then. This is now. Emily's voice rose. "Three days ago, you couldn't even run one hundred yards on the beach without falling over. This time there's not going to be any dolphins to drag your sorry ass back to the beach. Even

Rollie said one man couldn't do this mission. You'd need back up, and I don't think anyone here is crazy enough to put their life on the line for this."

"I can sneak in under cover of darkness, set the charges, and be back before anyone misses me. Emily, the guys on that boat killed my best friend and his family. And they're killing people and whales at their whim. How do you suggest we stop them? If you have any better ideas, I'm all ears."

Rosen turned away from him. She stared at a Diego Rivera painting that portrayed a young peasant woman holding lilies in her hand while breast-feeding a baby.

"I thought you were dead once. I can't go through that again."

Spinner grabbed her by the shoulders and spun her around to face him. "God damn it, Rosen. I don't have a death wish. I'm different now."

Emily looked into Spinner's deep blue eyes. "What's different? I watched you back there, Spinner. It's a good ol' boys club, brimming with machismo and testosterone."

He kissed her gently. She started to pull away, then kissed him back.

"You. That's what's different this time." He cupped her face in his hands. "I walked away from you once. I won't do it again."

They kissed again. "You're an idiot."

"I know. Now let's go look at those schematics."

# 61

Sandy Wainright sat at a table under a tarp that had been set up as an outdoor dining area. The structure had been erected hastily to accommodate the increased population of the small fishing camp. Several pangueros that Raúl knew from the fishing cooperative had arrived and offered to help in any way they could. The camp had turned into a small village. The new challenge was to conceal the increasing number of boats that crowded the small cove.

Sandy looked out and counted six: four pangas, Jake's boat, and the trimaran. The rest, including their research inflatable, had been hauled out and were hidden behind the dunes and covered with brush. They wanted to give the appearance that this was nothing more than a sleepy little fishing camp.

There was growing tension in the camp. Raúl and the other fishermen had decided to begin regular sweeps of the surrounding coastline, looking for new construction or a concentration of boats. They'd venture out every day and head in different directions, fishing as they searched. The large whaling ship continued to evade them.

Alejandro limped up to the table. He still looked weak. His cheeks were hollow and his face haggard. Pain and fatigue, coupled with being separated from his family, were taking their toll. He sat down heavily across from Sandy, opened his backpack, and retrieved a Nalgene water bottle. He took a long drink from the bottle.

"How're you holding up, Alex?"

"I guess as good as can be expected. This waiting game is really starting to wear on me."

"I think it's got everyone on edge."

"This is when I miss Carmen and Lili the most. This sitting around waiting is making me crazy. For all we know, the whalers could have already carried out the hunt and are on their way back to Japan."

"I think about that all the time. I don't dare ask Raúl again if he's heard from Alma Quintín. I can see the look in his eyes. Even he doesn't think she's going to call in. Any word from Spinner and Rosen?"

"No. They haven't checked in yet. I wonder what they're doing on the mainland."

"I wish I knew," said Sandy. "It makes me nervous that they're over there and we're here, kinda sitting on a powder keg."

"From what I know about Jake Spinner," Alejandro said with a wistful smile. "I think he's cooking up a plan that most likely involves a lot of mayhem."

"I just hope this isn't all for nothing."

Graham Neely approached them, coming from the direction of Jesús's shack. "Mind if I join you?"

"The more, the merrier," said Alejandro.

Graham slid in next to Sandy. "I just came from the communication center. Beau is having difficulty maintaining a connection to the satellite. The image feed keeps cutting out. He's trying to get it cleaned up before Spinner gets back." He looked back and forth between Alejandro and Sandy. "Any word from Jake and Rosen?"

"Nothing yet," said Alejandro.

"How about Raúl?"

"Still out on patrol," said Sandy. "If he'd heard anything from Alma Quintín, he would've called. That is, if he had reception."

Graham blew out a long breath. "You know, we've done all the drills we can do, gone over all possible scenarios until we're blue in the face. Right now, I'm pacing the cage."

"Alejandro, I was thinking," said Sandy. "Maybe we could use the inflatable for some recon work. It's just sitting there gathering sand."

"We have to be careful about fuel."

"She's fast and light. Doesn't eat a lot of gas. Another set of eyes on the water can't hurt."

"All right," Alejandro acquiesced. "I want regular reports."

Sandy turned to Graham. "How about it, Graham? Best antidote for cabin fever is a big stretch of open water."

"Sounds good to me."

"You both be careful," said Alejandro. "You see anything suspicious, just call it in. Do not engage. Get back to base ASAP."

"Aye, aye, captain." She turned back to Graham. "Sunrise. We'll head into a quadrant that hasn't been covered yet."

The sun sank further into the west until it was just above the water. The small capillary waves were tinged with streaks of silver and gold. Mullets jumped out of the water in the shallows. Marine birds began diving for fish, their bodies taking on a golden hue as they folded their wings against their bodies and bulleted into the water.

Just as darkness set in, the distant sound of an outboard motor carried across the water. Soon the silhouette of a panga appeared, a single light near the bow illuminating the water just in front of it.

"Looks like Raúl and Francisco are back," said Sandy.

As the panga slid onto the beach, Francisco tilted the motor to lift the prop. Once the panga came to rest, both men moved to the bow. Raúl jumped down deftly, and Francisco handed him a small ice chest. They trudged with the ice chest up the beach toward the group gathered at the table. The table was illuminated by a propane lantern hung from the canopy pole.

Sandy asked, "How was it?"

"Quiet," said Raúl. "Quieter than usual."

Alejandro asked, "How far did you get today?"

"This side of Isla Catalan," Raúl sounded tired. "Over 120 kilometers. Nothing. No whaling ship, no death camps."

Arturo pointed. "What's in the ice chest?"

"Yellowtail and red snapper," said Francisco. "Tonight, *pescado a la plancha.*"

"Raúl, Graham and I are thinking about helping out on the search grid with the RIB. She covers a lot of water and is pretty good on fuel conservation. What do you think?"

Raúl nodded in agreement. "We haven't been as far north as Isla San José yet. That would give us a chance to focus on more offshore sections."

Graham asked, "Do you think the whaling ship is anchored behind some island?"

"That would be a logical place," replied Raúl. "It can probably make fifteen to sixteen knots. It could be anywhere in the Gulf, from Isla Angel de la Guarda to Espíritu Santo."

"I'm going to go out on a limb and ask the question no one dares ask you," said Alejandro.

Raúl smiled weakly. "No word from Alma Quintín. I've left several messages for her to contact me, but she deactivated her message function." He looked around the table at the group of activists. "If she calls tonight, are all of you ready?"

After a slight hesitation, they all nodded. "Yeah, we're ready," said Graham. "About as ready as we're going to be."

Raúl shouldered his backpack and said, "It's been a long day. I'd like to see my wife and children before I fall asleep."

He walked across the beach toward Carlos's shack. Alisa and Julio were watching from the doorway. They sprinted out to greet him. Raúl dropped to one knee and hugged both children. He looked up to see Guadalupe drying a plate. She smiled warmly at her husband.

"Did you see them today, Papá? The whalers?"

"No, mija. It was a very quiet day. I didn't even see any whales or dolphins. I hope they're far away from the hunters."

"Me, too."

Raúl stood stiffly and walked toward the shack with his two children at his side.

The sound of his cell phone ringing startled him. The LED display glowed green in the dusky light.

"*Un momento*," he said to the children. "I need to take this call."

He walked toward the beach, just out of hearing range.

"Bueno," he said, his heart pounding in his chest.

"Raúl Campos?"

The frightened voice on the other end belonged to Alma Quintín. "Are you all right?"

"I must speak to you," said Alma "The hunt's been scheduled for two days from now. Can you come here tomorrow? There's someone else here who needs to speak to you."

"I can leave before first light, Alma."

"Come alone. Everyone on this coast is being watched. No one is safe right now."

"I will come. Alone. Can you tell me the location of the hunt now, so we have time to prepare?"

"No! We must meet face-to-face."

Alma disconnected, leaving Raúl to stare at the number on the phone. He sighed deeply, then proceeded up the beach to inform Guadalupe.

"Raúl, you can't go alone," Sandy said angrily. "What if it's a trap?"

Several others concurred. The group was crowded into Jesús's house after a hastily called meeting was announced. The air inside was humid and felt like it was electrically charged.

Raúl shook his head. "Alma insisted that I come alone."

"No way," said Sandy. "Graham and I are coming with you. There's at least some safety in numbers."

Raúl stood and leaned on the table, the brown muscles in his forearms tensed like steel coils. "This is probably our only opportunity to learn about the hunt. We won't get another chance. Two days. That's all we have. We have no choice but to do what Alma asks."

"We need to contact Spinner and Rosen," said Alejandro.

# 62

Spinner was going over the final placement of the explosive charges on the hull of the *Shodokai Maru* when the call came. Castellano, Emily, and Oliver Sweet looked on intently as he answered it. They had been studying the schematic for nearly three hours, trying to determine the maximum impact with the least amount of explosive.

"Spinner."

"Jake, it's Alejandro. Raúl got the call from Alma Quintín. The hunt is on."

"When?"

"Day after tomorrow."

"Where?"

"We don't know that yet," said Alejandro. "The Quintín woman wouldn't give information over the phone. She wants to tell Raúl in person."

"That doesn't sound good. What if the whalers got to her?"

"That's what we're thinking. She told him to come alone."

"What's he going to do?"

"He's going out at first light."

"Shit. This has all the makings of a trap."

"He wouldn't give in on this, Jake. He said we need that intel."

Spinner sighed deeply. "We're heading out first thing in the morning. We should be there by mid-afternoon."

"Good. I think having you and Em back will be good for morale. How's the foraging going?"

"We might have a few things for the cause. Let me talk to Raúl."

"He already went to bed. He was out all day on patrol. He came back long enough to see his family, eat something, and pass out."

"Alejandro, tell him I said to take the gun."

"I will, Jake. I will."

Alejandro disconnected. Spinner slipped the phone back in his pocket.

"Well," asked Rosen, "are you going to tell us?"

"Game on. Day after tomorrow. Alma Quintín called Raúl this evening. He's going alone to meet with her tomorrow to find out the location."

"That sounds fishy to me," said Rosen. "What if he's being set up?"

"Raúl is a smart guy. I think he'll know what he's walking into." Spinner let out a ragged breath. "Looks like it's going to be a long night."

He walked back to the table and stared down at the schematic of the *Shodokai Maru*. His brow furrowed as he traced his finger over the eight placement points. After several moments of silent contemplation, Spinner looked up at Castellano.

"Rollie, I think I can do this with thirty kilos of C-4. If the schematic isn't lying, the blast under the engine room should do the trick."

"Spinner, I'm sending Sweet along with you. And no bullshit about you doing the Gary Cooper thing. You can't pull this off by yourself. Hell, a week ago, you were more dead than alive and, on top of everything else, you ain't twenty-six years old anymore."

"Thanks for pointing that out to me. I can't ask you or Oliver to assist me any more than you already have. This isn't your fight."

"It is now." Castellano wheeled himself over to where Spinner stood and glowered at him. "Here's how this works, Jake. The ordnance, the equipment, the personnel, it's not a gift to a friend who wants to take revenge on a bunch of turd-hoppers that killed his friends. This is a business deal."

"What do you mean, a business deal?"

"You want my help? You're now on the payroll. I provide you with the materials and manpower; you come to work for me. I can deduct all the ordnance off your first few months' paychecks for some future assignment of my choosing."

"Wait a minute," Spinner held up his hands. "You know damn well that I don't play well with others."

"Yeah, you and everyone else I hire. You're all a bunch of god-damned free-wheeling individualists."

"It's not so bad, Jake," said Sweet. "The medical and dental is pretty good. Six weeks paid vacation."

"Oh, Christ." Spinner rolled his eyes. "Sweet, this is a bunch of activists trying to stop a whale hunt."

"I like dolphins as much as the next guy," said Sweet. "Hey, I either help you blow up a boat or I'm stuck babysitting a potential American presidential candidate traveling to Colombia for a photo-op about stopping the illegal drug trade."

"I see your point." Jake turned his gaze back toward Castellano.

"What can I say?" Castellano said with a palms-up shrug. "It pays the bills." Castellano returned Spinner's hard stare. "No negotiation on this one, Jake. Take it or leave it."

Spinner looked over at Rosen, who couldn't decide whether to be amused or worried. "Don't look at me, Spinner. They're your friends."

He smiled bitterly. "You know, you're going to want to shoot me after the first week of employment."

"We passed that point a long time before now, Spinner."

They worked late into the evening, planning the approach and deployment of the charges. Angelina came in with food and drinks for everyone. She gently chided the men to eat something, winking at Rosen as she left the room. Rosen regarded the quiet and gracious woman warmly. She suspected that Angelina's relationship with Rollie was more than a business arrangement.

By 10:30 p.m., Spinner could no longer see straight. Castellano had excused himself an hour before. He and Rosen bade Sweet goodnight and went back to their room. Spinner fell back on the bed sideways and closed his eyes. Rosen disappeared into the bathroom. When she returned, she was dressed in a sheer white, wrap-around dressing gown that revealed the inner curve of her breasts. She walked up to the bed. "Spinner?"

She heard soft snoring come from the motionless form on the bed.

Smiling ruefully, she said aloud, mostly to herself. "Let's see. Let him sleep. He's had a rough couple of weeks. He needs his rest. That would be the kind thing to do. But then . . . who knows when we'll have an opportunity in a place like this any time in the near future. Hell, in two days we all may be in jail— or dead."

A playful smile danced across her lips. She stepped forward, leaned down, and kissed Spinner gently on the lips.

One of the things that Rosen was discovering about Spinner was his innate ability to fall asleep anywhere and wake up quickly. Perhaps it was a carryover from his time in Special Forces, where downtimes were few and far between and you rested when you could. Wakefulness was a matter of survival.

She was pleasantly surprised that it didn't take a C-4 charge to bring Spinner back to the moment. When he opened his eyes and saw her sitting on the edge of the bed next to him, his eyes went from her face to the plunging neckline of her nightgown.

"Please tell me I'm not dreaming," said Jake. "Because if I am, it's the worst kind of cruel joke."

Emily touched his cheek. "No dream, Jake."

"God, you're beautiful."

"I hope you don't mind me waking you. But it would be such a shame to waste an opportunity in such a nice room."

Spinner's hand moved from her cheek down her neck until it rested on the nipple of her right breast. She felt an electrical surge that went from her breast to her loins. She closed her eyes and moaned.

"Wouldn't want to miss any of this," said Jake.

They made love with a passion that neither had experienced for a very long time. Perhaps it was because of the imminent danger they were facing. Rosen was pleasantly surprised to find out that Jake Spinner, despite his rough-around-the-edges nature, was a gentle and attentive lover.

At one point, Spinner rolled off Rosen and lay on his back, breathing heavily and bathed in sweat. His arm lay across her chest.

"Thank God," he said after a moment, exhaling deeply.

"What?"

"I'm just relieved."

"About what?"

"That damn small animal vet left all my parts working."

Rosen laughed, rolled over and kissed him. "Christ, Spinner. I was worried we were going to be permanently stuck together."

She lay next to him, listening to his even, slow breathing and watching the deep rise and fall of his chest. He passed out mid-sentence while answering her question about his friendship with Roland Castellano. She leaned in and pressed herself against him, kissing him on the cheek.

"It's okay, Jake. It was a hell of a day."

Rosen did not know how long she'd been asleep, but she woke with a start. She felt a strange sensation at the back of her neck and a feeling of uneasiness. Her hand moved to her left and she felt Spinner's warm body. He was dead asleep. She had the overwhelming feeling that someone—or something—was watching them. She slowly sat up and propped herself up on her elbows. She looked toward the large picture window. The darkness outside was backlit from a waxing moon, causing the shadows to be long and distorted. It was then she saw the face staring in at her. Her breath caught in her throat.

The jaguar was huge. From her angle, the head appeared disproportionate to its body. Even against the ash-colored background, Rosen caught a glint of yellow eyes fixed on her. The mottled pattern of the big cat's fur made it appear to dance in and out of the light. She heard her heart hammering against her chest wall, but dared not speak.

The jaguar lowered its great head and slowly moved it from side to side, never once taking its gaze from Rosen. She had never seen anything so beautiful and yet so savagely wild. She desperately wanted to shake Spinner awake to verify what she was seeing, but she remained frozen in position. On some level, she knew as soon as she moved, the big cat would disappear into the contrasting shadows.

Then the cat did something that took her by surprise. It rubbed its massive face against the glass, just like a house cat would rub against a sofa. Their eyes locked in a primordial stare. She felt a strange energy in her chest—it was more of a gentle, expanding heat that warmed her chest cavity. In her mind's eye, she was transformed, running through the jungle undergrowth in the dappled moonlight. Suddenly, her vision evaporated, and she was jolted back to the present as the cat's head whipped around, obviously alerted by an unfamiliar sound in the night. The jaguar turned to look at her one last time, then padded across the compound until it blended in with the foliage and was gone.

Rosen fell backward on the bed and blew out a huge breath. "Oh . . . my . . . God," she whispered. "What was that all about?"

Sleep pretty much eluded her the rest of the night. She got out of bed and went to the desk, After turning on the small lamp, she thought about getting her tape recorder out of the backpack to record the events that had just transpired. Instead, she decided on her notebook. For some reason, it seemed more appropriate to write the words on paper. It was a better way to solidify the memory—from brain to hand to paper. She turned and looked at Spinner, who had not stirred. She opened the notebook, and the words flowed from her pen.

She picked up her wristwatch. 4:45. She closed her journal, stood, and stretched. She might have gotten an hour, maybe two of sleep. But right now, her sensory system was working overtime. She had an overwhelming sensation of hyper-awareness. Her hearing and her vision seemed to be ramped up. She heard the ticking of her wristwatch. She heard the sound of Spinner breathing, and she heard the sounds of the pre-dawn jungle as if she were standing in the middle of it.

Rosen showered alone and dressed quietly. She would come back and wake Spinner in an hour. He needed all the rest and healing he could get given the daunting and possibly deadly task that he was soon to face. She slipped from the bedroom and tiptoed to the library. The house was quiet and mostly dark. Only a few low illumination lights helped her to navigate. Rosen opened the library door and slipped inside, closing it behind her. Angelina was helping Castellano transfer from a large leather office chair into his wheelchair, then kissing him on the forehead. When they heard the door click, they both looked up and smiled at her.

"Oh, I'm so sorry. I thought everyone was still asleep."

"No, please," replied Castellano. "Please come in. We always rise early around here. I find this is the best time of day to get my head cleared and get a good start on the day."

"Emily, may I interest you in some coffee?" Angelina's face was slightly flushed, but her composure remained unflappable.

"Yes, thank you. I didn't sleep well last night and decided to come down here and do a little research." Rosen swept her arms about the room. "This place is amazing. Oh, that is—if you don't mind?"

"Of course not, Emily. That's what the library is for. Consider this your home any time you'd like to come." Rollie turned his chair toward the bookshelf that was behind his desk. "Tell me what you're looking for, and I can direct your search."

"I'll be back shortly with some coffee and fruit juices." Angelina excused herself.

Rosen watched as Castellano's gaze followed her out of the room.

"I like her," Emily said. "You can tell that she is a very kind person."

Castellano smiled. "Would you believe she was once one of the top operatives for the Mexican secret service? She could kill a person with an emery board or any number of common household items."

Rosen looked incredulous. "You're kidding?"

"I met her five years ago while she was serving on the president's security detail. I eventually persuaded her to come and take over operations at Las Altas. She pretty much runs the entire organization now. Still goes out for the occasional field assignment, just to keep her edge."

"I'm impressed with everything and everyone I've met here."

"One favor," said Castellano. "When you write about the dolphin and whale hunt, which I know you will, please don't mention your time here at Las Altas. The success of our organization and our presence here depends on keeping a low profile."

Rosen eyed Castellano to see if his request masked a veiled threat. That was not what she saw in his face. She nodded. "Your secret's safe with me, Rollie."

"Besides, Las Altas could benefit from someone of your talent and unique ability to tell a story that gets down to the heart of the matter."

Rosen laughed. "Are you offering me a job?"

"Perhaps some freelance work. It's an idea I've been mulling over."

"Rollie, I don't do pieces with a slant."

"I'm not asking you to, Emily. I want an honest account of what's going on. The world doesn't seem to get enough of the real story anymore. We tend to be in places that can go hot long before any of the rest of the news cycle gets hold of them. This could be a means that lets you do what you do best. Tell me what you'd like to be paid, and let's see if we can work something out."

"I'll certainly give it some thought."

He laughed. "I'm sorry. We got off track. What was it you'd like to look up here in the library? If you can't find it, we have other sources."

"Well, this may sound a little weird. I want to look up some information about jaguars."

She went on to describe in detail her encounter with the great cat earlier that morning, including the sensations it provoked in her. Castellano listened intently, his hands steepled under his chin, nodding and smiling. After she finished, He sat quietly, then turned back toward the bookshelf, rolling his wheelchair down several sections. He scanned the books.

"Ah, here we go. *Ancient Meso-American Cultures and Mythology,* in particular pertaining to Mayan and Aztec symbology and ceremonies."

He stood awkwardly, his legs shaking as he arose to a full-standing posture. Rosen rose to help him, but he waved her off. "It's okay. I'm good."

With one hand he steadied himself on the chair, with the other he reached up and grabbed a thick volume from the shelf. He cradled the book under his arm and sat down. Placing the book in his lap, he wheeled himself back to where Rosen sat. He slid it across the table to her.

"In the times of the Aztecs and the Mayans, the jaguar would be your *'nagual.'*"

"What's that?"

"It means 'spirit companion.' In the Meso-American cultures, the jaguar was supposed to have protected the shamans from evil spirits as they moved between earth and the spiritual world. It has the ability to move as freely between the two worlds as it does between trees and water, daytime and nighttime. The jaguar was associated with warriors and hunters. It's a symbol of strength, courage, and spiritual power. It was also known as a shape shifter."

"Wow. That just gave me the chills. While I was watching the jaguar, she appeared to be moving in and out of the light. And she was standing still! Like her fur was changing as I watched."

"There are times when people here feel a presence, but can't see her. Later, they discover tracks just feet from where they stood."

Angelina returned with a tray of coffee, tea and fresh juices. She distributed the drinks and then took a seat next to Castellano.

"Emily had a visitor last night, Angie."

"Oh?" Angelina eyebrows rose as she took a sip of coffee.

"The jaguar came to her window and rubbed its head against the glass."

"Really? That's amazing!" Angelina's eyes were wide. "I've been here nearly five years and have only caught fleeting glimpses of that cat."

Castellano handed Rosen the book. "You're very lucky, Emily. Very few people on this planet get to experience what you just did. I'm envious."

"The last four weeks have been an eye opener for me. I've been introduced to a world I never knew existed. Now, I can't seem to get enough of it."

"Tell us, please," said Angelina, "how you came to know Jake Spinner."

Rosen took a sip of coffee and closed her eyes. The taste and the aroma were exquisite. Opening her eyes, she said, "It all started when I was reassigned to Baja to cover a travel piece about cartel activities and their effect on local tourism."

Rosen related a complex story about meeting the researchers and eventually bearing witness to the slaughter at San Mateo Cove. She told about tracking Spinner down after the hunt and about the assassins that broke into the shack to kill him. Angelina and Rollie sat in rapt attention as she described how she and Spinner had removed Alejandro from the hospital in Insurgentes. She then spoke of Spinner's ordeal on the *Shodokai Maru* and how his life was saved by some of the very dolphins he had freed from the barricade back at San Mateo cove. Castellano shook his head in wonder, and Angelina dabbed at her eyes.

Emily paused, staring out the window as the ground fog began to lift from the jungle foliage. Her voice caught in her throat as she gathered her thoughts.

"Something happened to Jake after he washed up on the beach," Rosen said. "He was different. I wouldn't have believed it if I hadn't seen it with my own eyes. Those dolphins wouldn't leave until he got up from his sickbed and limped down to the water's edge. They knew what he'd done for them. I know they did."

Angelina touched Emily's arm. "I think you've picked the right fight, Emily."

Rosen smiled bitterly. "Yeah, we just have to figure a way to keep Spinner from giving it up for the team."

"Let's see what we can do to level the playing field," said Castellano.

Rosen looked down at the tome in front of her. "I'll get this back to you before I leave."

"If you can't find what you want in that, there's a half shelf of related books over there."

"Thank you," said Emily, "for this and for everything you've done for us."

Castellano was pensive. He bit his lip and looked down at his hands. When he looked up, his eyes reflected a deep sorrow. "You know, for a lot of these men and women who've been in combat theaters, the holidays are pretty rough. A lot of the guys that served check themselves out between the week of Christmas and New Year's. For the past few years, I've been waiting for that call that I never wanted to get. The one that said that Jake Spinner had taken his own life."

Castellano stopped for a moment to get his emotions in check. "The last time I saw Jake, he looked terrible. He'd lost a lot of weight, and he'd been living inside a bottle of tequila. He was no longer the man I remembered from Special Forces. I think the loss of his comrades, his wife leaving him, and the pain—both emotional and physical—had him on oblivion's short list."

Rosen sat very still.

"Spinner saved my life, "Rollie continued. "Our armored vehicle hit an IED. The Hummer was on fire. Jake took some shrapnel to his gut and still managed to pull me from the wreckage and carry me to safety. We were both a month away from the end of our tour. All the others in our unit had been killed three days before. It was amazing we were still alive."

"That must have been horrible."

Castellano shifted his weight in his chair and took a deep breath. He looked around the room as if he were searching for a way to find the words to continue. "As you can see, I don't talk about this much. Angelina's heard it," he glanced up lovingly at his partner, "but not many others."

"I'm honored that you would tell me," said Emily.

"At first, all I wanted to do was die. My legs were useless, and the pain was beyond control. We helped each other through the long and painful rehabilitation process. Spinner got out after eight months. The extent of my wounds kept me in rehab for another twelve. He came to see me while I was still in, but I could see the change in him. He wasn't adjusting well to the civilian world. He started drinking and, after his wife left him, he went to Mexico and didn't look back."

Rosen swallowed hard. "I didn't know the extent of what you both had to go through. Spinner hasn't talked much about his past."

Castellano smiled. "Two years ago, when he came to see me, he looked like he was already knocking at death's door. I just wanted to let you know, when I saw Spinner yesterday something was different. I saw some of the light back in his eyes. I hadn't seen that for a very long time. I have a feeling you had something to do with that."

"I'm not sure who saved who here. We're both damaged goods."

Castellano smiled again. "Ernest Hemingway once said, 'The world breaks everyone, and afterward some people are stronger at the broken places.'"

Rosen leaned forward and touched Castellano on the arm. "I'm really glad I bugged Spinner to come along. Thank you."

"You're welcome here anytime, Emily."

The door to the study opened and Jake Spinner walked in, wild-eyed, his hair askew, wearing a bathrobe over a pair of flannel pajama bottoms. Rosen thought he looked adorable.

"What the hell?" He looked a bit dazed and confused. "Do you have any idea what time it is?"

"5:30, by my watch," replied Emily, winking at Castellano.

"Why didn't you wake me up?" Spinner scratched his head. "We need to get going. *¡Andele! ¡Andele!*"

"I made a judgment call, Jake. You needed to sleep, and I needed to catch up with Rollie and Angelina."

"Great. We have a whale hunt to stop."

"There's plenty of time to get you both back to the fishing camp," said Castellano. "When's the last time you slept in a bed and got more than four hours of sleep, Spinner?"

"You passed out, Jake," Rosen said. "With what we're going to be going up against in the next few days, you're going to need to get all the rest you can. So sue me."

"Can you believe this, Rollie?" Jake looked at his old friend plaintively.

"Jesus, Spinner, get over it. She's right and you damn well know it. You're just too pig-headed to admit it. You'd be a lot healthier if you listened to her."

"Everyone's against me."

Angelina tried not to laugh. "If it's any consolation, Jake, breakfast is about to be served. We have a wide variety of egg dishes, fruit, and yogurt for your dining pleasure. We're also serving up *pan francés*. I have it on good authority that it's one of your favorite dishes."

"Oh." Jake looked around the room and noticed his mode of attire. "Guess I better get ready then." He quickly left the room.

Castellano laughed. "French toast gets him every time."

Just when Rosen thought life couldn't get any better, breakfast was served. She didn't know if it was the ambiance of the beautiful veranda at sunrise, or the exquisite layout of food that rivaled any hotel or restaurant in New York City. Beautifully arranged plates of food from American breakfast favorites, such as omelets, bacon, and French toast to traditional Mexican dishes like huevos rancheros and chilaquiles were set next to their table. She and Spinner sat with Castellano and Oliver Sweet. Angelina joined them after making sure the preparations were going smoothly.

Castellano watched the subtle interactions of affection between Rosen and Spinner and a smile grew on his face. He and Spinner talked animatedly about old times and some of the crazy things they did back in the day.

Spinner tasted the French toast. "God, this is good." He pointed his fork at Rosen. "Whatever you do, Em, you can't tell anyone at the fish camp about this meal. There'll be mutiny for sure."

She felt a sudden twitch of anxiety. She had momentarily forgotten about what they were going back for. She looked across the compound. The early morning fog was lifting off the ground, causing shafts of sunlight to illuminate sections of the forest. High in the canopy, the local parrots and toucans were waking up and letting the world know about it. She took a deep breath and tried to absorb the sights, sounds, and smells of this magical place.

A man dressed in jungle fatigues walked briskly toward them from across the compound. He wore aviator Ray-Bans and a ball cap. As he drew closer, Rosen recognized Snake, the wild-eyed pilot who had flown them here.

"Morning, y'all," he said as he came up the steps. Passing by the long table, he noticed the spread of tempting food. "Damn, that looks good."

"Grab a plate and help yourself," said Castellano.

Moments later, Snake pulled up a chair and sat next to Oliver Sweet. One of the servers brought him food and coffee, and he dug into his meal. Between bites, he said to Castellano, "Boss, the helo is almost loaded with everything on the manifest." He looked at Spinner and Rosen. "We're ready when you are. We'll be a little heavy for takeoff, so I recommend you go light on the French toast." He winked at Rosen, causing her to laugh.

Spinner asked, "Even the inflatable?"

"Yep. We had to do some creative placement of the C-4. You may have to sit on some of it for the ride over. Sorry, but this is a non-smoking flight."

"The final solution for a terminal case of hemorrhoids," Spinner said.

Snake laughed. "Hey, that's right, Captain." He looked at Rosen again. "He's a right funny guy." He handed the manifest over to Spinner. "Check this out, mate. Make sure that we got everything on your shopping list."

Spinner held the manifest and squinted at the items listed. "Looks good, Snake. Thanks."

Snake put a large forkful of scrambled eggs in his mouth, then washed it down with a gulp of coffee. He looked at his watch. "Well, best be getting back to make sure everything is lashed down." He stood. "Thanks for breakfast."

Rosen watched as the chopper pilot headed back into the trees toward the landing pad near the rear of the compound. Spinner looked at his watch, and put his cloth napkin on the table. "Time to go, Em."

"I was afraid you were going to say that."

Angelina reached across the table and touched Emily's hand. "Please consider this your home. Come back any time you wish."

A short time later, Spinner and Rosen stood in the great room with their meager belongings at their feet. They had changed into clothes that Angelina had brought from the commissary.

Roland Castellano was in the next room on the phone finalizing the logistics for Spinner and his team. Angelina had excused herself momentarily to check in with her staff. Rosen marveled at the efficiency of everyone she had met in her short stay at Las Altas. Oliver Sweet had gone to the helicopter to make sure all the equipment matched the manifest.

"I want to come back here." Rosen leaned forward and kissed Spinner. "For some down time. Can we do that?"

"Yeah, we can. I can't remember the last time I was this relaxed. And I don't have a right to . . ."

"Don't go there, Jake. If anyone deserves a little R and R, it's you."

Castellano rolled his wheelchair back into the room. "Sweet will be here momentarily. We'll get you to the chopper straight away."

Rosen approached Castellano and bent to give him a hug. Rollie held up a hand. "Just a minute. I believe you need a good and proper send off." He struggled to his feet, taking several seconds to regain his balance.

"Okay, now we can do this."

From across the compound, a covered golf cart approached. At the wheel sat Oliver Sweet, dressed in jungle fatigues. He barreled up the hard-packed driveway and stopped abruptly at the foot of the steps, grinning. "Taxi?"

Spinner and Rosen walked down the steps and placed their belongings in the back of the golf cart. Rosen climbed into the front seat. Sweet said, "Let's go find something to blow up."

# 63

Hiro Yoshimatsu woke up in his luxury suite in Cabo San Lucas and slipped out of bed without disturbing Susan. He showered and dressed while the rest of the city slept. It was nearly midnight when confirmation came that the refrigerator trucks would arrive later today. Two trucks were coming by ferry from Topolobampo and would arrive in La Paz by late afternoon. The other two would arrive that evening, having traveled all the way down the peninsula after crossing the border at Tijuana.

Yoshimatsu felt an uneasiness that he wasn't used to. He and Susan hadn't made love in a week. She had employed all of her seductive methods, but he was unable to match her ardor. He was distracted.

He felt like he was on the verge of losing control of the operation. It had been plagued with obstacles from the onset. He was forced to deal with the incompetent Figueroa and his hired thugs. Many of the "loose ends" had not been handled in a timely fashion, or even worse, were completely bungled. The death of Gustavo Silvano and his family never should have made it to the local tabloids. Alejandro Cabrillo should have died on the road. Something deep in his core told him that he had not seen the last of the director of the Institute of Marine Mammals. Figueroa was now running scared, thinking that Cabrillo could possibly get to his brother-in-law, the President of Mexico.

At least, he didn't have to worry about Jake Spinner any more.

Yoshimatsu went into the kitchen and did something he hadn't done for himself in a very long time. He fixed a cup of hot tea. He took it out onto the terrace. The air was chilly. He stared east at the waters of the Gulf of California as the first rays of sun reflected on the water. Once this dirty business was concluded, he'd head back to Tokyo and spend some time with his family. He hadn't seen his children in more than two months. He found himself actually missing his wife. He suspected that she knew on some level about him and Susan, but she had never confronted him about it. From time to time, he noticed a deep sadness in her eyes. Perhaps he'd take her on holiday to Paris. She loved art and music.

Yoshimatsu was brought out of his reverie by his cell phone. He looked at the LED display. It was Kanamura.

"Yes? What is the mood of the village?"

"Quiet," replied Kanamura. "There were no desertions last night. Yesterday one of the fishermen attempted to leave, but we convinced him that it would be to his and his family's benefit if he remained and finished out his contractual agreement."

"I assume we have enough people to man the boats for the hunt and to process the animals on the beach?"

"If we utilize some of the crew members from the *Shodokai Maru,* we should be able to finish the operation in one to two days. And the refrigerator trucks? Are they on schedule?"

"They should arrive by late afternoon." Yoshimatsu paused, inhaling deeply. "Ako, I have been experiencing some troubling thoughts. This operation must proceed smoothly and without mistakes. We will not get another chance. Our friend, Figueroa, is losing his nerve, and I am concerned he is going to panic and expose us."

"Do you wish me to arrange for him to have an accident?"

"Possibly. He is due to meet with me this morning. I will have a better sense of what to do with him after I can look into his eyes."

"And what of Sato?"

"If we are successful, Sato will be of no consequence."

"I am ready, whatever the outcome, Hiro-san."

"I have decided that I will preside over the hunt," said Yoshimatsu. "I will be on one of the banger boats, coordinating the attack. You will be in charge of shore operations and security, Ako."

"The cove will be secured from the road leading to the barricades, and the barricade netting on the outside will allow no animals to escape. I'll have guards posted on the barricade and I'll coordinate operations from that location. Rest assured, the barricade will be much more efficient and secure this time."

"Once we get the first group into the pens, I want the processing to commence. I want this to run like a factory operation. The banger boats will go back out once the first wave of the animals is behind the barricade."

"Everything is proceeding according to plan, Hiro-san. The construction on the barricades is almost complete. We should have most of the main structure finished by tomorrow, if I can somehow convince the crew to work faster."

"I know you will find a way. Is there any word on the whereabouts of Cabrillo and the other two biologists?"

"No. Not since they were seen leaving the docks from San Jacinto. I believe they have gone. With Spinner dead and Cabrillo severely injured, I am sure they no longer have any desire to be activists. Even the video they posted on the media is no longer getting airtime."

"Ah, the short attention span of the general populace," said Yoshimatsu. "What would we do without them?"

His cell phone beeped again. Another call was coming in. Yoshimatsu glanced at the LED display and a slight smile crossed his lips. "I have to go. It seems one of our buyers from China would like an update." He ended the conversation and began another. "Hello, Mr. Li. I have some good news for you."

# 64

Sandy and Graham stood at the shoreline, watching in frustration as Raúl loaded gas and supplies into his panga. The morning air was cool and laden with moisture. Raúl, mad at himself that he had not arisen earlier, was hastily throwing items into the boat. Sandy had hardly slept last night, worrying about his upcoming trip to see Alma Quintín.

"I know you're worried about my safety," Raúl said, apologetically. "I deeply appreciate that. But having one or both of you accompanying me will not serve our cause. I was instructed to come alone. If I break my word to Alma, we may lose our only chance to find out where the hunt is to be held."

"I have a really bad feeling about this, Raúl. You could be walking into a trap. The Quintín woman could be lying to you. Maybe they got to her already. What if they're holding one of her family members hostage?"

"She's right," agreed Graham. "She could have very easily informed the whalers that you were out there nosing around. They could have coerced her into arranging a meeting with you. There's a lot of empty ocean and desert between here and their fishing camp. Pretty easy to make someone just up and disappear."

"I have considered all of this." Raúl, tossed his backpack into the panga. "As I told my wife and children this morning, you're going to have to trust me. I was the one who looked into Alma's eyes. Those were not the eyes of a betrayer."

"At least wait until Jake and Emily get back," pleaded Sandy. "I'd feel a lot better about this if Spinner went along with you. He has a nose for trouble."

"Spinner won't be back until late this afternoon. We're almost out of time. Besides, in case you haven't noticed, Señor Jake doesn't have a calming effect on most people."

"That's a fact," said Graham.

Sandy gave Graham an annoyed look. "You're not helping here."

"This might help you feel better." Raúl turned his back to them as he lifted his shirt and revealed Spinner's pistol, which was tucked into the waistband of his jeans. "Jake Spinner is already accompanying me."

Their eyes grew wide at the sight of the ominous semi-automatic.

"I hope I don't have to use it. But use it I will, should the need arise."

He smiled weakly and untied the bowline from the large rock. He tossed it onto the bow. "Don't worry. I'll be back before dark."

Sandy hugged him. "Be careful. I don't want to have to send out a search party."

Raúl shook Graham's hand. "We all have our jobs to do. Keep practicing."

They pushed the boat until the sand loosened its grip on the hull. The panga glided on the water. Raúl deftly leapt onto the bow and made his way back to the console. The motor caught on the second turn of the key. As he backed out, he pulled his cap down over his forehead and pushed the throttle forward. The panga accelerated out of the cove.

The activists spent most of that morning practicing their drills and assembling butyric acid stink bombs. Alejandro called a meeting of the group leaders to go over last-minute details. Francisco and his team had already begun assembling the ramming devices for the bows of the boats that would attack the barricade. The design was simple. A V-shaped metal frame would be fitted over the bow. The scoop was designed to cut through nylon netting and shatter up to four-by-four pieces of lumber. Although Arturo was scheduled to go out on the boats too, he still spent hours organizing supplies for a makeshift field hospital to handle any injuries incurred in the impending confrontation.

Sandy and Paola made last-minute phone calls to plead for assistance. Earlier, Paola had made several attempts to contact the office of the President of Mexico, to inform him about what was about to transpire. Each time, her call was transferred to a generic message service. So far, there had been little response from the outside media. The nonprofits they were able to reach offered moral support and wished them well. No physical assistance was offered.

"Any luck, Paola?"

"No. Not a peep. No response from the president's office. I think there are way too many layers in government."

Sandy placed her cell phone on the table and sighed. "That was a complete waste of time." She stood up and looked out at the blue-green water in the bay. "Maybe Graham and I should go out today to do a search grid. Beats the hell out of sitting around here waiting."

"You know Alejandro called all boats in after Raúl left," Paola said.

"I know, I know. We need to conserve fuel for the hunt. I'm going crazy."

Graham walked up the dune and approached the canopy. He flopped down in one of the folding chairs that had been borrowed from the trimaran. "Are we having fun yet?"

"I think Sandy needs a boat ride," said Paola. "I think all of us could use one."

"I didn't know I'd be sitting on my thumbs this long," Graham said, agitated.

Sandy asked, "How's your team shaping up?"

"Everyone's sick of making butyric acid bombs. Brittany and Diane are complaining of shoulder soreness from throwing the bottles. They're practiced out and, frankly, I've had enough for now. I need a break. I'm thinking about going for a swim. Anyone care to join me?"

Sandy smiled. "Not a bad idea, but I didn't bring a swimsuit on this trip."

Graham's grin was diabolical. "Who said anything about a swimsuit?"

Sandy and Paola looked at Graham, their brows furrowed, and they broke into a laugh.

Graham looked stricken, then finally laughed along with them. "Just kidding. You two looked like you needed a smile."

Sandy raised one eyebrow and grinned. "What would you have done if we had said yes?"

Graham shrugged. "Hadn't thought that far into the future."

"That's typical," said Paola. She yawned, then stood. "I'm going to take a nap. I'll see you later." She trudged back down the low dune and disappeared into her tent which was set up not far from Carlos's shack.

"I hope she didn't leave on my account."

"I wouldn't worry about it," Sandy said.

They sat in silence for a few moments, Sandy staring at the bay in front of her. Graham watched as a tawny-colored lizard skirted across the dune and dove headlong into the sand.

"Did you see that? That lizard was literally swimming through the sand!"

"Fringe-toed lizard, I suspect," replied Sandy, without taking her eyes off the building whitecaps in the distance. "The scales on their feet and legs are modified so they can move through the sand like they're swimming."

Graham looked at her. "Impressive. Whale researcher, dolphin rescuer, and budding herpetologist."

"I was born and raised in Iowa. I came out west to the University of Arizona to study marine biology and never looked back. I love the ocean and just about everything in the desert. Finding a place where those two worlds collide was a dream come true for me. Jacques Cousteau once called the Gulf of California 'the aquarium of the world.' I can't imagine being anywhere else."

"It is magnificent. I've never seen so much stark beauty as in these waters and isolated beaches. I could spend a year down here exploring."

"Be careful, Graham. Baja will surely get under your skin."

Graham laughed. He looked at her, his deep blue eyes reflecting the sea. "So, got anyone waiting for you stateside?"

Sandy looked at his tan and bearded face, unsure where the line of questioning was leading. "No. I dated a guy in grad school for nearly a year, but we ended up parting ways. Most of the time, I was too wrapped up in my studies. Relationships take a lot of time and energy."

"That, they do."

"So, what's your story? I'll bet you have a string of sweet young things at your beck and call back home."

"What's that supposed to mean?"

"Ah, c'mon, Neely. I saw how the young coeds that came with you on the sailboat looked at you."

"Not my type. Don't get me wrong, Sandy. They're beautiful and intelligent young women. The truth is, I recently came out of a broken engagement, and I've been a little gun-shy about jumping into another relationship."

"I'm sorry, Graham. If you don't mind me asking, her choice or yours?"

Graham hesitated and turned away momentarily, staring out at the blue-green water. "No, I don't mind." He turned back toward her, the sadness in his eyes revealing the anguish involved in his decision. "I was the one to call it off. We were to be married in June. I had passed the bar and was going to practice environmental law in San Francisco. Something kept pulling at me. I wasn't ready to settle down. Frankly, the thought of a sixty-hour work week, a mortgage, and financial responsibility scared the shit out of me. I wanted to make a difference in the world. It made for some tense times between us. I wasn't meeting her criteria as a good marriage candidate. I suppose neither one of us wanted to be the one to break it off, but I finally had to do it. Hardest thing I've ever done."

"I'm sorry to hear about that, Graham. It must have been tough."

Neely drew in a deep breath, then exhaled. He smiled slightly. "So, I signed on with the Cetus Alliance. They wanted to use my knowledge of legal and environmental issues to help them when they went to court. But I really wanted to be on the front lines. Thanks to you, here I am."

"I thought most of you were volunteers," said Sandy.

"I do a combination of pro bono and per diem work for them. This venture is on my dime."

"Well, we're really glad that you came down here. I wish there were more people like you out there."

"What's your plan after this is all over?"

Sandy shrugged. "I don't know. The Minister of Fisheries has shut down the institute. Someone tried to put a hit on Alex. Paola and I are under suspension, and I'm not sure there are going to be any whales to study if they get their way. Not a very bright picture I'm painting, is it?"

Graham touched her on the shoulder. "Well, I guess we're going to have to make sure that those assholes don't succeed."

# 65

Before Raúl Campos landed the boat on the beach, he cut the motor, stopping about a quarter mile offshore. He pulled out a set of old binoculars, looking for something—anything—that looked out of place. Fernando's dilapidated panga was lying on its side several feet above the high tide line. Raúl scanned the beach several times, and, taking a deep breath, he turned the ignition, engaged the throttle, and pointed his panga toward the shore.

He beached the boat on the sand and tied the bowline to a concrete block that was exposed halfway up the beach. No one had come out to help him land the panga. He hadn't expected anyone. He trudged up the beach to the shack and knocked on the closed wooden door.

He waited nearly a minute before Fernando answered. He didn't look happy to see Raúl. Alma's husband squinted up and down the beach, then said, "Come inside."

Raúl entered the cool darkness of the fishing shack. He noticed the old curtains were drawn. He stood in the main room while Fernando disappeared into the back bedroom.

Several moments later, Alma Quintín appeared at the doorway, their infant son slung on her hip. Right away, Raúl noticed a large red stain on Alma's sleeve. "Raúl Campos, come with me."

He followed her into the only other room in the house. On the bed were piles of clothing, clean diapers, and toys. A young man stared at Raúl in abject terror from an old mattress next to the bed. He was an indio in his late teens, possibly early twenties. He wore a bandage across his forehead with a bloody spot on the left side. Both of his hands were wrapped in gauze and, even in the dimly lit shack, Raúl could see they were swollen and discolored.

"My nephew, Teo," Alma said. "He's my brother Santiago's son. Santiago and his wife have not been seen for nearly three weeks. The whalers told Teo that his parents were working on the mainland for a few weeks and would return shortly. He hasn't heard from them." She turned and spoke to Teo in their native language. She turned back to Raúl. "I told him you were here to help us."

"When someone wants to make an example of you to the rest of the village," she said, the anger in her voice barely controlled, "this is what happens. He was caught trying to leave, and they did this to him. They bashed in his head and broke both of his hands."

"Who did this to him?"

"Kanamura. He is called El Jefe in the village."

"How did he get here?"

"Several boys brought him here last night. They were afraid he was going to be killed. Since they broke his hands, he can no longer work. He was of no use to them. The boys left him here and kept going across the desert. They no longer wish to do the devil's work. He needs medical attention. You must take him with you, Raúl Campos!"

Raúl shook his head. "He needs to go to a hospital. The fishing camp where we're staying is not equipped to care for him."

Alma grabbed Raúl's arm and squeezed tightly. "If they come here, they will kill him. And if they find out we're hiding him, God help us."

Fernando said acidly, "I told you helping these pendejos would come to nothing but grief, Alma. Now, you've put the baby and us in danger."

"Shut up, you old woman," snapped Alma. "I am sick of your whining." She turned on him, causing him to take a reflexive step backward. "You should be out there with Raúl and the others trying to stop the hunt. You should make them leave and never come back! This is our home, Fernando. We live here! We fish here as our ancestors did." Her eyes were wide with rage. Her husband glared at her for a moment, then realized that anything he said would invoke a rapid and vociferous response. Fernando swore under his breath and walked outside into the bright sunlight.

Alma and Raúl turned their attention to the injured Teo. Upon closer inspection, Raúl could see a deep bruise along his left ribcage. He looked from Teo to Alma and said, "I'll take him with me."

He turned back to the young indio. "Teo, what I am about to ask you is very important. Do you know where the next hunt is to be held?"

"Sí." The boy nodded weakly.

Raúl reached into the large pocket in his backpack and produced a worn nautical chart that looked as if it would fall apart when he unfolded it. He returned to the bed and kneeled down next to Teo. Raúl and Alma gently assisted the injured young man to a sitting position. Raúl spread the map out on Teo's lap, pointing to the rugged coastline. "Can you show me?"

Teo nodded and stared down at the chart. He grimaced and closed his eyes, shuddering in pain. Raúl thought that the young man was about to pass out. Teo took several ragged breaths, nodded, and said "Okay."

He traced his shaking finger along the rugged coastline of the map of eastern Baja California Sur. His finger stopped at a small cove north of their position.

"There," Teo said.

Raúl squinted at the location in the dim light. He read the words El Infierno and wondered if this location was chosen partly because of the name or if it was a cruel coincidence.

Alma looked at the map. "Do you know this place?"

Raúl shook his head. "I've been up and down this coastline more times than I can remember, but I have no memory of this cove."

Teo coughed raggedly and indicated that he wanted to lie down. They gently helped him to lie down. It was several moments before the young indio was able to speak again.

Finally, Teo said. "It's well protected. You won't be able to see the barricade until you are very close. The cove is shallow, and there are rocky walls on either side to set the anchors for the barricade."

Raúl touched the boy on the shoulder. "Bueno, mí amígo. ¡Hiciste bien! You did good." He looked at Alma and nodded. "I need to make a phone call."

She nodded. Raúl stood and rummaged through his backpack until he found the small leather bag from which he produced several small packets of herbs and other medicinal items. He handed the traditional medicines to Alma. "Boil these in water for two minutes, then let it steep for four minutes. Then have Teo drink it down."

"What is it?"

"My wife is a curandera. This will help to ease the pain and prepare him for the boat ride back to San Vicente."

"Who is your wife?" Alma eyed the contents suspiciously.

"Guadalupe Torres Campos de Corona."

Alma's eyebrows lifted. "I've heard of her. The coastal people speak well of her."

Raúl went outside into the blinding sunlight. Squinting, he saw Fernando leaning against his old panga, smoking a hand-rolled cigarette. The grizzled fisherman cast a disdainful glance at Raúl and gazed back to the sea.

Raúl pulled his cell phone from his pocket and punched in the number. After what seemed to be a very long time, the phone rang on the other end. He recognized Alejandro's voice, but the reception was erratic.

"Alejandro?"

"Yes? Raúl? I'm having trouble hearing you."

"Un momento." He moved away from the shack closer to the beach. "Can you hear me now?"

"Better. Were you able to meet with Alma?"

"I'm with her now. The location for the next hunt is Punta El Infierno. It's a protected cove that's easily cordoned off from both sides. Tell Arturo to make ready. I'm bringing him a patient."

"Alma? Is she injured?"

"No. It's her nephew. He was very badly beaten by the whalers when he tried to leave. I think they might have killed his parents."

"Díos mío. Ten cuidado, Raúl. Gather up the boy and get out of there quickly."

"I will. But there are a few matters I must see to first. I should be back by the end of the day. I'm sending you the coordinates now. Let me know when you get them." He disconnected and texted the coordinates to Alejandro's phone.

A moment later, Alejandro texted back. "Got it."

Raúl looked at Fernando, who was still leaning against the boat next to him. He sensed that Alma's husband was straining to hear any part of the conversation.

Raúl took a deep breath, exhaled, and joined Fernando. He leaned against the boat with him and stared out at the Gulf of California. The afternoon winds were forming whitecaps in the middle of the channel. It was going to be a rough ride back to San Vicente. Neither spoke. The only sound was the rush of rolling waves crashing onto the sand.

Finally, Raúl broke the silence. "We are both people of the sea. It flows through our veins like a great current. The waves carry the beat of our hearts. We have lived here, fished her waters to feed our families, and died here." He looked at the fisherman. "Fernando, I need to ask you a question, and I want you to look me in the eye when you answer."

Fernando turned slowly and looked at him.

"Will you tell the whalers that we are coming?"

Fernando bristled. "I bear no good will toward them."

"But having knowledge that the hunt is going to be interrupted could mean a lot of money to the person who brought them this valuable information."

Fernando did not take his gaze from Raúl. "I am a poor fisherman. But I would never sell out my family to those *culeros*."

Raúl nodded. "Will you help us?"

Fernando turned away and faced the ocean once more. "I can't. I will say nothing about you or your group stopping the hunt. My obligation is to Alma and Israel."

"I understand, Fernando. Thank you."

Raúl walked back inside and began helping Alma get Teo ready for the long boat ride back. He noticed that Teo was breathing a little easier, the lines of pain in his forehead relaxing. Together, they got the young indio up and sat him on a chair in the kitchen to catch his breath.

"Alma, I need to ask you a question."

She looked at Raúl, lifting her chin slightly.

"Can Fernando be trusted?"

"He's more afraid of me than the whalers." She smiled slightly, holding up a kitchen knife. "Besides, he doesn't fancy being separated from his *cajones* in the middle of the night."

Raúl fashioned a makeshift litter out of a blanket and, with help from Alma and Fernando, carried Teo out to the boat. Before they lifted him into the boat, Alma leaned down and kissed her nephew on the forehead. She then placed some money and a folded note in his shirt pocket.

"You stay in La Paz until this is over," Alma instructed. "I called my friend Leticia. You can stay with her."

"But I want to stay and fight," pleaded the young indio. "I think they killed my mother and father."

Alma touched his cheek. "You've already helped, Teo. More than you know."

The young man cried out when they attempted to lift him over the gunwale and into the panga. Raúl made a quick assessment of the sea conditions and decided that keeping him near the back of the boat would make for a smoother ride. They'd be traveling against the current and wind for the return trip. It was going to be a long ride to San Vicente.

Once they had Teo settled, Raúl moved forward and jumped onto the sand.

"¡Vaya con Díos! Be well, Raúl Campos."

"¡Muchas gracias! You and your family should get away from here for a few days until things calm down."

Alma's face was immediately transformed into a mask of anger. "Where are you going to be Raúl? Are you leaving?"

He smiled and shook his head.

"That's what I thought you'd say. You worry about stopping the hunt. We'll be fine here."

With Fernando's help, Raúl pushed the panga into the shallows, then climbed in and made his way back to the console.

He looked over at Teo. "Ready?"

"Ready."

Raúl turned over the motor and the engine hummed to life. He pushed the throttle into reverse and the panga glided backward, incoming chop washing over the stern. Before leaving, he looked over his shoulder and waved to Alma and Fernando. The boat rolled over the swells and began to parallel the shoreline.

"He's a fool," Fernando said bitterly. "Nothing good will come of this. The whalers will slice through them like they do the dolphins."

Alma cast a disgusted look at her husband. She turned and walked back toward the beach shack. At the door, she turned back to face him. "What happened to you, Fernando? When did you become a frightened child? Tomorrow, many people may die. They'll die because they believe in something. Because they will not give in to people who use brutality to force their will on others."

"It's a fight they cannot win!"

"Says you. If you don't want to help, then stay out of my way."

Fernando looked at his wife, his brow furrowing. "What are you thinking, you crazy woman?"

"The people in the village need to know. They need to be able to choose to fight the invaders. I think they have had more than enough of these culeros."

Raúl was twenty minutes out when, over the noise of the motor, he heard the ringing of his cell phone. He slowed and answered it.

Alma's voice came across as emphatic. "Raúl, you have to slow down. Now."

"Why, Alma? I'm worried about Teo."

"I'm sending some help." She hung up.

Raúl cut the motor and looked behind them. Three pangas were fast approaching. Soon, Fernando brought his boat alongside Raul's. Seated at the bow was another fisherman, his wife, and two small children The other two fishing vessels each held a fisherman with his family.

Raúl looked straight at Fernando. "Change of heart?"

"Persuasive wife."

Raúl gave him a thumbs up and nodded.

# 66

Alfonso Figueroa stepped out of the black limousine and walked into the upscale lobby of the Plaza Los Cabos Hotel. His destination was the penthouse suite where Hirokan Yoshimatsu had been directing his operations for several weeks.

Figueroa had just endured a blistering verbal assault from his brother-in-law, President Emilio Duarte. The president had asked questions that Figueroa had barely been able to dodge. The Consortium needed to be gone, whether they completed the hunt or not. If Duarte and his cabinet found out about the presence of the Consortium, Figueroa's options would not be good. He could be facing an extended stay as a guest of the Mexican penal system. Worse yet, since this was an election year, his life could very well be in danger. Family ties only go so far.

And then there was the matter of Alejandro Cabrillo. Alejandro and the researchers were the only ones who could tie Figueroa to the Japanese whaling operation. Yoshimatsu had promised him this problem would be handled. Now no one knew where Cabrillo was. No one knew where Sandy Wainright was. No one knew the location of Paola Jiménez. Even attempts at locating Alejandro's wife and daughter had been futile. On the eve of the impending whale hunt, Figueroa could not shake the feeling that these researchers might show up and expose his duplicity.

He rode the elevator to the fifth floor, fidgeting nervously. The elevator car slowed, then stopped, a soft chime announcing his arrival. The doors slid open and Figueroa found himself face-to-face with Ako Kanamura, Yoshimatsu's right-hand man and enforcer. The large man's face was expressionless, almost placid. But there was something about him that sent a cold chill up Figueroa's spine. It was the eyes. No light came from them. The pupils seemed almost black, as if the light of day was being sucked into them like two black holes.

"Mr. Yoshimatsu is expecting you," Kanamura said. He turned and walked ahead of Figueroa—a gesture not lost on the Minister of Fisheries.

Kanamura opened the door to the suite, and Figueroa stepped inside. Yoshimatsu stood with his back to Figueroa, his hands clasped behind his back. Off to one side, at the wet bar, stood a tall, skeletal, Japanese man, dressed in a gray suit and sipping on a half-full glass of scotch. Yoshimatsu's administrative assistant sat on a sofa, her black cocktail dress contrasting sharply with its white leather. Her long, shapely legs were crossed provocatively.

Yoshimatsu turned and smiled at the Minister of Fisheries. "Ah, Minister Figueroa, it is good to see you. To what do we owe this honor?"

"We need to talk," Figueroa said, looking nervously between the woman and the skinny gray-suited man. "In private."

"Forgive me," said Yoshimatsu. "This is my colleague, Sato Izumi, and of course you have met my assistant, Miss Lawrence. What you say to me, you can say to them."

Figueroa fidgeted, catching the hint of a smile at the corners of Sato's thin-lipped mouth. It was not a friendly smile.

"We must shut down the operation immediately," said the Minister. "The president has called for an investigation of the recent whale hunt. I can no longer provide protection for your group in Mexican waters. I'm being summoned to Mexico City tomorrow to meet with him. He will be sending an investigative team to Baja. I'll be forced to reveal my involvement. The only way to avoid this scandal is for you and your men to leave these waters immediately."

Figueroa noticed something fleeting cross Yoshimatsu's eyes. Simmering rage, perhaps? Just as quickly, it was gone.

"My friend," said Yoshimatsu magnanimously, "we have very good news. The trucks have arrived and are moving into place. As we speak, the banger boats are being deployed to round up the dolphins, and my associate, Mr. Kanamura, has the local villagers ready for the final hunt. Without any further distractions, the trucks should be loaded and headed for the border, and the ship should be out of Mexican waters by midnight tomorrow." Yoshimatsu smiled again. "And, of course, you will be paid the balance, as stated in our agreement. The funds will be transferred to the bank in the Turks and Caicos that you specified."

"I am very concerned that there are too many loose ends that are no longer under control."

"I assure you, Minister, that every contingency has been accounted for. The operation will proceed flawlessly."

"Where is Cabrillo? You gave me your word that he would be found and silenced. He and the other two scientists have the information and proof to ruin me. I could lose everything."

Yoshimatsu stepped closer. "Not everything, Minister. I would like you to think of your family for a moment. This is not a time to lose your nerve. The world is a very dangerous place. You can never know when tragedy may strike."

Yoshimatsu glared at Figueroa. The features of his face remained placid, but the look in his eyes made Figueroa want to turn and run.

"Now is not the time to show weakness, my friend." Yoshimatsu's tone softened. He placed a hand on Figueroa's shoulder. "Do not worry about Director Cabrillo. His general health and his worry for the well-being of his own family will discourage him from trying to stop us. And without Jake Spinner, the activists have no leader. There is no way they can organize in time to interfere with our operation."

He walked Figueroa to the door. "I assure you, by tomorrow night, there will be no trace that we were ever here. You will have the final payment in your account. We will fill our supplier's demands. I'm sure you can find a way to put off El Presidente for one more day. After all, he is family."

"Tomorrow midnight, no later," said Figueroa.

"Of course. I am as ready to be done with this part of the world as you are to have me leave. We must fulfill our contract. It is what honorable men do."

Figueroa nodded slowly and was shown out by Kanamura.

When Kanamura returned, he went to the bar and poured himself a shot of whiskey. Yoshimatsu turned back to the ocean and again clasped his hands behind his back.

"What would you have me do with the esteemed Minister?"

Yoshimatsu was pensive. "Once the hunt is concluded and the *Shodokai Maru* is back in international waters, I believe it is time for Minister Figueroa to suffer a most unfortunate accident."

"It will be the last thing I do before I board the plane for Yokohama," Kanamura said.

# 67

Alejandro was going over the list of final team assignments for the upcoming hunt when his cell phone rang. The number looked vaguely familiar. He knew it was not his wife. Her number was burned into his memory, no matter how much his brain had been scrambled or his body had been wracked with injury. An inner voice told him not to answer it, but his curiosity overcame his sense of caution. He pressed the answer button.

"Bueno."

"Alejandro Cabrillo?" The voice on the other end was familiar. Alex immediately regretted answering the call.

"This is Minister Figueroa. Where are you?"

"Safe."

"Are you all right?"

"Other than a fractured fibula, a collapsed lung, and multiple contusions—never better," Alejandro spoke without emotion. "Thanks for asking."

"What happened to you?"

"I fell off a ladder."

"I'm sorry to hear that," Figueroa sounded sympathetic. "We must talk, Alejandro. There are some new developments concerning the video that you've been sending out. I may be able to provide some assistance to you and your colleagues."

There was a brief pause, but Alejandro could sense the desperation in Figueroa's voice. "Just what type of assistance are you suggesting?" Alejandro was barely able to contain the anger that was building like a pressure cooker in his chest. "If I remember correctly, you dismissed me and my colleagues without following proper administrative protocols when we gave you that video. Which begs the question. What are you trying to hide, Minister Figueroa?"

405

"I'm offering you a chance to restore your previous positions without penalty. Your attitude and disrespect are not helping your colleagues' and your positions."

Alejandro took a deep breath. More than anything, he wanted to tear into Figueroa and tell him they knew about his involvement with the Japanese syndicate. He knew that Figueroa was supplying information to the whalers to enable them to harvest whales and dolphins. He desperately wanted to tell Figueroa that he suspected him of putting out a contract to have him killed, but he knew that if he said anything now, the plan to stop the upcoming hunt could be jeopardized. He quickly thought of a ruse. "Tell me what you have."

"I can't reveal the information over the phone. The information is sensitive and would expose some individuals high up in the echelons of the government. We must meet face-to-face. As soon as possible."

"I'm presently out of the country. Up in the states getting my broken leg taken care of and enjoying a little down time with my family. It would take me several days to get back. But I'll try to make a reservation and catch a plane back to Mexico City in a few days."

"Not Mexico City. It's better that we meet in La Paz, at the institute. As soon as possible. Tell your wife and daughter that something pressing is calling you back to La Paz. I'll happily pay your plane fare."

"I don't think I can book a flight for today. I'll see what I can do tomorrow."

"Time is of the essence! Call me as soon as you have your reservations."

"What about Sandy and Paola? Do you want them to hear this information as well?

"Oh, yes, they should be there. What I have to say is important to all of you and your work at the institute."

"Very well. I'll be in touch."

Alejandro disconnected and stared at the phone for several minutes. When Sandy and Graham approached, Sandy could see that Alejandro was seething.

"Alex, what's going on?" She slid into the chair opposite him.

"I just received a most interesting call."

"Who from?"

"His Excellency, the Minister of Fisheries, Alfonso Figueroa," Alex's words rolled off his tongue with measured sarcasm.

"What the hell does he want?"

"He wants to know where we are. He wants us to come in."

"That son of a bitch!" Sandy turned to Graham. "We think he's the one who made arrangements for Alejandro to have 'an accident.'" She made the quotation sign with her fingers. "We're pretty damn sure that he's been feeding the Japanese mafia information on where to find and kill the whales."

"He says he wants to meet with us to discuss some new developments regarding the whalers and who they're connected to. He says he has information that will help us get reinstated to our former positions."

Graham asked, "What did you tell him?"

"I told him that I was out of country at the moment. On a family trip to recuperate in the States, to be exact," said Alejandro. "I don't want him to think that any of us are anywhere near the hunt."

Sandy looked sidelong at Alejandro. "What do you think he has up his sleeve?"

"In times like these, I try to channel Jake Spinner. What's Figueroa's motivation?"

"He's in deep shit and wants to cover his tracks," said Sandy. "He doesn't want any witnesses when it all comes crashing down."

"Exactly. That's why he encouraged me to bring you and Paola."

"You're not going to meet with him, are you?" Sandy's eyes widened at the implications.

"Oh, I plan on meeting with him. But not until after we stop the hunt tomorrow. And then, on my terms."

"Alex, you know he'll bring muscle to finish you off. You need to just leave this to the higher-ups. He'll burn himself."

"Besides, you're not in the best physical condition to defend yourself, should the need arise, as I'm sure it will," said Graham, his gaze wandering down to Alejandro's broken leg.

Alejandro stared at Graham. "This leg is of no matter. Figueroa's going down, and I plan on being there when he does."

They heard the chopper's approach long before it appeared from around the point. It swung into the cove, hovering momentarily before landing on a fairly flat stretch of sand. While the rotors were still spinning, Emily Rosen sprang from the open cabin and landed lightly on the sand. Jake Spinner and Oliver Sweet followed.

They approached the group of people who had come to meet them. Spinner had his duffel slung over one shoulder and a canvas satchel over the other.

"Took you long enough," Sandy said, smiling. She and Rosen embraced.

"We brought party favors," said Rosen.

Spinner approached Alejandro and Graham and shook their hands.

"Good to see you, Jake," said Alejandro.

"Alejandro, Graham, Sandy—meet Oliver Sweet. He's going to provide a bit of external support to our cause."

They all shook Sweet's hand. Sandy was taken aback by how her hand was dwarfed by that of the big man.

"Welcome," Alejandro said. "We can use all the help we can get."

"Thought I'd get a little beach time and see about helping y'all save some big fish."

"Actually, they're not fish." Sandy stopped herself when she saw the big ear-to-ear grin on Sweet's face. "Okay, got me. I didn't realize we'd have a funny man in our midst."

"Oh, I'm not the funny one," said Sweet. "That would be my partner, Snake. But I need to let you all in on a little secret." He looked around, then leaned in. "I think he's—well, you know—crazy." Sweet twirled his index finger in a circular motion at his temple.

Sandy regarded Sweet, then looked over at Rosen. "Crazy?"

Emily nodded solemnly. "Totally batshit."

"It's okay," Spinner reassured them. "These guys will fit right in."

The pilot stepped out of the cockpit and looked around. He was grizzled, wore reflective Ray-Ban aviator glasses and had an old Florida Marlins ball cap reversed on his head. He peered at the group.

"Hey, God damn it! Who's gonna help me unload all this shit?"

Sandy glanced at Rosen. "Snake, I presume?"

"In the flesh. Be careful. I don't think he's had his shots."

"Graham, can you grab some of your crew? We have some fairly heavy ordnance that needs to be offloaded." Spinner said. He turned to look at Alejandro. "Jesús and Carlos about?"

"I think they're working on the boats. I'll send someone to get them."

Spinner walked over to the fishing shack and dropped his duffel next to the building. "Where's Beau?"

"Inside at the command center," said Sandy.

He began walking toward Jesús's shack. "Good. I have something that I think he's going to like." Rosen, Sandy, Graham, and Alejandro fell into step behind him.

The members of Graham's group were gathered around the table. Beau sat hunkered over his computer. When he looked up and saw Spinner, his face turned crimson.

"I have some bad news, Mr. Spinner. I haven't been able to maintain a satellite visual of the mother ship. I just don't have the juice. There's blackout times, and when I pick up the signal again, it's moved."

Spinner reached into his satchel and produced a red thumb drive. He tossed it to Beau who caught it in both hands.

"Compliments of Anika Probst"

Beau was suspicious. "Who's Anika Probst?"

"Your new best friend. Check it out."

Beau picked up the memory stick and inserted it into the USB port. It took several seconds for the computer to register the new files. He looked up at Spinner, his eyes wide. "Where did you get this?"

"Let's just say, there are some folks out there who spend their days and nights figuring out how to stay one step ahead of the competition."

"This shit is high level surveillance equipment. We're talking military grade."

Spinner half-smiled. "Type in these co-ordinates." He handed Beau a slip of paper with latitude and longitude written on it. "Let's see if you can find that whaler now."

Beau focused on the screen in front of him. His fingers flew across the keys as he struggled to keep up with the encryption code instructions. Several tense moments passed. The only sound in the room was the frenetic tapping of the computer keys.

"Damn it!" Beau swore as he hit a wrong keystroke and the program went into momentary error alerts.

"Relax, kid," said Spinner. "You can do this."

Beau took a deep breath and began typing again. A moment later, a satellite image of the Gulf of California appeared on the computer screen. He adjusted the image and location, finally zooming in on the image of the *Shodokai Maru*.

"Got it!" He zoomed in even further until he could actually see a pixelated image of the crew members on the deck. "This is amazing! The resolution is— Damn! I can almost see what they had for lunch."

"Anika said to call her if you have any problems. She can be reached by Skype. She said she left a link in a folder with her name on it."

Beau peered at the screen. "There it is." He clicked on the link and a box appeared with Anika's face on it. "She's hot."

"Focus, Beau. Your job, for the next twenty-four hours, is to not let that ship get out of your sight. Can you do this for me?"

Beau nodded solemnly. "You can count on me, sir."

Spinner placed his hand on Beau's shoulder. "I know I can."

Jake and the others returned to the helicopter where Jesús, Carlos, and Francisco were already unloading crates and bags onto the beach. Brad and Graham had joined in and were assisting Sweet and Snake with some of the heavier items. Most of the inhabitants of the fishing camp, curious to see what

Spinner and Rosen had brought back from their foraging mission, gathered around to get a look at the equipment. A large wooden crate and a smaller one next to it caught everyone's attention.

Brad, the young surfer dude from San Diego, stood over a crate and looked at Snake. "Where do you want this?"

"Oh, you can bring that over here," Snake said, without looking up.

Brad bent and lifted the crate, grunting from the weight. He carried it unsteadily to where Snake was checking the manifest and set the crate down roughly on the sand. "What the hell do you have in there? Gold bullion?"

Snake peered over his aviator glasses, then flipped the latches on the crate. He tossed a brick to Brad, who nearly dropped it.

"That would be C-4, Sonny."

Brad's eyes went wide. "C-4? Like the C-4 that—you know—explodes?"

"Is there any other kind? No worries, Dude. It won't explode without a blasting cap. You can shoot it and it won't explode. Back in 'Nam, the troops burned cubes of it to heat up their rations."

Brad cast a wary eye at Snake, then gingerly handed him the C-4 brick.

Spinner walked over to the crates and inspected them. Sweet joined him and, unable to contain their curiosity any longer, Alejandro and the others approached.

Alejandro pointed to the larger crate. "What's this?"

"RIB," said Sweet. "Rubber Inflatable Boat with a 150 horse Yamaha four-stroke outboard."

Graham asked, "Are you going to add this to the fleet?"

Sweet cast a glance at Spinner, seeking an indication from him of how much information to reveal.

"Not exactly," said Spinner. "But let's just say for now that the less you know, the better it will be for all of you if this whole thing goes south." He turned to Graham. "Now, over here is something I think you might find useful." He walked over to four stacked metal boxes and flipped the latch and opened one. In the box, arranged like black eggs, were row upon row of round metal objects.

Graham's eyes widened. "Hand grenades?"

"In a sense," said Spinner, picking one of the black objects out of the box and hefting it in his hand. "Tear gas." He tossed it over to Graham who caught it easily. "Think Morgan and the others could handle these?"

"Easier to throw than a bottle of butyric acid." Graham tested the weight of the tear gas grenade in his hand.

"Good. Let everyone know that there'll be a brief tutorial about how to use these things." Spinner looked at his watch "Sixteen hundred hours. One hour from now."

Graham's smile was devious. "I'll make sure everyone is there."

"When you pull the pin, here," Spinner indicated the small pin on the tear gas grenade he held in his hand, "you have five seconds to throw it. This is not the time to turn to your neighbor and ask them how their date went last night. Get rid of it. This thing goes off in your boat at that range, you'll all be blind."

Spinner looked at their solemn faces, seeing the fear in their eyes. That was a healthy thing, he thought. He'd be a lot more worried if the volunteers had looked more relaxed.

"Each boat will have eight of these," Spinner continued. "Use your throws wisely. Timing is of the essence. If you throw too soon, they can pick them up and fling them back at you. So, you have to pull the pin, count two, and throw. The closer you are the better."

He looked around at the group of activists. "Any questions?"

"I have a question," said Arturo. "A lot of the bad guys are going to have guns. What do we do if they start shooting at us?"

"Evasive maneuvers. Get out of there. You may only get one throw. Don't risk your life or your team's safety. We're working on a plan to neutralize the shooters on the barricade."

Jake motioned to Snake and Sweet, who brought forward a large wooden crate and set it on the sand. Spinner walked over and flipped the lid. He pulled out a Kevlar vest and a helmet and held them up.

"Everyone manning the boats is to wear these. They won't necessarily stop all bullets coming at you, but they're better than nothing. This is not a request. Nobody goes out on the water without them. Sweet and Snake will help you get sized up."

A sound like a swarm of angry bees came off the water. The gathering looked seaward and saw a panga round the point and head straight for them. A moment later, three more pangas appeared, headed in on the same tack. In the front boat, Raúl Campos stood at the console.

"Looks like the armada has arrived," said Sweet.

"I'll be damned," said Spinner. "He brought some of the pangueros with him."

Raúl cut the engine at the last moment and simultaneously lifted the motor. The panga glided onto the beach and stopped short in the sand. The other three pangas landed in a similar fashion. The group on the beach broke into thunderous applause.

"Now, that's what I call an entrance," said Arturo.

"We have a wounded man here." Raúl motioned for Arturo to come forward.

"Can he walk?" Arturo rushed to the panga and peered down at the injured Teo. "I need some help here!" Arturo called out. Several activists rushed to the side of the panga and gathered around the young man. Carefully, they lifted him out, placed him on a makeshift stretcher, and carried him to Jesús and Dora's house.

"You've been busy." Spinner shook Raúl's hand.

"Thought you could use the help," said Raúl. "Jake Spinner, this is Fernando Quintín, Manuel Soto, Ruben Diaz, and Luis Acosta.

Jake shook each man's hand. He turned to Fernando. "Are you—?"

"Yes," said Fernando. "I'm the husband of Alma Quintín, the most troublesome woman I have ever come across."

Spinner smiled again. "Welcome, all of you. Who's the kid?"

"Alma's nephew, Teo," said Raúl. "He tried to get away from the village. The whalers beat him badly. He told us where and when the next hunt is going to be."

"Who did this to him?"

"A man named Kanamura. Have you heard of him? He is El Jefe to the whalers."

Spinner's face took on the look of hard granite. "Yeah. I know him."

"Jake, I think you need to listen to Manuel, Ruben, and Luis. Until yesterday, they were still in Puerto Nacimiento. They escaped with their families in the dead of night when the guards were changing. They can tell you a lot about the whalers and what we're facing tomorrow."

"Good. I look forward to it."

Oliver Sweet stepped up and stood beside Jake. "Boss, we need to get the boat inflated and the ordnance loaded. We've got a long boat ride ahead of us."

Spinner nodded. "I'll be right there."

# 68

Kanamura was on the phone in the other room of the penthouse suite, his voice measured, but with a level of quiet intensity that told Yoshimatsu something had gone awry. When Yoshimatsu entered the living room, he could see the anger in Kanamura's black eyes.

"What do you mean they're gone? How did they get past the guards?" He listened for a moment as his underling attempted a weak explanation. "I don't care for your excuses. There are enough of you stationed there to keep the village in check. Double the guard. No one else leaves! Is that clear? We will discuss this further when I arrive."

Kanamura clicked off. He gazed up at Yoshimatsu.

"What is it?" Yoshimatsu already knew the answer but waited to hear it from his second in command.

"Three more boat drivers with their families escaped in the night. My men never saw them, never even heard them. They said this morning three of the boats were missing. They must have paddled out in the dead of night when the guards were in another part of the village, then started the motors when they were clear."

Yoshimatsu turned away, his fists clenched tightly at his sides. "How many boats does that leave us?"

"Counting the banger boats, eight in all. I will deal with their incompetence, Hiro-san. All of them."

There was a long pause before Yoshimatsu spoke. "That will have to wait. We need every available man for the hunt tomorrow. I will speak with Captain Watabe about using as many of the crew as he can spare from their duties on board the *Shodokai Maru*." He turned back to face Kanamura. "There will be no disciplinary action taken yet. After the hunt, you can deal with them as you see fit. For now, we require every available man to complete the operation."

Kanamura nodded.

"One more thing. Don't speak of this new development to Sato. I will deal with him later. Right now, I do not want to be distracted by his meddling."

"Where will he be during the hunt?"

"It seems my esteemed colleague has a problem with small boats and sea sickness, but he insisted on being present at the hunt. He wishes to oversee the culling at the cove."

Kanamura stood. "With your permission, Hiro-San, I will return to Puerto Nacimiento to oversee the readiness of the boat crews and transport trucks."

"I'm putting my faith in your ability to manage the boat crews and the timely loading of the processed meat and animals destined for our buyers. We have a great deal riding on the outcome of this operation, both to our customers at home and our foreign investors."

"Nothing will get in the way of our operation, Hiro-san."

Yoshimatsu nodded and forced a brief smile. "This country has proven to be a most troubling one. Never before have I encountered such incompetence. I blame myself for the unfortunate choice of Minister Figueroa as an ally. I should have known from the start that he's a man of many grandiose words but short on delivery of his promises. His planning is sloppy, his contractors are clumsy brutes, and he's unable to control his people. Tomorrow night, I'll be glad to be heading back to Yokahama with the venture brought to a successful conclusion."

Kanamura bowed deeply to his superior. He walked past Susan on his way to the front door. He looked at her with his cold, black eyes just long enough to send a chill the length of her spine. Kanamura was a man she never wanted to meet alone—anywhere.

After Kanamura walked out the door, Susan returned to the patio where Yoshimatsu, his hands still clasped behind his back, watched the late afternoon sun paint dramatic shadows on the mountains.

She approached tentatively, then lightly placed a hand on his shoulder. He reluctantly turned his attention away from the calming seas. He felt alarm as he saw the look of deep concern on her face.

"You are troubled, my love. What is it?"

She took a deep breath. "For the past seven years, I've been your friend, lover, and confidante in all things business and personal. I have always stood by you and always will. But this time, I feel very afraid. It seems this operation has been cursed from the start. I'm worried about you going out on the boats tomorrow. Perhaps I'm over-reacting, but this operation has been one disaster after another."

Yoshimatsu touched her cheek lightly. "I am moved that you are so worried about me," he said, smiling. He kissed her gently on the lips. "Everything will be fine, my dear Susan. We have enough men to carry out the operation. Do not concern yourself with Figueroa. He is weak, but he will not give us away. He is in too deep. By the time his brother-in-law finds out about our operation, the *Shodokai Maru* will be in international waters and the captive animals will be on planes destined for their new homes in Dubai, China, Korea, and Russia."

"Hiro-san, you have enough whale meat in that ship to prove to the Consortium that you are still the undisputed leader of the Pacific Rim associates. Even Sato can't argue, given the harvest you've collected here."

"The world is changing, Susan. Western countries are losing the desire to display whales and dolphins to the public. In the United States and Europe, many marine parks are retiring their animals to sanctuaries, stating that the animals deserve to live out their lives in peace. The rise of marine parks in China and other parts of Asia are the new markets. People will come out by the millions to see dolphins, swim in the water with them, pet them, and watch them do tricks. We are on the cusp of a multi-billion-dollar enterprise. And I can tell you, we will not encounter the resistance that we have faced here."

Susan hugged him. "Promise me you'll be careful tomorrow."

Yoshimatsu smiled again. "After the operation is completed, I will meet you in New York where we will embark on our flight to Vienna for a much-needed vacation. There is nothing to worry about."

After a late afternoon supper, Yoshimatsu placed several calls to his potential buyers, assuring them that their orders would be filled tomorrow. A buyer in Dubai, who had ordered four young bottlenose dolphins, inquired about the possible delivery of two additional short-finned pilot whales. After Yoshimatsu disconnected, he kissed Susan goodbye and made his way to the roof where the helicopter was waiting for him. Kanamura and Sato were already in their seats. Sato nodded to Yoshimatsu in a manner that indicated he was rather irritated about having to wait. Hiro climbed aboard and strapped himself into the forward seat. He then placed headphones over his ears.

Sato leaned forward and spoke into his own headset. "Is everything all right?"

"Yes, yes," said Yoshimatsu jovially. "Everything—and everyone—is in place. As soon as we arrive, we will deploy the banger boats. Several large pods were sighted this morning, and the teams are already heading toward the positions where they were last seen."

The pilot spun up the rotors, and the helicopter flew north over a metallic blue sea. Nearly an hour later, it banked and began to descend. The pilot made radio contact and, suddenly, a ship appeared out of the darkness, its bridge and helipad lit up to guide the helicopter to a safe landing.

After setting down, Yoshimatsu and Sato made their way to the bridge where Captain Watabe awaited their arrival. Yoshimatsu felt a damp chill in the air but did not shiver. He was fueled by the excitement of the upcoming hunt. Watabe bowed to the two Consortium executives and stood at attention.

Yoshimatsu returned the bow and then shook Watabe's hand. "Is everything ready?"

"Yes, Yoshimatsu-san. Tomorrow morning your boat will be ready so that you can join the rest of the fleet. Sato-san, we have another to take you to the containment and processing area."

"Very good," said Sato. "I'm looking forward to the capture and processing."

"You will have a very good seat from the boat inside the barricade," said Captain Watabe.

Kanamura's cell phone rang. He picked up and listened. "Very good." Kanamura disconnected and looked at Yoshimatsu. "Hiro-san, the trucks are arriving at the cove, as we speak."

"How many?" Yoshimatsu asked.

"All four made it," Kanamura said. "They will begin setting up the processing stations shortly."

"Are the boats from the village ready?" Yoshimatsu half-held his breath for an answer he didn't want to hear.

"They are awaiting your orders, sir. There will be one member of my team that will accompany the boatmen to their targets. I will take my place at the cove shortly to supervise the operation there. We will be awaiting your arrival, Hiro-san."

"Very good, Ako." Yoshimato turned to the three men. "Preparations are complete for tomorrow's hunt."

# 69

Emily Rosen sat at the dinner table in the home of Jesús and Dora, which had been transformed into a makeshift command center. She leaned over her laptop, headphones on, listening to interviews she'd recorded earlier. From time to time, she stopped the video long enough to jot down a few notes.

Frustrated with the seemingly endless waiting before the hunt, she decided to put her time and skills to work recording a log of the events leading up to and through the ordeal they were about to face.

She had already interviewed most of the people who were involved directly in stopping the hunt, from the researchers to the volunteers to the fishermen. Raúl acted as translator for the non-English-speaking members of the group.

Rosen, with Paola's assistance, interviewed some of the wives who made up the support group for the camp. Their shy but eloquent statements about their ties to the sea and the need to protect the oceans for their children truly moved Emily.

She closed the laptop and removed her headphones. She leaned back in the wooden chair and stretched, feeling the joints in her neck and shoulders pop noisily. She went over to where Beau sat staring bleary-eyed at the image of the *Shodokai Maru* on his computer screen.

"Hey," said Rosen, sidling up next to him and looking at the screen. "When was the last time you took a break?"

"I don't know." Beau blinked hard, then rubbed his eyes. "Around noon, I think."

"That was nearly four hours ago. Unless you have a catheter strapped to your leg, your back teeth have got to be floating right about now."

"I can't leave. If I lose that ship, Mr. Spinner's gonna kill me."

"I seriously doubt that. Don't take Spinner too literally, Beau."

"Besides, I don't think I can stand up. My legs are stuck in this position."

417

"That's it. Up you go. Go pee and stretch your legs and get outside for a while. Dora and Guadalupe are whipping up dinner as we speak. Go get some chow. I'll watch the show for a while."

"I don't know. Are you sure?"

"No problem. That ship moves one inch, I'll come running."

Beau stood, his face a mask of pain. "Damn! My feet fell asleep."

He straightened up. "I'm okay now. I'll be back in a few minutes."

"Take your time. We're good here."

Beau walked unsteadily toward the door. He turned around and looked at Emily. "Thanks."

Rosen was watching the updated still images of crew members on the *Shodokai Maru* when Jake Spinner walked in. He was surprised to see her hunkered down over the computer terminal that Beau had refused to vacate for food, water, or the call of nature. He strode over to where she sat and stood behind her.

"Before you say anything," Emily said, without looking up, "I told him to take a break. The kid hasn't eaten or peed in nearly four hours."

"Why'd he do that?"

"He was afraid you might think he was slacking, Spinner."

"I never told him that he couldn't take a break."

"He's a kid, Jake. He doesn't know you like I do. He looks up to you. He doesn't want to let you down." Rosen looked straight at him. "He's going to take everything you say literally."

"Oh." Spinner looked confused, his forehead furrowing, as if he was experiencing a strange new emotion.

"Remember, most of these kids never spent any time in the military."

"You're right, Em. I've been riding everyone a little hard, I guess."

"I know you have good intentions and that you want to keep all of them safe. Just give them a chance, Jake. They won't let you down."

She turned her attention back to the computer screen.

"Seen anything?" Spinner leaned in, bringing his face closer to hers to get a better look.

"Not much. There appears to be more people on deck now. What they're doing I couldn't tell you."

He studied the screen. "We're getting ready to interview the newly arrived fishermen from Puerto Nacimiento over at Carlos's place. I thought you might want to sit in on this one."

"Can you hold on until Beau gets back?"

"No problem. Dora and Guadalupe are serving them up some food right now."

He kissed her on the top of the head and walked out just as Beau hurriedly stepped inside, a plate of food in one hand and two bottles of water in the other. He looked contrite when he saw Jake.

"Mr. Spinner, I only took time to hit the head and grab some food. I swear, that's all."

"It's okay, Beau. We all need a little downtime. Staring at a computer screen all day long can make your brain and your ass go numb." He walked by Beau, then stopped, turned, and looked at the young man. "Good work, Beau. Let me know if you see anything that seems out of the ordinary. Now, go eat your fish tacos. And call me Jake. Mr. Spinner was my father."

Rosen joined Spinner and the others in Carlos's shack. The newly-arrived fishermen sat at the table with Raúl and the researchers. Oliver Sweet stood in the background with Graham Neely. Rosen noticed that several of the fishermen and their family members couldn't take their eyes off the towering black man.

In the late afternoon light, faces of the fishermen looked like they'd been carved out of some ancient rubbed wood. They were all probably in their mid-to-late-forties, but their faces reflected a lifetime of scorching sun, stinging salt, wind, poverty, and gnawing hunger. Even the children looked somber, peering out quietly from their mothers' laps, their eyes wide and cautious.

Raúl introduced them to Emily. In Spanish, he told them that Spinner would be asking them questions about the impending hunt, and Emily Rosen would be telling their stories to the world. At first, they looked nervously back and forth at each other. One of the fishermen, Ruben Diaz, said they were afraid the government would come looking for them if they spoke, or, worse yet, the whalers would come to take their revenge.

"Tell them no one's going to hurt them anymore," said Spinner. "Tomorrow, this all ends."

Raúl translated, and the three fishermen nodded and looked uneasily at Rosen.

"You can ask your questions," Raúl said, turning to Spinner.

"Raúl, my Spanish is rudimentary at best and I don't want any misunderstandings. The outcome of this operation may very well depend on the information we gather here. So, if you will do the honors—"

Spinner began a line of questioning that Rosen recognized as military intel-gathering techniques. He asked the fishermen how many men were stationed in the village and how they maintained order among the inhabitants of Puerto Nacimiento.

Over the next hour, the three fishermen and their wives gave accounts of forced labor, threats, and beatings. Manuel Soto described how once, when he had refused to go out on a night hunt, he was dragged out of his home in the middle of the night and severely beaten.

All three said the whalers constantly held their families at verbal ransom, threatening them with physical violence and even death. They painted a picture of intimidation and fear. Spinner felt pangs of guilt when he learned that the situation in the village grew worse after his actions interrupted the first whale hunt.

"Who was in charge?" Spinner asked. "*¿Quiénes eran el Jefe?*"

Ruben Diaz spoke up. "We call him '*El Diablo de Japón.*'" He described a large man with dead-looking eyes. He drew his hand down the right side of his face in a gesture indicating a scar, and Spinner immediately knew he was talking about Kanamura.

"Yeah, we've met."

Rosen saw the lines around Spinner's mouth tighten and his eyes take on the color of a gray sea just before a storm. Even though his posture had not changed, the cold anger emanating from his body was evident. A chill ran down her spine.

"Is he in the village now?"

Ruben said that he came and went, but he was usually present when more severe forms of discipline had to be meted out. Most of the time he left the village in charge of his subordinates—thugs who had ties to the Sinaloa Cartel on the mainland. He said he knew this, because one of them—in a state of drunkenness—had told the fishermen that he worked for people who could give them lucrative work as drug mules once the whalers left. The thugs also described in detail the methods they employed to make people disappear.

Rosen felt her own anger escalate as the fishermen told their stories. She noticed the looks of shock and horror on the faces of those gathered around the table as they realized the savagery of the people they were dealing with.

Spinner listened intently. He produced a chart of the area, a satellite map of El Infierno Cove. Rosen noted that he had marked several locations, using symbols to note the containment barricade and the positions of sentries.

Spinner asked, "Have any of you been to El Infierno?"

Manuel Soto looked at Spinner, then turned to Raúl. "Sí." He explained that after his beating, he was sent to work on the barricade.

"Is this accurate?" Spinner pushed the chart across the table and handed him a pencil.

Manuel studied the chart and then began correcting Spinner's symbols, adding more details to several key locations around the cove. Spinner's heart sank when he saw that there were additional armed guards posted on the barricade and along the rocks on either side of the cove. Manuel drew several Xs above the cove itself at higher elevations. They were going for a lot more fortifications than had been present at San Mateo Cove. The whalers were taking no chances with this hunt. Spinner cast a glance at Sweet and held up one open hand, then added two more fingers. Sweet nodded grimly.

Spinner pointed to a swath that Manuel had drawn near the eastern end of the lagoon. "¿Troques?"

"Sí Señor," said Manuel. "Para los delfines, vivos y muertos."

Spinner studied the changes that Manuel had made to the chart. He heaved a great sigh. "This changes things." He sat back and stared at it for a full minute without speaking, his fingers interlaced over the bridge of his crooked nose. "How many fishermen are participating in the hunt tomorrow?"

Ruben, Manuel, and Luis conferred, counting off the names of the ones they were fairly certain would be running boats the next day.

"Seis pangas, señor," replied Luis. "Con dieciocho o veinte pangueros."

"Can the village fishermen be turned?"

Luis shrugged. "No sé, Señor. No sé."

Alejandro asked, "What are you thinking, Jake?"

"I don't know. I was thinking of some way to get the word to them to fall out at the last moment, veer their boats away, and take away some of the whalers' ability to push the whales into the nets."

"Warning them of what's coming could work against us," said Raúl.

Spinner blew out a long breath. "It all boils down to who pulls your strings."

Brittany, one of the young Cetus volunteers, burst in through the door. She looked apologetically at Graham, then turned to Spinner.

"Mr. Spinner, I'm sorry to interrupt, but you'd better come quick." She was breathing hard. "Beau sent me to get you. Something's happening on the whaler."

Spinner looked at Oliver Sweet and both headed for the door. Emily grabbed her laptop and satchel and fell in behind them.

When they arrived at Jesús's home, Beau was standing over the computer, the glow from the screen bathing his face in a ghostly light.

"What have you got, Beau?" Spinner asked.

"You told me to get you if something came up. A few minutes ago, a helicopter landed on the deck and several men got out. I magnified the image and recorded it. This is what I came up with."

The enlarged image revealed three figures emerging from the helicopter. They were headed up to the bridge.

Spinner leaned in. "Can you magnify the image more?"

Beau clicked on a key until the images almost filled the screen. Spinner strained his eyes to discern the blurry, pixelated image.

Sweet leaned in to get a look. "Got an ID?"

"When I was taken to the *Maru*, I saw that helicopter on the foredeck. Yoshimatsu's on that ship." Spinner clapped Beau on the back. "You did good, Beau. Real good."

Spinner turned his gaze to Oliver Sweet. "Feel up to a little midnight cruise?"

"Damn straight."

Spinner turned back to the image on the computer screen and burned it into his brain. "I'm coming for you, assholes."

# 70

The last reddish rays of the sunset were fading in the west as the indigo canopy of night crept slowly earthward. The RIB was sitting in the water at the tide line, loaded with the explosives and dive gear.

Rosen watched as Spinner made the final check on the SCUBA diving rebreather. There wasn't much to say at this point. Rosen remained silent as the two men prepared for the mission. It was all matter-of-fact, each man checking and rechecking gear. Conversation was kept to a minimum.

Oliver Sweet, dressed in a black, neoprene dive suit peeled down to the waist, placed a long, waterproof bag into the RIB. His massive sculpted torso gleamed with sweat from the exertion of loading the boat.

"That's about everything, I do believe. How're you doing over there, Jake?"

"Been a while since I checked out a rebreather," Spinner said. "I think we're good to go."

He retrieved his wetsuit from the inflatable, stripped naked, and put it on, tying the arms of the wetsuit around his waist as Sweet had done. Working in a full wetsuit in sub-tropical Mexico could overheat a person in no time.

"Wait a minute," said Sweet. He reached into a dry bag and located a small container. He tossed it to Spinner. "Time to paint up that lily-white face of yours, Jake."

Spinner laughed. He took two fingers and dipped them into the greasepaint, smearing the camouflage paint over his face, neck, and hands. When he was done, only the whites of his eyes were visible behind the mask.

"That's a good look on you," Sweet said. "You could almost pass for one of the brothers."

A small entourage of people walked toward them. In the gathering darkness, Spinner recognized Raúl, Sandy, Paola, Graham, and Arturo. Alejandro brought up the rear, slowed by his lame right leg in the sand.

Raúl reached into the waistband of his trousers and produced Spinner's Beretta. "I think you may need this more than I do."

"Thanks." Spinner took the pistol and slipped it into his dry bag.

"Wish I was going with you guys," said Graham. "Nothing I'd like better than to see that damn ship light up the night sky."

"You're needed here more," said Spinner. "Tomorrow, you all are going to be the ones to throw the wrench into the works. Remember, they don't think we're going to be there. Get in, throw the bombs, and then move back. Alex, keep everyone back until you get the word. Do not go in until the sentries have been neutralized."

Snake, who up until then, had been sitting on a wooden crate nearby, smoking a cigar said, "Boss, it sure seems like a waste of a good helicopter to keep me on the beach for the fireworks."

"I thought Castellano told you to get your ass back there after you unloaded us. He didn't say anything about using his asset in the operation."

"Can't leave yet," Snake flashed a gap-toothed grin. "Got a problem with the stabilizer that needs to be checked out. Won't be able to complete repairs until tomorrow afternoon."

"You know he's going to ride my ass about that."

"Better yours than mine," said Snake.

Alejandro stepped forward. "Good luck, Jake, Ollie."

"I'll be in regular radio contact with Beau to make sure the *Shodokai Maru* is still where she's supposed to be." Spinner turned toward Rosen. "I guess we're ready."

"I really hate this shit, Spinner. It seems like all we ever do is say goodbye to each other."

"Keep your head down tomorrow. They have more firepower than last time and Yoshimatsu will do whatever it takes to finish the hunt. Keep back and try to disrupt the banger boats as they drive the animals in. I'll get there as soon as I can. If everything goes according to plan, Ollie is going to lay down a line of fire to get us to the barricade."

Rosen suddenly understood the significance of the elongated waterproof bag that Sweet had placed into the RIB.

"Don't let him do anything stupid," Rosen called over to Sweet. "He has a penchant for that, you know."

Sweet grinned. "Yes, ma'am."

Spinner pointed a thumb toward Sweet. "Yeah, but who's going to watch him?"

"Gotta fly, Jake. Kiss the girl quick."

Rosen leapt into Spinner's embrace. Their kiss was long and passionate with the desperation of not knowing if they would ever see each other again. When Spinner set her down, her cheeks and chin were smeared black from the tears and greasepaint. Spinner smiled.

"I love you, Em."

"Damn you, Spinner. You come back to me, or I swear I'll hunt you down and kick your ass." She kissed him gently one last time, then abruptly let him go.

Together, the two men pushed from either side of the bow until the sand released its grip on the inflatable. They jumped in as the RIB glided backward into the bay. Sweet went to the stern and set the shaft of the outboard into the water. He fired up the motor. They disappeared into the darkness. Rosen stayed on the beach looking seaward until the last sounds of the outboard had faded into the night.

Sandy sidled up to her and put a hand on her shoulder. "You okay?"

Rosen quickly wiped her eyes with one hand. "I'm a first-class fool. I'm in love with an alcoholic, PTSD, adrenaline-junkie who seems to be hell-bent on killing himself in the most grandiose manner imaginable."

"Well, nobody's perfect, Rosen."

She snorted, then began to laugh. "The hell of it is—when he leaves like that, I feel like someone just used a dull knife to cut out a large chunk of my heart."

"Love stinks." Sandy gave Emily a sidelong hug.

Raúl approached them and, seeing how distraught Emily was, stopped in his tracks. "Is this not a good time?"

"No, it's fine Raúl. Too little sleep and a case of nerves. I'm okay," said Rosen.

"Alejandro wants each of the teams to meet one more time and go over the plan."

Raúl headed for Jesús's fishing shack. Emily and Sandy watched his back as he trudged up the beach.

"If it's any consolation," Sandy said, turning back to Rosen, "I haven't been able to sleep much either. The idea of someone shooting at me again—well, not the stuff of sweet dreams, if you know what I mean."

Back at the shack, Alejandro made each group tick off their assignments for the hunt. Each member recited their individual responsibility, safety precautions, and what to do in case of a crippled boat, injuries, or other possible scenarios.

Alejandro turned to Arturo, who was sitting next to Paola. "Tell me about the emergency field hospital setup."

"I have instructed Dora in basic triage, CPR, and first aid techniques," said Arturo. "If necessary, I will come back in from the hunt to treat more serious injuries and get them ready for transport to the hospital in La Paz. Snake has volunteered the helicopter for emergency evacuations of the seriously wounded." He glanced at Paola. "If it's okay with the group, I'd like to at least do my part with Paola to stop the whalers."

Snake had been sitting in the back of Jesús's shack, sipping on a lukewarm beer. He said to Alejandro, "If there is an emergency, call me ASAP. We'll coordinate between the wounded and Arturo and get them to La Paz."

"The boats launch at 0400 hours, roughly an hour and a half before sunrise," said Alejandro. "The whalers should be herding their catch toward El Infierno Cove by mid-morning. Our objective is to disrupt the boats far enough out to scatter the whales and avoid the shooters stationed on the cliffs at the cove."

As the group dispersed, Snake walked up to the table where Alejandro sat talking to Sandy and Graham.

"'Scuse me, Boss," he half-squinted at Alejandro. "But I didn't get a good sense of where you're plannin' on being during this little *soirée* tomorrow."

Alejandro looked aggravated. "I'm going to coordinate the teams from here," he said. "I wouldn't be of much use on a boat, as you can see."

"Can't see much from this beach," mused Snake. "What say you to a little helicopter ride tomorrow morning? Might be a good way to see what you're up against, and I can't think of a better vantage point to call the shots."

"I thought Spinner said you had to get the helicopter back tomorrow," said Sandy, looking suspiciously at the Cajun.

"A few hours, one way or the other, ain't going to make much difference. Besides, I'd kinda like to see what's goin' on over there. Having a helicopter as your mobile command post ain't something those bastard whalers are expecting."

"Why are you doing this? You don't owe us anything," said Sandy.

"You're right about that, darlin'," Snake said. "But I just can't let y'all go on out there and have all the fun."

Alejandro asked, "What's your fuel situation? What if we need an emergency evacuation?"

"Already figured that in," Snake scratched at his weeklong beard growth. "I believe I have enough for two or three good passes, then a touchdown one or two times to pick up wounded before we have to skedaddle outta there."

"Okay," said Alejandro. "I'm in."

"Just one last thing," Snake said, his eyes flickering in the lantern's light. "There will be no puking in my helicopter."

Alejandro half-smiled. "I'll try to remember that."

# 71

Oliver Sweet steered the RIB in a northwesterly direction while Spinner sat hunkered down on the deck, his back supported by the pontoon. He kept an eye on the GPS in one hand, while his cell phone, protected by a waterproof case, was in the other. In another waterproof case, a VHF radio hung from a lanyard around his neck.

Fortunately, there were stars overhead that gave subtle illumination to the seascape. Otherwise, they'd be bouncing around in total blackness. Late afternoon winds building out of the west had whipped the ocean into a churning maelstrom of six-foot rollers. Both men wore wet suits, but, even so, along with all the gear in the boat, they were thoroughly soaked. They barely spoke as Sweet tried to maintain course while tacking against the waves. Spinner kept his eyes glued to the GPS, yelling out instructions over the sound of the motor and the wind when Ollie needed to make course corrections.

The plan was to bring the inflatable boat to within a mile of the *Shodokai Maru* and then swim the explosive devices to the mother whaling ship. The last leg was to be underwater on SCUBA. Each man would be carrying a satchel of C-4 and detonators. Once they got to the hull, Ollie would attach explosives near mid-ship and Spinner would concentrate his charges below the engine room and near the stern.

Sweet cast a glance at Spinner. He didn't appear to be in any distress, but here was a man about to go into a combat situation when, not even two weeks ago, he had been shot twice and almost died at sea. The swim was going to be arduous by any standards, but now the Gulf of California had decided to add in a gargantuan rinse cycle. Yet, Castellano had said you could not find a better man to have your back when everything turned to shit.

Spinner held up a hand. "Twenty degrees starboard," he yelled, above the sound of the motor and wind.

Sweet made a slight course correction and the RIB churned ahead. Due to the change in conditions, they would not arrive at the location of the whaling ship until after midnight.

After another hour had passed, Spinner pulled out his cell phone and bent down low over it to make a call. His fingers were stiff from the cold water, and he could barely hear over the sound of the wind.

When Beau finally picked up, Spinner could hardly hear him. "You have to speak up! I can't hear you!"

"How about now?" Beau yelled into the phone. In the fishing shack, all the lights had been turned out and everyone was asleep or, at least, trying to sleep. Several people grumbled in their beds and turned over. A few of the Cetus Alliance activists sat up in their sleeping bags and attempted to listen in.

"Better. Status?"

"No movement. I repeat, no movement!"

"Thanks, Beau. Keep me posted." Spinner disconnected.

He raised his head and peered at Oliver Sweet and gave him a thumbs up. "She hasn't moved."

Ollie brought the boat around into the face of a wave that threatened to broach them. The wave passed beneath the boat and the propeller caught again after it connected with the water. As the boat slammed into the trough, Spinner hung onto the boat handles.

The ride was wet and cold. Time seemed to drag on until both men were lulled into a state of near stupor. At one point, Spinner felt his entire body cramp. He tried to straighten his legs but they didn't respond. Finally, he had to manually push his knees straight into the floor of the RIB.

Oliver Sweet was beginning to feel the effects of the pounding waves, spray, and cold. Picking up on his discomfort, Spinner slowly came to all fours and then onto one knee.

"How 'bout I drive for awhile?"

"Nah, I'm good, Jake."

"Bullshit. Your face looks like someone put a scorpion in your skivvies. Besides, I could use a change of scenery."

Sweet nodded. They traded places. Jake handed him the cell phone and VHF radio.

"Stay on that heading," said Sweet. "I'll keep an eye out from here." He sat back and leaned against the inflatable chamber and tried to stretch out in the cramped boat. "Next time I volunteer for an assignment like this, you have my permission to shoot me."

"Next time." A half-smile crossed Spinner's salt-stung lips.

When Spinner next looked at his watch, two more hours had passed. He and Sweet both observed that the seas were starting to calm, the winds dying down to a mild breeze. Sweet had made the last call to Beau forty minutes earlier and was informed that the *Shodokai Maru* was still anchored in the same location.

They skirted an island bordered by steep cliffs and concealed themselves and their boat in the black shadow of the island. Sweet moved forward and located the anchor. Holding the coils of rope in one hand, he lowered it to the bottom.

Spinner killed the motor and let the RIB drift against the anchor's resistance in the blackness. After the noise of the wind and the waves and the motor straining against the angry sea, the relative calmness of the sea was unnerving. Spinner checked his GPS coordinates against Beau's most recent satellite position.

"By my reading, we're about a mile from the *Maru*," Jake said quietly.

"We're on the same page," said Sweet.

Silently, the two men began to prepare their equipment. A small inner tube was inflated and dropped over the side. The charges were placed in a mesh net within the tube. They donned their rebreathers, fins, and masks, and slipped into the black water. Spinner felt the cold flush of water between his skin and the wetsuit and immediately felt he was being dragged downward. He inflated his Buoyancy Compensator Device until his head rested comfortably above the water's surface. Oliver Sweet came alongside Spinner and both men held onto the inner tube for a moment.

"Ready?"

"Ready." Spinner tied the GPS to the inner tube with the LED face toward him. "That way," he pointed.

They kicked their legs and methodically pushed the inner tube laden with explosives into the darkness.

*The matriarch sensed a presence in the water. The group of dolphins had been resting in a shallow bay on the leeward side of the island. It was not as if she had tasted the essence of the man on the currents funneling into the bay. It was more a sense that he was nearby. And there was a feeling of dread. The man was moving toward the killing ship.*

*The young calf who rested at her side picked up on his mother's sudden tension. He nuzzled against her for assurance, patting and touching his pectoral fin to hers.*

*Galvanized into action, the female emitted a series of sharp whistles, alerting the rest of the matriarchal subgroup. Leading the other dolphins, she swam off in the direction of the Ship of Death.*

The winds had died down to almost nothing. Because of this, they swam more easily through the capillary waves. Although physically stronger than he was two weeks ago, the long swim was taking a toll on Spinner. His legs cramped continually, causing them to have to stop long enough for Spinner to stretch his hamstrings and calf muscles.

Oliver Sweet looked at him. "You okay, Jake?"

"Yeah, just ducky," Spinner said through gritted teeth, as he pulled the tip of his fin toward his chest. "I picked one hell of a time to quit drinking."

"Do you need to rest?" Although he didn't say as much, Spinner knew that Oliver Sweet had some concerns about his ability to carry out the mission.

"No. I'm okay. Keep going."

The masks they wore were fitted with audio capabilities, enabling them to talk to one another underwater in the darkness while they set the charges. Right now, the microphones were turned off to save the batteries. These would only be activated after they were on final approach to the mother ship. Once they arrived at their target, they had twenty minutes to place the explosives and get clear of the ship. Any number of things could go wrong. If Spinner were anywhere near the props if the ship started up, he would quickly be turned into chum. They had no idea how many guards would be posted on the night watch. Spinner figured security would be beefed up with Yoshimatsu on board. Even though they were operating under the blanket of darkness, an errant shot into the water could mean a painful death.

Spinner massaged his calf muscle, and they resumed finning, pushing the loaded inner tube toward the mother ship.

They hadn't traveled fifteen minutes when a disturbance in the water up ahead made them stop.

"What the fuck? Did you see that?"

"Just something splashing up ahead is all I could see."

A scythe-like fin cut the surface of the water a few meters off to Sweet's left. He spun quickly to face the menace. Another fin appeared in front of Spinner, then disappeared into the black sea.

"God damn it! Sharks!" Sweet spun all the way around in panic. "I fucking hate sharks!"

Spinner felt something brush against his thigh, sending his heart into his throat. Then he heard them. The distinctive whistles and clicks of bottlenose dolphins. He didn't know how or why, but inwardly he knew the old matriarch and her family had found them.

"It's okay, Ollie. They're friends of mine."

"Friends of yours? You keep some very strange company, Spinner."

"They're bottlenose dolphins. After I jumped off the *Maru*, they found me. I was just about shark bait when they intervened. They carried me on their backs to shore."

"You're shittin' me." Sweet turned around quickly as a dolphin made another pass.

"True story. If it wasn't for them, I would have been part of the food chain."

Then something very strange happened. The dolphins grouped together and began swimming frantically back and forth in front of the men and the inner tube. Several times, a dolphin would surface and push the inner tube backward with its rostrum, their whistles growing more frantic.

"What the hell?" He tried to push the inner tube forward, but with each stroke of his fins, the dolphins pushed harder against the inner tube.

"Hold on, Ollie," Spinner said, releasing his grip from the inner tube. "I think I know what they're trying to get us to do. They're trying to protect us from that ship."

"Now how would they know about that ship?"

Spinner put the regulator in his mouth and began to breathe. He let some of the air out of his BCD and slowly sank below the surface. Sweet, who was both terrified and curious, said, "Oh, no you don't." He followed Spinner down.

Spinner hovered in a horizontal attitude about eight feet down. Sweet could barely make him out in the darkness, but he could sense the many large forms surrounding him in a tight circle, some just below him. Sweet had a flashlight attached to his BCD but dared not turn it on. As his eyes grew accustomed to the darkness, he was able to see a little more clearly due to light cast by the stars overhead.

Now he could make out the forms of dolphins. A large dolphin hung suspended in the water not more than a foot or two from Spinner's face. Sweet observed a younger dolphin just beneath her and assumed it was her calf. The water was filled with whistles, chirps and clicks. Spinner didn't move. He almost looked like he was sleeping.

Sweet felt as if he had just been transported to an alien world, a witness to a first contact between two completely different species. He felt an odd sensation—a pinging, at his sternum—and realized the dolphins were echolocating on him. Mesmerized by the chorus of sounds, he was overcome by something he had never before experienced.

Spinner stirred and moved slightly, rising about six inches in the water, then sinking back down. The large dolphin moved forward slowly, resting her melon under Spinner's outstretched hand. The calf came close and did the same.

Then, with a powerful flip of her large flukes, the female shot forward, the other dolphins following like an array of fusiform missiles being launched into the blackness. The high-pitched vocalizations faded into the night.

Spinner and Sweet rose to the surface and removed their regulators. Sweet eyed Spinner. "What did I just see?"

"Don't tell me how, but that old girl and her sisters knew we were here. They were trying to keep us from going too close to the whaler."

"How do you know that?"

"Because she told me."

Sweet stared at Spinner for a moment then burst into a low deep laugh. "Jesus H. Christ. I'm on a suicide mission in the middle of the night, in the middle of the ocean with Dr. Fucking Doolittle."

Spinner resumed pushing the inner tube. Sweet joined in, and together they swam with a renewed urgency.

After several minutes of finning, Sweet said, "Hey? We make it out of here, can you teach me to do that?"

"You'll have to get in line. Raúl's daughter and Rosen asked me first."

Ako Kanamura stood at the railing of the *Shodokai Maru's* bow, staring down at the large forms swimming in and out of the shadows. Some of the crew members had informed him earlier that some large sharks were hanging around the whaling ship, awaiting the next flensing and processing.

He pulled a pack of cigarettes out of his pocket and lit one. He was irritable tonight. It was something he didn't experience often. He was a man who was always prepared for any situation. He'd work out the details long before the operation took place. Just like his boss, he didn't like surprises. The tension in his neck and shoulders only seemed to exacerbate his irritation.

Something was wrong. He could feel it. It was an intangible sensation, a niggling at the edges of his consciousness. Searching his memory, he reviewed the details. The plan was unfolding as Yoshimatsu had predicted. Still, he worried.

He was to supervise the entire operation from the cove. For the last twelve years, he had remained at Yoshimatsu's side—no matter the occasion. He felt uncomfortable about not being able to protect the man to whom he had pledged his loyalty so many years before.

Yoshimatsu and that reptile, Izumi, would be on the banger boats herding a large pod of dolphins that had been discovered yesterday. These four banger boats would be deployed from the *Shodokai Maru* in a few hours. Kanamura was to make sure the other four boats from Puerto Nacimiento would be on their way, each carrying an armed guard to keep the locals in line.

The situation in the village was deteriorating rapidly. There were more desertions every day. The longer they remained here, the greater the risk of discovery.

And then there was the matter of Minister Alfonso Figueroa. He hadn't been heard from in the past twenty-four hours. Kanamura had known that the Fisheries Minister could lose his nerve anytime. He had seen Figueroa's type again and again—all swagger and self-importance, but quick to turn when their positions were at risk.

The water below erupted into a churning caldron. In the dim light, Kanamura saw a glint of silver. At least the ship was safe here. No one in their right mind would come near this ship in the dark, given the deadly predators that had become incidental guardians. Still, Kanamura couldn't shake the feeling that something was about to go horribly wrong.

The silhouette of the *Shodokai Maru* finally came into view. It was nearly imperceptible in the darkness. The only way they detected it was the break in continuity of stars on the horizon. There was just a large empty black space at the confluence of the sky and the sea.

"Down from here," said Spinner. "Do you see running lights?"

"Yeah, I think so," said Ollie. "Wheelhouse, do you think?"

"My guess."

The two men reached into the inner tube and removed the satchels that carried the explosives. Spinner immediately felt the weight of the explosive devices pulling him downward. He quickly filled his BCD with more air until his head was just above surface level. After Sweet had secured his bag of explosives with detonators, he produced his combat knife and punctured the inner tube from underneath. They activated the mask communication system, released air from the BCDs and descended to thirty feet.

Once they achieved neutral buoyancy, they set their compasses to the coordinates of the ship and swam in that direction. Their pace was steady, but Spinner was already feeling the strain from the additional weight of the C-4 charges.

"How're you doing, Spinner?" Ollie spoke into the mask com.

"Slow below the surface, *poco a poco*."

It took nearly twenty-five minutes before they arrived at the massive hull of the *Shodokai Maru*. They were near the bow of the ship, its outline barely visible in the darkness.

Above them, several low-intensity lights illuminated patches of water. Fish swam in and out of the light, searching for prey that had been attracted to the light for the same reason.

"Stay away from the light," Spinner said.

"Synchronizing. I have 0043."

Spinner looked at his watch, then reset it. "0043," he said into the mic. "We meet back at the stern at 0113."

"Affirmative."

They began swimming down the length of the whaling ship. Spinner felt a constant downward pull on his body from the weight of the explosives. His legs were starting to cramp again. They had not gone far when they both noticed movement in the shadows ahead of them.

"Did you see that? Did the dolphins follow us to the boat?"

Spinner peered into the shimmering curtain of darkness. "Those aren't dolphins." His voice was tense. "Those are sharks. A lot of sharks."

"Oh, shit," said Sweet. "Where the hell did all those sharks come from?"

"Best easy meal for miles around. They're feeding off the remains of the butchered whales."

"What do we do now?"

"Keep your finning even and slow," said Spinner. "No flailing or jerky movements. If one gets too close, punch it in the nose."

"Seriously? You want me to cold cock a shark?"

"And one more thing. No bleeding."

"Right."

They drew closer together and swam in slow, broad fin strokes, turning their heads and scanning the sides, above and below. Spinner was no expert on sharks, but, in the gloom, he recognized hammerheads and some smaller sharks—probably blues or silkies. They were swimming slowly in and out of the shadow cast by the *Shodokai Maru*. A large form materialized out of the darkness and slowly headed for them. Ollie and Jake froze in the water column.

The shark was huge, passing within ten feet of them, its caudal fin moving back and forth slowly. Spinner knew instinctively that he was face-to-face with the largest tiger shark he had ever seen. He eyeballed the distance between the dorsal fin and the caudal fin and mentally calculated fourteen feet total length.

The shark passed them and disappeared into the blackness. Spinner realized he had been holding his breath—not the smartest thing to do at thirty feet. He exhaled quickly into his rebreather and attempted to breathe normally.

"I think my balls just disappeared into my body cavity and are heading north toward my throat," Ollie said.

"Given our present situation," Spinner said, as a six-foot shortfin mako shark swam in front of him, "that might not be a bad thing."

They moved along the hull as the sharks passed by, curious about the new arrivals. Several times, individuals would swim by close enough to touch, but then they would veer off. The men arrived at the section of the hull where Sweet was to place his charges. "Don't be trying to be no shark whisperer, Jake. Set those damn charges and let's get the fuck out of here."

"No worries there. See you at the stern."

Spinner continued slow finning toward the noise that was building. When he thought the noise was at its loudest level, he stopped. He knew he was below the engine room. Even though the ship's engines weren't running, the generators were still carrying out basic ship functions. He spun slowly in a 360-degree circle, checking for any unwanted visitors. For now, the sharks were keeping their distance.

He retrieved the first charge from the satchel. The magnets held it fast to the hull. He activated the charge and set the timer. The detonation was scheduled for the following evening, once the *Shodokai Maru* was en route back to Japan.

He was about to swim to the second placement when he felt that old familiar prickling at the base of his neck. He spun around and saw an immense form fill his field of vision. The tiger shark passed within inches of him, nearly causing him to lose his grip on the C-4 charge.

The shark melted into the darkness again. Spinner figured that the shark was testing him, sizing him up. He wondered if this was the shark that had tried to turn him into lunch a few weeks ago and now wanted to come in for the final course.

"Ah, shit!"

Out of his peripheral vision on the left, Spinner caught movement. He turned just in time to see the giant shark accelerating toward him. Instinctively, he brought the bag of explosives up in front of him, clasped firmly in both hands. The shark was upon him, so Spinner did the only thing he could do given his situation. He smashed the bag of C-4 into the shark's snout.

The impact pushed him back against the hull. The shark, not expecting such a solid blow to a highly sensitive area, immediately veered off to the side and disappeared into the night.

Sweet's voice came over the mask communicator. "Spinner, are you okay?" His tone smacked of someone who was seconds away from losing it.

"I'm okay. That tiger shark was thinking I might be tonight's blue plate special. I convinced him otherwise."

"Oh, that's just great," said Sweet. "Now, he's probably coming to this side of the buffet for dark meat."

Spinner performed some deep breathing exercises and regained his composure. He moved across the underside of the hull to the starboard side. He could still hear the thrumming of the auxiliary engines. He lifted the two charges out of their bag and pushed them against the hull, placing detonators in them.

He set the timer for the second explosive and began moving toward the stern. Moments later the large propellers came into view. He moved to the ship's port side—but still out of sight from the surface—and waited.

After what seemed like an eternity, he checked his watch. Ollie was overdue by a minute.

"Hey, Sweet, you still with me?"

It took several seconds before Sweet replied. "Yeah, be there in a minute. Couldn't get the last timer to set. It's okay now."

Spinner saw a figure appear out of the dark sea. Sweet swam up to him. "Well, I've had about as much fun as I'm going to have here. Thanks for a lifetime of nightmares."

"I think we're going to have to throw out our wetsuits," said Spinner.

"True that."

They checked their GPS for the return route and began swimming toward the RIB. Their pace was much quicker on the way back, but Spinner couldn't keep himself from checking behind him every few minutes, anticipating a large mouth with lots of serrated teeth closing in on him.

Finally, Sweet broke the silence. "Hey, Jake?"

"Yeah?"

"Castellano and Rosen were right. Hanging around with you is no picnic."

# 72

The sound of footsteps on the steel deck snapped Kanamura back to the present. One of the *Maru's* crew members approached tentatively. The young man bowed perfunctorily.

"Sir, it is time. Your transport is awaiting."

Kanamura glanced at his watch. It was 2:00 a.m. He followed the crewman back to the stern and descended to the lower deck. A group of men were gathered there, all wearing foul weather jackets and life vests. The deck reeked of coagulated blood, blubber, and rendered flesh. Kanamura spotted Yoshimatsu speaking to Captain Watabe. Sato Izumi stood nearby, his skeletal face pallid under the harsh lights. He was clearly seasick.

"Are you ready?"

"I have some concerns, Hiro-san. If I'm to manage the proceedings at the cove, then you are left exposed out at sea."

"It is all right, my friend. Once the animals are safely in the pens, I will join you for the rest of the operation. I want to supervise the hunt from the boat. I need you at the cove to make sure everyone is ready, from the processing and transport trucks, to the flensing and transport teams on the ground. I trust you—and you alone—to make the operation work flawlessly."

Kanamura looked from Yoshimatsu to Izumi, who suddenly turned another shade of green. Groaning, he bolted toward the rail and promptly emptied his stomach contents over the rail.

"This should prove to be an interesting day," Yoshimatsu mused.

Kanamura turned toward Watabe. "Captain, I want you to post extra guards until sunrise. Have them keep close watch on the sea and especially any strange activity near the ship"

Watabe looked at Kanamura questioningly. "We're in the middle of the Gulf of California, at night. Have you seen the waters around the ship? It's teeming

437

with sharks. No one would be foolhardy enough to attempt to approach the ship under those conditions."

"Just a feeling," said Kanamura. He looked at his superior, and their eyes met.

Yoshimatsu turned back to the captain. "Captain, I have known this man for a very long time. I trust his instincts. Think of it as a minor, but necessary, precaution."

Watabe bowed. "Yes, sir. I will post extra guards."

"Good luck, gentlemen," said Yoshimatsu. "In a few days, we will all be wealthy men, having completed a monumental, yet lucrative, task."

Izumi rejoined the group and Yoshimatsu and the others moved to the platform where the launches awaited. A sleek launch was waiting for Kanamura. It would deliver him to the cove quickly to oversee operations before the banger boats arrived.

Yoshimatsu climbed into the banger boat. The crew was to be composed of the driver, the banger, and an armed crew member from the *Maru*. Sato Izumi was to be in another banger boat. Yoshimatsu had insisted that Sato be able to assess the situation from another vessel. Besides, he didn't wish to watch Sato puking his guts out for the duration of the hunt.

Kanamura climbed into the launch. It was going to be a long, cold, and bumpy ride.

# 73

Emily Rosen walked into Jesús's fishing shack. The only light was the illumination from Beau's computer screen. She had finally given up on getting any sleep after tossing and turning for several hours. Her mind was reeling and it wouldn't let her rest. Spinner and Sweet's dangerous mission and the upcoming hunt had consumed her thoughts.

Sleeping bodies were scattered throughout the small cabin. She had to watch her step as she navigated her way around the somnolent forms on the floor. Beau was sitting at the kitchen table, hunkered down over the computer. His hair was tousled, and his head rested in his hands.

Spinner's last transmission was at 11:42 p.m. They had located the *Shodokai Maru* and were one mile away from their target about to make the arduous swim. That was nearly four hours ago.

She approached the table and saw that Beau had drifted off to sleep. She looked down at the screen, but couldn't make out any images. Worried, she gently shook Beau's shoulder.

He snapped awake as if he'd been hit with an electric charge. "What the—?"

"It's okay, Beau. It's me, Emily. I was just checking to see if you heard anything from Spinner and Sweet?"

Beau looked around in confusion. His eyes were red and his eyelids looked swollen. "Jesus, I think I'm hallucinating. How long was I out?"

"Not sure. I couldn't sleep, so I thought I'd keep you company. Any word?"

Beau rubbed his eyes and yawned. "Nada. Nothing since before midnight."

"You want me to spell you for a bit? Maybe a little sack time before the main event?"

"That's okay, Emily. I'm okay now. Thanks. After today, I'll sleep for a week."

He peered at the screen and then made some adjustments to the settings for the satellite image. The program had the equivalent of night vision optics, so even in the dark, an image of the *Shodokai Maru* materialized out of the ether.

"Still there," said Beau. "Whatever Mr. Spinner and Mr. Sweet were planning on doing to that boat, it's still there."

Rosen stared at the image of the whaling ship. "Where the hell are you, Spinner?"

After Rosen had fetched a fresh cup of black coffee for Beau, she walked the distance to Carlos's cabin. Lights were on and it looked like there was activity within. She knocked lightly. Carlos answered the door.

Seated at the kitchen table were the core members of the group. Dora and Cecelia were in the kitchen making tortillas and cooking eggs. The rich smell of coffee filled the small room.

Sandy looked up from her coffee. "Couldn't sleep either?"

Rosen shook her head. "Too wired."

Dora placed a steaming cup of coffee in Emily's hands. She smiled at Jesús's wife and thanked her. She took a sip. "I'm not sure I really need this right now."

"Any word from Jake?" Alejandro was worried.

"Not since before midnight. I just checked in with Beau. The *Shodokai Maru* is still there."

"Do you think something happened to them? Maybe they were spotted," said Graham.

"No, they weren't seen," said Emily. "Jake Spinner is very good at one thing. The U.S. government trained him specifically for these kinds of operations. They may have had problems with the devices."

"I still don't understand why they're not blowing that ship out of the water where she sits," said Arturo. "That would put an end to this mess once and for all."

"Three reasons," said Emily. "First, Jake wants the *Shodokai Maru* to be as far away as possible before he detonates the charges. He doesn't want any of the village fishermen nearby when the boat detonates. Second, if it goes down in deep water, it's going to be very difficult to determine what caused it to sink. Third, he doesn't want any of us to be implicated should the authorities come after us. If the Mexican authorities link any of us to the operation, it's going to be a long stretch in a Mexican prison."

The atmosphere in the room grew somber as the weight of the implications of their plan fully sunk in.

"Since no one else wants to address the elephant in the room, I guess that leaves it up to me," said Graham. "Just how are we going to get past the armed guards? They're going to be shooting at us—real bullets. We may be able to slow the boats, but as soon as we get close to the pens, they're going to slice through us like butter."

"Jake told me he had that all worked out," said Emily.

Sandy looked exasperated. "Well, did he provide you with any details, Emily? I'm not used to going into a dangerous situation on blind faith."

"I'm sorry, Sandy. Sometimes Spinner is a little short on details. I believe he and Sweet have a plan. We're just going to have to accept it as fact that they've got all the contingencies covered."

"No wonder most of us didn't get any sleep," said Arturo.

"So, we stick to the plan," said Alejandro.

By 4:00 a.m., the entire camp was awake and bustling with activity. The boats were fueled and loaded with the butyric acid bombs and tear gas grenades. Each activist met with their respective teams and went over their assignments one last time. Excitement coursed through the camp, masking the fear and anxiety of the events to unfold in the next few hours.

Francisco and several other fishermen were still making last minute changes on the additional reinforcements to the boats. The lights from the machine shop had been burning throughout the night as they worked feverishly to modify the pangas. Sheets of metal salvaged from old car hoods had been attached to the gunwales to provide some protection, albeit scant, to the activists throwing the tear gas and butyric acid. The vessels had taken on a surreal appearance. They now resembled Chinese junks more than Mexican fishing boats. The outboards were checked and extra cans of gas were stored under the seats.

Rosen busied herself checking through her photographic equipment one last time, making sure all batteries were charged. All cameras and lenses were wrapped in waterproof bags and arranged for easy access in a large, zippered, waterproof duffel, courtesy of Castellano and Las Altas.

She felt a tight knot in her gut unlike any she had experienced before. She wondered if this was what Spinner felt every time just before he was to go into battle. She knew, if she didn't keep herself busy, that feeling could be all consuming. Dora brought her a plate of eggs, beans, and tortillas. She could only down a few bites. Her stomach was doing too many flip-flops to eat.

Satisfied she had done all she could to safeguard her photographic equipment, Rosen shouldered the duffel and walked out into the pre-dawn light back to Jesús's fishing shack and stepped inside the cramped space. All the teams were already crammed into the room. Some of the occupants engaged in last minute conversations, but the atmosphere was solemn.

Diane, one of the young women from Cetus Alliance, was in the corner talking to Graham and Sandy. She looked distraught. Graham placed a hand on her shoulder in reassurance. She nodded.

Raúl moved through the crowd to stand near Beau, who still sat at the kitchen table. Rosen joined them.

Raúl looked at her and smiled. "How are you holding up?"

"I don't mind telling you, I'm scared shitless," said Emily.

"If it's any consolation, so am I."

From the front, Alejandro called out, "Attention everyone!" Several people whistled and others hushed their neighbors. The room went silent. He looked around the room. "Are all teams ready?" He looked to the different team leaders. "Spinner and Sweet are already out there in Orca 1. Graham? Sandy?"

Sandy spoke up. "Orca 2 is ready. I'm the designated driver. Graham and Brittany will be throwing the bombs. After Spinner secures the barrier, we'll move in close and help pull it down. Once inside the barrier, our job is to help move the dolphins toward the breaches in the nets."

Alejandro nodded. He turned his attention to Raúl and Rosen. "Orca 3?"

"*This Side Up* will flank the banger boats and scatter the dolphins and whales in front of them," said Raúl. "Morgan will be throwing for us and Emily will be recording."

Alejandro went down the list of assignments for the remaining teams. Orca 4 was composed of Arturo, Jesús, and Paola. Brad, Carlos, and Francisco were Orca 5. Fernando Quintín, Manuel Soto, and Diane were Orca 6. The last, Orca 7, was Ruben Diaz and Luis Acosta. Only the boats retrofitted with extra shielding were to commit to the attack on the barrier. The others were to hang back until the barrier came down. Alejandro hesitated for a moment, making eye contact with everyone in the room.

"Remember. Under no circumstances do any of you approach the barrier until Spinner and Sweet have secured it. I do not want anyone risking their lives needlessly."

Alejandro moved his gaze around the fishing shack. "I'll be coordinating from the air, thanks to Mr. Robideaux, who has generously loaned us the use of his helicopter."

All eyes turned to Snake leaning against the back wall of the shack. He tipped his hat and smiled laconically.

Alejandro said, "Keep all your radios tuned to channel twenty-one. Snake and I will keep you apprised of developments on the water as they happen." He scanned the room again. "Any questions? Now's the time to ask. If anyone here is having second thoughts about going on this mission, now's the time to speak up. No one will think badly of you if you want to sit this one out."

Everyone looked around the inside of the shack. Several people fidgeted, but no one raised a hand or stepped forward. Alejandro said. "I just wanted to tell all of you that I'm honored and grateful to have the chance to work with some of the finest people I've ever met. Good luck, everyone. And be careful out there."

The crowd dispersed and began moving toward the door. Rosen caught up with Sandy, who was talking to Alejandro. They both looked grim. She asked, "Is this a bad time?"

"No," said Alejandro. "Diane has backed out. We need to try and fill her spot."

Rosen grimaced. "Is she okay?"

"She got a bad case of nerves at the last minute," said Sandy. "She's very frightened about going out there."

"She can hang back with Beau and coordinate communications," said Alejandro. "I don't want anyone out there who might freeze up at the wrong time."

Sandy asked, "Whose team is she on?"

"Orca 6 with Fernando and Manuel," replied Alejandro. "They're going to have to make do: one driver, one thrower. On a more positive note, I found out that Manuel played some minor league baseball on the mainland a few years back. His throwing arm will be a welcome addition."

Emily pulled a small video camera from her pack and handed it to Alejandro. "You're going to have a bird's eye view of the cove, the banger boats, just about everything. This all needs to be recorded, if you can find some time."

Alejandro nodded. "I can do that. But I could use a quick lesson."

Rosen showed him the on-off control and the indicator lights for record and standby. She demonstrated how to use the telephoto zoom. "You're going to be in a moving, shaking helicopter. Find someplace to steady your shot."

"I think I have this."

Rosen hugged him. "Be careful up there, Alex. Remember who's waiting for you when you get down. Your wife and daughter want to see you in one piece."

"I'm putting myself in Snake's capable hands. Watch yourself out there. And good luck, Emily."

They hugged each other. Rosen broke the embrace and turned to her friend Sandy who said, "Em! Kick some ass out there, girlfriend. Last one on the beach buys the margaritas."

"You're on."

Everyone donned kevlar vests, helmets, and life preservers. The teams made their way down to the beach where the boats were lined up, their bows resting on the sand. There was a flurry of activity as last-minute items were stowed. The newly expanded Cetus Alliance pushed the boats into the water and jumped in the retrofitted pangas, the inflatable, and Jake Spinner's cruiser. The drivers assumed their positions and fired up the motors.

Alejandro watched as the boats headed out to sea. The wives and children of the fishermen stood on the sand in a cluster, watching the departure of their loved ones, their faces stony. Moments later, the boats left the cove, forming a chevron pattern on the water, with Sandy, Graham, and Brittany—Team Orca 2—in the lead.

# 74

From his position on the bow, Yoshimatsu became caught up in the thrill of the hunt. The sea ahead of him roiled with dolphins as far as he could see. Panicked dolphins blasted by the boat, raising rooster tails in the water from their powerful flukes. Groups of four to five dolphins flew out of the water in long arcing leaps, desperate to put as much distance between themselves and the terrifying noise that pursued them.

The whale hunters had located a vast superpod of common dolphins two hours after sunrise. They had traveled north along the coast when a spotter boat had called in the sighting. The whalers estimated that more than four hundred animals were traveling south. Once the drive began, a large group of Pacific bottlenose dolphins were swept up in the stampede. The banger boats fanned out and began their pursuit. The men in the bows began rhythmically banging on the steel pipes that projected down into the water using steel hammers. The formation of boats looked like a large seine net that pushed the panicked animals in front of the deafening sounds.

Many of the dolphins had young with them. Moms and calves were forced to travel near the surface because the little ones needed to breathe more often. Other large pelagic creatures, such as manta rays, sharks, and sea turtles, could dive down into deeper water to escape the horrific noise.

One of the spotter boats had called to report the sighting of a family of short-finned pilot whales on the north end of Isla Lobos. Yoshimatsu ordered one boat to peel off from the flotilla and pursue the black whales.

Once the dolphins were in the pens, the work of wrangling the ones for shipment would take place. This would be very difficult and dangerous. The dolphins would already be stressed and exhausted from the effects of the drive. Many would succumb in the pens, but Yoshimatsu was confident that there would be a good selection of young and desirable live animals for oceanariums, just based on the sheer numbers.

After those were transported to the trucks and secured, the remaining dolphins would be driven onto the beach where the flensing teams would slaughter them, and the meat would be processed and loaded into the refrigerator trucks.

Yoshimatsu barely heard his phone ring. He looked down and saw that the call was from Kanamura. Earlier Kanamura had called from Puerto Nacimiento and informed Yoshimatsu that four more whalers and their families had snuck out under cover of darkness. Because their resources were stretched thin, Kanamura's men could not keep a continuous watch on the whole village. Many of the boatmen and remaining villagers were to be conscripted to perform the dirty work on the beach. If everything went according to plan, by day's end there would be nothing left except remains for the desert scavengers.

Yoshimatsu stepped to the back of the boat to put some distance between his ears and the mind-numbing banging.

"Where are you? Speak loudly!"

"I am at the cove," said Kanamura. Yoshimatsu could barely hear him over the din. "Everyone is in place."

"Are the guards posted in the hills surrounding the cove?"

"Yes. All observation points to the cove are covered by two or three of Figueroa's men. There is no way anyone can get through by coming cross-country."

"Very good," said Yoshimatsu. "Have everyone ready. We are pushing a great many animals toward the cove. We should be there by midmorning."

Yoshimatsu signed off. Kanamura placed his cell phone in his pocket and surveyed the cove. He looked at the curved shoreline of the beach where, just back from the tide line, two large, eighteen-wheel refrigerator trucks were disguised as supermercado trucks from a Mexican grocery chain. Several smaller trucks with canvas sides painted in desert camouflage were parked down near the water's edge. Plastic tarps were spread out near the water's edge where the flensing of the animals was to take place. In the shallows were two smaller holding pens. These would be employed to hold the live dolphins before they were loaded onto the trucks bound for foreign aquariums.

Kanamura knew, because of how quickly they had to move, that there would be a high number of animal deaths due to shock and injury. It was a good thing the scouting boats had located a large pod. He didn't understand why there was such furor in other nations about the capture and consumption of marine mammals. To him, they were just another food source provided by the sea. He thought the sympathy that Western societies had for the whales and dolphins was frivolous and hypocritical. In the United States alone, tens of millions of livestock were killed every year for food, yet they were being condemned for taking a few hundred whales and dolphins for food and entertainment.

Kanamura's cell phone rang. It was one of the banger boat operators. The captain of the launch informed him that they had caught up with the pod of pilot whales and were now driving them toward the cove, along with several other large animals. He reported several turtles and two young whale sharks were also being driven toward the nets. It was shaping up to be a very lucrative day.

Kanamura disconnected and began shouting orders to the attendants gathered around the various stations of the killing cove. Galvanized by Kanamura's orders, they readied themselves for the approaching animals. Finally, Kanamura looked up to the hills and cliffs surrounding El Infierno Cove. He called the lead sentry just to make sure everything was in place. That irritating tingle that resided between his shoulder blades was still there. It hadn't gotten worse, but it had never left him.

When the lead assassin from the Zetas answered, he spoke. "This is Kanamura. Give me your status."

The mercenary, whose name was Huertas, was a large Mexican whose last job had been with the Sinaloa Cartel as a wet work specialist. He'd been trained by the Americans at Fort Bragg, but the cartels paid better than the CIA. A skilled assassin, Huertas was as lethal working with a knife as he was with a high-powered sniper rifle.

"Everyone is in position," said Huertas, with just a hint of a Spanish accent. "We have snipers covering the road into El Infierno and the cliffs and desert on either side of the cove. No one can get in or out without us seeing them. We have easy access to the seaward side of the cove in case anyone tries to attack the barrier wall."

"Good. If you see anything that is not part of the landscape, you know what to do. Understood?"

"Understood," acknowledged Huertas. "No one will penetrate our positions."

Kanamura clicked off. He breathed deeply and inhaled the humid, salty air. Perhaps he was being a little paranoid. Maybe the operation was finally going to come off as originally planned. He just wished he knew where Figueroa was right now. He was the only loose end.

Kanamura turned his attention out to sea. He scanned the horizon for signs of the boats and the massive movement of hundreds of animals being driven toward the nets.

# 75

Spinner and Sweet arrived at their designated location an hour before sunrise. Once they'd gotten back to the RIB, Spinner had contacted Beau by phone and told him to bring up an image of El Infierno cove and the surrounding geography. It took Beau several minutes to access the image. He finally said, "Got it!"

"Beau, I need a scan of the perimeter of the cove. Use infrared and look for sentries. They'll probably be posted at elevations that provide views of targets both in the cove and approaching from the desert."

Several minutes went by as Beau scrutinized the screen. "I have three placements that I can tell for sure."

"I need you to be really sure about this. If the intel is bad, then people are going to die."

"Let me check one more time, Jake. Hang on."

"I'm not going anywhere."

Several more agonizing moments passed. Finally, Beau spoke up. "I've checked every meter of the area surrounding the cove. We have three placements, all on bluffs or elevations. I've got three bad guys on the southern bluff, two on the east ridge, and two more on the west set of hills just past the dunes. I'm sending you the coordinates now, with a real-time photo download."

Jake motioned to Oliver Sweet. "He's sending an image now. Get your laptop ready."

Sweet nodded and pulled his laptop from his waterproof dry bag. "Okay. Good to go here."

"Go ahead and send," said Spinner.

Sweet opened up the file and stared at the screen. Beau had highlighted the figures and the coordinates. Sweet enlarged the image and looked up at Spinner. "Got it."

"You did real good, Beau," said Spinner. "Real good. That intel should give us just the edge we're going to need."

"Jake, can I ask you a question?"

"Sure. What is it?"

"Was your mission a success? I mean the *Shodokai Maru*. It's still there."

"Yeah, I know. After you sign off, keep a close watch on that ship. In a few hours, if everything goes according to plan, you just may get to see something really interesting. Did everyone get off the beach this morning?"

"They're on their way."

"So am I. Keep me posted. Spinner out."

Spinner eased the inflatable onto the beach three miles south of El Infierno Cove. He and Sweet were both dressed in desert camouflage. Their faces still bore the greasepaint from the night before. Sweet retrieved his Accuracy International AX50 sniper rifle from the waterproof case and fitted the scope and suppressor into place. His .40 caliber Glock semi-auto was strapped to his right leg. He donned his Kevlar vest and then shouldered his backpack. Inside, were extra magazines, water, a radio, and a GPS.

Spinner looked at the ominous black rifle. "That's a hell of a peashooter."

Sweet patted the rifle. "This here is Loretta. She's a big girl, but she's got some legs on her. Good up to 2,000 yards."

Spinner let out a low whistle. "How many rounds in a mag?"

"Five .50-caliber rounds. Loretta has another special talent. She just loves to take out engine blocks."

"I guess I don't need to tell you to watch your ass out there."

"No, but thanks for the sentiment just the same." Oliver grinned tersely. He held up his cell phone. "I got you on speed dial."

Spinner nodded. He extended his hand. "It's been a pleasure."

"Indeed, it has." Oliver grasped Jake's hand. "I'll see you down on that beach. Make sure you have lots of Dos Equis on ice when I get there."

"You got it. Good luck, Ollie."

"You, too." The big man rolled off the RIB's pontoon and hit the sand running. Spinner watched him move up the beach, AX50 in hand. Sweet ducked into some darkened mangroves that formed an apron in front of a series of small dunes and soon was invisible in the shadows that preceded the dawn.

Spinner jumped out and pushed the inflatable into deeper water, then climbed back in the boat and turned the ignition. The outboard coughed to life, idling in a low growl. He swung the tiller and the RIB accelerated back out to sea.

Oliver Sweet heard the sound of the inflatable's motor fade away. He turned once to look back, but it was still too dark to see anything—especially a black RIB on dark water. He jogged at an easy pace, steadily moving up the hill. He chose a path between the dunes, staying in the troughs to avoid detection. He had to time his pace so that he could outrun the sunrise but not blunder into a trap. Even though the morning air was cool, Sweet found himself sweating profusely from the humidity and the strain of his load.

His plan was simple. Get up the ridge before the sun hit it and then approach from the southeast. The first line of sentries would be looking directly into the sun. Once they were down, the sentries who were positioned in the hills behind the cove were next. After he neutralized the two sentries on the northwest dunes, he would set his sights on the barricade and on the trucks. The guards near the trucks and on the barricade would be the last to go since they didn't have much chance of getting clear shots at the activists.

He felt a change underfoot as the ground transitioned from sand to volcanic rock. The going was slowed as the angle of incline increased. One wrong step and he would set loose a cascade of sharp lava rocks and gravel. Any stumble or unnatural sound would bring fire down onto his position. As he climbed higher, he felt the weight of the sniper rifle with each step.

An outcropping of lava loomed about twenty meters above his position. He located the remnants of a worn game trail and followed the zigzag pattern until he was able to traverse his way across the face of the slope and duck under the cover of the black rocks. He did a quick recon of the area in all directions. Looking to the east, he saw a faint glimmer of light behind the mountains. Dawn was on its way. He moved cautiously around the lava outcropping until he had a view of the slope ahead. The steep trail finally terminated in a series of jagged rock formations around the summit. The good news: he had lots of places to hide. The bad news: so did the sentries.

Sweet removed a set of night vision goggles from his backpack and fitted them onto his head. He couldn't detect anything on his first scan. As he swung his gaze up the slope, a movement caught his attention and he tensed.

Something had just disappeared behind a set of boulders seventy yards ahead and off to his left. He focused his gaze on the rocks and waited. A moment later, two blazing eyes were staring down at him. His heart skipped a beat as he realized that the eyes of the phantom belonged to a very large coyote. The canid did not appear to be in any particular hurry. It moved in and out of the low-growing scrub like a wraith, nosing under bushes and rocks for unwary prey. That meant that the sentries were not standing guard nearby. Sweet relaxed a notch, re-shouldered his pack, and began picking his way up the slope.

Some thirty minutes later, he topped the ridge. He spotted a tumble of boulders forty yards ahead and moved in the shadows until he was crouched among them. The light had changed to that pre-dawn gray that gave the landscape a flat appearance. From his position, Sweet could barely make out the far point of the mesa that looked down on El Infierno Cove. He reached into his pack and retrieved his GPS. He checked his coordinates against the ones that Beau had given them back at the boat.

The sentries were close.

From his vantage point, he couldn't see them. To make matters worse, there was little cover. He checked over his shoulder. The sky in the east had now blushed to a pink glow on the horizon.

Sweet pulled the night vision goggles over his eyes once more and scanned the surroundings in the direction of the coordinates. He thought he should be seeing something from this range. Perhaps they were hunkered down among the rocks.

He was about to make his move out into the open when a sound caused him to freeze in his tracks. The undeniable crunch of boots on lava gravel on the other side of the boulders was coming his way. Silently, Sweet drew his combat knife from its sheath. He crouched in a position that would give him the maximum impact if he were forced to subdue the intruder. He knew his mission would be over before it began if the guard wasn't taken out silently. And what if there was more than one? So far, the footfalls told him there was only one intruder.

The footsteps stopped. Sweet had a fleeting moment of panic, thinking he'd been discovered. He heard the all-too-familiar sound of urine splashing against rock. Then he heard a voice come over a VHF radio in Spanish.

"Ramón, what's your position?"

Oliver heard the sound of a zipper and then a shuffling on the other side of the boulders as the sentry hurriedly adjusted his clothing and reached for his radio.

The sentry called in his location in Spanish. "South end of the ridge. Nothing to report. All clear."

Without making a sound, Sweet retreated further behind the boulders. Unless the guard stumbled upon him accidentally, he wouldn't engage the man now.

He heard the crunch of gravel again and waited as the footsteps passed by several feet from his position. In the gray dawn Sweet briefly saw a pair of desert combat boots stop as the guard perused the area. Then he moved out of Oliver's sight.

He waited until he could no longer hear the sentry's footfall before venturing out of his place of concealment. He found a vantage point where he could observe the guard's progress as he worked his way along the spine of the ridge. It was getting easier to see now, and Sweet had no difficulty following the sentry's path.

After several minutes, he was rewarded for his patience. The guard stepped down onto a flat platform of dirt. Two men rose from their positions and began talking to him.

Sweet had located his first targets.

# 76

Spinner's boat, *This Side Up*, was the lead boat. Emily Rosen stood at the bow scanning the horizon. The sun had just peeked over the mountains in the east, casting a silvery sheen on the water. Flashes of mauve reflected on its surface. Under any other circumstances, it would have been a sunrise to remember, but Rosen, Raúl, and Morgan had no time to reflect on the beauty that lay before them. They were heading into the killing fields.

Sandy and Graham in one boat and Jesús in another flanked them on either side. The other pangas moved in a chevron formation that stretched out for nearly half a mile.

They had been traveling for nearly two hours. Information supplied by Beau from the fishing camp revealed that the whalers and their prey were ahead. Because the banger boats had to maintain a formation in order to direct the movement of the dolphins, their travel speed was considerably slower than the activists.

For the past twenty minutes, Rosen had been looking for signs of the approaching whale boats. Morgan, the tall young woman from the Cetus Alliance, stood just behind her, eyes fixed on the ocean ahead. Both of the women wore jackets over their kevlar vests to fend off the morning chill. At the helm, Raúl accelerated in the direction of the oncoming vessels while maintaining radio contact with the other Orca Teams.

Once Alejandro spotted the fleet from the helicopter, he would instruct the activists' boats to split into two groups. Then they would attack the fleet from either side. The plan was to attack swiftly and accurately, landing as many tear gas grenades and butyric acid bombs as possible onto the decks of the whaler's boats as they could, then move out to scatter the pods of dolphins. Hopefully, they could get the small cetaceans turned back out to sea.

Morgan yelled to Emily over the din of motor noise and wind. "See anything yet?"

Rosen shook her head. "No. With all this bouncing around, I can't make out if those are dolphins, boats, or just waves."

Spinner's boat had been fitted with upright steel plating on the bow as well as on starboard and port amidships. Morgan would be behind these makeshift barriers to launch her bombs. Emily would take a position next to her, readying each projectile and handing it to Morgan. In between throws, Emily would be recording video and shooting photos of the hunt in real time. Rosen looked down at the prow. Thanks to Francisco, the bow of Spinner's boat had now become a deadly ramming device with two metal pieces that formed a fork at the waterline. If they could get in close enough, *This Side Up* would take down the barricade.

"Alejandro and Snake have made visual contact," yelled Raúl from the console. "The fleet should be coming into view soon."

Raúl spoke into the radio. "Orca 2, 4, 5, and 6—move out!"

"Roger that," replied Sandy.

The other boat captains acknowledged, and three boats peeled off behind Sandy and Graham and headed west. Raúl peered into the distance. He glimpsed something moving on the horizon line.

"Emily! One o'clock! I see movement."

Rosen and Morgan turned. Suddenly, the whaleboats came into view. There were eight vessels, all spread across a large swath of water. They were moving in a chevron formation of their own.

Rosen caught movement in the water. She readjusted the optics on the binoculars and searched again.

"Oh, my God."

"Is that what I think it is?" Morgan asked, as Rosen handed her the binoculars. "Jesus! The water's full of dolphins."

One hundred meters in front of the whale boats, the water was churning with flukes and leaping forms as hundreds of panicked dolphins stampeded toward them.

"Better get ready," Raúl said.

The helicopter roared past the ragtag armada of activists. From the helicopter, Alejandro saw the chevron formation of the banger boats as the whalers herded the massive group of cetaceans toward the cove. He stared down at the maelstrom of panicked animals speeding ahead, trying to distance themselves from the horrific sounds that were creating an auditory hell all around them.

"Sons of bitches," muttered Snake into his headset. "That just ain't right."

"Snake, can you get me in closer? I need to get this on video."

Snake leaned over and loosened Alejandro's harness. "You need a little more wiggle room to shoot pictures," he said into the mic. "Those bastards start shooting at us, you pull back in, ya hear?"

Alejandro nodded. Watching the hapless animals racing ahead, landing on each other as they fled, brought up a primal rage within him. He activated the video camera and began recording.

"I need to be closer."

"Thought you'd never ask. Hang on." Snake banked the helicopter and they swooped down low over the whalers.

The first pass was a total failure as Alejandro, in his nervousness, had forgotten to hit the record button. Snake banked the helicopter around for another pass. This time, Alejandro made sure the video was recording. They dove down on the banger boats approaching from behind. Alejandro began recording, seeing angry faces gesturing up at him and waving guns. Some of the boats veered erratically, momentarily caught off guard by the closeness of the helicopter.

Alejandro heard a high-pitched whine, followed by the *thunks* of several bullets into the fuselage.

"We're taking fire!" Snake yelled. "Pulling up. Hang on!"

Alejandro withdrew into the cabin as Snake pulled an evasive move that took them out of the line of fire. He took the helicopter higher while Alejandro put the video camera aside and called the activists.

Hirokan Yoshimatsu had seen the helicopter approaching, and his first thought was that Figueroa had betrayed them and sent the Armada de Mexico to expose their operation. But when the helicopter passed overhead the second time, there was no mistaking the tall, dark-haired man filming them. It was Alejandro Cabrillo. Very much alive.

Yoshimatsu shouted above the din, "Shoot them out of the sky!" Both the federale and the man at the helm began firing. But when the helicopter moved out of range, Yoshimatsu swore and returned his attention to the hunt. He yelled at the banger, "Keep banging, you idiot!" They needed to focus on driving the dolphins toward the cove, now less than two miles away.

The Japanese whaler at the helm peered toward the horizon and then swore. Yoshimatsu looked at him, and the whaler pointed ahead. In the distance, two sets of boats were vectoring toward their position at top speed.

"Don't stop! Keep them moving!" Yoshimatsu yelled into the radio.

"You okay for a few rounds?" Rosen asked Morgan. "I need to get some video."

"Yeah, I'm good, Em," said Morgan. "But you're out in the open. There's not much cover from the bow."

"Trust me, I won't be there long."

Rosen scrambled forward, her camera bag slung over one shoulder. She ducked behind a low steel plate that had been fastened to the bow railing. Lying on her side behind the flimsy metal plate, she pulled her camera and telephoto lens from the pack. Next to her, she placed a second camera and lens, this one designated for wide-angle shots and video. She brought the camera up and rested the lens against the steel plate. She pressed the trigger, and the camera clicked images in rapid-fire succession.

The scene playing out in front of her was horrific. As far as she could see, hundreds of panicked common dolphins were launching themselves out of the water, churning the sea into froth as they tried to escape the overwhelming banging noise. From her position on the bow, the banging was incredibly loud and distracting. She could only imagine what the hapless dolphins were experiencing under water with all sound amplified.

She snapped a picture as eight common dolphins flew out of the water in front of one of the banger boats. Impossible to track any one individual, all Rosen could see was leap upon leap, sometimes in excess of fifteen horizontal feet as the dolphins fled from their would-be captors.

She caught several glimpses of females with their calves, leaping in synchrony. Several times, she saw the same dolphin jump without her calf at her side. Interspersed among the smaller dolphins were larger gray to black dolphins with stockier bodies. These were bottlenose dolphins, who also were being driven toward the killing cove. A family of short-finned pilot whales, their scythe-like black dorsal fins and bulbous heads surfacing frenetically, zigzagged through the water in search of an escape route. But there was no escaping the wall of sound that pushed them forward.

"Positions!" Raúl yelled, "We're going in."

He gunned the throttle, and the boat roared ahead straight toward the banger boats. *This Side Up* parted the dolphins like a scene from *The Ten Commandments*. Raúl steered the cruiser toward the bow of a hunter's boat, then veered at the last moment to make a run broadside. "Now!"

Morgan pulled the pin on the tear gas grenade, rose from behind the steel barrier and threw. Her arm was a blur. Rosen could barely see the grenade as it arced toward the banger boat. It landed against the stern of the whaler and ricocheted into the water. The crew of the banger boat looked stunned, not realizing what she had thrown.

"Damn it!" Morgan swore as *This Side Up* shot past the whaler.

"Coming back around!" Raúl turned the wheel hard. "Throw the stink bomb next time!"

Morgan nodded and reached into the box that held the butyric acid bombs. She hefted one in her hand as the cruiser came around for another pass. Morgan remained crouched behind the steel plate as they gained on the slower moving whaler.

Rosen peeked over the steel barrier and began shooting video and stills. Looking through the viewfinder, she saw that the crew members were looking for something to deter the attackers. One of the men in the back drew an Uzi machine pistol and began firing at them.

"Stay down!" Raúl executed a series of evasive moves to avoid the gunfire. He heard several bullets thud into the hull of the cruiser. He swerved quickly, exposing them to the whaler's port side. "Now!"

Morgan rose up and, in one lightning move, let the bottle of butyric acid fly. It was a straight-line shot, and the bomb exploded against the console. Immediately, the boat slowed as the crew was overcome by the acrid stench. Panicked, several rushed to clean it up. Rosen watched as one crew member dropped what he was doing, leaned over the side and puked.

The man in the back of the boat aimed the Uzi and fired a burst. Partially blinded, his shots went wild, stitching across the water in front of the boat.

Rosen yelled back to Morgan, "Nice shot!"

Morgan pumped her fist in the air. But their jubilation was short lived. The crew on the whaler galvanized and began furiously cleaning up the residue while covering their eyes and noses with bandanas. Someone produced a large bailing bucket and doused the deck in seawater. The whaler accelerated again, and another crew member began banging on the pipe.

Turning again, Raúl said, "Coming about!"

Morgan reached for another tear gas canister and crouched low. "One more time," she said.

Raúl maneuvered closer to the banger boat. The guard standing at the stern, having splashed water on his burning eyes, aimed the Uzi pistol at them. A spray of bullets belched from the machine pistol. The bullets clanked into the steel barrier. Rosen saw indentations appear in the steel plating. Her backpack jumped as two slugs ripped through the canvas. She instinctively ducked down, covering her head.

Raúl yelled, "Get back here, Em!"

She crawled back next to Morgan's position. Breathless, she crouched as Raúl maneuvered *This Side Up* in a series of zigzag moves. Due to the choppiness of the water, most of the assailant's gunfire went wild. Raúl turned the wheel sharply as a line of bullets stitched across the transom of Jake's boat.

"Sorry, Jake," Raúl muttered. The whaler presented a broadside target. Raúl judged the distance between the two vessels.

"Ready, Morgan. Now!"

The lithe redhead pulled the pin on the tear gas grenade, paused a split second and came up, arm cocked. Her arm whipped forward in a lightening movement and the grenade arced toward the banger boat. Rosen barely had enough time to bring her camera up to capture the grenade's flight.

The throw was perfect. The tear gas grenade exploded on contact with the banger boat's console. Bluish white smoke filled the boat's interior, creating a roiling cloud. The men in the boat began to shout, and it suddenly swerved to port. Rosen caught a glimpse of the armed man, his hands over his face as he was consumed by the blinding smoke.

Morgan yelled jubilantly, "How do you like that, motherfuckers!" Without hesitating, she grabbed another butyric acid bomb and launched it. The bottle shattered against the banger boat's motor. Even at this distance, Rosen picked up traces of the noxious substance. Inside that boat, the air must have been suffocating.

"You're my new hero," Rosen said, as she fired off a series of photos of the crippled whaler. "Hell of a shot!"

"Hang on," said Raúl. "Some of the other boats need help."

He turned the wheel sharply, and *This Side Up* accelerated toward the rest of the whaling fleet.

# 77

"They're all armed!"

Alejandro's voice was barely audible over the din of the helicopter's motor. "They just took shots at us. Keep moving. Don't give them a target. We'll try and distract them from up here."

Graham turned to Sandy and Brittany. "They're all carrying. They've already taken shots at Alejandro and Snake. Stay low. Throw only when you have a clear shot."

Sandy yelled, "Hold on! We're going in!" She whipped the sleek inflatable sharply and they sped toward a banger boat that was driving a large pod of dolphins and pilot whales toward them. As the inflatable drew closer, the dolphins sounded and went deep. The banger boat came to bear on the inflatable. Over the whine of the rigid-hull inflatable's motor, Sandy heard the high-pitched whine as several bullets whizzed overhead followed by the report from the rifle.

Sandy's reflexes kicked in. She deftly changed direction and brought the boat to bear on the bow of the banger boat. At the last minute, the whaler swerved to avoid colliding with the inflatable, presenting Graham and Brittany with a broadside target. The move was so quick and violent, that it sent the occupants of the banger boat sprawling. Graham and Brittany sprang up from their cover and launched two tear gas grenades. Both found their targets and smoke billowed from the sputtering banger boat.

Sandy quickly accelerated the inflatable away. Several hundred yards ahead, she saw one of the pangas from the fishing camp dead in the water, black smoke pouring from the outboard. She brought her binoculars up to her eyes and strained to see who the occupants were. Fernando Quintín and Manuel Soto were frantically trying to kill the fire that had erupted when a bullet had struck the motor. Bearing down on them was one of the banger boats from the *Shodokai Maru*. Sandy tried to steady the up-and-down movement of the binoculars. She drew a sharp breath when she realized that the man standing at the bow and directing the captain to ram the crippled panga was none other than Yoshimatsu.

"Graham!"

"Yeah, I see them!"

"Get them on the radio! Tell them to get off that boat!"

He grabbed the radio and tried to call Fernando and Manuel, but the two men were so busy trying to squelch the fire, they didn't see the banger boat bearing down on them.

"Jump, god damn it!"

*We're not going to make it in time,* Sandy thought.

Seconds before the whale boat broadsided the panga, Fernando looked up and pointed. The two men dove into the water and disappeared beneath the surface.

The banger boat rammed the panga, splitting it in half. The motor exploded in a ball of flame that was quickly extinguished by the wash from the whaler.

Sandy bellowed, "No!"

High-pitched whines of bullets cut the air around them like angry wasps. Yoshimatsu and his men had turned their attention and firepower toward Sandy's inflatable. She veered several times to throw them off. A loud crack behind her told her they'd taken a hit. She turned quickly to see the fiberglass covering for the outboard motor was in shreds. Graham jumped back to inspect.

"It's okay!"

Sandy executed another series of quick course changes, and the banger boat lost its line-of-sight ability to fire. By now, the whalers were past the destroyed panga and were attempting to catch up with the wave of dolphins that were fleeing from the terrifying boats. Ahead, Sandy could see the entrance to the cove. Men moved around the barrier frenetically. The dolphins were driven toward a large open-net gate controlled by two small tenders.

She sped toward the remains of Fernando's panga, slowing as she approached the wreckage. Debris from the boat was scattered across the surface, but there was no sign of either Fernando or Manuel.

"I don't see them," said Brittany.

"Keep looking!"

Sandy throttled back the inflatable and scanned the surface for survivors. Bits of smoking fiberglass and life vests lay smoldering at the surface. Her heart sank as the thought came through like a shot to the chest. The whaler had run the two fishermen down.

She edged the inflatable past a section of the over-turned panga. A bloodied hand was holding onto what remained of the keel. Sandy's breath caught in her throat as she eased the inflatable around the remains of the fishing boat. Manuel was barely hanging onto the keel, his clothes in tatters. In his other arm, he supported the limp body of Fernando. He was bleeding profusely from a wound on his scalp.

Graham immediately kicked off his shoes and plunged into the water. In two quick strokes, he was at the boat, helping to buoy Fernando up. Sandy cut the motor and drifted over to the wrecked panga. Graham gently took Fernando from Manuel, placed him in a rescue hold and swam the unconscious fisherman over to the inflatable. Brittany and Sandy helped to lift him in, no easy task due to his girth. Graham went back and grabbed hold of Manuel, who was too weak to swim.

"I've got you. Hang on."

He soon had Manuel holding onto the tie lines while he climbed into the inflatable. He then grabbed Manuel by the back of the trousers and lifted him into the boat.

Graham soon realized the extent of Fernando's injuries. Besides the head wound, Fernando's right femur was fractured. A splinter of bone was protruding through his torn and bloodied trouser leg. Manuel had cuts and abrasions everywhere, and when Graham gently palpated his shoulders, he winced and gritted his teeth.

"I think you dislocated your shoulder." He turned his gaze to Sandy. "We need to get them to a hospital. Now."

She nodded grimly and reached for her radio to call Alejandro and Snake.

"We have wounded here, Alex. They're going to need to be air-evacked to La Paz or, at least, to the fishing camp so Arturo can stabilize them."

"Call Arturo. Tell him to break off from the attack. We need to get the wounded out of here."

"I can set her down on the beach a couple of clicks south of here," Snake added. "Just give me your location and ETA."

"I'll call you right back," Sandy said.

Several of the activists' boats were attempting to place themselves between the herd of panicked dolphins and El Infierno Cove. She saw a banger boat engulfed in smoke as Carlos, Francisco, and Brad tried to get away from another armed banger boat in pursuit. A volley of bullets stitched the water around their speeding panga. The five remaining banger boats had regrouped and continued to push the massive herd of dolphins toward the entrance of the cove.

Anguished, she watched the first wave of dolphins funnel into the cove.

Jesús throttled back as another hail of bullets laced the water in front of his panga. Arturo shielded Paola as several rounds chunked into the makeshift steel-plating barrier. The panga had taken severe damage from the automatic fire. It was a miracle that none of the occupants had been hit. They had only managed to land one butyric acid bomb, which exploded on the stern of the banger boat. As long as the banger boat moved forward, the stench was carried off on the wind.

They watched helplessly as the banger boats herded the dolphins into the killing cove. Although the activists had managed to turn away many of the dolphins, there were still several hundred that were now moving into the cove.

"If we go in there now, it'll be suicide," Arturo said.

Paola slapped her open hand on the seat. "We can't just sit here!"

"He's right," said Jesús. "Unless Spinner can bring down the barrier when he gets here, we'd be making ourselves easy targets."

A frantic voice came over the radio. It was Sandy. "Jesús, we have wounded here that need to be attended to. You need to fall back and bring Arturo."

"Who is it?" Jesús asked as Arturo and Paola moved closer to the radio to hear.

"Fernando Quintín and Manuel Soto. Their boat got rammed. Fernando is pretty bad. He's got a head injury and a broken leg. He's going to need to get to a hospital. Manuel's got a dislocated shoulder and a bunch of lacerations and bruises. They need to be stabilized. Snake and Alejandro are going to get them to the hospital in La Paz."

"We'll be there as soon as we can," said Arturo.

"Give me the coordinates." Jesús's face was grim.

"I'll have Snake call them in to you," Sandy said. "Are you all right?"

"Mad as hell that we couldn't stop them," said Arturo. "We get any closer, it'll be a bloodbath."

"It already is." Paola looked at the entrance to the cove.

"I am sorry, Paola," said Jesús. "But we have to go."

"Where's Spinner?" Paola looked out to sea. "He should've been here by now."

# 78

Jake Spinner saw the black smoke on the horizon and felt his stomach churn. He pushed the RIB to its limits, but the motor was sputtering. The fuel line was clogged, and Jake's repeated attempts hadn't been able to clear it.

"Come on, god damn it!" He hoped he wasn't too late.

Another plume of smoke appeared in the distance. He retrieved a set of binoculars from the duffel bag and focused on the scene ahead.

The activists were in trouble. Several pangas were already disabled. They sat on the water with smoke pouring from their motors. Two whaling vessels, consumed in smoke, were trying to move ahead. In front of them, the activists buzzed around the whaling ships like angry hornets. Over the sputtering din of the motor, Spinner heard the rhythmic banging of the steel pipes from the whale boats.

He spied *This Side Up*. She was closing in on one of the banger boats. He could hear intermittent small arms fire. Jake let out a primal yell. His zodiac shot forward, headed toward a mass of panicked dolphins.

Emily Rosen looked up from her position as they flanked the lead banger boat. She managed to shoot several pictures with her camera. *This Side Up* had taken more damage from the gunfire coming from the whaler. Rosen had seen the man on the bow that had been shooting at them. Fortunately, due to the chop that had been building, most of the shots did not connect with their boat. When she enlarged the image on her LED screen, Rosen's heart almost stopped. The man at the bow shooting at them was Hirokan Yoshimatsu.

"Raúl! It's Yoshimatsu!" Rosen pointed emphatically at the banger boat.

Raúl nodded and pushed the throttle. She set the camera down and slid back to where Morgan was crouched, a tear gas grenade in her hand, poised for another throw.

463

Rosen slid in next to her and picked one up. "Mind if I join you?" Emily asked. "Love it," said Morgan.

"There's a miserable son-of-a-bitch on the bow of that whaler. Hundred bucks right now if you bean him with that grenade."

"You're on." Morgan chanced a look over the top of the barrier. "You know who he is?"

"Yoshimatsu. He's running this *Little Shop of Horrors*. Stop him, we stop the whole operation."

The high-pitched whine of bullets whizzed over their heads. Reflexively, Emily and Morgan ducked down, even though the bullets had long since passed.

"Call it, Raúl!" Rosen felt the boat lurch as he made quick adjustments to avoid the fire from the men on the whaler.

"Now!"

Emily and Morgan rose quickly and hurled the tear gas canisters at the banger boat. The whaler at the helm saw them and made an abrupt evasive maneuver. The canisters landed behind the boat, not finding their intended target.

More shots laced the water in front of them as Yoshimatsu fired on them again. Bullets splintered the deck of This Side Up. Rosen and Morgan dove down to the floor and curled into fetal positions as the deck erupted. Raúl peeled off and fell back out of range. Yoshimatsu's banger boat plowed ahead, driving the mass of whales toward the cove which was now in sight.

"Anyone hit?" Raúl couldn't see either woman.

Rosen felt like she was in a dream. Everything moved in slow motion except for her heartbeat, which pounded in her ears. She felt something slick on her cheek and put her hand up to it. When she drew her hand away, she saw blood on her fingertips.

Morgan, who had her head in her hands, was shaking badly. When she finally looked up her eyes reflected horror.

"Oh, my God! Rosen, you're hit!"

It took Rosen several seconds to realize that she had been grazed by one of the bullets. Then the realization hit her. If the bullet had hit another half-inch to the left, she'd be dead. Suddenly, at the far edge of her narrowed vision, she saw something black moving fast toward them and the line of banger boats. As the speeding vessel drew closer, she recognized the driver. His face was blackened with grease paint, and, at first glance, she thought she was looking at one of the Four Horsemen of the Apocalypse reincarnate.

Spinner had seen the banger boat open up on *This Side Up*, and he pushed the RIB to its limits. He sent out a silent prayer that Emily and the others were okay. He didn't take his eyes off the boat, straining to see signs of life aboard.

As he drew closer, he saw Raúl waving his arms wildly.

Drawing alongside, Raúl stepped forward and caught the bowline that Spinner had tossed to him. When the RIB was tethered to *This Side Up*, Spinner quickly jumped aboard.

"Are you okay?" Jake looked around at the devastation that was his boat.

"We're okay, Jake," said Raúl.

Spinner's eyes were wild. It took him a couple of seconds to see Emily and Morgan hunkered down. Morgan was dressing a wound on Rosen's face. Spinner rushed to her side.

"Took you long enough," Rosen said.

"Jesus, Em, I'm so sorry. The damn fuel line clogged, and I didn't have a spare." His face looked grim. "I should've been here sooner."

She touched his grizzled cheek. "Better late than never."

"Are you okay, Em?"

"Never been shot before. Definitely dodged the proverbial bullet this time."

Spinner looked at Morgan who was visibly rattled from the firefight. "You okay?"

She nodded weakly. "I think so."

"We can't get any closer, Jake," said Raúl. "We're lucky no one's been killed. So far."

"What have we got?"

"We were able to slow them down for a while," Raúl continued. "Some of the dolphins were scattered and got away. But the whalers closed ranks and kept most of the pods moving. Fernando and Manuel were rammed and were injured. Arturo and Paola are tending to them until Snake can fly them to the hospital in La Paz."

Spinner looked out at the whaling fleet moving toward the cove. He sighed deeply and then turned back to Raúl and the others. "Em, are you okay to drive?"

"Sure. What's the plan?"

"I want you and Morgan to take the RIB back to the fishing camp. Raúl, call everyone back in."

Rosen sat up straight, her back arching. "Are you kidding?"

"It's about to get mean, Em. I can't risk losing anyone."

"And what do you think you're going to do?" Rosen's anger rose in her voice.

"I'm going into that cove." Spinner cast a narrow gaze toward El Infierno. "I made a promise to some friends."

"And you think you're going in there all by yourself?" Rosen was barely able to contain herself.

"He won't be going alone," said Raúl.

Rosen glared defiantly at the two men. "Hell no. I'm going with you."

"Rosen, they have high-powered guns. They'll be shooting at us."

"Then give me a gun, god damn it! I made the same promise, Spinner. And by God, neither you nor anyone else will deny me my right."

Spinner stared at her, then turned to Morgan. "You did great, Morgan. Time for you to sit this one out."

Morgan nodded.

"Stay here with the RIB. The rest of the group will be along shortly to get you back to base camp."

They assisted Morgan into the inflatable and made sure she was comfortable. Spinner left her a radio, water, and a thermal blanket from *This Side Up*'s emergency kit.

"We'll call Arturo and they'll be out shortly. Stay put."

Morgan looked up at Rosen. "Kick some ass for me, Em."

Rosen nodded grimly. "You got it."

Spinner untied the bowline and Raúl fired up the engine. Spinner and Rosen moved to the bow as Raúl brought *This Side Up* on plane and sped toward the whaling fleet.

# 79

Oliver Sweet moved behind a small cluster of brittlebush plants and dropped into a prone position. It had taken him nearly a half hour to get close enough to see all three of the cartel assassins. The men were focused on what was going on below them in the cove. From this distance the deafening din from the banger boats echoed throughout the hills. Occasionally, one of the gunmen would turn and look in Sweet's direction, scanning for anyone who might be foolish enough to attempt an approach from the desert.

Sweet froze, his breath held tight in his chest. The assassin was staring right at him. Sweet focused the sights on him. He saw the lines on the man's face and the dark sunglasses that shielded his eyes. The man's brown skin glistened with sweat from the heat reflecting off the black lava rocks.

He leaned forward and stared directly at the spot where Sweet lay camouflaged. Sweet knew that this one had to go first. He made a mental note of the other two assassins' positions and added some pressure to the trigger. Even with the suppressor, the report from the sniper rifle would alert the other two sentry posts. He listened to the cadence of the banger pipes and attempted to sync his shots with the bangers.

The man removed his sunglasses and squinted at the low-lying bushes. He took two steps forward, then put the glasses back on. Sweet slowed his breathing and gently squeezed the trigger.

Through the scope, Sweet saw the dark sunglasses split in two and a red hole appear between the assassin's eyes. His head snapped backward as he was lifted off his feet. He landed hard on his back, creating a small cloud of dust.

The other two assassins turned to see their fallen colleague, looking momentarily confused. Sweet sighted in on the man on the right and fired again. The bullet caught him in the middle of the chest, and he was flung backward. The third man dove to the ground, shielding himself from Sweet's fire by hiding behind his fallen colleague's corpse.

Through the scope, Oliver saw the assassin fumbling for his cell phone. There was no clear shot to the head for the kill. If he managed to make that call, this party would be over before it even started. Then Sweet saw the man's leg move. From the knee down, it was exposed. Sweet adjusted the scope, breathed out and pulled the trigger.

The bullet caught the assassin right below the knee. The man rolled away in pain grabbing his injured leg and rocked forward. Sweet fired again. This time, the shot hit home, punching through the man's throat.

He shouldered his rifle and jogged toward the bodies. Drawing his .40-caliber Glock, he approached the three immobilized assassins. He holstered his semi-automatic when he saw that they were all dead.

He quickly surveyed the area. Looking down into the cove, he saw why the assassins had been so interested in the goings-on below. The water was being thrashed by hundreds of panicked dolphins. Reaching for his binoculars, he scanned the desert behind the cove. From his vantage point he saw that the barricade at the entrance to the cove was more strongly fortified than Spinner had thought. Spanning the width of the barricade were five thick telephone poles, which had been sunk into the sand. Two one-by-twelve planks made up the breadth of the boardwalk, and they were secured to the upright posts. Breaking through the barricade was going to be a miracle of the first order.

He scanned until he saw his next four targets. Two Zeta mercenaries were crouched on a low ridge about one hundred meters back from El Infierno. They were perched on the edge of the ridge. The two men were fixated on the spectacle unfolding in the Cove of Death. Sweet soon located the other two assassins, standing watch on a sand dune above the cove's west side. They stood conspicuously out in the open on the top of the highest dune. They must have felt pretty secure in their position, Sweet thought. They didn't expect any resistance coming from the cove side.

Oliver took a moment to check the barricade on the cove. Four armed men were standing guard. There was one on each end of the barricade, and two held the middle, separated by roughly fifty meters. All of the guards standing on that catwalk needed to be neutralized before Spinner and the other activists could assault the barricade.

He dragged the dead assassins and rolled them into a shallow depression just back from the edge of the cliff. Taking advantage of the depression, he set up his AX50, placing extra magazines, binoculars, radio, and backpack within easy reach. From this vantage point, he had an optimal view of the comings and goings of the whalers' operation below.

At the rear of the cove, two eighteen-wheelers were parked. Sweet noted the large refrigeration units on top. Several smaller military-style trucks with canvas tarps, like troop carriers, were parked closer to the water's edge.

Sweet counted six men, three of them Japanese, standing around large blue tarps that were stretched out on the sand. Several were casually smoking, waiting for word to begin the slaughter. This must be the flensing station where the animals' bodies would be dragged after they were killed in the shallows, either by drowning or stabbing. Sweet felt a deep revulsion at the core of his being. He had heard that the whalers would first impale the dolphins behind their blowhole with a sharpened spike, then insert wooden plugs in the dying animals' blowhole to suffocate them. Odd, he thought, that he felt sickened by what was to befall these gentle creatures, but he felt no remorse whatsoever for the impending fate of their captors.

There were already several dozen animals trapped inside the sorting pen. Although Sweet didn't know the species, he noticed that there were several different sizes and shapes of dolphins swimming frantically along the perimeter of El Infierno inlet.

Oliver set the binoculars aside and positioned the rifle. A breeze was blowing across the ridge from east to west. He adjusted the windage knob on his scope to compensate. The scope gave him a reading in one corner of its digital display. Even though it was still early morning, the sun was already causing the lava-blackened landscape to shimmer in the rising heat. Sweet adjusted the range aspect of the trajectory. Under normal circumstances, he would have a spotter who would give him feedback regarding wind conditions, distance to target, and angle of declination. Today, here on this ridge, he just had to wing it.

The radio he had taken off one of the dead assassins crackled and a voice came over the speaker. The man spoke in Spanish.

"Post two checking in," said the voice. "All quiet on the south ridge."

Sweet hesitated, then picked up the radio. His mind raced as he sought to find a proper response. "Bueno." Then he commanded in Spanish. "Stay alert." He set the radio down.

Looking through his scope, Sweet saw the man on the radio looking in his direction. He adjusted the vertical field to compensate for bullet drop and sighted in once more. The rangefinder read 1,200 yards. Sweet had taken longer shots than this before, but under less adverse conditions.

The man in Sweet's sights was now talking to his colleagues and pointing toward his position on the ridge. Sweet took a deep breath and placed a small amount of pressure on the trigger. He let his breath out slowly and squeezed. The rifle recoiled, but Sweet had sufficient control to keep his eye on the target. A second later, he saw a red stain appear on the assassin's chest. Panicked, his associate scrambled to find cover.

Sweet picked his next target. The second assassin was reaching for the radio. Sweet ejected the spent cartridge. He felt the heat as it passed close to his face. He squeezed the trigger, and the man dropped, radio still in his outstretched hand. Sweet ejected the magazine and jammed a fresh one into place.

He then turned his sights to the two cove guards on the dunes to the west. This was a longer shot, pushing the range limits of the sniper rifle. He sighted in on the first of these two assassins and fired. The man fell back, then began to tumble down the dune. The second guard attempted to run back and hide behind the crest of the dune. Sweet caught him at the apex of the sand dune, and the man fell onto the other side.

Oliver reached for his radio. The VHF channel was already programmed. "Orca 1, this is Osprey. Do you copy?"

"Go ahead." Jake Spinner's voice crackled.

Sweet unscrewed the suppressor from his sniper rifle. There was no need for stealth any longer.

"Osprey is on the nest. I repeat. Osprey is on the nest."

# 80

S pinner shouted to the others, "It's a go! Head for the cove!"

Rosen yelled ahead to Jake, "Ollie?"

Spinner nodded. "We have a window." He radioed the rest of the assault team. "All teams converge on the cove. Converge on the cove!"

Spinner looked back at Raúl. "You bring that peashooter?"

Raúl reached down and produced his old rifle. He unwrapped it and tossed the rifle to Spinner, who caught it in one hand.

Spinner raised the rifle to his shoulder and cocked it. He looked back. "Em, can you pick out Yoshimatsu's boat?"

"No problem."

She picked up Raúl's binoculars and scanned the sea in front of them. The second wave of dolphins had now reached the entrance of the cove, and the banger boats surrounded them as they crowded into the opening. Once near the barricades, the boats peeled off and circled around to prevent more dolphins from escaping. In the distance, Rosen could still hear the incessant banging on the pipes.

"Got him! He's in the front of that cluster of boats on the outside. The boats behind are covering his ass. They're all armed."

"Stay back there with Raúl, Em. Under no circumstances do you leave that spot. Are we together on this?"

Rosen gave Spinner the look that, given other circumstances, might have made him laugh. "Yeah, right. Why do I even bother?"

He crawled to the bow and rested the barrel of the rifle over the top of the sheet metal guard. This rifle was a lot more cumbersome than the M4 he had carried in Iraq and Afghanistan.

Out of his peripheral vision, Spinner spied the remaining activists' boats speeding toward the entrance to the cove. They closed the distance quickly, but the banger boats were still herding the swarm of terrified cetaceans in tight formation.

Sandy's voice came over the radio. "Orca 1, this is Orca 2. We're coming in on your three."

Rosen looked to starboard and saw Sandy's inflatable speeding toward the banger boats. Sandy stood behind the wheel while Graham and Brittany crouched in the bow. Behind them, Orca 5, with Brad, Carlos, and Francisco, blasted through the waves. Orca 4, with Alejandro at the bow and Carlos at the wheel were close behind. Alejandro had replaced Arturo after Snake landed the helicopter on the beach. Snake ferried Arturo away in the helicopter where he tended to Fernando and Manuel's wounds on their way to La Paz.

Emily observed Paola at the bow with Alejandro. Both were poised to throw butyric acid and tear gas bombs.

*Four boats,* she thought. *Four boats were all that stood between the dolphins and a slaughter.*

*This Side Up* closed the distance between the three banger boats. Rosen saw a Japanese whaler, who was wearing a red shirt, turn, and point at them. Then something strange happened. A native fisherman tried to wrest control of the wheel from the captain. A struggle ensued with both men fighting fiercely. Red shirt stepped up and shot the indio point blank in the back and heaved him over the side.

"Jesus!" Rosen pointed at the boat. "Did you see that?"

"I think the fishermen from Puerto Nacimiento have had enough of their overlords," said Spinner, sighting down the length of the barrel. "And I've had just about enough of them, too."

Her eyes were still transfixed on the banger boat, so the report of the rifle made Rosen jump. Red shirt flew backward. His legs caught on the gunwale, and he flipped into the water.

Raúl called out, "Nice shot!"

"Nice rifle," Spinner said.

The captain of the boat, panicked that one of the activists' boats had fired on them, started yelling for the other two whalers to move to the back and take up positions. The indio crewman took this as his cue and dove off the boat headlong. The other whaler, a stocky Mexican man in a federale uniform, stepped to the back, an Uzi machine pistol in his hands.

Jake leveled the rifle and fired again, spinning the federale around and knocking him against the wheelhouse. As they descended upon the banger boat, Spinner saw his chance. He squeezed the trigger and the gas tank ruptured. Spinner ejected the shell and fired again, deliberately aiming for the steel housing on the back of the boat. The bullet ricocheted and, a second later, the rear of the banger boat erupted in flames.

Hirokan Yoshimatsu heard the explosion and turned to see his trailing boat engulfed in flames, dead in the water. He saw the approaching boat speeding toward them. "Kill them!"

The captain picked up the radio and ordered a second boat to break formation and go after the attacking vessel.

Yoshimatsu was surprised at the ferocity of the attacking activists. Armed with stink bombs and tear gas grenades, they made nuisances of themselves. They would be in for a deadly surprise once they got within firing range of the barricade.

He wondered how they'd managed to get a hold of tear gas canisters and how they had known the exact location of the hunt. Right now, it was imperative that they all be silenced. He would not tolerate any further interference from this rabble. The hunt must be completed, no matter what the cost.

He watched as the second boat peeled off and headed straight toward *This Side Up*. Most of the other activists' boats were Mexican fishing boats. This was a sport fishing model that was coming at the banger boat at full speed. Yoshimatsu saw its bow had been modified with a vertical fork and the gunwales had been reinforced with steel plating. Something else about it tugged at his memory, but he couldn't retrieve it.

The whaler opened fire on the approaching boat. Yoshimatsu saw two of his men step to the bow and begin firing on the incoming vessel. Then a single shot rang out from the cruiser, and one of them crumpled and fell into the water. The second deckhand, losing his nerve, retreated from the bow and moved back to a position by the wheelhouse. The captain made a quick course correction to avoid being rammed as a woman stood and hurled grenades.

The banger boat became engulfed in thick white smoke, obscuring the captain and crew member from Yoshimatsu's view. Smoke hung ghost-like on the water. A sickening crunch reverberated across the water as steel connected with fiberglass, then Yoshimatsu saw an image that came straight out of his worst nightmare. The cruiser emerged from the smoke, and the figure at the bow was pointing a rifle directly at him.

Yoshimatsu suddenly knew where he'd seen that boat before. It was the one Spinner had used to break up the first dolphin hunt. Then he realized the man in the bow was none other than Jake Spinner.

"You're supposed to be dead!" He brought up his pistol and began firing.

"Get me next to that boat, Raúl!" Spinner yelled. He leveled the rifle and fired. The bullet ricocheted off the hull next to Yoshimatsu, driving him to the deck. Jake ejected the spent shell from the chamber. "I'm out!"

Rosen retrieved the box of cartridges that Raúl had on the console. She sprinted to the bow and slid in next to Spinner just as Yoshimatsu came up firing again. Spinner pulled her down and covered her with his body as several bullets slammed into the metal plating.

The Plexiglas window in front of Raúl shattered as Yoshimatsu fired another burst. Rosen saw that the dolphin herd was beginning to disperse. With the whale boats distracted and unable to bang on the steel pipes, the animals—no longer being driven—were breaking away and heading back out to sea.

Spinner jammed six bullets into the feed. He nodded to Emily and came up firing, again driving Yoshimatsu to the deck. Closing in on the boat, Spinner handed the rifle to Rosen. He pulled back the bolt and slammed it home. "Cock. Aim. Shoot."

"Spinner, what the hell are you doing?"

"I'm going to kill that son of a bitch."

Yoshimatsu came up firing and bullets thudded into the hull of *This Side Up*, forcing Raúl to drop down below the wheel. He continued to close the distance between the boats. Rosen brought the rifle up, aimed and fired. She felt a sudden sharp pain as the rifle recoiled into her shoulder. Her shot went high but was sufficient to make Yoshimatsu duck down.

"Pull the butt in tight. Squeeze the trigger while you exhale. All you need to do is make him keep his head down until I can get on that boat."

"Spinner, this is insane. Let's hit him with tear gas and butyric acid and come back and get him later."

Spinner shook his head. "This ends here. Now."

Raúl yelled, "Get ready for impact!"

Rosen looked at Spinner and nodded. "Go!"

She came up and fired. The bullet splintered the gunwale close to Yoshimatsu. Wide-eyed, he ducked down quickly. The two boats collided, knocking Rosen off balance. Spinner braced, then sprang to his feet and leapt onto the banger boat. He rolled and came up, drawing the Beretta from his waistband. He quickly disappeared around the wheelhouse.

Rosen peered over the sight of the rifle and searched the bow for any sign of Yoshimatsu. He was nowhere to be seen. The whaler was still moving, but she noticed that its course was erratic. Both boats were now veering away from the cove.

Spinner stopped short of the wheelhouse entrance. He knew the pilot of the vessel was waiting for him. There was only one way to get to Yoshimatsu, and it would leave him exposed. He needed a diversion. He slunk back until he was again visible to Emily. He motioned to her with his hands. She understood what he wanted.

Reaching for the last tear gas grenade, she hefted it in her hand and tossed it to Spinner underhanded. He caught it and moved around the corner of the wheelhouse once again.

He inched forward until he was close enough to attempt a bank shot into the cabin. The wheelhouse door was open, banging back and forth with the rhythm of the waves. Several feet forward, lay the inert form of one of the whalers. He'd been shot in the back. Spinner recognized the dead man as one of the villagers from Puerto Nacimiento. An ill-fated mutiny at a costly price. Spinner knew Yoshimatsu was hunkered down, lying in wait for him near the bow. He hoped the smoke from the tear gas would give him enough cover to close the distance between them.

He waited just long enough for the door to swing wide, then he pulled the pin. He banked the grenade off the door and it bounced inside. A second later, there was a muffled explosion in the wheelhouse. The captain came running out the door, pistol in one hand and shielding his face with the other. He fired blindly in Spinner's direction. Spinner leveled the pistol and fired. The captain slammed against the door and crumpled to the deck. Spinner clambered up onto the wheelhouse roof and flattened himself on the deck. Eyes stinging from the tear gas, he could barely see Yoshimatsu's figure crouched behind a storage box on the bow. Yoshimatsu looked left and right while trying to wipe the tear gas from his eyes.

Spinner launched himself from the wheelhouse roof. He hit Yoshimatsu with the full force of his weight, bringing up his elbow into the man's chin. Yoshimatsu pitched backward, the Uzi pistol flying from his hands. Spinner crashed to the deck as Yoshimatsu went down against the bow. The whaler scrambled for the pistol, but Spinner grabbed him by both legs. Yoshimatsu turned and kicked Spinner viciously in the face. Spinner let go of one leg but managed to hang onto the other one and twist it hard at the knee. Yoshimatsu cried out in pain.

Spinner stood and rounded on the Japanese magnate. He picked up the Uzi and flung it over the side. Yoshimatsu stood up surprisingly fast despite his injured knee. He glared balefully at Spinner. The two men sized each other up.

"I find it somewhat irritating," said Yoshimatsu, assuming a fight stance position, "that you just don't stay dead."

"It's over, Yoshimatsu. You and your whale poachers are done."

Yoshimatsu laughed. "You can't stop me. Your pathetic group of animal lovers cannot penetrate the barrier to the cove. I have snipers positioned on the catwalk and above in the hills overlooking the cove. All you can do is watch while we finish our work here."

"You may want to take another look. Your perimeter is not as secure as you think."

Yoshimatsu's expression of triumphant rage faltered momentarily. "You're lying."

Spinner retrieved a pair of binoculars from the dead captain's body and tossed them to the wary Yoshimatsu. "Have a look for yourself. And don't worry—I'm not going to kill you—yet."

Yoshimatsu put the binoculars to his eyes and scanned the hills behind El Infierno Inlet. He was expecting to see standing guards. At first, he couldn't see anyone. Then his attention was drawn to the bodies splayed out on the sand. He checked all three locations around the cove. All of the assassins were dead.

He brought the binoculars down, his face filled with blind rage.

"We're going in." Spinner's voice was ice cold. "And there's not a god damn thing you can do about it."

Yoshimatsu eyed him. "I believe you to be an honorable man, Jake Spinner. You would not just shoot me down like a dog. You want to know how it turns out, just you and me. A chance for me—or you—to die with honor."

"Like the honorable deaths you gave to Macario Silvano and his parents? How about the honorable deaths you murdering bastards gave to those dolphins and whales?"

Yoshimatsu stared. Perhaps it was a trick of the morning light, but it looked like Spinner's eyes had changed from deep ocean-blue to gray.

"Lose the knife." Spinner motioned the gun toward Yoshimatsu's ankle.

Yoshimatsu's lips curled into a cruel smile. He reached down and removed a drop-point Japanese dagger from his sock. He tossed it aside. "And now, you will reciprocate?"

Spinner set his pistol on the deck behind him. "Bring it."

Both men stared at each other, then began circling each other slowly. Spinner looked for weak points in Yoshimatsu's physique. He was shorter by a couple of inches, but he was stockier of build. He might have once been a wrestler. His movements were cat-like, despite the new injury to his knee. His legs moved with the potential energy of coiled springs. Spinner knew that he needed to guard his weak spots. His left shoulder and right lower quadrant were still healing from the bullet wounds he'd sustained just weeks ago.

Yoshimatsu launched himself at Spinner and delivered two rapid fire punches. Spinner blocked the first one, but the second one glanced off the left side of his cheek. He rocked back on his heels for a second, then recovered and brought his guard up.

Yoshimatsu spun in a full roundhouse kick, catching Spinner on the right side. Spinner slammed against the wheelhouse, feeling the full shock of the blow over his still-healing wound. Yoshimatsu saw Spinner flinch and went on the attack, his dark eyes blazing.

Spinner spun and presented his left side as Yoshimatsu's kick connected with his hip. He jabbed left and landed a solid blow to Yoshimatsu's face, knocking the tycoon backward. He stopped to wipe the blood that was now running freely down his nose.

By now, Raúl had brought *This Side Up* alongside the Japanese whaler. He and Rosen watched the deadly duel unfold.

Yoshimatsu saw that a red stain had appeared on the right side of Spinner's tee shirt. He focused his attack on the old wound. He threw a combination of punches and kicks at Spinner. Jake was able to deflect all but one blow. He was slammed backward against the wheelhouse again.

"Jake!" Emily ran forward and grabbed the rail.

By now, Raúl had taken back possession of the rifle. He aimed the rifle at Yoshimatsu's head. "I can take him out, Jake."

"No!" Jake's face was a mask of rage. "I got this."

Spinner grabbed his side and stood straight, grimacing all the while. He looked Yoshimatsu in the face while watching his hips with his peripheral vision, anticipating a kick. Yoshimatsu closed in. Spinner moved back and forth, one hand protecting his right side, the other in front of his face. Yoshimatsu's eyes flickered, and Spinner caught the slightest bit of rotation in his hips. The Yakuza operative spun and kicked out violently with his left leg. Spinner dropped his torso and kicked out, catching Yoshimatsu full force in the groin. Rosen heard the audible sound of air rushing from Yoshimatsu's lungs.

Yoshimatsu staggered backward and fought to regain his stance. Spinner was on him. He landed two crushing blows to Yoshimatsu's face, sending him to the deck. Yoshimatsu was now on his hands and knees. Blood flowed freely from his face. He tried to stand but Spinner flattened him with a hard right to the cheek.

Spinner stood over him. Yoshimatsu reached into the back waistband of his trousers and pulled out another knife. He lunged at Spinner, grazing his leg. Spinner wrested the knife away from him, then punched him to the deck. In one move Spinner lifted the whale killer above his head and slammed his back over the gunwale.

Rosen heard a horrible wet snap followed by the most penetratingly primal scream she'd ever heard. Spinner picked up his pistol and walked purposefully back to where Yoshimatsu lay screaming.

"I can't feel my legs! I can't feel my legs!"

Spinner brought the Beretta up and pointed the pistol right between the Yakuza's eyes. Rosen and Raúl looked on in horror at the man they thought they knew.

"Jake, don't," Rosen pleaded. "He's not worth it."

Just then the radio crackled and the panicked voice of Sandy came over the speaker. "Orca 3! We have a problem. Orca 5 is pinned down by gunfire and can't move. They need assistance immediately."

"Jake, we need to go," said Emily. "Carlos and Francisco are getting hammered."

She watched as the rage began to drain from Spinner's face. He shoved the pistol in the back waistband of his pants and turned away from Yoshimatsu.

Yoshimatsu screamed, "This is not a death of honor! Finish me!"

"Later." Spinner's voice was devoid of any emotion. He walked to the port side gunwale and leapt onto *This Side Up*.

# 81

Raúl handed the rifle to Spinner before he took the wheel. Spinner kneeled at the bow with Emily next to him. The boat sped back toward the fray.

The drive had changed configuration. Many of the small whales and dolphins had slipped through the curtain of deafening sound created by the banger boats. Spinner pulled the binoculars up and looked ahead. He saw the panga that had been manned by Carlos, Francisco and Brad, but none of them were visible. From a short distance away, one of the remaining whalers was firing automatic weapons at it. Splinters were being peeled away as the three assailants blasted it. Two of the shooters were Japanese. One of them was a tall, skinny man with a skeletal face. The other was the boat driver. The third man wore the uniform of a Mexican federal police officer. He was firing his machine pistol into the hull of the destroyed panga.

Spinner handed the binoculars to Rosen. "Stay down, Em." He brought the rifle to bear. "Get me a little closer, can you Raúl?"

"Tell me when."

"You'll know."

"It's your boat."

"I can't see anyone moving in the panga," Rosen said. "I hope to God we're not too late."

Several hundred yards away, Sandy and Graham circled as close as they dared. Occasionally, one or two of the assailants on the whaling boat would direct fire at the inflatable, preventing them from rescuing any of the panga's occupants.

Suddenly bullets whizzed overhead as the assassins on the whaling boat turned their attention to Spinner and his team.

Spinner sighted down the barrel and picked a target. "Keep an eye out, would you, Em?"

Rosen scanned the scenario through the binoculars. "We're taking fire from the boat driver and the federale."

Bullets chinked into the bow and ricocheted off the steel plating. Rosen and Spinner ducked.

"Damn it!" Rosen said.

Spinner came up and leveled the rifle once more. Emily had just brought the binoculars up when the report from Spinner's rifle cracked beside her. A red blotch appeared on the helmsman's chest, and he was thrown backward.

"The Mexican guy and the Japanese guy are kinda pissed now."

"Who's worse?" Spinner yanked the bolt back and ejected a spent shell.

"The Mexican guy has the automatic."

Spinner took aim and squeezed the trigger. The first shot caught the federale in the left shoulder. He spun and went to his knees then rose again, attempting to fire at the oncoming boat. Spinner fired again, hitting the phony federale in the chest.

"The Japanese guy doesn't look so mad now," Rosen said, peering through the binoculars.

Spinner ejected the spent round. "What does he look like?"

"Like he's got a diaper full."

The man in the whaling boat crouched down to avoid the deadly fire coming from the oncoming boat.

Spinner directed Raúl to head over to the shot-up panga. It had been splintered from the hail of bullets that had penetrated its hull. The cover on the outboard was hanging in shreds. Emily held her breath, fearing a gruesome sight.

"Francisco! Carlos!" Raúl called out. "Brad!"

Carlos's head appeared first, his eyes wide. Then Francisco came up, looking disoriented. Brad peered over the gunwale last. His right shoulder oozed blood. All three were soaking wet.

"Are you okay?" Spinner called out.

"We're okay," said Carlos. "Brad took a bullet to his shoulder."

"I'm fine," said Brad. "But the panga isn't. They shot the motor to shit."

"How the hell did you manage to survive that?" Rosen was incredulous at the amount of damage their boat had received in the firefight.

"We laid face down on the bottom of the boat," said Francisco. "It was below the water line."

"You better climb aboard," said Jake. "Bring that gas tank and those plastic bottles with you."

"What do you want to do, Jake?" Raúl helped the three men into the boat.

"I want that banger boat on the bottom of the sea."

"I was hoping you were going to say that. Hang on."

*This End Up* accelerated toward the whaler. Spinner set the rifle down and drew his pistol. He rolled onto his back grimacing at the newly-opened wound on his right side. "Get ready to toss a couple of tear gas grenades."

"Spinner, you're bleeding again. We need to get you to Arturo."

"Not now, Em." Spinner turned to Carlos and Francisco. "Fill up a couple of those bottles with petrol and stick a rag in the end."

They set about emptying some of the gas from the fuel tank into the plastic water bottles. As they drew closer to the whaler, everyone was on high alert for the lone occupant of the boat. As they approached, Raúl retrieved the Krag and trained the rifle on the whale banger. Spinner pulled his gun.

"You in the boat. You have thirty seconds to show yourself. Drop your weapons and come out with your hands up. We will not shoot you. Thirty seconds and we blow up your boat. Starting now." Spinner looked at his watch. All eyes were glued to the whaling boat.

In the distance, the sounds of boats racing on the water diminished as the last two surviving banger boats reached the barricade, driving the rest of the dolphins and small whales into the cove. A small skiff pulled ropes drawing the nets together and quickly closed the barricade.

"Twenty seconds," said Spinner. "We don't have all day."

The tall Japanese man with the skeletal face came out from behind the wheelhouse. He carried a semi-automatic pistol in one hand.

"Drop the gun! Now!" Spinner stood, his pistol aimed directly at the Japanese man's head.

"I would rather die honorably than to give up to rabble like you." Sato Izumi looked defiant.

"What is it with you people and your damned honor? You have no honor. Here's how this is going to go down, dickhead. I'm going to count to three. If I get to three and you haven't dropped that gun, I'm going to shoot you in the face."

"If I drop the gun, then what?" Sato's gun was unwavering.

"You're going to swim for it. Because we're going to blow up your boat."

"I'll drown out here!"

"You might. I didn't. But I had some help from some friends. I don't think they're going to be as forthcoming with your rescue."

The lines of Sato's forehead deepened, and his gun arm faltered slightly. "One."

"I'm just an observer here!"

"Bullshit. Guilt by association. Two."

"Wait! Wait!" He tossed the gun forward, and it clattered onto the deck. He raised his hands over his head. Spinner climbed onto the whaler's boat and forcefully slammed Sato against the wheelhouse. He frisked the Yakuza operative and found a sharp throwing knife tucked into the waistband under his shirt.

"Honor, my ass." He tossed the knife overboard. "Francisco, Carlos. Set the charges."

Francisco and Carlos clambered onto the boat and went to the stern while Spinner kept his gun pointed at Sato.

"You'll never get away with this. The arms of the Consortium reach into many places you could never imagine. They will find you."

Spinner gave him a world-weary look. "Tell me where the remaining gun placements are, and where I can expect the most resistance at the barrier, and I'll let you go. Your boss is lying on the deck of a boat a couple of miles back with his back broken. You can go join him. If you can get past the sharks."

"I don't know anything! I swear it!"

"Talk to me, god damn it! Or I'll drown you myself."

"There are two guards on either end. Just above the catwalk. They have AK-47s."

"Tell me something I don't already know." Spinner's teeth were clenched.

"Who else?"

"Kanamura," said Sato.

"Kanamura? He's on the barricade?"

Spinner thought of that fateful night on the *Shodokai Maru*. He remembered the look on Kanamura's face as he drew the knife blade across Macario's throat. The memory brought a new wave of rekindled rage spewing to the surface.

Sato nodded nervously. "He and four Mexican mercenaries from the cartel are on the boardwalk. They're all armed."

"We're ready here, Jake," Carlos said from the back of the whaler.

"I—can't swim," said Sato. "I never learned."

"No time like the present, I always say." Spinner motioned to the water with his pistol. "Japan is that way."

Sato walked hesitatingly toward the gunwale. He looked at Spinner beseechingly.

"Consider yourself lucky. Before I went over the side, your boss's lackey pumped two slugs into me."

Sato looked at Spinner and then the rest of the crew. "You will all die today."

While Spinner pointed the pistol at his head, Sato Izumi turned and stepped off the boat into the chill water. He came up sputtering and thrashing.

Spinner turned to Carlos. "Torch it."

# 82

*The male short-finned pilot whale skirted the inside of the barricade, searching desperately for an escape. He was one of two males that had been traveling with a maternal subgroup of females and their calves, when the constant and terrifying noise drove them toward this cove. The wound on his right flank stung, the result of a lance jab from a man on the barricade. He had positioned himself between the man and a young pilot whale. The incessant banging had stopped momentarily, but the water reverberated with the frantic calls of his kind and of the others. Several smaller dolphins had been so severely stressed from the drive hunt that they floated listlessly at the surface, unable to move.*

*This was not the first encounter with humans for the sixteen-foot pilot whale. Originally captured and procured by the U.S. Navy, the whale had been trained to patrol harbors at night and neutralize potential terrorists seeking to attack ships at anchor. After he had turned on one of his trainers, the pilot whale was released off the coast of San Diego. He gradually made his way south until he was able to join a pod of females. He knew he was a very special whale. The Navy had trained him to be a killer.*

*The younger male was positioned behind him, creating a protective shield between the females and their calves and the men on the barrier. The males spyhopped intermittently, searching for an opening to lead the pod back out to sea. The whales submerged and tested the netting under the catwalks with their rostrums. The nets held firm.*

On the shore, the flensers stood on the giant blue plastic tarps, readying their knives. The freezer units on top of the eighteen-wheelers were working overtime. From the catwalk, some of the Japanese crewman and Mexican cartel members began to climb into skiffs to drive the dolphins and whales to the beach.

Ako Kanamura was standing on the catwalk issuing orders when he heard the explosion. He turned quickly to see a distant whaler boat explode in a conflagration of burning debris which blossomed out in all directions. He realized it was Sato Izumi's boat. He peered through a pair of binoculars to see four boats racing toward the barricade. An inflatable boat and two steel-reinforced pangas flanked a larger vessel that resembled a deep-water fishing trawler. Standing at the bow of the trawler was Jake Spinner, very much alive.

He shouted to the cove guards. "Get ready!"

Kanamura looked up and down the ranks of the alert men on the catwalk. In the bay behind them, the water was being churned to foam by trapped and panicked bottlenose and common dolphins. A pod of fifteen short-finned pilot whales were frantically cruising the nets along the inside of the perimeter, searching for an opening. Some of the whalers on the barricade beat the water with oars to drive them back.

A sudden explosive exhalation caught Kanamura off guard. A huge black head arose from the water near his feet at the edge of the catwalk. The pilot whale emitted frantic vocalizations from its blowhole. Kanamura brought his foot up and kicked the whale viciously in the rostrum.

The whale let out a loud high-pitched squeal, turned, and disappeared into the dark water. The other pilot whales followed in a thrashing of flukes.

Kanamura quickly scanned the hills above the cove. There was no sign of the sentries. Something wasn't right. Kanamura could sense it. He was about to call Huertos, the lead guard, on the radio when his cell phone rang. Annoyed, he looked down at the number. It was Yoshimatsu.

"Hiro-san, where are you?"

The voice on the other end didn't sound like Yoshimatsu. The man was speaking through clenched teeth. "I-I'm on the banger boat. My back is broken. Spinner did this to me. Everyone else is dead."

"Can you move?"

"I can't feel my legs."

"I'm sending someone for you. He'll take you back to the *Shodokai Maru*."

"Where is Sato?" Yoshimatsu asked.

"Sato's boat just exploded. I don't know if he made it."

"Spinner is coming." Yoshimatsu gasped in pain. "Kill him!"

"Yes, Hiro-san."

Kanamura disconnected and looked around. The Japanese crewman who had delivered him to El Infierno in the speedboat stood nearby. He motioned him over.

"I want you to take the boat. Pick up Yoshimatsu-san. Get him back to the *Shodokai Maru* as fast as you can. He requires medical attention."

"How will you get back?"

"I'll return on that boat that is coming towards us." Kanamura's lips curled into a sinister grin. "Jake Spinner's head will be tied to the bow."

The crewman took off running along the catwalk toward the speedboat tied near the west end of the cove. Kanamura watched him run past two of the barricade guards. He looked up onto the rocky promontory above the cove where another armed sentry stood at full attention, staring out at the approaching boats. Suddenly, the guard was yanked backward, as if pulled by a giant invisible hand. Then Kanamura heard the rifle blast. He saw the sentries looking around in confusion.

Kanamura heard the whine of another bullet and then its impact behind him. The sentry on the east end of the cove pitched forward, a gaping hole in the front of his chest. Again, he heard the delayed report from the sniper rifle. He ran along the catwalk and found cover behind a metal storage box. Some of the barricade guards started to run toward the periphery of the catwalk.

"Hold your positions!"

On the shoreline, the flensing crew began to panic. One by one the sniper began to systematically shoot out the tires on the eighteen-wheelers. Bullets riddled the body of one of the transport trucks. A slug hit its gas tank, and the truck ignited, exploding in a spectacular burst of metal and flaming rubber.

Another shot ripped the tire of the remaining transport truck. Kanamura strained his vision to find the source of the sniper fire. He saw a brief muzzle flash coming from the top of the east ridge. He pointed. "Up there! Shoot up there!"

The Mexican cartel assassins turned their weapons toward the ridge and began firing indiscriminately. The last of the conscripted fishermen from Puerto Nacimiento were leaving their stations and running for cover. Kanamura spotted one clambering up onto the rocks at the cove's edge. He pulled his semi-automatic pistol and leveled it at the fleeing indio. He fired twice, and the man tumbled down the steep rocks and fell into the sea.

Kanamura turned to the rest of the men on the barricade. "I will kill any man who deserts his post!"

Up on the ridge, Oliver Sweet ducked as several bullets whizzed overhead. Several more slugs kicked up plumes of black dust around him. The cove sentries were firing blindly. Most of their weapons didn't have the range or accuracy to reach his position. He calmly ejected the spent magazine and inserted a fresh one. He looked and saw that four boats were closing the distance and realized he had only seconds to protect the activists from being slaughtered. He rolled back into a prone position and took aim.

"I can see a little more persuasion is in order." He squeezed the trigger.

On the barricade, another guard went down several yards from Kanamura. The assassin was literally lifted off his feet and hurled into the water outside the barrier. Kanamura moved quickly several yards down the catwalk. He shifted his glance to the oncoming boats. They'd be on them in minutes.

On the beach, the flensing crew had taken cover in or under anything that would provide them the tiniest bit of protection from the death raining down from the ridge. One flenser had found a rifle lying near one of the downed guards. He picked it up and fired a volley at the ridge. In response, the air whined with a *thwip* and the flenser went down. The blast from the sniper rifle echoed back through the hills and arroyos. It sent collective terror through the rest of the processing crew. Some covered their heads and began to run for the dunes behind the cove.

Kanamura moved up and down the barricade line. "Steady. Pick your targets. Do not shoot the man in the lead boat. Leave him to me."

Descending on the barrier, in a chevron formation, *This Side Up* led the charge, flanked by Orca 2 on one side, and Orca 7 on the other, manned by Ruben and Luis. Orca 4, manned by Jesus and Alejandro, was coming up fast from behind. Alejandro had replaced Arturo after the veterinarian and Paola had fallen back to tend to the wounded.

Alejandro's voice came over the radio. "Sorry to be late to the fiesta. Where do you want us, Jake?"

"West end of the barricade. Orca 7, Ruben and Luis, aim for the east. Watch yourselves. There's still active shooters on the catwalk."

"Thanks for the heads up. See you in the cove."

Spinner looked through the binoculars and saw the destruction Oliver Sweet had wrought on the cove guards and Yoshimatsu's operation. One of the eighteen-wheelers and a smaller transport truck were on fire. Black smoke lifted off the beach and swirled around the cove, cutting off visibility from the ridge.

Spinner hit the radio call button. "Osprey, this is Orca 3. We are inbound. Do you copy?"

He heard crackling and static before the familiar sound of Oliver Sweet's voice came over the speaker.

"Orca, this is Osprey. Visibility on the cove sucks right now. Having trouble locating targets. Be advised, there are still three shooters on the barricade."

"Copy, Osprey. Orca 2, 3, 4, and 7 are going in."

"Watch yourself, Orca."

Suddenly they heard the sound of engines revving. A sleek launch burst through the smoke cloud and came directly at them. Spinner turned his binoculars on the boat's driver who, upon seeing the approaching echelon formation of four boats, veered away suddenly.

"What do you think, Jake?" Raúl asked. "Want to pursue?"

Spinner shook his head. "Let him go. They're not going anywhere."

The launch sped east. Spinner knew exactly where it was going. Yoshimatsu had called in to be picked up.

The three accompanying boats fanned out from *This Side Up* and headed for different sections of the barricade. In the pall of black smoke hanging over the water, Spinner could barely see the barricade.

Spinner handed the rifle to Raúl, who turned the wheel over to Francisco. "Head the boat straight for the middle," Raúl instructed. "Don't stop until you break through."

Francisco nodded, and Raúl moved to the bow with Spinner and Rosen.

The plan was to have *This Side Up* and the two retrofitted pangas ram the barrier simultaneously. Sandy and Graham would blast into the lagoon to drive the dolphins and whales back out to sea through the openings created.

Spinner reached into his satchel and retrieved his last three magazines. He loaded one into each pocket and slammed a third fresh mag into the Beretta.

He looked over at Rosen. Her Canon camera hung loosely around her neck. Her faced was smudged with dirt, sweat, and dried blood. She'd never looked so beautiful. He touched her cheek.

"Get this down for posterity, Em."

She nodded. "Don't do anything stupid."

"If I don't get a chance to tell you . . . "

Emily put a finger to his swollen lip. "Tell me when it's all over."

The smoke now covered the entire catwalk. The only sound that could be heard was the roar of the boats' motors as they sped forward on a collision course with the barricade.

"Hang on!" Raúl yelled over the din of the engines.

# 83

Kanamura had lost sight of the boats in the smoke that now hung over the entire scene. They sounded like a mass of angry hornets descending on his position. He had seen some attachments on the bows of the pangas and realized they were designed for ramming the barricade.

"Fire at will!"

The two barricade guards opened up, pouring a fusillade of bullets through the smoke. Gunfire erupted from one of the incoming boats. One of the guards cried out, then fell backward into the water.

When a vessel appeared out of the haze, Kanamura only had a moment to read *This Side Up* on its prow before it plowed full speed into the barricade's central section, causing a sickening squeal of splintered lumber, exploding fiberglass, and bent steel. The barricade crumpled with a sickening crunch as metal jaws splintered lumber and shredded netting. In the next instant, a panga also rammed the barricade, hitting one of the guards, flinging him into the water. The one-by-twelve planks cracked in two with the panga's full weight.

Suddenly, two pangas—one on each side of the cruiser—slammed into the barricade, sending shockwaves through the catwalk. Kanamura was thrown off balance and nearly fell into the water. A shot rang out and another cove guard fell into the water.

Francisco threw the throttle into reverse and backed away. He accelerated a second time, further shattering the planking and pulling up netting.

The activists crouched down until the last moment to avoid the gunfire directed at them. When Spinner looked up, he saw an image through the smoke. One of the cove sentries was aiming at him. Jake fired, and the assassin tumbled into the water.

489

A large gap finally opened up wide enough for the next boat to pass through. Just then, a silver blur blasted through the opening, and Rosen caught a brief glimpse of Sandy's rigid hull inflatable roaring into El Infierno Cove.

Spinner jumped off his boat and landed on the catwalk. He peered into the haze, searching for his target. A Japanese assailant ran at him from out of the smoky haze wielding a large flensing knife. Spinner raised his pistol and shot him in the chest.

He heard shouts and someone crying out in pain from one of the other pangas. He saw the outline of Orca 4. It had punched halfway through the barricade, but was also hung up on the planking and netting. A vicious fight was in progress as three whalers attacked Alejandro and Jesús. Armed only with spare oars, Carlos, Francisco, and Brad jumped off *This Side Up* and ran along the catwalk. They attacked the whalers, all of whom were wielding long flensing knives and clubs. Armed only with the oars, the activists were at a disadvantage.

Spinner ran toward the panga, closed in on one of the attackers, spun him around, and pistol-whipped him across the face. The man pitched sidelong and landed in the water. A second whaler came out of the haze thrusting his flensing knife at Spinner.

Jake leveled the pistol at the assailant's head. "Really?" The whaler stopped dead in his tracks, his eyes wide.

The whaler stared at the gun then dropped the flensing lance and dove into the water.

Francisco and Carlos succeeded in neutralizing the last whaler with a series of blows with the oars. Immediately, Brad and Francisco began pulling debris away from the boat. Spinner grabbed a length of netting and pulled it free from the stern.

Francisco yelled, "Put it in reverse and hit it again! The opening's not big enough!"

Jesús backed the panga up several yards, then hit full throttle. It crashed through the remainder of the barricade.

Spinner peered through the smoke and saw the outline of a large man holding a Samurai sword in two hands. He moved purposely toward Kanamura.

After Sandy and Graham blasted through the opening created by *This Side Up*, they sped to the center of the cove where Sandy slowed to a near stop to assess the situation. They needed to move the terrified animals toward the openings in the barricade. Herding dolphins and whales was dangerous. If

Sandy miscalculated her maneuvering or speed, she could inadvertently drive them into each other or into the shallows where the flensers were waiting.

The animals were milling about the lagoon in great confusion, swimming haphazardly in all directions. Many of the small whales performed spy-hopping behavior, lifting their heads out of the water in an attempt to orient themselves in the chaos of panicked dolphin vocalizations, gunfire, and engine noise.

In the thick smoke that hung over the cove, it was hard to see. The water churned with dorsal fins as Sandy carefully maneuvered the RIB in a tacking pattern toward the openings in the barricade.

Sandy heard the motor before they saw the skiff. It appeared out of the haze with three Japanese men carrying blunt clubs and flensing knives, heading straight for them.

Struggling to steer, she reached with one hand and hefted the emergency oar that had been lashed to the gunwale. "Graham!" She tossed it high and Graham caught it. Brittany reached for the last butyric acid bomb and showed it to Sandy.

"Make it count, Brit."

The skiff swung in close to the inflatable. Sandy pulled the wheel in an evasive maneuver to avoid a direct collision. The skiff closed in again and the man in the bow leapt for the RIB. Sandy pulled hard to starboard, and he hit the side of the inflatable and bounced into the water.

The skiff came around for another pass. Another man had moved to the bow. He held a long, razor sharp flensing knife attached to a six-foot pole. The boats collided. He and Graham parried blows, the blade clacking off the oar. The whaler brought the blade down and it caught Graham across the forearm, causing a deep gash. Graham swung at him with the paddle, but his reach fell short. Suddenly, Brittany stood up and threw the butyric acid bottle at the skiff. It exploded against the whaler's chest, enveloping him in a rancid cloud. Both whalers began to cough and wretch as the skiff turned away from the inflatable.

Sandy saw the blood running freely down Graham's arm. "Brittany! Take the wheel!"

Sandy reached under the console and located the first aid kit. She rushed to Graham who was staring at the gaping wound on his forearm.

"Hang on, Graham. I'll get this bandaged." Sandy quickly dabbed the wound and applied a pressure bandage. "You're going to need stitches, Neely."

"Thanks, Sandy."

"Stay away from sharp knives for a while, okay?"

The inflatable suddenly lurched and came to a jarring halt. The motor whined, then sputtered as the propeller caught in the sand.

Brittany's eyes were wide with fear. "What did I do?"

Sandy yelled, "Turn it off! Turn it off! We're too shallow!"

Brittany turned off the motor. "Sorry! I'm sorry!"

"Not your fault. It's just too shallow."

"I'm going in." Graham swung his long legs over the side and landed in mid-thigh-deep water. He pushed the inflatable. "It won't budge. Can you lift the motor?"

Sandy tried to hoist the motor. "It's stuck."

Graham took a deep breath and dove under. The water was turbid, making a visual inspection difficult. He felt his way around the shaft of the outboard until he located the prop, then dug furiously, scooping sand away from it. The more sand he scooped, the more it filled in the furrow created by his hands.

He came up for air, sputtering. "I think the prop might be bent. It's buried in the sand." He jiggled the shaft of the motor, attempting to dislodge any particles of sand still stuck in the lift mechanism. "Try it again."

Sandy engaged the electronic motor lift. The motor whined but the shaft remained immovable.

Graham gave Sandy a resigned look, then dove down again and scraped more handfuls of sand away from the prop. This time, he was able to move the shaft back and forth several inches. He resumed digging furiously, scooping handfuls of sand away like a possessed gopher. The bandage on his forearm, now soaking wet, was leaking blood freely into the water around him. The intense effort was causing his lungs to burn. Unable to stay under any longer, he burst to the surface.

He stood up, put his back to the transom and began to push as hard as he could. His feet slipped, finding no purchase in the shifting sand. The boat moved forward several inches. Graham cried out through clenched teeth. "Get out and push!"

Sandy jumped overboard. Brittany leapt over the opposite side. Together they pushed for all they were worth. The inflatable moved a foot, then two. Seconds later, it was floating free. Graham fell backwards into the water as the boat slid ahead. Sandy and Brittany quickly climbed back in.

The wind changed direction, and the smoke began to lift. Sandy peered ahead into the swirling smoke, and her eyes widened in fright.

"Oh, shit."

Wading toward the inflatable were four whalers armed with clubs and flensing knives. Seeing Sandy's frozen posture, Graham leaned around the boat and saw what had transfixed her.

"Hand me the paddle," he said quietly.

"Graham, you need to get in the boat. Now."

"Give me the paddle."

Without taking her eyes off the advancing whalers, Sandy handed it to him. He sloshed through the water, assuming a waist-deep stance at the bow of the boat.

"Get that motor started." Graham held the paddle like a baseball bat. The assailants closed in, forming a semi-circle around him.

Sandy hurriedly turned the ignition. The motor sputtered and died. "Come on! Come on, damn you!"

Suddenly, another gust of wind lifted the pall of smoke, revealing the beach and the dunes beyond. Black smoke curled skyward from the burning trucks. Something caught Sandy's attention on top of the dune behind the cove. Human figures stood lined up. They were all carrying rakes, pitchforks, shovels, and machetes. The line of people, both men and women, let out a spine-chilling war cry, then they careened down the slope toward the beach.

The remaining villagers—the ones who had been conscripted for the whalers' grisly endeavor—turned on their tormentors and began to fight back. Some of the whalers broke and tried to run, but they were quickly chased down and beaten where they fell.

The four whalers who had surrounded the RIB saw their escape route had been cut off. Led by a fiery india wielding a machete and a marlin spike, villagers from Puerto Nacimiento were already wading out toward them. The whalers turned back toward the inflatable, panic on their faces. They waded toward the boat, eyeing their only possible means of escape. Graham swung hard and caught one across the side of the head. A Mexican assailant advanced on Graham and thrust his flensing knife. Graham ducked to the side as the attacker lost his footing and went down. Graham brought the paddle down hard against the man's head.

The two remaining whalers were suddenly engulfed by a swarm of angry villagers, who began to beat their tormentors mercilessly. They beat them for the fathers, brothers, and sons who had been tortured or killed.

Behind him, he heard the RIB's motor roar to life.

"Graham! We have to get these dolphins back out to sea!"

The petite india looked up, her hair and clothes soaking wet. She nodded to Graham once, then held up a fist in solidarity with Sandy and Brittany. Graham clambered into the boat and they accelerated toward groups of stunned dolphins. Ruben and Luis had cleared a path in the breach they had created and were waving them forward.

"God damn it, Spinner, just shoot the son of a bitch!" Rosen said.

Spinner aimed the Beretta at Kanamura's head. The assassin didn't flinch.

"You won't shoot me, Spinner," Kanamura said. "Your hate for me is far greater than that. You want to look into my eyes when you kill me."

Kanamura laid his Samurai sword and pistol down on the planking and stood defiantly. "Men like us, this is how we measure ourselves."

Spinner let out a long breath, then lowered the semi-automatic, never taking his eyes off Kanamura. He set his gun down and straightened up. He gauged the distance between them. The platform was supported by a single post, which stood between them.

Rosen put down the gaff she was holding and jumped lightly onto the catwalk. She needed to get close to Jake. She turned her head and looked at Raúl, the message in her eyes clear. Raúl nodded, raised the rifle to his shoulder, and aimed at Kanamura's chest.

Spinner and Kanamura got to the platform at the same time. They circled each other, looking for weaknesses. Kanamura took notice of the bloodstain on Spinner's shirt. He flashed the slightest of smiles.

"You continue to surprise me, Jake Spinner. You survived not only two of my bullets, but you managed to overcome the ocean herself. Impressive."

Spinner circled Kanamura, watching how he weighted his feet, the length of his steps, and where his center of gravity rode. Kanamura moved like a large and very deadly snake.

The wind changed once more, and smoke obscured the catwalk and platform where they faced off.

"I don't have a clear shot," Raúl said.

"Shit." Rosen moved along the catwalk toward the two men, disappearing in a wall of smoke.

Spinner and Kanamura were almost on each other. The only thing separating them now was the thick wooden post. Spinner tried not to think about the pain in his right side. He knew that was where Kanamura would be focusing his attack.

They dodged and weaved around the post for several seconds. Kanamura made a move and advanced toward Spinner. He led with several punches, which Spinner blocked with his arms. Kanamura then lashed out with a vicious kick toward Spinner's injured side. Jake spun and caught Kanamura with a full roundhouse kick to the jaw with the heel of his foot. Kanamura went back on his heels, shook his head, and wiped his mouth. The blood on his hand made him smile.

He came at Spinner and hit him with a flurry of punches to the head and stomach. Spinner was able to deflect most of them, but one jab tagged him with a glancing blow to the side of his head. Another punch landed solidly on Spinner's right side, causing him to cry out in pain.

Kanamura, seeing his advantage, continued his barrage of blows. A thrusting kick caught Spinner just above the eye and he stumbled backward. Kanamura kicked out again, but Spinner answered with a kick and swept Kanamura's locked knee. The knee joint cracked with a sickening sound. The assassin screamed, crumpled, and went down hard.

Spinner felt a sharp pain in his right side, making his breath come in gasps. He was having trouble seeing out of his swollen left eye. He knew his right side couldn't take much more abuse.

Kanamura stood painfully, favoring his right leg. He circled Spinner slowly keeping his right leg protected. Spinner dropped his right arm to protect his injured side. This left him with only his weakened left arm to deliver the blows.

Kanamura charged, surprisingly quickly considering his leg injury. The two men collided with a thud of flesh pounding into flesh. Kanamura caught Spinner in the chest with a hard right. Spinner's left fist came up under Kanamura's chin in a vicious uppercut. Kanamura's head snapped back, and Spinner brought his right fist down on Kanamura's cheekbone. The assassin's left hand caught Spinner squarely in his wound. Both men crumpled to the deck, writhing in pain. Spinner rolled onto his knees then came to a half-kneeling position. He brought his left hand up and hammered Kanamura in the face again. Kanamura returned the blow, and Spinner went down again.

Kanamura tried to stand. He was unsteady, but straightened up to his full height, then advanced on Spinner, who was still struggling to get up. He stood over him, blood dripping freely from his face. Spinner struggled to his knees once more. Kanamura prepared to deliver the blow that would snap Spinner's neck.

From out of the smoke, Rosen appeared in a blur. She launched herself at Kanamura, landing squarely on his back and pitching him forward over Spinner. The three went down in a jumbled heap. Rosen hung on for all she was worth, her fingers desperately probing for Kanamura's eye sockets. She dug in with her nails and Kanamura screamed. He pulled her hands away and head-butted her. Stunned, Rosen let go. Kanamura rounded on her, punched her and threw her aside like a rag doll.

With his last reserves of strength, Spinner stood. He began pummeling Kanamura's face. Teeth and bones cracked under his desperate blows. Kanamura punched Spinner in the face, but Spinner did not relent. In a final blow, Kanamura hit him in the right side. Spinner went down on the deck and didn't move.

Kanamura got up slowly, wincing. His face was unrecognizable, his cheekbone crushed. Blood dripped freely down his chin and made large spatters on the wooden deck.

He turned and walked through the hanging smoke to the remaining segment of catwalk. He bent painfully, picked up his Samurai sword, and limped back to the platform. He had to stop and rest due to the pain in his leg and face. He reached Spinner, who remained inert on the deck. Kanamura rolled Spinner over and with great effort, pulled him up to his knees.

"I want you to see your death coming," Kanamura said, his voice barely recognizable while attempting to talk through a mouthful of broken teeth.

Rosen, who had come to, rolled over, and saw Kanamura poised with the Samurai sword, about to deliver the killing blow to Spinner. She yelled, "No!"

Spinner looked defiantly at Kanamura. "Go fuck yourself."

Kanamura brought the blade back.

From his good eye, Spinner spied a large black shadow just under the surface of the water, approaching fast.

"Incoming," said Jake, almost inaudibly.

Kanamura paused, his gaze following Spinner's.

Suddenly, the water next to the platform exploded as a huge black missile shot out of the sea. Instinctively, Spinner dropped down flat and rolled away. As Kanamura turned, two-and-a-half tons of angry male pilot whale breached and slammed into the assassin, snapping his neck with a wet crack. He fell sideways into the water, and the massive pilot whale landed on top of him. The great splash rocked the platform, separating it from the rest of the catwalk.

When Spinner looked up again, he saw Rosen holding onto the platform, her eyes wild. He looked back at the deck and saw one of Kanamura's shoes, his Samurai sword, and a cell phone, the only reminders of his presence.

Spinner rolled onto his back. He closed his eyes, breathing heavily. He then began to laugh softly, grimacing in pain. Suddenly, Rosen was at his side, hugging him.

"Rosen, what the hell were you thinking?"

"In case you hadn't noticed, Spinner, you were getting your ass handed to you."

"Bullshit." Spinner coughed painfully. "I had him just where I wanted."

"Yeah, right." She squeezed him.

Spinner winced again. "Ouch."

The smoke began to lift, slowly unveiling the destruction in the cove. There were shouts and confusion all around them. Several pangas and Sandy's RIB moved through El Infierno inlet, herding straggling dolphins through the breaks in the barricade. The whales and dolphins were escorted back out to sea.

"Can you stand?" Rosen asked.

"Won't know until we try, I guess."

She put her shoulder under Spinner's left arm, and with great effort helped him up.

"God damn it, that hurts."

"Stop being a baby. You know, you could have avoided all this if you had just shot the fucker in the first place. Men. Macho jerks, the whole lot of you."

Spinner stood, still leaning heavily on her. "Jesus, I really need to start working out."

*The male pilot whale pushed the human's body down into the sand and head-butted the corpse several times. Satisfied the man wasn't going to move, the pilot whale rose to the surface and began to emit high-pitched whistles and squeaks to guide the other members of the subgroup through the breach in the barricade. One by one, the members of the family swam by Kanamura's limp form as they headed back out to sea. All around them, dolphins were speed-swimming toward the open water. The other male pilot whale swam up to the corpse, regarded it briefly, then joined the rest of the pod.*

# 84

The winds had shifted once more, carrying the smoke cloud to the east. The barricade was in tatters, three gaping holes now evident. In the cove, the last of the dolphins were being gently enticed to go through the openings to their freedom.

Spinner and Rosen limped along the only remaining segment of catwalk toward *This Side Up*. Raúl stood at the stern, his face lined with deep concern when he saw the two bloodied figures stumbling toward him.

"Jake! Emily! Are you all right?"

"We're good." Rosen looked at Spinner. "We're good."

"I'm so sorry. I couldn't get a clear shot due to the smoke. I was afraid I would shoot one of you." As he saw them more closely, Raúl's expression changed to horror. Making the sign of the cross, he whispered, "Dios mío."

Raúl looked directly at Spinner. "Kanamura?"

"You didn't see it?"

Raúl shook his head. "The smoke was too thick."

Rosen smiled. "He was bitch-slapped by a two-ton pilot whale."

"Man, I would've paid good money to see that," said Brad.

They assisted Rosen and Spinner into the boat, sitting them down on a bench seat. Blankets were draped over their shoulders. The thrumming sound of helicopter rotors was heard over the ridge.

Snake maneuvered the helicopter to a stretch of beach upwind from the burning vehicles. As soon as he touched down, two figures stepped out quickly carrying medical supplies. Arturo and Paola immediately set up an emergency treatment clinic on the beach for the wounded.

Francisco ferried *This Side Up* and gently guided it into the shallows. A crowd of people were gathered there. The surviving whalers and cartel assassins were sitting on the ground, their hands on their heads. Several villagers from Puerto Nacimiento stood guard over the thugs with the guns they had confiscated.

Many of the villagers appeared to be in a state of shock as the aftereffects of combat began to sink in. Several cried softly by themselves, others stood in small circles, talking quietly, trying to make some sense of what they had just gone through.

Raúl and the others helped Rosen and Spinner to the sand. They limped toward the aid station.

When Arturo looked up and saw Jake, his eyes went wide. He shook his head slowly. "Patching you up is becoming a full-time vocation."

"I missed your bedside manner, doc." Spinner forced a smile.

"Well, come on over and let's have a look at you."

Spinner held up a hand. "I'm okay. Take care of Em and some of the others who are worse off than me."

"Spinner, take a look around. You are the worst one."

"I'm okay. I just need to sit for a few minutes."

Snake walked up to the group and surveyed the destruction all around the cove. He gave a low whistle. "Jesus H. Christ! I leave for a couple of hours and look at the mess you made."

Alejandro limped toward Jake and Emily. He was barely able to put weight on his right leg. He and Jesús had opened up the breach on the west side of the cove, pulling down the nets and support posts, and creating a large opening for the dolphins' escape.

Jake stood, and the two men embraced.

"We did it, Jake," Alejandro's eyes were brimming. "We did it."

Spinner nodded. "That we did."

Graham stepped up with Sandy at his side, and Arturo unwrapped his sodden bandages. "I heard you were swinging for the fence out there," Arturo said. "Taking on four bad guys with a boat paddle?"

Graham blushed. "If it hadn't been for Sandy's expert driving and for the villagers' intervention, I'd be lying at the bottom of that cove right now."

Paola looked at her friend and they exchanged a knowing look.

"You opened this arm up pretty good," said the vet. "I'm going to have to do two sets of stitches to close this. I'm going to give you something for pain now. When we get back to the fishing camp, I can suture it up properly."

A figure appeared at the crest of the dune at the back of the cove. He waved, then took giant strides down the dune face, creating cascades of sand in a sliding mini-avalanche. When he got to the bottom of the dune, Oliver Sweet jogged toward them, his sniper rifle in one hand.

He saw Spinner sitting on an old plastic milk crate.

Rosen walked to Sweet and hugged him fiercely. The big man said something to her, then walked toward Spinner, who rose painfully. He grinned at Sweet.

"So, where's the cold Dos Equis, Spinner?"

"I've been kinda busy. Couldn't make it to El Pulpo."

"Jake, you look like shit."

"You should see me from this side."

Sweet embraced Spinner. "How'd we do, Boss?"

"Nice job, Ollie." Spinner grimaced." You saved a lot of lives today." Jake looked at Arturo with his good eye. "How are Fernando and Manuel?"

A deep sadness passed across Arturo's face. "Manuel will be fine. Fernando didn't make it. His head injuries were too severe. I'm sorry. I was told his widow was here. I need to inform her."

Spinner lowered his head. "Damn. I'm so sorry."

"Nothing anyone of us could have done. No one could have survived that impact. He died on the table in the La Paz hospital."

Raúl, who had been standing in the background, stepped forward. "No. I should be the one to tell her."

A diminutive woman, her clothes soaking wet and her hair disheveled, stood near the water's edge talking with members of her village. She looked around at the gathered crowd, hoping to see a familiar face. Her eyes fell on Raúl. Recognizing him, she handed her machete and spike to the man next to her and walked over and hugged him.

He held her close for a long moment before standing back and looking into her eyes. "Thank you for what you and your people did today. If you hadn't intervened, a lot of good people would be injured or dead."

"The People of the Desert Sea won today." Alma looked up at him, in fearful anticipation.

Raúl gently placed his hands on Alma's shoulders. "There was an accident at sea. Fernando's and Manuel's panga was rammed by one of the whaleboats. We got him to shore and transported him to the hospital in La Paz. The doctors could not revive him."

Her eyes welled with tears. She buried her head in his shoulder. The other villagers, realizing what had just happened, gathered around Alma to console her.

She pulled away from Raúl and looked at him, tears running tracks down her cheeks. "Did he . . . "

Raúl looked directly in her eyes. "Your husband was a hero today, Alma. They went after the whale boat while under heavy gunfire. Because of their actions, we were able to stop the head of the whaling operation and destroy his boat. I'll sing Fernando's praises for the rest of my life. He will not be forgotten."

"His son will grow up knowing his father died a hero."

Snake, who had been standing nearby with his worn baseball hat in his hands, stepped forward. "Ma'am, I can take you in the helicopter to La Paz to be with your husband."

He turned back and looked at Spinner. "I think I've got enough fuel for one more run."

Spinner nodded. "Whatever you need, Alma."

Moments later, the helicopter lifted off the sand carrying Alma Quintín to say her goodbyes to Fernando.

Rosen studied the ragtag group of activists, villagers, and fishermen. Everyone bore the marks of conflict, from the haunted looks of post-battle fatigue to various wounds and bruises. She stared out to the sea beyond the cove. The last of the dolphins and pilot whales were a barely visible thin line of black shapes on the horizon, rising and falling in unison.

The ringing of a cell phone snapped the group back to reality. Everyone looked toward Alejandro. Surprised, he pulled it out of his pocket and listened. The voice on the other end made him cringe.

"Cabrillo, you need to listen to me." Alfonso Figueroa sounded menacing. "It is of the utmost importance that we meet. Now. The Department of Justice has issued warrants for all of your arrests. You, Sandy, and Paola are to answer for your involvement with the illegal whale hunt."

"Which one? The last one, or the one we just stopped?"

There was a brief moment of heavy silence as Figueroa tried to comprehend Alejandro's meaning. "What?"

"Hold, please." Alejandro put him on hold, clicked the camera to video mode, and then panned the debris-laden cove. He pushed send and texted the video.

He switched back on to talk. "I just sent you a video file. Stand by."

A moment later, Figueroa swore. "Where is this?"

"Why don't you tell me?"

"Listen and listen well, Alejandro. You and your colleagues are in serious trouble. Unless you meet with me and release the old videotape and all of your footage from this whale hunt, the repercussions for you, your colleagues—even your families—will be devastating. This is now a matter of national security. Your involvement will bring down harsh retribution from the highest offices in the Mexican government. Remember who my connections are."

"I'll come in. But I get to choose the place of our meeting. I want a public place. No hidden offices, no clandestine locations. That's my one condition. Or no deal."

There was another pause on the other end of the line. "Very well. Where?"

"The soccer stadium in La Paz. Day after tomorrow. Sunrise."

"The three of you are to come alone. This is a most sensitive matter and must be handled with the utmost discretion."

"I understand."

Figueroa rung off.

Alejandro looked at the phone and then looked up at the group. All eyes were focused on him.

"It seems the Minister of Fisheries is threatening Sandy, Paola, and me with serious reprisals if we don't surrender our information and video tapes. He wants to meet us. Alone. Day after tomorrow morning at dawn."

"Like hell you will," said Spinner. "It's a setup."

"If they silence you three and take away the evidence, then this hunt never happened," said Rosen. "Call him back, and tell him to shove it."

"She's right," said Sandy. "We need to get this information out to the public. Otherwise, everything we've been fighting for will be for nothing."

"In order to kill the beast, you have cut off the head," said Alejandro. "Unless we stop Figueroa once and for all, this could happen again."

"Figueroa has just one thing on his mind," Spinner said. "And that's to make you and the data disappear. You're walking into a trap, sure as I'm sitting here."

Alejandro smiled. "I think I have an idea."

# 85

Yoshimatsu had tried to find a way to take his own life, but he couldn't even crawl the shortest distance due to excruciating pain. When the crewman dispatched by Kanamura found Yoshimatsu, he was lying on the deck of the banger boat soaked in urine and feces. With great effort, the crewman was able to drag him onto the speedboat and lay him on the floor. Yoshimatsu, in his painful delirium, saw a sodden Sato Izumi sitting near him. Sato's eyes were crimson, and he bent over and vomited seawater.

Once he was in the infirmary, the ship's medical officer got an IV started on Yoshimatsu and did his best to clean him up. Yoshimatsu screamed whenever the med tech attempted to move his useless legs. Hours later, Hirokan Yoshimatsu lay on a gurney in the *Shodokai Maru*'s infirmary. The intense pain he had been experiencing had been tamped down by the morphine drip now attached to his right arm.

He heard the deep thrum of the engines below him and realized he must have passed out for a while. The ship was moving now. He looked around the infirmary. Izumi was lying on his back in a bunk by the wall. He was covered in blankets and his face was ashen. Yoshimatsu thought he was dead until he noticed a slight rise and fall of his chest.

Yoshimatsu's overwhelming urge to die had been replaced by a building, seething rage that distracted from the excruciating pain in his back and legs. He would live to see Jake Spinner pay for what he'd done. If Kanamura hadn't finished Spinner off, Yoshimatsu would use every resource available to the Consortium to find that dog and hunt him down. No place on the planet would be safe for him. Yoshimatsu would relish the day when he could look into Spinner's face and watch him die in the most exquisitely painful way.

As this feeling surged through him, it replaced pain with a sense of power. Yes, this was what would fuel his recovery. He would recuperate to exact his vengeance on Jake Spinner.

The door to the infirmary opened and Captain Watabe stepped inside. His face was grim but he tried his best to conceal it. He spoke to the med tech in low tones, then approached the gurney.

"Sir, we are underway. I have contacted the hospital in Puerto Vallarta. They will have an ambulance waiting for you. The hospital will stabilize you, and then you will be transported back to Tokyo where the best doctors will take over."

"How long?" Yoshimatsu was barely able to get the words out.

"Seven hours if the sea remains calm."

Yoshimatsu reached out and grabbed Captain Watabe's forearm. "The hunt. How many boats came back?"

"Just the one you were on, Hiro-san." Watabe looked down at the floor. He didn't want to see the rage in the shipping magnate's face.

"And the trucks?"

Watabe shook his head. "The crewman who brought you back told me someone was attacking them from the hills. They killed the sentries and destroyed the vehicles."

Yoshimatsu closed his eyes and turned his head toward the wall.

"Sir, our refrigerators and ice lockers are full to the brim with whale meat, marlin, and tuna. This has been a very successful operation already."

Yoshimatsu's upper torso and arms erupted into a spasm of flailing and thrashing as he lashed out with the only moving parts left of his crushed body. An inhuman howl rose from his mouth as he arched his neck and head into the pillow. The tirade brought Sato Izumi bolt upright in his bunk, staring wildly around him. The med tech rushed over, thinking that Yoshimatsu was undergoing a grand mal seizure.

The med tech tried to give the business tycoon another shot of morphine, then realized that Yoshimatsu wasn't experiencing a seizure. He stepped out of the way until the tirade ceased, leaving Yoshimatsu spent and bathed in sweat.

Just then, Yoshimatsu's cell phone on the tray table next to the gurney began to ring. Captain Watabe picked it up and looked at the LED readout. Izumi sat on the edge of his bunk, eager to hear the news.

"It's Kanamura," said Watabe. He put the phone to speaker mode and presented it to Yoshimatsu.

Yoshimatsu grabbed the phone. "Ako! Did you kill him? Did you kill Spinner?"

"Your boy is hagfish food on the bottom of the sea," said a familiar voice.

"Spinner! I will hunt you down! I won't rest until I watch you die!"

"Good luck with that. Right now, you're sitting on about 50 kilos of C-4 attached to your hull. And by my watch, it's scheduled to blow in about thirty seconds."

Yoshimatsu's face contorted, and his eyes went wide. He looked around the room at the terrified looks on the faces of the others listening.

"Oh . . . and consider this a little parting gift from the Silvano family and the good people of Puerto Nacimiento. Sayonara, pendejos!"

Yoshimatsu looked at Captain Watabe, his mouth trying to form words. Suddenly, four explosions rocked the *Shodokai Maru*, the last one directly underneath them in the engine room. The ship listed and the floor split with a screeching tear of metal. Yoshimatsu and the others were incinerated as the room was enveloped by a conflagration of fire and debris.

Later, reports from observers as far north as Cabo San Lucas on the southern tip of Baja and Topolobampo on the mainland Mexican coast stated that they saw an immense explosion light up the night sky on the horizon. The Mexican Navy dispatched a search and rescue boat in the early morning hours to search for survivors. When they arrived at the site, the only evidence that a ship had sunk was some debris and a small oil slick. One of the pieces of flotsam recovered was a scorched life ring with part of the lettering in Japanese characters. The letters spelled out "-*kai Maru*." When the first officer checked the depth of their location, he turned to the captain of the Navy rescue boat and told him that the boat had sunk in an area where the depth of the seabed was in excess of 4,000 feet.

# 86

Alejandro limped through the archway leading onto the soccer field. The air was damp and chilly, but he didn't feel it. In the east, the first rays of light painted the small flat clouds in deep hues of orange and vermilion. The palm trees that lined the outside of the stadium were silhouetted against the breathtakingly fiery sunrise.

Alejandro's heart pounded in his chest as he walked toward the four figures standing in the middle of the field. In the dim light, he saw that three of the men wore the uniforms of Mexican Federal Police. These federales carried semi-automatic weapons. The fourth man was dressed in a black jacket and jeans, his hands hidden in his jacket pockets.

Figueroa demanded, "Where are the other two? Where are Jiménez and Wainright?"

Alejandro pointed to the three assassins. "Who are they? I thought this transaction was between you and me, Figueroa."

"Do you think they'll be able to hide from me? I have access to the highest levels of the Mexican government. You could have saved them and yourself a great deal of suffering."

Alejandro slowly shook his head. "This wasn't about any kind of amnesty for me or my colleagues. You're just looking to destroy all evidence and witnesses to your collaboration with the Japanese mafia."

In the early morning light, Alejandro saw Figueroa's expression change and his shoulders go rigid.

Alejandro raised his voice. "Those videos won't help you, Figueroa. It's too late. They've already gone public."

"You should never have interfered, Alejandro. You've tossed away your career, your family, and now your life and the lives of your colleagues. I'll take those videos now. In return, I promise my men will kill you quickly." Figueroa walked toward Alejandro, flanked by the three cartel assassins. "I will have the videos. Now."

Alejandro reached into his back pocket and retrieved two thumb drives. He tossed them onto the ground in front of Figueroa. The Minister of Fisheries picked them up and dusted them off. He placed the thumb drives in his coat pocket.

"See? That wasn't so hard now, was it?" Figueroa's smile was sinister. "Don't worry, Alejandro. Your wife and daughter and colleagues will be joining you shortly. You have my word."

"Not today," Alejandro's face was a portrait in stone.

The assassins raised their pistols at him. He stared at Figueroa unwaveringly. Figueroa took a step away from him. Suddenly, red laser dots appeared on the chests and heads of Figueroa's henchmen. Figueroa looked down at his own chest to see an ominous red laser dot over his heart. The three henchmen immediately threw their guns to the ground.

Figueroa's attention was drawn to motion at the entrances around the upper levels of the stadium. The arena began filling with people. Men and women fanned out in a giant circle looking down at the scene playing out on the field. Then, one by one, the people began stomping their feet and banging their hands against the stadium seats in a rhythmic drumming that echoed throughout the arena. Figueroa's gaze came to rest on the center portal. Standing in front of members of his cabinet, staring down at him, was his brother-in-law, President Emilio Duarte. Armed men in black uniforms flanked Duarte, their rifles aimed at Figueroa and his henchmen. Several armed Mexican federal police came out of the tunnels at ground level and walked toward the gathering at the center of the soccer field.

Alejandro walked up to Figueroa, reached into his pocket and took back the two thumb drives.

"Like I said," Alejandro looked directly into Figueroa's eyes, "not today."

He looked at the faces in the crowd. The drumming noise was so loud that all other city sounds were drowned out. He saw the fishermen and women from Puerto Nacimiento. Alma Quintín stood among them, her face wet with tears. He saw Raúl, Sandy, Paola, and Arturo. In another section, he recognized the faces of Carlos, Jesús, and Francisco, all representing San Vicente fishing camp.

Conspicuously absent from the crowd were Oliver Sweet, Snake, Emily Rosen, and Jake Spinner.

# Epilogue

An anonymous call to one of his aides had tipped off President Emilio Duarte and his cabinet about the battle at El Infierno Inlet. The Mexican Navy was dispatched. When they arrived, they found a handful of Japanese crewmen and several men dressed like federales. Several bodies were discovered in the area surrounding the cove. Charred trucks rimmed the cove's tideline. Along the perimeter of the inlet they saw fragments of a barricade floating near the shoreline in shreds of netting and fractured lumber.

The caller told El Presidente of the beating and suspected killing of members of a local coastal tribe and how they had been coerced into hunting the whales. The woman on the phone told them of an upcoming meeting set up by Figueroa to forcibly extract the incriminating evidence from the researchers who had discovered their plan for the hunt.

The Japanese government denied any claims of whaling activities in the area, but was soon embarrassed by the release of videos showing the two hunts. This ultimately resulted in increased international pressure on the Japanese to abandon the brutal and inhumane massacre of whales and dolphins.

Alfonso Figueroa was tried by a Mexican court and sentenced to twenty years in a federal penitentiary in Jalisco. He was found in his cell one day hanging by a canvas belt. This was strange, as prisoners were not allowed to have potentially lethal objects in their cells. Speculation was that his brother-in-law had decided that Figueroa was too much of a liability to his administration and had arranged for him to have an accident. Others said it was the work of Las Zetas in retribution for their losses.

Alisa Campos Mora sat on the transom of Jake Spinner's boat, her legs dangling in the water. She was dressed in a wetsuit and was busy fitting a mask and snorkel to her face. Next to her, Jake Spinner and Emily Rosen were both similarly clad. Alisa's parents, Raúl and Guadalupe, stood at the stern with son Julio, excitement on their faces.

In the water, fusiform shapes moved back and forth just feet below them. Several dorsal fins appeared and came right toward them, disappearing under the boat at the last moment. The dolphins vocalized in trills and whistles with each pass.

Alisa watched in awe. "What do you think they're saying, *Tio* Jake?"

"I think you've been invited to swim with them."

"I'm nervous."

"It's okay. I have it on good experience that they won't hurt you. Just stay close to Emily and me. Remember, let the dolphins choose the encounter. If they get close to you, don't touch their blowholes, eyes, or flukes. Keep your hands in but you can touch elbows with their pec fins. Keep your hands at your sides at first."

Emily asked, "Are you ready?"

Alisa nodded. The threesome donned their masks and snorkels and slid into the water.

The visibility was good for the area—nearly fifty feet. Alisa looked down and saw colorful fish swimming on the reef. She squealed with delight into her snorkel when a green sea turtle rose off the reef and began to swim along beneath them.

The dolphins approached out of the shimmering green curtain of water. Led by the old female, they swam as a group, eyeing the three humans who were holding hands and drifting with the gentle current.

The matriarch with the distinctive marks on her rostrum swam toward them. At her side the baby male dolphin with the star pattern on his head swam under her pectoral fin. He was eyeing the smaller human between the two larger ones. The family of bottlenose dolphins came to a stop several feet away. They began to issue a series of whistles and clicks. Emily felt her sternum vibrate as the dolphins probed with their pulsed echolocations. She shivered even though she was wearing a wetsuit.

The female drifted slowly toward Jake, staying just out of arm's reach. With his free hand, Jake slowly reached out toward the dolphin. The matriarch hesitated, briefly regarding Jake's outstretched hand. Then she drifted in until her rostrum came under Spinner's hand. Jake nodded to Alisa. Alisa let go of Jake's hand and tentatively reached out. The female dolphin moved forward until the young girl's hand rested on her head. The mother dolphin began to vocalize, causing Alisa's hand to vibrate. Alisa giggled through the mouthpiece of her snorkel.

Rosen looked into the matriarch's eye and blinked back tears. The little male bottlenose, sensing all was safe, came out from beneath his mother and approached her. He tipped his head and regarded Emily, first from one side, then rolling over and studying her from an inverted position. He began to flutter his pectoral fin at her. Rosen bent her elbow and slowly presented it to the young dolphin. Ever so gently, the dolphin tap-tapped Emily's elbow with his pectoral fin. Now, it was Rosen's turn to giggle like a schoolgirl.

The little dolphin took off in a flurry of bubbles and shot back to the maternal subgroup. Circling them in a blur of motion, he came back around and did a dead stop in front of Alisa. Alisa looked at Jake, and he nodded. Alisa slowly glided toward the young dolphin. He spun like a dervish around the twelve-year-old girl, getting almost close enough to touch before wheeling away with exaggerated sweeps of his flukes.

The rest of the subgroup approached, and dolphins and humans began to swim and dive down together in a slow dance of green water and beams of light. It was an otherworldly ballet of two species, choreographed by the family of dolphins.

The connection was older than time, Rosen thought, and probably had been going on for millennia. She wondered how the message had gotten lost. And, in that moment, she knew she would dedicate the rest of her life to spreading that very message.

The minutes they spent among the dolphin pod seemed timeless. It was as if everything else in the world had stopped and there was only this. All too soon, the dolphins' postures changed, and they began to swim with a slight agitation to their movements.

Spinner understood this behavior and watched as the dignified female approached him. She came forward until she was close enough to touch. Her baby was once again at her side. Spinner bowed his head and the matriarch touched her rostrum to his forehead. They hung in that position in the water column for several seconds. She drifted back as the young dolphin came forward and nuzzled Jake's hand. She issued a series of whistles and the other dolphins began circling. Spinner reached out and, one by one, the pod passed under his hand and then swam slowly into the shimmering green curtain. The matriarch regarded the three humans, then—with several powerful kicks of her flukes—she disappeared into the void followed by the others.

Back on *This Side Up*, Raúl and Guadalupe were nearly beside themselves with excitement as Alisa clambered back onto the boat with an enormous grin on her face. Guadalupe, seeing her daughter's happiness, swept her up in her arms.

"That was the best thing ever!" Alisa said.

"That's how I feel when I'm around them, too," said Emily. She saw the gratitude on the faces of Alisa's parents.

Alisa continued to regale her parents about the experience. Later, she sat on the bow of the boat with Jake on one side and her father on the other. A pastel sunset was forming in the west. Splashed against a canvas of gold sky were lavender clouds edged with burnt orange. Just above the horizon, a corona of white rays from the sun fanned out through the clouds.

Spinner heard the laughter coming from the galley as Rosen and Guadalupe prepared the dinner of yellowtail that Raúl had caught earlier. Spinner felt the pain of his wounds—and the years of abuse—begin to melt away. He couldn't remember a time when he felt so at peace.

Alisa looked at her father. "I know what I want to do with my life."

She turned and looked at Spinner. "I want to protect the dolphins and whales. I want to save the oceans."

Spinner grinned. "Why do you think I took you swimming with the dolphin family? That's what I told them. I wanted to introduce them to you."

Raúl took his daughter's hand. "You know, if you want to save the dolphins, you will have to study hard to get to university."

"I know, Papá. I will study very hard."

Raúl looked at his daughter wistfully. "University is very expensive. We don't have a lot of extra money."

Alisa looked downcast and a little guilty, realizing the impact of her father's statement and the extra burden it would place on her parents.

"You know, every dolphin researcher needs a good boat in order to conduct their studies." Spinner stared out at the blaze of colors on the western horizon. "I think this boat might do the trick, don't you?"

Raúl cast a sidelong glance at him. "What are you talking about, Jake?"

"I can't think of anyone better to take over *This Side Up* than you and your family."

"Gracias, Jake, but I can't afford such a fine boat."

"It's not for sale, my friend. It's a gift to you and your family."

"This is your livelihood, your life!"

"I got a new job. Besides, where I'm going, there's no place to haul a boat along. Think about it, Raúl. Now you have two boats. You can hire one out, and you can use this one. With some modifications done by Francisco, you can increase the storage capacity and the distance you travel."

"Jake, I don't know what to say," Raúl said, tears filling his eyes.

"Besides, the dolphins know this boat. I think this is a pretty good place for Alisa to start her education. I truly believe she and her generation will finally take steps to let these animals live in peace and maybe even save the planet along the way."

Alisa turned and hugged Jake tightly around the neck. "Thank you, Tío Jake."

"The next time I come through," Spinner pulled away from her and looked at her, "you can take me to visit the dolphin family."

Raúl touched his friend's shoulder. "Yes, any time. Thank you, my friend."

After dinner, Spinner and Rosen stood on the bow of *This Side Up* staring at the canopy of stars that now shone like brilliant diamonds tossed across a black satin cloth.

"That was a great meal," said Spinner. "I didn't know you could cook."

"Don't get too used to it," said Rosen. "I'm not sure I have the temperament."

"Hell, I don't mind. I'll cook if you like."

Rosen smiled. "That was a wonderful thing you did for Raúl and his family."

"There are no boats where we're going," Jake said. "At least not this kind."

"And where are *we* going, Mr. Spinner?"

"Castellano called earlier today. He wants us to come back to Las Altas for a few days to debrief. Then he's got an assignment for you. I'm coming along for comic relief."

"And when were you going to tell me about this?" Rosen asked, feigning anger.

"How about now? Hot off the press."

"And where, pray tell, are we going?"

"Rollie asked me not to spoil it for you. He said my life would hang in the balance if I leaked the intel before you're fully briefed."

"Spinnnnerrrrr!" Rosen said in a warning tone.

"Okay! Okay. I can't tell you outright, but I can give you a hint. Think really big animals. Really. Big. Animals." Spinner paused dramatically between each word and extended his arms a little wider with each one.

Rosen wrinkled her nose and pondered the question. "Big animals? Africa?"

Spinner shrugged. "Better bone up on your Swahili. But you didn't hear it from me."

"Hmm. Africa could be fun."

"I'm not sure that Castellano has fun on his mind, but, if that's where he's sending you, I'm coming, too."

Alejandro Cabrillo reopened the Instituto de Mamíferos Marinos. Students from several countries came to the renowned research center to study sea lions, dolphins, and whales in the Gulf of California.

Within two years, Sandy Wainright finished her post-doctorate and took a teaching position at the University of California at Santa Cruz, specializing in dolphin communication. Graham Neely took a position at the National Resource Defense Council in Washington, D.C. He has been seen in Sandy's company on a regular basis, and they are very active in marine mammal conservation.

Arturo and Paola were married the following year and opened their own veterinary clinic in La Paz. They coordinate local agencies and fishermen with marine mammal rescue operations up and down the coast of Baja.

Raúl Campos brought local fishermen together and helped to form a cooperative for sustainable fisheries and environmental management. He works closely with the new Minister of Fisheries in Mexico City. He still fishes regularly with his daughter Alisa.

Alma Quintín became a strong advocate for indigenous people of the gulf, pushing for educational reforms in the coastal *ejidos* and championing causes that would promote ecotourism in the southern Gulf of California.

Emily Rosen was shortlisted for a Pulitzer Prize for her exposé about illegal whale hunting in Mexico. The original piece appeared in *Esquire* with interviews and excerpts showcased in the *New York Times*, *Los Angeles Times*, and the *Washington Post*. She currently lists her profession as "freelance journalist."

Jake Spinner's whereabouts are unknown. He remains a "person of interest" to law enforcement authorities in Mexico, the United States, and Japan.

On the 15th of every month, a sum of money is deposited to the Alisa Campos Mora Educational Fund by a benefactor who chooses to remain anonymous.

# AFTERWORD

I chose Mexico for the location of this story mainly because of my familiarity and affinity with Baja and the Gulf of California. I have been fortunate to interact with the people and observe the wildlife of Baja and mainland Mexico for decades.

The fishing camp at San Vicente is a product of my imagination, but is drawn from actual fishing camps. The pueblos of San Jacinto and Puerto Nacimiento are also fictitious villages, fashioned after villages I have visited in Mexico. The indigenous people of that region, the Kumeyaay, are the direct descendants of the Cochimí who lived along the east coast of the Baja peninsula until the 1800s.

For the last three decades, Mexico has been at the forefront of marine mammal conservation, establishing protected areas for migrating whales in three lagoons on the Pacific side and creating several large reserves in the Gulf of California. Mexico City has recently banned the presence of any dolphinariums within the city limits. In 2017, Mexico created the *Archipiélago de Revillagigedo* National Park, which spans more than 57,000 square miles, making it the largest fully protected marine reserve in North America.

The U.S. Navy has been training marine mammals since the Vietnam War. Sea lions, dolphins, and pilot whales have been trained to both place and remove mines in harbors and to neutralize submerged enemy combatants who enter harbors under stealth. Before I wrote the SOFAR Trilogy, I interviewed a Navy war veteran whose job during the Vietnam War was to train dolphins for these missions. Knowing I was writing that series, he anonymously allowed me to peruse the original training manual. I must add that I'm not a big fan of exploiting cetaceans in this way. There are several documented accounts of pilot whales turning on their trainers and acting aggressively toward snorkelers and divers, on occasion resulting in the death of the person. There is speculation that some pilot whales which had been trained for warfare were later released into the wild. My interviews with pangueros (fishermen) in Loreto Bay revealed that pilot whales can be unpredictable with divers and snorkelers.

A number of dolphin and whale species have been listed as critically endangered. There is increasing public outcry against capturing and killing of cetaceans for food and entertainment. Countries like Japan, Norway, Iceland, the Solomon Islands, and the Faroe Islands still practice inhumane methods of slaughtering cetaceans for food and harvesting them for oceanariums.

Commercial whaling is still carried out by the Japanese under the guise of "scientific research." Meat from endangered and protected species is packaged and sold in Japanese markets throughout Asia. In recent times—especially among the younger generations—the consumption of whale meat is becoming less popular. Work by Ric O'Barry's Dolphin Project continues to shed light on the cruel practice of the annual hunt in Taiji, Japan.

Although the topic of sentience in non-human species has long been controversial among scientists, many recent studies have revealed the complexity of emotional and cultural lives of dolphins and whales. Scientists, such as Dr. Diana Reiss, Dr. Kathleen Dudzinski, and Dr. Denise Herzing, have broken new ground in dolphin communication and recognition of self (a true sign of intelligence). There is still much to learn concerning cetacean societies and their connections to the web of life in the oceans of our blue planet.

John R. Gentile
Tucson, Arizona

# ACKNOWLEDGMENTS

I have read that writing is a lonely profession. Most of the time, it's just the self-sequestered writer, their desk, a chair, and a computer (sometimes accompanied by a cup of Earl Grey or something stronger). It is true that I have spent many hours dwelling in my own alternate universe staring at a computer screen and tapping away without speaking with anyone. Having said that, after returning from the beyond, I have been very fortunate to have a circle of friends and family who have painstakingly read my manuscripts and given me invaluable advice along the way. These individuals come from varied and unique walks of life. From each one, I have received sage counsel to finally bring this project to completion.

I would like to thank Todd Anderson, podcaster and voice-over specialist, for his in-depth critique of the overall flow of the story—especially when I needed help regarding the use of technology from a Gen Z standpoint. To Nancy Buchanan, retired college librarian and editor, whose editing and Spanish translations added immensely to the feel of Baja, Mexico, I give my deepest thanks. To Lucinda Davis, Debbie Ensign, and Joia Wheeler, thank you for your enthusiastic comments regarding the pacing of the story. Many thanks to Dr. Timothy Fagan, internist, archivist, and friend, who scrutinized the manuscript and always kept me honest regarding all things medical. To Steve Iverson, historian, thank you for your meticulous edits in the early drafts. And to my friend, Paul Maseman, pilot, former merchant mariner, dog whisperer, and optical technician extraordinaire, I am deeply indebted to you for your well thought out advice on aspects of flight, ships, and how things work, in general.

Special thanks to my long-time friend Jonathan Hanson, naturalist, author, editor, and adventurer, who read the finished manuscript and provided much welcomed feedback.

I am indebted to Sharon Miller, author and editor, who painstakingly edited and formatted the manuscript and provided excellent advice that helped fine-tune the story. Many thanks to Leah Rubin for the final proofread of the manuscript.

Finally, I owe the biggest debt to my amazingly talented and beautiful wife, Katie Iverson. Without her enduring and patient assistance, I don't think this book would have been possible. Her background as a marine biologist and naturalist were essential in creating realistic scenarios and characters. Her talents as an artist and photographer are showcased in the book cover for *Baja Redemption*. I have been told that I am "not a man of few words." Katie's careful editing and scrutiny of the manuscript have not only helped sculpt the story, but also moved it along at a heart-racing pace. To you, my love, you are the best!

# ABOUT THE AUTHOR

John R. Gentile, an Arizona native, has a diverse background that includes SCUBA diving, sea kayaking, rock climbing, and wildlife photography. For ten years, he and his marine biologist wife, Katie Iverson, observed and photographed a population of bottlenose dolphins in the Gulf of California. He and Katie have kayaked with orcas in British Columbia, traveled to the headwaters of the Amazon in Peru, photographed the wildlife in Tanzania, circumnavigated the continent of Australia, and led trips to Baja California, Mexico, to observe dolphins and whales. His writing incorporates epic storytelling with likable yet flawed characters, insightful moments with wildlife, and just a touch of mysticism. *Baja Redemption,* an eco-thriller, is his fourth novel and the first book in the *Guardians of Gaia* series.

Please visit John's website at johnrgentile.com for information about upcoming writing projects and to view his wildlife photography gallery.